BATTLEFIELDS BEYOND TOMORROW

ABOUT THE EDITORS

CHARLES G. WAUGH is a leading authority on science fiction and fantasy who has published more than 120 anthologies and single-author collections. He lives with his family in Winthrop, Maine.

MARTIN H. GREENBERG, who has been called "the king of the anthologists," now has some 200 to his credit. Greenberg is professor of regional analysis and political science at the University of Wisconsin–Green Bay, where he teaches a course in American foreign and defense policy. He is also coeditor, with Charles G. Waugh and others, of *Baker's Dozen: 13 Short Fantasy Novels* and *Baker's Dozen: 13 Short Science Fiction Novels*, and, with Bill Pronzini and others, of *Baker's Dozen: 13 Short Mystery Novels* and *101 Mystery Stories*.

BATTLEFIELDS BEYOND TOMORROW

Science Fiction War Stories

Edited by Charles G. Waugh
and Martin H. Greenberg

With an Introduction by Robert Silverberg

BONANZA BOOKS
New York

First published in 1987 by Bonanza Books, distributed by Crown Publishers, Inc., 225 Park Avenue South, New York, New York 10003, by arrangement with Charles G. Waugh and Martin H. Greenberg.

Printed and Bound in the United States of America

Library of Congress Cataloging-in-Publication Data

Battlefields beyond tomorrow.
    1. Science fiction, American.   2. War stories, American.   I. Waugh, Charles.   II. Greenberg, Martin Harry.
PS648.S3B36   1987   813'.0876'08358   87-10264
ISBN 0-517-64105-4

h g f e d c b a

Book design by Clair Moritz

ACKNOWLEDGMENTS

Clarke—Copyright 1951 by Street & Smith Publications, Inc.; renewed © 1979 by Arthur C. Clarke. Reprinted by permission of the Scott Meredith Literary Agency, Inc., 845 Third Avenue, New York, New York 10022.

Green—Copyright © 1964 by New Worlds Science Fiction. Reprinted by permission of the author.

Herbert—Copyright © 1965 by Galaxy Publishing Corporation. Reprinted by permission of Kirby McCauley, Ltd.

Card—Copyright © 1977, 1985 by Orson Scott Card. Reprinted by permission of Barbara Bova, Literary Agent.

Haldeman—Copyright © 1972 by Condé Nast Publications, Inc. Reprinted by permission of Kirby McCauley, Ltd.

Moudy—Copyright © 1965 by Ziff-Davis Publishing Company; reprinted by permission of Virginia Kidd, Literary Agent for the Estate of Walter Moudy.

Carter—Copyright 1946 by Street & Smith Publications, Inc.; copyright renewed. Reprinted by permission of the author.

Saberhagen—Copyright © 1974, 1981 by Fred Saberhagen. Originally published as "Inhuman Error." Reprinted by permission of the author.

Drake—Copyright © 1979 by David Drake. Reprinted by permission of Kirby McCauley, Ltd.

CONTENTS

INTRODUCTION

Certainly it seems now that nothing could have been more obvious to the people of the earlier twentieth century than the rapidity with which war was becoming impossible. And as certainly they did not see it. They did not see it until the atomic bombs burst in their fumbling hands. Yet the broad facts must have glared upon any intelligent mind. All through the nineteenth and twentieth centuries the amount of energy that men were able to command was continually increasing. There was no increase whatever in the ability to escape. Every sort of passive defense, armor, fortifications, and so forth was being outmastered by the tremendous increase on the destructive side.

It could easily be an extract from some broad historical survey of the twentieth century published a year or two ago. But in fact the passage I have just quoted comes from a work of science fiction some three quarters of a century old: *The World Set Free,* by H. G. Wells, written in 1913. It is a remarkable example of the visionary power of Wells—to me the greatest of all science fiction writers—in two distinct ways.

One is the prediction of atomic weaponry itself, thirty years before Hiroshima. Wells opens the novel with a lecture by a professor of physics who shows a container of uranium oxide to his audience and declares that it contains "a source of power so potent that a man might carry in his hand the energy of light for a year, fight a fleet of battleships or drive one of our giant liners across the Atlantic. . . . Every scrap of solid matter in the world would become an available reservoir of concentrated force." From that ominous beginning Wells goes on to imagine the terrible atomic war of 1959:

For the whole world was flaring then into a monstrous phase of destruction. Power after power about the armed globe sought to anticipate attack by aggression. They went to war in a delirium of panic, in order to use their bombs first. China and Japan had assailed Russia and destroyed Moscow, the United States had attacked Japan, India was in anarchistic revolt with Delhi a pit of fire spouting death and flame; the redoubtable King of the Balkans was mobilizing. It must have been plain at last to every one in those days that the world was slipping headlong to anarchy. By the spring of 1959 from nearly two hundred centers, and every week added to their number, roared the unquenchable crimson conflagrations of the atomic bombs; the flimsy fabric of the world's credit had vanished, industry was completely disorganized and every city, every thickly populated area, was starving or trembled on the edge of starvation. Most of the capital cities of the world were burning; millions of people had already perished, and over great areas government was at an end.

Certainly Wells's was a vivid and preternaturally prophetic vision of the great nightmare of the late twentieth century. But, however impressive Wells's feat of imagination in foretelling global devastation by uranium-based atomic bombs may seem, I think it is in another aspect of these passages that Wells's true genius as a science fiction writer can be found. Not only was he astute enough to see the atomic bomb coming (and able to see the destruction it could wreak), but he was capable of perceiving the military stalemate that the invention of weapons too terrible to use might produce. ("Certainly it seems now that nothing could have been more obvious to the people of the earlier twentieth century than the rapidity with which war was becoming impossible.") His insight into the psychology of nuclear warfare extended even to predicting the preemptive strike. ("Power after power about the armed globe sought to anticipate attack by aggression. They went to war in a delirium of panic, in order to use their bombs first.")

Wells's remarkable visionary achievements in *The World Set Free* are superior examples of what the subspecies of science fiction that deals with the future of war can do by way of shaping our understanding of the problems that lie ahead. Even though he fell short of seeing the full horror of nuclear war—he does not take into account at all the matter of radioactive contamination—he offered his readers not only a clever guess at the next major development in the technique of warfare, but also a shrewd and sadly accurate sketch of the logical consequences of that development. That *sense of consequences* is the unique contribution of the best science fiction. To understand the special nature of the speculative thought that is science fiction, we need only contrast Wells's hypothetical view of the future with one expressed half a century earlier by another great writer, Victor Hugo.

Hugo, writing in 1864 to the French balloonist Nadar, expressed the belief that mankind's conquest of the air would bring an end to war. The development of aircraft, Hugo thought, would create a total deterrent to warfare by bringing about "the immediate, absolute, instantaneous, universal and perpetual abolition of frontiers. Armies would vanish, and with them the whole business of war, exploitation, and subjugation. It would be an immense peaceful revolution. It would mean the liberation of mankind."

A pleasing fantasy—but one that was not borne out by reality. Hugo had enough of the speculative turn of mind to be able to look beyond the obvious prediction (that an age of aviation lay just ahead) to a possible consequence (that the coming of aircraft would make war impossible). An interesting thought, yes, but not one that appears to have been soundly grounded in a knowledge of the human predilection for belligerence. It remained for a far greater speculative thinker, Wells, to see that greater technology would bring more destructive war—and *then* to reach Hugo's conclusion that monstrous weapons might provide the ultimate deterrent, but only after we had seen them in action.

The use of speculative fantasy—or science fiction, if you will—to peer into the future of warfare has a venerable literary tradition. According to the British scholar I. F. Clarke, the primary authority on the field, the earliest known account of a future war is an anonymous story published in 1763, *The Reign of George VI, 1900–1925*. Not much of a visionary work, this: it transplants eighteenth-century battle techniques to the twentieth century and shows us the heroic King George VI leading his troops up and down the battlefields of Europe:

The Russian army had a superiority of above sixty thousand men, consequently their numbers were two to one; but no dangers could depress the heart of George. Having . . . secured the rear and wings of his army from being surrounded, he placed his artillery in the most advantageous manner; and dividing his front into two lines, at the head of the first he began the attack, after his artillery had played on the enemy an hour, with great success. The Russian infantry, animated by the presence of their Czar under whom they had so often conquered, repulsed him with some losses. . . . George flew like lightning to his weakened troops, and, placing himself at the head of six regiments of dragoons, made such a furious attack on the eager Russians as threw them into disorder with great success.

Such is the author of *King George VI*'s description of the battle of Vienna in May of 1918—kings and czars contending in person on the battlefield at the heads of armies of thirty thousand or sixty thousand. Whereas in the real world of May 1918, millions of troops were colliding in the terrible climactic battles of World War I while airplanes dueled overhead and vast cannons hurled their projectiles against cities many miles away.

Yet quaintness of this sort is the exception, rather than the rule, in the literature of future war. Though prescience on the level of H. G. Wells has of course been rare, many writers have offered thoughtful and useful speculations on the shape of wars to come—such books as *The Battle of Dorking* in 1871; William Le Queux's *The Invasion of 1910*, written in 1907; Edward Shanks's *The People of the Ruins* (1920); and even George Orwell's 1949 classic, *1984*, in which a perpetual war is waged among three superpowers primarily for the purpose of helping them to maintain control over their own citizens.

Many of these books and stories have been frankly propagandistic in intent: attempts at awakening people to clear and present danger. One typical early example of that is the pamphlet *A History of the Sudden and Terrible Invasion of England by the French in the Month of May, 1852*, published in England a few months before the date of the predicted invasion. It tells how a fleet of fourteen French steamers crosses the English Channel while Parliament is still debating the fine points of international law; before a declaration of war can be issued, the French have landed and within two weeks crushed all opposition. A generation later came Chesney's famous *Battle of Dorking*, in which an unprepared England was invaded by the Germans. The popularity of this book, writes I. F. Clarke, "helped to launch a new type of purposive fiction in which the whole aim was either to terrify the reader by a clear and merciless demonstration of the consequences to be expected from a country's shortcomings, or to prove the rightness of national policy by describing the course of a victorious war in the near future." Clarke calls books of this type "the new literature of anxiety and belligerent nationalism." Such polemics in favor of military preparedness have been common ever since: the most recent novel of the impending Communist takeover of the United States reached my hands only last week.

A related form is the fantasy of national revenge—a school of fiction much practiced in France, for example, after the humiliating defeat at the hands of Germany in 1871. Books such as *The Battle of Berlin in 1875* showed the angry French liberating the Germans from their own rulers, telling them, "Our sole desire is to break those iron fetters that oppress you and set you free." The first shots of World War I, it could be said, were fired in the pages of works of this sort.

The blatant fantasy of national revenge is much more scarce today: neither the Germans nor the Japanese indulged conspicuously in writing such works after 1945, nor have the Palestinians who decry the creation of the state of Israel chosen fiction as the preferred form for their demand for vengeance. But nationalistic fervor is far from extinct, and such themes do emerge, however subtly concealed, in much of today's speculative fiction.

Basically, though, most stories of future war do not embody an underlying warlike intent. Except for a minority of crusaders and jingoes, the writers of fiction are generally a peaceable sort. To advocate war is not their purpose. To speculate about the possible forms it may take—with, perhaps, the effect of heading off some of the worst calamities before they become real—is more central to their aims.

And, not to be forgotten, of course, is that speculative fiction of this sort is also written to entertain—as we see in the stories collected here.

BATTLEFIELDS BEYOND TOMORROW

Arthur C. Clarke
SUPERIORITY

In making this statement—which I do of my own free will—I wish first to make it perfectly clear that I am not in any way trying to gain sympathy, nor do I expect any mitigation of whatever sentence the Court may pronounce. I am writing this in an attempt to refute some of the lying reports broadcast over the prison radio and published in the papers I have been allowed to see. These have given an entirely false picture of the true cause of our defeat, and as the leader of my race's armed forces at the cessation of hostilities I feel it my duty to protest against such libels upon those who served under me.

I also hope that this statement may explain the reasons for the application I have twice made to the Court, and will now induce it to grant a favor for which I can see no possible grounds of refusal.

The ultimate cause of our failure was a simple one: despite all statements to the contrary, it was not due to lack of bravery on the part of our men, or to any fault of the Fleet's. We were defeated by one thing only—by the inferior science of our enemies. I repeat—by the *inferior* science of our enemies.

When the war opened we had no doubt of our ultimate victory. The combined fleets of our allies greatly exceeded in number and armament those which the enemy could muster against us, and in almost all branches of military science we were their superiors. We were sure that we could maintain this superiority. Our belief proved, alas, to be only too well founded.

At the opening of the war our main weapons were the long-range homing torpedo, dirigible ball-lightning and the various modifications of the Klydon beam. Every unit of the Fleet was equipped with these and though the enemy possessed similar weapons their installations were generally of lesser power. Moreover, we had behind us a far greater military Research Organization, and with this initial advantage we could not possibly lose.

The campaign proceeded according to plan until the Battle of the Five Suns. We won this, of course, but the opposition proved stronger than we had expected. It was realized that victory might be more difficult, and more delayed, than had first been imagined. A conference of supreme commanders was therefore called to discuss our future strategy.

Present for the first time at one of our war conferences was Professor-General Norden, the new Chief of the Research Staff, who had just been appointed to fill the gap left by the death of Malvar, our greatest scientist. Malvar's leadership had been responsible, more than any other single factor, for the efficiency and power of our weapons. His loss was a very serious blow, but no one doubted the brilliance of his successor— though many of us disputed the wisdom of appointing a theoretical scientist to fill a post of such vital importance. But we had been overruled.

I can well remember the impression Norden made at that conference. The military advisers were worried, and as usual turned to the scientists for help. Would it be possible to improve our existing weapons, they asked, so that our present advantage could be increased still further?

Norden's reply was quite unexpected. Malvar had often been asked such a question—and he had always done what we requested.

"Frankly, gentlemen," said Norden, "I doubt it. Our existing weapons have practically reached finality. I don't wish to criticize my predecessor, or the excellent work done by the Research Staff in the last few generations, but do you realize that there has been no basic change in armaments for over a century? It is, I am afraid, the result of a tradition that has become conservative. For too long, the Research Staff has devoted itself to perfecting old weapons instead of developing new ones. It is fortunate for us that our opponents have been no wiser: we cannot assume that this will always be so."

Norden's words left an uncomfortable impression, as he had no doubt intended. He quickly pressed home the attack.

"What we want are *new* weapons—weapons totally different from any that have been employed before. Such weapons can be made: it will take time, of course, but since assuming charge I have replaced some of the older scientists by young men and have directed research into several unexplored fields which show great promise. I believe, in fact, that a revolution in warfare may soon be upon us."

We were skeptical. There was a bombastic tone in Norden's voice that made us suspicious of his claims. We did not know, then, that he never promised anything that he had not already almost perfected in the laboratory. *In the laboratory*—that was the operative phrase.

Norden proved his case less than a month later, when he demonstrated the Sphere of Annihilation, which produced complete disintegration of matter over a radius of several hundred meters. We were intoxicated by the power of the new weapon, and were quite prepared to overlook one fundamental defect—the fact that it *was* a sphere and hence destroyed its rather complicated generating equipment at the instant of formation. This meant, of course, that it could not be used on warships but only on guided missiles, and a great program was started to convert all homing torpedoes to carry the new weapon. For the time being all further offensives were suspended.

We realize now that this was our first mistake. I still think that it was a natural one, for it seemed to us then that all our existing weapons had become obsolete overnight, and we already regarded them as almost primitive survivals. What we did not appreciate was the magnitude of the task we were attempting, and the length of time it would take to get the revolutionary super-weapon into battle. Nothing like this had happened for a hundred years and we had no previous experience to guide us.

The conversion problem proved far more difficult than anticipated. A new class of torpedo had to be designed, as the standard model was too small. This meant in turn that only the larger ships could launch the weapon, but we were prepared to accept this penalty. After six months, the heavy units of the Fleet were being equipped with the Sphere. Training maneuvers and tests had shown that it was operating satisfactorily and we were ready to take it into action. Norden was already being hailed as the architect of victory, and had half promised even more spectacular weapons.

Then two things happened. One of our battleships disappeared completely on a training flight, and an investigation showed that under certain conditions the ship's long-range radar could trigger the Sphere immediately it had been launched. The modification needed to overcome this defect was trivial, but it caused a delay of another month and was the source of much bad feeling between the naval staff and the scientists. We were ready for action again—when Norden announced that the radius of effectiveness of the Sphere had now been increased by ten, thus multiplying by a thousand the chances of destroying an enemy ship.

So the modifications started all over again, but everyone agreed that the delay would be worth it. Meanwhile, however, the enemy had been emboldened by the absence of further attacks and had made an unexpected onslaught. Our ships were short of torpedoes, since none had been coming from the factories, and were forced to retire. So we lost the systems of Kyrane and Floranus, and the planetary fortress of Rhamsandron.

It was an annoying but not a serious blow, for the recaptured systems had been unfriendly, and difficult to administer. We had no doubt that we could restore the position in the near future, as soon as the new weapon became operational.

These hopes were only partially fulfilled. When we renewed our offensive, we had to do so with fewer of the Spheres of Annihilation than had been planned, and this was one reason for our limited success. The other reason was more serious.

While we had been equipping as many of our ships as we could with the irresistible weapon, the enemy had been building feverishly. His ships were of the old pattern with the old weapons—but they now outnumbered ours. When we went into action, we found that the numbers ranged against us were often 100 percent greater than expected, causing target confusion among the automatic weapons and resulting in higher losses than anticipated. The enemy losses were higher still, for once a Sphere had reached its objective, destruction was certain, but the balance had not swung as far in our favor as we had hoped.

Moreover, while the main fleets had been engaged, the enemy had launched a daring attack on the lightly held systems of Eriston, Duranus, Carmanidora and Pharanidon—recapturing them all. We were thus faced with a threat only fifty light-years from our home planets.

There was much recrimination at the next meeting of the supreme commanders. Most of the complaints were addressed to Norden—Grand Admiral Taxaris in particular maintaining that thanks to our admittedly irresistible weapon we were now considerably worse off than before. We should, he claimed, have continued to build conventional ships, thus preventing the loss of our numerical superiority.

Norden was equally angry and called the naval staff ungrateful bunglers. But I could tell that he was worried—as indeed we all were—by the unexpected turn of events. He hinted that there might be a speedy way of remedying the situation.

We now know that Research had been working on the Battle Analyzer for many years, but at the time it came as a revelation to us and perhaps we were too easily swept off our feet. Norden's argument, also, was seductively convincing. What did it matter, he said, if the enemy had twice as many ships as we—if the efficiency of ours could be doubled or even trebled? For decades the limiting factor in warfare had been not mechanical but biological—it had become more and more difficult for any single mind, or group of minds, to cope with the rapidly changing complexities of battle in three-dimensional space. Norden's mathematicians had analyzed some of the classic engagements of the past, and had shown that even when we had been victorious we had often operated our units at much less than half of their theoretical efficiency.

The Battle Analyzer would change all this by replacing the operations staff with electronic calculators. The idea was not new, in theory, but until now it had been no more than a utopian dream. Many of us found it difficult to believe that it was still anything but a dream: after we had run through several very complex dummy battles, however, we were convinced.

It was decided to install the Analyzer in four of our heaviest ships, so that each of the main fleets could be equipped with one. At this stage, the trouble began—though we did not know it until later.

The Analyzer contained just short of a million vacuum tubes and needed a team of five hundred technicians to maintain and operate it. It was quite impossible to accommodate the extra staff aboard a battleship, so each of the four units had to be accompanied by a converted liner to carry the technicians not on duty. Installation was also a very slow and tedious business, but by gigantic efforts it was completed in six months.

Then, to our dismay, we were confronted by another crisis. Nearly five thousand highly skilled men had been selected to serve the Analyzers and had been given an intensive course at the Technical Training Schools. At the end of seven months, 10 per cent of them had had nervous breakdowns and only 40 per cent had qualified.

Once again, everyone started to blame everyone else. Norden, of course, said that the Research Staff could not be held responsible, and so incurred the enmity of the Personnel and Training Commands. It was finally decided that the only thing to do was to use two instead of four Analyzers and to bring the others into action as soon as men could be trained. There was little time to lose, for the enemy was still on the offensive and his morale was rising.

The first Analyzer fleet was ordered to recapture the system of Eriston. On the way, by one of the hazards of war, the liner carrying the technicians was struck by a roving mine. A warship would have survived, but the liner with its irreplaceable cargo was totally destroyed. So the operation had to be abandoned.

The other expedition was, at first, more successful. There was no doubt at all that the Analyzer fulfilled its designers' claims, and the enemy was heavily defeated in the first engagements. He withdrew, leaving us in possession of Saphran, Leucon and Hexanerax. But his Intelligence Staff must have noted the change in our tactics and the inexplicable presence of a liner in the heart of our battlefleet. It must have noted, also, that our first fleet had been accompanied by a similar ship—and had withdrawn when it had been destroyed.

In the next engagement, the enemy used his superior numbers to launch an overwhelming attack on the Analyzer ship and its unarmed consort. The attack was made without regard to losses—both ships were, of course, very heavily protected—and it succeeded. The result was the virtual decapitation of the Fleet, since an effectual transfer to the old operational methods proved impossible. We disengaged under heavy fire, and so lost all our gains and also the systems of Lormyia, Ismarnus, Beronis, Alphanidon and Sideneus.

At this stage, Grand Admiral Taxaris expressed his disapproval of Norden by committing suicide, and I assumed supreme command.

The situation was now both serious and infuriating. With stubborn conservatism and complete lack of imagination, the enemy continued to advance with his old-fashioned and inefficient but now vastly more numerous ships. It was galling to realize that if we had only continued building, without seeking new weapons, we would have been in a far more advantageous position. There were many acrimonious conferences at which Norden defended the scientists while everyone else blamed them for all that had happened. The difficulty was that Norden had proved every one of his claims: he had a perfect excuse for all the disasters that had occurred. And we could not now turn back—the search for an irresistible weapon must go on. At first it had been a luxury that would shorten the war. Now it was a necessity if we were to end it victoriously.

We were on the defensive, and so was Norden. He was more than ever determined to re-establish his prestige and that of the Research Staff. But we had been twice disappointed, and would not make the same mistake again. No doubt Norden's twenty thousand scientists would produce many further weapons: we would remain unimpressed.

We were wrong. The final weapon was something so fantastic that even now it seems difficult to believe that it ever existed. Its innocent, noncommittal name—The Exponential Field—gave no hint of its real potentialities. Some of Norden's mathematicians had discovered it during a piece of entirely theoretical research into the properties of space, and to everyone's great surprise their results were found to be physically realizable.

It seems very difficult to explain the operation of the Field to the layman. According to the technical description, it "produces an exponential condition of space, so that a finite distance in normal, linear space may become infinite in pseudo-space." Norden gave an analogy which some of us found useful. It was as if one took a flat disk of rubber—representing a region of normal space—and then pulled its center out to infinity. The circumference of the disk would be unaltered—but its "diameter" would be infinite. That was the sort of thing the generator of the Field did to the space around it.

As an example, suppose that a ship carrying the generator was surrounded by a ring of hostile machines. If it switched on the Field, *each* of the enemy ships would think that it—and the ships on the far side of the circle—had suddenly receded into nothingness. Yet the circumference of the circle would be the same as before: only the journey to the center would be of infinite duration, for as one proceeded, distances would appear to become greater and greater as the "scale" of space altered.

It was a nightmare condition, but a very useful one. Nothing could reach a ship carrying the Field: it might be englobed by an enemy fleet yet would be as inaccessible as if it were at the other side of the Universe. Against this, of course, it could not fight back without switching off the Field, but this still left it at a very great advantage, not only in defense but in offense. For a ship fitted with the Field could approach an enemy fleet undetected and suddenly appear in its midst.

This time there seemed to be no flaws in the new weapon. Needless to say, we looked for all the possible objections before we committed ourselves again. Fortunately the equipment was fairly simple and did not require a large operating staff. After much debate, we decided to rush it into production, for we realized that time was running short and the war was going against us. We had now lost about the whole of our initial gains and enemy forces had made several raids into our own solar system.

We managed to hold off the enemy while the Fleet was reequipped and the new battle techniques were worked out. To use the field operationally it was necessary to locate an enemy formation, set a course that would intercept it, and then switch on the generator for the calculated period of time. On releasing the Field again—if the calculations had been accurate—one would be in the enemy's midst and could do great damage during the resulting confusion, retreating by the same route when necessary.

The first trial maneuvers proved satisfactory and the equipment seemed quite reliable. Numerous mock attacks were made and the crews became accustomed to the new technique. I was on one of the test flights and can vividly remember my impressions as the Field was switched on. The ships around us seemed to dwindle as if on the surface of an expanding bubble: in an instant they had vanished completely. So had the stars—but presently we could see that the Galaxy was still visible as a faint band of light around the ship. The virtual radius of our pseudo-space was not really infinite, but some hundred thousand light-years, and so the distance to the farthest stars of our system had not been greatly increased—though the nearest had of course totally disappeared.

These training maneuvers, however, had to be canceled before they were completed owing to a whole flock of minor technical troubles in various pieces of equipment, notably the communications circuits. These were annoying, but not important, though it was thought best to return to Base to clear them up.

At that moment the enemy made what was obviously intended to be a decisive attack against the fortress planet of Iton at the limits of our Solar System. The Fleet had to go into battle before repairs could be made.

The enemy must have believed that we had mastered the secret of invisibility—as in a sense we had. Our ships appeared suddenly out of nowhere and inflicted tremendous damage—for a while. And then something quite baffling and inexplicable happened.

I was in command of the flagship *Hircania* when the trouble started. We had been operating as independent units, each against assigned objectives. Our detectors observed an enemy formation at medium range and the navigating officers measured its distance with great accuracy. We set course and switched on the generator.

The Exponential Field was released at the moment when we should have been passing through the center of the enemy group. To our consternation, we emerged into normal space at a distance of many hundred miles—and when we found the enemy, he had already found us. We retreated, and tried again. This time we were so far away from the enemy that he located us first.

Obviously, something was seriously wrong. We broke communicator silence and tried to contact the other ships of the Fleet to see if they had experienced the same trouble. Once again we failed—and this time the failure was beyond all reason, for the communication equipment appeared to be working perfectly. We could only assume, fantastic though it seemed, that the rest of the Fleet had been destroyed.

I do not wish to describe the scenes when the scattered units of the Fleet struggled back to Base. Our casualties had actually been negligible, but the ships were completely demoralized. Almost all had lost touch with one another and had found that their ranging equipment showed inexplicable errors. It was obvious that the Exponential Field was the cause of the troubles, despite the fact that they were only apparent when it was switched off.

The explanation came too late to do us any good, and Norden's final discomfiture was small consolation for the virtual loss of the war. As I have explained, the Field generators produced a radial distortion of space, distances appearing greater and greater as one approached the center of the artificial pseudo-space. When the Field was switched off, conditions returned to normal.

But not quite. It was never possible to restore the initial state *exactly*. Switching the Field on and off was equivalent to an elongation and contraction of the ship carrying the generator, but there was a hysteretic effect, as it were, and the initial condition was never quite reproducible, owing to all the thousands of electrical changes and movements of mass aboard the ship while the Field was on. These asymmetries and distortions were cumulative, and though they seldom amounted to more than a fraction of one percent, that was quite enough. It meant that the precision ranging equipment and the tuned circuits in the communication apparatus were thrown completely out of adjustment. Any single ship could never detect the change—only when it compared its equipment with that of another vessel, or tried to communicate with it, could it tell what had happened.

It is impossible to describe the resultant chaos. Not a single component of one ship could be expected with certainty to work aboard another. The very nuts and bolts were no longer interchangeable, and the supply position became quite impossible. Given time, we might even have overcome these difficulties, but the enemy ships were already attacking in thousands with weapons which now seemed centuries behind those that we had invented. Our magnificent Fleet, crippled by our own science, fought on as best it could until it was overwhelmed and forced to surrender. The ships fitted with the Field were still invulnerable, but as fighting units they were almost helpless. Every time they switched on their generators to escape from enemy attack, the permanent distortion of their equipment increased. In a month, it was all over.

This is the true story of our defeat, which I give without prejudice to my defense before this Court. I make it, as I have said, to counteract the libels that have been circulating against the men who fought under me, and to show where the true blame for our misfortunes lay.

Finally, my request, which as the Court will now realize, I make in no frivolous manner and which I hope will therefore be granted.

The Court will be aware that the conditions under which we are housed and the constant surveillance to which we are subjected night and day are somewhat distressing. Yet I am not complaining of this: nor do I complain of the fact that shortage of accommodation has made it necessary to house us in pairs.

But I cannot be held responsible for my future actions if I am compelled any longer to share my cell with Professor Norden, late Chief of the Research Staff of my armed forces.

SINGLE COMBAT

The Curtain Rises:

Blue Rigel came vaulting over the high tops of the snow-capped mountains, dispelling the deep shadows in the cleft, and the Day of Tribute was at hand. Kala Brabant, six-foot-nine of coal-black skin stretched taut over stringy muscles and prominent bones, stood in the door of the king's cave and watched the people of the Saa'Hualla tribe beginning to stir.

Behind him he heard Ahmist, his Number One wife, kicking the three lesser wives out of their bed in the inner room. It was time to make Kala's breakfast, which he insisted be unduly well cooked, and afterward start preparing food for the numerous expected guests of the king.

Kala stepped outside, into the cold breeze blowing off the shoulder of the Home Mountain, and made a brisk tour of the guards at their stockade posts. The Caves of Kala sat within a large pocket in a sheer face of rock, impossible to approach from the back, and the previous chiefs had built and maintained a high wall across the entrance from the valley. This fortress had not been overrun within the memory of the Saa'Hualla.

A good base from which to conquer a planet, considering the job had to be done with spear and sword.

He met Grabo, the general of his army, as he approached his cave again, and exchanged good-mornings.

"Have any warriors in the tribes taken the oath to kill the king this tribute day, Grabo?" Kala asked after the formal pleasantries.

"None of which I have heard, O King."

"Good. We will need all our warriors for the coming campaign against the Willikazee. And I do not like this useless killing of my own folk. I am glad they realize I cannot be beaten."

"Mighty is the king," responded Grabo mechanically, and left to hunt his own breakfast.

Mighty is the king! thought Kala as he ate his thoroughly cooked meat. *Yes, mighty is the Earthman posing as a Saa'Hualla, mighty is the man who uses parapowers against primitive savages. Mighty is the Slaughterer of Warriors, the Killer of Great Men, the Maker of Widows. And how sick at the stomach he is of the whole bloody mess!*

But regrets were a luxury in which he could ill afford to indulge. There was, as always, too much to do.

He attended to some routine details connected with the day's festivities and then had his great chair pulled out of its corner in his cave and set up outside. He was barely ready when Birananga, one of his two living fathers-in-law, presented himself and two bearers loaded with gifts for his king and son-in-law. It was time to start the political dickering that would consume most of his day. Birananga was chief of a small people to the southeast, one of the few local tribes who had fallen under his authority without the use of force. To the west of both their kingdoms was the large and powerful tribe of the Sinnedocks, whose fat king had acknowledged the overlordship of Kala only after a bloody and terrible battle. He needed to bind a little tighter the bonds of fealty he held over the Sinnedocks, and according to the complicated kinship line he and their fat old king would become relatives if married to sisters. Birananga had a daughter, the apple of his aging eye, who had just reached mating age. If a marriage between her and the old king could be arranged, enabling him to say his "family" ruled this area of the world, it would greatly ease the chafe by acknowledging overlordship.

By the time he had half argued, half bullied his father-in-law into reluctant assentation the next chief was waiting to present the chafe of acknowledging overlordship.

For the rest of the morning he worked hard at consolidating his already large empire, pitting his tremendous knowledge and keen mind against their native shrewdness and stubborn greed. Like any other overlord he held power primarily through the strength of his sword, but high-pressure politics, to which these primitives were unaccustomed, saved many hours of battle and many gallons of blood.

Blood. The thought of the number of men he had killed personally, and countless others killed in battles he had started, came home again for the hundredth time, with its usual sickening force. He felt physically ill where he sat, and for a moment was afraid he would lose his breakfast, in front of all those assembled guests. He took control of his sympathetic nervous system for a moment, forced down his rising gorge, and calmed himself physically. For mental relief he used a trick he had employed often in this three years on this planet, divorced himself from the scene around him and imagined that he was flying upward into the blue sky, rising far enough into space to permit him to see the faint light of old Sol twinkling in the heavens eleven hundred light-years away. But this relief, too, failed, for the thought came that it was less than half that distance in the opposite direction to the home world of the enemy, the Flish.

Memory One:

Professor Kala Brabant, head of the classical poetry department at Ruanda University, turned his back on the recruiter from United Government and walked to the window, stood staring out at the blue water of Lake Tanganyika. His small grandchildren were playing in the water near the edge, their ebony skins glittering with droplets jeweled by sunlight. The quiet hum of expensive appliances told him that Temi was in her new control room, preparing dinner for himself and the grandchildren they were babysitting. This was home, this sprawling white house on the shores of the Long Lake, and his mountain cabin just below the snowline, a half-hour's ride by aircar, provided a place of refuge from all wordly cares. There he had his books, his tapes, the huge collection of unviewed films he had just purchased from the estate of a dead friend; there awaited serenity and contentment.

The short, stout little Oriental waited patiently. He possessed degrees as imposing as Kala's, and most of them dealt with understanding and handling people. U.G. used only the best for recruiters, and he was the best of the best.

Kala turned from the window, wringing his hands in deep agitation. "But why me?" he echoed the immemorial cry of man. "I'm a teacher, a philosopher and poet, not a spy. How could I possibly help you? And if I could, why should I?"

Instead of answering, the smaller man dug a relaxer out of his pocket, flicked off the cover, and inserted it in a nostril. He breathed deeply for a moment, then cleared his throat and said, "Why you? That's an easy one, Professor. You are the only man we have found who is fully qualified for the job. Nowhere among the forty billion Earthmen here and on the other twenty-nine planets we have colonized is there a Negro tall enough and slim enough for the necessary reconversion, who is also a psionic adept and possesses the necessary high intelligence. That is why I must—why I *shall*—convince you to accept the assignment."

"I am not even convinced of the need."

"Professor Brabant, most of the facts are known to you, but perhaps it is necessary to see them in their proper relation to each other. First, we now live to be two hundred Eryears, on the average, and recent advances promise still longer lives in the future. Despite this, the drive in man to procreate has not weakened, and every family wants children. They are one of the subjective building blocks on which a happy life is based. With a new generation every thirty years this means our population doubles approximately every eighty-five years, and *Lebensraum* is the single greatest need of the human race. The only possible place that room may be secured is by colonization of other planets, which the phase-shifted makes practicable. With thirty planets under our control we have, at the moment, plenty of room. But, sir, U.G. does not plan for today, or tomorrow, or a hundred years from now. If the human race learned one single lesson from communism, it was that the future must be planned a thousand years in advance. This we have done, and you, Professor, are an important part of that plan."

"But what you ask is ridiculous! To become a fighter at my age, a warrior king among primitive savages! The entire idea is repulsive in the extreme."

"That may be true, but it is vital and necessary. We are committed, by agreements with the other intelligent life-forms too strong to be broken, never to colonize a world which contains an intelligent race below Grade Three civilization. There are nine such worlds now known, and we are seeking to lift their level to Three, and at the same time orient them toward Earth. All, of course, in strict secrecy. One day they shall choose their neighbors, and it must be ourselves.

"The Flish know this even better than we, and are far ahead of us in advance planning. Slowly but surely they are winning over uncommitted worlds, developing primitive societies into capable cultures oriented in *their* direction. They do not own a single warship, have never invaded by force a single world. Yet they are conquering the galaxy, world by world and star by star. And they must be stopped! Or ten thousand years from now Earth will stand alone, and the long twilight of the dignity of the individual will be upon us."

"I've heard of the Flish, of course. Everyone has. But aren't they fully human, so much so it's even speculated Earth and Flish unions might be fertile? What is so dreadful about them?"

"Just this, Professor; the word 'Flish' is either singular or plural and the Flish are both. They live a mutual mental symbiosis with each other that our brains, though we are their equal in parapowers, cannot duplicate. Their lives as individuals are secondary to the group life and the group mind, and such is their power the mental matrix they extend will cover an entire planet. Communism sought to accomplish the same object in the physical world, and we rejected the attempt. Individual freedom of choice, within an ordered society, is our heritage. If we wish to preserve it—to prove that individuals voluntarily working together can accomplish as much as a hiveworker—then we must fight the Flish."

The last small tribal chief finally presented his gifts and reswore his allegiance as the women were stacking heaped platters of food on the great tables his steward had caused to be erected in front of the caves. It was time for the noon meal. Afterward the games, and then the bloody climax of the day, when by tribal law too long standing and powerful for even he, who had changed so much, to oppose, any warrior of any subject tribe could challenge the king to a duel by combat, and assume his crown if he won.

Kala ate sparingly of the plentiful food, it being almost too raw for his digestion, and passed the time talking animatedly with his guests, those same lesser kings who had that morning sworn an obedience enforceable only by might and power.

Grabo appeared at the side of the table and caught his eye. With an almost imperceptible motion of his head he indicated the king's cave, and Kala muttered to his vassals that he would be back and rose and went into the shadowed interior. It was deserted at the moment, his wives working outside. In the house of the king there were no children.

Grabo appeared a moment later, his long form looming large in the shadows. "O King, it has come to my ears there may be a challenger after all. There is a young warrior in the tribe of Nil'Abola who has won much fame in combat during the past year, and some of his friends say he is anxious to try the greatest game of all. It is said he is a cunning man, though very young, and they expect him to hold back if there are other challengers, permitting you to tire yourself on them. It would be well to be wary of him."

"Say you he has won all his fame as a warrior within the past year?"

"It is so, O King. A very young man indeed, but still, one who has not lost a fight. He would be chief of the Nil'Abola now, save that he chose instead to fight you and perhaps gain a kingdom."

Kala glanced sharply at Grabo, but the shorter man was looking out of the cave into the sunlight. Could Grabo, who had seen him down the greatest of Saa'Hualla warriors with ease, be losing faith in him? Well, it little mattered what this primitive general thought. Kala was invincible, and knew it, and not all the people gathered outside could take him unless they were very lucky indeed.

Kala's hand rose and clutched the great power crystal at his throat as he turned away and strode toward the door. In the sleeve of his hide jacket were two smaller penetration crystals, and in the belt at his waist were a series of six of the glittering bits of glass, two blue amplifiers, two red clarivoys, and two colorless pulsers. The latter he had never used, for they brought madness instead of death. Most of his many kills had been made with the help of the two distorters in the hilt of his curved sword, though his brain could immobilize a nonpsionic opponent without aid. The distorters, controlled by his mind, powered by the white crystal, and amplified by the blue ones in his belt, could burst a thousand bloodvessels in a man's brain in a few microseconds. He had plunged the curving sword into the heart of many a man dead before he could fall, in order to fool the watchers, but had yet actually to kill a man with it.

Kala Brabant paused in the door a few seconds before stepping out. In earthly measurements that door was over seven feet high, and there was only just adequate room for him to pass erect. Still, he was a little shorter than the average Saa'Hualla, who stood a full seven feet tall.

Memory Two:

He stood naked before the full-length mirror in his hospital room, staring at the dazed disbelief in his own face. The final operation of the series had just been completed, the relatively minor one of killing all hair cells on his body, and he would soon be leaving. This was the first time the doctors had let him see himself.

Knowing verbally what they were doing was no panacea for the shock of seeing the reality of the transformation. They had broken both his femurs and inserted three-inch sections of artificial bone, and later performed the same operation on the humerus bones. The attaching muscles had been extended until they were long threads of hard fiber clinging close to the mutilated bones they served. They had starved him down to tendon and ligament thinness, added pigment to his skin until he was black as coal itself, changed the shape of his eyes, and colored his teeth. Still, these were minor changes and could be reversed when his five-year tour of duty was over. No one could give him back the two fingers they had cut off, or the two toes. The fourth metacarpals and fifth metacarpals had been removed completely, and the adjoining carpals and calcaneum bones trimmed to match the slimmer appearance of the Saa'Hualla. Bald-headed, thin-limbed, four-fingered, and four-toed, he had emerged from the last operation a Saa'Hualla in all but name and background. And the name was so similar that he was using his given name here!

His curse was that he was one of the few people on Earth who closely enough resembled the Saa'Hualla to make finishing surgery possible. He had been proud of his Batutsi heritage, proud of his height, proud of the color of his skin, which he had considered black until he saw his first movies of the Saa'Hualla. His Hamitic ancestory had given him the lean facial structure, thin lips, and high cheekbones common to these primitives, and the accursed doctors had done the rest. And now his wife waited alone in the house in Usumbura, grandchildren he had never seen swam in the blue waters of Lake Tanganyika, and his little cabin below the snowline stood empty and silent.

He straightened his shoulders and moved forward, aware that Grabo might misinterpret his hesitation as cowardice. Well, he would be right. They could not have picked a worse coward than Kala Brabant, and he had tried to tell them this, but they had laughed at his protestations, those high men of the United Government, laughed and clapped him on the back and sent him in to the psychologists, who confirmed every word he had said. And still it hadn't mattered. With the amplifying crystals and what they taught him of control he had become an impossible opponent to anyone not equally equipped. So far there had been no call for bravery—only butchery—but if it ever came he was sorely afraid it would find him lacking.

He resumed his place at the table and dawdled with his food a little longer, and then the feast was blessedly over and it was time for the games.

As he was leading his kingly guests toward the hides which had been spread on the ground in a choice location Kala sensed another presence at his back and half turned his head. Ahmist was striding along just behind him. Without moving her thin lips, and with her voice pitched just loud enough to reach his sensitive ears, she said, "The one who will challenge you is named Listra, and I have arranged with Grabo that he will be challenged to a game of whips, and in such a manner that he may not refuse."

Kala felt a smile twitch at his lips, but did not look back, and after a moment more Ahmist took another direction. He had known that she loved him, in her own primitive way, but this was the first time she had actively interfered in his affairs. He wondered how Temi, his wife of a quarter century waiting alone in Usumbura, would have reacted under like circumstances.

Kala and his guests made themselves comfortable on the hides and the games began. The usual contests in running, jumping, spear-casting, and swordplay were held, with rich prizes for the winning warriors. Kala found himself repressing a smile when his prize corps of bowmen gave an exhibition of fancy shooting, and his guest stared with amazement and dismay. The bow and arrow was a relatively new weapon and had been given scant attention in the arts of war. It would receive more in the future.

There was a commotion to the left of the seated royalty and voices raised in anger. A moment later two figures strode through the seated spectators and approached the royal seat. At the head, looking very angry, Kala recognized O'Sirinaga, one of his best warriors, a man well over seven feet tall and a little heavier and stronger than most Saa'Hualla. The man trailing him was much smaller, shorter even than Kala, and walked with an insolent, shoulder-swinging swagger very unusual among these long-striding people. He was unusually thick-lipped, and his face was a good deal more full than customary. In fact, to be a member of a race made primarily of skin, bone, and ligament, he was almost fat.

O'Sirinaga knelt before him and presented his case in swift, angry phrases. He had been insulted by this pretended warrior from the Nil'Abola and demanded satisfaction. Since dueling between warriors was forbidden on this day he requested the games to be halted long enough to enable him to avenge the insult by laying a few whipmarks across the back of this young imitation of a fighter.

Listra listened to the insults with almost bored inattention, and when questioned by Kala as to whether or not the charge was true he shrugged his well-fleshed shoulders with careless disdain. "If you deny him the opportunity to obtain a few more scars, O King, some other fool will take his place. I have not insulted his ancestors, but since he wishes to fight I would not dream of denying him the privelege. Let us have no more talk."

"Bring the whips," said Kala to a court attendant, and a short moment later they were laid in his hands. He checked them carefully, then presented one to each man, and clapped his hands to indicate the fight might begin.

O'Sirinaga backed away until he was just out of range, cracked his bone-tipped whip in the air a few times, then laid it on the ground behind him and advanced on the smaller man, who had not moved since he walked into the cleared area. He was holding his whip carelessly in front of him, his large eyes fixed on his opponent, not in a position to strike the larger man without first throwing the long whip behind him.

O'Sirinaga struck, the long braided thong whipping through the air so fast the tip was invisible, the bone barb aimed for the eye of the smaller man. But it struck empty air. In a motion so fast the eyes were unable to follow him, the smaller man leaped forward, driving ahead like a springing animal, and his whip was suddenly reversed, the cutting body trailing the ground behind him, the heavy butt gripped like a club in his hand. Before O'Sirinaga could draw in his whip for another stroke, before he could take more than a single step backward, the Nil'Abola warrior was upon him, and the heavy butt crashed down on his head. The big warrior went down and out, knocked unconscious in the first thirty seconds of the fight.

The constant background chatter of the spectators, the cries of the children and the gossiping of women were suddenly halted, and a vast and oppressive silence hung over the assembled people. It was broken by a sharp crack and the sodden sound of leather biting into flesh. Twice more Listra raised his whip and laid long deep cuts across the back of the unconscious man, and then the small warrior tossed the whip across the bleeding body and walked insolently away.

There were cries of outrage from the people of Saa'Hualla, and several of the men leaped to their feet, ready to continue the duel. Kala motioned them down. It scarcely mattered. In a few more hours the young warrior would be dead anyway.

But it was true he was going to regret killing this young man a great deal less than many others he had dispatched to their ancestors.

The rest of the primitive physical games ran their courses. When the last down warrior was carried off he felt satisfied with the day's work. His conquer-with-force-and-rule-with-law tactics were working well, as they had worked in that great empire built by the swords of Rome so long ago. He had a close-knit group of subchiefs, each of whom willingly subordinated his personal interests to the interests of the people as a whole. And each seemed reasonably content to run his own small area, without aspiring too highly to the post held by Kala.

All too soon the field was clear and the people were beginning to straggle back toward the caves, where the huge cooking pots were filled and waiting. The appointed time had come, and old Nakabawa, the high priest, rose to perform his duty, his wrinkled, ancient face turned toward the lowering sun. He droned the words of the ancient ritual in a hasty and careless voice, obviously unaware that a potential challenger lurked among the Nil'Abola. When he finished and Listra stepped forward, drawing his sword, there was a concerted gasp from the audience and those walking toward the cooking pots hurriedly returned to their seats. The day's entertainment was not over. Kala, The Great King, had still another man to kill.

Listra spoke his challenge, sword in hand, and Kala drew his blade and responded in kind. The formalities for this particular event were simple and soon over. The rules of combat were known to everyone, down to the small children. There remained only the killing to be done, and the event was over for another year.

The Sun is Setting:

Kala walked forward to the edge of the barren ground, a man no longer young, a man to whom the thrill of combat was a stomach-turning experience fit for only the immature. As he reached the last of the grass something flickered by his foot and he glanced downward in time to see a tiny burrowing animal disappear into its hole. The poor creature must have been caught away from its home when the first of the huge crowd had appeared, and had been hiding among the grassblades in fear and trembling ever since.

There was a small stinging sensation on his right ankle, just above his hide shoe, but he ignored the urge to scratch and kept walking. Getting accustomed to insects had been one of his more agonizing adjustments. They were very bad during the warm weather.

For the first time he raised his lowered head and stared his foe in the face. Listra was leaning comfortably on his sword, watching him come, and on the younger man's face was a small smile of satisfaction. He seemed very relaxed and sure of himself for a young and relatively inexperienced warrior going up against the most formidable adversary who had ever appeared among the Saa'Hualla. A very good man, undoubtedly, one whom it would have been worthwhile to save. Too bad it couldn't be.

Nakabawa stepped backward from between the two men and droned a few more words of ritual. At the conclusion he retreated until he was out of the danger area and sat down to watch the fight. The contestants were free to begin at any time.

Kala heaved a mental sigh, raised his sword, saluted the setting sun, and lunged toward his young opponent, the deadly blade glinting in the slanting rays of light, the two jewels in its hilt flashing their own separate color of emerald green. He also activated the crystal at his throat and sent a surge of power into the belt amplifiers, and from there to the distorters in the hilt. The invisible beam leaped ahead of the sword, guided in its general direction by the blade but controlled by the mind of the man behind it. The disruptive force, capable of penetrating a man's skull without visible sign and turning the brain cells into a bloody jelly, crossed the space between man and sword in less than a microsecond. . . . and was met and stopped by an impenetrable barrier of counterforce.

Kala was already leaning forward, stretching out his arm in the long stroke that would sink the sword into the heart of the erect corpse. In those agonizing milliseconds before he could stop the thrusting blade, while his eyes saw the sword of Listra coming easily upward to parry the fast thrust, realization came.

It was obvious, so very obvious. How stupid he had been, and how wrong. *How conceited, little Superman, how complacent, tall fool! And are you lost, idiot Earthman?* Kala shifted the blunted power of his first thrust, dropped the distorters, sent the full power of his amplified mind into the cerebral centers of his own brain, and jumped his time-sense to its highest possible range.

He looked out of his own eyes and saw the sword in his extended hand not yet reaching the apex of its thrust, saw the hard small muscles in his bony arm in the slow act of tensing to stop the forward movement, and then abandoned his eyes entirely and used only the parasenses. He needed the use of null-time in order to sort his sudden new understanding of the situation, and analyze his own part in it.

The first and most obvious fact his lazy senses had not revealed was that Listra was no more a Saa'Hualla than himself. And the second and equally obvious, which had been beating unheeded on his sensibilities since he first laid eyes on the swaggering young warrior, was that Listra was not a man. Kala was dueling to the death with a woman!

I hated and regretted the physiological changes necessary to change me into a Saa'Hualla. How much more so must it have hurt a young and undoubtedly pretty girl! Good-bye to that great artifice of feminine beauty, the hair, kiss farewell the soft bloody flesh of severed breasts with long strands of milk gland ducts dangling beneath, cry long over buttocks stretched and slimmed to thin covers of long hard muscle, bid good-bye to womanhood! And if he knew the Flish surgeons they had not stopped there. Underneath those hide trousers would be plastic male sex organs, undetectable from the real except by function. The only feminine attribute remaining was one which even they would have had a hard time concealing, the width of pelvic bones. And this they had hidden by that braggadacio swagger, the exaggerated movement which served to draw the observer's attention to the shoulders.

And why go to so much trouble, when a man would have been far easier to convert? Why the extra work, time, trouble, expense? That, too, was fairly obvious in the person of Listra. Nowhere on her hands was there an ornament, from her neck hung no necklace, in her sword was no glitter of glass. She was a natural psionic, one of those rare individuals so gifted that crystals could not amplify or aid her. She did not need the massed power of the hive-mind, could be sent alone to an alien world, could fight strange humans, pitiful creatures who had never known the oneness of a billion selves, and conquer them without the supporting comfort of an infinity of minds linked tightly to her own. She was also death, death attired in a long thin suit of flesh, death for Kala Brabant, puny Earthman.

And that death was already in his blood.

With my great power crystal to amplify my weak mind, with laminated layers of silicone doted by the impurities which focus and condense, with those artificial aids of man which bring me up out of nothingness I too am a mighty power of destruction, I too draw upon that power which is above force and twist it to my will, I too am a god. But I am a stupid man above all things, and only an idiot like myself would have ignored that scramble of tiny claws, the small life scuttling to its newly dug hole, the flealike carrier who abandoned the bounding body and leaped, compelled by a will beyond his understanding, toward a man's ankle, and landed and clung and bit and chewed until he penetrated the tough black skin and ejected from their snug home within its tiny jaws the swarm of alien life which now pulsed and throbbed and grew within the stinging wound.

A Trip Inside, While Time Passes:

Kala used a few milliseconds to refocus his attention on the optic nerve and glanced at the current timescene. His sword was within a few inches of Listra's and there appeared to be no danger of a counterthrust before he could assume full body control.

He moved his center of consciousness out of the brain and into the bloodstream, streaking along the tubular passageways with the swiftness of thought itself. An instant later his consciousness was at the scene of combat. The battle had been raging for several minutes and his soldiers were fighting valiantly but steadily giving ground, the entire affair having been overlooked by his higher consciousness until this moment. That tiny insect had released a flood of unicellular protozoa into the capillaries nearest the dermis, flagellate infusorians which he recognized at once as being closely akin to the dreaded *Trypanosoma rhodesiense* of his own African highlands. But these voracious strangers ate, grew, and reproduced with a speed no earthly life could possibly match. They were disposing of red blood cells at a prodigious rate, and his hard-fighting guard of granular leucocytes were unable to stop them escaping into the surrounding tissues and finding unguarded bloodvessels, from where they were swiftly making their way throughout his body. True, the macrophages in the liver and lymph nodes would get many of them, but those which got through and continued their meal of red cells were going to cause him a serious problem in the near future.

His automatic control system had already started routing more leucocytes to the infected area, but he assumed control of the situation long enough to start every valiant warrior in the nearest pint of blood toward the danger scene. It was going to be necessary virtually to block off this area from circulation, since it was obvious the invaders ate and reproduced four times as fast as a leucocyte could encompass and neutralize a single enemy, and the only way to do it was with their stacked white bodies.

Fast though they moved in response to his direct will it was going to be several full seconds before enough leucocytes arrived to start the blocking action, and he could not wait. Regretfully, he detached a small portion of his consciousness and left it at the scene to direct operations, then returned his primary attention to the mental battle he had started.

A Trip Outside, Outside Time:

He felt the beginning of the wave as his sword touched Listra's, the mighty battering power of a mind perhaps unique in the galaxy, certainly the most powerful of which he had ever heard. She was hurling the full power of her distorting force at his cerebellum; if he couldn't block it the fight was over. If he could, she had a measure of his amplified strength.

Kala marshaled all his forces, disregarding all other crystals and concentrating through the white power source on his neck to build a wall against the force of her thrust. For the few microseconds it lasted it was close, but fortunately for him it took less power to defend than to attack, and after that instant of vain effort she withdrew, leaving only a small portion of her power still beating constantly at his defenses. But even that small thrust was enough that he had to leave another portion of his consciousness, and a little of his strength, to defend against her.

Kala Brabant considered the use of his pulsers, the givers of madness. They amplified and transmitted on specific wavelengths and in frequencies so high as to be almost beyond count, and they shattered the currents flowing in the delicate neural network of the brain, those currents which were human consciousness. He hesitated now, knowing that it was impossible for a natural psionic, working without crystals, to transmit in pulses. And somewhere in the lower levels of his mind a voice screamed. *That's a woman out there Under that stygian skin hiding behind the smooth expanse of breastless chest is the heart of a woman Maybe she has kids at home maybe a husband maybe a lover who waits and gazes sighing at blue moons on darkened worlds Maybe Another Time Another Place we could be friends. . . . Lovers. . . .*

But then he remembered she was a Flish, in mental communion with every other Flish agent on the planet. He had been thinking of her in earthly terms, and they did not apply. An ant among ants is an ant.

Kala activated the pulsers, sent the beam at her brain.

Forgive me Temi Ahmist lesser wives forgive the killing of a woman!

The swords had met, parted with a clash of steel and spark of fire, and his arm was drawing back to hew the second blow that would put the mindless woman out of her lack of consciousness of misery *she blocked the pulsers!*

He felt the opposing wall as solid, almost tangible in its sense of presence, and the pulsating thrusts should have penetrated and disrupted, sliding through in those almost infinitely small moments of time when her longer wavelength was out of tune with his own. But they didn't. Her defense was so powerful it absorbed each individual pulsation, letting it penetrate a short distance before it was neutralized and destroyed.

The Battle Rages on All Fronts:

She had parried his stroke and was aiming one of her own. He knew that she, too, was concentrating most of her forces in the mental battles, since their hyper-time parapowers allowed them to move and countermove a hundred times while even the fastest swordsman struck once, but still, if either forgot the sharp-edged tools of death long enough to let one penetrate, on that instant the battle was lost.

He began to move his sword to the position which would catch her stroke, satisfied himself that it was too late for her to change without giving him an opening that would be fatal, and, keeping his guard up against her next probe, moved half his conscious mind to the fleabite on his ankle. A few of the reinforcements he had summoned were beginning to straggle in, but most were still seconds away and the battle was rapidly being lost. More and more of the invading protozoa, long tails lashing, were breaking through the leucocytes and escaping into the central bloodstream, eating red cells by the millions wherever they swam. Unless he finished the other two battles soon and concentrated his forces on these hungry invaders he was a dead man.

Still, he had minutes here. Outside he had only seconds or less.

He brought nine tenths of his awareness back to the exchange of arrows taking place in the ether and discovered that he was conscious of *Darkness, Vastness, Infinity. . . . Lost Suns, Darkening Nebula, Dying Light. . . . A Universe Marcescent, Quiescent, Exanimate. . . .* SIZE. *. . . Insignificant, Meaningless, Man. . . .*

He drew away from the contagion of depression, wondering what had happened to his defense, called upon it, threw it up full strength, and discovered what even the best parapowers on Earth had not been able to tell him. Thought alone, without force or hint of force, was very hard to block. He was still conscious of her depressing projections, still aware of *Darkness. . . .* He drew as much consciousness away from the sensation as he could spare, wondering why she was willing to project harmless thought at all, and discovered that his guard had become lax, her sword was sliding over his own and toward his lower abdomen. He twisted his lean hip aside a fraction of a second too late and received a shallow gash on one buttock, and received as well the reason she projected harmless thought.

But two could play at that game. He weakened his defense a little and put part of his power into a counterattack, hurling at her hairless head a barrage of disconnected fragments of poetry, song, and nonsense, enough to throw her non-Earth-oriented mind off balance if she should try to understand *Hold that! Hold that! Hold that line! . . . She walks in beauty. . . . Go, Tiger! . . . Cloudless climes . . . Edina! Scotia's Darling seat! All Hail! . . . When you were a tadpole and I was a fish. . . . O a'ye hymeneal powers! . . . Side by side in the oozing tide. . . . Three-score-fyfteen, a bloomin' bride, This night with seventy-four is ty'd. . . . Sae sed, Sae dune; Ye standers hearde. . . .*

He hurled Byron, Burns, and Carroll at her strong barrier and knew he was getting through when her next stroke faltered. He rejoiced that he had at last found a weapon which worked against her and ignored the clamoring darkness in his mind, sending her music notes, dead love songs, English poetry, all the dregs of a mind educated on every culture but his own. And he turned his weakness against her by sending images of *sex loveliness womanhood babies happiness joy.*

She hit back with *Blackness Lightlessness Nothingness, Quintessence of. . . . Vastness Openness. . . .* SPACE! *. . . Arbourg, Arbeg, Arb, Ar. . . . Sound Symbol Sign Death! Death! . . . Blood Flow Life Go Deep Woe. . . .* But he absorbed without trying to understand, absorbed and sank and buried the alien concepts.

The Stroke Is Given, Death Hovers O'er:

Her next stroke was almost feeble. He brought his brain back to normal time, for better coordination between body and mind, and put most of his faculties into the physical duel. He easily parried the weak thrust, leaped to one side, hit the edge of her sword with his free hand and forced it downward a few inches while he brought his own swinging toward her from the side. On an impulse he could neither define nor explain Kala changed his mind at the last instant and turned the blade so that the flat side smacked into her hip. He continued his motion to the side and at the same time hurled himself forward, anticipating her backward leap, and brought the sword toward her head, flat side forward, for a knockout blow.

It was impossible for her to parry, but she ducked very swiftly and the flat side whistled over her head. And then he was suddenly breathless, out of position, unable to move backward or stop his stroke in time to parry, and knew he had lingered too long outside. The enemy in his blood had done its work and his muscles were weak from oxygen star-vation. He was slowly dying where he stood.

He saw the bright blade flashing toward him, the elongated face smil-ing now in the moment of death, suddenly all female, not a trace of maleness in its soft shadows and fleshy planes, and he wondered, as the sharp point entered his thin chest and pushed toward his heart, how all the gathered savages could fail to see he was being killed by a woman.

The Final Scene:

Grabo stared at the gush of blood from the punctured heart, running up the sword to the hilt, stared as the body of Kala Brabant hit the ground, dead before he fell, stared at the suddenly stricken look on the face of the intelligent and sensitive young woman who had just committed the deed and thought *Fool of a soft intellectual, idiot of a higher education, great man and benefactor of humanity, how still you lie! If only I could have told you, shared your triumphs, despairs, plans, sorrows! If only this unworthy shadow of your greatness could have died for you. . . .*

Nakabawa stepped forward, to do his sad duty and present the new king with the sword of the fallen man, as custom of centuries dictated. He picked it up, gazed at the unbloodied surface with a face as expres-sionless as the wrinkled parchment it resembled, shifted the blade to his hand and held it hilt-foremost to the victor, who had regained her com-posure and accepted it in stony silence.

Nakabawa turned, casting an expressionless glance at the sun, still visible as a rim of light above the distant mountaintops, and started to turn away. And Grabo the backup man moved forward, drawing his sword from its scabbard, the blade glinting in the dying light.

"I challenge the king to combat!"

The Curtain Closes.

FRANK HERBERT

COMMITTEE OF THE WHOLE

1   **W**ith an increasing sense of unease, Alan Wallace studied his client as they neared the public hearing room on the second floor of the Old Senate Office Building. The guy was too relaxed.

"Bill, I'm worried about this," Wallace said. "You could damn well lose your grazing rights here in this room today."

They were almost into the gantlet of guards, reporters and TV cameramen before Wallace got his answer.

"Who the hell cares?" Custer asked.

Wallace, who prided himself on being the Washington-type lawyer—above contamination by complaints and briefs, immune to all shock—found himself tongue-tied with surprise.

They were into the ruck then and Wallace had to pull on his bold face, smiling at the press, trying to soften the sharpness of that necessary phrase:

"No comment. Sorry."

"See us after the hearing if you have any questions, gentlemen," Custer said.

The man's voice was level and confident.

He has himself over-controlled, Wallace thought. Maybe he was just joking. . . . a graveyard joke.

The marble-walled hearing room blazed with lights. Camera platforms had been raised above the seats at the rear. Some of the smaller UHF stations had their cameramen standing on the window ledges.

The subdued hubbub of the place eased slightly, Wallace noted, then picked up tempo as William R. Custer—"The Baron of Oregon" they called him—entered with his attorney, passed the press tables and crossed to the seats reserved for them in the witness section.

Ahead and to their right, that one empty chair at the long table stood waiting with its aura of complete exposure.

"Who the hell cares?"

That wasn't a Custer-type joke, Wallace reminded himself. For all his cattle-baron pose, Custer held a doctorate in agriculture and degrees in philosophy, math, and electronics. His western neighbors called him "The Brain."

It was no accident that the cattlemen had chosen him to represent them here.

Wallace glanced covertly at the man, studying him. The cowboy boots and string tie added to a neat dark business suit would have been affectation on most men. They merely accented Custer's good looks—the sunburned, windblown outdoorsman. He was a little darker of hair and skin than his father had been, still light enough to be called blond, but not as ruddy and without the late father's drink-tumescent veins.

But then young Custer wasn't quite thirty.

Custer turned, met the attorney's eyes. He smiled.

"Those were good patent attorneys you recommended, Al," Custer said. He lifted his briefcase to his lap, patted it. "No mincing around or mealy-mouthed excuses. Already got this thing on the way." Again he tapped the briefcase.

He brought that damn light gadget here with him? Wallace wondered. Why? He glanced at the briefcase. Didn't know it was that small . . . but maybe he's just talking about the plans for it.

"Let's keep our minds on this hearing," Wallace whispered. "This is the only thing that's important."

Into a sudden lull in the room's high noise level, the voice of someone in the press section carried across them: "greatest political show on earth."

"I brought this as an exhibit," Custer said. Again, he tapped the briefcase. It did bulge oddly.

Exhibit? Wallace asked himself.

It was the second time in ten minutes that Custer had shocked him. This was to be a hearing of a subcommittee of the Senate Interior and Insular Affairs Committee. The issue was Taylor grazing lands. What the devil could that . . . gadget have to do with the battle of words and laws to be fought here?

"You're supposed to talk over all strategy with your attorney," Wallace whispered. "What the devil do you. . . ."

He broke off as the room fell suddenly silent.

Wallace looked up to see the subcommittee chairman, Senator Haycourt Tiborough, stride through the wide double doors followed by his coterie of investigators and attorneys. The Senator was a tall man who had once been fat. He had dieted with such savage abruptness that his skin had never recovered. His jowls and the flesh on the back of his hands sagged. The top of his head was shiny bald and ringed by a three-quarter tonsure that had purposely been allowed to grow long and straggly so that it fanned back over his ears.

The Senator was followed in close lock step by syndicated columnist Anthony Poxman, who was speaking fiercely into Tiborough's left ear. TV cameras tracked the pair.

If Poxman's covering this one himself instead of sending a flunky, it's going to be bad, Wallace told himself.

Tiborough took his chair at the center of the committee table facing them, glanced left and right to assure himself the other members were present.

Senator Spealance was absent, Wallace noted, but he had party organization difficulties at home and the Senior Senator from Oregon was, significantly, not present. Illness, it was reported.

A sudden attack of caution, that common Washington malady, no doubt. He knew where his campaign money came from . . . but he also knew where the votes were.

They had a quorum, though.

Tiborough cleared his throat, said: "The committee will please come to order."

The Senator's voice and manner gave Wallace a cold chill. We were nuts trying to fight this one in the open, he thought. Why'd I let Custer and his friends talk me into this? You can't butt heads with a United States Senator who's out to get you. The only way's to fight him on the inside.

And now Custer suddenly turning screwball.

Exhibit!

"Gentlemen," said Tiborough, "I think we can . . . that is, today we can dispense with preliminaries . . . unless my colleagues . . . if any of them have objections."

Again, he glanced at the other senators—five of them. Wallace swept his gaze down the line behind that table—Plowers of Nebraska (a horse trader), Johnstone of Ohio (a parliamentarian—devious), Lane of South Carolina (a Republican in Democrat disguise), Emery of Minnesota (new and eager—dangerous because he lacked the old inhibitions) and Meltzer of New York (poker player, fine old family with traditions).

None of them had objections.

They've had a private meeting—both sides of the aisle—and talked over a smooth streamroller procedure, Wallace thought.

It was another ominous sign.

"This is a subcommittee of the United States Senate Committee on Interior and Insular Affairs," Tiborough said, his tone formal. "We are charged with obtaining expert opinion on proposed amendments to the Taylor Grazing Act of 1934. Today's hearing will begin with testimony and . . . ah, questioning of a man whose family has been in the business of raising beef cattle in Oregon for three generations."

Tiborough smiled at the TV cameras.

The son-of-a-bitch is playing to the galleries, Wallace thought. He glanced at Custer. The cattleman sat relaxed against the back of his chair, eyes half lidded, staring at the Senator.

"We call as our first witness today Mr. William R. Custer of Bend, Oregon," Tiborough said. "Will the clerk please swear in Mr. Custer."

Custer moved forward to the "hot seat," placed his briefcase on the table. Wallace pulled a chair up beside his client, noted how the cameras turned as the clerk stepped forward, put the Bible on the table and administered the oath.

Tiborough ruffled through some papers in front of him, waiting for full attention to return to him, said: "This subcommittee . . . we have before us a bill, this is a United States Senate Bill entitled SB-1024 of the current session, an act amending the Taylor Grazing Act of 1934 and, the intent is, as many have noted, that we would broaden the base of the advisory committees to the Act and include a wider public representation."

Custer was fiddling with the clasp of his briefcase.

How the hell could that light gadget be an exhibit here? Wallace asked himself. He glanced at the set of Custer's jaw, noted the nervous working of a muscle. It was the first sign of unease he'd seen in Custer. The sight failed to settle Wallace's own nerves.

"Ah, Mr. Custer," Tiborough said. "Do you—did you bring a preliminary statement? Your counsel. . . ."

"I have a statement," Custer said. His big voice rumbled through the room, requiring instant attention and the shift of cameras that had been holding tardily on Tiborough, expecting an addition to the question.

Tiborough smiled, waited, then: "Your attorney—is your statement the one your counsel supplied the committee?"

"With some slight additions of my own," Custer said.

Wallace felt a sudden qualm. They were too willing to accept Custer's statement. He leaned close to his client's ear, whispered: "They know what your stand is. Skip the preliminaries."

Custer ignored him, said: "I intend to speak plainly and simply. I oppose the amendment. Broaden the base and wider public representation are phases of the amendment. Broaden the base and wider public representation are phases of politician double talk. The intent is to pack the committees, to put control of them into the hands of people who don't know the first thing about the cattle business and whose private intent is to destroy the Taylor Grazing Act itself."

"Plain, simple talk," Tiborough said. "This committee . . . we welcome such directness. Strong words. A majority of this committee . . . we have taken the position that the public range lands have been too long subjected to the tender mercies of the stockmen advisors, that the lands . . . stockmen have exploited them to their own advantage."

The gloves are off, Wallace thought. I hope Custer knows what he's doing. He's sure as hell not accepting advice.

Custer pulled a sheaf of papers from his briefcase and Wallace glimpsed shiny metal in the case before the flap was closed.

Christ! That looked like a gun or something!

Then Wallace recognized the papers—the brief he and his staff had labored over—and the preliminary statement. He noted with alarm the penciled markings and marginal notations. How could Custer have done that much to it in just twenty-four hours?

Again, Wallace whispered in Custer's ear: "Take it easy, Bill. The bastard's out for blood."

Custer nodded to show he had heard, glanced at the papers, looked up directly at Tiborough.

A hush settled on the room, broken only by the scraping of a chair somewhere in the rear, and the whirr of cameras.

2   "First, the nature of these lands we're talking about," Custer said. "In my state. . . ." He cleared his throat, a mannerism that would have indicated anger in the old man, his father. There was no break in Custer's expression, though, and his voice remained level. ". . . in my state, these were mostly Indian lands. This nation took them by brute force, right of conquest. That's about the oldest right in the world, I guess. I don't want to argue with it at this point."

"Mr. Custer."

It was Nebraska's Senator Plowers, his amiable farmer's face set in a tight grin. "Mr. Custer, I hope. . . ."

"Is this a point of order?" Tiborough asked.

"Mr. Chairman," Plowers said, "I merely wished to make sure we weren't going to bring up that old suggestion about giving these lands back to the Indians."

Laughter shot across the hearing room. Tiborough chuckled as he pounded his gavel for order.

"You may continue, Mr. Custer," Tiborough said.

Custer looked at Plowers, said: "No, Senator, I don't want to give these lands back to the Indians. When they had these lands, they only got about three hundred pounds of meat a year off eighty acres. We get five hundred pounds of the highest grade protein—premium beef—from only ten acres."

"No one doubts the efficiency of your factory-like methods," Tiborough said. "You can . . . we know your methods wring the largest amount of meat from a minimum acreage."

Ugh! Wallace thought. That was a low blow—implying Bill's overgrazing and destroying the land value.

"My neighbors, the Warm Springs Indians, use the same methods I do," Custer said. "They are happy to adopt our methods because we use the land while maintaining it and increasing its value. We don't permit the land to fall prey to natural disasters such as fire and erosion. We don't. . . ."

"No doubt your methods are meticulously correct," Tiborough said. "But I fail to see where. . . ."

"Has Mr. Custer finished his preliminary statement yet?" Senator Plowers cut in.

Wallace shot a startled look at the Nebraskan. That was help from an unexpected quarter.

"Thank you, Senator," Custer said. "I'm quite willing to adapt to the chairman's methods and explain the meticulous correctness of my operation. Our lowliest cowhands are college men, highly paid. We travel ten times as many jeep miles as we do horse miles. Every outlying division of the ranch—every holding pen and grazing supervisor's cabin is linked to the central ranch by radio. We use the. . . ."

"I concede that your methods must be the most modern in the world," Tiborough said. "It's not your methods as much as the results of those methods that are at issue here. We. . . ."

He broke off at a disturbance by the door. An Army colonel was talking to the guard there. He wore Special Services fourragere—Pentagon.

Wallace noted with an odd feeling of disquiet that the man was armed —a .45 at the hip. The weapon was out of place on him, as though he had added it suddenly on an overpowering need . . . emergency.

More guards were coming up outside the door now—Marines and Army. They carried rifles.

The colonel said something sharp to the guard, turned away from him and entered the committee room. All the cameras were tracking him now. He ignored them, crossed swiftly to Tiborough, and spoke to him.

The Senator shot a startled glance at Custer, accepted a sheaf of papers the colonel thrust at him. He forced his attention off Custer, studied the papers, leafing through him. Presently, he looked up, stared at Custer.

A hush fell over the room.

"I find myself at a loss, Mr. Custer," Tiborough said. "I have here a copy of a report. . . . it's from the Special Services branch of the Army . . . through the Pentagon, you understand. It was just handed to me by, ah . . . the colonel here."

He looked up at the colonel, who was standing, one hand resting lightly on the holstered .45. Tiborough looked back at Custer and it was obvious the Senator was trying to marshal his thoughts.

"It is," Tiborough said, "that is . . . this report supposedly . . . and I have every confidence it is what it is represented to be . . . here in my hands . . . they say that . . . uh, within the last, uh, few days they have, uh, investigated a certain device . . . weapon they call it, that you are attempting to patent. They report. . . ." He glanced at the papers, back to Custer, who was staring at him steadily. ". . . this, uh, weapon, is a thing that . . . it is extremely dangerous."

"It is," Custer said.

"I . . . ah, see." Tiborough cleared his throat, glanced up at the colonel, who was staring fixedly at Custer. The Senator brought his attention back to Custer.

"Do you in fact have such a weapon with you, Mr. Custer?" Tiborough asked.

"I have brought it as an exhibit, sir."

"Exhibit?"

"Yes, sir."

Wallace rubbed his lips, found them dry. He wet them with his tongue, wished for the water glass, but it was beyond Custer. Christ! That stupid cowpuncher! He wondered if he dared whisper to Custer. Would the senators and that Pentagon lackey interpret such an action as meaning he was part of Custer's crazy antics?

"Are you threatening this committee with your weapon, Mr. Custer?" Tiborough asked. "If you are, I may say special precautions have been taken . . . extra guards in this room and we . . . that is, we will not allow ourselves to worry too much about any action you may take, but ordinary precautions are in force."

Wallace could no longer sit quietly. He tugged Custer's sleeve, got an abrupt shake of the head. He leaned close, whispered: "We could ask for a recess, Bill. Maybe we. . . ."

"Don't interrupt me," Custer said. He looked at Tiborough. "Senator, I would not threaten you or any other man. Threats in the way you mean them are a thing we no longer can indulge in."

"You . . . I believe you said this device is an exhibit," Tiborough said. He cast a worried frown at the report in his hands. "I fail . . . it does not appear germane."

Senator Plowers cleared his throat. "Mr. Chairman," he said.

"The chair recognizes the Senator from Nebraska," Tiborough said, and the relief in his voice was obvious. He wanted time to think.

"Mr. Custer," Plowers said, "I have not seen the report, the report my distinguished colleague alludes to; however, if I may . . . is it your wish to use this committee as some kind of publicity device?"

"By no means, Senator," Custer said. "I don't wish to profit by my presence here. . . . not at all."

Tiborough had apparently come to a decision. He leaned back, whispered to the colonel, who nodded and returned to the outer hall.

"You strike me as an eminently reasonable man, Mr. Custer," Tiborough said. "If I may. . . ."

"May I," Senator Plowers said. "May I, just permit me to conclude this one point. May we have the Special Services report in the record?"

"Certainly," Tiborough said. "But what I was about to suggest. . . ."

"May I," Plowers said. "May I, would you permit me, please, Mr. Chairman, to make this point clear for the record?"

Tiborough scowled, but the heavy dignity of the Senate overcame his irritation. "Please continue, Senator. I had thought you were finished."

"I respect . . . there is no doubt in my mind of Mr. Custer's truthfulness," Plowers said. His face eased into a grin that made him look grandfatherly, a kindly elder statesman. "I would like, therefore, to have him explain how this . . . ah, weapon, can be an exhibit in the matter before our committee."

Wallace glanced at Custer, saw the hard set to the man's jaw, realized the cattleman had gotten to Plowers somehow. This was a set piece.

Tiborough was glancing at the other senators, weighing the advisability of high-handed dismissal . . . perhaps a star chamber session. No . . . they were all too curious about Custer's device, his purpose here.

The thoughts were plain on the Senator's face.

"Very well," Tiborough said. He nodded to Custer. "You may proceed, Mr. Custer."

"During last winter's slack season," Custer said, "two of my men and I worked on a project we've had in the works for three years—to develop a sustained-emission laser device."

Custer opened his briefcase, slid out a fat aluminum tube mounted on a pistol grip with a conventional appearing trigger.

"This is quite harmless," he said. "I didn't bring the power pack."

"That is . . . this is your weapon?" Tiborough asked.

"Calling this a weapon is misleading," Custer said. "The term limits and oversimplifies. This is also a brush-cutter, a substitute for a logger's saw and axe, a diamond cutter, a milling machine . . . and a weapon. It is also a turning point in history."

"Come now, isn't that a bit pretentious?" Tiborough asked.

"We tend to think of history as something old and slow," Custer said. "But history is, as a matter of fact, extremely rapid and immediate. A President is assassinated, a bomb explodes over a city, a dam breaks, a revolutionary device is announced."

"Lasers have been known for quite a few years," Tiborough said. He looked at the papers the Colonel had given him. "The principle dates from 1956 or thereabouts."

"I don't wish it to appear that I'm taking credit for inventing this device," Custer said. "Nor am I claiming sole credit for developing the sustained-emission laser. I was merely one of a team. But I do hold the device here in my hand, gentlemen."

"Exhibit, Mr. Custer," Plowers reminded him. "How is this an exhibit?"

"May I explain first how it works?" Custer asked. "That will make the rest of my statement much easier."

Tiborough looked at Plowers, back to Custer. "If you will tie this all together, Mr. Custer," Tiborough said. "I want to . . . the bearing of this device on our—we are hearing a particular bill in this room."

"Certainly, Senator," Custer said. He looked at his device. "A ninety-volt radio battery drives this particular model. We have some that require less voltage, some that use more. We aimed for a construction with simple parts. Our crystals are common quartz. We shattered them by bringing them to a boil in water and then plunging them into ice water . . . repeatedly. We chose twenty pieces of very close to the same size—about one gram, slightly more than fifteen grains each."

Custer unscrewed the back of the tube, slid out a round length of plastic trailing lengths of red, green, brown, blue and yellow wire.

Wallace noted how the cameras of the TV men were centered on the object in Custer's hands. Even the senators were leaning forward, staring.

We're gadget crazy people, Wallace thought.

"The crystals were dipped in thinned household cement and then into iron filings," Custer said. "We made a little jig out of a fly-tying vise and opened a passage in the filings at opposite ends of the crystals. We then made some common celluloid—nitrocellulose, acetic acid, gelatin, and alcohol—all very common products, and formed it in a length of garden hose just long enough to take the crystals end to end. The crystals were inserted in the hose, the celluloid poured over them and the whole thing was seated in a magnetic waveguide while the celluloid was cooling. This centered and aligned the crystals. The waveguide was constructed from wire salvaged from an old TV set and built following the directions in the Radio Amateur's Handbook."

Custer re-inserted the length of plastic into the tube, adjusted the wires. There was an unearthly silence in the room with only the cameras whirring. It was as though everyone were holding his breath.

"A laser requires a resonant cavity, but that's complicated," Custer said. "Instead, we wound two layers of fine copper wire around our tube, immersed it in the celluloid solution to coat it and then filed one end flat. This end took a piece of mirror cut to fit. We then pressed a number eight embroidery needle at right angles into the mirror end of the tube until it touched the side of the number one crystal."

Custer cleared his throat.

Two of the senators leaned back. Plowers coughed. Tiborough glanced at the banks of TV cameras and there was a questioning look in his eyes.

"We then determined the master frequency of our crystal series," Custer said. "We used a test signal and oscilloscope, but any radio amateur could do it without the oscilloscope. We constructed an oscillator of that master frequency, attached it at the needle and a bare spot scraped in the opposite edge of the waveguide."

"And this . . . ah . . . worked?" Tiborough asked.

"No." Custer shook his head. "When we fed power through a voltage multiplier into the system we produced an estimated four hundred joules emission and melted half the tube. So we started all over again."

"You are going to tie this in?" Tiborough asked. He frowned at the papers in his hands, glanced toward the door where the colonel had gone.

"I am, sir, believe me," Custer said.

"Very well, then," Tiborough said.

"So we started all over again," Custer said. "But for the second celluloid dip we added bismuth—a saturate solution, actually. It stayed gummy and we had to paint over it with a sealing coat of the straight celluloid. We then coupled this bismuth layer through a pulse circuit so that it was bathed in a counter wave—180 degrees out of phase with the master frequency. We had, in effect, immersed the unit in a thermoelectric cooler that exactly countered the heat production. A thin beam issued from the unmirrored end when we powered it. We have yet to find something that thin beam cannot cut."

"Diamonds?" Tiborough asked.

"Powered by less than two hundred volts, this device could cut our planet in half like a ripe tomato," Custer said. "One man could destroy an aerial armada with it, knock down ICBMs before they touched atmosphere, sink a fleet, pulverize a city. I'm afraid, sir, that I haven't mentally catalogued all the violent implications of this device. The mind tends to boggle at the enormous power focused in. . . ."

"Shut down those TV cameras!"

It was Tiborough shouting, leaping to his feet and making a sweeping gesture to include the banks of cameras. The abrupt violence of his voice and gesture fell on the room like an explosion. "Guards!" he called. "You there at the door. Cordon off that door and don't let anyone out who heard this fool!" He whirled back to face Custer. "You irresponsible idiot!"

"I'm afraid, Senator," Custer said, "that you're locking the barn door many weeks too late."

For a long minute of silence Tiborough glared at Custer. Then: "You did this deliberately, eh?"

3   "**S**enator, if I'd waited any longer, there might have been no hope for us at all."

Tiborough sat back in his chair, still keeping his attention fastened on Custer. Plowers and Johnstone on his right had their heads close together whispering fiercely. The other senators were dividing their attention between Custer and Tiborough, their eyes wide and with no attempt to conceal their astonishment.

Wallace, growing conscious of the implications in what Custer had said, tried to wet his lips with his tongue. Christ! he thought. This stupid cowpoke has sold us all down the river!

Tiborough signaled an aide, spoke briefly with him, beckoned the colonel from the door. There was a buzzing of excited conversation in the room. Several of the press and TV crew were huddled near the windows on Custer's left, arguing. One of their number—a florid-faced man with gray hair and horn-rimmed glasses—started across the room toward Tiborough, was stopped by a committee aide. They began a low-voiced argument with violent gestures.

A loud curse sounded from the door. Poxman, the syndicated columnist, was trying to push past the guards there.

"Poxman!" Tiborough called. The columnist turned. "My orders are that no one leaves," Tiborough said. "You are not an exception." He turned back to face Custer.

The room had fallen into a semblance of quiet, although there still were pockets of muttering and there was the sound of running feet and a hurrying about in the hall outside.

"Two channels went out of here live," Tiborough said. "Nothing much we can do about them, although we will trace down as many of their viewers as we can. Every bit of film in this room and every sound tape will be confiscated, however." His voice rose as protests sounded from the press section. "Our national security is at stake. The President has been notified. Such measures as are necessary will be taken."

The colonel came hurrying into the room, crossed to Tiborough, quietly said something.

"You should've warned me!" Tiborough snapped. "I had no idea that. . . ."

The colonel interrupted with a whispered comment.

"These papers . . . your damned report is not clear!" Tiborough said. He looked around at Custer. "I see you're smiling, Mr. Custer. I don't think you'll find much to smile about before long."

"Senator, this is not a happy smile," Custer said. "But I told myself several days ago you'd fail to see the implications of this thing." He tapped the pistol-shaped device he had rested on the table. "I told myself you'd fall back into the old, useless pattern."

"Is that what you told yourself, really?" Tiborough said.

Wallace, hearing the venom in the Senator's voice, moved his chair a few inches farther away from Custer.

Tiborough looked at the laser projector. "Is that thing really disarmed?"

"Yes, sir."

"If I order one of my men to take it from you, you will not resist?"

"Which of your men will you trust with it, Senator?" Custer asked.

In the long silence that followed, someone in the press section emitted a nervous guffaw.

"Virtually every man on my ranch has one of these things," Custer said. "We fell trees with them, cut firewood, make fence posts. Every letter written to me as a result of my patent application has been answered candidly. More than a thousand sets of schematics and instructions on how to build this device have been sent out to varied places in the world."

"You vicious traitor!" Tiborough rasped.

"You're certainly entitled to your opinion, Senator," Custer said. "But I warn you I've had time for considerably more concentrated and considerably more painful thought than you've applied to this problem. In my estimation, I had no choice. Every week I waited to make this thing public, every day, every minute, merely raised the odds that humanity would be destroyed by. . . ."

"You said this thing applied to the hearings on the grazing act," Plowers protested, and there was a plaintive note of complaint in his voice.

"Senator, I told you the truth," Custer said. "There's no real reason to change the act, now. We intend to go on operating under it—with the agreement of our neighbors and others concerned. People are still going to need food."

Tiborough glared at him. "You're saying we can't force you to. . . ." He broke off at a disturbance in the doorway. A rope barrier had been stretched there and a line of Marines stood with their backs to it, facing the hall. A mob of people was trying to press through. Press cards were being waved.

"Colonel, I told you to clear that hall!" Tiborough barked.

The colonel ran to the barrier. "Use your bayonets if you have to!" he shouted.

The disturbance subsided at the sound of his voice. More uniformed men could be seen moving in along the barrier. Presently, the noise receded.

Tiborough turned back to Custer. "You make Benedict Arnold look like the greatest friend the United States ever had," he said.

"Cursing me isn't going to help you," Custer said. "You are going to have to live with this thing; so you'd better try understanding it."

"That appears to be simple," Tiborough said. "All I have to do is send twenty-five cents to the Patent office for the schematics and then write you a letter."

"The world already was headed toward suicide," Custer said. "Only fools failed to realize. . . ."

"So you decided to give us a little push," Tiborough said.

"H. G. Wells warned us," Custer said. "That's how far back it goes, but nobody listened. 'Human history becomes more and more a race between education and catastrophe,' Wells said. But those were just words. Many scientists have remarked the growth curve on the amount of raw energy becoming available to humans—and the diminishing curve on the number of persons required to use that energy. For a long time now, more and more violent power was being made available to fewer and fewer people. It was only a matter of time until total destruction was put into the hands of single individuals."

"And you didn't think you could take your government into your confidence."

"The government already was committed to a political course diametrically opposite the one this device requires," Custer said. "Virtually every man in the government has a vested interest in not reversing that course."

"So you set yourself above the government?"

"I'm probably wasting my time," Custer said, "but I'll try to explain it. Virtually every government in the world is dedicated to manipulating something called the 'mass man.' That's how governments have stayed in power. But there is no such man. When you elevate the nonexistent 'mass man' you degrade the individual. And obviously it was only a matter of time until all of us were at the mercy of the individual holding power."

"You talk like a commie!"

"They'll say I'm a goddamn capitalist pawn," Custer said. "Let me ask you, Senator, to visualize a poor radio technician in a South American country. Brazil, for example. He lives a hand-to-mouth existence, ground down by an overbearing, unimaginative, essentially uncouth ruling oligarchy. What is he going to do when this device comes into his hands?"

"Murder, robbery and anarchy."

"You could be right," Custer said. "But we might reach an understanding out of ultimate necessity—that each of us must cooperate in maintaining the dignity of all."

Tiborough stared at him, began to speak musingly: "We'll have to control the essential materials for constructing this thing . . . and there may be trouble for a while, but. . . ."

"You're a vicious fool."

In the cold silence that followed, Custer said: "It was too late to try that ten years ago. I'm telling you this thing can be patchworked out of a wide variety of materials that are already scattered over the earth. It can be made in basements and mud huts, in palaces and shacks. The key item is the crystals, but other crystals will work, too. That's obvious. A patient man can grow crystals . . . and this world is full of patient men."

"I'm going to place you under arest," Tiborough said. "You have outraged every rule—"

"You're living in a dream world," Custer said. "I refuse to threaten you, but I'll defend myself from any attempt to oppress or degrade me. If I cannot defend myself, my friends will defend me. No man who understands what this device means will permit his dignity to be taken from him."

Custer allowed a moment for his words to sink in, then: "And don't twist those words to imply a threat. Refusal to threaten a fellow human is an absolute requirement in the day that has just dawned on us."

"You haven't changed a thing!" Tiborough raged. "If one man is powerful with that thing, a hundred are. . . ."

"All previous insults aside," Custer said, "I think you are a highly intelligent man, Senator. I ask you to think long and hard about this device. Use of power is no longer the deciding factor because one man is as powerful as a million. Restraint—self-restraint is now the key to survival. Each of us is at the mercy of his neighbor's good will. Each of us, Senator—the man in the palace and the man in the shack. We'd better do all we can to increase that good will—not attempting to buy it, but simply recognizing that individual dignity is the one inalienable right of. . . ."

"Don't you preach to me, you commie traitor!" Tiborough rasped. "You're a living example of. . . ."

"Senator!"

It was one of the TV cameramen in the left rear of the room.

"Let's stop insulting Mr. Custer and hear him out," the cameraman said.

"Get that man's name," Tiborough told an aide. "If he. . . ."

"I'm an expert electronic technician, Senator," the man said. "You can't threaten me now."

Custer smiled, turned to face Tiborough.

"The revolution begins," Custer said. He waved a hand as the Senator started to whirl away. "Sit down, Senator."

Wallace, watching the Senator obey, saw how the balance of control had changed in this room.

"Ideas are in the wind," Custer said. "There comes a time for a thing to develop. It comes into being. The spinning jenny came into being because that was its time. It was based on countless ideas that had preceded it."

"And this is the age of the laser?" Tiborough asked.

"It was bound to come," Custer said. "But the number of people in the world who're filled with hate and frustration and violence has been growing with terrible speed. You add to that the enormous danger that this might fall into the hands of just one group or nation or. . ." Custer shrugged. "This is too much power to be confined to one man or group with the hope they'll administer wisely. I didn't dare delay. That's why I spread this thing now and announced it as broadly as I could."

Tiborough leaned back in his chair, his hands in his lap. His face was pale and beads of perspiration stood out on his forehead.

"We won't make it."

"I hope you're wrong, Senator," Custer said. "But the only thing I know for sure is that we'd have had less chance of making it tomorrow than we have today."

ENDER'S GAME

"**W**hatever your gravity is when you get to the door, remember—the enemy's gate is *down*. If you step through your own door like you're out for a stroll, you're a big target and you deserve to get hit. With more than a flasher." Ender Wiggins paused and looked over the group. Most were just watching him nervously. A few understanding. A few sullen and resisting.

First day with this army, all fresh from the teacher squads, and Ender had forgotten how young new kids could be. He'd been in it for three years, they'd had six months—nobody over nine years old in the whole bunch. But they were his. At eleven, he was half a year early to be a commander. He'd had a toon of his own and knew a few tricks, but there were forty in his new army. Green. All marksmen with a flasher, all in top shape, or they wouldn't be here—but they were all just as likely as not to get wiped out first time into battle.

"Remember," he went on, "they can't see you till you get through that door. But the second you're out, they'll be on you. So hit that door the way you want to be when they shoot at you. Legs go under you, going straight *down*." He pointed at a sullen kid who looked like he was only seven, the smallest of them all. "Which way is down, greenoh!"

"Toward the enemy door." The answer was quick. It was also surly, as if to say, Yeah, yeah, now get on with the important stuff.

"Name, kid?"

"Bean."

"Get that for size or for brains?"

Bean didn't answer. The rest laughed a little. Ender had chosen right. The kid *was* younger than the rest, must have been advanced because he was sharp. The others didn't like him much, they were happy to see him taken down a little. Like Ender's first commander had taken him down.

"Well, Bean, you're right onto things. Now I tell you this, nobody's gonna get through that door without a good chance of getting hit. A lot of you are going to be turned into cement somewhere. Make sure it's your legs. Right? If only your legs get hit, then only your legs get frozen, and in nullo that's no sweat." Ender turned to one of the dazed ones. "What're legs for? Hmmm?"

Blank stare. Confusion. Stammer.

"Forget it. Guess I'll have to ask Bean here."

"Legs are for pushing off walls." Still bored.

"Thanks, Bean. Get that, everybody?" They all got it, and didn't like getting it from Bean. "Right. You can't *see* with legs, you can't *shoot* with legs, and most of the time they just get in the way. If they get frozen sticking straight out you've turned yourself into a blimp. No way to hide. So how do legs go?"

A few answered this time, to prove that Bean wasn't the only one who knew anything. "Under you. Tucked up under."

"Right. A shield. You're kneeling on a shield, and the shield is your own legs. And there's a trick to the suits. Even when your legs are flashed you can *still* kick off. I've never seen anybody do it but me— but you're all gonna learn it."

Ender Wiggins turned on his flasher. It glowed faintly green in his hand. Then he let himself rise in the weightless workout room, pulled his legs under him as though he were kneeling, and flashed both of them. Immediately his suit stiffened at the knees and ankles, so that he couldn't bend at all.

"Okay, I'm frozen, see?"

He was floating a meter above them. They all looked up at him, puzzled. He leaned back and caught one of the handholds on the wall behind him, and pulled himself flush against the wall.

"I'm stuck at a wall. If I had legs, I'd use legs, and string myself out like a string *bean,* right?"

They laughed.

"But I don't have legs, and that's *better,* got it? Because of this." Ender jackknifed at the waist, then straightened out violently. He was across the workout room in only a moment. From the other side he called to them. "Got that? I didn't use hands, so I still had use of my flasher. *And* I didn't have my legs floating five feet behind me. Now watch it again."

He repeated the jackknife, and caught a handhold on the wall near them. "Now, I don't just want you to do that when they've flashed your legs. I want you to do that when you've still got legs, because it's better. And because they'll never be expecting it. All right now, everybody up in the air and kneeling."

Most were up in a few seconds. Ender flashed the stragglers, and they dangled, helplessly frozen, while the others laughed. "When I give an order, you move. Got it? When we're at a door and they clear it, I'll be giving you orders in two seconds, as soon as I see the setup. And when I give the order you better be out there, because whoever's out there first is going to win, unless he's a fool. I'm not. And you better not be, or I'll have you back in the teacher squads." He saw more than a few of them gulp, and the frozen ones looked at him with fear. "You guys who are hanging there. You watch. You'll thaw out in about fifteen minutes, and let's see if you can catch up to the others."

For the next half hour Ender had them jackknifing off walls. He called a stop when he saw that they all had the basic idea. They were a good group, maybe. They'd get better.

"Now you're warmed up," he said to them, "we'll start working."

Ender was the last one out after practice, since he stayed to help some of the slower ones improve on technique. They'd had good teachers, but like all armies they were uneven, and some of them could be a real drawback in battle. Their first battle might be weeks away. It might be tomorrow. A schedule was never printed. The commander just woke up and found a note by his bunk, giving him the time of his battle and the name of his opponent. So for the first while he was going to drive his boys until they were in top shape—all of them. Ready for anything, at any time. Strategy was nice, but it was worth nothing if the soldiers couldn't hold up under the strain.

He turned the corner into the residence wing and found himself face to face with Bean, the seven-year-old he had picked on all through practice that day. Problems. Ender didn't want problems right now.

"Ho, Bean."

"Ho, Ender."

Pause.

"Sir," Ender said softly.

"We're not on duty."

"In my army, Bean, we're always on duty." Ender brushed past him.

Bean's high voice piped up behind him. "I know what you're doing, Ender, sir, and I'm warning you."

Ender turned slowly and looked at him. "Warning me?"

"I'm the best man you've got. But I'd better be treated like it."

"Or what?" Ender smiled menacingly.

"Or I'll be the worst man you've got. One or the other."

"And what do you want? Love and kisses?" Ender was getting angry now.

Bean was unworried. "I want a toon."

Ender walked back to him and stood looking down into his eyes. "I'll give a toon," he said, "to the boys who prove they're worth something. They've got to be good soldiers, they've got to know how to take orders, they've got to be able to think for themselves in a pinch, and they've got to be able to keep respect. That's how I got to be a commander. That's how you'll get to be a toon leader. Got it?"

Bean smiled. "That's fair. *If* you actually work that way, I'll be a toon leader in a month."

Ender reached down and grabbed the front of his uniform and shoved him into the wall. "When I say I work a certain way, Bean, then that's the way I work."

Bean just smiled. Ender let go of him and walked away, and didn't look back. He was sure, without looking, that Bean was still watching, still smiling, still just a little contemptuous. He might make a good toon leader at that. Ender would keep an eye on him.

Captain Graff, six foot two and a little chubby, stroked his belly as he leaned back in his chair. Across his desk sat Lieutenant Anderson, who was earnestly pointing out high points on a chart.

"Here it is, Captain," Anderson said. "Ender's already got them doing a tactic that's going to throw off everyone who meets it. Doubled their speed."

Graff nodded.

"And you know his test scores. He thinks well, too."

Graff smiled. "All true, all true, Anderson, he's a fine student, shows real promise."

They waited.

Graff sighed. "So what do you want me to do?"

"Ender's the one. He's got to be."

"He'll never be ready in time, Lieutenant. He's eleven, for heaven's sake, man, what do you want, a miracle?"

"I want him into battles, every day starting tomorrow. I want him to have a year's worth of battles in a month."

Graff shook his head. "That would have his army in the hospital."

"No, sir He's getting them into form. And we need Ender."

"Correction, Lieutenant. We need somebody. You think it's Ender."

"All right, I think it's Ender. Which of the commanders if it isn't him?"

"I don't know, Lieutenant." Graff ran his hands over his slightly fuzzy bald head. "These are children, Anderson. Do you realize that? Ender's army is nine years old. Are we going to put them against the older kids? Are we going to put them through hell for a month like that?"

Lieutenant Anderson leaned even farther over Graff's desk. "Ender's test scores, Captain!"

"I've seen his bloody test scores! I've watched him in battle, I've listened to tapes of his training sessions. I've watched his sleep patterns, I've heard tapes of his conversations in the corridors and in the bathrooms, I'm more aware of Ender Wiggins than you could possibly imagine! And against all the arguments, against his obvious qualities, I'm weighing one thing. I have this picture of Ender a year from now, if you have your way. I see him completely useless, worn down, a failure, because he was pushed farther than he or any living person could go. But it doesn't weigh enough, does it, Lieutenant, because there's a war on, and our best talent is gone, and the biggest battles are ahead. So give Ender a battle every day this week. And then bring me a report."

Anderson stood and saluted. "Thank you, sir."

He had almost reached the door when Graff called his name. He turned and faced the captain.

"Anderson," Captain Graff said. "Have you been outside, lately I mean?"

"Not since last leave, six months ago."

"I didn't think so. Not that it makes any difference. But have you ever been to Beaman Park, there in the city? Hmm? Beautiful park. Trees. Grass. No nullo, no battles, no worries. Do you know what else there is in Beaman Park?"

"What, sir?" Lieutenant Anderson asked.

"Children," Graff answered.

"Of course, children," said Anderson.

"I mean children. I mean kids who get up in the morning when their mothers call them and they go to school and then in the afternoons they go to Beaman Park and play. They're happy, they smile a lot, they laugh, they have fun. Hmmm?"

"I'm sure they do, sir."

"Is that all you can say, Anderson?"

Anderson cleared his throat. "It's good for children to have fun, I think, sir. I know I did when I was a boy. But right now the world needs soldiers. And this is the way to get them."

Graff nodded and closed his eyes. "Oh, indeed, you're right, by statistical proof and by all the important theories, and dammit they work and the system is right but all the same Ender's older than I am. He's not a child. He's barely a person."

"If that's true, sir, then at least we all know that Ender is making it possible for the others of his age to be playing in the park."

"And Jesus died to save all men, of course." Graff sat up and looked at Anderson almost sadly. "But we're the ones," Graff said, "we're the ones who are driving in the nails."

Ender Wiggins lay on his bed staring at the ceiling. He never slept more than five hours a night—but the lights went off at 2200 and didn't come on again until 0600. So he stared at the ceiling and thought.

He'd had his army for three and a half weeks. Dragon Army. The name was assigned, and it wasn't a lucky one. Oh, the charts said that about nine years ago a Dragon Army had done fairly well. But for the next six years the name had been attached to inferior armies, and finally, because of the superstition that was beginning to play about the name, Dragon Army was retired. Until now. And now, Ender thought, smiling, Dragon Army was going to take them by surprise.

The door opened quietly. Ender did not turn his head. Someone stepped softly into his room, then left with the sound of the door shutting. When soft steps died away Ender rolled over and saw a white slip of paper lying on the floor. He reached down and picked it up.

"Dragon Army against Rabbit Army, Ender Wiggins and Carn Carby, 0700."

The first battle. Ender got out of bed and quickly dressed. He went rapidly to the rooms of each of his toon leaders and told them to rouse their boys. In five minutes they were all gathered in the corridor, sleepy and slow. Ender spoke softly.

"First battle, 0700 against Rabbit Army. I've fought them twice before but they've got a new commander. Never heard of him. They're an older group, though, and I know a few of their old tricks. Now wake up. Run, doublefast, warmup in workroom three."

For an hour and a half they worked out, with three mock battles and calisthenics in the corridor out of the nullo. Then for fifteen minutes they all lay up in the air, totally relaxing in the weightlessness. At 0650 Ender roused them and they hurried into the corridor. Ender led them down the corridor, running again, and occasionally leaping to touch a light panel on the ceiling. The boys all touched the same light panel. And at 0658 they reached their gate to the battleroom.

The members of toons C and D grabbed the first eight handholds in the ceiling of the corridor. Toons A, B, and E crouched on the floor. Ender hooked his feet into two handholds in the middle of the ceiling, so he was out of everyone's way.

"Which way is the enemy's door?" he hissed.

"Down! they whispered back, and laughed.

"Flashers on." The boxes in their hands glowed green. They waited for a few seconds more, and then the grey wall in front of them disappeared and the battleroom was visible.

Ender sized it up immediately. The familiar open grid of most early games, like the monkey bars at the park, with seven or eight boxes scattered through the grid. They called the boxes *stars*. There were enough of them, and in forward enough positions, that they were worth going for. Ender decided this in a second, and he hissed, "Spread to near stars. E hold!"

The four groups in the corners plunged through the forcefield at the doorway and fell down into the battleroom. Before the enemy even appeared through the opposite gate Ender's army had spread from the door to the nearest stars.

Then the enemy soldiers came through the door. From their stance Ender knew they had been in a different gravity, and didn't know enough to disorient themselves from it. They came through standing up, their entire bodies spread and defenseless.

"Kill 'em, E!" Ender hissed, and threw himself out the door knees first, with his flasher between his legs and firing. While Ender's group flew across the room the rest of Dragon Army lay down a protecting fire, so that E group reached a forward position with only one boy frozen completely, though they had all lost the use of their legs—which didn't impair them in the least. There was a lull as Ender and his opponent, Carn Carnby, assessed their positions. Aside from Rabbit Army's losses at the gate, there had been few casualties, and both armies were near full strength. But Carn had no originality—he was in a four-corner spread that any five-year-old in the teacher squads might have thought of. And Ender knew how to defeat it.

He called out, loudly, "E covers A, C down. B, D angle east wall." Under E toon's cover, B and D toons lunged away from their stars. While they were still exposed, A and C toons left their stars and drifted toward the near wall. They reached it together, and together jackknifed off the wall. At double the normal speed they appeared behind the enemy's stars, and opened fire. In a few seconds the battle was over, with the enemy almost entirely frozen, including the commander, and the rest scattered to the corners. For the next five minutes, in squads of four, Dragon Army cleaned out the dark corners of the battleroom and shepherded the enemy into the center, where their bodies, frozen at impossible angles, jostled each other. Then Ender took three of his boys to the enemy gate and went through the formality of reversing the one-way field by simultaneously touching a Dragon Army helmet at each corner. Then Ender assembled his army in vertical files near the knot of frozen Rabbit Army soldiers.

Only three of Dragon Army's soldiers were immobile. Their victory margin—38 to 0—was ridiculously high, and Ender began to laugh.

Dragon Army joined him, laughing long and loud. They were still laughing when Lieutenant Anderson and Lieutenant Morris came in from the teachergate at the south end of the battleroom.

Lieutenant Anderson kept his face stiff and unsmiling, but Ender saw him wink as he held out his hand and offered the stiff, formal congratulations that were ritually given to the victor in the game.

Morris found Carn Carby and unfroze him, and the thirteen-year-old came and presented himself to Ender, who laughed without malice and held out his hand. Carn graciously took Ender's hand and bowed his head over it. It was that or be flashed again.

Lieutenant Anderson dismissed Dragon Army, and they silently left the battleroom through the enemy's door—again part of the ritual. A light was blinking on the north side of the square door, indicating where the gravity was in that corridor. Ender, leading his soldiers, changed his orientation and went through the forcefield and into gravity on his feet. His army followed him at a brisk run back to the workroom. When they got there they formed up into squads, and Ender hung in the air, watching them.

"Good first battle," he said, which was excuse enough for a cheer, which he quieted. "Dragon Army did all right against Rabbits. But the enemy isn't always going to be that bad. And if that had been a good army we would have been smashed. We still would have won, but we would have been smashed. Now let me see B and D toons out here. Your takeoff from the stars was way too slow. If Rabbit Army knew how to aim a flasher, you all would have been frozen solid before A and C even got to the wall."

They worked out for the rest of the day.

That night Ender went for the first time to the commanders' mess hall. No one was allowed there until he had won at least one battle, and Ender was the youngest commander ever to make it. There was no great stir when he came in. But when some of the other boys saw the Dragon on his breast pocket, they stared at him openly, and by the time he got his tray and sat at an empty table, the entire room was silent, with the other commanders watching him. Intensely self-conscious, Ender wondered how they all knew, and why they all looked so hostile.

Then he looked above the door he had just come through. There was a huge scoreboard across the entire wall. It showed the win/loss record for the commander of every army; that day's battles were lit in red. Only four of them. The other three winners had barely made it—the best of them had only two men whole and eleven mobile at the end of the game. Dragon Army's score of thirty-eight mobile was embarrassingly better.

Other new commanders had been admitted to the commanders' mess hall with cheers and congratulations. Other new commanders hadn't won thirty-eight to zero.

Ender looked for Rabbit Army on the scoreboard. He was surprised to find that Carn Carby's score to date was eight wins and three losses. Was he that good? Or had he only fought against inferior armies? Whichever, there was still a zero in Carn's mobile and whole columns, and Ender looked down from the scoreboard grinning. No one smiled back, and Ender knew that they were afraid of him, which meant that they would hate him, which meant that anyone who went into battle against Dragon Army would be scared and angry and less competent. Ender looked for Carn Carby in the crowd, and found him not too far away. He stared at Carby until one of the other boys nudged the Rabbit commander and pointed to Ender. Ender smiled again and waved slightly. Carby turned red, and Ender, satisfied, leaned over his dinner and began to eat.

At the end of the week Dragon Army had fought seven battles in seven days. The score stood 7 wins and 0 losses. Ender had never had more than five boys frozen in any game. It was no longer possible for the other commanders to ignore Ender. A few of them sat with him and quietly conversed about game strategies that Ender's opponents had used. Other much larger groups were talking with the commanders that Ender had defeated, trying to find out what Ender had done to beat them.

In the middle of the meal the teacher door opened and the groups fell silent as Lieutenant Anderson stepped in and looked over the group. When he located Ender he strode quickly across the room and whispered in Ender's ear. Ender nodded, finished his glass of water, and left with the lieutenant. On the way out, Anderson handed a slip of paper to one of the older boys. The room became very noisy with conversation as Anderson and Ender left.

Ender was escorted down corridors he had never seen before. They didn't have the blue glow of the soldier corridors. Most were wood paneled, and the floors were carpeted. The doors were wood, with nameplates on them, and they stopped at one that said "Captain Graff, supervisor." Anderson knocked softly, and a low voice said, "Come in."

They went in. Captain Graff was seated behind a desk, his hands folded across his pot belly. He nodded, and Anderson sat. Ender also sat down. Graff cleared his throat and spoke.

"Seven days since your first battle, Ender."

Ender did not reply.

"Won seven battles, one every day."

Ender nodded.

"Scores unusually high, too."

Ender blinked.

"Why?" Graff asked him.

Ender glanced at Anderson, and then spoke to the captain behind the desk. "Two new tactics, sir. Legs doubled up as a shield, so that a flash doesn't immobilize. Jackknife takeoffs from the walls. Superior strategy, as Lieutenant Anderson taught, think places, not spaces. Five toons of eight instead of four of ten. Incompetent opponents. Excellent toon leaders, good soldiers."

Graff looked at Ender without expression. Waiting for what, Ender wondered. Lieutenant Anderson spoke up.

"Ender, what's the condition of your army?"

Do they want me to ask for relief? Not a chance, he decided. "A little tired, in peak condition, morale high, learning fast. Anxious for the next battle."

Anderson looked at Graff. Graff shrugged slightly and turned to Ender.

"Is there anything you want to know?"

Ender held his hands loosely in his lap. "When are you going to put us up against a good army?"

Graff's laughter rang in the room, and when it stopped, Graff handed a piece of paper to Ender.

"Now," the captain said, and Ender read the paper: "Dragon Army against Leopard Army, Ender Wiggins and Pol Slattery, 2000."

Ender looked up at Captain Graff. "That's ten minutes from now, sir."

Graff smiled. "Better hurry, then, boy."

As Ender left he realized Pol Slattery was the boy who had been handed his orders as Ender left the mess hall.

He got to his army five minutes later. Three toon leaders were already undressed and lying naked on their beds. He sent them all flying down the corridors to rouse their toons, and gathered up their suits himself. When all his boys were assembled in the corridor, most of them still getting dressed, Ender spoke to them.

"This one's hot and there's no time. We'll be late to the door, and the enemy'll be deployed right outside our gate. Ambush, and I've never heard of it happening before. So we'll take our time at the door. A and B toons, keep your belts loose, and give your flashers to the leaders and seconds of the other toons."

Puzzled, his soldiers complied. By then all were dressed, and Ender led them at a trot to the gate. When they reached it the forcefield was already on one-way, and some of his soldiers were panting. They had had one battle that day and a full workout. They were tired.

Ender stopped at the entrance and looked at the placement of the enemy soldiers. Some of them were grouped not more than twenty feet out from the gate. There was no grid, there were no stars. A big empty space. Where were most of the enemy soldiers? There should have been thirty more.

"They're flat against this wall," Ender said, "where we can't see them."

He took A and B toons and made them kneel, their hands on their hips. Then he flashed them, so that their bodies were frozen rigid.

"You're shields," Ender said, and then had boys from C and D kneel on their legs and hook both arms under the frozen boys' belts. Each boy was holding two flashers. Then Ender and the members of E toon picked up the duos, three at a time, and threw them out the door.

Of course, the enemy opened fire immediately. But they mainly hit the boys who were already flashed, and in a few moments pandemonium broke out in the battleroom. All the soldiers of Leopard Army were easy targets as they lay pressed flat against the wall or floated, unprotected, in the middle of the battleroom; and Ender's soldiers, armed with two flashers each, carved them up easily. Pol Slattery reacted quickly, ordering his men away from the wall, but not quickly enough—only a few were able to move, and they were flashed before they could get a quarter of the way across the battleroom.

When the battle was over Dragon Army had only twelve boys whole, the lowest score they had ever had. But Ender was satisfied. And during the ritual of surrender Pol Slattery broke form by shaking hands and asking, "Why did you wait so long getting out of the gate?"

Ender glanced at Anderson, who was floating nearby. "I was informed late," he said. "It was an ambush."

Slattery grinned, and gripped Ender's hand again. "Good game."

Ender didn't smile at Anderson this time. He knew that now the games would be arranged against him, to even up the odds. He didn't like it.

It was 2150, nearly time for lights out, when Ender knocked at the door of the room shared by Bean and three other soldiers. One of the others opened the door, then stepped back and held it wide. Ender stood for a moment, then asked if he could come in. They answered, of course, of course, come in, and he walked to the upper bunk, where Bean had set down his book and was leaning on one elbow to look at Ender.

"Bean, can you give me twenty minutes?"

"Near lights out," Bean answered.

"My room," Ender answered. "I'll cover for you."

Bean sat up and slid off his bed. Together he and Ender padded silently down the corridor to Ender's room. Bean entered first, and Ender closed the door behind them.

"Sit down," Ender said, and they both sat on the edge of the bed, looking at each other.

"Remember four weeks ago, Bean? When you told me to make you a toon leader?"

"Yeah."

"I've made five toon leaders since then, haven't I? And none of them was you."

Bean looked at him calmly.

"Was I right?" Ender asked.

"Yes, sir," Bean answered.

Ender nodded. "How have you done in these battles?"

Bean cocked his head to one side. "I've never been immobilized, sir, and I've immobilized forty-three of the enemy. I've obeyed orders quickly, and I've commanded a squad in mop-up and never lost a soldier."

"Then you'll understand this." Ender paused, then decided to back up and say something else first.

"You know you're early, Bean, by a good half year. I was, too, and I've been made a commander six months early. Now they've put me into battles after only three weeks of training with my army. They've given me eight battles in seven days. I've already had more battles than boys who were made commander four months ago. I've won more battles than many who've been commanders for a year. And then tonight. You know what happened tonight."

Bean nodded. "They told you late."

"I don't know what the teachers are doing. But my army is getting tired, and I'm getting tired, and now they're changing the rules of the game. You see, Bean, I've looked in the old charts. No one has ever destroyed so many enemies and kept so many of his own soldiers whole in the history of the game. I'm unique—and I'm getting unique treatment."

Bean smiled. "You're the best, Ender."

Ender shook his head. "Maybe. But it was no accident that I got the soldiers I got. My worst soldier could be a toon leader in another army. I've got the best. They've loaded things my way—but now they're loading it all against me. I don't know why. But I know I have to be ready for it. I need your help."

"Why mine?"

"Because even though there are some better soldiers than you in Dragon Army—not many, but some—there's nobody who can think better and faster than you." Bean said nothing. They both knew it was true.

Ender continued, "I need to be ready, but I can't retrain the whole army. So I'm going to cut every toon down by one, including you. With four others you'll be a special squad under me. And you'll learn to do some new things. Most of the time you'll be in the regular toons just like you are now. But when I need you. See?"

Bean smiled and nodded. "That's right, that's good, can I pick them myself?"

"One from each toon except your own, and you can't take any toon leaders."

"What do you want us to do?"

"Bean, I don't know. I don't know what they'll throw at us. What would you do if suddenly our flashers didn't work, and the enemy's did? What would you do if we had to face two armies at once? The only thing I know is—there may be a game where we don't even try for score. Where we just go for the enemy's gate. That's when the battle is technically won—four helmets at the corners of the gate. I want you ready to do that any time I call for it. Got it? You take them for two hours a day during regular workout. Then you and I and your soldiers, we'll work at night after dinner."

"We'll get tired."

"I have a feeling we don't know what tired is." Ender reached out and took Bean's hand, and gripped it. "Even when it's rigged against us, Bean. We'll win."

Bean left in silence and padded down the corridor.

Dragon Army wasn't the only army working out after hours now. The other commanders had finally realized they had some catching up to do. From early morning to lights out soldiers all over Training and Command Center, none of them over fourteen years old, were learning to jackknife off walls and use each other as living shields.

But while other commanders mastered the techniques that Ender had used to defeat them, Ender and Bean worked on solutions to problems that had never come up.

There were still battles every day, but for a while they were normal, with grids and stars and sudden plunges through the gate. And after the battles, Ender and Bean and four other soldiers would leave the main group and practice strange maneuvers. Attacks without flashers, using feet to physically disarm or disorient an enemy. Using four frozen soldiers to reverse the enemy's gate in less than two seconds. And one day Bean came to workout with a 300-meter cord.

"What's that for?"

"I don't know yet." Absently Bean spun one end of the cord. It wasn't more than an eighth of an inch thick, but it could have lifted ten adults without breaking.

"Where did you get it?"

"Commissary. They asked what for. I said to practice tying knots."

Bean tied a loop in the end of the rope and slid it over his shoulders.

"Here, you two, hang on to the wall here. Now don't let go of the rope. Give me about fifty yards of slack." They complied, and Bean moved about ten feet from them along the wall. As soon as he was sure they were ready, he jackknifed off the wall and flew straight out, fifty yards. Then the rope snapped taut. It was so fine that it was virtually invisible, but it was strong enough to force Bean to veer off at almost a right angle. It happened so suddenly that he had inscribed a perfect arc and hit the wall hard before most of the other soldiers knew what had happened. Bean did a perfect rebound and drifted quickly back to where Ender and the others waited for him.

Many of the soldiers in the five regular squads hadn't noticed the rope, and were demanding to know how it was done. It was impossible to change direction that abruptly in nullo. Bean just laughed.

"Wait till the next game without a grid! They'll never know what hit them."

They never did. The next game was only two hours later, but Bean and two others had become pretty good at aiming and shooting while they flew at ridiculous speeds at the end of the rope. The slip of paper was delivered, and Dragon Army trotted off to the gate, to battle with Griffin Army. Bean coiled the rope all the way.

When the gate opened, all they could see was a large brown star only fifteen feet away, completely blocking their view of the enemy's gate.

Ender didn't pause. "Bean, give yourself fifty feet of rope and go around the star." Bean and his four soldiers dropped through the gate and in a moment Bean was launched sideways away from the star. The rope snapped taut, and Bean flew forward. As the rope was stopped by each edge of the star in turn, his arc became tighter and his speed greater, until when he hit the wall only a few feet away from the gate, he was barely able to control his rebound to end up behind the star. But he immediately moved all his arms and legs so that those waiting inside the gate would know that the enemy hadn't flashed him anywhere.

Ender dropped through the gate, and Bean quickly told him how Griffin Army was situated. "They've got two squares of stars, all the way around the gate. All their soldiers are under cover, and there's no way to hit any of them until we're clear to the bottom wall. Even with shields, we'd get there at half strength and we wouldn't have a chance."

"They moving?" Ender asked.

"Do they need to?"

"I would." Ender thought for a moment. "This one's tough. We'll go for the gate, Bean."

Griffin Army began to call out to them.

"Hey, is anybody there!"

"Wake up, there's a war on!"

"We wanna join the picnic!"

They were still calling when Ender's army came out from behind their star with a shield of fourteen frozen soldiers. William Bee, Griffin Army's commander, waited patiently as the screen approached, his men waiting at the fringes of their stars for the moment when whatever was behind the screen became visible. About ten yards away the screen suddenly exploded as the soldiers behind it shoved the screen north. The momentum carried them south twice as fast, and at the same moment the rest of Dragon Army burst from behind their star at the opposite end of the room, firing rapidly.

William Bee's boys joined battle immediately, of course, but William Bee was far more interested in what had been left behind when the shield disappeared. A formation of four frozen Dragon Army soldiers was moving headfirst toward the Griffin Army gate, held together by another frozen soldier whose feet and hands were hooked through their belts. A sixth soldier hung to his waist and trailed like the tail of a kite. Griffin Army was winning the battle easily, and William Bee concentrated on the formation as it approached the gate. Suddenly the soldier trailing in back moved—he wasn't frozen at all! And even though William Bee flashed him immediately, the damage was done. The formation drifted to the Griffin Army gate, and their helmets touched all four corners simultaneously. A buzzer sounded, the gate reversed, and the frozen soldier in the middle was carried by momentum right through the gate. All the flashers stopped working, and the game was over.

The teachergate opened and Lieutenant Anderson came in. Anderson stopped himself with a slight movement on his hands when he reached the center of the battleroom. "Ender," he called, breaking protocol. One of the frozen Dragon soldiers near the south wall tried to call through jaws that were clamped shut by the suit. Anderson drifted to him and unfroze him.

Ender was smiling.

"I beat you again, sir," Ender said.

Anderson didn't smile. "That's nonsense, Ender," Anderson said softly. "Your battle was with William Bee of Griffin Army."

Ender raised an eyebrow.

"After that maneuver," Anderson said, "the rules are being revised to require that all of the enemy's soldiers must be immobilized before the gate can be reversed."

"That's all right," Ender said. "It could only work once, anyway." Anderson nodded, and was turning away when Ender added, "Is there going to be a new rule that armies be given equal positions to fight from?"

Anderson turned back around. "If you're in one of the positions, Ender, you can hardly call them equal, whatever they are."

William Bee counted carefully and wondered how in the world he had lost when not one of his soldiers had been flashed and only four of Ender's soldiers were even mobile.

And that night as Ender came into the commanders' mess hall, he was greeted with applause and cheers, and his table was crowded with respectful commanders, many of them two or three years older than he was. He was friendly, but while he ate he wondered what the teachers would do to him in his next battle. He didn't need to worry. His next two battles were easy victories, and after that he never saw the battleroom again.

It was 2100 and Ender was a little irritated to hear someone knock at his door. His army was exhausted, and he had ordered them all to be in bed after 2030. The last two days had been regular battles, and Ender was expecting the worst in the morning.

It was Bean. He came in sheepishly, and saluted.

Ender returned his salute and snapped, "Bean, I wanted everybody in bed."

Bean nodded but didn't leave. Ender considered ordering him out. But as he looked at Bean it occurred to him for the first time in weeks just how young Bean was. He had turned eight a week before, and he was still small and—no, Ender thought, he wasn't young. Nobody was young. Bean had been in battle, and with a whole army depending on him he had come through and won. And even though he was small, Ender could never think of him as young again.

Ender shrugged and Bean came over and sat on the edge of the bed. The younger boy looked at his hands for a while, and finally Ender grew impatient and asked, "Well, what is it?"

"I'm transferred. Got orders just a few minutes ago."

Ender closed his eyes for a moment. "I knew they'd pull something new. Now they're taking—where are you going?"

"Rabbit Army."

"How can they put you under an idiot like Carn Carby!"

"Carn was graduated. Support squads."

Ender looked up. "Well, who's commanding Rabbit then?"

Bean held his hands out helplessly.

"Me," he said.

Ender nodded, and then smiled. "Of course. After all, you're only four years younger than the regular age."

"It isn't funny," Bean said. "I don't know what's going on here. First all the changes in the game. And now this. I wasn't the only one transferred, either, Ender. Ren, Peder, Brian, Wins, Younger. All commanders now."

Ender stood up angrily and strode to the wall. "Every damn toon leader I've got!" he said, and whirled to face Bean. "If they're going to break up my army, Bean, why did they bother making me a commander at all?"

Bean shook his head. "I don't know. You're the best, Ender. Nobody's ever done what you've done. Nineteen battles in fifteen days, sir, and you won every one of them, no matter what they did to you."

"And now you and the others are commanders. You know every trick I've got, I trained you, and who am I supposed to replace you with? Are they going to stick me with six greenohs?"

"It stinks, Ender, but you know that if they gave you five crippled midgets and armed you with a roll of toilet paper you'd win."

They both laughed, and then they noticed that the door was open.

Lieutenant Anderson stepped in. He was followed by Captain Graff.

"Ender Wiggins," Graff said, holding his hands across his stomach.

"Yes, sir," Ender answered.

"Orders."

Anderson extended a slip of paper. Ender read it quickly, then crumpled it, still looking at the air where the paper had been. After a few moments he asked, "Can I tell my army?"

"They'll find out," Graff answered. "It's better not to talk to them after orders. It makes it easier."

"For you or for me?" Ender asked. He didn't wait for an answer. He turned quickly to Bean, took his hand for a moment, and then headed for the door.

"Wait," Bean said. "Where are you going? Tactical or Support School?"

"Command School," Ender answered, and then he was gone and Anderson closed the door.

Command School, Bean thought. Nobody went to Command School until they had gone through three years of Tactical. But then, nobody went to Tactical until they had been through at least five years of Battle School. Ender had only had three.

The system was breaking up. No doubt about it, Bean thought. Either somebody at the top was going crazy, or something was going wrong with the war—the real war, the one they were training to fight in. Why else would they break down the training system, advance somebody— even somebody as good as Ender—straight to Command School? Why else would they ever have an eight-year-old greenoh like Bean command an army?

Bean wondered about it for a long time, and then he finally lay down on Ender's bed and realized that he'd never see Ender again, probably. For some reason that made him want to cry. But he didn't cry, of course.

Training in the preschools had taught him how to force down emotions like that. He remembered how his first teacher, when he was three, would have been upset to see his lip quivering and his eyes full of tears.

Bean went through the relaxing routine until he didn't feel like crying anymore. Then he drifted off to sleep. His hand was near his mouth. It lay on his pillow hesitantly, as if Bean couldn't decide whether to bite his nails or suck on his fingertips. His forehead was creased and furrowed. His breathing was quick and light. He was a soldier, and if anyone had asked him what he wanted to be when he grew up, he wouldn't have known what they meant.

There's a war on, they said, and that was excuse enough for all the hurry in the world. They said it like a password and flashed a little card at every ticket counter and customs check and guard station. It got them to the head of every line.

Ender Wiggins was rushed from place to place so quickly he had no time to examine anything. But he did see trees for the first time. He saw men who were not in uniform. He saw women. He saw strange animals that didn't speak, but that followed docilely behind women and small children. He saw suitcases and conveyor belts and signs that said words he had never heard of. He would have asked someone what the words meant, except that purpose and authority surrounded him in the persons of four very high officers who never spoke to each other and never spoke to him.

Ender Wiggins was a stranger to the world he was being trained to save. He did not remember ever leaving Battle School before. His earliest memories were of childish war games under the direction of a teacher, of meals with other boys in the grey and green uniforms of the armed forces of his world. He did not know that the grey represented the sky and the green represented the great forests of his planet. All he knew of the world was from vague references to "outside."

And before he could make any sense of the strange world he was seeing for the first time, they enclosed him again within the shell of the military, where nobody had to say There's a war on anymore because no one within the shell of the military forgot it for a single instant of a single day.

They put him in a spaceship and launched him to a large artificial satellite that circled the world.

This space station was called Command School. It held the ansible.

On his first day Ender Wiggins was taught about the ansible and what it meant to warfare. It meant that even though the starships of today's battles were launched a hundred years ago, the commanders of the starships were men of today, who used the ansible to send messages to the computers and the few men on each ship. The ansible sent words as they were spoken, orders as they were made. Battleplans as they were fought. Light was a pedestrian.

For two months Ender Wiggins didn't meet a single person. They came to him namelessly, taught him what they knew, and left him to other teachers. He had no time to miss his friends at Battle School. He only had time to learn how to operate the stimulator, which flashed battle patterns around him as if he were in a starship at the center of the battle. How to command mock ships in mock battle by manipulating the keys on the stimulator and speaking words into the ansible. How to recognize instantly every enemy ship and the weapons it carried by the pattern that the simulator showed. How to transfer all that he learned in the nullo battles at Battle School to the starship battles at Command School.

He had thought the game was taken seriously before. Here they hurried him through every step, were angry and worried beyond reason every time he forgot something or made a mistake. But he worked as he had always worked, and learned as he had always learned. After a while he didn't make any more mistakes. He used the simulator as if it were a part of himself. Then they stopped being worried and gave him a teacher.

Maezr Rackham was sitting cross-legged on the floor when Ender awoke. He said nothing as Ender got up and showered and dressed, and Ender did not bother to ask him anything. He had long since learned that when something unusual was going on, he would often find out more information faster by waiting than by asking.

Maezr still hadn't spoken when Ender was ready and went to the door to leave the room. The door didn't open. Ender turned to face the man sitting on the floor. Maezr was at least forty, which made him the oldest man Ender had ever seen close up. He had a day's growth of black and white whiskers that grizzled his face only slightly less than his close-cut hair. His face sagged a little and his eyes were surrounded by creases and lines. He looked at Ender without interest.

Ender turned back to the door and tried again to open it.

"All right," he said, giving up. "Why's the door locked?"

Maezr continued to look at him blankly.

Ender became impatient. "I'm going to be late. If I'm not supposed to be there until later, than tell me so I can go back to bed." No answer. "Is it a guessing game?" Ender asked. No answer. Ender decided that maybe the man was trying to make him angry, so he went through a relaxing exercise as he leaned on the door, and soon he was calm again. Maezr didn't take his eyes off Ender.

For the next two hours the silence endured, Maezr watching Ender constantly, Ender trying to pretend he didn't notice the old man. The boy became more and more nervous, and finally ended up walking from one end of the room to the other in a sporadic pattern.

He walked by Maezr as he had several times before, and Maezr's hand shot out and pushed Ender's left leg into his right in the middle of a step. Ender fell flat on the floor.

He leaped to his feet immediately, furious. He found Maezr sitting calmly, cross-legged, as if he had never moved. Ender stood poised to fight. But the other's immobility made it impossible for Ender to attack, and he found himself wondering if he had only imagined the old man's hand tripping him up.

The pacing continued for another hour, with Ender Wiggins trying the door every now and then. At last he gave up and took off his uniform and walked to his bed.

As he leaned over to pull the covers back, he felt a hand jab roughly between his thighs and another hand grab his hair. In a moment he had been turned upside down. His face and shoulders were being pressed into the floor by the old man's knee, while his back was excruciatingly bent and his legs were pinioned by Maezr's arm. Ender was helpless to use his arms, and he couldn't bend his back to gain slack so he could use his legs. In less than two seconds the old man had completely defeated Ender Wiggins.

"All right," Ender gasped. "You win."

Maezr's knee thrust painfully downward.

"Since when," Maezr asked in a soft, rasping voice, "do you have to tell the enemy when he has won?"

Ender remained silent.

"I surprised you once, Ender Wiggins. Why didn't you destroy me immediately afterward? Just because I looked peaceful? You turned your back on me. Stupid. You have learned nothing. You have never had a teacher."

Ender was angry now. "I've had too many damned teachers, how was I supposed to know you'd turn out to be a—" Ender hunted for a word. Maezr supplied one.

"An enemy, Ender Wiggins," Maezr whispered. "I am your enemy, the first one you've ever had who was smarter than you. There is no teacher but the enemy, Ender Wiggins. No one but the enemy will ever tell you what the enemy is going to do. No one but the enemy will ever teach you how to destroy and conquer. I am your enemy, from now on. From now on I am your teacher."

Then Maezr let Ender's legs fall to the floor. Because the old man still held Ender's head to the floor, the boy couldn't use his arms to compensate, and his legs hit the plastic surface with a loud crack and a sickening pain that made Ender wince. Then Maezr stood and let Ender rise.

Slowly the boy pulled his legs under him, with a faint groan of pain, and he knelt on all fours for a moment, recovering. Then his right arm flashed out. Maezr quickly danced back and Ender's hand closed on air as his teacher's foot shot forward to catch Ender on the chin.

Ender's chin wasn't there. He was lying flat on his back, spinning on the floor, and during the moment that Maezr was off balance from his kick Ender's feet smashed into Maezr's other leg. The old man fell on the ground in a heap.

What seemed to be a heap was really a hornet's nest. Ender couldn't find an arm or a leg that held still long enough to be grabbed, and in the meantime blows were landing on his back and arms. Ender was smaller —he couldn't reach past the old man's flailing limbs.

So he leaped back out of the way and stood poised near the door.

The old man stopped thrashing about and sat up, cross-legged again, laughing. "Better, this time, boy. But slow. You will have to be better with a fleet than you are with your body or no one will be safe with you in command. Lesson learned?"

Ender nodded slowly.

Maezr smiled. "Good. Then we'll never have such a battle again. All the rest with the simulator. I will program your battles, I will devise the strategy of your enemy, and you will learn to be quick and discover what tricks the enemy has for you. Remember, boy. From now on the enemy is more clever than you. From now on the enemy is stronger than you. From now on you are always about to lose."

Then Maezr's face became serious again. "You will be about to lose, Ender, but you will win. You will learn to defeat the enemy. He will teach you how."

Maezr got up and walked toward the door. Ender stepped back out of the way. As the old man touched the handle of the door, Ender leaped into the air and kicked Maezr in the small of the back with both feet. He hit hard enough that he rebounded onto his feet, as Maezr cried out and collapsed on the floor.

Maezr got up slowly, holding on to the door handle, his face contorted with pain. He seemed disabled, but Ender didn't trust him. He waited warily. And yet in spite of his suspicion he was caught off guard by Maezr's speed. In a moment he found himself on the floor near the opposite wall, his nose and lip bleeding where his face had hit the bed. He was able to turn enough to see Maezr open the door and leave. The old man was limping and walking slowly.

Ender smiled in spite of the pain, then rolled over onto his back and laughed until his mouth filled with blood and he started to gag. Then he got up and painfully made his way to the bed. He lay down and in a few minutes a medic came and took care of his injuries.

As the drug had its effect and Ender drifted off to sleep he remembered the way Maezr limped out of his room and laughed again. He was still laughing softly as his mind went blank and the medic pulled the blanket over him and snapped off the light. He slept until the pain woke him in the morning. He dreamed of defeating Maezr.

The next day Ender went to the simulator room with his nose bandaged and his lip still puffy. Maezr was not there. Instead, a captain who had worked with him before showed him an addition that had been made. The captain pointed to a tube with a loop at one end. "Radio. Primitive, I know, but it loops over your ear and we tuck the other end into your mouth like this."

"Watch it," Ender said as the captain pushed the end of the tube into his swollen lip.

"Sorry. Now you just talk."

"Good. Who to?"

The captain smiled. "Ask and see."

Ender shrugged and turned to the simulator. As he did a voice reverberated through his skull. It was too loud for him to understand, and he ripped the radio off his ear.

"What are you trying to do, make me deaf?"

The captain shook his head and turned a dial on a small box on a nearby table. Ender put the radio back on.

"Commander," the radio said in a familiar voice.

Ender answered, "Yes."

"Instructions, sir?"

The voice was definitely familiar. "Bean?" Ender asked.

"Yes, sir."

"Bean, this is Ender."

Silence. And then a burst of laughter from the other side. Then six or seven more voices laughing, and Ender waited for silence to return. When it did, he asked, "Who else?"

A few voices spoke at once, but Bean drowned them out. "Me, I'm Bean, and Peder, Wins, Younger, Lee, and Vlad."

Ender thought for a moment. Then he asked what the hell was going on. They laughed again.

"They can't break up the group," Bean said. "We were commanders for maybe two weeks, and here we are at Command School, training with the simulator, and all of a sudden they told us we were going to form a fleet with a new commander. And that's you."

Ender smiled. "Are you boys any good?"

"If we aren't, you'll let us know."

Ender chuckled a little. "Might work out. A fleet."

For the next ten days Ender trained his toon leaders until they could maneuver their ships like precision dancers. It was like being back in the battleroom again, except that now Ender could always see everything, and could speak to his toon leaders and change their orders at any time.

One day as Ender sat down at the control board and switched on the simulator, harsh green lights appeared in the space—the enemy.

"This is it," Ender said. "X, Y, bullet, C, D, reserve screen, E, south loop, Bean, angle north."

The enemy was grouped in a globe, and outnumbered Ender two to one. Half of Ender's force was grouped in a tight, bulletlike formation, with the rest in a flat circular screen—except for a tiny force under Bean that moved off the simulator, heading behind the enemy's formation. Ender quickly learned the enemy's strategy: whenever Ender's bullet formation came close, the enemy would give way, hoping to draw Ender inside the globe where he would be surrounded. So Ender obligingly fell into the trap, bringing his bullet to the center of the globe.

The enemy began to contract slowly, not wanting to come within range until all their weapons could be brought to bear at once. Then Ender began to work in earnest. His reserve screen approached the outside of the globe, and the enemy began to concentrate his forces there. Then Bean's force appeared on the opposite side, and the enemy again deployed ships on that side.

Which left most of the globe only thinly defended. Ender's bullet attacked, and since at the point of attack it outnumbered the enemy overwhelmingly, he tore a hole in the formation. The enemy reacted to try to plug the gap, but in the confusion the reserve force and Bean's small force attacked simultaneously, with the bullet moved to another part of the globe. In a few more minutes the formation was shattered, most of the enemy ships destroyed, and the few survivors rushing away as fast as they could go.

Ender switched the simulator off. All the lights faded. Maezr was standing beside Ender, his hands in his pockets, his body tense. Ender looked up at him.

"I thought you said the enemy would be smart," Ender said.

Maezr's face remained expressionless. "What did you learn?"

"I learned that a sphere only works if your enemy's a fool. He had his forces so spread out that I outnumbered him whenever I engaged him."

"And?"

"And," Ender said, "you can't stay committed to one pattern. It makes you too easy to predict."

"Is that all?" Maezr asked quietly.

Ender took off his radio. "The enemy could have defeated me by breaking the sphere earlier."

Maezr nodded. "You had an unfair advantage."

Ender looked up at him coldly. "I was outnumbered two to one."

Maezr shook his head. "You have the ansible. The enemy doesn't. We include that in the mock battles. Their messages travel at the speed of light."

Ender glanced toward the simulator. "Is there enough space to make a difference?"

"Don't you know?" Maezr asked. "None of the ships was ever closer than thirty thousand kilometers to any other."

Ender tried to figure the size of the enemy's sphere. Astronomy was beyond him. But now his curiosity was stirred.

"What kind of weapons are on those ships? To be able to strike so fast?"

Maezr shook his head. "The science is too much for you. You'd have to study many more years than you've lived to understand even the basics. All you need to know is that the weapons work."

"Why do we have to come so close to be in range?"

"The ships are all protected by forcefields. A certain distance away the weapons are weaker and can't get through. Closer in the weapons are stronger than the shields. But the computers take care of all that. They're constantly firing in any direction that won't hurt one of our ships. The computers pick targets, aim; they do all the detail work. You just tell them when and get them in a position to win. All right?"

"No." Ender twisted the tube of the radio around his fingers. "I have to know how the weapons work."

"I told you, it would take—"

"I can't command a fleet—not even on the simulator—unless I know." Ender waited a moment, then added, "Just the rough idea."

Maezr stood up and walked a few steps away. "All right, Ender. It won't make any sense, but I'll try. As simply as I can." He shoved his hands into his pockets. "It's this way, Ender. Everything is made up of atoms, little particles so small you can't see them with your eyes. These atoms, there are only a few different types, and they're all made up of even smaller particles that are pretty much the same. These atoms can be broken, so that they stop being atoms. So that this metal doesn't hold together anymore. Or the plastic floor. Or your body. Or even the air. They just seem to disappear, if you break the atoms. All that's left is the pieces. And they fly around and break more atoms. The weapons on the ships set up an area where it's impossible for atoms of anything to stay together. They all break down. So things in that area—they disappear."

Ender nodded. "You're right, I don't understand it. Can it be blocked?"

"No. But it gets wider and weaker the farther it goes from the ship, so that after a while a forcefield will block it. OK? And to make it strong at all, it has to be focused, so that a ship can only fire effectively in maybe three or four directions at once."

Ender nodded again, but he didn't really understand, not well enough. "If the pieces of the broken atoms go breaking more atoms, why doesn't it just make everything disappear?"

"Space. Those thousands of kilometers between the ships, they're empty. Almost no atoms. The pieces don't hit anything, and when they finally do hit something, they're so spread out they can't do any harm." Maezr cocked his head quizzically. "Anything else you need to know?"

"Do the weapons on the ships—do they work against anything besides ships?"

Maezr moved in close to Ender and said firmly, "We only use them against ships. Never anything else. If we used them against anything else, the enemy would use them against us. Got it?"

Maezr walked away, and was nearly out the door when Ender called to him.

"I don't know your name yet," Ender said blandly.

"Maezr Rackham."

"Maezr Rackham," Ender said, "I defeated you."

Maezr laughed.

"Ender, you weren't fighting me today," he said. "You were fighting the stupidest computer in the Command School, set on a ten-year-old program. You don't think I'd use a sphere, do you?" He shook his head. "Ender, my dear little fellow, when you fight me you'll know it. Because you'll lose." And Maezr left the room.

Ender still practiced ten hours a day with his toon leaders. He never saw them, though, only heard their voices on the radio. Battles came every two or three days. The enemy had something new every time, something harder—but Ender coped with it. And won every time. And after every battle Maezr would point out mistakes and show Ender that he had really lost. Maezr only let Ender finish so that he would learn to handle the end of the game.

Until finally Maezr came in and solemnly shook Ender's hand and said, "That, boy, was a good battle."

Because the praise was so long in coming, it pleased Ender more than praise had ever pleased him before. And because it was so condescending, he resented it.

"So from now on," Maezr said, "we can give you hard ones."

From then on Ender's life was a slow nervous breakdown.

He began fighting two battles a day, with problems that steadily grew more difficult. He had been trained in nothing but the game all his life, but now the game began to consume him. He woke in the morning with new strategies for the simulator and went fitfully to sleep at night with the mistakes of the day preying on him. Sometimes he would wake up in the middle of the night crying for a reason he didn't remember. Sometimes he woke with his knuckles bloody from biting them. But every day he went impassively to the simulator and drilled his toon leaders until the battles, and drilled his toon leaders after the battles, and endured and studied the harsh criticism that Maezr Rackham piled on him. He noted that Rackham perversely criticized him more after his hardest battles. He noted that every time he thought of a new strategy the enemy was using it within a few days. And he noted that while his fleet always stayed the same size, the enemy increased in numbers every day.

He asked his teacher.

"We are showing you what it will be like when you really command. The ratios of enemy to us."

"Why does the enemy always outnumber us?"

Maezr bowed his grey head for a moment, as if deciding whether to answer. Finally he looked up and reached out his hand and touched Ender on the shoulder. "I will tell you, even though the information is secret. You see, the enemy attacked us first. He had good reason to attack us, but that is a matter for politicians, and whether the fault was ours or his, we could not let him win. So when the enemy came to our worlds, we fought back, hard, and spent the finest of our young men in the fleets. But we won, and the enemy retreated."

Maezr smiled ruefully. "But the enemy was not through, boy. The enemy would never be through. They came again, with more numbers, and it was harder to beat them. And another generation of young men was spent. Only a few survived. So we came up with a plan—the big men came up with the plan. We knew that we had to destroy the enemy once and for all, totally, eliminate his ability to make war against us. To do that we had to go to his home worlds—his home world, really, since the enemy's empire is all tied to his capital world."

"And so?" Ender asked.

"And so we made a fleet. We made more ships than the enemy ever had. We made a hundred ships for every ship he had sent against us. And we launched them against his twenty-eight worlds. They started leaving a hundred years ago. And they carried on them the ansible, and only a few men. So that someday a commander could sit on a planet somewhere far from the battle and command the fleet. So that our best minds would not be destroyed by the enemy."

Ender's question had still not been answered. "Why do they outnumber us?"

Maezr laughed. "Because it took a hundred years for our ships to get there. They've had a hundred years to prepare for us. They'd be fools, don't you think, boy, if they waited in old tugboats to defend their harbors. They have new ships, great ships, hundreds of ships. All we have is the ansible, that and the fact that they have to put a commander with every fleet, and when they lose—and they will lose—they lose one of their best minds every time."

Ender started to ask another question.

"No more, Ender Wiggins. I've told you more than you ought to know as it is."

Ender stood angrily and turned away. "I have a right to know. Do you think this can go on forever, pushing me through one school and another and never telling me what my life is for? You use me and the others as a tool, someday we'll command your ships, someday maybe we'll save your lives, but I'm not a computer, and I have to *know!*"

"Ask me a question, then, boy," Maezr said, "and if I can answer, I will."

"If you use your best minds to command the fleets, and you never lose any, then what do you need me for? Who am I replacing, if they're all still there?"

Maezr shook his head. "I can't tell you the answer to that, Ender. Be content that we will need you, soon. It's late. Go to bed. You have a battle in the morning."

Ender walked out of the simulator room. But when Maezr left by the same door a few moments later, the boy was waiting in the hall.

"All right, boy," Maezr said impatiently, "what is it? I don't have all night and you need to sleep."

Ender wasn't sure what his question was, but Maezr waited. Finally Ender asked softly, "Do they live?"

"Does who live?"

"The other commanders. The ones now. And before me."

Maezr snorted. "Live. Of course they live. He wonders if they live." Still chuckling, the old man walked off down the hall. Ender stood in the corridor for a while, but at last he was tired and he went off to bed. They live, he thought. They live, but he can't tell me what happens to them.

That night Ender didn't wake up crying. But he did wake up with blood on his hands.

Months wore on with battles every day, until at last Ender settled into the routine of the destruction of himself. He slept less every night, dreamed more, and he began to have terrible pains in his stomach. They put him on a very bland diet, but soon he didn't even have an appetite for that. "Eat," Maezr said, and Ender would mechanically put food in his mouth. But if nobody told him to eat he didn't eat.

One day as he was drilling his toon leaders the room went black and he woke up on the floor with his face bloody where he had hit the controls.

They put him to bed then, and for three days he was very ill. He remembered seeing faces in his dreams, but they weren't real faces, and he knew it even while he thought he saw them. He thought he saw Bean sometimes, and sometimes he thought he saw Lieutenant Anderson and Captain Graff. And then he woke up and it was only his enemy Maezr Rackham.

"I'm awake," he said to Maezr.

"So I see," Maezr answered. "Took you long enough. You have a battle today."

So Ender got up and fought the battle and he won it. But there was no second battle that day, and they let him go to bed earlier. His hands were shaking as he undressed.

During the night he thought he felt hands touching him gently, and he dreamed he heard voices saying, "How long can he go on?"

"Long enough."

"So soon?"

"In a few days, then he's through."

"How will he do?"

"Fine. Even today, he was better than ever."

Ender recognized the last voice as Maezr Rackham's. He resented Rackham's intruding even in his sleep.

He woke up and fought another battle and won.

Then he went to bed.

He woke up and won again.

And the next day was his last day in Command School, though he didn't know it. He got up and went to the simulator for the battle.

Maezr was waiting for him. Ender walked slowly into the simulator room. He step was slightly shuffling, and he seemed tired and dull. Maezr frowned.

"Are you awake, boy?" If Ender had been alert, he would have cared more about the concern in his teacher's voice. Instead, he simply went to the controls and sat down. Maezr spoke to him.

"Today's game needs a little explanation, Ender Wiggins. Please turn around and pay strict attention."

Ender turned around, and for the first time he noticed that there were people at the back of the room. He recognized Graff and Anderson from Battle School, and vaguely remembered a few of the men from Command School—teachers for a few hours at some time or another. But most of the people he didn't know at all.

"Who are they?"

Maezr shook his head and answered, "Observers. Every now and then we let observers come in to watch the battle. If you don't want them, we'll send them out."

Ender shrugged. Maezr began his explanation. "Today's game, boy, has a new element. We're staging this battle around a planet. This will complicate things in two ways. The planet isn't large, on the scale we're using, but the ansible can't detect anything on the other side of it—so there's a blind spot. Also, it's against the rules to use weapons against the planet itself. All right?"

"Why, don't the weapons work against planets?"

Maezr answered coldly, "There are rules of war, Ender, that apply even in training games."

Ender shook his head slowly. "Can the planet attack?"

Maezr looked nonplussed for a moment, then smiled. "I guess you'll have to find that one out, boy. And one more thing. Today, Ender, your opponent isn't the computer. I am your enemy today, and today I won't be letting you off so easily. Today is a battle to the end. And I'll use any means I can to defeat you."

Then Maezr was gone, and Ender expressionlessly led his toon leaders through maneuvers. Ender was doing well, of course, but several of the observers shook their heads, and Graff kept clasping and unclasping his hands, crossing and uncrossing his legs. Ender would be slow today, and today Ender couldn't afford to be slow.

A warning buzzer sounded, and Ender cleared the simulator board, waiting for today's game to appear. He felt muddled today, and wondered why people were there watching. Were they going to judge him today? Decide if he was good enough for something else? For another two years of grueling training, another two years of struggling to exceed his best? Ender was twelve. He felt very old. And as he waited for the game to appear, he wished he could simply lose it, lose the battle badly and completely so that they would remove him from the program, punish him however they wanted, he didn't care, just so he could sleep.

Then the enemy formation appeared, and Ender's weariness turned to desperation.

The enemy outnumbered him a thousand to one, the simulator glowed green with them, and Ender knew that he couldn't win.

And the enemy was not stupid. There was no formation that Ender could study and attack. Instead the vast swarms of ships were constantly moving, constantly shifting from one momentary formation to another, so that a space that for one moment was empty was immediately filled with formidable enemy force. And even though Ender's fleet was the largest he had ever had, there was no place he could deploy it where he would outnumber the enemy long enough to accomplish anything.

And behind the enemy was the planet. The planet, which Maezr had warned him about. What difference did a planet make, when Ender couldn't hope to get near it? Ender waited, waited for the flash of insight that would tell him what to do, how to destroy the enemy. And as he waited, he heard the observers behind him begin to shift in their seats, wondering what Ender was doing, what plan he would follow. And finally it was obvious to everyone that Ender didn't know what to do, that there was nothing to do, and a few of the men at the back of the room made quiet little sounds in their throats.

Then Ender heard Bean's voice in his ear. Bean chuckled and said, "Remember, the enemy's gate is *down*." A few of the other toon leaders laughed and Ender thought back to the simple games he had played and won in Battle School. They had put him against hopeless odds there, too. And he had beaten them. And he'd be damned if he'd let Maezr Rackham beat him with a cheap trick like outnumbering him a thousand to one. He had won a game in Battle School by going for something against the rules—he had won by going against the enemy's gate.

And the enemy's gate was down.

Ender smiled, and realized that if he broke this rule they'd probably kick him out of school, and that way he'd win for sure: He would never have to play a game again.

He whispered into the microphone. His six commanders each took a part of the fleet and launched themselves against the enemy. They pursued erratic courses, darting off in one direction and then another. The enemy immediately stopped his aimless maneuvering and began to group around Ender's six fleets.

Ender took off his microphone, leaned back in his chair, and watched. The observers murmured out loud, now. Ender was doing nothing—he had thrown the game away.

But a pattern began to emerge from the quick confrontations with the enemy. Ender's six groups lost ships constantly as they brushed with each enemy force—but they never stopped for a fight, even when for a moment they could have won a small tactical victory. Instead they continued on their erratic course that led, eventually, down. Toward the enemy planet.

And because of their seemingly random course the enemy didn't realize it until the same time that the observers did. By then it was too late, just as it had been too late for William Bee to stop Ender's soldiers from activating the gate. More of Ender's ships could be hit and destroyed, so that of the six fleets only two were able to get to the planet, and those were decimated. But those tiny groups *did* get through, and they opened fire on the planet.

Ender leaned forward now, anxious to see if his guess would pay off. He half expected a buzzer to sound and the game to be stopped, because he had broken the rule. But he was betting on the accuracy of the simulator. If it could simulate a planet, it could simulate what would happen to a planet under attack.

It did.

The weapons that blew up little ships didn't blow up the entire planet at first. But they did cause terrible explosions. And on the planet there was no space to dissipate the chain reaction. On the planet the chain reaction found more and more fuel to feed it.

The planet's surface seemed to be moving back and forth, but soon the surface gave way in an immense explosion that sent light flashing in all directions. It swallowed up Ender's entire fleet. And then it reached the enemy ships.

The first simply vanished in the explosion. Then, as the explosion spread and became less bright, it was clear what happened to each ship. As the light reached them they flashed brightly for a moment and disappeared. They were all fuel for the fire of the planet.

It took more than three minutes for the explosion to reach the limits of the simulator, and by then it was much fainter. All the ships were gone, and if any had escaped before the explosion reached them, they were few and not worth worrying about. Where the planet had been there was nothing. The simulator was empty.

Ender had destroyed the enemy by sacrificing his entire fleet and breaking the rule against destroying the enemy planet. He wasn't sure whether to feel triumphant at his victory or defiant at the rebuke he was certain would come. So instead he felt nothing. He was tired. He wanted to go to bed and sleep.

He switched off the simulator, and finally heard the noise behind him.

There were no longer two rows of dignified military observers. Instead there was chaos. Some of them were slapping each other on the back; some of them were bowed, head in hands; others were openly weeping. Captain Graff detached himself from the group and came to Ender. Tears streamed down his face, but he was smiling. He reached out his arms, and to Ender's surprise he embraced the boy, held him tightly, and whispered, "Thank you, thank you, thank you, Ender."

Soon all the observers were gathered around the bewildered child, thanking him and cheering him and patting him on the shoulder and shaking his hand. Ender tried to make sense of what they were saying. Had he passed the test after all? Why did it matter so much to them?

Then the crowd parted and Maezr Rackham walked through. He came straight up to Ender Wiggins and held out his hand.

"You made the hard choice, boy. But heaven knows there was no other way you could have done it. Congratulations. You beat them, and it's all over."

All over. Beat them. "I beat *you,* Maezr Rackham."

Maezr laughed, a loud laugh that filled the room. "Ender Wiggins, you never played me. You never played a *game* since I was your teacher."

Ender didn't get the joke. He had played a great many games, at a terrible cost to himself. He began to get angry.

Maezr reached out and touched his shoulder. Ender shrugged him off. Maezr then grew serious and said, "Ender Wiggins, for the last months you have been the commander of our fleets. There were no games. The battles were real. Your only enemy was *the* enemy. You won every battle. And finally today you fought them at their home world, and you destroyed their world, their fleet, you destroyed them completely, and they'll never come against us again. You did it. You."

Real. Not a game. Ender's mind was too tired to cope with it all. He walked away from Maezr, walked silently through the crowd that still whispered thanks and congratulations to the boy, walked out of the simulator room and finally arrived in his bedroom and closed the door.

He was asleep when Graff and Maezr Rackham found him. They came in quietly and roused him. He awoke slowly, and when he recognized them he turned away to go back to sleep.

"Ender," Graff said. "We need to talk to you."

Ender rolled back to face them. He said nothing.

Graff smiled. "It was a shock to you yesterday, I know. But it must make you feel good to know you won the war."

Ender nodded slowly.

"Maezr Rackham here, he never played against you. He only analyzed your battles to find out your weak spots, to help you improve. It worked, didn't it?"

Ender closed his eyes tightly. They waited. He said, "Why didn't you tell me?"

Maezr smiled. "A hundred years ago, Ender, we found out some things. That when a commander's life is in danger he becomes afraid, and fear slows down his thinking. When a commander knows that he's killing people, he becomes cautious or insane, and neither of those help him do well. And when he's mature, when he has responsibilities and an understanding of the world, he becomes cautious and sluggish and can't do his job. So we trained children, who didn't know anything but the game, and never knew when it would become real. That was the theory, and you proved that the theory worked."

Graff reached out and touched Ender's shoulder. "We launched the ships so that they would all arrive at their destination during these few months. We knew that we'd probably have only one good commander, if we were lucky. In history it's been very rare to have more than one genius in a war. So we planned on having a genius. We were gambling. And you came along and we won."

Ender opened his eyes again and they realized that he was angry. "Yes, you won."

Graff and Maezr Rackham looked at each other. "He doesn't understand," Graff whispered.

"I understand," Ender said. "You needed a weapon, and you got it, and it was me."

"That's right," Maezr answered.

"So tell me," Ender went on, "how many people lived on that planet that I destroyed."

They didn't answer him. They waited awhile in silence, and then Graff spoke. "Weapons don't need to understand what they're pointed at, Ender. We did the pointing, and so we're responsible. You just did your job."

Maezr smiled. "Of course, Ender, you'll be taken care of. The government will never forget you. You served us all very well."

Ender rolled over and faced the wall, and even though they tried to talk to him, he didn't answer them. Finally they left.

Ender lay in his bed for a long time before anyone disturbed him again. The door opened softly. Ender didn't turn to see who it was. Then a hand touched him softly.

"Ender, it's me, Bean."

Ender turned over and looked at the little boy who was standing by his bed.

"Sit down," Ender said.

Bean sat. "That last battle, Ender. I didn't know how you'd get us out of it."

Ender smiled. "I didn't. I cheated. I thought they'd kick me out."

"Can you believe it! We won the war. The whole war's over, and we thought we'd have to wait till we grew up to fight in it, and it was us fighting it all the time. I mean, Ender, we're little kids. I'm a little kid, anyway." Bean laughed and Ender smiled. Then they were silent for a little while, Bean sitting on the edge of the bed, Ender watching him out of half-closed eyes.

Finally Bean thought of something else to say.

"What will we do now that the war's over?" he said.

Ender closed his eyes and said, "I need some sleep, Bean."

Bean got up and left and Ender slept.

Graff and Anderson walked through the gates into the park. There was a breeze, but the sun was hot on their shoulders.

"Abba Technics? In the capital?" Graff asked.

"No, in Biggock County. Training division," Anderson replied. "They think my work with children is good preparation. And you?"

Graff smiled and shook his head. "No plans. I'll be here for a few more months. Reports, winding down. I've had offers. Personnel development for DCIA, executive vice-president for U and P, but I said no. Publisher wants me to do memoirs of the war. I don't know."

They sat on a bench and watched leaves shivering in the breeze.

Children on the monkey bars were laughing and yelling, but the wind and the distance swallowed their words. "Look," Graff said, pointing. A little boy jumped from the bars and ran near the bench where the two men sat. Another boy followed him, and holding his hands like a gun he made an explosive sound. The child he was shooting at didn't stop. He fired again.

"I got you! Come back here!"

The other little boy ran on out of sight.

"Don't you know when you're dead?" The boy shoved his hands in his pockets and kicked a rock back to the monkey bars. Anderson smiled and shook his head. "Kids," he said. Then he and Graff stood up and walked on out of the park.

Joe W. Haldeman

HERO

1   "**T**onight we're going to show you eight silent ways to kill a man." The guy who said that was a sergeant who didn't look five years older than I. Ergo, as they say, he couldn't possibly ever have killed a man, not in combat, silently or otherwise.

I already knew eighty ways to kill people, though most of them were pretty noisy. I sat up straight in my chair and assumed a look of polite attention and fell asleep with my eyes open. So did most everybody else. We'd learned that they never schedule anything important for these after-chop classes.

The projector woke me up and I sat through a short movie showing the "eight silent ways." Some of the actors must have been brainwipes, since they were actually killed.

After the movie a girl in the front row raised her hand. The sergeant nodded at her and she rose to parade rest. Not bad looking, but kind of chunky about the neck and shoulders. Everybody gets that way after carrying a heavy pack around for a couple of months.

"Sir"—we had to call sergeants "sir" until graduation—"most of those methods, really, they looked . . . kind of silly."

"For instance?"

"Like killing a man with a blow to the kidneys, from an entrenching tool. I mean, when would you *actually* just have an entrenching tool, and no gun or knife? And why not just bash him over the head with it?"

"He might have a helmet on," he said reasonably.

"Besides, Taurans probably don't even *have* kidneys!"

He shrugged. "Probably they don't." This was 1997, and we'd never seen a Tauran: hadn't even found any pieces of Taurans bigger than a scorched chromosome. "But their body chemistry is similar to ours, and we have to assume they're similarly complex creatures. They *must* have weaknesses, vulnerable spots. You have to find out where they are.

"That's the important thing." He stabbed a finger at the screen. "That's why those eight convicts got caulked for your benefit . . . you've got to find out how to kill Taurans, and be able to do it whether you have a megawatt laser or just an emery board."

She sat back down, not looking too convinced.

"Any more questions?" Nobody raised a hand.

"O.K.—tench-hut!" We staggered upright and he looked at us expectantly.

"Screw you, sir," came the tired chorus.

"Louder!"

"SCREW YOU, SIR!"

One of the army's less-inspired morale devices.

"That's better. Don't forget, predawn maneuvers tomorrow. Chop at 0330, first formation, 0400. Anybody sacked after 0340 gets one stripe. Dismissed."

I zipped up my coverall and went across the snow to the lounge for a cup of soya and a joint. I'd always been able to get by on five or six hours of sleep, and this was the only time I could be by myself, out of the army for a while. Looked at the newsfax for a few minutes. Another ship got caulked, out by Aldebaran sector. That was four years ago. They were mounting a reprisal fleet, but it'll take four years more for them to get out there. By then, the Taurans would have every portal planet sewed up tight.

Back at the billet, everybody else was sacked and the main lights were out. The whole company'd been dragging ever since we got back from the two-week lunar training. I dumped my clothes in the locker, checked the roster and found out I was in bunk 31. Damn it, right under the heater.

I slipped through the curtain as quietly as possible so as not to wake up my bunkmate. Couldn't see who it was, but I couldn't have cared less. I slipped under the blanket.

"You're late, Mandella," a voice yawned. It was Rogers.

"Sorry I woke you up," I whispered.

"'Sallright." She snuggled over and clasped me spoon-fashion. She was warm and reasonably soft. I patted her hip in what I hoped was a brotherly fashion. "Night, Rogers."

"G'night, Stallion." She returned the gesture, a good deal more point-edly.

Why do you always get the tired ones when you're ready and the randy ones when you're tired? I bowed to the inevitable.

2 "**A**wright, let's get some *back* inta that! Stringer team! Move it up—move up!"

A warm front had come in about midnight and the snow had turned to sleet. The permaplast stringer weighed five hundred pounds and was a bitch to handle, even when it wasn't covered with ice. There were four of us, two at each end, carrying the plastic girder with frozen fingertips. Rogers and I were partners.

"Steel!" the guy behind me yelled, meaning that he was losing his hold. It wasn't steel, but it was heavy enough to break your foot. Every-body let go and hopped away. It splashed slush and mud all over us.

"Damn it, Petrov," Rogers said, "why didn't you go out for Star Fleet, or maybe the Red Cross? This damn thing's not that damn heavy." Most of the girls were a little more circumspect in their speech.

"Awright, get a *move* on, stringers—Epoxy team! Dog 'em! Dog 'em!"

Our two epoxy people ran up, swinging their buckets. "Let's go, Mandella. I'm freezin'."

"Me, too," the girl said earnestly.

"One—two—heave!" We got the thing up again and staggered to-ward the bridge. It was about three-quarters completed. Looked as if the Second Platoon was going to beat us. I wouldn't give a damn, but the platoon that got their bridge built first got to fly home. Four miles of muck for the rest of us, and no rest before chop.

We got the stringer in place, dropped it with a clank, and fitted the static clamps that held it to the rise-beams. The female half of the epoxy team started slopping glue on it before we even had it secured. Her partner was waiting for the stringer on the other side. The floor team was waiting at the foot of the bridge, each one holding a piece of the light stressed permaplast over his head, like an umbrella. They were dry and clean. I wondered aloud what they had done to deserve it, and Rogers suggested a couple of colorful, but unlikely possibilities.

We were going back to stand by the next stringer when the Field First—he was named Dougelstein, but we called him "Awright"—blew a whistle and bellowed, "Awright, soldier boys and girls, ten minutes. Smoke 'em if you got 'em." He reached into his pocket and turned on the control that heated our coveralls.

Rogers and I sat down on our end of the stringer and I took out my weed box. I had lots of joints, but we weren't allowed to smoke them until after night-chop. The only tobacco I had was a cigarro butt about three inches long. I lit it on the side of the box; it wasn't too bad after the first couple of puffs. Rogers took a puff to be sociable, but made a face and gave it back.

"Were you in school when you got drafted?" she asked.

"Yeah. Just got a degree in Physics. Was going after a teacher's certificate."

She nodded soberly. "I was in Biology. . . ."

"Figures." I ducked a handful of slush. "How far?"

"Six years, bachelor's and technical." She slid her boot along the ground, turning up a ridge of mud and slush the consistency of freezing ice milk. "Why the hell did this have to happen?"

I shrugged. It didn't call for an answer, least of all the answer that the UNEF kept giving us. Intellectual and physical elite of the planet, going out to guard humanity against the Tauran menace. It was all just a big experiment. See whether we could goad the Taurans into ground action.

Awright blew the whistle two minutes early, as expected, but Rogers and I and the other two stringers got to sit for a minute while the epoxy and floor teams finished covering our stringer. It got cold fast, sitting there with our suits turned off, but we remained inactive, on principle.

I really didn't see the sense of us having to train in the cold. Typical army half-logic. Sure, it was going to be cold where we were going; but not ice-cold or snow-cold. Almost by definition, a portal planet remained within a degree or two of absolute zero all the time, since collapsars don't shine—and the first chill you felt would mean that you were a dead man.

Twelve years before, when I was ten years old, they had discovered the collapsar jump. Just fling an object at a collapsar with sufficient speed, and it pops out in some other part of the galaxy. It didn't take long to figure out the formula that predicted where it would come out; it just traveled along the same "line"—actually an Einsteinian geodesic—it would have followed if the collapsar hadn't been in the way—until it reaches another collapsar field, whereupon it reappears, repelled with the same speed it had approaching the original collapsar. Travel time between the two collapsars is exactly zero.

It made a lot of work for mathematical physicists, who had to redefine simultaneity, then tear down general relativity and build it back up again. And it made the politicians very happy, because now they could send a shipload of colonists to Fomalhaut for less than it once cost to put a brace of men on the Moon. There were a lot of people the politicians would just love to see on Fomalhaut, implementing a glorious adventure instead of stirring up trouble at home.

The ships were always accompanied by an automated probe that followed a couple of million miles behind. We knew about the portal planets, little bits of flotsam that whirled around the collapsars; the purpose of the drone was to come back and tell us in the event that a ship had smacked into a portal planet at .999 of the speed of light.

That particular catastrophe never happened, but one day a drone did come limping back alone. Its data were analyzed, and it turned out that the colonists' ship had been pursued by another vessel and destroyed. This happened near Aldebaran, in the constellation Taurus, but since "Aldebaranian" is a little hard to handle, they named the enemy Taurans.

Colonizing vessels thenceforth went out protected by an armed guard. Often the armed guard went out alone, and finally the colonization effort itself slowed to a token trickle. The United Nations Exploratory and Colonization Group got shortened to UNEF, United Nations Exploratory Force, emphasis on the "force."

Then some bright lad in the General Assembly decided that we ought to field an army of footsoldiers to guard the portal planets of the nearer collapsars. This led to the Elite Conscription Act of 1996 and the most rigorously selected army in the history of warfare.

So here we are, fifty men and fifty women, with IQ's over 150 and bodies of unusual health and strength, slogging elitely through the mud and slush of central Missouri, reflecting on how useful our skill in building bridges will be, on worlds where the only fluid will be your occasional standing pool of liquid helium.

3 About a month later, we left for our final training exercise; maneuvers on the planet Charon. Though nearing perihelion it was still more than twice as far from the sun as Pluto.

The troopship was a converted "cattlewagon," made to carry two hundred colonists and assorted bushes and beasts. Don't think it was roomy, though, just because there were half that many of us. Most of the excess space was taken up with extra reaction mass and ordnance.

The whole trip took three weeks, accelerating at 2 Gs halfway; decelerating the other half. Our top speed, as we roared by the orbit of Pluto, was around one twentieth of the speed of light—not quite enough for relativity to rear its complicated head.

Three weeks of carrying around twice as much weight as normal . . . it's no picnic. We did some cautious exercises three times a day, and remained horizontal as much as possible. Still, we had several broken bones and serious dislocations. The men had to wear special supporters. It was almost impossible to sleep, what with nightmares of choking and being crushed, and the necessity of rolling over periodically to prevent blood pooling and bedsores. One girl got so fatigued that she almost slept through the experience of having a rib rub through to the open air.

I'd been in space several times before, so when we finally stopped decelerating and went into free fall, it was nothing but a relief. But some people had never been out, except for our training on the Moon, and succumbed to the sudden vertigo and disorientation. The rest of us cleaned up after them, floating through the quarters with sponges and inspirators to suck up globules of partly-digested "Concentrate, High-protein, Low-residue, Beef Flavor (Soya)."

A shuttle took us down to the surface in three trips. I waited for the last one, along with everybody else who wasn't bothered by free fall.

We had a good view of Charon, coming down from orbit. There wasn't much to see, though. It was just a dim, off-white sphere with a few smudges on it. We landed about two hundred meters from the base. A pressurized crawler came out and mated with the ferry, so we didn't have to suit up. We clanked and squeaked up to the main building, a featureless box of grayish plastic.

Inside, the walls were the same inspired color. The rest of the company was sitting at desks, chattering away. There was a seat next to Freeland.

"Jeff—feeling better?" He still looked a little pale.

"If the gods had meant for man to survive in free fall, they would have given him a cast-iron glottis. Somewhat better. Dying for a smoke."

"Yeah."

"*You* seemed to take it all right. Went up in school, didn't you?"

"Senior thesis in vacuum welding, yeah, three weeks in Earth orbit." I sat back and reached for my weed box, for the thousandth time. It still wasn't there, of course. The Life Support Unit didn't want to handle nicotine and THC.

"Training was bad enough," Jeff groused, "but *this* crap—"

"I don't know." I'd been thinking about it. "It might just all be worth it."

"Hell, no—this is a *space* war, let Star Fleet take care of it . . . they're just going to send us out and either we sit for fifty years on some damn ice cube of a portal planet, or we get. . . ."

"Well, Jeff, you've got to look at it the other way, too. Even if there's only one chance in a thousand that we'll be doing some good, keeping the Taurans. . . ."

* * *

"Tench-hut!" We stood up in a raggety-ass fashion, by twos and threes. The door opened and a full major came in. I stiffened a little. He was the highest-ranking officer I'd ever seen. He had a row of ribbons stitched into his coveralls, including a purple strip meaning he'd been wounded in combat, fighting in the old American army. Must have been that Indochina thing, but it had fizzled out before I was born. He didn't look that old.

"Sit, sit." He made a patting motion with his hand. Then he put his hands on his hips and scanned the company with a small smile on his face. "Welcome to Charon. You picked a lovely day to land; the temperature outside is a summery eight point one five degrees Absolute. We expect little change for the next two centuries or so." Some of us laughed half-heartedly.

"You'd best enjoy the tropical climate here at Miami Base, enjoy it while you can. We're on the center of sunside here, and most of your training will be on darkside. Over there, the temperature drops to a chilly two point zero eight.

"You might as well regard all the training you got on Earth and the Moon as just a warm-up exercise, to give you a fair chance of surviving Charon. You'll have to go through your whole repertory here: tools, weapons, maneuvers. And you'll find that, at these temperatures, tools don't work the way they should, weapons don't want to fire. And people move v-e-r-y cautiously."

He studied the clipboard in his hand. "Right now, you have forty-nine women and forty-eight men. Two deaths, one psychiatric release. Having read an outline of your training program, I'm frankly surprised that so many of you pulled through.

"But you might as well know that I won't be displeased if as few as fifty of you graduate from this final phase. And the only way not to graduate is to die. Here. The only way anybody gets back to Earth—including me—is after a combat tour.

"You will complete your training in one month. From here you go to Stargate collapsar, a little over two lights away. You will stay at the settlement on Stargate I, the largest portal planet, until replacements arrive. Hopefully, that will be no more than a month; another group is due here as soon as you leave.

"When you leave Stargate, you will be going to a strategically important collapsar, set up a military base there, and fight the enemy, if attacked. Otherwise, maintain the base until further orders.

"The last two weeks of your training will consist of constructing such a base, on darkside. There you will be totally isolated from Miami Base: no communication, no medical evacuation, no resupply. Sometime before the two weeks are up, your defense facilities will be evaluated in an attack by guided drones. They will be armed.

"All of the permanent personnel here on Charon are combat veterans. Thus, all of us are forty to fifty years of age, but I think we can keep up with you. Two of us will be with you at all times, and will accompany you at least as far as Stargate. They are Captain Sherman Stott, your company commander, and Sergeant Octavio Cortez, your first sergeant. Gentlemen?"

Two men in the front row stood easily and turned to face us. Captain Stott was a little smaller than the major, but cut from the same mold; face hard and smooth as porcelain, cynical half-smile, a precise centimeter of beard framing a large chin, looking thirty at the most. He wore a large, gunpowder-type pistol on his hip.

Sergeant Cortez was another story. His head was shaved and the wrong shape; flattened out on one side where a large piece of skull had obviously been taken out. His face was very dark and seamed with wrinkles and scars. Half his left ear was missing and his eyes were as expressive as buttons on a machine. He had a moustache-and-beard combination that looked like a skinny white caterpillar taking a lap around his mouth. On anybody else, his schoolboy smile might look pleasant, but he was about the ugliest, meanest-looking creature I'd ever seen. Still, if you didn't look at his head and considered the lower six feet or so, he could pose as the "after" advertisement for a body-building spa. Neither Stott nor Cortez wore any ribbons. Cortez had a small pocketlaser suspended in a magnetic rig, sideways, under his left armpit. It had wooden grips that were worn very smooth.

"Now, before I turn you over to the tender mercies of these two gentlemen, let me caution you again.

"Two months ago there was not a living soul on this planet, a working force of forty-five men struggled for a month to erect this base. Twenty-four of them, more than half, died in the construction of it. This is the most dangerous planet men have ever tried to live on, but the places you'll be going will be this bad and worse. Your cadre will try to keep you alive for the next month. Listen to them . . . and follow their example; all of them have survived here for longer than you'll have to. Captain?" The captain stood up as the major went out the door.

"Tench-*hut!*" The last syllable was like an explosion and we all jerked to our feet.

"Now I'm only gonna say this *once* so you better listen," he growled. "We *are* in a combat situation here and in a combat situation there is only *one* penalty for disobedience and insubordination." He jerked the pistol from his hip and held it by the barrel, like a club. "This is an Army model 1911 automatic *pistol* caliber .45 and it is a primitive, but effective, weapon. The sergeant and I are authorized to use our weapons to kill to enforce discipline, don't make us do it because we will. We *will."* He put the pistol back. The holster snap made a loud crack in the dead quiet.

"Sergeant Cortez and I between us have killed more people than are sitting in this room. Both of us fought in Vietnam on the American side and both of us joined the United Nations International Guard more than ten years ago. I took a break in grade from major for the privilege of commanding this company, and First Sergeant Cortez took a break from sub-major, because we are both *combat* soldiers and this is the first *combat* situation since 1974.

"Keep in mind what I've said while the First Sergeant instructs you more specifically in what your duties will be under this command. Take over, Sergeant." He turned on his heel and strode out of the room, with the little smile on his face that hadn't changed one millimeter during the whole harangue.

The First Sergeant moved like a heavy machine with lots of ball bearings. When the door hissed shut he swiveled ponderously to face us and said, "At ease, siddown," in a surprisingly gentle voice. He sat on a table in the front of the room. It creaked—but held.

"Now the captain talks scary and I look scary, but we both mean well. You'll be working pretty closely with me, so you better get used to this thing I've got hanging in front of my brain. You probably won't see the captain much, except on maneuvers."

He touched the flat part of his head. "And speaking of brains, I still have just about all of mine, in spite of Chinese efforts to the contrary. All of us old vets who mustered into UNEF had to pass the same criteria that got you drafted by the Elite Conscription Act. So I suspect all of you are smart and tough—but just keep in mind that the captain and I are smart and tough *and* experienced."

He flipped through the roster without really looking at it. "Now, as the captain said, there'll be only one kind of disciplinary action, on maneuvers. Capital punishment. But normally *we* won't have to kill you for disobeying. Charon'll save us the trouble.

"Back in the billeting area, it'll be another story. We don't much care what you do inside, but once you suit up and go outside, you've gotta have discipline that would shame a Centurian. There will be situations where one stupid act could kill us all.

"Anyhow, the first thing we've gotta do is get you fitted to your fighting suits. The armorer's waiting at your billet; he'll take you one at a time. Let's go."

4

"Now I know you got lectured and lectured on what a fighting suit can do, back on Earth." The armorer was a small man, partially bald, with no insignia of rank on his coveralls. Sergeant Cortez told us to call him "sir," since he was a lieutenant.

"But I'd like to reinforce a couple of points, maybe add some things your instructors Earthside weren't clear about, or couldn't know. Your First Sergeant was kind enough to consent to being my visual aid. Sergeant?"

Cortez slipped out of his coveralls and came up to the little raised platform where a fighting suit was standing, popped open like a man-shaped clam. He backed into it and slipped his arms into the rigid sleeves. There was a click and the thing swung shut with a sigh. It was bright green with CORTEZ stenciled in white letters on the helmet.

"Camouflage, Sergeant." The green faded to white, then dirty gray. "This is good camouflage for Charon, and most of your portal planets," said Cortez, from a deep well. "But there are several other combinations available." The gray dappled and brightened to a combination of greens and browns: "Jungle." Then smoothed out to a hard light ochre: "Desert." Dark brown, darker, to a deep flat black: "Night or space."

"Very good, Sergeant. To my knowledge, this is the only feature of the suit which was perfected after your training. The control is around your left wrist and is admittedly awkward. But once you find the right combination, it's easy to lock in.

"Now, you didn't get much in-suit training Earthside because we didn't want you to get used to using the thing in a friendly environment. The fighting suit is the deadliest personal weapon ever built, and with no weapon it is easier for the user to kill himself through carelessness. Turn around, Sergeant.

"Case in point." He tapped a square protuberance between the shoulders. "Exhaust fins. As you know the suit tries to keep you at a comfortable temperature no matter what the weather's like outside. The material of the suit is as near to a perfect insulator as we could get, consistent with mechanical demands. Therefore, these fins get *hot*— especially hot, compared to darkside temperatures—as they bleed off the body's heat.

"All you have to do is lean up against a boulder of frozen gas; there's lots of it around. The gas will sublime off faster than it can escape from the fins; in escaping, it will push against the surrounding 'ice' and fracture it . . . and in about one hundredth of a second, you have the equivalent of a hand grenade going off right below your neck. You'll never feel a thing.

"Variations on this theme have killed eleven people in the past two months. And they were just building a bunch of huts.

"I assume you know how easily the waldo capabilities can kill you or your companions. Anybody want to shake hands with the sergeant?" He stepped over and clasped his glove. "He's had lots of practice. Until *you* have, be extremely careful. You might scratch an itch and wind up bleeding to death. Remember, semi-logarithmic respose: two pounds' pressure exerts five pounds' force; three pounds gives ten; four pounds, twenty-three; five pounds, forty-seven. Most of you can muster up a grip of well over a hundred pounds. Theoretically, you could rip a steel girder in two with that, amplified. Actually, you'd destroy the material of your gloves and, at least on Charon, die very quickly. It'd be a race between decompression and flash-freezing. You'd be the loser.

"The leg waldos are also dangerous, even though the amplification is less extreme. Until you're really skilled, don't try to run, or jump. You're likely to trip, and that means you're likely to die.

"Charon's gravity is three-fourths of Earth normal, so it's not too bad. But on a really small world, like Luna, you could take a running jump and not come down for twenty minutes, just keep sailing over the horizon. Maybe bash into a mountain at eighty meters per second. On a small asteroid, it'd be no trick at all to run up to escape velocity and be off on an informal tour of intergalactic space. It's a slow way to travel.

"Tomorrow morning, we'll start teaching you how to stay alive inside of this infernal machine. The rest of the afternoon and evening, I'll call you one at a time to be fitted. That's all, Sergeant."

Cortez went to the door and turned the stopcock that let air into the air lock. A bank of infrared lamps went on to keep the air from freezing inside it. When the pressures were equalized, he shut the stopcock, unclamped the door and stepped in, clamping it shut behind him. A pump hummed for about a minute, evacuating the air lock, then he stepped out and sealed the outside door. It was pretty much like the ones on Luna.

"First I want Private Omar Almizar. The rest of you can go find your bunks. I'll call you over the squawker."

"Alphabetical order, sir?"

"Yep. About ten minutes apiece. If your name begins with Z, you might as well get sacked."

That was Rogers. She probably *was* thinking about getting sacked.

5 The sun was a hard white point directly overhead. It was a lot brighter than I had expected it to be; since we were eighty AUs out, it was only 1/6400th as bright as it is on Earth. Still, it was putting out about as much light as a powerful streetlamp.

"This is considerably more light than you'll have on a portal planet,"

Captain Stott's voice crackled in our collective ear. "Be glad that you'll be able to watch your step."

We were lined up, single file, on a permaplast sidewalk connecting the billet and the supply hut. We'd practiced walking inside, all morning, and this wasn't any different except for the exotic scenery. Though the light was rather dim, you could see all the way to the horizon quite clearly, with no atmosphere in the way. A black cliff that looked too regular to be natural stretched from one horizon to the other, passing within a kilometer of us. The ground was obsidian-black, mottled with patches of white, or bluish, ice. Next to the supply hut was a small mountain of snow in a bin marked OXYGEN.

The suit was fairly comfortable, but it gave you the odd feeling of being simultaneously a marionette and a puppeteer. You apply the impulse to move your leg and the suit picks it up and magnifies it and moves your leg for you.

"Today we're only going to walk around the company area and nobody will *leave* the company area." The captain wasn't wearing his .45, but he had a laser-finger like the rest of us. And his was probably hooked up.

Keeping an interval of at least two meters between each person, we stepped off the permaplast and followed the captain over the smooth rock. We walked carefully for about an hour, spiraling out, and finally stopped at the far edge of the perimeter.

"Now everybody pay close attention. I'm going out to that blue slab of ice"—it was a big one, about twenty meters away—"and show you something that you'd better know if you want to live."

He walked out a dozen confident steps. "First I have to heat up a rock—filters down." I slapped the stud under my armpit and the filter slid into place over my image converter. The captain pointed his finger at a black rock the size of a basketball and gave it a short burst. The glare rolled a long shadow of the captain over us and beyond. The rock shattered into a pile of hazy splinters.

"It doesn't take long for these to cool down." He stooped and picked up a piece. "This one is probably twenty or twenty-five degrees. Watch." He tossed the "warm" rock on the ice slab. It skittered around in a crazy pattern and shot off the side. He tossed another one, and it did the same.

"As you know you are not quite *perfectly* insulated. These rocks are about the temperature of the soles of your boots. If you try to stand on a slab of hydrogen the same thing will happen to you. Except that the rock is *already* dead.

"The reason for this behavior is that the rock makes a slick interface with the ice—a little puddle of liquid hydrogen—and rides a few molecules above the liquid on a cushion of hydrogen vapor. This makes the rock, or *you,* a frictionless bearing as far as the ice is concerned and you *can't* stand up without any friction under your boots.

"After you have lived in your suit for a month or so you *should* be able to survive falling down, but right *now* you just don't know enough. Watch."

The captain flexed and hopped up onto the slab. His feet shot out from under him and he twisted around in midair, landing on hands and knees. He slipped off and stood on the ground.

"The idea is to keep your exhaust fins from making contact with the frozen gas. Compared to the ice they are as hot as a blast furnace and contact with any weight behind it will result in an explosion."

After that demonstration, we walked around for another hour or so, and returned to the billet. Once through the air lock, we had to mill around for a while, letting the suits get up to something like room temperature. Somebody came up and touched helmets with me.

"William?" She had MC COY stenciled above her faceplate.

"Hi, Sean. Anything special?"

"I just wondered if you had anyone to sleep with tonight."

That's right; I'd forgotten, there wasn't any sleeping roster here. Everybody just chose his own partner. "Sure, I mean, uh, no . . . no, I haven't asked anybody, sure, if you want to. . . ."

"Thanks, William. See you later." I watched her walk away and thought that if anybody could make a fighting suit look sexy, it'd be Sean. But even Sean couldn't.

Cortez decided we were warm enough and led us to the suit room where we backed the things into place and hooked them up to the charging plates—each suit had a little chunk of plutonium that would power it for several years, but we were supposed to run on fuel cells as much as possible. After a lot of shuffling around, everybody finally got plugged in and we were allowed to unsuit, ninety-seven naked chickens squirming out of bright green eggs. It was *cold*—the air, the floor, and especially the suits—and we made a pretty disorderly exit toward the lockers.

I slipped on tunic, trousers and sandals and was still cold. I took my cup and joined the line for soya, everybody jumping up and down to keep warm.

"How c-cold, do you think, it is, M-Mandella?" That was McCoy.

"I don't, even want, to think, about it." I stopped jumping and rubbed myself as briskly as possible, while holding a cup in one hand. "At least as cold as Missouri was."

"Ung . . . wish they'd, get some damn heat in, this place." It always affects the small girls more than anybody else. McCoy was the littlest one in the company, a waspwaist doll barely five feet high.

"They've got the airco going. It can't be long now."

"I wish I, was a big, slab of, meat like, you."

I was glad she wasn't.

6   **W**e had our first casualty on the third day, learning how to dig holes.

With such large amounts of energy stored in a soldier's weapons, it wouldn't be practical for him to hack out a hole in the frozen ground with the conventional pick and shovel. Still, you can launch grenades all day and get nothing but shallow depressions—so the usual method is to bore a hole in the ground with the hand laser, drop a timed charge in after it's cooled down and, ideally, fill the hole with stuff. Of course, there's not much loose rock on Charon, unless you've already blown a hole nearby.

The only difficult thing about the procedure is getting away. To be safe, we were told, you've got to either be behind something really solid, or be at least a hundred meters away. You've got about three minutes after setting the charge, but you can't just spring away. Not on Charon.

The accident happened when we were making a really deep hole, the kind you want for a large underground bunker. For this, we had to blow a hole, then climb down to the bottom of the crater and repeat the procedure again and again until the hole was deep enough. Inside the crater we used charges with a five-minute delay, but it hardly seemed enough time—you really had to go slow, picking your way up the crater's edge.

Just about everybody had blown a double hole; everybody but me and three others. I guess we were the only ones paying really close attention when Bovanovitch got into trouble. All of us were a good two hundred meters away. With my image converter turned up to about forty power, I watched her disappear over the rim of the crater. After that I could only listen in on her conversation with Cortez.

"I'm on the bottom, Sergeant." Normal radio procedure was suspended for these maneuvers; only the trainee and Cortez could broadcast.

"O.K., move to the center and clear out the rubble. Take your time. No rush until you pull the pin."

"Sure, Sergeant." We could hear small echoes of rocks clattering; sound conduction through her boots. She didn't say anything for several minutes.

"Found bottom." She sounded a little out of breath.

"Ice, or rock?"

"Oh, it's rock, Sergeant. The greenish stuff."

"Use a low setting, then. One point two, dispersion four."

"God darn it, Sergeant, that'll take forever."

"Yeah, but that stuff's got hydrated crystals in it—heat it up too fast and you might make it fracture. And we'd just have to leave you there, girl."

"O.K., one point two dee four." The inside edge of the crater flickered red with reflected laser light.

"When you get about half a meter deep, squeeze it up to dee two."

"Roger." It took her exactly seventeen minutes, three of them at dispersion two. I could imagine how tired her shooting arm was.

"Now rest for a few minutes. When the bottom of the hole stops glowing, arm the charge and drop it in. Then *walk* out. Understand? You'll have plenty of time."

"I understand, Sergeant. Walk out." She sounded nervous. Well, you don't often have to tiptoe away from a twenty microton tachyon bomb. We listened to her breathing for a few minutes.

"Here goes." Faint slithering sound of the bomb sliding down.

"Slow and easy now, you've got five minutes."

"Y-yeah. Five." Her footsteps started out slow and regular. Then, after she started climbing the side, the sounds were less regular; maybe a little frantic. And with four minutes to go—

"Crap!" A loud scraping noise, then clatters and bumps.

"What's wrong, Private?"

"Oh, crap." Silence. "Crap!"

"Private, you don't wanna get shot, you *tell me what's wrong!*"

"I . . . I'm stuck, damn rockslide . . . DO SOMETHING I can't move. I can't move I, I—"

"Shut up! How deep?"

"Can't move my crap, my damn legs HELP ME—"

"Then damn it use your arms—push!—you can move a ton with each hand." Three minutes.

Then she stopped cussing and started to mumble, in Russian, I guess, a low monotone. She was panting and you could hear rocks tumbling away.

"I'm free." Two minutes.

"Go as fast as you can." Cortez's voice was flat, emotionless.

At ninety seconds she appeared crawling over the rim. "Run, girl . . . you better run." She ran five or six steps and fell, skidded a few meters and got back up, running; fell again, got up again—

It looked like she was going pretty fast, but she had only covered about thirty meters when Cortez said, "All right, Bovanovitch, get down on your stomach and lie still." Ten seconds, but she didn't hear him, or she wanted to get just a little more distance, and she kept running, careless leaping strides and at the high point of one leap there was a flash and a rumble and something big hit her below the neck and her headless body spun off end over end through space, trailing a red-black spiral of flash-frozen blood that settled gracefully to the ground, a path of crystal powder that nobody disturbed while we gathered rocks to cover the juiceless thing at the end of it.

That night Cortez didn't lecture us, didn't even show up for night-chop. We were all very polite to each other and nobody was afraid to talk about it.

I sacked with Rogers; everybody sacked with a good friend, but all she wanted to do was cry, and she cried so long and so hard that she got me doing it, too.

7   "**F**ire team A—move out!" The twelve of us advanced in a ragged line toward the simulated bunker. It was about a kilometer away, across a carefully prepared obstacle course. We could move pretty fast, since all of the ice had been cleared from the field, but even with ten days' experience we weren't ready to do more than an easy jog.

I carried a grenade launcher, loaded with tenth-microton practice grenades. Everybody had their laser-fingers set at point oh eight dee one; not much more than a flashlight. This was a *simulated* attack—the bunker and its robot defender cost too much to be used once and thrown away.

"Team B follow. Team leaders, take over."

We approached a clump of boulders at about the halfway mark, and Potter, my team leader, said "Stop and cover." We clustered behind the rocks and waited for team B.

Barely visible in their blackened suits, the dozen men and women whispered by us. As soon as they were clear, they jogged left, out of our line of sight.

"Fire!" Red circles of light danced a half-click downrange, where the bunker was just visible. Five hundred meters was the limit for these practice grenades; but I might luck out, so I lined the launcher up on the image of the bunker, held it at a 45° angle and popped off a salvo of three.

Return fire from the bunker started before my grenades even landed. Its automatic lasers were no more powerful than the ones we were using, but a direct hit would deactivate your image converter, leaving you blind. It was setting down a random field of fire, not even coming close to the boulders we were hiding behind.

Three magnesium-bright flashes blinked simultaneously, about thirty meters short of the bunker. "Mandella! I thought you were supposed to be *good* with that thing."

"Damn it, Potter—it only throws half a click. Once we get closer, I'll lay 'em right on top, every time."

"*Sure* you will." I didn't say anything. She wouldn't be team leader forever. Besides, she hadn't been such a bad girl before the power went to her head.

Since the grenadeier is the assistant team leader, I was slaved into Potter's radio and could hear B team talk to her.

"Potter, this is Freeman. Losses?"

"Potter here—no, looks like they were concentrating on you."

"Yeah, we lost three. Right now we're in a depression about eighty, a hundred meters down from you. We can give cover whenever you're ready."

"O.K., start." Soft click: "A team follow me." She slid out from behind the rock and turned on the faint pink beacon beneath her power-pack. I turned on mine and moved out to run alongside of her and the rest of the team fanned out in a trailing wedge. Nobody fired while B team laid down a cover for us.

All I could hear was Potter's breathing and the soft *crunch-crunch* of my boots. Couldn't see much of anything, so I tongued the image con-verter up to a log two intensification. That made the image kind of blurry but adequately bright. Looked like the bunker had B team pretty well pinned down; they were getting quite a roasting. All of their return fire was laser; they must have lost their grenadier.

"Potter, this is Mandella. Shouldn't we take some of the heat off B team?"

"Soon as I can find us good enough cover. Is that all right with you? Private?" She'd been promoted to corporal for the duration of the exer-cise.

We angled to the right and laid down behind a slab of rock. Most of the others found cover nearby, but a few had to just hug the ground.

"Freeman, this is Potter."

"Potter, this is Smithy. Freeman's out; Samuels is out. We only have five men left. Give us some cover so we can get. . . ."

"Roger, Smithy."—*click*—"Open up, A team. The B's are really hur-tin'."

I peeked out over the edge of the rock. My rangefinder said that the bunker was about three hundred fifty meters away, still pretty far. I aimed just a smidgeon high and popped three, then down a couple of degrees and three more. The first ones overshot by about twenty meters, then the second salvo flared up directly in front of the bunker. I tried to hold on that angle and popped fifteen, the rest of the magazine, in the same direction.

I should have ducked down behind the rock to reload, but I wanted to see where the fifteen would land, so I kept my eyes on the bunker while I reached back to unclip another magazine. . . .

When the laser hit my image converter there was a red glare so intense it seemed to go right through my eyes and bounce off the back of my skull. It must have been only a few milliseconds before the converter overloaded and went blind, but the bright green afterimage hurt my eyes for several minutes.

Since I was officially "dead," my radio automatically cut off and I had to remain where I was until the mock battle was over. With no sensory input besides the feel of my own skin—and it ached where the image converter had shone on it—and the ringing in my ears, it seemed like an awfully long time. Finally, a helmet clanked against mine:

"You O.K., Mandella?" Potter's voice.

"Sorry, I died of boredom twenty minutes ago."

"Stand up and take my hand." I did so and we shuffled back to the billet. It must have taken over an hour. She didn't say anything more, all the way back—it's a pretty awkward way to communicate—but after we'd cycled through the air lock and warmed up, she helped me undo my suit. I got ready for a mild tongue-lashing, but when the suit popped open, before I could even get my eyes adjusted to the light, she grabbed me around the neck and planted a wet kiss on my mouth.

"Nice shooting, Mandella."

"Huh?"

"The last salvo before you got hit—four direct hits; the bunker decided it was knocked out, and all we had to do was walk the rest of the way."

"Great." I scratched my face under the eyes and some dry skin flaked off. She giggled.

"You should see yourself, you look like. . . ."

"All personnel report to the assembly area." That was the captain's voice. Bad news.

She handed me a tunic and sandals. "Let's go."

The assembly area/chop hall was just down the corridor. There was a row of roll-call buttons at the door; I pressed the one beside my name. Four of the names were covered with black tape. That was good, we hadn't lost anybody else during today's maneuvers.

The captain was sitting on the raised dais, which at least meant we didn't have to go through the tench-hut bullshit. The place filled up in less than a minute; a soft chime indicated the roll was complete.

Captain Stott didn't stand up. "You did *fairly* well today, nobody got killed and I expected some to. In that respect you exceeded my expectations but in *every* other respect you did a poor job.

"I am glad you're taking good care of yourselves because each of you represents an investment of over a million dollars and one fourth of a human life.

"But in this simulated battle against a *very* stupid robot enemy, thirty-seven of you managed to walk into laser fire and be killed in a *sim*ulated way and since dead people require no food *you* will require no food, for the next three days. Each person who was a casualty in this battle will be allowed only two liters of water and a vitamin ration each day."

We knew enough not to groan or anything, but there were some pretty disgusted looks, especially on the faces that had singed eyebrows and a pink rectangle of sunburn framing their eyes.

"Mandella."

"Sir?"

"You are far and away the worst burned casualty. Was your image converter set on normal?"

Oh, crap. "No, sir. Log two."

"I see. Who was your team leader for the exercise?"

"Acting Corporal Potter, sir."

"Private Potter, did you order him to use image intensification?"

"Sir, I . . . I don't remember."

"You don't. Well as a memory exercise you may join the dead people. Is that satisfactory?"

"Yes, sir."

"Good. Dead people get one last meal tonight, and go on no rations starting tomorrow. Are there any questions?" He must have been kidding. "All right. Dismissed."

I selected the meal that looked as if it had the most calories and took my tray over to sit by Potter.

"That was a quixotic damn thing to do. But thanks."

"Nothing. I've been wanting to lose a few pounds anyway." I couldn't see where she was carrying any extra.

"I know a good exercise," I said. She smiled without looking up from her tray. "Have anybody for tonight?"

"Kind of thought I'd ask Jeff. . . ."

"Better hurry, then. He's lusting after Uhuru." Well, that was mostly true. Everybody did.

"I don't know. Maybe we ought to save our strength. That third day. . . ."

"Come on," I scratched the back of her hand lightly with a fingernail. "We haven't sacked since Missouri. Maybe I've learned something new."

"Maybe you have." She tilted her head up at me in a sly way. "O.K."

Actually, she was the one with the new trick. The French corkscrew, she called it. She wouldn't tell me who taught it to her, though. I'd like to shake his hand.

8

The two weeks' training around Miami Base eventually cost us eleven lives. Twelve, if you count Dahlquist. I guess having to spend the rest of your life on Charon, with a hand and both legs missing, is close enough to dying.

Little Foster was crushed in a landslide and Freeland had a suit malfunction that froze him solid before we could carry him inside. Most of the other deaders were people I didn't know all that well. But they all hurt. And they seemed to make us more scared rather than more cautious.

Now darkside. A flier brought us over in groups of twenty, and set us down beside a pile of building materials, thoughtfully immersed in a pool of helium II.

We used grapples to haul the stuff out of the pool. It's not safe to go wading, since the stuff crawls all over you and it's hard to tell what's underneath; you could walk out onto a slab of hydrogen and be out of luck.

I'd suggested that we try to boil away the pool with our lasers, but ten minutes of concentrated fire didn't drop the helium level appreciably. It didn't boil, either; helium II is a "superfluid," so what evaporation there was had to take place evenly, all over the surface. No hot spots, so no bubbling.

We weren't supposed to use lights, to "avoid detection." There was plenty of starlight, with your image converter cranked up to log three or four, but each stage of amplification meant some loss of detail. By log four, the landscape looked like a crude monochrome painting, and you couldn't read the names on people's helmets unless they were right in front of you.

The landscape wasn't all that interesting, anyhow. There were half a dozen medium-sized meteor craters—all with exactly the same level of helium II in them—and the suggestion of some puny mountains just over the horizon. The uneven ground was the consistency of frozen spiderwebs; every time you put your foot down, you'd sink half an inch with a squeaking crunch. It could get on your nerves.

It took most of a day to pull all the stuff out of the pool. We took shifts napping, which you could do either standing up, sitting, or lying on your stomach. I didn't do well in any of those positions, so I was anxious to get the bunker built and pressurized.

We couldn't build the thing underground—it'd just fill up with helium II—so the first thing to do was to build an insulating platform, a permaplast-vacuum sandwich three layers tall.

I was an acting corporal, with a crew of ten people. We were carrying the permaplast layers to the building site—two people can carry one easily—when one of "my" men slipped and fell on his back.

"Damn it, Singer, watch your step." We'd had a couple of deaders that way.

"Sorry, Corporal. I'm bushed, just got my feet tangled up."

"Yeah, just watch it." He got back up all right, and with his partner placed the sheet and went back to get another.

I kept my eye on him. In a few minutes he was practically staggering, not easy to do with that suit of cybernetic armor.

"Singer! After you set that plank, I want to see you."

"O.K." He labored through the task and mooched over.

"Let me check your readout." I opened the door on his chest to expose the medical monitor. His temperature was two degrees high; blood pressure and heart rate both elevated. Not up to the red line, though.

"You sick or something?"

"Hell, Mandella, I feel O.K., just tired. Since I fell I've been a little dizzy."

I chinned the medic's combination. "Doc, this is Mandella. You wanna come over here for a minute?"

"Sure, where are you?" I waved and he walked over from poolside.

"What's the problem?" I showed him Singer's readout.

He knew what all the other little dials and things meant, so it took him a while. "As far as I can tell, Mandella . . . he's just hot."

"Hell, I coulda told you that," said Singer.

"Maybe you better have the armorer take a look at his suit." We had two people who'd taken a crash course in suit maintenance; they were our "armorers."

I chinned Sanchez and asked him to come over with his tool kit.

"Be a couple of minutes, Corporal. Carryin' a plank."

"Well, put it down and get on over here." I was getting an uneasy feeling. Waiting for him, the medic and I looked over Singer's suit.

"Uh-oh," Doc Jones said. "Look at this." I went around to the back and looked where he was pointing. Two of the fins on the heat exchanger were bent out of shape.

"What is wrong?" Singer asked.

"You fell on your heat exchanger, right?"

"Sure, Corporal—that's it, it must not be working right."

"I don't think it's working at *all*," said Doc.

Sanchez came over with his diagnostic kit and we told him what had happened. He looked at the heat exchanger, then plugged a couple of jacks into it and got a digital readout from a little monitor in his kit. I didn't know what it was measuring, but it came out zero to eight decimal places.

Heard a soft click, Sanchez chinning my private frequency. "Corporal, this guy's a deader."

"What? Can't you fix the damn thing?"

"Maybe . . . maybe I could, if I could take it apart. But there's no way. . . ."

"Hey! Sanchez?" Singer was talking on the general freak. "Find out what's wrong?" He was panting.

Click. "Keep your pants on, man, we're working on it." *Click.* "He won't last long enough for us to get the bunker pressurized. And I can't work on the heat exchanger from outside of the suit."

"You've got a spare suit, haven't you?"

"Two of 'em, the fit-anybody kind. But there's no place . . . say. . . ."

"Right. Go get one of the suits warmed up." I chinned the general freak. "Listen, Singer, we've gotta get you out of that thing. Sanchez has a spare untit, but to make the switch, we're gonna have to build a house around you. Understand?"

"Huh-uh."

"Look, we'll just make a box with you inside, and hook it up to the life-support unit. That way you can breathe while you make the switch."

"Soun's pretty compis . . . complicated t'me."

"Look, just come along. . . ."

"I'll be all right, man, jus' lemme res'. . . ."

I grabbed his arm and led him to the building site. He was really weaving. Doc took his other arm and between us, we kept him from falling over.

"Corporal Ho, this is Corporal Mandella." Ho was in charge of the life-support unit.

"Go away, Mandella, I'm busy."

"You're going to be busier." I outlined the problem to her. While her group hurried to adapt the LSU—for this purpose, it need only be an air hose and heater—I got my crew to bring around six slabs of permaplast, so we could build a big box around Singer and the extra suit. It would look like a huge coffin, a meter square and six meters long.

We set the suit down on the slab that would be the floor of the coffin. "O.K., Singer, let's go."

No answer.

"Singer!" He was just standing there. Doc Jones checked his readout.

"He's out, man, unconscious."

* * *

My mind raced. There might just be room for another person in the box. "Give me a hand here." I took Singer's shoulders and Doc took his feet, and we carefully laid him out at the feet of the empty suit.

Then I laid down myself, above the suit. "O.K., close 'er up."

"Look, Mandella, if anybody goes in there, it oughta be me."

"No, Doc. *My* job. My man." That sounded all wrong. William Mandella, boy hero.

They stood a slab up on edge—it had two openings for the LSU input and exhaust—and proceeded to weld it to the bottom plank with a narrow laser beam. On Earth, we'd just use glue, but here the only fluid was helium, which has lots of interesting properties, but is definitely not sticky.

After about ten minutes we were completely walled up. I could feel the LSU humming. I switched on my suit light—the first time since we landed on darkside—and the glare made purple blotches dance in front of my eyes.

"Mandella, this is Ho. Stay in your suit at least two or three minutes. We're putting hot air in, but it's coming back just this side of liquid." I lay and watched the purple fade.

"O.K., it's still cold, but you can make it." I popped my suit. It wouldn't open all the way, but I didn't have too much trouble getting out. The suit was still cold enough to take some skin off my fingers and butt as I wiggled out.

I had to crawl feet-first down the coffin to get to Singer. It got darker fast, moving away from my light. When I popped his suit a rush of hot stink hit me in the face. In the dim light his skin was dark red and splotchy. His breathing was very shallow and I could see his heart palpitating.

First I unhooked the relief tubes—an unpleasant business—then the bio sensors, and then I had the problem of getting his arms out of their sleeves.

It's pretty easy to do for yourself. You twist this way and turn that way and the arm pops out. Doing it from the outside is a different matter: I had to twist his arm and then reach under and move the suit's arm to match—and it takes muscle to move a suit around from the outside.

Once I had one arm out it was pretty easy: I just crawled forward, putting my feet on the suit's shoulders, and pulled on his free arm. He slid out of the suit like an oyster slipping out of its shell.

I popped the spare suit and after a lot of pulling and pushing, managed to get his legs in. Hooked up the bio sensors and the front relief tube. He'd have to do the other one himself, it's too complicated. For the nth time I was glad not to have been born female; they have to have two of those damned plumber's friends, instead of just one and a simple hose.

I left his arms out of the sleeves. The suit would be useless for any kind of work, anyhow; waldos have to be tailored to the individual.

His eyelids fluttered. "Man . . . della. Where . . . the hell. . . ."

I explained, slowly, and he seemed to get most of it. "Now I'm gonna close you up and go get into my suit. I'll have the crew cut the end off this thing and I'll haul you out. Got it?"

He nodded. Strange to see that—when you nod or shrug in a suit, it doesn't communicate anything.

I crawled into my suit, hooked up the attachments and chinned the general freak. "Doc, I think he's gonna be O.K. Get us out of here now."

"Will do." Ho's voice. The LSU hum was replaced by a chatter, then a throb; evacuating the box to prevent an explosion.

One corner of the seam grew red, then white and a bright crimson beam lanced through, not a foot away from my head. I scrunched back as far as I could. The beam slid up the seam and around three corners, back to where it started. The end of the box fell away slowly, trailing filaments of melted 'plast.

"Wait for the stuff to harden, Mandella."

"Sanchez, I'm not that stupid."

"Here you go." Somebody tossed a line to me. That *would* be smarter than dragging him out by myself. I threaded a long bight under his arms and tied it behind his neck. Then I scrambled out to help them pull, which was silly—they had a dozen people already lined up to haul.

Singer got out all right and was actually sitting up while Doc Jones checked his readout. People were asking me about it and congratulating me when suddenly Ho said "Look!" and pointed toward the horizon.

It was a black ship, coming in fast. I just had time to think it wasn't fair, they weren't supposed to attack until the last few days, and then the ship was right on top of us.

9   **W**e all flopped to the ground instinctively, but the ship didn't attack. It blasted braking rockets and dropped to land on skids. Then it skied around to come to a rest beside the building site.

Everybody had it figured out and was standing around sheepishly when the two suited figures stepped out of the ship.

A familiar voice crackled over the general freak. "Every *one* of you saw us coming in and not *one* of you responded with laser fire. It wouldn't have done any good but it would have indicated a certain amount of fighting spirit. You have a week or less before the real thing and since the sergeant and *I* will be here *I* will insist that you show a little more will to live. Acting Sergeant Potter."

"Here, sir."

"Get me a detail of twelve men to unload cargo. We brought a hundred small robot drones for *tar*get practice so that you might have at least a fighting chance, when a live target comes over.

"Move *now;* we only have thirty minutes before the ship returns to Miami."

I checked, and it was actually more like forty minutes.

Having the captain and sergeant there didn't really make much difference; we were still on our own, they were just observing.

Once we got the floor down, it only took one day to complete the bunker. It was a gray oblong, featureless except for the air-lock blister and four windows. On top was a swivel-mounted bevawatt laser. The operator—you couldn't call him a "gunner"—sat in a chair holding dead-man switches in both hands. The laser wouldn't fire as long as he was holding one of those switches. If he let go, it would automatically aim for any moving aerial object and fire at will. Primary detection and aiming was by means of a kilometer-high antenna mounted beside the bunker.

It was the only arrangement that could really be expected to work, with the horizon so close and human reflexes so slow. You couldn't have the thing fully automatic, because in theory, friendly ships might also approach.

The aiming computer could choose up to twelve targets, appearing simultaneously—firing at the largest ones first. And it would get all twelve in the space of half a second.

The installation was partly protected from enemy fire by an efficient ablative layer that covered everything except the human operator. But then they *were* dead-man switches. One man above guarding eighty inside. The army's good at that kind of arithmetic.

Once the bunker was finished, half of us stayed inside at all times—feeling very much like targets—taking turns operating the laser, while the other half went on maneuvers.

About four clicks from the base was a large "lake" of frozen hydrogen; one of our most important maneuvers was to learn how to get around on the treacherous stuff.

It really wasn't too difficult. You couldn't stand up on it, so you had to belly down and slide.

If you had somebody to push you from the edge, getting started was no problem. Otherwise, you had to scrabble with your hands and feet, pushing down as hard as was practical, until you started moving, in a series of little jumps. Once started, you would keep going until you ran out of ice. You could steer a little bit by digging in, hand and foot, on the appropriate side, but you couldn't slow to a stop that way. So it was a good idea not to go too fast, and to be positioned in such a way that your helmet didn't absorb the shock of stopping.

We went through all the things we'd done on the Miami side; weapons practice, demolition, attack patterns. We also launched drones at irregular intervals, toward the bunker. Thus, ten or fifteen times a day, the operators got to demonstrate their skill in letting go of the handles as soon as the proximity light went on.

I had four hours of that, like everybody else. I was nervous until the first "attack," when I saw how little there was to it. The light went on, I let go, the gun aimed and when the drone peeped over the horizon—*zzt!* Nice touch of color, the molten metal spraying through space. Otherwise not too exciting.

So none of us were worried about the upcoming "graduation exercise," thinking it would be just more of the same.

Miami Base attacked on the thirteenth day with two simultaneous missiles streaking over opposite sides of the horizon at some forty kilometers per second. The laser vaporized the first one with no trouble, but the second got within eight clicks of the bunker before it was hit.

We were coming back from maneuvers, about a click away from the bunker. I wouldn't have seen it happen if I hadn't been looking directly at the bunker the moment of the attack.

The second missile sent a shower of molten debris straight toward the bunker. Eleven pieces hit, and, as we later reconstructed it, this is what happened.

The first casualty was Uhuru, pretty Uhuru inside the bunker, who was hit in the back and head and died instantly. With the drop in pressure, the LSU went into high gear. Friedman was standing in front of the main airco outlet and was blown into the opposite wall hard enough to knock him unconscious; he died of decompression before the others could get him to his suit.

Everybody else managed to stagger through the gale and get into their suits, but Garcia's suit had been holed and didn't do him any good.

By the time we got there, they had turned off the LSU and were welding up the holes in the wall. One man was trying to scrape up the unrecognizable mess that had been Uhuru. I could hear him sobbing and retching. They had already taken Garcia and Friedman outside for burial. The captain took over the repair detail from Potter. Sergeant Cortez led the sobbing man over to a corner and came back to work on cleaning up Uhuru's remains, alone. He didn't order anybody to help and nobody volunteered.

10

As a graduation exercise, we were unceremoniously stuffed into a ship—*Earth's Hope,* the same one we rode to Charon—and bundled off to Stargate at a little more than 1 G.

The trip seemed endless, about six months subjective time, and boring, but not as hard on the carcass as going to Charon had been. Captain Stott made us review our training orally, day by day, and we did exercises every day until we were worn to a collective frazzle.

Stargate I was like Charon's darkside, only more so. The base on Stargate I was smaller than Miami Base—only a little bigger than the one we constructed on darkside—and we were due to lay over a week to help expand the facilities. The crew there was very glad to see us; especially the two females, who looked a little worn around the edges.

We all crowded into the small dining hall, where Submajor Williamson, the man in charge of Stargate I, gave us some disconcerting news:

"Everybody get comfortable. Get off the tables, though, there's plenty of floor.

"I have some idea of what you just went through, training on Charon. I won't say it's all been wasted. But where you're headed, things will be quite different. Warmer."

He paused to let that soak in.

"Aleph Aurigae, the first collapsar ever detected, revolves around the normal star Epsilon Aurigae, in a twenty-seven-year orbit. The enemy has a base of operations, not on a regular portal planet of Aleph, but on a planet in orbit around Epsilon. We don't know much about the planet: just that it goes around Epsilon once every seven hundred forty-five days, is about three fourths the size of Earth, and has an albedo of 0.8, meaning it's probably covered with clouds. We can't say precisely how hot it will be, but judging from its distance from Epsilon, it's probably rather hotter than Earth. Of course, we don't know whether you'll be working ... fighting on lightside or darkside, equator or poles. It's highly unlikely that the atmosphere will be breathable—at any rate, you'll stay inside your suits.

"Now you know exactly as much about where you're going as I do. Questions?"

"Sir," Stein drawled, "now we know where we're goin' ... anybody know what we're goin' to do when we get there?"

Williamson shrugged. "That's up to your captain—and your sergeant, and the captain of *Earth's Hope,* and *Hope*'s logistic computer.

We just don't have enough data yet, to project a course of action for you. It may be a long and bloody battle, it may be just a case of walking in to pick up the pieces. Conceivably, the Taurans might want to make a peace offer"—Cortez snorted—"in which case you would simply be part of our muscle, our bargaining power." He looked at Cortez mildly. "No one can say for sure."

The orgy that night was kind of amusing, but it was like trying to sleep in the middle of a raucous beach party. The only area big enough to sleep all of us was the dining hall; they draped a few bedsheets here and there for privacy, then unleashed Stargate's eighteen sex-starved men on our women, compliant and promiscuous by military custom— and law—but desiring nothing so much as sleep on solid ground.

The eighteen men acted as if they were compelled to try as many permutations as possible, and their performance was impressive—in a strictly quantitative sense, that is.

The next morning—and every other morning we were on Stargate I—we staggered out of bed and into our suits, to go outside and work on the "new wing." Eventually, Stargate would be tactical and logistic headquarters for the war, with thousands of permanent personnel, guarded by half-a-dozen heavy cruisers in *Hope*'s class. When we started, it was two shacks and twenty people; when we left, it was four shacks and twenty people. The work was a breeze, compared to dark-side, since we had all the light we needed, and got sixteen hours inside for every eight hours' work. And no drone attacks for a final exam.

When we shuttled back up to the *Hope,* nobody was too happy about leaving—though some of the more popular females declared it'd be good to get some rest—Stargate was the last easy, safe assignment we'd have before taking up arms against the Taurans. And as Williamson had pointed out the first day, there was no way of predicting what that would be like.

Most of us didn't feel too enthusiastic about making a collapsar jump, either. We'd been assured that we wouldn't even feel it happen, just free fall all the way.

I wasn't convinced. As a physics student, I'd had the usual courses in general relativity and theories of gravitation. We only had a little direct data at that time—Stargate was discovered when I was in grade school —but the mathematical model seemed clear enough.

The collapsar Stargate was a perfect sphere about three kilometers in radius. It was suspended forever in a state of gravitational collapse that should have meant its surface was dropping toward its center at nearly the speed of light. Relativity propped it up, at least gave it the illusion of being there . . . the way all reality becomes illusory and observer-oriented when you study general relativity, or Buddhism.

At any rate, there would be a theoretical point in spacetime when one end of our ship was just above the surface of the collapsar, and the other end was a kilometer away—in our frame of reference. In any sane universe, this would set up tidal stresses and tear the ship apart, and we would be just another million kilograms of degenerate matter on the theoretical surface, rushing headlong to nowhere for the rest of eternity; or dropping to the center in the next trillionth of a second. You pays your money and you takes your frame of reference.

But they were right. We blasted away from Stargate I, made a few course corrections and then just dropped, for about an hour.

Then a bell rang and we sank into our cushions under a steady two gravities of deceleration. We were in enemy territory.

11 **W**e'd been decelerating at two gravities for almost nine days when the battle began. Lying on our couches being miserable, all we felt were two soft bumps, missiles being released. Some eight hours later, the squawkbox crackled: "Attention, all crew. This is the captain." Quinsana, the pilot, was only a lieutenant, but was allowed to call himself captain aboard the vessel, where he outranked all of us, even Captain Stott. "You grunts in the cargo hold can listen, too.

"We just engaged the enemy with two fifty-bevaton tachyon missiles, and have destroyed both the enemy vessel and another object which it had launched approximately three microseconds before.

"The enemy has been trying to overtake us for the past one hundred seventy-nine hours, ship time. At the time of the engagement, the enemy was moving at a little over half the speed of light, relative to Aleph, and was only about thirty AU's from *Earth's Hope*. It was moving at .47c relative to us, and thus we would have been coincident in spacetime"— rammed!—"in a little more than nine hours. The missiles were launched at 0719 ship's time, and destroyed the enemy at 1540, both tachyon bombs detonating within a thousand clicks of the enemy objects."

The two missiles were a type whose propulsion system itself was only a barely-controlled tachyon bomb. They accelerated at a constant rate of 100 Gs, and were traveling at a relativistic speed by the time the nearby mass of the enemy ship detonated them.

"We expect no further interference from enemy vessels. Our velocity with respect to Aleph will be zero in another five hours; we will then begin to journey back. The return will take twenty-seven days." General moans and dejected cussing. Everybody knew all that already, of course; but we didn't care to be reminded of it.

* * *

So after another month of logycalisthenics and drill, at a constant 2 Gs, we got our first look at the planet we were going to attack. Invaders from outer space, yes, sir.

It was a blinding white crescent basking two AU's from Epsilon. The captain had pinned down the location of the enemy base from fifty AU's out, and we had jockeyed in on a wide arc, keeping the bulk of the planet between them and us. That didn't mean we were sneaking up on them—quite the contrary; they launched three abortive attacks—but it put us in a stronger defensive position. Until we had to go to the surface, that is. Then only the ship and its Star Fleet crew would be reasonably safe.

Since the planet rotated rather slowly—once every ten and one half days—a "stationary" orbit for the ship had to be one hundred fifty thousand clicks out. This made the people in the ship feel quite secure, with six thousand miles of rock and ninety thousand miles of space between them and the enemy. But it meant a whole second's time lag in communication between us on the ground and the ship's battle computer. A person could get awful dead while that neutrino pulse crawled up and back.

Our vague orders were to attack the base and gain control while damaging a minimum of enemy equipment. We were to take at least one enemy alive. We were under no circumstances to allow *ourselves* to be taken alive, however. And the decision wasn't up to us; one special pulse from the battle computer, and that speck of plutonium in your power plant would fission with all of .01% efficiency, and you'd be nothing but a rapidly expanding, very hot plasma.

They strapped us into six scoutships—one platoon of twelve people in each—and we blasted away from *Earth's Hope* at 8 Gs. Each scoutship was supposed to follow its own carefully random path to our rendezvous point, one hundred eight clicks from the base. Fourteen drone ships were launched at the same time, to confound the enemy's anti-spacecraft system.

The landing went off almost perfectly. One ship suffered minor damage, a near miss boiling away some of the ablative material on one side of the hull, but it'd still be able to make it and return, as long as it kept its speed down while in the atmosphere.

We zigged and zagged and wound up first ship at the rendezvous point. There was only one trouble. It was under four kilometers of water.

I could almost hear that machine, ninety thousand miles away, grinding its mental gears, adding this new bit of data. We proceeded just as if we were landing on solid ground: braking rockets, falling, skids out, hit the water, skip, hit the water, skip, hit the water, sink.

It would have made sense to go ahead and land on the bottom—we were streamlined, after all, and water just another fluid—but the hull wasn't strong enough to hold up a four-kilometer column of water. Sergeant Cortez was in the scoutship with us.

"Sarge, tell that computer to *do* something! We're gonna get. . . ."

"Oh, shut up, Mandella. Trust in th' lord." "Lord" was definitely lower-case when Cortez said it.

There was a loud bubbly sigh, then another and a slight increase in pressure on my back that meant the ship was rising. "Flotation bags?" Cortez didn't deign to answer, or didn't know.

That must have been it. We rose to within ten or fifteen meters of the surface and stopped, suspended there. Through the port I could see the surface above, shimmering like a mirror of hammered silver. I wondered what it could be like, to be a fish and have a definite roof over your world.

I watched another ship splash in. It made a great cloud of bubbles and turbulence, then fell—slightly tailfirst—for a short distance before large bags popped out under each delta wing. Then it bobbed up to about our level and stayed.

Soon all of the ships were floating within a few hundred meters of us, like a school of ungainly fish.

"This is Captain Stott. Now listen carefully. There is a beach some twenty-eight clicks from your present position, in the direction of the enemy. You will be proceeding to this beach by scoutship and from there will mount your assault on the Tauran position." That was *some* improvement; we'd only have to walk eighty clicks.

We deflated the bags, blasted to the surface and flew in a slow, spread-out formation to the beach. It took several minutes. As the ship scraped to a halt I could hear pumps humming, making the cabin pressure equal to the air pressure outside. Before it had quite stopped moving, the escape slot beside my couch slid open. I rolled out onto the wing of the craft and jumped to the ground. Ten seconds to find cover— I sprinted across loose gravel to the "treeline," a twisty bramble of tall sparse bluish-green shrubs. I dove into the briar path and turned to watch the ships leave. The drones that were left rose slowly to about a hundred meters, then took off in all directions with a bone-jarring roar. The real scoutships slid slowly back into the water. Maybe that was a good idea.

It wasn't a terribly attractive world, but certainly would be easier to get around in than the cryogenic nightmare we were trained for. The sky was a uniform dull silver brightness that merged with the mist over the ocean so completely as to make it impossible to tell where water ended and air began. Small wavelets licked at the black gravel shore, much too slow and graceful in the three-quarters Earth normal gravity. Even from fifty meters away, the rattle of billions of pebbles rolling with the tide was loud in my ears.

The air temperature was 79° Centigrade, not quite hot enough for the sea to boil, even though the air pressure was low compared to Earth's. Wisps of steam drifted quickly upward from the line where water met land. I wondered how long a man would survive, exposed here without a suit. Would the heat or the low oxygen—partial pressure one-eighth Earth normal—kill him first? Or was there some deadly microorganism that would beat them both. . . .

"This is Cortez. Everybody come over and assemble by me." He was standing on the beach a little to the left of me, waving his hand in a circle over his head. I walked toward him through the shrubs. They were brittle, unsubstantial, seemed paradoxically dried-out in the steamy air. They wouldn't offer much in the way of cover.

"We'll be advancing on a heading .05 radians east of north. I want Platoon One to take point. Two and Three follow about twenty meters behind, to the left and right. Seven, command platoon, is in the middle, twenty meters behind Two and Three. Five and Six, bring up the rear, in a semicircular closed flank. Everybody straight?" Sure, we could do that "arrowhead" maneuver in our sleep. "O.K., let's move out."

I was in Platoon Seven, the "command group." Captain Stott put me there not because I was expected to give any commands, but because of my training in physics.

The command group was supposedly the safest place, buffered by six platoons: people were assigned to it because there was some tactical reason for them to survive at least a little longer than the rest. Cortez was there to give orders. Chavez was there to correct suit malfuncts. The senior medic, Doc Wilson—the only medic who actually had an MD— was there and so was Theodopolis, the radio engineer: our link with the captain, who had elected to stay in orbit.

The rest of us were assigned to the command group by dint of special training or aptitude that wouldn't normally be considered of a "tactical" nature. Facing a totally unknown enemy, there was no way of telling what might prove important. Thus I was there because I was the closest the company had to a physicist. Rogers was biology. Tate was chemistry. He could crank out a perfect score on the Rhine extrasensory perception test, every time. Bohrs was a polyglot, able to speak twenty-one languages fluently, idiomatically. Petrov's talent was that he had tested out to have not one molecule of xenophobia in his psyche. Keating was a skilled acrobat. Debby Hollister—"Lucky" Hollister—showed a remarkable aptitude for making money, and also had a consistently high Rhine potential.

12

When we first set out, we were using the "jungle" camouflage combination on our suits. But what passed for jungle in these anemic tropics was too sparse; we looked like a band of conspicuous harlequins trooping through the woods. Cortez had us switch to black, but that was just as bad, as the light from Epsilon came evenly from all parts of the sky, and there were no shadows except us. We finally settled on the dun-colored desert camouflage.

The nature of the countryside changed slowly as we walked north, away from the sea. The throned stalks, I guess you could call them trees, came in fewer numbers but were bigger around and less brittle; at the base of each was a tangled mass of vine with the same blue-green color, which spread out in a flattened cone some ten meters in diameter. There was a delicate green flower the size of a man's head near the top of each tree.

Grass began to appear some five clicks from the sea. It seemed to respect the trees' "property rights," leaving a strip of bare earth around each cone of vine. At the edge of such a clearing, it would grow as timid blue-green stubble; then, moving away from the tree, would get thicker and taller until it reached shoulder-high in some places, where the separation between two trees was unusually large. The grass was a lighter, greener shade than the trees and vines. We changed the color of our suits to the bright green we had used for maximum visibility on Charon. Keeping to the thickest part of the grass, we were fairly inconspicuous.

I couldn't help thinking that one week of training in a South American jungle would have been worth a hell of a lot more than all those weeks on Charon. We wouldn't be so understrength, either.

We covered over twenty clicks each day, buoyant after months under 2 Gs. Until the second day, the only form of animal life we saw was a kind of black worm, finger-sized with hundreds of cilium legs like the bristles of a stiff brush. Rogers said that there obviously had to be some sort of larger creature around, or there would be no reason for the trees to have thorns. So we were doubly on guard, expecting trouble both from the Taurans and the unidentified "large creatures."

Potter's Second Platoon was on point; the general freak was reserved for her, since point would likely be the first platoon to spot any trouble.

"Sarge, this is Potter," we all heard. "Movement ahead."

"Get down then!"

"We are. Don't think they see us."

"First Platoon, go up to the right of point. Keep down. Fourth, get up to the left. Tell me when you get in position. Sixth Platoon, stay back and guard the rear. Fifth and Third, close with the command group."

Two dozen people whispered out of the grass, to join us. Cortez must have heard from the Fourth Platoon.

"Good. How about you, First . . . O.K., fine. How many are there?"

"Eight we can see." Potter's voice.

"Good. When I give the word, open fire. Shoot to kill."

"Sarge . . . they're just animals."

"Potter—if you've known all this time what a Tauran looks like, you should've told us. Shoot to kill."

"But we need. . . ."

"We need a prisoner, but we don't need to escort him forty clicks to his home base and keep an eye on him while we fight. Clear?"

"Yes. Sergeant."

"O.K. Seventh, all you brains and weirds, we're going up and watch. Fifth and Third, come along to guard."

We crawled through the meter-high grass to where the Second Platoon had stretched out in a firing line.

"I don't see anything," Cortez said.

"Ahead and just to the left. Dark green."

They were only a shade darker than the grass. But after you saw the first one, you could see them all, moving slowly around some thirty meters ahead.

"Fire!" Cortez fired first, then twelve streaks of crimson leaped out and the grass wilted back, disappeared and the creatures convulsed and died trying to scatter.

"Hold fire, hold it!" Cortez stood up. "We want to have something left—Second Platoon, follow me." He strode out toward the smoldering corpses, laser finger pointed out front, obscene divining rod pulling him toward the carnage . . . I felt my gorge rising and knew that all the lurid training tapes, all the horrible deaths in training accidents, hadn't prepared me for this sudden reality . . . that I had a magic wand that I could point at a life and make it a smoking piece of half-raw meat; I wasn't a soldier nor even wanted to be one nor ever would want. . . .

"O.K., Seventh, come on up."

While we were walking toward them, one of the creatures moved, a tiny shudder, and Cortez flicked the beam of his laser over it with an almost negligent gesture. It made a hand-deep gash across the creature's middle. It died, like the others, without emitting a sound.

They were not quite as tall as humans, but wider in girth. They were covered with dark green, almost black fur; white curls where the laser had singed. They appeared to have three legs and an arm. The only ornament to their shaggy heads was a mouth, wet black orifice filled with flat black teeth. They were thoroughly repulsive but their worst feature was not a difference from human beings but a similarity . . . wherever the laser had opened a body cavity, milk-white glistening veined globes and coils of organs spilled out, and their blood was dark clotting red.

"Rogers, take a look. Taurans or not?"

Rogers knelt by one of the disemboweled creatures and opened a flat plastic box, filled with glistening dissecting tools. She selected a scalpel. "One way we might be able to find out." Doc Wilson watched over her shoulder as she methodically slit the membrane covering several organs.

"Here." She held up a blackish fibrous mass between two fingers, parody of daintiness through all that armor.

"So?"

"It's grass, Sergeant. If the Taurans can eat grass and breathe the air, they certainly found a planet remarkably like their home." She tossed it away. "They're animals, Sergeant, just damn animals."

"I don't know," Doc Wilson said. "Just because they walk around on all fours, threes maybe, and are able to eat grass. . . ."

"Well, let's check out the brain." She found one that had been hit on the head and scraped the superficial black char from the wound. "Look at that."

It was almost solid bone. She tugged and ruffled the hair all over the head of another one. "What the hell does it use for sensory organs? No eyes, or ears, or. . . ." She stood up. "Nothing in that head but a mouth and ten centimeters of skull. To protect nothing, not a damn thing."

"If I could shrug, I'd shrug," the doctor said. "It doesn't prove anything—a brain doesn't have to look like a mushy walnut and it doesn't have to be in the head. Maybe that skull isn't bone, maybe *that's* the brain, some crystal lattice. . . ."

"Yeah, but the stomach's in the right place, and if those aren't intestines I'll eat—"

"Look," Cortez said, "this is all real interesting, but all we need to know is whether that thing's dangerous, then we've gotta move on, we don't have all—"

"They aren't dangerous," Rogers began. "They don't. . . ."

"Medic! DOC!" Somebody was waving his arms, back at the firing line. Doc sprinted back to him, the rest of us following.

"What's wrong?" He had reached back and unclipped his medical kit on the run.

"It's Ho, she's out."

Doc swung open the door on HO's biomedical monitor. He didn't have to look far. "She's dead."

"Dead?" Cortez said. "What the hell. . . ."

"Just a minute." Doc plugged a jack into the monitor and fiddled with some dials on his kit. "Everybody's biomed readout is stored for twelve hours. I'm running it backwards, should be able to—there!"

"What?"

"Four and a half minutes ago—must have been when you opened fire...."

"Well?"

"Massive cerebral hemorrhage. No...." He watched the dials. "No ... warning, no indication of anything out of the ordinary; blood pressure up, pulse up, but normal under the circumstances ... nothing to ... indicate...." He reached down and popped her suit. Her fine oriental features were distorted in a horrible grimace, both gums showing. Sticky fluid ran from under her collapsed eyelids and a trickle of blood still dripped from each ear. Doc Wilson closed the suit back up.

"I've never seen anything like it. It's as if a bomb went off in her skull."

"Oh crap," Rogers said, "she was Rhine-sensitive, wasn't she."

"That's right." Cortez sounded thoughtful. "All right, everybody listen. Platoon leaders, check your platoons and see if anybody's missing, or hurt. Anybody else in Seventh?"

"I ... I've got a splitting headache, Sarge," Lucky said.

Four others had bad headaches. One of them affirmed that he was slightly Rhine-sensitive. The others didn't know.

"Cortez, I think it's obvious," Doc Wilson said, "that we should give these ... monsters wide berth, especially shouldn't harm any more of them. Not with five people susceptible to whatever apparently killed Ho."

"Of course, damn it, I don't need anybody to tell me that. We'd better get moving. I just filled the captain in on what happened; he agrees that we'd better get as far away from here as we can, before we stop for the night.

"Let's get back in formation and continue on the same bearing. Fifth Platoon, take over point; Second, come back to the rear. Everybody else, same as before."

"What about Ho?" Lucky asked.

"She'll be taken care of. From the ship."

After we'd gone half a click, there was a flash and rolling thunder. Where Ho had been, came a wispy luminous mushroom cloud boiling up to disappear against the gray sky.

13

We stopped for the "night"—actually, the sun wouldn't set for another seventy hours—atop a slight rise some ten clicks from where we had killed the aliens. But they weren't aliens, I had to remind myself—*we* were.

Two platoons deployed in a ring around the rest of us, and we flopped down exhausted. Everybody was allowed four hours'sleep and had two hours' guard duty.

Potter came over and sat next to me. I chinned her frequency.

"Hi, Marygay."

"Oh, William," her voice over the radio was hoarse and cracking. "God, it's so horrible."

"It's over now. . . ."

"I killed one of them, the first instant, I shot it right in the, in the . . ."

I put my hand on her knee. The contact made a plastic click and I jerked it back, visions of machines embracing, copulating. "Don't feel singled out, Marygay, whatever guilt there is, belongs evenly to all of us . . . but a triple portion for Cor. . . ."

"You privates quit jawin' and get some sleep. You both pull guard in two hours."

"O.K., Sarge." Her voice was so sad and tired I couldn't bear it. I felt if I could only touch her I could drain off the sadness like a ground wire draining current but we were each trapped in our own plastic world.

"G'night, William."

"Night." It's almost impossible to get sexually excited inside a suit, with the relief tube and all the silver chloride sensors poking you, but somehow this was my body's response to the emotional impotence, maybe remembering more pleasant sleeps with Marygay, maybe feeling that in the midst of all this death, personal death could be soon, cranking up the pro-creative derrick for one last try . . . lovely thoughts like this and I fell asleep and dreamed that I was a machine, mimicking the functions of life, creaking and clanking my clumsy way through the world, people too polite to say anything but giggling behind my back, and the little man who sat inside my head pulling the levers and clutches and watching the dials, he was hopelessly mad and was storing up hurts for the day. . . .

"Mandella—wake up, damn it, your shift!"

I shuffled over to my place on the perimeter to watch for God knows what . . . but I was so weary I couldn't keep my eyes open. Finally I tongued a stimtab, knowing I'd pay for it later.

For over an hour I sat there, scanning my sector left, right, near, far; the scene never changing, not even a breath of wind to stir the grass.

Then suddenly the grass parted and one of the three-legged creatures was right in front of me. I raised my finger but didn't squeeze.

"Movement!"

"Movement!"

"HOLD YOUR FIRE. Don't shoot!"

"Movement."

"Movement." I looked left and right and as far as I could see, every perimeter guard had one of the blind dumb creatures standing right in front of him.

Maybe the drug I'd taken to stay awake made me more sensitive to whatever they did. My scalp crawled and I felt a formless *thing* in my mind, the feeling you get when somebody has said something and you didn't quite hear it, want to respond but the opportunity to ask him to repeat it is gone.

The creature sat back on its haunches, leaning forward on the one front leg. Big green bear with a withered arm. Its power threaded through my mind, spiderwebs, echo of night terrors, trying to communicate, trying to destroy me, I couldn't know.

"All right, everybody on the perimeter, fall back, slow. Don't make any quick gestures . . . anybody got a headache or anything?"

"Sergeant, this is Hollister." Lucky.

"They're trying to say something . . . I can almost . . . no, just. . . ."

"Well?"

"All I can get is that they think we're . . . think we're . . . well, *funny.* They aren't afraid."

"You mean the one in front of you isn't. . . ."

"No, the feeling comes from all of them, they're all thinking the same thing. Don't ask me how I know, I just do."

"Maybe they thought it was funny, what they did to Ho."

"Maybe. I don't feel like they're dangerous. Just curious about us."

"Sergeant, this is Bohrs."

"Yeah."

"The Taurans have been here at least a year—maybe they've learned how to communicate with these . . . overgrown teddy-bears. They might be spying on us, might be sending back. . . ."

"I don't think they'd show themselves, if that were the case," Lucky said. "They can obviously hide from us pretty well when they want to."

"Anyhow," Cortez said, "if they're spies, the damage has been done. Don't think it'd be smart to take any action against them. I know you'd all like to see 'em dead for what they did to Ho, so would I, but we'd better be careful."

I didn't want to see them dead, but I'd just as soon not see them in any condition. I was walking backwards slowly, toward the middle of camp. The creature didn't seem disposed to follow. Maybe he just knew we were surrounded. He was pulling up grass with his arm and munching.

"O.K., all of you platoon leaders, wake everybody up, get a roll count. Let me know if anybody's been hurt. Tell your people we're moving out in one minute."

I don't know what Cortez expected, but of course the creatures just followed right along. They didn't keep us surrounded; just had twenty or thirty following us all the time. Not the same ones, either. Individuals would saunter away, new ones would join the parade. It was pretty obvious that *they* weren't going to tire out.

We were each allowed one stimtab. Without it, no one could have marched an hour. A second pill would have been welcome after the edge started to wear off, but the mathematics of the situation forbade it: we were still thirty clicks from the enemy base; fifteen hours' marching at the least. And though one could stay awake and energetic for a hundred hours on the 'tabs, aberrations of judgment and perception snowballed after the second 'tab, until *in extremis* the most bizarre hallucinations would be taken at face value, and a person would fidget for hours, deciding whether to have breakfast.

Under artificial stimulation, the company traveled with great energy for the first six hours, was slowing by the seventh, and ground to an exhausted halt after nine hours and nineteen kilometers. The teddy-bears had never lost sight of us and, according to Lucky, had never stopped "broadcasting." Cortez's decision was that we would stop for seven hours, each platoon taking one hour of perimeter guard. I was never so glad to have been in the Seventh Platoon, as we stood guard the last shift and thus were the only ones to get six hours of uninterrupted sleep.

In the few moments I lay awake after finally lying down, the thought came to me that the next time I closed my eyes could well be the last. And partly because of the drug hangover, mostly because of the past day's horrors, I found that I really just didn't give a damn.

14

Our first contact with the Taurans came during my shift.

The teddy-bears were still there when I woke up and replaced Doc Jones on guard. They'd gone back to their original formation, one in front of each guard position. The one who was waiting for me seemed a little larger than normal, but otherwise looked just like all the others. All the grass had been cropped where he was sitting, so he occasionally made forays to the left or right. But he always returned to sit right in front of me, you would say staring if he had had anything to stare with.

We had been facing each other for about fifteen minutes when Cortez's voice rumbled:

"Awright, everybody wake up and get hid!"

I followed instinct and flopped to the ground and rolled into a tall stand of grass.

"Enemy vessel overhead." His voice was almost laconic.

Strictly speaking, it wasn't really overhead, but rather passing somewhat east of us. It was moving slowly, maybe a hundred clicks per hour, and looked like a broomstick surrounded by a dirty soap bubble. The creature riding it was a little more human-looking than the teddy-bears, but still no prize. I cranked my image amplifier up to forty log two for a closer look.

He had two arms and two legs, but his waist was so small you could encompass it with both hands. Under the tiny waist was a large horse-shoe-shaped pelvic structure nearly a meter wide, from which dangled two ling skinny legs with no apparent knee joint. Above that waist his body swelled out again, to a chest no smaller than the huge pelvis. His arms looked surprisingly human, except that they were too long and undermuscled. There were too many fingers on his hands. Shoulderless, neckless; his head was a nightmarish growth that swelled like a goiter from his massive chest. Two eyes that looked like clusters of fish eggs, a bundle of tassles instead of a nose, and a rigidly open hole that might have been a mouth sitting low down where his Adam's apple should have been. Evidently the soap bubble contained an amenable environment, as he was wearing absolutely nothing except a ridged hide that looked like skin submerged too long in hot water, then dyed a pale orange. "He" had no external genitalia, nor anything that might hint of mammary glands.

Obviously, he either didn't see us, or thought we were part of the herd of teddy-bears. He never looked back at us, but just continued in the same direction we were headed, .05 rad east of north.

"Might as well go back to sleep now, if you can sleep after looking at *that* thing. We move out at 0435." Forty minutes.

Because of the planet's opaque cloud cover, there had been no way to tell, from space, what the enemy base looked like or how big it was. We only knew its position, the same way we knew the position the scout-ships were supposed to land on. So it could easily have been underwater too, or underground.

But some of the drones were reconnaissance ships as well as decoys; and in their mock attacks on the base, one managed to get close enough to take a picture. Captain Stott beamed down a diagram of the place to Cortez—the only one with a visor in his suit—when we were five clicks from the base's "radio" position. We stopped and he called all of the platoon leaders in with the Seventh Platoon to confer. Two teddy-bears loped in, too. We tried to ignore them.

"O.K., the captain sent down some pictures of our objective. I'm going to draw a map; you platoon leaders copy." They took pads and styli out of their leg pockets, while Cortez unrolled a large plastic mat. He gave it a shake to randomize any residual charge, and turned on his stylus.

"Now, we're coming from this direction." He put an arrow at the bottom of the sheet. "First thing we'll hit is this row of huts, probably billets, or bunkers, but who the hell knows . . . our initial objective is to destroy these buildings—the whole base is on a flat plain; there's no way we could really sneak by them."

"Potter here. Why can't we jump over them?"

"Yeah, we could do that, and wind up completely surrounded, cut to ribbons. We take the buildings.

"After we do that . . . all I can say is that we'll have to think on our feet. From the aerial reconnaissance, we can figure out the function of only a couple of buildings—and that stinks. We might wind up wasting a lot of time demolishing the equivalent of an enlisted man's bar, ignoring a huge logistic computer because it looks like . . . a garbage dump or something."

"Mandella here," I said. "Isn't there a spaceport of some kind— seems to me we ought to. . . ."

"I'll *get* to that, damn it. There's a ring of these huts all around the camp, so we've got to break through somewhere. This place'll be closest, less chance of giving away our position before we attack.

"There's nothing in the whole place that actually looks like a weapon. That doesn't mean anything, though; you could hide a bevawatt laser in each of those huts.

"Now, about five hundred meters from the huts, in the middle of the base, we'll come to this big flower-shaped structure." Cortez drew a large symmetrical shape that looked like the outline of a flower with seven petals. "What the hell this is, your guess is as good as mine. There's only one of them, though, so we don't damage it any more than we have to. Which means . . . we blast it to splinters if I think it's dangerous.

"Now, as far as your spaceport, Mandella, is concerned—there just isn't one. Nothing.

"That cruiser the *Hope* caulked had probably been left in orbit, like ours has to be. If they have any equivalent of a scoutship, or drone missiles, they're either not kept here or they're well hidden."

"Bohrs here. Then what did they attack with, while we were coming down from orbit?"

"I wish we knew, Private.

"Obviously, we don't have any way of estimating their numbers, not directly. Recon pictures failed to show a single Tauran on the grounds of the base. Meaning nothing, because it *is* an alien environment. Indirectly, though . . . we can count the number of broomsticks.

"There are fifty-one huts, and each has at most one broomstick. Four don't have one parked outside, but we located three at various other parts of the base. Maybe this indicates that there are fifty-one Taurans, one of whom was outside the base when the picture was taken."

"Keating here. Or fifty-one officers."

"That's right—maybe fifty thousand infantrymen stacked in one of these buildings. No way to tell. Maybe ten Taurans, each with five broomsticks, to use according to his mood.

"We've got one thing in our favor, and that's communications. They evidently use a frequency modulation of megahertz electromagnetic radiation."

"Radio!"

"That's right, whoever you are. Identify yourself when you speak. So, it's quite possible that they can't detect our phased-neutrino communications. Also, just prior to the attack, the *Hope* is going to deliver a nice dirty fission bomb; detonate it in the upper atmosphere right over the base. That'll restrict them to line-of-sight communication for some time; even those will be full of static."

"Why don't . . . Tate here . . . why don't they just drop the bomb right in their laps? Would save us a lot of. . . ."

"That doesn't even deserve an answer, Private. But the answer is, they might. And you better hope they don't. If they caulk the base, it'll be for the safety of the *Hope*. *After* we've attacked, and probably before we're far enough away for it to make much difference.

"We keep that from happening by doing a good job. We have to reduce the base to where it can no longer function; at the same time, leave as much intact as possible. And take one prisoner."

"Potter here. You mean, at least one prisoner."

"I mean what I say. One only. Potter . . . you're relieved of your platoon. Send Chavez up."

"All right, Sergeant." The relief in her voice was unmistakable.

Cortez continued with his map and instructions. There was one other building whose function was pretty obvious; it had a large steerable dish antenna on top. We were to destroy it as soon as the grenadiers got in range.

The attack plan was very loose. Our signal to begin would be the flash of the fission bomb. At the same time, several drones would converge on the base, so we could see what their antispacecraft defenses were. We would try to reduce the effectiveness of those defenses without destroying them completely.

Immediately after the bomb and the drones, the grenadiers would vaporize a line of seven huts. Everybody would break through the hole into the base . . . and what would happen after that was anybody's guess.

Ideally, we'd sweep from that end of the base to the other, destroying certain targets caulking all but one Tauran. But that was unlikely to happen, as it depended on the Taurans' offering very little resistance.

On the other hand, if the Taurans showed obvious superiority from the beginning, Cortez would give the order to scatter: everybody had a different compass bearing for retreat—we'd blossom out in all directions, the survivors to rendezvous in a valley some forty clicks east of the base. Then we'd see about a return engagement, after the *Hope* softened the base up a bit.

"One last thing," Cortez rasped. "Maybe some of you feel the way Potter evidently does, maybe some of your men feel that way . . . that we ought to go easy, not make this so much of a bloodbath. Mercy is a luxury, a weakness we can't afford to indulge in at this stage of the war. *All* we know about the enemy is that they have killed seven hundred and ninety-eight humans. They haven't shown any restraint in attacking our cruisers, and it'd be foolish to expect any this time, this first ground action.

"*They* are responsible for the lives of all of your comrades who died in training, and for Ho, and for all the others who are surely going to die today. I can't *understand* anybody who wants to spare them. But that doesn't make any difference. You have your orders, and what the hell, you might as well know, all of you have a posthypnotic suggestion that I will trigger by a phrase, just before the battle. It will make your job easier."

"Sergeant. . . ."

"Shut up. We're short on time; get back to your platoons and brief them. We move out in five minutes."

The platoon leaders returned to their men, leaving Cortez and the ten of us, plus three teddy-bears, milling around, getting in the way.

15

We took the last five clicks very carefully, sticking to the highest grass, running across occasional clearings. When we were five hundred meters from where the base was supposed to be, Cortez took the Third Platoon forward to scout, while the rest of us laid low.

Cortez's voice came over the general freak: "Looks pretty much like we expected. Advance in a file, crawling. When you get to the Third Platoon, follow your squad leader to the left, or right."

We did that and wound up with a string of eighty-three people in a line roughly perpendicular to the direction of attack. We were pretty well hidden, except for the dozen or so teddy-bears that mooched along the line munching grass.

There was no sign of life inside the base. All of the buildings were windowless, and a uniform shiny white. The huts that were our first objective were large featureless half-buried eggs, some sixty meters apart. Cortez assigned one to each grenadier.

We were broken into three fire teams: Team A consisted of platoons Two, Four, and Six; Team B was One, Three, and Five; the command platoon was Team C.

"Less than a minute now—filters down!—when I say 'fire', grenadiers take out your targets. God help you if you miss."

There was a sound like a giant's belch and a stream of five or six iridescent bubbles floated up from the flower-shaped building. They rose with increasing speed to where they were almost out of sight, then shot off to the south, over our heads. The ground was suddenly bright and for the first time in a long time, I saw my shadow, a long one pointed north. The bomb had gone off prematurely. I just had time to think that it didn't make too much difference; it'd still make alphabet soup out of their communications. . . .

"Drones!" A ship came screaming in just above tree level, and a bubble was in the air to meet it. When they contacted, the bubble popped and the drone exploded into a million tiny fragments. Another one came from the opposite side and suffered the same fate.

"FIRE!" Seven bright glares of 500-microton grenades and a sustained concussion that I'm sure would have killed an unprotected man.

"Filters up." Gray haze of smoke and dust. Clods of dirt falling with a sound like heavy raindrops.

"Listen up:

> " 'Scots, wha hae wi' Wallace bled;
> Scots, wham Bruce has aften led,
> Welcome to your gory bed,
> Or to victory!' "

I hardly heard him, for trying to keep track of what was going on in my skull. I knew it was just posthypnotic suggestion, even remembered the session in Missouri when they'd implanted it, but that didn't make it any less compelling. My mind reeled under the strong pseudo-memories; shaggy hulks that were Taurans—not at all what we now knew they looked like—boarding a colonist's vessel, eating babies while mothers watched in screaming terror—the colonists never took babies; they wouldn't stand the acceleration—then raping the women to death with huge veined purple members—ridiculous that they would feel desire for humans—holding the men down while they plucked flesh from their living bodies and gobbled it. . . . a hundred grisly details as sharply remembered as the events of a minute ago, ridiculously overdone and logically absurd; but while my conscious mind was reflecting the silliness, somewhere much deeper, down in that sleeping giant where we keep our real motives and morals, something was thirsting for alien blood, secure in the conviction that the noblest thing a man could do would be to die killing one of those horrible monsters. . . .

I knew it was all purest soya, and I hated the men who had taken such obscene liberties with my mind, but still I could hear my teeth grinding, feel cheeks frozen in a spastic grin, bloodlust . . . a teddy-bear walked in front of me, looking dazed. I started to raise my laserfinger, but somebody beat me to it and the creature's head exploded in a cloud of gray splinters and blood.

Lucky groaned, half-whining, "Dirty . . . filthy bastards." Lasers flared and crisscrossed and all of the teddy-bears fell dead.

"Watch it, damn it," Cortez screamed. *"Aim* those things they aren't toys!

"Team A, move out—into the craters to cover B."

Somebody was laughing and sobbing. "What the crap is wrong with *you, Petrov?"* First time I could remember Cortez cussing.

I twisted around and saw Petrov, behind and to my left, lying in a shallow hole, digging frantically with both hands, crying and gurgling.

"Crap," Cortez said. "Team B! past the craters ten meters, get down in a line. Team C—into the craters with A."

I scrambled up and covered the hundred meters in twelve amplified strides. The craters were practically large enough to hide a scoutship, some ten meters in diameter. I jumped to the opposite side of the hole and landed next to a fellow named Chin. He didn't even look around when I landed, just kept scanning the base for signs of life.

"Team A—past Team B ten meters, down in line." Just as he finished, the building in front of us burped and a salvo of the bubbles fanned out toward our lines. Most people saw it coming and got down, but Chin was just getting up to make his rush and stepped right into one.

It grazed the top of his helmet, and disappeared with a faint pop. He took one step backwards and toppled over the edge of the crater, trailing an arc of blood and brains. Lifeless, spreadeagled, he slid halfway to the bottom, shoveling dirt into the perfectly symmetrical hole where the bubble had chewed through plastic, hair, skin, bone and brain indiscriminately.

"Everybody hold it. Platoon leaders, casualty report . . . check . . . check, check . . . check, check, check . . . check. We have three deaders. Wouldn't be *any* if you'd have kept low. So everybody grab dirt when you hear that thing go off. Team A, complete the rush."

They completed the maneuver without incident. "O.K. Team C, rush to where B . . . hold it! Down!"

Everybody was already hugging the ground. The bubbles slid by in a smooth arc about two meters off the ground. They went serenely over our heads and, except for one that made toothpicks out of a tree, disappeared in the distance.

"B, rush past A ten meters. C, take over B's place. You B grenadiers see if you can reach the Flower."

Two grenades tore up the ground thirty or forty meters from the structure. In a good imitation of panic, it started belching out a continuous stream of bubbles—still, none coming lower than two meters off the ground. We kept hunched down and continued to advance.

Suddenly, a seam appeared in the building, widened to the size of a large door, and Taurans came swarming out.

"Grenadiers, hold your fire. B team, laser fire to the left and right, keep 'em bunched up. A and C, rush down the center."

One Tauran died trying to turn through a laser beam. The others stayed where they were.

In a suit, it's pretty awkward to run and try to keep your head down, at the same time. You have to go from side to side, like a skater getting started; otherwise you'll be airborne. At least one person, somebody in A team, bounced too high and suffered the same fate as Chin.

I was feeling pretty fenced-in and trapped, with a wall of laser fire on each side and a low ceiling that meant death to touch. But in spite of myself, I felt happy, euphoric at finally getting the chance to kill some of those villainous baby-eaters.

They weren't fighting back, except for the rather ineffective bubbles —obviously not designed as an antipersonnel weapon—and they didn't retreat back into the building, either. They just milled around, about a hundred of them, and watched us get closer. A couple of grenades would caulk them all, but I guess Cortez was thinking about the prisoner.

"O.K., when I say 'go', we're going to flank 'em. B team will hold fire . . . Second and Fourth to the right, Sixth and Seventh to the left. B team will move forward in line to box them in.

"Go!" We peeled off to the left. As soon as the lasers stopped, the Taurans bolted, running in a group on a collision course with our flank.

"A Team, down and fire! Don't shoot until you're sure of your aim— if you miss you might hit a friendly. And fer Chris'sake save me one!"

It was a horrifying sight, that herd of monsters bearing down on us. They were running in great leaps—the bubbles avoiding them—and they all looked like the one we saw earlier, riding the broomstick; naked except for an almost transparent sphere around their whole bodies, that moved along with them. The right flank started firing, picking off individuals in the rear of the pack.

Suddenly a laser flared through the Taurans from the other side, somebody missing his mark. There was a horrible scream and I looked down the line to see someone, I think it was Perry, writhing on the ground, right hand over the smoldering stump of his left arm, seared off just below the elbow. Blood sprayed through his fingers and the suit, its camouflage circuits scrambled, flickered black-white-jungle-desert-green-gray. I don't know how long I stared—long enough for the medic to run over and start giving aid—but when I looked up the Taurans were almost on top of me.

My first shot was wild and high, but it grazed the top of the leading Tauran's protective bubble. The bubble disappeared and the monster stumbled and fell to the ground, jerking spasmodically. Foam gushed out of his mouth-hole, first white, then streaked with red. With one last jerk he became rigid and twisted backwards, almost to the shape of a horse-shoe. His long scream, a high-pitched whistle, stopped just as his comrades trampled over him and I hated myself for smiling.

It was slaughter, even though our flank was outnumbered five to one. They kept coming without faltering, even when they had to climb over the drift of bodies and parts of bodies that piled up high, parallel to our flank. The ground between us was slick red with Tauran blood—all God's children got hemoglobin—and, like the teddy-bears, their guts looked pretty much like guts to my untrained eye. My helmet reverberated with hysterical laughter while we cut them to gory chunks. I almost didn't hear Cortez.

"Hold your fire—I said HOLD IT damn it! *Catch* a couple of the bastards, they won't hurt you."

I stopped shooting and eventually so did everybody else. When the next Tauran jumped over the smoking pile of meat in front of me, I dove to tackle him around those spindly legs.

It was like hugging a big, slippery balloon. When I tried to drag him down, he just popped out of my arms and kept running.

We managed to stop one of them by the simple expedient of piling half-a-dozen people on top of him. By that time the others had run through our line and were headed for the row of large cylindrical tanks that Cortez had said were probably for storage. A little door had opened in the base of each one.

"We've *got* our prisoner," Cortez shouted. *"Kill!"*

They were fifty meters away and running hard, difficult targets. Lasers slashed around them, bobbing high and low. One fell, sliced in two, but the others, about ten of them, kept going and were almost to the doors when the grenadiers started firing.

They were still loaded with 500-mike bombs, but a near miss wasn't enough—the concussion would just send them flying, unhurt in their bubbles.

"The buildings! Get the damn buildings!" The grenadiers raised their aim and let fly, but the bombs only seemed to scorch the white outside of the structures until, by chance, one landed in a door. That split the building just as if it had a seam; the two halves popped away and a cloud of machinery flew into the air, accompanied by a huge pale flame that rolled up and disappeared in an instant. Then the others all concentrated on the doors, except for potshots at some of the Taurans; not so much to get them as to blow them away before they could get inside. They seemed awfully eager.

All this time, we were trying to get the Taurans with laser fire, while they weaved and bounced around trying to get into the structures. We moved in as close to them as we could without putting ourselves in danger from the grenade blasts—that was still too far away for good aim.

Still, we were getting them one by one, and managed to destroy four of the seven buildings. Then, when there were only two aliens left, a nearby grenade blast flung one of them to within a few meters of a door. He dove in and several grenadiers fired salvos after him, but they all fell short, or detonated harmlessly on the side. Bombs were falling all around, making an awful racket, but the sound was suddenly drowned out by a great sigh, like a giant's intake of breath, and where the building had been was a thick cylindrical cloud of smoke, solid-looking, dwindling away into the stratosphere, straight as if laid down by a ruler. The other Tauran had been right at the base of the cylinder; I could see pieces of him flying. A second later, a shock wave hit us and I rolled helplessly, pinwheeling, to smash into the pile of Tauran bodies and roll beyond.

I picked myself up and panicked for a second when I saw there was blood all over my suit—when I realized it was only alien blood, I relaxed but felt unclean.

"*Catch* the bastard! Catch him!" In the confusion, the Tauran—now the only one left alive—had got free and was running for the grass. One platoon was chasing after him, losing ground, but then all of B team ran over and cut him off. I jogged over to join in the fun.

There were four people on top of him, and fifty people watching.

"Spread out, damn it! There might be a thousand more of them waiting to get us in one place." We dispersed, grumbling. By unspoken agreement we were all sure that there were no more live Taurans on the face of the planet.

Cortez was walking toward the prisoner while I backed away. Suddenly the four men collapsed in a pile on top of the creature . . . even from my distance I could see the foam spouting from his mouth-hole. His bubble had popped. Suicide.

"Damn!" Cortez was right there. "Get off that bastard." The four men got off and Cortez used his laser to slice the monster into a dozen quivering chunks. Heartwarming sight.

"That's all right, though, we'll find another one—everybody! Back in the arrowhead formation. Combat assault, on the Flower."

Well, we assaulted the Flower, which had evidently run out of ammunition—it was still belching, but no bubbles—and it was empty. We just scurried up ramps and through corridors, fingers at the ready, like kids playing soldier. There was nobody home.

The same lack of response at the antenna installation, the "Salami," and twenty other major buildings, as well as the forty-four perimeter huts still intact. So we had "captured" dozens of buildings, mostly of incomprehensible purpose, but failed in our main mission; capturing a Tauran for the xenologists to experiment with. Oh, well, they could have all the bits and pieces of the creatures they'd ever want. That was something.

After we'd combed every last square centimeter of the base, a scoutship came in with the real exploration crew, Star Fleet scientists. Cortez said, "All right, snap out of it," and the hypnotic compulsion fell away.

At first it was pretty grim. A lot of the people, like Lucky and Marygay, almost went crazy with the memories of bloody murder multiplied a hundred times. Cortez ordered everybody to take a sedtab, two for the ones most upset. I took two without being specifically ordered to do so.

Because it *was* murder, unadorned butchery—once we had the antispacecraft weapon doped out, we weren't in any danger. The Taurans didn't seem to have any conception of person-to-person fighting. We just herded them up and slaughtered them, in the first encounter between mankind and another intelligent species. What might have happened if we had sat down and tried to communicate? Maybe it was the second encounter, counting the teddy-bears. But they got the same treatment.

I spent a long time after that, telling myself over and over that it hadn't been *me* who so gleefully carved up those frightened, stampeding creatures. Back in the Twentieth Century, they established to everybody's satisfaction that "I was just following orders" was an inadequate excuse for inhuman conduct . . . but what can you do when the orders come from deep down in that puppet master of the unconscious?

Worst of all was the feeling that perhaps my actions weren't all that inhuman. Ancestors only a few generations back would have done the same thing, even to their fellowmen, without any hypnotic conditioning.

So I was disgusted with the human race, disgusted with the army, and horrified at the prospect of living with myself for another century or so . . . well, there was always brainwipe.

The ship that the lone Tauran survivor had escaped in had got away, clean, the bulk of the planet shielding it from *Earth's Hope* while it dropped into Aleph's collapsar field. Escaped to home, I guessed, wherever that was, to report what twenty men with hand-weapons could do to a hundred fleeing on foot, unarmed.

I suspected that the next time humans met Taurans in ground combat, we would be more evenly matched. And I was right.

WALTER F. MOUDY

THE SURVIVOR

There was a harmony in the design of the arena which an artist might find pleasing. The curved granite walls which extended upward three hundred feet from its base were polished and smooth like the sides of a bowl. A fly, perhaps a lizard, could crawl up those glistening walls—but surely not a man. The walls encircled an egg-shaped area which was precisely three thousand meters long and two thousand one hundred meters wide at its widest point. There were two large hills located on either side of the arena exactly midway from its center to its end. If you were to slice the arena crosswise, your knife would dissect a third, tree-studded hill and a small, clear lake; and the two divided halves would each be the exact mirror image of the other down to the smallest detail. If you were a farmer you would notice the rich flat soil which ran obliquely from the two larger hills toward the lake. If you were an artist you might find pleasure in contemplating the rich shades of green and brown presented by the forested lowlands at the lake's edge. A sportsman seeing the crystalline lake in the morning's first light would find his fingers itching for light tackle and wading boots. Boys, particularly city boys, would yearn to climb the two larger hills because they looked easy to climb, but not too easy. A general viewing the topography would immediately recognize that possession of the central hill would permit dominance of the lake and the surrounding lowlands.

There was something peaceful about the arena that first morning. The early-morning sun broke through a light mist and spilled over the central hill to the low dew-drenched ground beyond. There were trees with young, green leaves, and the leaves rustled softly in rhythm with the wind. There were birds in those trees, and the birds still sang, for it was spring, and they were filled with the joy of life and the beauty of the morning. A night owl, its appetite satiated now by a recent kill, perched on a dead limb of a large sycamore tree and, tucking its beak in its feathers, prepared to sleep the day away. A sleek copperhead snake, sensing the sun's approach and anticipating its soothing warmth, crawled from beneath the flat rock where it had spent the night and sought the comfort of its favorite rock ledge. A red squirrel chattered nervously as it watched the men enter the arena from the north and then, having decided that there was danger there, darted swiftly to an adjacent tree and disappeared into the security of its nest.

There were exactly one hundred of them. They stood tall and proud in their uniforms, a barely perceptible swaying motion rippling through their lines like wheat stirred by a gentle breeze. If they anticipated what was to come, they did not show it. Their every movement showed their absolute discipline. Once they had been only men—now they were killers. The hunger for blood was like a taste in their mouths; their zest for destruction like a flood which raged inside them. They were finely honed and razor keen to kill.

Their general made his last inspection. As he passed down the lines the squad captains barked a sharp order and the men froze into absolute immobility. Private Richard Starbuck heard the rasp of the general's boots against the stones as he approached. There was no other sound, not even of men breathing. From long discipline he forced his eyes to maintain their focus on the distant point he had selected, and his eyes did not waver as the general paused in front of him. They were still fixed on that same imaginary point. He did not even see the general.

Private Richard Starbuck was not thinking of death, although he knew he must surely die. He was thinking of the rifle which he felt securely on his shoulder and of the driving need he had to discharge its deadly pellets into human flesh. His urge to kill was dominant, but even so he was vaguely relieved that he had not been selected for the assassination squad (the suicide squad the men called it); for he still had a chance, a slim chance, to live; while the assassination squad was consigned to inevitable death.

A command was given and Private Starbuck permitted his tense body to relax. He glanced at his watch. Five-twenty-five. He still had an hour and thirty-five minutes to wait. There was a tenseness inside him which his relaxed body did not disclose. They taught you how to do that in training. They taught you lots of things in training.

* * *

The TV screen was bigger than life and just as real. The color was true and the images three-dimensional. For a moment the zoom cameras scanned the silent deserted portions of the arena. The sound system was sensitive and sharp and caught the sound made by a squirrel's feet against the bark of a black oak tree. Over one hundred cameras were fixed on the arena; yet so smooth was the transition from one camera to the next that it was as though the viewer was floating over the arena. There was the sound of marching feet, and the pace of the moving cameras quickened and then shifted to the north where one hundred men were entering the arena in perfect unison, a hundred steel-toed boots striking the earth as one. For a moment the cameras fixed on the flashing boots and the sensitive sound system recorded the thunder of men marching to war. Then the cameras flashed to the proud face of their general; then to the hard, determined faces of the men; then back again to the thundering boots. The cameras backed off to watch the column execute an abrupt halt, moved forward to focus for a moment on the general's hawklike face, and then, with the general, inspected the troops one by one, moving down the rigid lines of men and peering intently at each frozen face.

When the "at ease" order was given, the camera backed up to show an aerial view of the arena and then fixed upon one of the control towers which lined the arena's upper periphery before sweeping slowly downward and seeming to pass into the control tower. Inside the tower a distinguished gray-haired man in his mid-forties sat beside a jovial, fat-jawed man who was probably in his early fifties. There was an expectant look on their faces. Finally the gray-haired man said:

"Good morning, ladies and gentlemen, I'm John Ardanyon—"

"And I'm Bill Carr," the fat-jawed man said.

"And this is it—yes, this is the big one, ladies and gentlemen. The 2050 edition of the Olympic War Games. This is the day we've all been waiting for, ladies and gentlemen, and in precisely one hour and thirty-two minutes the games will be under way. Here to help describe the action is Bill Carr who is known to all of you sports fans all over the world. And with us for this special broadcast are some of the finest technicians in the business. Bill?"

"That's right, John. This year the NSB has spared no expense to insure our viewing public that its 2050 game coverage will be second to none. So stay tuned to this station for the most complete, the most immediate coverage of any station. John?"

"That's right, Bill. This year NSB has installed over one hundred specially designed zoom cameras to insure complete coverage of the games. We are using the latest sonic sound equipment—so sensitive that it can detect the sound of a man's heart beating at a thousand yards. Our camera crew is highly trained in the recently developed transitional-zone technique which you just saw so effectively demonstrated during the fade-in. I think we can promise you that this time no station will be able to match the immediacy of NSB."

"Right, John. And now, less than an hour and a half before the action begins, NSB is proud to bring you this prerecorded announcement from the President of the United States. Ladies and gentlemen, the President of the United States."

There was a brief flash of the White House lawn, a fade-out, and then:

"My fellow countrymen. When you hear these words, the beginning of the fifth meeting between the United States and Russia in the Olympic War Games will be just minutes away.

"I hope and pray that we will be victorious. With the help of God, we shall be.

"But in our longing for victory, we must not lose sight of the primary purpose of these games. In the long run it is not whether we win or lose but that the games were played. For, my fellow citizens, we must never forget that these games are played in order that the frightening spectre of war may never again stalk our land. It is better that a few should decide the nation's fate, than all the resources of our two nations should be mobilized to destroy the other.

"My friends, many of you do not remember the horror of the Final War of 1998. I can recall that war. I lost my father and two sisters in that war. I spent two months in a class-two fallout shelter—as many of you know. There must never be another such war. We cannot—we shall not—permit that to happen.

"The Olympic War Games are the answer—the only answer. Thanks to the Olympic War Games we are at peace. Today one hundred of our finest fighting men will meet one hundred Russian soldiers to decide whether we shall be victorious or shall go down to defeat. The loser must pay the victor reparations of ten billion dollars. The stakes are high.

"The stakes are high, but, my fellow citizens, the cost of total war is a hundred times higher. This miniature war is a thousand times less costly than total war. Thanks to the Olympic War Games, we have a kind of peace.

"And now, in keeping with the tradition established by the late President Goldstein, I hereby declare a national holiday for all persons not engaged in essential services from now until the conclusion of the games.

"To those brave men who made the team I say: the hope and the prayers of the nation go with you. May you emerge victorious."

There was a fade-out and then the pleasant features of John Ardanyon appeared. After a short, respectful silence, he said:

"I'm sure we can all agree with the President on that. And now, here is Professor Carl Overmann to explain the computer system developed especially for NSB's coverage of the 2050 war games."

"Thank you, Mr. Ardanyon. This year, with the help of the Englewood system of evaluating intangible factors, we hope to start bringing you reliable predictions at the ten-percent casualty level. Now, very briefly, here is how the Englewood system works. . . ."

Private Richard Starbuck looked at his watch. Still forty more minutes to wait. He pulled back the bolt on his rifle and checked once more to make sure that the first shell was properly positioned in the chamber. For the third time in the past twenty minutes he walked to one side and urinated on the ground. His throat seemed abnormally dry, and he removed his canteen to moisten his lips with water. He took only a small swallow because the rules permitted only one canteen of water per man, and their battle plan did not call for early possession of the lake.

A passing lizard caught his attention. He put his foot on it and squashed it slowly with the toe of his right boot. He noticed with mild satisfaction that the thing had left a small blood smear at the end of his boot. Oddly, however, seeing the blood triggered something in his mind, and for the first time he vaguely recognized the possibility that he could be hurt. In training he had not thought much about that. Mostly you thought of how it would feel to kill a man. After a while you got so that you wanted to kill. You came to love your rifle, like it was an extension of your own body. And if you could not feel its comforting presence, you felt like a part of you was missing. Still a person could be hurt. You might not die immediately. He wondered what it would be like to feel a misshapen chunk of lead tearing through his belly. The Russians would x their bullets too, probably. They do more damage that way.

It might not be so bad. He remembered a time four years ago when he had thought he was dying, and that had not been so bad. He remembered that at the time he had been more concerned about bleeding on the Martins' new couch. The Martins had always been good to him. Once they had thought they could never have a child of their own, and they had about half adopted him because his own mother worked and was too busy to bake cookies for him and his father was not interested in fishing or basketball or things like that. Even after the Martins had Cassandra, they continued to treat him like a favorite nephew. Mr. Martin took him fishing and attended all the basketball games when he was playing. And that was why when he wrecked the motor scooter and cut his head he had been more concerned about bleeding on the Martins' new couch than about dying, although he had felt that he was surely dying. He remembered that his first thought upon regaining consciousness was one of self-importance. The Martins had looked worried and their nine-year-old daughter, Cassandra, was looking at the blood running down his face and was crying. That was when he felt he might be dying. Dying had seemed a strangely appropriate thing to do, and he had felt an urge to do it well and had begun to assure them that he was all right. And, to his slight disappointment, he was.

Private Richard Starbuck, formerly a star forward on the Center High basketball team, looked at his watch and wondered, as he waited, if being shot in the gut would be anything like cutting your head on the pavement. It was funny he should have thought of that now. He hadn't thought of the Martins for months. He wondered if they would be watching. He wondered, if they did, if they would recognize the sixteen-year-old boy who had bled on their living room couch four years ago. He wondered if he recognized that sixteen-year-old boy himself.

Professor Carl Overmann had finished explaining the marvels of the NSB computer system; a mousy little man from the sociology department of a second rate university had spent ten minutes assuring the TV audience that one of the important psychological effects of the TV coverage of the games was that it allowed the people to satisfy the innate blood lust vicariously and strongly urged the viewers to encourage the youngsters to watch; a minister had spent three minutes explaining that the miniature war could serve to educate mankind to the horrors of war; an economics professor was just finishing a short lecture on the economic effects of victory or defeat.

"Well, there you have it, ladies and gentlemen," Bill Carr said when the economics professor had finished. "You all know there's a lot at stake for both sides. And now—what's that? You what? Just a minute, folks. I think we may have another NSB first." He looked off camera to his right. "Is he there? Yes, indeed, ladies and gentlemen, NSB has done it again. For the first time we are going to have—well, here he is, ladies and gentlemen, General George W. Caldwell, chief of the Olympic War Games training section. General, it's nice to have you with us."

"Thank you, Bill. It's good to be here."

"General, I'm sure our audience already knows this, but just so there will be no misunderstanding, it's not possible for either side to communicate to their people in the arena now. Is that right?"

"That's right, Bill, or I could not be here. An electronic curtain, as it were, protects the field from any attempt to communicate. From here on out the boys are strictly on their own."

"General, do you care to make any predictions on the outcome of the games?"

"Yes, Bill, I may be going out on a limb here, but I think our boys are ready. I can't say that I agree with the neutral-money boys who have the

United States a six-to-five underdog. I say we'll win."

"General, there is some thought that our defeat in the games four years ago was caused by an inferior battle plan. Do you care to comment on that?"

"No comment."

"Do you have any explanation for why the United States team has lost the last two games after winning the first two?"

"Well, let me say this. Our defeat in '42 could well have been caused by overconfidence. After all, we had won the first two games rather handily. As I recall we won the game in '38 by four survivors. But as for our defeat in '46—well, your estimate on that one is as good as mine. I will say this: General Hanley was much criticized for an unimaginative battle plan by a lot of so-called experts. Those so-called experts—those armchair generals—were definitely wrong. General Hanley's battle strategy was sound in every detail. I've studied his plans at considerable length, I can assure you."

"Perhaps the training program—?"

"Nonsense. My own exec was on General Hanley's training staff. With only slight modifications it's the same program we used for this year's games."

"Do you care to comment on your own battle plans, General?"

"Well, Bill, I wouldn't want to kill the suspense for your TV audience. But I can say this: we'll have a few surprises this year. No one can accuse us of conservative tactics, I can tell you that."

"How do you think our boys will stack up against the Russians, General?"

"Bill, on a man to man basis, I think our boys will stack up very well indeed. In fact, we had men in the drop-out squads who could have made our last team with no trouble at all. I'd say this year's crop is probably twenty percent improved."

"General, what do you look for in selecting your final squads?"

"Bill, I'd say that more than anything else we look for desire. Of course, a man has to be a good athlete, but if he doesn't have that killer instinct, as we say, he won't make the team. I'd say it's desire."

"Can you tell us how you pick the men for the games?"

"Yes, Bill, I think I can, up to a point. We know the Russians use the same system, and, of course, there has been quite a bit written on the subject in the popular press in recent months.

"Naturally, we get thousands of applicants. We give each of them a tough screening test—physical, mental, and psychological. Most applicants are eliminated in the first test. You'd be surprised at some of the boys who apply. The ones who are left—just under two thousand for this year's games—are put through an intensive six-month training course. During this training period we begin to get our first drop-outs, the men who somehow got past our screening system and who will crack under pressure.

"Next comes a year of training in which the emphasis is on conditioning."

"Let me interrupt here for just a moment, General, if I may. This conditioning—is this a type of physical training?"

The general smiled tolerantly. "No, Bill, this is a special type of conditioning—both mental and physical. The men are conditioned to war. They are taught to recognize and to hate the enemy. They are taught to react instantly to every possible hostile stimuli. They learn to love their weapons and to distrust all else."

"I take it that an average training day must leave the men very little free time."

"Free time!" The general now seemed more shocked than amused. "Free time indeed. Our training program leaves no time free. We don't coddle our boys. After all, Bill, these men are training for war. No man is permitted more than two hours' consecutive sleep. We have an average of four alerts every night.

"Actually the night alerts are an important element in our selection as well as our training program. We have the men under constant observation, of course. You can tell a lot about how a man responds to an alert. Of course, all of the men are conditioned to come instantly awake with their rifles in their hands. But some would execute a simultaneous roll-away movement while at the same time cocking and aiming their weapons in the direction of the hostile sound which signaled the alert."

"How about the final six months, General?"

"Well, Bill, of course, I can't give away all our little tricks during those last six months. I can tell you in a general sort of way that this involved putting battle plans on a duplicate of the arena itself."

"And these hundred men who made this year's team—I presume they were picked during the last six months training?"

"No, Bill, actually we only made our final selection last night. You see, for the first time in two years these men have had some free time. We give them two days off before the games begin. How the men react to this enforced inactivity can tell us a lot about their level of readiness. I can tell you we have an impatient bunch of boys out there."

"General, it's ten minutes to game time. Do you suppose our team may be getting a little nervous down there?"

"Nervous? I suppose the boys may be a little tensed up. But they'll be all right just as soon as the action starts."

"General, I want to thank you for coming by. I'm sure our TV audience has found this brief discussion most enlightening."

"It was my pleasure, Bill."

"Well, there you have it, ladies and gentlemen. You heard it from the man who should know—Lieutenant General George W. Caldwell himself. He picks the United States team to go all the way. John?"

"Thank you, Bill. And let me say that there has been considerable sentiment for the United States team in recent weeks among the neutrals. These are the men who set the odds—the men who bet their heads but never their hearts. In fact at least one oddsmaker in Stockholm told me last night that he had stopped taking anything but six-to-five bets, and you pick 'em. In other words, this fight is rated just about even here just a few minutes before game time."

"Right, John, it promises to be an exciting day, so stay tuned to this station for full coverage."

"I see the troops are beginning to stir. It won't be long now. Bill, while we wait I think it might be well, for the benefit of you younger people, to tell the folks just what it means to be a survivor in one of these games. Bill?"

"Right, John. Folks, the survivor, or survivors as the case may be, will truly become a *Survivor*. A *Survivor,* as most of you know, is exempt from all laws; he has unlimited credit; in short, he can literally do no wrong. And that's what those men are shooting for today. John."

"Okay, Bill. And now as our cameras scan the Russian team, let us review very briefly the rules of the game. Each side has one hundred men divided into ten squads each consisting of nine men and one squad captain. Each man has a standard automatic rifle, four hand grenades, a canteen of water, and enough food to last three days. All officers are armed with side arms in addition to their automatic rifles. Two of the squads are armed with air-cooled light machine guns, and one squad is armed with a mortar with one thousand rounds of ammunition. And those, ladies and gentlemen, are the rules of the game. Once the games begin the men are on their own. There are no more rules—except, of course, that the game is not over until one side or the other has no more survivors. Bill?"

"Okay, John. Well, folks, here we are just seconds away from game time. NSB will bring you live each exciting moment—so stand by. We're waiting for the start of the 2050 Olympic War Games. Ten seconds now. Six. Four, three, two, one—the games are underway, and look at 'em go!"

The cameras spanned back from the arena to give a distant view of the action. Squad one reeled off from the main body and headed toward the enemy rear at a fast trot. They were armed with rifles and grenades. Squads two, three, and four went directly toward the high hill in the American sector where they broke out entrenching tools and began to dig in. Squads five and six took one of the light machine guns and marched at double time to the east of the central hill where they concealed themselves in the brush and waited. Squads seven through ten were held in reserve where they occupied themselves by burying the ammunition and other supplies at predetermined points and in beginning the preparation of their own defense perimeters.

The cameras swung briefly to the Russian sector. Four Russian squads had already occupied the high hill in the Russian sector, and a rifle squad was being rushed to the central hill located on the north-south dividing line. A Russian machine gun squad was digging in to the south of the lake to establish a base of fire on the north side of the central hill.

The cameras returned to the American squads five and six, which were now deployed along the east side of the central hill. The cameras moved in from above the entrenched machine gunner, paused momentarily on his right hand, which was curved lovingly around the trigger guard while his middle finger stroked the trigger itself in a manner almost obscene, and then followed the gunner's unblinking eyes to the mist-enshrouded base of the central hill where the point man of the Russian advance squad was cautiously testing his fate in a squirming, crawling advance on the lower slopes of the hill.

"This could be it!" Bill Carr's booming voice exploded from the screen like a shot. "This could be the first skirmish, ladies and gentlemen. John, how does it look to you?"

"Yes, Bill, it looks like we will probably get our first action in the east-central sector. Quite a surprise, too, Bill. A lot of experts felt that the American team would concentrate its initial push on control of the central hill. Instead, the strategy appears to be—at least as it appears from here—to concede the central hill to the Russian team but to make them pay for it. You can't see it on your screens just now, ladies and gentlemen, but the American mortar squad is now positioned on the north slope of the north hill and is ready to fire."

"All right, John. Folks, here in our booth operating as spotter for the American team is Colonel Bullock of the United States Army. Our Russian spotter is Brigadier General Vorsilov, who will from time to time give us his views on Russian strategy. Colonel Bullock, do you care to comment?"

"Well, I think it's fairly obvious, Bill, that—"

His words were interrupted by the first chilling chatter of the American light machine gun. Tracer bullets etched their brilliant way through the morning air to seek and find human flesh. Four mortar rounds, fired in rapid succession, arched over the low hill and came screaming a tale of death and destruction. The rifle squad opened fire with compelling accuracy. The Russian line halted, faltered, reformed, and charged up the central hill. Three men made it to the sheltering rocks on the hill's upper slope. The squad captain and six enlisted men lay dead or dying on the lower slopes. As quickly as it had begun the firing ended.

"How about that!" Bill Carr exclaimed. "First blood for the American team. What a fantastic beginning to these 2050 war games, ladies and gentlemen. John, how about that?"

"Right, Bill. Beautifully done. Brilliantly conceived and executed with marvelous precision. An almost unbelievable maneuver by the American team that obviously caught the Russians completely off guard. Did you get the casualty figures on that first skirmish, Bill?"

"I make it five dead and two seriously wounded, John. Now keep in mind, folks, these figures are unofficial. Ed, can you give us a closeup on that south slope?"

The cameras scanned the hill first from a distance and then zoomed in to give a closeup of each man who lay on the bleak southern slope. The Russian captain was obviously dead with a neat rifle bullet through his forehead. The next man appeared to be sleeping peacefully. There was not a mark visible on his body; yet he too was dead as was demonstrated when the delicate sonic sound system was focused on his corpse without disclosing the whisper of a heart beat. The third man was still living, though death was just minutes away. For him it would be a peaceful death, for he was unconscious and was quietly leaking his life away from a torn artery in his neck. The camera rested next upon the shredded corpse of the Russian point man who had been the initial target for so many rifles. He lay on his stomach, and there were nine visible wounds in his back. The camera showed next a closeup view of a young man's face frozen in the moment of death, blue eyes, lusterless now and pale in death, framed by a face registering the shock of war's ultimate reality, his lips half opened still as if to protest his fate or to ask for another chance. The camera moved next to a body lying fetal-like near the top of the hill hardly two steps from the covering rocks where the three surviving squad members had found shelter. The camera then moved slowly down the slope seeking the last casualty. It found him on a pleasant, grassy spot beneath a small oak tree. A mortar fragment had caught him in the lower belly and his guts were spewed out on the grass like an overturned bucket of sand. He was whimpering softly, and with his free left hand was trying with almost comic desperation to place his entrails back inside his belly.

"Well, there you have it, folks," Bill Carr said. "It's official now. You saw it for yourselves thanks to our fine camera technicians. Seven casualties confirmed. John, I don't believe the American team has had its first casualty yet, is that right?"

"That's right, Bill. The Russian team apparently was caught completely off guard."

"Colonel Bullock, would you care to comment on what you've seen so far?"

"Yes, Bill, I think it's fair to say that this first skirmish gives the

American team a decided advantage. I would like to see the computer's probability reports before going too far out on a limb, but I'd say the odds are definitely in favor of the American team at this stage. General Caldwell's election not to take the central hill has paid a handsome dividend here early in the games."

"General Vorsilov, would you care to give us the Russian point of view?"

"I do not agree with my American friend, Colonel Bullock," the general said with a crisp British accent. "The fourth Russian squad was given the mission to take the central hill. The central hill has been taken and is now controlled by the Russian team. Possession of the central hill provides almost absolute dominance of the lake and surrounding low land. Those of you who have studied military history know how important that can be, particularly in the later stages of the games. I emphatically do not agree that the first skirmish was a defeat. Possession of the hill is worth a dozen men."

"Comments, Colonel Bullock?"

"Well, Bill, first of all, I don't agree that the Russian team has possession of the hill. True they have three men up there, but those men are armed with nothing but rifles and hand grenades—and they are not dug in. Right now the central hill is up for grabs. I—"

"Just a minute, Colonel. Pardon this interruption, but our computer has the first probability report. And here it is! The prediction is for an American victory with a probability rating of 57.2 How about that, folks? Here early in the first day the American team, which was a decided underdog in this year's games has jumped to a substantial lead."

Colonel Bullock spoke: "Bill, I want you to notice that man there—over there on the right-hand side of your screen. Can we have a closeup on that? That's a runner, Bill. A lot of the folks don't notice little things like that. They want to watch the machine gunners or the point man, but that man there could have a decided effect on the outcome of these games, Bill."

"I presume he's carrying a message back to headquarters, eh Colonel?"

"That's right, Bill, and a very important message, I'll warrant. You see an attack on the central hill from the east or south sides would be disastrous. The Russians, of course, hold the south hill. From their positions there they could subject our boys to a blistering fire from the rear on any attack made from the south. That runner was sent back with word that there are only three Russians on the hill. I think we can expect an immediate counterattack from the north as soon as the message has been delivered. In the meantime, squads five and six will maintain their positions in the eastern sector and try to prevent any reinforcements of the Russian position."

"Thank you, Colonel, for that enlightening analysis, and now, folks —" He broke off when the runner to whom the Colonel referred stumbled and fell.

"Wait a minute, folks. He's been hit! He's down! The runner has been shot. You saw it here, folks. Brilliant camera work. Simply great, John, how about that?"

"Simply tremendous, Bill. A really great shot. Ed, can we back the cameras up and show the folks that action again? Here it is in slow motion, folks. Now you see him (who is that, Colonel? Ted Krogan? Thank you, Colonel) here he is, folks, Private Ted Krogan from Milwaukee, Wisconsin. Here he is coming around the last clump of bushes —now watch this, folks—he gets about half way across the clearing—and there it is, folks, you can actually see the bullet strike his throat—a direct hit. Watch this camera close up of his face, you'll see him die in front of your eyes. And there he goes—he rolls over and not a move. He was dead before he hit the ground. Bill, did any of our cameras catch where that shot came from?"

"Yes, John, the Russians have slipped a two man sniper team in on our left flank. This could be serious, John. I don't think our boys know the runner was hit."

"Only time will tell, Bill. Only time will tell. Right now, I believe we have our first lull. Let's take thirty seconds for our stations to identify themselves."

Private Richard Starbuck's first day was not at all what he had expected. He was with the second squad, one of the three squads which were dug in on the north hill. After digging his foxhole he had spent the day staring at the south and central hills. He had heard the brief skirmish near the central hill, but he had yet to see his first Russian. He strained so hard to see something that sometimes his eyes played tricks on him. Twice his mind gave movement to a distant shadow. Once he nearly fired at the sudden sound of a rabbit in the brush. His desire to see the enemy was almost overpowering. It reminded him of the first time Mr. Martin had taken him fishing on the lake. He had been thirteen at the time. He had stared at that still, white cork for what had seemed like hours. He remembered he had even prayed to God to send a fish along that would make the cork go under. His mind had played tricks on him that day too, and several times he had fancied the cork was moving when it was not. He was not praying today, of course—except the intensity of his desire was something like a prayer.

He spent the entire first day in a foxhole without seeing anything or hearing anything except an occasional distant sniper's bullet. When the sun went down, he brought out his rations and consumed eighteen hundred calories. As soon as it was dark, his squad was to move to the south slope and prepare their defensive positions. He knew the Russians would be similarly occupied. It was maddening to know that for a time the enemy would be exposed and yet be relatively safe because of the covering darkness.

When it was completely dark, his squad captain gave the signal, and the squad moved out to their predetermined positions and began to dig in. So far they were still following the battle plan to the letter. He dug his foxhole with care, building a small ledge half way down on which to sit and placing some foliage on the bottom to keep it from becoming muddy, and then he settled down to wait. Somehow it was better at night. He even found himself wishing that they would not come tonight. He discovered that he could wait.

Later he slept. How long, he did not know. He only knew that when he awoke he heard a sound of air parting followed by a hard, thundering impact that shook the ground. His first instinct was to action, and then he remembered that there was nothing he could do, so he hunched down as far as possible in his foxhole and waited. He knew real fear now—the kind of fear that no amount of training or conditioning can eliminate. He was a living thing whose dominant instinct was to continue living. He did not wish to die hunched down in a hole in the ground. The flesh along his spine quivered involuntarily with each fractional warning whoosh which preceded the mortar's fall. Now he knew that he could die, knew it with his body as well as with his mind. A shell landed nearby, and he heard a shrill, womanlike scream. Bill Smith had been hit. His first reaction was one of relief. It had been Bill Smith and not he. But why did he have to scream? Bill Smith had been one of the toughest men in the squad. There ought to be more dignity than that. There ought to be a better way of dying than lying helpless in a hole and waiting for chance or fate in the form of some unseen, impersonal gunner, who probably was firing an assigned pattern anyhow, to bring you life or death.

In training, under conditions of simulated danger, he had grown to rely upon the solidarity of the squad. They faced danger together; together they could whip the world. But now he knew that in the end war was a lonely thing. He could not reach out into the darkness and draw courage from the huddled forms of his comrades from the second squad. He took no comfort from the fact that the other members of the squad were just as exposed as he. The fear which he discovered in himself was a thing which had to be endured alone, and he sensed now that when he died, that too would have to be endured alone.

"Well, folks, this is Bill Carr still bringing you our continuous coverage of the 2050 Olympic War Games. John Ardanyon is getting a few hours' sleep right now, but he'll be back at four o'clock.

"For the benefit of those viewers who may have tuned in late, let me say again that NSB will bring continuous coverage. Yes sir, folks, this year, thanks to our special owl-eye cameras, we can give you shots of the night action with remarkable clarity.

"Well, folks, the games are almost eighteen hours old, and here to bring you the latest casualty report is my old friend Max Sanders. Max?"

"Thank you, Bill, and good evening, ladies and gentlemen. The latest casualty reports—and these are confirmed figures. Let me repeat—these are confirmed figures. For the Russian team: twenty-two dead, and eight incapacitated wounded. For the American team: seventeen dead, and only six incapacitated wounded."

"Thank you, Max. Folks, our computer has just recomputed the odds, and the results are—what's this? Folks, here is a surprise. A rather unpleasant surprise. Just forty-five minutes ago the odds on an American victory were 62.1. Those odds, ladies and gentlemen, have just fallen to 53.0. I'm afraid I don't understand this at all. Professor Overmann, what do you make of this?"

"I'm afraid the computer has picked up a little trouble in the southwestern sector, Bill. As I explained earlier, the computer's estimates are made up of many factors—and the casualty reports are just one of them. Can you give us a long shot of the central hill, Ed? There. There you see one of the factors which undoubtedly has influenced the new odds. The Russian team has succeeded in reinforcing their position on the central hill with a light machine gun squad. This goes back to the first American casualty earlier today when the messenger failed to get word through for the counterattack.

"Now give me a medium shot of the American assassination squad. Back it up a little more, will you, Ed? There, that's it. I was afraid of that. What has happened, Bill, is that, unknowingly, the American squad has been spotted by the Russian reserve guard. That could mean trouble."

"I see. Well, that explains the sudden drop in the odds, folks. Now the question is, can the American assassination squad pull it off under this handicap? We'll keep the cameras over here, folks, until we have an answer. The other sectors are relatively quiet now except for sporadic mortar fire."

For the first time since the skirmish which had begun the battle, the cameras were able to concentrate their sustained attention on one small area of the arena. The assassination squad moved slowly, torturously slow, through the brush and the deep grass which dotted the southwest sector. They had successfully infiltrated the Russian rear. For a moment the camera switched to the Russian sentry who had discovered the enemy's presence and who was now reporting to his captain. Orders were given and in a very few minutes the light machine gun had been brought back from the lake and was in position to fire on the advancing American squad. Two Russian reserve squads were positioned to deliver a deadly crossfire on the patrol. To the men in the arena it must have been pitch dark. Even on camera there was an eerie, uneasy quality to the light that lent a ghostlike effect to the faces of the men whose fates had been determined by an unsuspected meeting with a Russian sentry. Death would have been exceedingly quick and profitless for the ten-man squad had not a Russian rifleman fired his rifle prematurely. As it was, the squad captain and six men were killed in the first furious burst of fire. The three survivors reacted instantly and disappeared into the brush. One died there noiselessly from a chest wound inflicted in the ambush. Another managed to kill two Russian infantrymen with hand grenades before he died. In the darkness the Russian captain became confused and sent word to his general that the entire squad had been destroyed. The general came to inspect the site and was instantly killed at short range by the lone surviving member of the assassination squad. By a series of fortuitous events the squad had accomplished its primary purpose. The Russian general was dead, and in less than two seconds so was the last man in the assassination squad.

"Well, there you have it, ladies and gentlemen. High drama here in the early hours of the morning as an American infantry squad cuts down the Russian general. Those of you who have watched these games before will know that some of the most exciting action takes place at night. In a few minutes we should have the latest probability report, but until then, how do you see it, Colonel Bullock?"

"Bill, I think the raiding squad came out of that very well indeed. They were discovered and boxed in by the enemy, yet they still fulfilled their primary mission—they killed the Russian general. It's bound to have an effect."

"General Vorsilov, do you care to comment, sir?"

"I think your computer will confirm that three for ten is a good exchange, even if one of those three happens to be a general. Of course, we had an unlucky break when one of our soldiers accidentally discharged his weapon. Otherwise we would have suffered no casualties. As for the loss of General Sarlov, no general has ever survived the games, and I venture to say no general ever will. The leadership of the Russian team will now descend by predetermined selection to the senior Russian captain."

"Thank you, General. Well, folks, here is the latest computer report. This is going to disappoint a lotta people. For an American victory, the odds now stand at 49.1. Of course, let me emphasize, folks, that such a small difference at this stage is virtually meaningless.

"Well, we seem to have another lag, folks. While our cameras scan the arena, let me remind you that each morning of the games NSB will be bringing you a special capsule re-run of the highlights of the preceding night's action.

"Well, folks, things seem to be a little quiet right now, but don't go away. In the games, anything can happen and usually does. We lost ten good men in that last action, so maybe this is a good time to remind you ladies and gentlemen that this year NSB is giving to the parents of each one of these boys a special tape recording of the action in the arena complete with sound effects and a brand-new uniflex projector. Thus each parent will be able to see their son's participation in the games. This is a gift that I'm sure will be treasured throughout the years.

"NSB would like to take this opportunity to thank the following sponsors for relinquishing their time so we could bring you this special broadcast. . . ."

Private Richard Starbuck watched the dawn edge its way over the arena. He had slept perhaps a total of two hours last night, and already a feeling of unreality was invading his senses. When the roll was called, he answered with a voice which surprised him by its impersonalness: "Private Richard Starbuck, uninjured, ammunition expended; zero." Three men did not answer the roll. One of the three was the squad captain. That meant that Sergeant Collins was the new squad captain. Through discipline and habit he broke out his breakfast ration and forced himself to eat. Then he waited again.

Later that morning he fired his first shot. He caught a movement on the central hill, and this time it was not a shadow. He fired quickly, but he missed, and his target quickly disappeared. There was heavy firing in the mid-eastern sector, but he was no longer even curious as to what was going on unless it affected his own position. All day long he fired whenever he saw something that could have been a man on either of the Russian-held hills. Sometimes he fired when he saw nothing because it made him feel better. The Russians returned the fire but neither side appeared to be doing any real damage against a distant, well-entrenched enemy.

Toward evening Captain Collins gave orders for him to take possession of Private Bill Smith's foxhole. It seemed like a ridiculous thing to do in broad daylight when in a couple more hours he could accomplish the same thing in almost perfect safety. They obviously intended for him to draw fire to expose the Russian positions. For a moment he hesitated, feeling the hate for Collins wash over him like a flood. Then he grasped his rifle, leaped from his hole, and ran twenty yards diagonally down the hill to Smith's foxhole. It seemed to him as if the opposing hills had suddenly come alive. He flung himself face first to the ground and landed grotesquely on top of the once tough body of Private Bill Smith.

He felt blood trickling down his arm, and for a moment he thought he had been hit, but it was only a scratch from a projecting rock. His own squad had been firing heavily, and he heard someone say: "I got one. B'god, I got one." He twisted around in the foxhole trying to keep his head safely below the surface, and then he saw what it was that had made Bill Smith scream. The mortar had wrenched his left arm loose at the elbow. It dangled there now, hung in place only by a torn shirt and a small piece of skin. He braced himself and began to edge the body up past him in the foxhole. He managed to get below it and heave it over the side. He heard the excited volley of shots which followed the body's tumbling course down the hill. Somehow in his exertions he had finished wrenching the arm loose from the body. He reached down and threw that too over the side of the foxhole. And now this particular bit of earth belonged to him. He liked it better than his last one. He felt he had earned it.

The night brought a return of the mortar fire. This time he didn't care. This time he could sleep, although there was a slight twitching motion on the left side of his face and he woke up every two hours for no reason at all.

"Good morning, ladies and gentlemen, this is John Ardanyon bringing you the start of the third day of the 2050 Olympic War Games.

"And what a night it's been, ladies and gentlemen. In a moment we'll bring you the highlights of last night's action, but first here is Bill Carr to bring you up to date on the vital statistics."

"Thank you, John. Folks, we're happy to say that in the last few hours the early trend of the night's action has been reversed and the American team once again has a substantial lead. Squads five and six were wiped out in an early-evening engagement in the mid-eastern sector, but they gave a good account of themselves. The Russians lost eleven men and a light machine gun in their efforts to get this thorn out of their side. And I'm happy to say the American light machine gun carried by squad six was successfully destroyed before the squad was overrun. But the big news this morning is the success of the American mortar and sniper squads. Our mortars accounted for six dead and two seriously wounded as opposed to only two killed and one wounded by the Russian mortars. Our sniper squad, working in two-man teams, was successful in killing five men; whereas we only lost one man to enemy sniper action last night. We'll have a great shot coming up, folks, showing Private Cecil Harding from Plainview, New Jersey, killing a Russian captain in his sleep with nothing more than a sharp rock."

"Right, Bill, but before we show last night's highlights, I'm sure the folks would like to know that the score now stands forty-two fighting men for the American team as opposed to only thirty-seven for the Russians. Computer-wise that figures out to a 52.5 probability for the American team. I'm sure that probability figure would be higher if the Russians were not positioned on that central hill."

"And here now are the high spots of the night's action. . . ."

On the morning of the third day, word was spread that the American general had been killed. Private Richard Starbuck did not care. He realized now that good generalship was not going to preserve his life. So far chance seemed the only decisive factor. The mortar fire grew heavier, and the word was given to prepare for an attack on the hill. He gripped his rifle, and as he waited, he hoped they would come. He wanted to see, to face his enemy. He wanted to feel again that man had the power to control his own destiny.

A few minutes after noon it began to rain, a chilling spring rain that drizzled slowly and soaked in next to the skin. The enemy mortar ceased firing. The man in the foxhole next to his was laughing somewhat hysterically and claiming he had counted the Russian mortar fire and that they had now exploded eight hundred of their thousand rounds. It seemed improbable; nevertheless Private Starbuck heard the story spread from foxhole to foxhole and presently he even began to believe it himself.

Toward evening, the sun came out briefly, and the mortars commenced firing again. This time, however, the shells landed on the far side of the hill. There was an answering fire from the American mortar, although it seemed a senseless duel when neither gunner could get a fix on the other. The duel continued after nightfall, and then, suddenly, there was silence from the American sector. In a few minutes, his worst fears were confirmed when a runner brought orders to fall back to new positions. An unhappy chance round had knocked out the American mortar.

There were five men left in his squad. They managed to withdraw from the south slope of the hill without further losses. Their new general, Captain Paulson, had a meeting of his surviving officers in Private Starbuck's hearing. The situation was not good, but before going into purely defensive positions, two things must be accomplished. The enemy machine gun and mortar must be destroyed. Squads seven and eight, who had been in reserve for a time and who had suffered the fewest casualties, were assigned the task. It must be done tonight. If the enemy's heavy weapons could be destroyed while the Americans still maintained possession of their remaining light machine gun, their position would be favorable. Otherwise their chances were fading. The mortar shells for the now useless American mortar were to be destroyed immediately to prevent their possible use by the enemy. And, the general added almost as an afterthought, at sunrise the second squad will attack and take the central hill. They would be supported by the light machine gun if, by then, the enemy mortar had been put out of action. Questions? There were many, but none were asked.

"Colonel Bullock, this is an unusual development. Would you tell us what General Paulson has in mind?"

"Well, Bill, I think it must be pretty obvious even to the men in the field that the loss of the American mortar has drastically changed the situation. An unfortunate occurrence, unfortunate indeed. The probability report is now only 37.6 in favor of the Amerian team. Of course, General Paulson doesn't have a computer, but I imagine he's arrived at pretty much the same conclusion.

"The two squads—seven and eight, I believe—which you see on your screens are undoubtedly being sent out in a desperation attempt— no, not desperation—in a courageous attempt to destroy the enemy mortar and light machine gun. It's a good move. I approve. Of course, you won't find this one in the books, but the fact is that at this stage of the game, the pre-determined battle plans are of ever-decreasing importance."

"General Vorsilov?"

"The Americans are doing the only thing they can do, Mr. Carr, but it's only a question of time now. You can rest assured that the Russian team will be alert to this very maneuver."

"Well, stand by, folks. This is still anybody's game. The games are not over yet—not by a long shot. Don't go away. This could be the key maneuver of the games. John?"

"While we're waiting, Bill, I'm sure the folks would like to hear a list of the new records which have already been set in this fifth meeting between the United States and Russia in the Olympic War Games. Our first record came early in the games when the American fifth and sixth squads startled the world with a brilliant demonstration of firepower and shattering the old mark set back in 2042 by killing seven men in just. . . ."

On the morning of the fifth day Private Starbuck moved out as the point man for the assault on the central hill. He had trained on a replica of the hill hundreds of times, and he knew it as well as he knew the back of his own hand. Squad seven had knocked out the enemy mortar last night, so they had the support of their own light machine gun for at least part of the way. Squad eight had failed in their mission and had been killed to the last man. Private Starbuck only hoped the Russian machine gun was not in position to fire on the assault team.

At first it was like maneuvers. Their own machine gun delivered a blistering fire twenty yards ahead of them and the five squad members themselves fired from the hip as they advanced. There was only occasional and weak counterfire. They were eight yards from the top, and he was beginning to hope that, by some miracle spawned by a grotesque god, they were going to make it. Then it came. Grenades came rolling down from above, and a sustained volley of rifle-fire came red hot from the depths of hell. He was hit twice in the first volley. Once in the hip, again in the shoulder. He would have gotten up, would have tried to go forward, but Captain Collins fell dead on top of him and he could not. A grenade exploded three feet away. He felt something jar his cheek and knew he had been hit again. Somehow it was enough. Now he could die. He had done enough. Blood ran down his face and into his left eye, but he made no attempt to wipe it away. He would surely die now. He hoped it would be soon.

"It doesn't look too good, folks. Not good at all. Colonel Bullock?"

"I'm afraid I have to agree, Bill. The American probability factor is down to 16.9, and right now I couldn't quarrel with the computer at all. The Russians still have sixteen fighting men, while the Americans are down to nine. The American team will undoubtedly establish a defense position around the light machine gun on the north hill, but with the Russians still in control of the central hill and still in possession of their own machine gun, it appears pretty hopeless. Pretty hopeless indeed."

He owed his life during the next few minutes to the fact that he was able to maintain consciousness. The firing had ceased all about him, and for a time he heard nothing, not even the sound of distant gun fire. This is death, he thought. Death is when you can't hear the guns any longer. Then he heard the sound of boots. He picked out a spot in the sky and forced his eyes to remain on that spot. He wished to die in peace, and they might not let him die in peace. After a while the boots moved on.

He lost consciousness shortly after that. When he awoke, it was dark. He was not dead yet, for he could hear the sounds of guns again. Let them kill each other. He was out of it. It really was not such a bad way to die, if only it wouldn't take so long. He could tolerate the pain, but he hated the waiting.

While he waited, a strange thing happened. It was as though his spirit passed from his body and he could see himself lying there on the hill. Poor forlorn body to lie so long upon a hill. Would they write poems and sing songs about Private Richard Starbuck like they did four years ago for Sergeant Ernie Stevens? No, no poems for this lonely body lying on a hill waiting to die. Sergeant Stevens had killed six men before he died. So far as he knew he had killed none.

In the recruiting pamphlet they told you that your heirs would receive one hundred thousand dollars if you died in the games. Was that why he signed up? No, no, he was willing to die now, but not for that. Surely he had had a better reason than that. Why had he done such a crazy thing? Was it the chance to be a survivor? No, not that either. Suddenly he realized something the selection committee had known long ago: he had volunteered for no other reason than the fact there was a war to be fought, and he had not wanted to be left out.

He thought of the cameras next. Had they seen him on TV? Had all the girls, all the people in his home town been watching? Had his dad watched? Had Mr. and Mrs. Martin and their daughter watched? Had they seen him when he had drawn fire by changing foxholes? Were they watching now to see if he died well?

Toward morning, he began to wonder if he could hold out. There was only one thing left for him to do and that was to die as quietly and peacefully as possible. Yet it was not an easy thing to do, and now his wounds were beginning to hurt again. Twice he heard the boots pass nearby, and each time he had to fight back an impulse to call out to them so they could come hurry death. He did not do it. Someone might be watching, and he wanted them to be proud of him.

At daybreak there was a wild flurry of rifle and machine gun fire, and then, suddenly, there was no sound, no movement, nothing but silence. Perhaps now he could die.

The sad, dejected voice of Bill Carr was saying ". . . all over. It's all over, folks. We're waiting now for the lights to come on in the arena— the official sign that the games are over. It was close—but close only counts in horse-shoes, as the saying goes. The American team made a fine last stand. They almost pulled it off. I make out only three Russian survivors, John. Is that right?"

"Just three, Bill, and one of those is wounded in the arm. Well, ladies and gentlemen, we had a very exciting finish. We're waiting now for the arena lights to come on. Wait a minute! Something's wrong! The lights are not coming on! I thought for a moment the official scorer was asleep at the switch. Bill, can you find out what the situation is? This damned computer still gives the American team a 1.4 probability factor."

"We've located it, John. Our sonic sound system has located a lone American survivor. Can you get the cameras on the central hill over there? There he is, folks. Our spotters in the booth have just identified him as Private Richard Starbuck from Centerville, Iowa. He seems badly wounded, but he's still alive. The question is: can he fight? He's not moving, but his heart is definitely beating and we know where there's life, there's hope."

"Right, Bill. And you can bet the three Russian soldiers are a pretty puzzled group right now. They don't know what's happened. They can't figure out why the lights have not come on. Two minutes ago they were

shouting and yelling a victory chant that now seems to have been premature. Ed, give us a camera on that north hill. Look at this, ladies and
gentlemen. The three Russian survivors have gone berserk. Literally
berserk—they are shooting and clubbing the bodies of the American
dead. Don't go away, folks. . . ."

He began to fear he might not die. His wounds had lost their numbness and had begun to throb. He heard the sounds of guns and then of
boots. Why wouldn't they leave him alone? Surely the war was over. He
had nothing to do with them. One side or another had won—so why
couldn't they leave him alone? The boots were coming closer, and he
sensed that they would not leave him alone this time. A sudden rage
mingled with his pain, and he knew he could lie there no longer. For the
next few seconds he was completely and utterly insane. He pulled the
pin on the grenade which had been pressing against his side and threw it
blindly in the direction of the sound of the boots. With an instinct gained
in two years of intense training, he rolled to his belly and began to fire at
the blurred forms below him. He did not stop firing even when the
blurred shapes ceased to move. He did not stop firing until his rifle
clicked on an empty chamber. Only then did he learn that the blurred
shapes were Russian soldiers.

They healed his wounds. His shoulder would always be a little stiff,
but his leg healed nicely, leaving him without a trace of a limp. There
was a jagged scar on his jaw, but they did wonders with plastic surgery
these days and unless you knew it was there, you would hardly notice it.
They put him through a two-month reconditioning school, but it didn't
take, of course. They gave him ticker tape parades, medals, and the keys
to all the major cities. They warned him about the psychological dangers
of being a survivor. They gave him case histories of other survivors—
grim little anecdotes involving suicide, insanity, and various mental
aberrations.
And then they turned him loose.
For a while he enjoyed the fruits of victory. Whatever he wanted he
could have for the asking. Girls flocked around him, men respected him,
governments honored him, and a group of flunkies and hangers-on were
willing enough to serve his every whim. He grew bored and returned to
his home town.
It was not the same. He was not the same. When he walked down the
streets, mothers would draw close to their daughters and hurry on past.
If he shot pool, his old friends seemed aloof and played as if they were
afraid to win. Only the shopkeepers were glad to see him come in, for
whatever he took, the government paid for. If he were to shoot the
mayor's son, the government would pay for that, too. At home his own

mother would look at him with that guarded look in her eyes, and his dad was careful not to look him in the eyes at all.

He spent a lot of time in his room. He was not lonely. He had learned to live alone. He was sitting in his room one evening when he saw Cassandra, the Martins' fifteen-year-old daughter, coming home with some neighborhood kid from the early movie. He watched idly as the boy tried to kiss her goodnight. There was an awkwardness between them that was vaguely exciting. At last the boy succeeded in kissing her on the cheek, and then, apparently satisfied, went on home.

He sat there for a long time lighting one cigarette from the last one. There was a conflict inside his mind that once would have been resolved differently and probably with no conscious thought. Making up his mind, he stubbed his cigarette and went downstairs. His mother and father were watching TV. They did not look up as he walked out the front door. They never did any more.

The Martins were still up. Mr. Martin was tying brightly colored flies for his new fly rod and Mrs. Martin was reading. They both stiffened when he entered without knocking—alarm playing over their faces like a flickering fire light. He didn't pause, but walked on up stairs without looking at them.

Mrs. Martin got to her feet and stood looking up the stairway without moving. In her eyes there was the look of a jungle tiger who watches its mate pinned to a stake at the bottom of the pit. Mr. Martin sat staring at the brightly colored flies on his lap. For a moment there was silence. Then a girl's shrill screams announced to the Martins that war's reality was also for the very young.

PAUL CARTER

THE LAST OBJECTIVE

For uncounted aeons the great beds of shale and limestone had known the stillness and the darkness of eternity. Now they trembled and shuddered to the passage of an invader; stirred and vibrated in sleepy protest at a disturbance not of Nature's making.

Tearing through the masses of soft rock, its great duralloy cutters screaming a hymn of hate into the crumbling crust, its caterpillar treads clanking and grinding over gravel shard, fresh-torn from their age-old strata, lurched a juggernaut—one of the underground cruisers of the Combined Western Powers. It was squat, ugly; the top of its great cutting head full forty feet above the clattering treads, its square stern rocking and swaying one hundred and fifty feet behind the diamond-hard prow. It was angular, windowless; there were ugly lumps just behind the shrieking blades which concealed its powerful armament.

It had been built for warfare in an age when the sea and air were ruled by insensate rocket projectiles which flashed through the skies to spend their atomic wrath upon objectives which had long since ceased to exist; where infantry no longer was Queen of Battles, since the ravages of combat had wiped out the armies which began the war. And floods of hard radiation, sterilizing whole populations and making hideous mutational horrors of many of those who were born alive, had prevented the conscription of fresh armies which might have won the war.

The conflict had been going on for more than a generation. The causes had long been forgotten; the embattled nations, burrowing into the earth, knew only a fiery longing for revenge. The chaos produced by the first aerial attacks had enabled the survivors to hide themselves beyond the reach even of atomic bombs to carry on the struggle. Navies and armored divisions exchanged knowledge; strategy and tactics underwent drastic revamping. Psychology, once the major hope of mankind for a solution to the war problem, now had become perverted to the ends of the militarists, as a substitute for patriotism to motivate the men at war. In new ways but with the old philosophies, the war went on; and therefore this armored monster clawed its way through the earth's crust toward its objective.

On the "bridge" of the underground warship, a small turret in the center of its roof, Commander Sanderson clung to a stanchion as he barked orders to his staff through the intercom. The ship proper was swung on special mountings and gyro-stabilized to divorce it from the violent jolting of the lower unit, consisting of the drill, the treads and the mighty, earth-moving atomic engines. But still some of the lurching and jouncing of the treads was transmitted up through the storerooms through the crew's quarters to the bridge, and the steel deck underfoot swayed and shook drunkenly. However, men had once learned to accustom themselves to the fitful motions of the sea; and the hardened skipper paid no attention to the way his command pounded forward.

Commander Sanderson was a thickset man, whose hunched shoulders and bull neck suggested the prize ring. But he moved like a cat, even here inside this vibrating juggernaut, as he slipped from one command post to another, reading over the shoulders of unheeding operators the findings of their instruments. The Seismo Log was an open book to his practiced eye; his black brows met in a deep frown as he noticed a severe shock registered only two minutes previously, only a few hundred yards to starboard. He passed by the radio locator and the radioman; their jobs would come later, meantime radio silence was enforced on both sides. The thin little soundman adjusted his earphones as the "Old Man" came by: "No other diggers contacted, sir," he muttered automatically and continued listening. The optical technician leaped to his feet and saluted smartly as the Commander passed; he would have nothing to do unless they broke into a cavern, and so he rendered the military courtesy his fellows could not.

Sanderson halted beside the post of the environmental technician. This man's loosely described rating covered many fields; he was at once geologist, radarman, vibration expert, and navigator. It was his duty to deduce the nature of their surroundings and suggest a course to follow.

"Your report," demanded Sanderson.

"Igneous rock across our course at fifteen thousand feet, I believe, sir," he replied promptly. "It's not on the chart, sir—probably a new formation."

Sanderson swore. This meant volcanic activity—and, whether man-made or accidental, that spelled trouble. "Course?" he asked.

"Change course to one hundred seventy-five degrees—and half-speed, sir, if you please, until I can chart this formation more accurately."

Sanderson returned his salute, turned on his heel. "Mr. Culver!"

The young lieutenant-commander saluted casually. "Sir?"

Sanderson repressed another oath. He did not like the young executive officer with his lordly manners, his natty uniform and the coat of tan he had acquired from frequent ultraviolet exposure—a luxury beyond the means of most of the pasty-faced undermen. But duty is duty—"Change course to one seven five. Half-speed," he ordered.

"Aye, aye, sir." Culver picked up a microphone, jabbed a phone jack into the proper plug and pressed the buzzer.

Far below, near the clanking treads, Lieutenant Watson wiped the sweat from his brow—most of the ship was not as well insulated as the bridge, whose personnel must be at their physical peak at all times. He jumped as the intercom buzzed, then spoke into his chest microphone. "Navigation," he called.

"Bridge," came Culver's voice. "Change course to one seven five. Over."

"Navigation to bridge. Course one seven five, aye, aye," said Watson mechanically. Then: "What is it, Culver?"

"Environmental thinks it's lava."

"Damnation." The old lieutenant—one of the few able-bodied survivors of the surface stages of the war—turned to his aides. "Change course to one seven five."

Peterson, brawny Navigator Third Class, stepped up to a chrome handle projecting from a circular slot and shoved it to "175," then turned a small crank for finer adjustment. Slowly the pitch of the great blades shifted—the sound of their turning, muffled by layers of armor, abruptly changed in tone.

Chief Navigator Schmidt looked up from a pile of strata charts. "Ask the exec to have a copy of the new formation sent down here," he said, speaking as calmly as if he were a laboratory technician requesting a routine report. Schmidt was the psycho officer's pride and joy; he was the only person aboard the underground cruiser who had never been subjected to a mental manhandling as a result of that worthy's suspicions. He was slightly plump, pink-cheeked, with a straggling yellow moustache—just a little childish; perhaps that was why he had never cracked.

His request was transmitted; up on the bridge, the environmental technician threw a switch, cutting a remote repeater into the series of scanners which brought him his information. Chief Navigator Schmidt heard the bell clang, fed a sheet of paper into the transcriber, and sat back happily to watch the results.

The great drillhead completed its grinding turn; the blades tore into the rock ahead of it again.

"Navigation to bridge: bearing one seven five," reported Watson.

"Carry on," returned young Culver. He pulled out the phone jack, plugged it in elsewhere.

Ensign Clark stroked the slight, fuzzy black beard which was one of many ego-boosters for his crushing introversion, along with the tattoos on his arms and the book of physical exercises which he practiced whenever he thought he was alone. At Culver's buzz, he cursed the exec vigorously, then opened the circuit. "Power," he replied diffidently.

"Bridge to power: reduce speed by one-half. Over."

"Power to bridge: speed one-half—aye, aye." Clark put his hand over the mike, shouted at the non-rated man stationed at the speed lever. "You! Half-speed, and shake the lead out of your pants!"

The clanking of the treads slowed; simultaneously the whine of the blades rose, cutting more rapidly to compensate for the decreased pressure from behind the drill.

In the hot, steam-filled galley, fat Chief Cook Kelly lifted the lid from a kettle to sniff the synthetic stew. "What stinkin' slum—an' to think they kicked about the chow back in the Surface Wars."

"Chief, they say there was *real meat* in the chow then," rejoined Marconi, Food Chemist First Class.

"Why, Marc, even I can remember——" he was interrupted by the intercom's buzz.

"Attention, all hands!" came Culver's voice. "Igneous rock detected, probably a fresh lava-flow. We have changed our course. Action is expected within a few hours—stand by to go to quarters. Repeating——"

Kelly spat expertly. His face was impassive, but his hand trembled as he replaced the lid on the kettle. "We better hurry this chow up, Marc. Heaven only knows when we'll eat again."

Lieutenant Carpenter raised his hand, slapped the hysterical Private Worth twice.

"Now, shut up or I'll have the psych corpsmen go over you again," he snapped.

Worth dropped his head between his hands, said nothing.

Carpenter backed out the cell. "I'm posting a guard here," he warned. "One peep out of you and the boys will finish what they started."

He slammed the door for emphasis.

"Well, sir, you did it again," said the sentry admiringly. "He was throwing things when you got here, but you tamed him in a hurry."

"We've got to get these cells soundproofed," muttered Carpenter abstractedly, putting on his glasses. "The combat-detachment bunks are right next to them."

"Yeah, sir, I guess it's harder on the combat detachment than the rest of us. We've all got our watches and so forth, but they haven't got a thing to do until we hit an enemy city or something. They crack easy—like this Worth guy in here now."

Carpenter whirled on him. "Listen, corpsman, I'm too busy a man to be chasing up here to deal with every enlisted man in this brig—I've got the other officers to keep in line. And let's not be volunteering information to superiors without permission!" he hissed.

"I'm sorry, sir——" the guard began—but the lieutenant was gone!

The sentry smiled crookedly. "O.K., Mr. Carpenter, your big job is to keep the officers in line. I'm just wonderin' who's supposed to keep *you* out of this cell block."

Corporal Sheehan dealt the cards with sudden, jerky motions; his brow was furrowed, his face a study in concentration. One would have thought him a schoolboy puzzling over a difficult final examination.

Sergeants Fontaine and Richards snatched each card as it came, partly crushing the pasteboards as they completed their hands. Fat old Koch, Private First Class, waited until all the cards had been dealt, then grabbed the whole hand and clutched it against his broad stomach, glancing suspiciously at his fellow players.

Their conversation was in terse, jerky monosyllables—but around them other men of the combat detachment talked, loudly and incessantly. Private Carson sat in a corner, chain smoking in brief, nervous puffs. Coarse jokes and harsh laughter dominated the conversation. Nobody mentioned Culver's "alert" of a few minutes before.

"Three," grunted the obese Koch. Sheehan dealt him the cards swiftly.

"Hey!" Richards interrupted, before play could begin. "I didn't like that deal. Let's have a look at that hand."

"Know what you're callin' me?" retorted Sheehan, snatching the deck as Richards was about to pick it up.

"Yeah—I know what to call you, you lyin', yella cheat——"

Sheehan lurched to his feet, lashed out with a ham-like fist. Richards scrambled out of the way, bringing chair and table down with a crash. A moment later both men were on their feet and squared off.

Conversation halted; men drifted over toward the table even as Fontaine stepped between the two players. Koch had not yet fully reacted to the situation and was only halfway out of his chair.

"You fools!" shouted Fontaine. "You want the psych corpsmen on our necks again? That louse Carpenter said if there was another fight we'd all get it."

Corporal Sheehan's big fists unclenched slowly. "That low, stinkin'—"

"Sit down," said Koch heavily. "Fontaine's right. The psychs probably have a spy or two planted in this room." His eye rested briefly on Carson, still smoking silently alone in the corner, seemingly oblivious of the commotion.

"That Carson," muttered Richards, shifting the object of his anger. "I'll bet any money you want he's a stool for Carpenter."

"Always by himself," corroborated Sheehan. "What's the story about him—born in a lab somewhere, wasn't he?"

The others were moving away now that it was plain there was to be no fight. Koch picked up the cards, stacked them. "Carson may not even be human," he suggested. "The science profs have been workin' on artificial cannon-fodder for years, and you can be sure if they ever do make a robot they're not goin' to talk about it until it's been tried in combat."

Carson overheard part of his statement; smiled shortly. He rose and left the room.

"See?" Richards went on. "Probably puttin' all four of us on report right now."

Lieutenant Carpenter placed the wire recorder back inside its concealed niche, polished his glasses carefully, opened his notebook and made several entries in a neat schoolteacher's hand:

Friction betw. Sheehan, Richards worse—psych. reg. next time back to Gen. Psych. Hosp. New Chicago. No sign men susp. Koch my agent; K. planting idea of robots in crew's minds per order. Can reveal Carson whenever enemy knows Powers mfg. robots in quantity. Fontaine well integrated, stopped fight—recomm. transfer my staff to Sanderson.

He put the notebook away, began to climb the nearest metal ladder with the mincing, catlike tread which the whole crew had learned to hate.

The lone guard before the massive lead-and-steel door of the central chamber saluted as the lieutenant passed. His task was to safeguard the ship's most important cargo—its sole atomic bomb. Carpenter asked him several routine word-association questions before proceeding.

The lieutenant paused just once more in his progress upward. This was to play back the tape of another listening device, this one piped into the quarters of the men who serviced the mighty atomic engines. Making notes copiously, he proceeded directly to the bridge.

"Captain, my report," he announced, not without some show of pride.

"Later," said Sanderson shortly, without looking up from a rough strata-chart the environmental technician had just handed him.

"But it's rather important, sir. Serious trouble is indicated in the combat detachment——"

"It always is," retorted Sanderson in some heat. "Take your report to Culver; I'm busy."

Carpenter froze, then turned to the young lieutenant-commander. "If you will initial this, please——"

Culver repressed a shudder. He couldn't keep back the rebellious feeling that the ancient navies had been better off with their primitive chaplains than the modern underground fleets with their prying psychiatrists. Of course, he hastily told himself, that was impossible today—organized religion had long since ceased to sanction war and had been appropriately dealt with by the government.

The Seismo Log recorded a prolonged disturbance directly ahead, and as Sanderson began his rounds the environmental technician called to him. "Sudden fault and more igneous activity dead ahead, sir," he reported.

"Carry on," replied Sanderson. "Probably artificial," he muttered half to himself. "Lot of volcanism in enemy territory. . . . Mr. Culver!"

Culver hastily initialled the psycho officer's notebook and handed it back. "Sir?"

"Elevate the cutters twenty-five degrees—we're going up and come on the enemy from above."

The order was soon transmitted to navigation; Lieutenant Watson's efficient gang soon had the metallic behemoth inclined at an angle of twenty-five degrees and rising rapidly toward the surface. Chief Schmidt dragged out new charts, noted down outstanding information and relayed data topside.

The ship's body swung on its mountings as the treads assumed the new slant, preserving equilibrium throughout. An order from Ensign Clark of power soon had the ship driving ahead as fast as the cutters could tear through the living rock.

"Diggers ahead," the thin soundman called out suddenly, adjusting his earphones. He snapped a switch; lights flickered on a phosphorescent screen. "Sounds like about three, sir—one is going to intersect our course at a distance of about five thousand yards."

"Let him," grunted Sanderson. "Mr. Culver, you may level off now."

"Electronic activity dead ahead," and "Enemy transmitter dead ahead," the radio locator and radioman reported almost simultaneously, before Culver's quiet order had been carried out.

"Go to general quarters, Mr. Culver," ordered Sanderson quickly. The exec pressed a button.

Throughout the ship was heard the tolling of a great bell—slowly the strokes lost their ponderous beat, quickened in tempo faster and faster until they became a continuous pandemonium of noise; simultaneously the pitch increased. All of this was a trick devised by staff psych officers, believing it would produce a subconscious incentive to greater speed and urgency.

The observational and operational posts were already manned; now, as quickly as possible, reliefs took over the more grueling watches such as that of the environmental technician. Medical and psych corpsmen hurriedly unpacked their gear, fanned out through the ship. Ensign Clark's voice faltered briefly as he ordered the power consumption cut to a minimum. The great cruiser slowed to a crawl.

The galley was bedlam as Kelly and Marconi rushed from one kettle to the next, supervising the ladling of hot food into deep pans by the apprentices who had assembled in haste in response to Kelly's profane bellowing. Chow runners dashed madly out the door, slopping over the contents of the steaming dishes as they ran. "Battle breakfast" was on its way to the men; and even as the last load departed Kelly shut off all power into the galley and shrugged his squat form into a heavy coverall. Marconi snatched two empty trays, filled them, and the two men wolfed their meal quickly and then ran at full tilt down toward the combat detachment's briefing-room.

Here the scene was even more chaotic. Men helped one another hastily into coveralls, rubber-and-steel suits, metallic boots. They twisted each other's transparent helmets into place, buckled on oxygen tanks, kits of emergency rations, first aid equipment, and great nightmarish-looking weapons. Richards and Sheehan, their quarrel temporarily forgotten, wrestled with the latter's oxygen valve. Koch struggled mightily with the metal joints of his attack suit; Fontaine checked the readings of the dials on a long, tubular "heat ray" machine. Carson, fully outfitted, manipulated the ingenious device which brought a cigarette to his lips and lit it. He took a few puffs, pressed another lever to eject the butt, and wrenched his helmet into place with gloved hands. From now until the battle was over, the men would carry all their air on their backs, compressed in cylinders. Underneath the shouts and the rattling noises of the armor could be heard the screams of Private Worth from his cell next door. They were suddenly cut off; one of Lieutenant Carpenter's watchful corpsmen had silenced the boy.

And now there was nothing to do but wait. The combat detachment's confusion subsided; but a subdued clatter of shifting armor, helmets being adjusted, tightening of joints, the rattle of equipment, and tele-phoned conversation continued. The new bridge-watch checked their in-struments, then settled down to careful, strained waiting. Sanderson paced his rounds, hearing reports and issuing occasional orders. Culver stood by the intercom, told the crew all their superiors knew of the opposition as the information came in. Carpenter catfooted through the ship, followed at a discreet distance by four of his strong-arm men.

Ensign Clark was white with fear. He sat stiffly at his post like a prisoner in Death Row; the sweat rolled down his face and into his soft black beard. He tried to repeat the auto-suggestion formulae Carpenter had prescribed for him, but all that he could choke out was a series of earnest curses which a kinder age would have called prayers.

He jumped as if he had been shot at Culver's sudden announcement: "Attention all hands. Enemy digger believed to have sighted this ship. Prepare for action at close quarters." The voice paused, and then added: "Bridge to power: full speed ahead for the next half-hour, then bring the ship to a halt. We'll let the enemy carry the fight to us."

Clark automatically repeated "Full speed ahead," then cringed as the crewman slammed the lever over and the cruiser leaped forward with a shrill whine of its blades. "No!" he suddenly yelled, leaping out of his seat. "Not another inch—stop this ship!" He ran over to the speed lever, pushed at the crewman's hands. "I won't be killed, I won't, I *won't!*" The brawny crewman and the maddened officer wrestled desperately for a moment, then the crewman flung his superior on his back and stood over him, panting. "I'm sorry, sir."

Clark lay there whimpering for a few seconds, then made a quick grab inside his shirt and leveled a pistol at the towering crewman. "Get over there," he half-sobbed, "and stop this ship before I shoot you."

The white-uniformed psych corpsman flung open the door and fired, all in one motion. The crewman instinctively backed away as the little pellet exploded, shredding most of Clark's head into his cherished beard; the crewman stood over the body, making little wordless sounds.

"Go off watch," ordered Carpenter, coming into the room on the heels of his henchman. "Get a sedative from the medics." He gazed linger-ingly, almost appreciatively, on the disfigured face of the dead man be-fore covering it with the ensign's coat. Then he called Culver and told him briefly what had happened.

"I'll send a relief," promised the exec. "Tell him to reduce speed in another twenty minutes. That was quick thinking, Carpenter; the captain says you rate a citation." The psycho officer had failed to give the corpsman credit for firing the shot.

Sanderson caught Culver's eye, put a finger to his lips.

"Huh?" Culver paused, then got the idea. "Oh—and, say, Carpenter

—don't let the crew hear of this. It wouldn't do for them to know an officer was the first to crack." There was a very faint trace of sarcasm in his tone.

But Sanderson's warning was already too late. The power crewman who had witnessed Clark's death agonies talked before he was put to sleep; the medic who administered the sedative took it to the crew. By the time Carpenter had received the new order from Culver, his efficient corpsmen had disposed of Clark's body and the whole ship knew the story. It hit the combat detachment like a physical blow; their strained morale took a serious beating, and the officers grew alarmed.

"Pass the word to let them smoke," Sanderson finally ordered, after the great ship had shuddered to a halt and backed a short distance up the tunnel on his order. "Give them ten minutes—the enemy will take at least twice that to get here. Have Carpenter go down and administer drugs at his own discretion—maybe it will slow them for fighting, but if they crack they'll be of no use anyway."

And so for ten minutes the combat crewmen removed their helmets and relaxed, while the psychos moved unobtrusively throughout the room, asking questions here and there, occasionally giving drungs. Once they helped a man partially out of his armor for a hypo. Tension relaxed somewhat; the psych corpsmen could soothe as well as coerce.

Kelly and Marconi were engaged in a heated argument over the relative merits of synthetic and natural foods—a time-tested emotional release the two veterans used habitually. Koch was up to his ears in a more serious controversy—for Sheehan and Richards were practically at each other's throats again. Carson as usual said nothing, smoked continuously; even the level-headed Fontaine got up and paced the floor, his armor clanking as he walked. Three men had to be put to sleep. Then the ten-minute break was over and the strain grew even worse.

Carpenter spoke softly into the intercom. "Tell the commander that if battle is not joined in another hour I cannot prevent a mutiny. Culver, I *told* you not to leave that man on watch—if you had listened to me Ensign Clark need not have been liquidated."

Culver's lip curled; he opened his mouth to reply in his usual irritating manner—but at that moment the soundman flung the earphones off his head. The roar of shearing duralloy blades was audible several feet away as the phones bounced to the deck. "Enemy digger within one hundred feet and coming in fast!" the soundman shouted.

"Don't reverse engines!" Sanderson roared as Culver contacted the new power officer. "Turn on our drill, leaving the treads stationary—we'll call his bluff."

Culver issued the necessary order, then alerted the crew again. The great blades began to whirl once more; there was a brief shower of rocks, and they churned emptiness—their usual throbbing, tearing chant became a hair-raising shriek; the blast of air they raised kicked up a cloud of dust which blanketed the fresh-carved tunnel—"That's for their optical technician," explained Sanderson. "He'll be blind when he comes out—and we've a sharp gunnery officer down in fire control that will catch them by surprise."

The soundman gingerly picked up the headphones; the roar of the enemy's drill had dropped to a whisper—Sanderson's curious tactics evidently had him guessing, for he had slowed down.

The sound of the approaching drill was now audible without the benefit of electronic gear, as a muffled noise like the chewing of a great rat. Then came the chattering breakthrough, and Sanderson knew he had contacted the enemy, despite the dust clouds which baffled even the infra-red visual equipment.

Temporarily blind, confused by the whirling blades of their motionless opponent, the enemy hesitated for the precious seconds that meant the difference between victory and destruction.

As the enemy warhead broke through, the cruiser's whirling blades suddenly came to a quivering halt. Simultaneously the forward batteries opened fire.

Gone were the days of laboring, sweating gun-crews and ammunition loaders. All the stubby barrels were controlled from a small, semicircular control panel like an organ console. Lieutenant Atkins, a cool, competent, graying officer who had once been an instructor at the military academy, calmly pressed buttons and pulled levers and interestedly watched the results by means of various types of mechanical "eyes." And so it was that, when the sweep second-hand of his chronometer crossed the red line, Atkins' sensitive fingers danced over the keys and the ship rocked to the salvos of half its guns.

Magnified and echoed in the narrow tunnel, the crash of the barrage rolled and reverberated and shouted in an uninterrupted tornado of pure noise, roar upon roar—the light of the explosions was by contrast insignificant, a vicious reddish flare quickly snuffed in the dust. The ship jerked with each salvo; faint flashes and Olympian thunders tossed the great cruiser like a raft on the wild Atlantic. The fury of sound beat through the thick armor plate, poured and pounded savagely past the vaunted "soundproof" insulation. The decks lurched and reeled underfoot; instruments and equipment trembled with bone-shaking vibrations. Crash upon thunderous crash filled the air with new strains of this artillery symphony; and then Culver pressed a button. His voice could not be heard through the racket, but the sudden glow of a red light in the combat detachment's assembly room transmitted his order instantly— "Away landing party!"

* * *

And then the trap between the great, flat treads was sprung, and the mechanical monster spawned progeny, visible only by infra-red light in the underground gloom—the little doll-like figures in bulky, nightmarish costumes, dropping from a chain ladder to the broken shale underfoot, running and stumbling through the debris, falling and picking themselves up and falling again like so many children—Marconi and Kelly and Carson and Sheehan and Richards and Fontaine and Koch, tripping over the debris and fragments which the great machine had made.

And at last the enemy cruiser replied, even as the landing party picked its way through the obscuring dust and fanned out from its source. Though confused and blind, the men of the other ship, too, had been prepared for action, and thus new sounds were added to the din that were not of the attackers' making.

A titanic explosion rocked the carriage of Sanderson's cruiser; then another, and still another, strewing steel fragments indiscriminately among the men in the tunnel. The ferocity of the defense was less than the attack; much of their armament must have been destroyed on the first salvo—but what remained wrought havoc. Some quick-witted commander of the enemy must have anticipated the landing of a ground party, for fragmentation shells burst near the embattled cruisers, and here and there the armored figures began to twist and jerk and go down. Their comrades dropped into the partial protection of the broken rock and continued their advance.

Fontaine ran and crawled and scrambled and crouched over the tunnel floor, which was visible to his infra-red-sensitive helmet, and torn now even more by arrowing slivers of steel. His hand found a valve, twisted it to give him more oxygen for this most critical part of the struggle. He did not think much; he was too busy keeping alive. But a bitter thought flashed across his mind—*This part of war hasn't changed a bit*. He leaped over a strange and terrible object in which armor, blood, rock and flesh made a fantastic jigsaw puzzle which had lost its meaning. Once again he merely noted the item in his subconscious mind; he did not think.

Lieutenant Atkins' fingers still danced over the console; his face was exalted like that of a man playing a concerto. And into the symphony of death which he wove with subtle skill there crept fewer and fewer of the discords of the enemy's guns.

Sanderson paced the deck moodily, communicating briefly with his subordinates by means of lip reading which Culver swiftly translated into many-colored lights. Information came back to the bridge in the same manner. Sanderson smiled with grim satisfaction at the scarcity of dark lamps on the master damage control board. Those mighty walls could take a lot of punishment, and damage so far had been superficial

—one blast in the psycho ward; Private Worth would suffer Carpenter's displeasure no longer.

The helmeted monstrosities grew bolder in their advance as the counter-barrage slackened. Now there was but one battery in action, far to the left—all the thunder came from their own ship.

Fontaine rose from the little depression in which he had been crouching. Another man waved to him; from that outsized suit it would have to be Koch. The big man's armor was dented, the rubber portions torn—his steel right boot looked like a large, wrinkled sheet of tinfoil, and he dragged the leg behind him. But he saw Fontaine, pointed a gauntleted finger into the gloom. The enemy ship must be up there; yes, there was the flash of the one operating gun—Fontaine moved forward.

There was another, nearer flash; something exploded on Koch's chestplate, knocking him down. He moved, feebly, like a crushed insect, then lay still. Fontaine immediately slipped back into his hollow; for here was the enemy.

A man in a light, jointed metal suit of Asian make appeared from behind a boulder, slipped over to Koch's body to examine it, felt for Koch's weapons.

Fontaine unslung the long, bazooka-like heat-ray tube—an adaptation of very slow atomic disintegration—and pressed the firing stud. The weapon contributed no noise and no flare to the hellish inferno of the tunnel, but the Asiatic suddenly straightened up, took a step forward. That was all he had time for.

Accident and his jointed armor combined to keep his body standing. Fontaine made sure of his man by holding the heat ray on him until the enemy's armor glowed cherry-red, then released the stud. He came forward, gave the still-glowing figure a push. The body collapsed with a clatter across Koch. Fontaine pushed on—the dust was at last clearing slightly, and directly ahead loomed the enemy ship.

Another Asiatic appeared over a short ridge; too quick for the heat ray. Fontaine drew his pistol and fired. The pellet flared; another enemy went down.

Something whizzed over Fontaine's head; he ducked, ran for cover. Somebody was firing high-speed metallic slugs from an old-fashioned machine gun, and his partly rubber suit would not stop them. Miraculously he found himself unharmed in front of the enemy ship.

Its drill was torn and crumpled, blades lying cast off among the rocks; one of the treads was fouled, and the forward part of the carriage was smashed in completely. This war vehicle would obviously never fight again. Another volley of slugs chattered overhead, and Fontaine rolled back out of the way. *Snap judgment,* he told himself ironically in another rare flash of lucidity. *Maybe she'll never fight after this time, but she's got plenty of spirit right now.*

He dug a hole in the loose shale and tried to cover himself as much as possible, meanwhile surveying the layout. They couldn't know he was here, or his life would have been snuffed out; but he could neither advance nor retreat. He absently transmitted the prearranged "contact" signal back to the cruiser. Then he settled himself, soldier-wise, to wait as long as might be necessary.

Fontaine's "contact," and several others, returned to their ship as lights on a board. The landing party could proceed no further or they would encounter their own barrage. Sanderson immediately gave the "cease fire" order. The barrage lifted.

Culver shouted down an immediate flood of radio reports that broke the sudden, aching silence. "Lieutenant Atkins, you will continue action against the remaining enemy battery until you have destroyed it, or until I inform you that members of the task force have neutralized it."

"Aye, aye, sir." Atkins turned back to his guns, studied the image of the battered enemy ship which was becoming increasingly visible as the dust settled. He restored all the automatic controls to manual, pressed several buttons judiciously, and fingered a firing switch.

To Fontaine, crouching in his retreat under the enemy ship, the sudden silence which followed the barrage was almost intolerable. One moment the guns had thundered and bellowed overhead; the next there were a few echoes and reverberations and then all was over.

His ears sang for minutes; his addled brains slowly returned to a normal state. And he realized that the silence was not absolute. It was punctually broken by the crash of the remaining enemy battery, and soon at less frequent intervals by the cautious probing of Atkins' turrets. And between the blows of this duel of giants he could at last hear the whine of metal slugs over his head.

This weapon had him stumped. The Asiatic explosive bullets, such as the one that had killed Koch, only operated at fairly close quarters; the rubber suits were fairly good insulation against death rays; and the Asiatics had no heat ray. But with an antiquated machine gun an Asiatic could sit comfortably at a considerable distance from him and send a volley of missiles crunching through the flimsy Western armor to rip him apart in helpless pain. He raised his head very slightly and looked around. The detachment was well trained; he could see only three of his fellows and they were well concealed from the enemy. Under infra-red light—the only possible means of vision in the gloom of the tunnel—they looked like weird red ghosts.

Something gleamed ahead of him. He sighted along the heat ray, energized its coils. The mechanism hummed softly; the Asiatic jumped out of his hiding place and right into the machine gun's line of fire. The singing bits of metal punched a neat line of holes across his armor and knocked him down, twisting as he fell. Moments later the chattering stream stopped flowing, and Fontaine dashed for more adequate cover. Bullets promptly kicked up dust in little spurts in the hollow he had just vacated.

He searched the darkness, a weird, shimmering ghostland revealed to him by its own tremendous heat through his infra-red equipment. The ship and his armor were very well insulated; he had not been conscious of the stifling heat or the absolute night-gloom which would have made combat impossible for an unprepared, unprotected soldier of the Surface Wars.

Atkins' insistent batteries spoke; there was a great flash and a series of explosions at the enemy target to the left. Fontaine seized the opportunity to make a charge on the loosely piled boulders which, his practiced eye told him, sheltered the deadly machine gun. He fell and rolled out of the line of fire as the opposing gunner found him and swerved his weapon; then began to fire explosive pellets at the crude nest, showering it with a series of sharp reports. The enemy machine gun swung back and forth, raking the terrain in search of the invader.

Fontaine unloaded his heat ray, placed it in a well-sheltered crevice and worked it around until it was aimed at the enemy, then shorted the coils. The weapon throbbed with power; rocks began to glow, and the flying slugs poured down upon the menacing heat ray, trying to silence it. Meanwhile Fontaine, like uncounted warriors of all ages, began cautiously to work his way around to the left for a flank attack. Indeed, there were many things in war that had not changed.

"Fire control to bridge: enemy battery silenced," Atkins reported firmly.

"Secure fire control," Culver ordered, then turned on his heel. "The enemy's ordnance is destroyed, sir," he asserted. "Our combat crewmen are engaging the enemy in front of his ship."

"Send Mr. Atkins my congratulations," Sanderson replied promptly. "Then inform the combat detachment of the situation."

Culver turned back to the intercom—then started, as a siren wailed somewhere in the bowels of the ship. A station amidships was buzzing frantically; he plugged in the mike. "Bridge," he answered.

"Atomic-bomb watch to bridge: instruments show unprecedented activity of the bomb. Dangerous reaction predicted."

Culver fought to keep his voice down as he relayed the information. The bridge watch simply came to a dead stop; all eyes were on Sanderson.

Even the phlegmatic commander hesitated. Finally: "Prepare to abandon ship," he ordered, heavily.

At once the confusion which had accompanied the preparations of the combat detachment was repeated throughout the ship. Atomic bombs by this time were largely made of artificial isotopes and elements; the type which they carried had never been tested in combat—and radioactive elements can do strange and unpredictable things when stimulated. Mere concussion had started the trouble this time, and the mind of man was incapable of prophecying the results. The bomb might merely increase in the speed of its radioactive decay, flooding the ship and the bodies of its men with deadly gamma rays; it might release enormous heat and melt the cruiser into a bubbling pool of metal; it might blast both of the ships and mile on cubic mile of rocks out of existence—but all they could do was abandon the cruiser and hope for the best. All mankind was unable to do more.

Sanderson's forceful personality and Carpenter's prowling corpsmen prevented a panic. Men cursed as they struggled with obstinate clasps and joints. A few of Kelly's apprentices who had not gone into combat flung cases of concentrated food through the landing-trap to the tunnel floor. Culver packed the ship's records—logs, papers, muster sheets, inventories—into an insulated metal can for preservation. A picked force of atomic technicians in cumbersome lead suits vanished into the shielded bomb-chamber with the faint hope of suppressing the reaction.

Sanderson paused before sealing his helmet. "Mr. Culver, you will have all hands assemble in or near the landing-trap. We must advance, destroy the enemy and take refuge in his ship; it is our only hope."

Navigation buzzed; Culver made the necessary connection. "One moment, sir," he murmured to Sanderson. "Bridge."

The young exc could visualize old Lieutenant Watson's strained expression, his set jaw. "Navigation requests permission to remain aboard when ship is abandoned," Watson said slowly. "Chances of crew's survival would be materially increased if the ship reversed engines and departed this area—"

Sanderson was silent a long moment. "Permission granted," he finally answered in a low voice. He started to say more, caught Carpenter's eye and was silent.

But Culver could not maintain military formality in answering Watson's call. "Go ahead, Phil, and—thanks," he replied, almost in a whisper.

Carpenter stepped forward quickly. "This is no time for sentiment, Mr. Culver," he snapped. "Lieutenant Watson's behavior was a little naïve for an officer, but the important fact remains that his antiquated altruism may be the means of preserving the lives of more important personnel." He waved a sheaf of loose papers excitedly. "This report of mine, for example, on the psychiatric aspects of this battle will be invaluable to the Board—"

Crack!

All the wiry power of the young exc's rigidly trained body went into the punch; literally traveled through him from toe to fist and exploded on the psycho officer's jaw. Months of harsh discipline—psychological manhandling—the strain of combat—repressed emotions, never really unhampered since his childhood—the sense of the war's futility which had not been completely trained out of anyone—his poorly concealed hatred for Carpenter—all these subconscious impressions came boiling up and sped the blow—and his hand was incased in a metal glove.

Carpenter's head snapped back. His feet literally flew off the deck as his body described a long arc and slammed into the far wall. He sprawled there grotesquely like a discarded marionette. Miraculously his glasses were unbroken.

The iron reserve which Sanderson had kept throughout the battle left him with the disruption of his neat, disciplined little military cosmos. For a long time he was unable to speak or move.

Two tough-looking psych corpsmen closed in on the exec, who stood facing the fallen officer, his fists clenched. He twisted angrily as they grabbed his arms.

"Let him alone," Sanderson ordered, coming to his senses. They reluctantly released Culver.

"Mr. Culver," the skipper said very quietly, "I need you now. You will resume your duties until this crisis is over. But, if we come through this, I'm going to see that you're broken."

Culver faced him, anger draining out of him like the color from his flushed face. He saluted, turned back to the intercom to give out the last order Sanderson had issued. "Attention, all hands," he called mechanically. "Fall in at the landing-trap to abandon ship."

Sanderson beckoned to the two psych corpsmen. "Please take Lieutenant Carpenter to sick bay," he ordered. "Bring him around as soon as you can."

The Asiatic squatted crosslegged behind his shining pneumatic machine gun, frantically raking the rock-strewn ground before him. The air ahead shimmered and danced with heat; the other side of his crude stone shelter must be glowing whitely, and the sweat ran down his yellow face even though the tiny cooling motor within his armor hummed savagely as it labored to keep him from suffocating. He must destroy the offending heat ray or abandon his position.

A confused impression of rubber-and-metal armor was all he received as Fontaine rushed upon him from the side. The two men came together and went down with a loud clatter of armor, rolled over and over in quick, bitter struggle. Even in the Atomic Age there could be hand-to-hand combat.

It was an exhausting fight; the battle suits were heavy and awkward. They wrestled clumsily, the clank of their armor lending an incongruously comic note. The lithe Asiatic broke a hold, cleared his right hand. Fontaine rolled over to avoid the glittering knife his opponent had succeeded in drawing. Here beneath the crust a rip in his rubberized suit would spell disaster. The Asiatic jumped at him to follow up his advantage. Fontaine dropped back on his elbows, swung his feet around and kicked viciously.

The metal boot shattered the Asiatic's glass face-plate, nearly broke his neck from its impact. Shaken by the cruel blow to his face, blinded by blood drawn by the jagged glass, gasping from the foul air and the oppressive heat, he desperately broke away and ran staggering toward the right, misjudging the direction of his ship.

Fontaine estimated the number of explosive bullets he had left, then let his enemy go, knowing there would be no more danger from that quarter. He lay unmoving beside the abandoned machine gun, breathing heavily. His near-miraculous survival thus far deserved a few minutes' rest.

The enemy's landing-trap, like the Western one, was under the ship's carriage; instead of a chain ladder, a ramp had been let down. A terrific mêlée now raged around the ramp—Fontaine and his opponent had been so intent on their duel they had not seen the tide of battle wash past them. Here and there lay dead men of both sides; his recent enemy had soon been overcome and lay not a score of feet away, moving spasmodically. Battle-hardened as he was, Fontaine seriously debated putting the fellow out of his misery—death from armor failure was the worst kind in this war except radioactive poisoning—then carefully counted his explosive pellets again. Only six—he might need them. He dismissed the writhing Asiatic from his mind.

He looked up at the smashed hull of the enemy ship, and an idea came to him. They wouldn't be watching here, with their ship in danger of being boarded elsewhere.

He rose, moved quietly to the great right-hand tread. The flat links here were torn and disconnected; he seized a loose projection and hauled himself upward. Slipping and scrambling, using gauntleted hands and booted feet, he reached the top of the tread.

Directly above him was a jagged hole in the ship's carriage, about four feet long. He seized the edges and somehow managed to wriggle his way inside.

The interior was a shambles of smashed compartments, with men and metal uncleanly mated. Fontaine laboriously pushed his way forward, climbing over and around barriers flung up at the caprice of Atkins' guns. Once he was forced to expend one of the precious pellets; the recoil nearly flattened him at such close quarters, but he picked himself up and climbed through the still-smoking hole into a passageway which was buckled somewhat but still intact.

He looked carefully in both directions, then saw a ladder and began to ascend. It brought him into a small storage compartment which was still illuminated. He grunted in satisfaction; if he had reached the still-powered portion of the ship, he was going in the right direction.

He eased the door open three inches; air hissed—this compartment must be sealed off. He quickly passed through, closed the door, and cautiously tested the air—good; this part of the ship still had pure air and insulation. Confidently he continued forward and climbed another ladder toward the bridge.

He had to wait at one level until a sentry turned his back. Then he sprang, and his steel fingers sank into the Asiatic's throat. There was no outcry.

Faintly from below there came the sounds of a struggle; his comrades had successfully invaded the ship. Curiously, Fontaine tried his helmet radio. It had been put out of commission in his fight with the machine gunner outside.

There were no more sentries; that was odd. He proceeded with extreme caution as he came to the ladder leading up to the bridge. Here would be the brains of the Asiatic ship; his five remaining pellets could end the engagement now that the battle was raging on enemy territory.

He stumbled over something—a man's foot. He dragged the body out of the shadows which had concealed it.

"What the devil—"

The man had been another guard. His chest was shattered; an explosive pistol was clutched in his right hand. One pellet was missing from the chamber.

Wonderingly Fontaine climbed the ladder, halted at the door.

Lying at his feet was another sentry. The man's body was unmarked but his face bore signs of a painful death. A small supersonic projector lay near him.

Fontaine opened the door—and turned away, sick.

Somebody had turned on a heat ray at close quarters. Officers and enlisted men lay in charred horror. And in the center of the room the ship's commanding officer slumped on a bloodstained silken cushion. The man had committed honorable suicide with a replica of an ancient Japanese samurai sword.

In his left hand was a crumpled sheet of yellow paper, evidently a radiogram.

Fontaine took the scrap from the lax yellow fingers, puzzled over the Oriental characters.

Then he went outside, and closed the door, and sat down at the head of the ladder to await the coming of men who might be able to solve the mystery.

The last man scrambled down the swaying chains and dropped to the ground from the Western cruiser.

Lieutenants Watson and Atkins were alone in the ship.

"Why did you stay?" demanded Watson, throwing the starting switch. He had hastily rigged an extension from the power room to navigation. "Only one man is needed to operate the ship, in an emergency."

Lieutenant Atkins found a fine cigar in his uniform. "I've been saving this," he remarked, stripping off the cellophane wrapper lovingly. "The condemned man indulges in the traditional liberties."

"Answer my question," Watson insisted, advancing the speed lever.

Atkins pressed a glowing heating-coil "lighter" to the tip of the cigar. "Let me ask you this—why did *you* make this heroic gesture?"

Watson flushed. "You might as well ask—why fight at all?"

"You might," Atkins said, smiling slightly.

"I did this because our men come first!" Watson shouted almost in fury.

Atkins chuckled. "Forgive me, old friend—I find it hard to shake off the illusions I had back in the Last Surface War myself." He blew a huge cloud of smoke. "But, when Culver sent down the commander's congratulations to me for silencing that enemy battery, it struck me how empty all our battles and decorations are."

Watson shoved the speed lever to maximum; the cruiser rolled backward down the tunnel at a terrific velocity, no longer impeded by masses of rock. After a long silence he asked: "Atkins—what were *you* fighting for?"

Atkins looked him squarely in the eye. "Well, I managed to hypnotize myself into a superficial love of massed artillery—it's a perversion of my love for the symphony—used to conduct a small orchestra at the academy before it was dissolved and the funds allocated to a military band. I liked that orchestra; felt I was doing something constructive for once." He was silent for a while, smoking and reminiscing. Coming back to reality with a start, he went on hastily: "Of course, underneath it all I guess I was motivated just the way you were—to maintain the dead traditions of the service, to save our shipmates who would have died anyway, and to advance a cause which no longer exists."

Watson buried his head in his hands. "I fought because I thought it was the right thing to do."

Atkins softened. "So did I, my friend," he admitted. "But it's all over now—"

He paused to flick ashes from the cigar. "I saved something else for this," he went on irrelevantly. "Carpenter is gone now, Watson, so we can dispense with his psychopathic mummery. What a joke if he should ever know I had this aboard." He laughed lightly, producing a small, gold-stamped book bound in black leather. "This sort of thing is the only value left, for us," he asserted. "Let us pray."

And thus, a few minutes later, the two elderly officers died. It was not a great blast, as atomic explosions go, but ship and men and rock puffed and sparkled in bright, cleansing flame.

The bridge of the captured enemy ship looked fresh and clean. The remains of the Asiatic commander's gruesome self-destruction had been cleared away; blackened places about the room glistened with new paint. It was several hours after the battle.

Sanderson stood at attention reading a report to his surviving officers. Sergeant Fontaine, permitted to attend as the first witness to the baffling slaughter, fidgeted in the presence of so much gold braid. Private Carson, the strange child of the laboratory, present to assist Fontaine in guarding the disgraced executive officer, stood stolidly, a detached expression on his face.

"—and therefore the atomic explosion, when it did come, was hardly noticed here," the commander concluded his report. "Lieutenant Watson did his duty"—he glared covertly at Culver, manacled between Fontaine and Carson—"and if we can return safely to our Advance Base this will go down as one of the greatest exploits in the history of warfare."

He cleared his throat. "At ease," he said offhandedly, straightening his papers. The officers and crewmen relaxed, shifted position, as Sanderson went on more informally: "Before we discuss any future action, however, there is this business of the Asiatic warlords—their inexplicable suicide. Lieutenant Carpenter?"

The psycho officer stepped forward, caressing his bandaged jaw. "I have questioned the ten prisoners we took," he announced as clearly as he could through the bandages, "and my men have applied all of the standard means of coercion. I am firmly convinced that the Asiatic prisoners are as ignorant as we are of the reason for their masters' strange behavior."

Sanderson motioned him back impatiently. "Ensign Becker?"

The personnel officer rustled some sheets of paper. "I have checked the records carefully, sir," he asserted, "and Lieutenant-Commander Culver is the only man aboard this ship who understands written Asiatic."

Sanderson's gaze swept over all his officers. "Gentlemen, the executive officer was guilty of striking the psycho officer shortly before we abandoned ship—I witnessed the action. I want to know if you will accept as valid his translation of the radiogram which Sergeant Fontaine found on the body of the enemy leader."

"I object!" shouted Carpenter immediately. "Culver violated one of the *basic* principles of the officers' corps—he can't be completely *sane.*"

"True, perhaps," admitted Sanderson testily, "but, lieutenant, would you care to suggest a plan of action—*before* we discover why our late enemies killed themselves so conveniently?"

"Commander, are you trying to vindicate this man?" Carpenter demanded indignantly.

Sanderson looked at the psycho officer with an expression almost contemptuous. "You should know by this time, lieutenant, that I have never liked Mr. Culver," he snorted. "Unfortunately this could be a question of our own survival. If the officers present accept Culver's translation of the message, I shall act on it."

"But we came here to begin courtmartial proceedings—"

"That can wait," the skipper interrupted impatiently. "This is my command, Carpenter, and I wish you'd remember that. Well, gentlemen? A show of hands, please—" He paused to count. "Very well," he decided shortly. "Sergeant Fontaine, give the message to the prisoner."

Fontaine threw a snappy salute and handed the yellow scrap of paper silently to the exec. Carson loosened his grip somewhat; Culver began to work out the translation—

FROM Supreme Headquarters in Mongolia.
TO All field commanders.
SUBJECT Secret weapon X-39, failure of.

1. Research project X-39, a semi-living chemical process attacking all forms of protoplasm, was released on the South American front according to plan last night.
2. Secret weapon X-39 was found to be uncontrollable and is spreading throughout our own armies all over the world. In addition, infection centering on the secret research laboratories has covered at least one-third of Asia.
3. You are directed to—

"Well?" demanded Sanderson.

"That's all, sir," Culver replied quietly.

The room immediately exploded into conversation, all pretense at military discipline forgotten. The commander shouted for order. He stood even straighter than his normally stiff military bearing allowed; he was the picture of triumph and confidence.

"This interrupted message can be interpreted in only one way," he declared ringingly. "Ensign Becker, you will inform all hands that the enemy's suicide is worldwide and that *the war is over!*"

For a long, long moment there was dead silence. The last peace rumor had died when most of these men were children. It took much time for the realization to sink in that the senseless murder was over at last.

Then—cheering, laughing, slapping one another's backs, the officers gave way to their emotions. Many became hysterical; a few still stood dumbly, failing to comprehend what "peace" was.

Battle-hardened, stiffly militaristic Sanderson's face was wet with tears.

And then Lieutenant Carpenter screamed.

All eyes were riveted on the psycho officer, a hideous suspicion growing in their minds as he cringed in a corner and yelled meaninglessly, his whole body shaking with unutterable terror. They had all seen men afraid of death—but in Carpenter's mad eyes was reflected the essence of all the hells conceived in the ancient religions—he slavered, he whimpered, and suddenly his body began to *ripple.*

His fellow officers stood rooted to the deck in sheer fright as he *slid* rather than fell to a huddled heap that continued to sink down after he had fallen, spreading and flowing and finally *running like water.*

Sanderson stared in stunned horror at a pool of sticky yellow fluid that dripped through a bronze grating in the floor.

Culver grinned foolishly. "Yes, commander," he said airily, "you were right—the war is over."

Sanderson gingerly picked Carpenter's notebook out of the sodden pile of clothing and bandages and the broken glass of the psycho officer's spectacles. "Read the radiogram again," he ordered hoarsely, signaling the two crewmen to release their prisoner.

The exec rubbed his wrists to restore circulation as the handcuffs were removed. Then he picked up the crumpled paper, smoothed it out.

"Research Project X-39, a semi-living chemical process attacking all forms of protoplasm, was released—" Culver choked over the words. "Sir, I—"

And then, in a few terrible minutes of screams and curses and hideous dissolution, all the officers understood why the Asiatics had committed suicide.

Sergeant Fontaine for some reason kept his head. He fired four shots rapidly from his pistol; one missed Carson, the others found their mark in Sanderson, Culver, and Becker, who looked oddly grateful as their bodies jerked under the impact and they slumped in unholy disintegration.

Sanderson saluted solemnly with a dissolving arm.

Fontaine had one more pellet in his gun. He hesitated, looked inquiringly for a moment at the inscrutable Carson, then as he felt a subtle *loosening* under his skin he turned the weapon on himself and fired.

Private Carson puffed nervously at a cigarette, staring in shocked, horrible fascination at the weird carnage—then ran blindly, fleeing from he knew not what.

The terror flew on wings of light through the ruined enemy ship. Technicians, bridge watches, the ten enemy prisoners, psych corpsmen, navigators, combat crewmen—even the dead Oriental commanders joined the dissolving tide. Richards and Sheehan were the last to go; they hysterically accused each other of causing the horror, trying desperately to find some tangible cause for the Doom—they fought like great beasts, and fat Koch was not there to stop the fight—they struggled, and coalesced suddenly into one rippling yellow pool.

Carson, still incased in his armor, raced and clattered through the deserted ship—the sound of his passing was almost sacrilegious, like the desecration of a tomb. Everywhere silence, smashed walls, empty suits of armor, little bundles of wet clothing, and curious yellow stains. *Die, why can't you die?*

Carson, the strange one—separated by more than aloofness from his fellows—spawned in a laboratory, the culmination of thousands of experiments in the vain hope of circumventing the extremity of the slaughter by manufacturing men. His metabolism was subtly different from that of normal man; he *needed* nicotine in his system for some reason—that was why he chain-smoked—but tobacco was a narcotic; it could not protect protoplasm. *Why can't you die, Carson?* All through the ship, silence, wet clothing, little pools—not even the dead had escaped—nothing moved or lived except this running, half-mad man—or Thing—born in a laboratory, if one could say he *had* been "born."

A quick movement of his gloved hands sealed the round helmet on his shoulders. He ran and stumbled and climbed through passageways and down ladders; he fairly flew down the landing-ramp and soon disappeared in the black depths of the tunnel.

And the nighted cavern so recently hacked from the outraged crust was given back to the darkness and the silence it had always known.

Fred Saberhagen

WHAT DO YOU WANT ME TO DO TO PROVE IM HUMAN STOP

When the dreadnought *Hamilcar Barca* came out of the inhuman world of plus-space into the blue-white glare of Meitner's sun the forty men and women of the dreadnought's crew were taut at their battle stations, not knowing whether or not the whole berserker fleet would be around them as they emerged. But then they were in normal space, seconds of time were ticking calmly by, and there were only the stars and galaxies to be seen, no implacable, inanimate killers coming to the attack. The tautness eased a little.

Captain Liao, strapped firmly into his combat chair in the center of the dreadnought's bridge, had brought his ship back into normal space as close to Meitner's sun as he dared—operating on interstellar, faster-than-light, c-plus drive in a gravitational field this strong was dangerous, to put it mildly—but the orbit of the one planet in the system worth being concerned about was still tens of millions of kilometers closer to the central sun. It was known simply as Meitner's planet, and was the one rock in the system habitable in terms of gravity and temperature.

Before his ship had been ten standard seconds in normal space, Liao had begun to focus a remotely controlled telescope to bring the planet into close view on a screen that hung before him on the bridge. Luck had brought him to the same side of the sun that the planet happened to be on; it showed under magnification on the screen as a thin illuminated crescent, covered with fluffy-looking perpetual clouds. Somewhere beneath those clouds a colony of about ten thousand people dwelt, for the most part under the shelter of one huge ceramic dome. The colonists had begun work on the titanic project of converting the plant's ammonia atmosphere to a breathable one of nitrogen and oxygen. Meanwhile they held the planet as an outpost of some importance for the interstellar community of all Earth-descended men.

There were no flares of battle visible in space around the planet, but still Liao lost no time in transmitting a message on the standard radio and laser communications frequencies. "Meitner's planet, calling Meitner's. This is the dreadnought *Hamilcar Barca*. Are you under attack? Do you need immediate assistance?"

There came no immediate answer, nor could one be expected for several minutes, the time required for signals traveling at the speed of light to reach the planet, and for an answer to be returned.

Into Liao's earphones now came the voice of his Detection and Ranging officer. "Captain, we have three ships in view." On the bridge there now sprang to life a three-dimensional holographic presentation, showing Liao the situation as accurately as the dreadnought's far-ranging detection systems and elaborate combat computers could diagram it.

One ship, appearing as a small bright dot with attached numerical coordinates, was hanging relatively motionless in space, nearly on a line between *Hamilcar Barca* and Meitner's planet. The symbol chosen for it indicated that this was probably a sizable craft, though not nearly as massive as the dreadnought. The other two ships visible in the presentation were much smaller, according to the mass-detector readings on them. They were also both considerably closer to the planet, and moving toward it at velocities that would let them stand on it, if that was their intention, in less than a standard hour.

What these three ships were up to, and whether they were controlled by human beings or berserker machines, were not immediately apparent. After sizing up the situation for a few seconds, Liao ordered full speed toward the planet—full speed, of course, in the sense of that attainable while remaining in normal space and thus traveling much slower than light—and to each of the three ships in view he ordered the same message beamed: "Identify yourself, or be destroyed."

The threat was no bluff. One took no chances where berserker machines were concerned. They were an armada of robot spaceships and supporting devices built by some unknown and long-vanished race to fight in some interstellar war that had reached its forgotten conclusion while men on Earth were wielding spears against the sabertooth tiger. Though the war for which the berserker machines had been made was long since over, still they fought on across the galaxy, replicating and repairing themselves endlessly, learning new strategies and tactics, refining their weapons to cope with their chief new enemy, Earth-descended man. The sole known basic in their fundamental programming was the destruction of all life, wherever and whenever they could find it.

Waiting for replies from the planet and the three ships, Liao studied his instruments, and hoped fervently that the berserker fleet that was known to be on its way here had not already come and gone, leaving the helpless colony destroyed. "Drive, this is the captain. Can't you get a little more speed on?"

The answer came into his earphones. "No, sir, we're on the red line now. Another kilometer-per-second and we'll blow a power lamp, or worse. This is one heavy sun, and it's got some dirty space around it." The ship was running now on the same space-warping engines that carried it faster than light between the stars, but this deep within the huge gravitational well surrounding Meitner's sun the power that could be applied to them was severely restricted. The more so because here space was dirty, as the Drive officer had said, meaning the interplanetary matter to be encountered within this system was comparatively dense. It boiled down to the fact that Liao had no hope of overtaking the two small vessels that fled ahead of him toward the planet. They, as it were, skimmed over shoals of particles that the dreadnought must plow through, flirted with reefs of drive-wrecking gravitational potential that it must approach more cautiously, and rode more lightly the waves of the solar wind that streamed outward as always from a sun.

Now the minimum time in which the largest, nearest vessel might have replied to the dreadnought's challenge had elapsed. No reply had been received. Liao ordered the challenge repeated continuously.

The Communications officer was speaking. "Answer from the planet, Captain. It's coming in code. I mean the simple standard dot-dash code, sir, like emergency signals. There's a lot of noise around; maybe that's the only way they can get a signal through." Powerfully and crudely modulated dot-and-dash signals could carry intelligence through under conditions where more advanced forms of modulation were swamped by interference.

Already Communications had the decoded words flowing across a big screen on the bridge. DREADNOUGHT ARE WE EVER GLAD TO HEAR FROM YOU STOP ONE OF THE TWO LITTLE SHIPS CLOSING IN ON US MUST BE A BERSERKER STOP BETTER TRANSMIT TO US IN DOTDASH CODE STOP LOTS OF NOISE BECAUSE SUN IS FLARING WE COULDNT READ YOUR SIGNAL VERY WELL

The letter abruptly stopped flowing across the screen. The voice of the Communications officer said: "Big burst of noise, Captain; signals from the planet are going to be cut off entirely for a little while. This sun is a very active flare star . . . just a moment, sir. Now we're getting voice and video transmissions beamed to us from both small ships. But the signals from both ships are so garbled by noise we can't make anything out of them."

"Beam back to them in dot-dash; tell them they'll have to answer us that way. Repeat our warnings that they must identify themselves. And keep trying to find out what the ground wants to tell us." The captain turned his head to look over at his second officer in the adjoining combat chair. "What'd you think of that, Miller? 'One of the two little ships must be a berserker'?"

Miller, by nature a somewhat morose man, only shook his head gloomily, and saved his speech to make a factual report. "Sir, I've been working on identifying the two active ships. The one nearest the planet is so small it seems to be nothing but a lifeboat. Extrapolating backward from its present course indicates it may well have come from the third ship, the one that's drifting, a couple of hours ago.

"The second little ship is a true interstellar vessel; could be a one-man courier ship or even somebody's private yacht. Or a berserker, of course." The enemy came in all shapes and sizes.

Still no answer had been returned from the large, drifting ship, though the dreadnought was continuing to beam threatening messages to her, now in dot-dash code. Detection reported now that she was spinning slowly around her longest axis, consistent with the theory that she was some kind of derelict. Liao checked again on the state of communications with the planet, but they were still cut off by noise.

"But here's something, Captain. Dot-and-dash is coming in from the supposed courier. Standard code as before, coming at moderate manual speed."

Immediately more letters began to flow across the number one screen on the bridge: I AM METION CHONGJIN COMMANDING THE ONE MAN COURIER ETRURIA EIGHT DAYS OUT OF ESTEEL STOP CANNOT TURN ASIDE I AM CARRYING VITAL DEFENSE COMPONENT FOR COLONY STOP LIFEBOAT APPROX 12 MILLION KM TO MY PORT AND AHEAD IS SAID BY GROUND TO BE CLAIMING TO BE THE SHIP CARRYING THE DEFENSE COMPONENT THEREFORE IT MUST REALLY BE A BERSERKER STOP IT WILL PROBABLY REACH COLONY AND BOMB AND RAM IT BEFORE I GET THERE SO YOU MUST DESTROY IT REPEAT DESTROY THE BERSERKER QUOTE LIFEBOAT UNQUOTE MOST URGENT THAT YOU HIT IT SOON END MESSAGE.

Miller made a faint whistling noise. "Sounds fairly convincing, chief." During briefing back at base three standard days ago they had been informed of the fact that the colonists on Meitner's planet were awaiting shipment of a space inverter to complete and activate their defensive system of protective force-screens and beam-projecting weapons. Until the inverter could be brought from Esteel and installed the colony was virtually defenseless; the dreadnought had been dispatched to offer it some interim protection.

Liao was giving orders to Armament to lock the c-plus cannon of the main battery onto the lifeboat. "But fire only on my command." Turning back to Miller, he said: "Yes, fairly convincing. But the berserkers might have found out somehow that the space inverter was being rushed here. They might even have intercepted and taken over the courier carrying it. We can't see who we're talking to on that ship or hear his voice. It might have been a berserker machine that just tapped out that message to us."

The Communications officer was on again. "Bridge, we have the first coded reply from the lifeboat coming in now. Here it comes on your screen."

WE ARE HENRI SAKAI AND WINIFRED ISPAHAN CARRYING THE DEFENSE MATERIEL NAMELY SPACE INVERTER THEY NEED ON THE PLANET STOP OUR SHIP THE WILHELMINA FROM ESTEEL WAS SHOT UP BY THE BERSERKER TWO DAYS AGO WHEN IT ALMOST CAUGHT US STOP THE BERSERKER OR ANOTHER ONE IS HERE NOW ABOUT 11 MILLION KM TO OUR STARBOARD AND A LITTLE BEHIND US YOU MUST KEEP IT FROM GETTING TO US OR TO THE PLANET WHERE MAYBE IT COULD RAM THE DOME END MESSAGE.

"Communications," the captain snapped, "how is this coming through? I mean, does this also seem like someone sending manual code?"

"No, sir, this is very rapid and regular. But if you mean, Captain, does that prove they're not human, it doesn't. In a lifeboat the radio often has a voice-to-code converter built in."

"And conversely a berserker could send slowly and somewhat irregularly, like a man, if it wanted to. Thank you." The captain pondered in silence for a little while.

"Sir," Miller suggested, "maybe we'd better order both small ships to stop, until we can overtake and board them."

The captain turned his head to look at him steadily, but remained silent.

Miller, slightly flustered, took thought and then corrected himself. "Now I see the problem more fully, sir. You can't do that. If one of them is really carrying the space inverter you don't dare delay him for a minute. A berserker fleet may materialize in-system here at any moment, and is virtually certain to arrive within the next six to eight standard hours. Our ship alone won't be able to do more than hit and run when that happens. Our fleet can't get here for another day. The colony will never survive the interval without their space inverter installed."

"Right. Even if I sent a fast launch ahead to board and inspect those ships, the delay would be too much to risk. And now tell me this, Second—is this conceivably just some misunderstanding, and both of those ships are really manned by human beings?"

"Not a chance," the second officer answered promptly. "They both claim to be carrying the space inverter, and that can't be true. Those things just aren't ordered or built in duplicate or triplicate, and they both claim to be bringing it from the planet Esteel. . . . The next question is, can both of our little targets be berserkers? Trying to psych us into letting one of them get through? I'll keep trying to reach the ground, see if they can shed any more light on this."

"Good going."

In their earphones Communications said: "Here's more from the ship that calls itself *Etruria,* Bridge."

"Put it right on our screen."

REPEAT COLONY SAYS LIFEBOAT IS ALSO CLAIMING TO BE HUMAN ONE STOP THEY MUST BE A BERSERKER IMPERATIVE YOU STOP THEM WHAT DO YOU WANT ME TO DO TO PROVE IM HUMAN STOP REPEAT MY NAME IS ME-TION CHONGJIN IM ALONE ON BOARD HERE WIFE AND KIDS AT HOME ON ESTEEL IF THAT MEANS ANYTHING TO YOU STOP REPEAT HOW CAN I PROVE TO YOU IM HUMAN END MESSAGE.

"Easy," Captain Liao muttered to himself. "Father a human child. Compose a decent symphony. In the next forty minutes or so." That was approximately the time left before at least one of the ships would be able to reach the planet. Liao's mind was racing to formulate possible tests that could be applied in the present situation, but getting nowhere. Berserkers had awesome powers, not only as physical fighting machines, but as computers. He was not certain that a battery of psychologists with plenty of time to work in would be able to set up the kind of test he needed now.

Time passed. Hurtling through silence and near-emptiness at many kilometers per second, the ships very slowly changed the positions of their symbols in the huge holographic presentation on the bridge.

"Now more from the *Wilhelmina's* lifeboat, Captain."

"Run that on top of the screen, will you, and put any more that comes in from *Etruria* on the bottom."

HENRI AND WINIFRED HERE COLONY TELLS US OTHER SHIP IS CLAIMING TO BE FROM ESTEEL CARRYING DEFENSE COMPONENTS AND REQUESTING LAND-ING INSTRUCTIONS STOP IT MUST BE LYING IT MUST BE A BERSERKER MAYBE THE SAME ONE THAT ATTACKED OUR SHIP TWO DAYS AGO. . . .

The message ran on, and despite some irrelevancies and redundancies it soon outlined a story. The *Wilhelmina* (if the story was to be believed) had been on an interstellar cruise, carrying a number of young people on some kind of student exchange voyage or postgraduate trip. Somewhere on the outskirts of the solar system that contained the heavily industrial-ized planet Esteel, a courier ship bound out for Meitner's had ap-proached and hailed the *Wilhelmina,* had in fact commandeered her to complete the courier's mission. Berserkers were in pursuit of the courier and had already damaged her extensively.

. . . AND WE WERE ON OUR WAY HERE WITH THE INVERTER WHEN ONE OF THE BERSERKERS ALMOST CAUGHT UP AGAIN TWO STANDARD DAYS AGO STOP WILHELMINA WAS BADLY SHOT UP THEN CREW ALL KILLED WE ARE ONLY TWO LEFT ALIVE TWO HISTORY STUDENTS WE HAD TERRIBLE PROBLEMS ASTROGATING HERE BUT WE MADE IT STOP LIVING IN LIFEBOAT AND WORKING RIDDLED SHIP IN SPACESUITS YOU CANT STOP US NOW AFTER ALL WEVE BEEN THROUGH STOP YOU MUST DESTROY THE BERSERKER SHIP WE WILL REACH PLANET BEFORE IT DOES I THINK BUT IT WILL BE ABLE TO HIT THE DOME BEFORE THE SPACE INVERTER CAN BE INSTALLED STOP WE ARE GOING TO KEEP SENDING UNTIL YOU ARE CONVINCED WERE HUMAN. . . .

The message from the lifeboat went on, somewhat more repetitiously now. And at the same time on the bottom of the screen more words from the *Etruria* flowed in:

IVE TRIED TO CATCH THE BERSERKER LIFEBOAT AND SHOOT IT DOWN BUT I CANT ITS UP TO YOU TO STOP IT STOP WHAT DO YOU WANT ME TO DO TO PROVE IM HUMAN. . . .

The second officer sighed lightly to himself, wondering if, after all, he really wanted his own command.

"Communications, beam this out," the captain was ordering. "Tell them both to keep talking and give us their life histories. Birth, family, education, the works. Tell them both they'd better make it good if they want to live." On buttons on the arm of his chair he punched out an order for tea, and a moment later tea came to him there through a little door, hot in a capped cup with drinking tube attached. "I've got an idea, Second. You study the background this so-called Esteeler spaceman Metion Chongjin gives us. Think up someplace you might have known him. We'll introduce you to him as an old friend, see how he copes."

"Good idea, chief."

"Communications here again, Bridge. We've finally gotten another clear answer back from the ground. It's coming through now, we'll put it in the middle of your number one screen."

. . . IN ANSWER TO YOUR QUESTION NO THEY CANT BOTH BE BERSERKERS STOP AN HOUR AGO THERE WAS A BRIEF LETUP IN THE NOISE AND WE GOT ONE CLEAR LOOK AT A HUMAN MALE FACE ALIVE AND TALKING COGENTLY ANSWERING OUR QUESTIONS NO POSSIBILITY THAT WAS A BERSERKER BUT UNFORTUNATELY BOTH SUSPECT SHIPS WERE SENDING ON THE SAME FREQ AND WE DONT KNOW FROM WHICH ONE THAT VOICE AND PICTURE CAME BUT WE DO KNOW ONE OF THEM IS HUMAN. . . .

"Damnation, how they've botched things up. Why didn't they ask the two men to describe themselves, and see which description fit what they saw?"

"This is Communications again, Bridge. They may have tried asking that, sir, for all we know. We've lost contact with the ground again now, even on code. I guess the solar wind is heating up. Conditions in the ionosphere down there must be pretty fierce. Anyway, here's a little more from the *Etruria*."

WHAT DO YOU WANT ME TO DO TO PROVE IM HUMAN RECITE POETRY MARY HAD A LITTLE LAMB STOP SAY PRAYERS I NEVER MEMORIZED ANY OF THEM STOP OK I GIVE UP SHOOT US BOTH DOWN THEN END MESSAGE.

The second officer thumped a fist on the arm of his massive combat chair. "A berserker would say that, knowing that its fleet was coming, and the colony would be defenseless if we stopped the space inverter from getting to it."

Liao shrugged, and helped himself to a massive slug of tea. "But a human might say that too, being willing to die to give a colony a few more hours of life. A human might hope that given a few more hours some miracle might come along, like the human fleet getting here first after all. I'm afraid that statement didn't prove a thing."

"I . . . guess it didn't."

After another good slug of tea, Liao put in a call to Astrogation.

"Chief Astrogator here, sir."

"Barbara, have you been listening in on this? Good. Tell me, could those two supposed history students, probably knowing little science or technology, have brought that ship in here? Specifically, could they have astrogated for two days, maybe fifty or sixty light-years, without getting lost? I suppose the ship's autopilot was knocked out. They said they were living in the lifeboat and working the damaged ship in spacesuits."

"Captain, I've been pondering that claim too, and I just don't know. I can't say definitely that it would be impossible. If we knew just how badly that ship was damaged, what they had to work with, we could make a better guess."

The captain looked back at his situation hologram. The apparently inert hulk that he had been told was the *Wilhelmina* was considerably closer now, lying as it did almost in *Hamilcar Barca*'s path toward Meitner's planet. The dreadnought was going to pass fairly near the other ship within the next few minutes. "As to that, maybe we can find out something. Keep listening in, Barbara." Turning to the second officer, Liao ordered: "You're going to be taking over the bridge shortly, Miller. I want us to match velocities with that supposed hulk ahead, and then I'm going over to her, in hopes of learning something."

"It might be booby-trapped, Captain."

"Then we'll have an answer, won't we? But I don't suppose an answer will be found that easily. Also get me a reading on exactly how much time we have left to decide which ship we're going to fire on."

"I've already had the computers going on that, sir. As of now, thirty-two and a quarter minutes. Then the lifeboat will either be down in atmosphere or around on the other side of the planet, and out of effective range in either case. The courier will take a little longer to get out of effective range, but. . . ." He gestured helplessly.

"Yes, the courier being slower won't help us. We have to decide in thirty-two minutes."

"Chief, I just had an idea. If the lifeboat was the berserker, since it's closer to the planet, wouldn't it have tried before we got here to head off the courier from the planet . . . oh. No good. No offensive weapons on the lifeboat."

"Right, except perhaps it has one bloody big bomb, meant for the colony. While the courier ship doubtless has some light armament, enough to deal with the lifeboat if it got in range. Still nothing proved, either way."

In another minute the silent ship ahead was close enough for telescopes on the dreadnought to pick out her name by starlight. It was *Wilhelmina,* all right, emblazoned near one end of her cigarlike shape. The dreadnought matched velocities with her smoothly, and held position a couple of kilometers off. Just before getting into a launch with a squad of marines to go over and inspect her, Liao checked back with the bridge to see if anything was new.

"Better hear this before you go," Miller told him. "I just introduced myself to Chongjin as an old buddy. This is his reply, quote: 'I honestly don't remember your name if I ever knew it, stop. If this was a test I guess I passed hurrah now get on with it and stop that berserker on the lifeboat. . . .' and then the signal faded out again. Chief, our communication problems are getting steadily worse. If we're going to say anything more to either of those ships we'd better send it soon."

"How many minutes left, Second?"

"Just eighteen, sir."

"Don't waste any of 'em. The ship is yours."

"I relieve you, sir."

No signs of either life or berserker activity were apparent on the *Wilhelmina* as the launch crossed the space separating her from the dreadnought and docked, with a gentle clang of magnetic grapples. Now Liao could see that the reported damage was certainly a fact. Holes several meters in diameter had been torn in *Wilhelmina's* outer hull. Conditions inside could hardly be good.

Leaving one man with the launch, Liao led the rest of his small party in through one of the blasted holes, swimming weightlessly, propelling themselves by whatever they could grip. He had briefed the men to look for something, anything, that would prove or disprove the contention that humans had driven this ship during the two days since she had been damaged.

Fifteen and a half minutes left.

The damage inside was quite extensive as the condition of the hull had indicated. Their suit lights augmenting the sharp beams that Meitner's distant sun threw into the airless interior, the boarding party spread out, keeping in touch with their suit radios. This had undoubtedly been a passenger ship. Much of the interior was meant as living quarters, divided into single and double cabins, with accommodations for a couple of dozen people. What furnishings remained suggested luxury. So far, everything said by the lifeboat's occupant was being proved true, but Liao had as yet no clear evidence regarding that occupant's humanity. He could only hope the evidence was here, and that he would recognize it at first sight.

The interior of the ship was totally airless now, having been effectively opened to the stars by the repeated use of some kind of penetration weapon. The ruin was much cleaner than any similarly damaged structure on a planet's surface could be, loose debris having been carried out of the ship with escaping air, or separated from her when her drive took her outside of normal space and time, between the stars.

"Look here, Captain." The lieutenant in charge of the marine squad was beckoning to him.

Near the center of the slender ship the lieutenant had found a place where a wound bigger than any of the others had pierced in, creating in effect an enormous skylight over what had been one of the largest compartments on board. Probably it had been a lounge or refectory for the passengers and crew. Since the ship was damaged this ruined room had evidently provided the most convenient observation platform for whoever or whatever had been in control: a small, wide-angle telescope, and a tubular electronic spectroscope, battery-powered and made for use in vacuum, had been roughly but effectively clamped to the jagged upper edge of what had been one of the lounge's interior walls and now formed a parapet against infinity.

The lieutenant was swiveling the instruments on their mountings. "Captain, these look like emergency equipment from a lifeboat. Would a berserker machine have needed to use these, or would it have gear of its own?"

The captain stood beside him. "When a berserker puts a prize crew on a ship, it uses man-sized, almost android machines for the job. It's just more convenient for the machines that way, I suppose, more efficient. So they could quite easily use instruments designed for humans." He swung his legs to put his magnetic boots against the lounge's soft floor, so that they held him lightly to the steel deck beneath, and stared at the instruments, trying to force more meaning from them.

Men kept on searching the ship, probing everywhere, coming and going to report results (rather the lack of them) to Liao at his impromptu command post in what had been the lounge. Two marines had broken open a jammed door and found a small airless room containing a dead man who wore a spacesuit. Cause of death was not immediately apparent, but the uniform collar visible through the helmet's faceplate indicated that the man had been a member of *Wilhelmina*'s crew. And in an area of considerable damage near the lounge another, suitless, body was discovered wedged among twisted structural members. This corpse had probably been frozen near absolute zero for several days and exposed to vacuum for an equal length of time. Also its death had been violent. After all this it was hard to be sure, but Liao thought that the body had once been that of a young girl who had been wearing a fancy party dress when she met her end.

Liao could imagine a full scenario now, or rather two of them. Both began with the shipload of students, eighteen or twenty of them perhaps, enjoying their interstellar trip. Surely such a cruise had been a momentous event in their lives. Maybe they had been partying as they either entered or were about to leave the solar system containing the planet Esteel. And then, according to Scenario One, out of the deep night of space came the desperate pleas for help from the damaged and harried courier, hotly pursued by berserkers that were not expected to be in this part of the galaxy at all. The students would have had to remain on board the *Wilhelmina,* there being no place for them to get off, when she was commandeered to carry the space inverter on to Meitner's planet. Then urgent flight, and two days from Meitner's a berserker almost catching up, tracking and finding and shooting holes in *Wilhelmina,* somewhere in the great labyrinth of space and dust and stars and time, in which the little worlds of men were strange and isolate phenomena. And then the two heroic survivors, Henri and Winifred, finding a way to push on somehow.

Scenario Two diverged from that version early on, and was simpler and at first glance more credible. Instead of the *Wilhelmina* being hailed by a courier and pressed into military service, she was simply jumped by berserkers somewhere, her crew and passengers efficiently wiped out, her battered body driven on here ahead of the main berserker fleet in a ploy to forestall the installation of the space inverter and demolish the colony before any help could reach it. Scenario One was the more heroic and romantic, Two the more prosaic and businesslike. The trouble was that the real world was not committed to behaving in either style but went on its way indifferently.

A man was just now back from inspecting *Wilhelmina*'s control room. "Almost a total loss in there, sir, except for the drive controls and their directional settings. Artificial and the autopilot too. Drive itself seems all right, as far as I can tell without trying it."

"Don't bother. Thank you, mister."

Another man came to report, drifting upside down before the captain in the lack of gravity. "Starboard forward lifeboat's been launched, Captain. Others are still in place, no signs of having been lived in. Eight-passenger models."

"Thank you," Liao said courteously. These facts told him nothing new. Twelve minutes left now, before he must elect a target and give the command to fire. In his magnetic boots he stood before the telescope and spectroscope as their user had done, and looked out at the stars.

The slow rotation of the *Wilhelmina* brought the dreadnought into view, and Liao flicked his suit radio to the intership channel. "Bridge, this is Captain. Someone tell me just how big that space inverter is. Could two untrained people manhandle it and its packing into one of those little eight-passenger lifeboats?"

"This is the Armaments officer, sir," an answer came back promptly. "I used to work in ground installations, and I've handled those things. I could put my arms around the biggest space inverter ever made, and it wouldn't mass more than fifty kilograms. It's not the size makes 'em rare and hard to come by, it's the complexity. Makes a regular drive unit or artificial gravity generator look like nothing."

"All right. Thank you. Astrogation, are you there?"

"Listening in, sir."

"Good. Barbara, the regular astrogator's gear on this ship seems to have been wiped out. What we have then is two history students or whatever, with unknown astronomical competence, working their way here from someplace two days off, in a series of c-plus jumps. We've found their instruments, apparently all they used, simply telescope and spectroscope. You've been thinking it over, now how about it? Possible?"

There was a pause. "Possible, yes. I can't say more than that on what you've given me."

"I'm not convinced it's possible. With umpteen thousand stars to look at, their patterns changing every time you jump, how could you hope to find the one you wanted to work toward?" *Ten minutes.* Inspiration struck. "Listen! Why couldn't they have shoved off in the lifeboat, two days ago, and used its autopilot?"

Barbara's voice was careful as always. "To answer your last question first, chief, the lifeboat autopilots on civilian ships are usually not adjustable to give you a choice of goals; they just bring you out in the nearest place where you are likely to be found. No good for either people or berserkers intent on coming to Meitner's system. And if *Wilhelmina*'s drive is working it could take them between the stars faster than a lifeboat could.

"To answer your first question, the lifeboats carry aids for the amateur astrogator, such as spectral records of thousands of key stars, kept on microfilm. Also often provided is an electronic scanning spectroscope of the type you seem to have found there. The star records are indexed by basic spectral type, you know, types O, B, A, F, G, K, and so on. Type O stars, for example, are quite rare in this neck of the woods so if you just scanned for them you would cut down tremendously on the number of stars to be looked at closely for identification. There are large draw-backs to such a system of astrogation, but on the other hand with a little luck one might go a long way using it. If the two students are real people, though, I'll bet at least one of them knows some astronomy."

"Thank you," Liao said carefully, once again. He glanced around him. The marines were still busy, flashing their lights on everything and poking into every crevice. Eight minutes. He thought he could keep the time in his head now, not needing a chronometer.

People had lived in this lounge, or rec room, or whatever it had been, and enjoyed themselves. The wall to which the astrogation instruments were now fastened had earlier been decorated, or burdened, with numer-ous graffiti of the kinds students seemed always to generate. Many of the messages, Liao saw now, were in English, an ancient and honorable language still fairly widely taught. From his own schooldays he remem-bered enough to be able to read it fairly well, helping himself out with an occasional guess.

CAPTAIN AHAB CHASES ALEWIVES, said one message proceeding boldly across the wall at an easy reading height. The first and third words of that were certainly English, but the meaning of the whole eluded him. Captain Liao chases shadows, he thought, and hunches. What else is left?

Here was another:

<pre>
                              WORLD
                          WHOLE
                      THE
                    WISH
                 CLASSMATES
               NOBLE
           HIS
       AND
    OSS
</pre>

And then nothingness, the remainder of the message having gone when Oss and his noble classmates went and the upper half of this wall with them.

"Here, Captain! Look!" A marine was beckoning wildly.

The writing he was pointing to was low down on the wall and inconspicuous, made with a thinner writing instrument than most of the other graffiti had been. It said simply:

Henri & Winifred

Liao looked at it, first with a jumping hope in his heart and then with a sagging sensation that had rapidly become all too familiar. He rubbed at the writing with his suited thumb; nothing much came off. He said: "Can anyone tell me in seven minutes whether this was put here after the air went out of the ship? If so, it would seem to prove that Henri and Winifred were still around then. Otherwise it proves nothing. If the berserker had been here it could easily have seen those names and retained them in its effortless, lifeless memory, and used them when it had to construct a scenario.

"Where are Henri and Winifred now, that is the question," Liao said to the lieutenant, who came drifting near, evidently wondering, as they all must be, what to do next. "Maybe that was Winifred back there in the party dress."

The marine answered: "Sir, that might have been Henri, for all that I could tell." He went on directing his men, and waiting for the captain to tell him what else was to be done.

A little distance to one side of the names, an English message in the same script and apparently made with the same writing instrument went down the wall like this:

Oh
Be
A
Fine
Girl
Kiss
Me
Right
Now
Sweetie

Liao was willing to bet that particular message wasn't written by anyone wearing a space helmet. But no, he wouldn't make such a bet, not really. If he tried he could easily enough picture the two young people, rubbing faceplates and laughing, momentarily able to forget the dead wedged in the twisted girders a few meters away. Something about that message nagged at his memory, though. Could it be the first line of an English poem he had forgotten?

The slow turn of the torn ship was bringing the dreadnought into view again. "Bridge, this is Captain. Tell me anything that's new."

"Sir, here's a little more that came in clear from the lifeboat. I quote: 'This is Winifred talking now, stop. We're going on being human even if you don't believe us, stop.' Some more repetitious stuff, Captain, and then this: 'While Henri was navigating I would come out from the lifeboat with him and he started trying to teach me about the stars, stop. We wrote our names there on the wall under the telescope if you care to look you'll find them of course that doesn't prove anything does it if I had lenses for eyes I could have read those names there and remembered them. . . .' It cuts off there, chief, buried in noise."

"Second, confirm my reading of how much time we have left to decide."

"Three minutes forty seconds, sir. That's cutting it thin."

"Thanks." Liao fell silent, looking off across the universe. It offered him no help.

"Sir! Sir! I may have something here." It was the marine who had found the names, who was still closely examining the wall.

Looking at the wall where the man had aimed his helmet light, near the deck below the mounted instruments, Liao beheld a set of small grayish indented scratches, about half a meter apart.

"Sir, some machine coming here repeatedly to use the scopes might well have made these markings on the wall. Whereas a man or woman in a spacesuit would not have left such marks, in my opinion, sir."

"I see." Looking at the marks, that might have been made by anything, maybe furniture banged into the wall during that final party, Liao felt an irrational anger at the marine. But of course the man was only trying his best to help. He had a duty to put forward any possibly useful idea that came into his head. "I'm not sure these were made by a berserker, spaceman, but it's something to think about. How much time have we left, Second?"

"Just under three minutes. Standing by ready to fire at target of your choice, sir. Pleading messages still coming in intermittently from both ships, nothing new in them."

"All right." The only reasonable hope of winning was to guess and take the fifty-fifty chance. If he let both ships go on, the bad one was certain to ram the colony and destroy it before the other could deliver the key to the defenses and it could be installed. If he destroyed both ships, the odds were ten to one or worse that the berserker fleet would be here shortly and would accomplish the same ruin upon a colony deprived of any chance of defending itself.

Liao adjusted his throat muscles so that his voice when it came out would be firm and certain, and then he flipped a coin in his mind. Well, not really. There were the indented scratches on the bulkhead, perhaps not so meaningless after all, and there was the story of the two students' struggle to get here, perhaps a little too fantastic. "Hit the lifeboat," he said then, decisively. "Give it another two minutes, but if no new evidence turns up, let go at it with the main turret. Under no circumstances delay enough to let it reach the planet."

"Understand, sir," said Miller's voice. "Fire at the lifeboat two minutes from your order."

He would repeat the order to fire, emphatically, when the time was up, so that there could be no possible confusion as to where responsibility lay. "Lieutenant, let's get the men back to the launch. Continue to keep your eyes open on the way, for anything. . . ."

"Yes, sir."

The last one to leave the ruined lounge-observatory, Liao looked at the place once more before following the marines back through the ship. Oh, be a fine girl, Winifred, when the slug from the c-plus cannon comes. But if I have guessed wrong and it is coming for you, at least you'll never see it. Just no more for you. No more Henri and no more lessons about the stars.

The stars. . . .

Oh, be a fine girl. . . .

O, B, A, F, G, K. . . .

"Sir!"

"Cancel my previous order! Let the lifeboat land. Hit the *Etruria!* Unload on that bloody damned berserker with everything we've got, right now!"

"Yessir!"

Long before Liao got back to the launch the c-plus cannon volleyed. Their firing was invisible, and inaudible here in airlessness, but still he and the others felt the released energies pass twistingly through all their bones. Now the huge leaden slugs would begin skipping in and out of normal space, homing on their tiny target, far outracing light in their trajectories toward Meitner's planet. The slugs would be traveling now like de Broglie wavicles, one aspect matter with its mass magnified awesomely by Einsteinian velocity, one aspect waves of not much more than mathematics. The molecules of lead churned internally with phase velocities greater than that of light.

Liao was back on the dreadnought's bridge before laggard light brought the faint flash of destruction back.

"Direct hit, Captain." There was no need to amplify on that.

"Good shot, Arms."

And then, only a little later, a message got through the planet's ionospheric noise to tell them that the two people with the space inverter were safely down.

Within a few hours the berserker fleet appeared in the system, and found an armed and ready colony, with *Hamilcar Barca* hanging by for heavy hit-and-run support. The enemy skirmished briefly and then declined battle and departed. A few hours after that, the human fleet arrived, and put in for some refitting. And then Captain Liao had a chance to get down into the domed colony and talk to two people who wanted very much to meet him.

"So," he was explaining, soon after the first round of mutual congratulations had been completed, "when I at last recognized the mnemonic on the wall for what it was, I knew that not only had Henri and Winny been there but that he had in fact been teaching her something about astronomical spectroscopy at that very place beside the instruments—therefore after the ship was damaged."

Henri was shaking his youthful head, with the air of one still marveling at it all. "Yes, *now* I can remember putting the mnemonic thing down, showing Winny how to remember the order of spectral types. I guess we use mnemonics all the time without thinking about it much. Every good boy does fine, for the musical notes. Bad boys race our young girls—that one's in electronics."

The captain nodded. "Thirty days hath September. And 'Barbara Celarent' that the logicians still use now and then. Berserkers, with their perfect memories, probably don't even know what mnemonics are, much less need them. Anyway, if the berserker had been on the *Wilhelmina,* it would've had no reason to leave false clues. No way it could have guessed that I was coming to look things over."

Winifred took him by the hand. "Captain, you've given us our lives, you know. What can we ever do for you?"

"Well. For a start. . . ." He slipped into some English he had recently practiced. "You might be a fine girl, sweetie, and. . . ."

DAVID DRAKE

HANGMAN

The light in the kitchen alcove glittered on Lt. Schilling's blond curls; glittered also on the frost-spangled window beside her and from the armor of the tank parked outside. All the highlights looked cold to Capt. Danny Pritchard as he stepped closer to the infantry lieutenant.

"Sal—" Pritchard began. From the orderly room behind them came the babble of the radios ranked against one wall and, less muted, the laughter of soldiers waiting for action. "You can't think like a Dutchman any more. We're Hammer's Slammers, all of us. We're mercs. Not Dutch, not Frisians—"

"You're not," Lt. Schilling snapped, looking up from the cup of bitter chocolate she had just drawn from the urn. She was a short woman and lightly built, but she had the unerring instinct of a bully who is willing to make a scene for a victim who is not willing to be part of one. "You're a farmer from Dunstan, what d'you care about Dutch miners, whatever these bleeding French do to them. But a lot of us do care, Danny, and if you had a little compassion—"

"But Sal—" Pritchard repeated, only his right arm moving as he touched the blonde girl's shoulder.

"Get your hands off me, Captain!" she shouted, "That's over!" She shifted the mug of steaming chocolate in her hand. The voices in the orderly room stilled. Then, simultaneously, someone turned up the volume of the radios and at least three people began to talk loudly on unconnected subjects.

Pritchard studied the back of his hand, turned it over to examine the calloused palm as well. He smiled. "Sorry, I'll remember that," he said in a normal voice. He turned and stepped back into the orderly room, a brown-haired man of 34 with a good set of muscles to cover his moderate frame and nothing at all to cover his heart. Those who knew Danny Pritchard slightly thought him a relaxed man, and he looked relaxed even now. But waiting around the electric grate were three troopers who knew Danny very well indeed: The crew of The Plow, Pritchard's command tank.

Kowie drove the beast, a rabbit-eyed man whose fingers now flipped cards in another game of privy solitaire. His deck was so dirty that only familiarity allowed him to read the pips. Kowie's hands and eyes were just as quick at the controls of the tank, sliding its bulbous hundred and fifty metric tons through spaces that were only big enough to pass it. When he had to, he drove nervelessly through objects instead of going around. Kowie would never be more than a tank driver; but he was the best tank driver in the Regiment.

Rob Jenne was big and as blond as Lt. Schilling. He grinned up at Pritchard, his expression changing from embarrassment to relief as he saw that his captain was able to smile also. Jenne had transferred from combat cars to tanks three years back, after the Slammers had pulled out of Squire's World. He was sharp-eyed and calm in a crisis. Twice after his transfer Jenne had been offered a blower of his own to command if he would return to combat cars. He had refused both promotions, saying he would stay with tanks or buy back his contract, that there was no way he was going back to those open-topped coffins again. When a tank commander's slot came open, Jenne got it; and Pritchard had made the blond sergeant his own blower chief when a directional mine had retired the previous man. Now Jenne straddled a chair backwards, his hands flexing a collapsible torsion device that kept his muscles as dense and hard as they had been the day he was recruited from a quarry on Burlage.

Line tanks carry only a driver and the blower chief who directs the tank and its guns when they are not under the direct charge of the Regiment's computer. In addition to those two and a captain, command tanks have a Communications Technician to handle the multiplex burden of radio traffic focused on the vehicle. Pritchard's commo tech was Margritte DiManzo, a slender widow who cropped her lustrous hair short so that it would not interfere with the radio helmet she wore most of her waking hours. She was off-duty now, but she had not removed the bulky headgear which linked her to the six radios in the tank parked outside. Their simultaneous sound would have been unintelligible babbling to most listeners. The black-haired woman's training, both conscious and hypnotic, broke that babbling into a set of discrete conversations. When Pritchard reentered the room, Margritte was speaking to Jenne. She did not look up at her commander until Jenne's brightening expression showed her it was safe to do so.

Two commo people and a sergeant with Intelligence tabs were at consoles in the orderly room. They were from the Regiment's HQ Battalion, assigned to Sector Two here on Kobold but in no sense a part of the sector's combat companies: Capt. Riis' S Company—infantry—and Pritchard's own tanks.

Riis was the senior captain and in charge of the sector, a matter which neither he nor Pritchard ever forgot. Sally Schilling led his first platoon. Her aide, a black-haired corporal, sat with his huge boots up, humming as he polished the pieces of his field-stripped powergun. Its barrel gleamed orange in the light of the electric grate. Electricity was more general on Kobold than on some wealthier worlds, since mining and copper smelting made fusion units a practical necessity. But though the copper in the transmission cable might well have been processed on Kobold, the wire had probably been drawn off-world and shipped back here. Aurore and Friesland had refused to allow even such simple manufactures here on their joint colony. They had kept Kobold a market and a supplier of raw materials, but never a rival.

"Going to snow tonight?" Jenne asked.

"Umm, too cold," Pritchard said, walking over to the grate. He pretended he did not hear Lt. Schilling stepping out of the alcove. "I figure—"

"Hold it," said Margritte, her index finger curling out for a volume control before the duty man had time to react. One of the wall radios boomed loudly to the whole room. Prodding another switch, Margritte patched the signal separately through the link implanted in Pritchard's right mastoid. "—guns and looks like satchel charges. There's only one man in each truck, but they've been on the horn too and we can figure on more Frenchies here any—"

"Red Alert," Pritchard ordered, facing his commo tech so that she could read his lips. "Where is this?"

The headquarters radiomen stood nervously, afraid to interfere but unwilling to let an outsider run their equipment, however ably. "Red Alert," Margritte was repeating over all bands. Then, through Pritchard's implant, she said, "It's Patrol Sigma three-nine, near Haacin. Dutch civilians've stopped three outbound provisions trucks from Barthe's Company."

"Scramble First Platoon," Pritchard said, "but tell 'em to hold for us to arrive." As Margritte coolly passed on the order, Pritchard picked up the commo helmet he had laid on his chair when he followed Lt. Schilling into the kitchen. The helmet gave him automatic switching and greater range than the bio-electric unit behind his ear.

The wall radio was saying, "—need some big friendlies fast or it'll drop in the pot for sure."

"Sigma three-niner," Pritchard said, "this is Michael One."

"Go ahead, Michael One," replied the distant squad leader. Pritchard's commo helmet added an airy boundlessness to his surroundings without really deadening the ambient noise.

"Hold what you've got, boys," the tank captain said. "There's help on the way."

The door of the orderly room stood ajar the way Pritchard's crewmen had left it. The captain slammed it shut as he too ran for his tank. Behind in the orderly room, Lt. Schilling was snapping out quick directions to her own platoon and to her awakened commander.

The Plow was already floating when Danny reached it. Ice crystals, spewed from beneath the skirts by the lift fans, made a blue-white dazzle in the vehicle's running lights. Frost whitened the ladder up the high side of the tank's plenum chamber and hull. Pritchard paused to pull on his gloves before mounting. Sgt. Jenne, anchoring himself with his left hand on the turret's storage rack, reached down and lifted his captain aboard without noticeable effort. Side by side, the two men slid through the hatches to their battle stations.

"Ready," Pritchard said over the intercom.

"Movin' on," replied Kowie, and with his words the tank slid forward over the frozen ground like grease on a hot griddle.

The command post had been a district road-maintenance center before all semblance of central government on Kobold had collapsed. The orderly room and officers' quarters were in the supervisor's house, a comfortable structure with shutters and mottoes embroidered in French on the walls. Some of the hangings had been defaced by short-range gunfire. The crew barracks across the road now served the troopers on headquarters duty. Many of the Slammers could read the Dutch periodicals abandoned there in the break-up. The equipment shed beside the barracks garaged the infantry skimmers because the battery-powered platforms could not shrug off the weather like the huge panzers of M Company. The shed doors were open, pluming the night with heated air as the duty platoon ran for its mounts. Some of the troopers had not yet donned their helmets and body armor. Jenne waved as the tank swept on by; then the road curved and the infantry was lost in the night.

Kobold was a joint colony of Aurore and Friesland. When eighty years of French oppression had driven the Dutch settlers to rebellion, their first act was to hire Hammer's Slammers. The break between Hammer and Friesland had been sharp, but time has a way of blunting anger and letting old habits resume. The Regimental language was Dutch, and many of the Slammers' officers were Frisians seconded from their own service. Friesland gained from the men's experience when they returned home; Hammer gained company officers with excellent training from the Gröningen Academy.

To counter the Slammers, the settlers of Auroran descent had hired three Francophone regiments. If either group of colonists could have afforded to pay its mercenaries unaided, the fighting would have been immediate and brief. Kobold had been kept deliberately poor by its homeworlds, however; so in their necessities the settlers turned to those homeworlds for financial help.

And neither Aurore nor Friesland wanted a war on Kobold.

Friesland had let its settlers swing almost from the beginning, sloughing their interests for a half share of the copper produced and concessions elsewhere in its sphere of influence. The arrangement was still satisfactory to the Council of State, if Frisian public opinion could be mollified by apparent activity. Aurore was on the brink of war in the Zemla System. Her Parlement feared another proxy war which could in a moment explode full-fledged, even though Friesland had been weakened by a decade of severe internal troubles. So Aurore and Friesland reached a compromise. Then, under threat of abandonment, the warring parties were forced to transfer their mercenaries' contracts to the home worlds. Finally, Aurore and Friesland mutually hired the four regiments: the Slammers; Compagnie de Barthe; the Alaudae; and Phenix Moirots. Mercs from either side were mixed and divided among eight sectors imposed on a map of inhabited Kobold. There the contract ordered them to keep peace between the factions; prevent the importation of modern weapons to either side; and—wait.

But Col. Barthe and the Auroran leaders had come to a further, secret agreement; and although Hammer had learned of it, he had informed only two men—Maj. Steuben, his aide and bodyguard; and Capt. Daniel Pritchard.

Pritchard scowled at the memory. Even without the details a traitor had sold Hammer, it would have been obvious that Barthe had his own plans. In the other sectors, Hammer's men and their French counterparts ran joint patrols. Both sides scattered their camps throughout the sectors, just as the villages of either nationality were scattered. Barthe had split his sectors in halves, brusquely ordering the Slammers to keep to the west of the River Aillet because his own troops were mining the east of the basin heavily. Barthe's Company was noted for its minefields. That skill was one of the reasons they had been hired by the French. Since most of Kobold was covered either by forests or by rugged hills, armor was limited to roads where well-placed mines could stack tanks like crushed boxes.

Hammer listened to Barthe's pronouncement and laughed, despite the anger of most of his staff officers. Beside him, Joachim Steuben had grinned and traced the line of his cut-away holster. When Danny Pritchard was informed, he had only shivered a little and called a vehicle inspection for the next morning. That had been three months ago. . . .

The night streamed by like smoke around the tank. Pritchard lowered his face shield, but he did not drop his seat into the belly of the tank. Vision blocks within gave a 360° view of the tank's surroundings, but the farmer in Danny could not avoid the feeling of blindness within the impenetrable walls. Jenne sat beside his captain in a cupola fitted with a three-barrelled automatic weapon. He too rode with his head out of the hatch, but that was only for comradeship. The sergeant much preferred to be inside. He would button up at the first sign of hostile action. Jenne was in no sense a coward; it was just that he had quirks. Most combat veterans do.

Pritchard liked the whistle of the black wind past his helmet. Warm air from the tank's resistance heaters jetted up through the hatch and kept his body quite comfortable. The vehicle's huge mass required the power of a fusion plant to drive its lift motors, and the additional burden of climate control was inconsequential.

The tankers' face shields automatically augmented the light of the moon, dim and red because the sun it reflected was dim and red as well. The boosted light level displayed the walls of forest, the boles snaking densely to either side of the road. At Kobold's perihelion, the thin stems grew in days to their full six-meter height and spread a ceiling of red-brown leaves the size of blankets. Now, at aphelion, the chilled, sapless trees burned with almost explosive intensity. The wood was too dangerous to use for heating, even if electricity had not been common; but it fueled the gasogene engines of most vehicles on the planet.

Jenne gestured ahead. "Blowers," he muttered on the intercom. His head rested on the gun switch though he knew the vehicles must be friendly. The Plow slowed.

Pritchard nodded agreement. "Michael First, this is Michael One," he said. "Flash your running lights so we can be sure it's you."

"Roger," replied the radio. Blue light flickered from the shapes hulking at the edge of the forest ahead. Kowie throttled the fans up to cruise, then chopped them and swung expertly into the midst of the four tanks of the outlying platoon.

"Michael One, this is Sigma One," Capt. Riis' angry voice demanded in the helmet.

"Go ahead."

"Barthe's sent a battalion across the river. I'm moving Lt. Schilling into position to block 'em and called Central for artillery support. You hold your first platoon at Haacin for reserve and any partisans up from Portela. I'll take direct command of the rest of—"

"Negative, negative, Sigma One!" Pritchard snapped. The Plow was accelerating again, second in the line of five tanks. They were beasts of prey sliding across the landscape of snow and black trees at 80 kph and climbing. "Let the French through, Captain. There won't be fighting, repeat, negative fighting."

"There damned well *will* be fighting, Michael One, if Barthe tries to shove a battalion into my sector!" Riis thundered back. "Remember, this isn't your command or a joint command. *I'm* in charge here."

"Margritte, patch me through to Battalion," Pritchard hissed on intercom. The Plow's turret was cocked 30° to the right. It covered the forest sweeping by to that side and anything which might be hiding there. Pritchard's mind was on Sally Schilling, riding a skimmer through forest like that flanking the tanks, hurrying with her fifty men to try to stop a battalion's hasty advance.

The commo helmet popped quietly to itself. Pritchard tensed, groping for the words he would need to convince Lt. Col. Miezierk. Miezierk, under whom command of Sectors One and Two was grouped, had been a Frisian regular until five years ago. He was supposed to think like a merc, now, not like a Frisian; but. . . .

The voice that suddenly rasped, "Override, override!" was not Miezierk's. "Sigma One, Michael One, this is Regiment."

"Go ahead," Pritchard blurted. Capt. Riis, equally rattled, said, "Yes, *sir!*" on the three-way link.

"Sigma, your fire order is cancelled. Keep your troops on alert, but keep 'em the hell out of Barthe's way."

"But Col. Hammer—"

"Riis, you're not going to start a war tonight. Michael One, can your panzers handle whatever's going on at Haacin without violating the contract?"

"Yes, sir." Pritchard flashed a map briefly on his face shield to check his position. "We're almost there now."

"If you can't handle it, Captain, you'd better hope you're killed in action," Col. Hammer said bluntly. "I haven't nursed this regiment for twenty-three years to lose it because somebody forgets what his job is." Then, more softly—Pritchard could imagine the Colonel flicking his eyes side to side to gauge bystanders' reactions—he added, "There's support if you need it, Captain—if they're the ones who breach the contract."

"Affirmative."

"Keep the lid on, boy. Regiment out."

The trees had drunk the whine of the fans. Now the road curved and the tanks banked greasily to join the main highway from Dimo to Portela. The tailings pile of the Haacin Mine loomed to the right and hurled the drive noise back redoubled at the vehicles. The steel skirts of the lead tank touched the road metal momentarily, showering the night with orange sparks. Beyond the mine were the now-empty wheat fields and then the village itself.

Haacin, the largest Dutch settlement in Sector Two, sprawled to either side of the highway. Its houses were two- and three-story lumps of cemented mine tailings. They were roofed with tile or plastic rather than shakes of native timber, because of the wood's lethal flammability. The highway was straight and broad. It gave Pritchard a good view of the three cargo vehicles pulled to one side. Men in local dress swarmed about them. Across the road were ten of Hammer's khaki-clad infantry, patrol S-39, whose ported weapons half-threatened, half-protected the trio of drivers in their midst. Occasionally a civilian turned to hurl a curse at Barthe's men, but mostly the Dutch busied themselves with off-loading cartons from the trucks.

Pritchard gave a brief series of commands. The four line tanks grounded in a hedgehog at the edge of the village. Their main guns and automatics faced outward in all directions. Kowie swung the command vehicle around the tank which had been leading it. He cut the fans' angle of attack, slowing The Plow without losing the ability to accelerate quickly. The command vehicle eased past the squad of infantry, then grounded behind the rearmost truck. Pritchard felt the fans' hum through the metal of the hull.

"Who's in charge here?" the captain demanded, his voice booming through the command vehicle's public address system.

The Dutch unloading the trucks halted silently. A squat man in a parka of feathery native fur stepped forward. Unlike many of the other civilians, he was not armed. He did not flinch when Pritchard pinned him with the spotlight of the tank. "I am Paul van Oosten," the man announced in the heavy Dutch of Kobold. "I am Mayor of Haacin. But if you mean who leads us in what we are doing here, well . . . perhaps Justice herself does. Klaus, show them what these trucks were carrying to Portela."

Another civilian stepped forward, ripping the top off the box he carried. Flat plastic wafers spilled from it, glittering in the cold light: powergun ammunition, intended for shoulder weapons like those the infantry carried.

"They were taking powerguns to the beasts of Portela to use against us," van Oosten said. He used the slang term, "skepsels" to name the Francophone settlers. The Mayor's shaven jaw was jutting out in anger.

"Captain!" called one of Barthe's truck drivers, brushing forward through the ring of Hammer's men. "Let me explain."

One of the civilians growled and lifted his heavy musket. Rob Jenne rang his knuckles twice on the receiver of his tribarrel, calling attention to the muzzles as he swept them down across the crowd. The Dutchman froze. Jenne smiled without speaking.

"We were sent to pick up wheat the regiment had purchased," Barthe's man began. Pritchard was not familiar with Barthe's insigniae, but from the merc's age and bearing he was a senior sergeant. An unlikely choice to be driving a provisions truck. "One of the vehicles happened to be partly loaded. We didn't take the time to empty it because we were in a hurry to finish the run and go off duty—there was enough room and lift to handle that little bit of gear and the grain besides.

"In any case—" and here the sergeant began pressing, because the tank captain had not cut him off at the first sentence as expected—"you do not, and these fools *surely* do not, have the right to stop Col. Barthe's transport. If you have questions about the way we pick up wheat, that's between your CO and ours, Sir."

Pritchard ran his gloved index finger back and forth below his right eyesocket. He was ice inside, bubbling ice that tore and chilled him and had nothing to do with the weather. He turned back to Mayor van Oosten. "Reload the trucks," he said, hoping that his voice did not break.

"You can't!" van Oosten cried. "These powerguns are the only chance my village, my *people* have to survive when you leave. You know that'll happen, don't you? Friesland and Aurore, they'll come to an agreement, a *trade-off,* they'll call it, and all the troops will leave. It's our lives they're trading! The beasts in Dimo, in Portela if you let these go through, they'll have powerguns that *their* mercenaries gave them. And we—"

Pritchard whispered a prepared order into his helmet mike. The rearmost of the four tanks at the edge of the village fired a single round from its main gun. The night flared cyan as the 200 mm bolt struck the middle of the tailings pile a kilometer away. Stone, decomposed by the enormous energy of the shot, recombined in a huge gout of flame. Vapor, lava, and cinders spewed in every direction. After a moment, bits of high-flung rock began pattering down on the roofs of Haacin.

The bolt caused a double thunder-clap, that of the heated air followed by the explosive release of energy at the point of impact. When the reverberations died away there was utter silence in Haacin. On the distant jumble of rock, a dying red glow marked where the charge had hit. The shot had also ignited some saplings rooted among the stones. They had blazed as white torches for a few moments but they were already collapsing as cinders.

"The Slammers are playing this by rules," Pritchard said. Loudspeakers flung his quiet words about the village like the echoes of the shot; but he was really speaking for the recorder in the belly of the tank, preserving his words for a later Bonding Authority hearing. "There'll be no powerguns in civilian hands. Load every bit of this gear back in the truck. Remember, there's satellites up there—" Pritchard waved generally at the sky—"that see everything that happens on Kobold. If one powergun is fired by a civilian in this sector, I'll come for him. I promise you."

The mayor sagged within his furs. Turning to the crowd behind him, he said, "Put the guns back on the truck. So that the Portelans can kill us more easily."

"Are you mad, van Oosten?" demanded the gunman who had earlier threatened Barthe's sergeant.

"Are *you* mad, Kruse?" the mayor shouted back without trying to hide his fury. "D'ye doubt what those tanks would do to Haacin? And do you doubt this butcher—" his back was to Pritchard but there was no doubt as to whom the mayor meant—"would use them on us? Perhaps tomorrow we could have. . . ."

There was motion at the far edge of the crowd, near the corner of a building. Margritte, watching the vision blocks within, called a warning. Pritchard reached for his panic bar—Rob Jenne was traversing the tribarrel. All three of them were too late. The muzzle flash was red and it expanded in Pritchard's eyes as a hammer blow smashed him in the middle of the forehead.

The bullet's impact heaved the tanker up and backwards. His shattered helmet flew off into the night. The unyielding hatch coaming caught him in the small of the back, arching his torso over it as if he were being broken on the wheel. Pritchard's eyes flared with sheets of light. As reaction flung him forward again, he realized he was hearing the reports of Jenne's powergun and that some of the hellish flashes were real.

If the tribarrel's discharges were less brilliant than that of the main gun, then they were more than a hundred times as close to the civilians. The burst snapped within a meter of one bystander, an old man who stumbled backward into a wall. His mouth and staring eyes were three circles of empty terror. Jenne fired seven rounds. Every charge but one struck the sniper or the building he sheltered against. Powdered concrete sprayed from the wall. The sniper's body spun backwards, chest gobbled away by the bolts. His right arm still gripped the musket he had fired at Pritchard. The arm had been flung alone onto the snowy pavement. The electric bite of ozone hung in the air with the ghostly afterimages of the shots. The dead man's clothes were burning, tiny orange flames that rippled into smoke an inch from their bases.

Jenne's big left hand was wrapped in the fabric of Pritchard's jacket, holding the dazed officer upright. "There's another rule you play by," the sergeant roared to the crowd. "You shoot at Hammer's Slammers and you get your balls kicked between your ears. Sure as god, boys; sure as death." Jenne's right hand swung the muzzles of his weapon across the faces of the civilians. "Now, load the bleeding trucks like the captain said, heroes."

For a brief moment, nothing moved but the threatening powergun. Then a civilian turned and hefted a heavy crate back aboard the truck from which he had just taken it. Empty-handed, the colonist began to sidle away from the vehicle—and from the deadly tribarrel. One by one the other villagers reloaded the hijacked cargo, the guns and ammunition they had hoped would save them in the cataclysm they awaited. One by one they took the blower chief's unspoken leave to return to their houses. One who did not leave was sobbing out her grief over the mangled body of the sniper. None of her neighbors had gone to her side. They could all appreciate—now—what it would have meant if that first shot had led to a general firefight instead of Jenne's selective response.

"Rob, help me get him inside," Pritchard heard Margritte say.

Pritchard braced himself with both hands and leaned away from his sergeant's supporting arm. "No, I'm all right," he croaked. His vision was clear enough, but the landscape was flashing bright and dim with varicolored light.

The side hatch of the turret clanked. Margritte was beside her captain. She had stripped off her cold weather gear in the belly of the tank and wore only her khaki uniform. "Get back inside there," Pritchard muttered. "It's not safe." He was afraid of falling if he raised a hand to fend her away. He felt an injector prick the swelling flesh over his cheekbones. The flashing colors died away though Pritchard's ears began to ring.

"They carried some into the nearest building," the non-com from Barthe's Company was saying. He spoke in Dutch, having sleep-trained in the language during the transit to Kobold just as Hammer's men had in French.

"Get it," Jenne ordered the civilians still near the trucks. Three of them were already scurrying toward the house the merc had indicated. They were back in moments, carrying the last of the arms chests.

Pritchard surveyed the scene. The cargo had been reloaded, except for the few spilled rounds winking from the pavement. Van Oosten and the furious Kruse were the only villagers still in sight. "All right," Pritchard said to the truck drivers, "get aboard and get moving. And come back by way of Bitzen, not here. I'll arrange an escort for you."

The French non-com winked, grinned, and shouted a quick order to his men. The infantrymen stepped aside silently to pass the truckers. The French mercenaries mounted their vehicles and kicked them to life. Their fans whined and the trucks lifted, sending snow crystals dancing. With gathering speed, they slid westward along the forest-rimmed highway.

Jenne shook his head at the departing trucks, then stiffened as his helmet spat a message. "Captain," he said, "we got company coming."

Pritchard grunted. His own radio helmet had been smashed by the bullet, and his implant would only relay messages on the band to which it had been verbally keyed most recently. "Margritte, start switching for me," he said. His slender commo tech was already slipping back inside through the side hatch. Pritchard's blood raced with the chemicals Margritte had shot into it. His eyes and mind worked perfectly, though all his thoughts seemed to have razor edges on them.

"Use mine," Jenne said, trying to hand the captain his helmet.

"I've got the implant," Pritchard said. He started to shake his head and regretted the motion instantly. "That and Margritte's worth a helmet any day."

"It's a whole battalion," Jenne explained quietly, his eyes scanning the Bever Road down which Command Central had warned that Barthe's troops were coming. "All but the artillery—that's back in Dimo, but it'll range here easy enough. Brought in anti-tank battery and a couple calliopes, though."

"Slide us up ahead of Michael First," Pritchard ordered his driver. As The Plow shuddered, then spun on its axis, the captain dropped his seat into the turret to use the vision blocks. He heard Jenne's seat whirr down beside him and the cupola hatch snick closed. In front of Pritchard's knees, pale in the instrument lights, Margritte DiManzo sat still and open-eyed at her communications console.

"Little friendlies," Pritchard called through his loudspeakers to the ten infantrymen, "find yourselves a quiet alley and hope nothing happens. The Lord help you if you fire a shot without me ordering it." The Lord help us all, Pritchard thought to himself.

Ahead of the command vehicle, the beetle shapes of First Platoon began to shift position. "Michael First," Pritchard ordered sharply, "get back as you were. We're not going to engage Barthe, we're going to meet him." Maybe.

Kowie slid them alongside, then a little forward of the point vehicle of the defensive lozenge. They set down. All of the tanks were buttoned up, save for the hatch over Pritchard's head. The central vision block was a meter by 30 cm panel. It could be set for anything from a 360° view of the tank's surroundings to a one-to-one image of an object a kilometer away. Pritchard focused and ran the gain to ten magnifications, then thirty. At the higher power, motion curling along the snow-smoothed grainfields between Haacin and its mine resolved into men. Barthe's troops were clad in sooty-white coveralls and battle armor. The leading elements were hunched low on the meager platforms of their skimmers. Magnification and the augmented light made the skittering images grainy, but the tanker's practiced eye caught the tubes of rocket launchers clipped to every one of the skimmers. The skirmish line swelled at two points where self-propelled guns were strung like beads on the cord of men: anti-tank weapons, 50 mm powerguns firing high-intensity charges. They were supposed to be able to burn through the heaviest armor. Barthe's boys had come loaded for bear; oh yes. They thought they knew just what they were going up against. Well, the Slammers weren't going to show them they were wrong. Tonight.

"Running lights, everybody," Pritchard ordered. Then, taking a deep breath, he touched the lift on his seat and raised himself head and shoulders back into the chill night air. There was a hand light clipped to Pritchard's jacket. He snapped it on, aiming the beam down onto the turret top so that the burnished metal splashed diffused radiance up over him. It bathed his torso and face plainly for the oncoming infantry. Through the open hatch, Pritchard could hear Rob cursing. Just possibly Margritte was mumbling a prayer.

"Batteries at Dimo and Harfleur in Sector One have received fire orders and are waiting for a signal to execute," the implant grated. "If Barthe opens fire, Command Central will not, repeat, negative, use Michael First or Michael One to knock down the shells. Your guns will be clear for action, Michael One."

Pritchard grinned starkly. His face would not have been pleasant even if livid bruises were not covering almost all of it. The Slammers' central fire direction computer used radar and satellite reconnaissance to track shells in flight. Then the computer took control of any of the Regiment's vehicle-mounted powerguns and swung them onto the target. Central's message notified Pritchard that he would have full control of his weapons at all times, while guns tens or hundreds of kilometers away kept his force clear of artillery fire.

Margritte had blocked most of the commo traffic, Pritchard realized. She had let through only this message that was crucial to what they were about to do. A good commo tech; a very good person indeed.

The skirmish line grounded. The nearest infantryment were within fifty meters of the tanks and their fellows spread off into the night like lethal wings. Barthe's men rolled off their skimmers and lay prone. Pritchard began to relax when he noticed that their rocket launchers were still aboard the skimmers. The anti-tank weapons were in instant reach, but at least they were not being leveled for an immediate salvo. Barthe didn't want to fight the Slammers. His targets were the Dutch civilians, just as Mayor van Oosten had suggested.

An air cushion jeep with a driver and two officers aboard drew close. It hissed slowly through the line of infantry, then stopped nearly touching the command vehicle's bow armor. One of the officers dismounted. He was a tall man who was probably very thin when he was not wearing insulated coveralls and battle armor. He raised his face to Pritchard atop the high curve of the blower, sweeping up his reflective face shield as he did so. He was Lt. Col. Benoit, commander of the French mercenaries in Sector Two; a clean-shaven man with sharp features and a splash of gray hair displaced across his forehead by his helmet. Benoit grinned and waved at the muzzle of the 200 mm powergun pointed at him. Nobody had ever said Barthe's chief subordinate was a coward.

Pritchard climbed out of the turret to the deck, then slid down the bow slope to the ground. Benoit was several inches taller than the tanker, with a force of personality which was daunting in a way that height alone could never be. It didn't matter to Pritchard. He worked with tanks and with Col. Hammer; nothing else was going to face down a man who was accustomed to those.

"Sgt. Major Oberlie reported how well and. . . . firmly you handled their little affair, Captain," Benoit said, extending his hand to Pritchard. "I'll admit that I was a little concerned that I would have to rescue my men myself."

"Hammer's Slammers can be depended on to keep their contracts," the tanker replied, smiling with false warmth. "I told these squareheads that any civilian caught with a powergun was going to have to answer to me for it. Then we made sure nobody thinks we were kidding."

Benoit chuckled. Little puffs of vapor spurted from his mouth with the sounds. "You've been sent to the Gröningen Academy, have you not, Capt. Pritchard?" the older man asked. "You understand that I take an interest in my opposite numbers in this sector."

Pritchard nodded. "The Old Man picked me for the two year crash course on Friesland, yeah. Now and again he sends non-coms he wants to promote."

"But you're not a Frisian, though you have Frisian military training," the other mercenary continued, nodding to himself. "As you know, Captain, promotion in some infantry regiments comes much faster than it does in the . . . Slammers. If you feel a desire to speak to Col. Barthe some time in the future, I assure you this evening's business will not be forgotten."

"Just doing my job, Colonel," Pritchard simpered. Did Benoit think a job offer would make a traitor of him? Perhaps. Hammer had bought Barthe's plans for very little, considering their military worth. "Enforcing the contract, just like you'd have done if things were the other way around."

Benoit chuckled again and stepped back aboard his jeep. "Until we meet again, Capt. Pritchard," he said. "For the moment, I think we'll just proceed on into Portela. That's permissible under the contract, of course."

"Swing wide around Haacin, will you?" Pritchard called back. "The folks there're pretty worked up. Nobody wants more trouble, do we?"

Benoit nodded. As his jeep lifted, he spoke into his helmet communicator. The skirmish company rose awkwardly and set off in a counterclockwise circuit of Haacin. Behind them, in a column reformed from their support positions at the base of the tailings heap, came the truck-mounted men of the other three companies. Pritchard stood and watched until the last of them whined past.

Air stirred by the tank's idling fans leaked out under the skirts. The jets formed tiny deltas of the snow which winked as Pritchard's feet caused eddy currents. In their cold precision, the tanker recalled Col. Benoit's grin.

"Command Central," Pritchard said as he climbed his blower, "Michael One. Everything's smooth here. Over." Then, "Sigma One, this is Michael One. I'll be back as quick as fans'll move me, so if you have anything to say we can discuss it then." Pritchard knew that Capt. Riis must have been burning the net up, trying to raise him for a report or to make demands. It wasn't fair to make Margritte hold the bag now tha. Pritchard himself was free to respond to the sector chief; but neither did the Dunstan tanker have the energy to argue with Riis just at the moment. Already this night he'd faced death and Col. Benoit. Riis could wait another ten minutes.

The Plow's armor was a tight fit for its crew, the radios, and the central bulk of the main gun with its feed mechanism. The command vehicle rode glass-smooth over the frozen roadway, with none of the jouncing that a rougher surface might bring even through the air cushion. Margritte faced Pritchard over her console, her seat a meter lower than his so that she appeared a suppliant. Her short hair was the lustrous purple-black of a grackle's throat in sunlight. Hidden illumination from the instruments brought her face to life.

"Gee, Captain," Jenne was saying at Pritchard's side, "I wish you'd a let me pick up that squarehead's rifle. I know those groundpounders. They're just as apt as not to claim the kill credit themselves, and if I can't prove I stepped on the body they might get away with it. I remember on Paradise, me and Piet de Hagen—he was left wing gunner, I was right—both shot at a partisan. And then damned if Central didn't decide the slope had blown herself up with a hand grenade after we'd wounded her. So *neither* of us got the credit. You'd think—"

"Lord's *blood,* sergeant," Pritchard snarled, "are you so damned proud of killing one of the poor bastards who hired us to protect them?"

Jenne said nothing. Pritchard shrank up inside, realizing what he had said and unable to take the words back. "Oh, Lord, Rob," he said without looking up, "I'm sorry. It . . . I'm shook, that's all."

After a brief silence, the blond sergeant laughed. "Never been shot in the head myself, Captain, but I can see it might shake a fellow, yeah." Jenne let the whine of the fans stand for a moment as the only further comment while he decided whether he would go on. Then he said, "Captain, for a week after I first saw action I meant to get out of the Slammers, even if I had to sweep floors on Curwin for the rest of my life. Finally I decided I'd stick it. I didn't like the . . . rules of the game, but I could learn to play by them.

"And I did. And one rule is, that you get to be as good as you can at killing the people Col. Hammer wants killed. Yeah, I'm proud about that one just now. It was a tough snap shot and I made it. I don't care why we're on Kobold or who brought us here. But I know I'm supposed to kill anybody who shoots at us, and I will."

"Well, I'm glad you did," Pritchard said evenly as he looked the sergeant in the eyes. "You pretty well saved things from getting out of hand by the way you reacted."

As if he had not heard his captain, Jenne went on, "I was afraid if I stayed in the Slammers I'd turn into an animal, like the dogs we trained back home to kill rats in the quarries. And I was right. But it's the way I am now, so I don't seem to mind."

"You do care about those villagers, don't you?" Margritte asked Pritchard unexpectedly.

The captain looked down and found her eyes on him. They were the rich powder-blue of chicory flowers. "You're probably the only person in the Regiment who thinks that," he said bitterly. "Except for me. And maybe Col. Hammer. . . ."

Margritte smiled, a quick flash and as quickly gone. "There're rule-book soldiers in the Slammers," she said, "captains who'd never believe Barthe was passing arms to the Auroran settlements since he'd signed a contract that said he wouldn't. You aren't that kind. And the Lord knows Col. Hammer isn't, and he's backing you. I've been around you too long, Danny, to believe you like what you see the French doing."

Pritchard shrugged. His whole face was stiff with bruises and the drugs Margritte had injected to control them. If he'd locked the helmet's chin strap, the bullet's impact would have broken his neck even though the lead itself did not penetrate. "No, I don't like it," the brown-haired captain said. "It reminds me too much of the way the Combine kept us so poor on Dunstan that a thousand of us signed on for birdseed to fight off-planet. Just because it *was* off-planet. And if Kobold only gets cop from the worlds who settled her, then the French skim the best of that. Sure, I'll tell the Lord I feel sorry for the Dutch here."

Pritchard held the commo tech's eyes with his own as he continued, "But it's just like Rob said, Margritte: I'll do my job, no matter who gets hurt. We can't do a thing to Barthe or the French until they step over the line in a really obvious way. That'll mean a lot of people get hurt too. But that's what I'm waiting for."

Margritte reached up and touched Pritchard's hand where it rested on his knee. "You'll do something when you can," she said quietly.

He turned his palm up so that he could grasp the woman's fingers. What if she knew he was planning an incident, not just waiting for one? "I'll do something, yeah," he said. "But it's going to be too late for an awful lot of people."

Kowie kept The Plow at cruising speed until they were actually in the yard of the command post. Then he cocked the fan shafts forward, lifting the bow and bringing the tank's mass around in a curve that killed its velocity and blasted an arc of snow against the building. Someone inside had started to unlatch the door as they heard the vehicle approach. The air spilling from the tank's skirts flung the panel against the inner wall and skidded the man within on his back.

The man was Capt. Riis, Pritchard noted without surprise. Well, the incident wouldn't make the infantry captain any angrier than the rest of the evening had made him already.

Riis had regained his feet by the time Pritchard could jump from the deck of his blower to the fan-cleared ground in front of the building. The Frisian's normally pale face was livid now with rage. He was of the same somatotype as Lt. Col. Benoit, his French counterpart in the sector: tall, thin, and proudly erect. Despite the fact that Riis was only 27, he was Pritchard's senior in grade by two years. He had kept the rank he held in Friesland's regular army when Col. Hammer recruited him. Many of the Slammers were like Riis, Frisian soldiers who had transferred for the action and pay of a fighting regiment in which their training would be appreciated.

"You cowardly filth!" the infantryman hissed as Pritchard approached. A squad in battle gear stood within the orderly room beyond Riis. He pursed his fine lips to spit.

"Hey Captain!" Rob Jenne called. Riis looked up. Pritchard turned, surprised that the big tank commander was not right on his heels. Jenne still smiled from The Plow's cupola. He waved at the officers with his left hand. His right was on the butterfly trigger of the tribarrel.

The threat, unspoken as it was, made a professional of Riis again. "Come on into my office," he muttered to the tank captain, turning his back on the armored vehicle as if it were only a part of the landscape.

The infantrymen inside parted to pass the captains. Sally Schilling was there. Her eyes were as hard as her porcelain armor as they raked over Pritchard. That didn't matter, he lied to himself tiredly.

Riis' office was at the top of the stairs, a narrow cubicle which had once been a child's bedroom. The sloping roof pressed in on the occupants, though a dormer window brightened the room during daylight. One wall was decorated with a regimental battle flag—not Hammer's rampant lion but a pattern of seven stars on a white field. It had probably come from the unit in which Riis had served on Friesland. Over the door hung another souvenir, a big-bore musket of local manufacture. Riis threw himself into the padded chair behind his desk. "Those bastards were carrying powerguns to Portela!" he snarled at Pritchard.

The tanker nodded. He was leaning with his right shoulder against the door jamb. "That's what the folks at Haacin thought," he agreed. "If they'll put in a complaint with the Bonding Authority, I'll testify to what I saw."

"Testify, *testify!*" Riis shouted. "We're not lawyers, we're soldiers! You should've seized the trucks right then and—"

"No I should *not* have, Captain!" Pritchard shouted back, holding up a mirror to Riis' anger. "Because if I had, Barthe would've complained to the Authority himself, and we'd at least've been fined. At least! The contract says the Slammers'll cooperate with the other three units in keeping peace on Kobold. Just because we suspect Barthe is violating the contract doesn't give us a right to violate it ourselves. Especially in a way any *simpleton* can see is a violation."

"If Barthe can get away with it, we can," Riis insisted, but he settled back in his chair. He was physically bigger than Pritchard, but the tanker had spent half his life with the Slammers. Years like those mark men; death is never very far behind their eyes.

"I don't think Barthe can get away with it," Pritchard lied quietly, remembering Hammer's advice on how to handle Riis and calm the Frisian without telling him the truth. Barthe's officers had been in on his plans; and one of them had talked. Any regiment might have one traitor.

The tanker lifted down the musket on the wall behind him and began turning it in his fingers. "If the Dutch settlers can prove to the Authority that Barthe's been passing out powerguns to the French," the tanker mused aloud, "well, they're responsible for half Barthe's pay, remember. It's about as bad a violation as you'll find. The Authority'll forfeit his whole bond and pay it over to whoever they decide the injured parties are. That's about three years' gross earnings for Barthe, I'd judge—he won't be able to replace it. And without a bond posted, well, he may get jobs, but they'll be the kind nobody else'd touch for the risk and the pay. His best troops'll sign on with other people. In a year or so, Barthe won't have a regiment any more."

"He's willing to take the chance," said Riis.

"Col. Hammer isn't!" Pritchard blazed back.

"You don't know that. It isn't the sort of thing the Colonel could say—"

"Say?" Pritchard shouted. He waved the musket at Riis. Its breech was triple-strapped to take the shock of the industrial explosive it used for propellant. Clumsy and large, it was the best that could be produced on a mining colony whose home worlds had forbidden local manufacturing. "Say? I bet my life against one of these tonight that the Colonel wanted us to obey the contract. Do you have the guts to ask him flat out if he wants us to run guns to the Dutch?"

"I don't think that would be proper, Captain," said Riis coldly as he stood up again.

"Then try not to 'think it proper' to go do some bloody stupid stunt on your own—sir," Pritchard retorted. So much for good intentions. Hammer—and Pritchard—had expected Riis' support of the Dutch civilians. They had even planned on it. But the man seemed to have lost all his common sense. Pritchard laid the musket on the desk because his hands were trembling too badly to hang it back on the hooks.

"If it weren't for you, Captain," Riis said, "there's not a Slammer in this sector who'd object to our helping the only decent people on this planet the way we ought to. You've made your decision, and it sickens me. But I've made decisions too."

Pritchard went out without being dismissed. He blundered into the jamb, but he did not try to slam the door. That would have been petty, and there was nothing petty in the tanker's rage.

Blank-faced, he clumped down the stairs. His bunk was in a parlor which had its own door to the outside. Pritchard's crew was still in The Plow. There they had listened intently to his half of the argument with Riis, transmitted by the implant. If Pritchard had called for help, Kowie would have sent the command vehicle through the front wall buttoned up, with Jenne ready to shoot if he had to, to rescue his CO. A tank looks huge when seen close up. It is all howling steel and iridium, with black muzzles ready to spew death across a planet. On a battlefield, when the sky is a thousand, shrieking colors no god ever made and the earth beneath trembles and gouts in sudden mountains, a tank is a small world indeed for its crew. Their loyalties are to nearer things than an abstraction like "The Regiment."

Besides, tankers and infantrymen have never gotten along well together.

No one was in the orderly room except two radiomen. They kept their backs to the stairs. Pritchard glanced at them, then unlatched his door. The room was dark, as he had left it, but there was a presence. Pritchard said, "Sal—" as he stepped within and the club knocked him forward into the arms of the man waiting to catch his body.

The first thing Pritchard thought as his mind slipped toward oblivion was that the cloth rubbing his face was homespun, not the hard synthetic from which uniforms were made. The last thing Pritchard thought was that there could have been no civilians within the headquarters perimeter unless the guards had allowed them; and that Lt. Schilling was officer of the guard tonight.

Pritchard could not be quite certain when he regained consciousness. A heavy felt rug covered and hid his trussed body on the floor of a clattering surface vehicle. He had no memory of being carried to the truck, though presumably it had been parked some distance from the command post. Riis and his confederates would not have been so open as to have civilians drive to the door to take a kidnapped officer, even if Pritchard's crew could have been expected to ignore the breach of security.

Kidnapped. Not for later murder, or he would already be dead instead of smothering under the musty rug. Thick as it was, the rug was still inadequate to keep the cold from his shivering body. The only lights Pritchard could see were the washings of icy color from the night's doubled shock to his skull.

That bone-deep ache reminded Pritchard of the transceiver implanted in his mastoid. He said in a husky whisper which he hoped would not penetrate the rug, "Michael One to any unit, any unit at all. Come in please, any Slammer."

Nothing. Well, no surprise. The implant had an effective range of less than twenty meters, enough for relaying to and from a base unit, but unlikely to be useful in Kobold's empty darkness. Of course, if the truck happened to be passing one of M Company's night defensive positions.... "Michael One to any unit," the tanker repeated more urgently.

A boot slammed him in the ribs. A voice in guttural Dutch snarled, "Shut up, you, or you get what you gave Henrik."

So he'd been shopped to the Dutch, not that there had been much question about it. And not that he might not have been safer in French hands, the way everybody on this cursed planet thought he was a traitor to his real employers. Well, it wasn't fair; but Danny Pritchard had grown up a farmer, and no farmer is ever tricked into believing that life is fair.

The truck finally jolted to a stop. Gloved hands jerked the cover from Pritchard's eyes. He was not surprised to recognize the concrete angles of Haacin as men passed him hand to hand into a cellar. The attempt to hijack Barthe's powerguns had been an accident, an opportunity seized; but the crew which had kidnapped Pritchard must have been in position before the call from S-39 had intervened.

"Is this wise?" Pritchard heard someone demand from the background. "If they begin searching, surely they'll begin in Haacin."

The two men at the bottom of the cellar stairs took Pritchard's shoulders and ankles to carry him to a spring cot. It had no mattress. The man at his feet called, "There won't be a search, they don't have enough men. Besides, the beasts'll be blamed—as they should be for so many things. If Pauli won't let us kill the turncoat, then we'll all have to stand the extra risk of him living."

"You talk too much," Mayor van Oosten muttered as he dropped Pritchard's shoulders on the bunk. Many civilians had followed the captive into the cellar. The last of them swung the door closed. It lay almost horizontal to the ground. When it slammed, dust sprang from the ceiling. Someone switched on a dim incandescent light. The scores of men and women in the storage room were as hard and fell as the bare walls. There were three windows at street level, high on the wall. Slotted shutters blocked most of their dusty glass.

"Get some heat in this hole or you may as well cut my throat," Pritchard grumbled.

A woman with a musket cursed and spat in his face. The man behind her took her arm before the gunbutt could smear the spittle. Almost in apology, the man said to Pritchard, "It was her husband you killed."

"You're being kept out of the way," said a husky man—Kruse, the hothead from the hijack scene. His facial hair was pale and long, merging indistinguishably with the silky fringe of his parka. Like most of the others in the cellar, he carried a musket. "Without your meddling, there'll be a chance for us to . . . get ready to protect outselves, after the tanks leave and the beasts come to finish us with their powerguns."

"Does Riis think I won't talk when this is over?" Pritchard asked.

"I told you—" one of the men shouted at van Oosten. The heavy-set mayor silenced him with a tap on the chest and a bellowed, "Quiet!" The rising babble hushed long enough for van Oosten to say, "Captain, you will be released in a very few days. If you—cause trouble, then, it will only be an embarrassment to yourself. Even if your Colonel believes you were doing right, he won't be the one to bring to light a violation which was committed with—so you will claim—the connivance of his own officers."

The mayor paused to clear his throat and glower around the room. "Though in fact we had no help from any of your fellows, either in seizing you or in arming ourselves for our own protection."

"Are you all blind?" Pritchard demanded. He struggled with his elbows and back to raise himself against the wall. "Do you think a few lies will cover it all up? The only ships that've touched on Kobold in three months are the ones supplying us and the other mercs. Barthe maybe's smuggled in enough guns in cans of lube oil and the like to arm some civilians. He won't be able to keep that a secret, but maybe he can keep the Authority from proving who's responsible.

"That's with three months and pre-planning. If Riis tries to do anything on his own, that many of his own men are going to be short sidearms—they're all issued by serial number, Lord take it!—and a blind Mongoloid could get enough proof to sink the Regiment."

"You think we don't understand," said Kruse in a quiet voice. He transferred his musket to his left hand, then slapped Pritchard across the side of the head. "We understand very well," the civilian said. "All the mercenaries will leave in a few days or weeks. If the French have powerguns and we do not, they will kill us, our wives, our children. . . . There's a hundred and fifty villages on Kobold like this one, Dutch, and as many French ones scattered between. It was bad before, with no one but the beasts allowed any real say in the government; but now if they win, there'll be French villages and French mines—and slave pens. Forever."

"You think a few guns'll save you?" Pritchard asked. Kruse's blow left no visible mark in the tanker's livid flesh, though a better judge than Kruse might have noted that Pritchard's eyes were as hard as his voice was mild.

"They'll help us save ourselves when the time comes," Kruse retorted.

"If you'd gotten powerguns from French civilians instead of the mercs directly, you might have been all right," the captain said. He was coldly aware that the lie he was telling was more likely to be believed in this situation than it would have been in any setting he might deliberately have contrived. There had to be an incident, the French civilians *had* to think they were safe in using their illegal weapons. . . . "The Portelans, say, couldn't admit to having guns to lose. But anything you take from mercs—us or Barthe, it doesn't matter—we'll take back the hard way. You don't know what you're buying into."

Kruse's face did not change, but his fist drew back for another blow. The mayor caught the younger man's arm and snapped, "Franz, we're here to show him that it's not a few of us, it's every family in the village behind . . . our holding him," Van Oosten nodded around the room. "More of us than your colonel could dream of trying to punish," he added naively to Pritchard. Then he flashed back at Kruse, "If you act like a fool, he'll want revenge anyway."

"You may never believe this," Pritchard interjected wearily, "but I just want to do my job. If you let me go now, it—may be easier in the long run."

"Fool," Kruse spat and turned his back on the tanker.

A trap door opened in the ceiling, spilling more light into the cellar. "Pauli!" a woman shouted down the opening, "Hals is on the radio. There's tanks coming down the road, just like before!"

"The Lord's wounds!" van Oosten gasped. "We must—"

"They can't know!" Kruse insisted. "But we've got to get everybody out of here and back to their own houses. Everybody but me and him—"

a nod at Pritchard—"and this." The musket lowered so that its round black eye pointed straight into the bound man's face.

"No, by the side door!" van Oosten called to the press of conspirators clumping up toward the street. "Don't run right out in front of them." Cursing and jostling, the villagers climbed the ladder to the ground floor, there presumably to exit on an alley.

Able only to twist his head and legs, Pritchard watched Kruse and the trembling muzzle of his weapon. The village must have watchmen with radios at either approach through the forests. If Hals was atop the heap of mine tailings—where Pritchard would have placed his outpost if he were in charge, certainly—then he'd gotten a nasty surprise when the main gun splashed the rocks with Hell. The captain grinned at the thought. Kruse misunderstood and snarled, "If they *are* coming for you, you're dead, you treacherous bastard!" To the backs of his departing fellows, the young Dutchman called, "Turn out the light here, but leave the trap door open. That won't show on the street, but it'll give me enough light to shoot by."

The tanks weren't coming for him, Pritchard knew, because they couldn't have any idea where he was. Perhaps his disappearance had stirred up some patrolling, for want of more directed action; perhaps a platoon was just changing ground because of its commander's whim. Pritchard had encouraged random motion. Tanks that freeze in one place are sitting targets, albeit hard ones. But whatever the reason tanks were approaching Haacin, if they whined by in the street outside they would be well within range of his implanted transmitter.

The big blowers were audible now, nearing with an arrogant lack of haste as if bears headed for a beehive. They were moving at about 30 kph, more slowly than Pritchard would have expected even for a contact patrol. From the sound there were four or more of them, smooth and gray and deadly.

"Kruse, I'm serious," the Slammer captain said. Light from the trap door back-lit the civilian into a hulking beast with a musket. "If you—"

"Shut up!" Kruse snarled, prodding his prisoner's bruised forehead with the gun muzzle. "One more word, any word, and—"

Kruse's right hand was so tense and white that the musket might fire even without his deliberate intent.

The first of the tanks slid by outside. Its cushion of air was so dense that the ground trembled even though none of the blower's 170 tonnes was in direct contact with it. Squeezed between the pavement and the steel curtain of the plenum chamber, the air spurted sideways and rattled the cellar windows. The rattling was inaudible against the howling of the fans themselves, but the trembling shutters chopped facets in the play of the tank's running lights. Kruse's face and the far wall flickered in blotched abstraction.

The tank moved on without pausing. Pritchard had not tried to summon it.

"That power," Kruse was mumbling to himself, "that should be for us to use to sweep the beasts—" The rest of his words were lost in the growing wail of the second tank in the column.

Pritchard tensed within. Even if a passing tank picked up his implant's transmission, its crew would probably ignore the message. Unless Pritchard identified himself, the tankers would assume it was babbling thrown by the ionosphere. And if he did identify himself, Kruse—

Kruse thrust his musket against Pritchard's skull again, banging the tanker's head back against the cellar wall. The Dutchman's voice was lost in the blower's howling, but his blue-lit lips clearly were repeating, "One word. . . ."

The tank moved on down the highway toward Portela.

". . . and maybe I'll shoot you anyway," Kruse was saying. "That's the way to serve traitors, isn't it? *Mercenary!*"

The third blower was approaching. Its note seemed slightly different, though that might be the aftereffect of the preceding vehicles' echoing din. Pritchard was cold all the way to his heart, because in a moment he was going to call for help. He knew that Kruse would shoot him, knew also that he would rather die now than live after hope had come so near but passed on, passed on. . . .

The third tank smashed through the wall of the house.

The Plow's skirts were not a bulldozer blade, but they were thick steel and backed with the mass of a 150 tonne command tank. The slag wall repowdered at the impact. Ceiling joists buckled into pretzel shape and ripped the cellar open to the floor above. Kruse flung his musket up and fired through the cascading rubble. The boom and red flash were lost in the chaos, but the blue-green fire stabbing back across the cellar laid the Dutchman on his back with his parka aflame. Pritchard rolled to the floor at the first shock. He thrust himself with corded legs and arms back under the feeble protection of the bunk. When the sound of falling objects had died away, the captain slitted his eyelids against the rock dust and risked a look upward.

The collision had torn a gap ten feet long in the house wall, crushing it from street level to the beams supporting the second story. The tank blocked the hole with its gray bulk. Fresh scars brightened the patina of corrosion etched onto its skirts by the atmospheres of a dozen planets. Through the buckled flooring and the dust whipped into arabesques by the idling fans, Pritchard glimpsed a slight figure clinging lefthanded to the turret. Her right hand still threatened the wreckage with a submachinegun. Carpeting burned on the floor above, ignited by the burst that killed Kruse. Somewhere a woman was screaming in Dutch.

"Margritte!" Pritchard shouted. "Margritte! Down here!"

The helmeted woman swung up her face shield and tried to pierce the cellar gloom with her unaided eyes. The tank-battered opening had sufficed for the exchange of shots, but the tangle of structural members and splintered flooring was too tight to pass a man—or even a small woman. Sooty flames were beginning to shroud the gap. Margritte jumped to the ground and struggled for a moment before she was able to heave open the door. The Plow's turret swung to cover her, though neither the main gun nor the tribarrel in the cupola could depress enough to rake the cellar. Margritte ran down the steps to Pritchard. Coughing in the rock dust, he rolled out over the rubble to meet her. Much of the smashed sidewall had collapsed onto the street when the tank backed after the initial impact. Still, the crumpled beams of the ground floor sagged further with the additional weight of the slag on them. Head-sized pieces had splanged on the cot above Pritchard.

Margritte switched the submachinegun to her left hand and began using a clasp knife on her captain's bonds. The cord with which he was tied bit momentarily deeper at the blade's pressure.

Pritchard winced, then began flexing his freed hands. "You know, Margi," he said, "I don't think I've ever seen you with a gun before."

The commo tech's face hardened as if the polarized helmet shield had slipped down over it again. "You hadn't," she said. The ankle bindings parted and she stood, the dust graying her helmet and her foam-filled coveralls. "Captain, Kowie had to drive and we needed Rob in the cupola at the gun. That left me to—do anything else that had to be done. I did what had to be done."

Pritchard tried to stand, using the technician as a post on which to draw himself upright. Margritte looked frail, but with her legs braced she stood like a rock. Her arm around Pritchard's back was as firm as a man's.

"You didn't ask Capt. Riis for help, I guess," Pritchard said, pain making his breath catch. The line tanks had two-man crews with no one to spare for outrider, of course.

"We didn't report you missing," Margritte said, "even to First Platoon. They just went along like before, thinking you were in The Plow giving orders." Together, captain and technician shuffled across the floor to the stairs. As they passed Kruse's body, Margritte muttered cryptically, "That's four."

Pritchard assumed the tremors beginning to shake the woman's body were from physical strain. He took as much weight off her as he could and found his numbed feet were beginning to function reasonably well. He would never have been able to board The Plow without Sgt. Jenne's grip on his arm, however.

The battered officer settled in the turret with a groan of comfort. The seat cradled his body with gentle firmness, and the warm air blown across him was just the near side of heaven.

"Captain," Jenne said, "what d'we do about the slopes who grabbed you? Shall we call in an interrogation team and—"

"We don't do anything," Pritchard interrupted. "We just pretend none of this happened and head back to...." He paused. His flesh wavered both hot and cold as Margritte sprayed his ankles with some of the apparatus from the medical kit. "Say, how did you find me, anyway?"

"We shut off coverage when you—went into your room," Jenne said, seeing that the commo tech herself did not intend to speak. He meant, Pritchard knew, they had shut off the sound when their captain had said, "Sal." None of the three of them were looking either of the other two in the eyes. "After a bit, though, Margi noticed the carrier line from your implant had dropped off her oscilloscope. I checked your room, didn't find you. Didn't see much point talking it over with the remfs on duty, either.

"So we got satellite recce and found two trucks'd left the area since we got back. One was Riis', and the other was a civvie junker before that. It'd been parked in the woods out of sight, half a kay up the road from the buildings. Both trucks unloaded in Haacin. We couldn't tell which load was you, but Margi said if we got close, she'd home on your carrier even though you weren't calling us on the implant. Some girl we got here, hey?"

Pritchard bent forward and squeezed the commo tech's shoulder. She did not look up, but she smiled. "Yeah, always knew she was something," he agreed, "but I don't think I realized quite what a person she was until just now."

Margritte lifted her smile. "Rob ordered First Platoon to fall in with us," she said. "He set up the whole rescue." Her fine-fingered hands caressed Pritchard's calves.

But there was other business in Haacin, now. Riis had been quicker to act than Pritchard had hoped. He asked, "You say one of the infantry's trucks took a load here a little bit ago?"

"Yeah, you want the off-print?" Jenne agreed, searching for the flimsy copy of the satellite picture. "What the Hell would they be doing, anyhow?"

"I got a suspicion," his captain said grimly, "and I suppose it's one we've got to check out."

"Michael First-Three to Michael One," the radio broke in. "Vehicles approaching from the east on the hardball."

"Michael One to Michael First," Pritchard said, letting the search for contraband arms wait for this new development. "Reverse and form a line abreast beyond the village. Twenty meter intervals. The Plow'll take the road." More weapons from Riis? More of Barthe's troops when half his sector command was already in Portela? Pritchard touched switches beneath the vision blocks as Kowie slid the tank into position. He split the screen between satellite coverage and a ground-level view at top magnification. Six vehicles, combat cars, coming fast. Pritchard swore. Friendly, because only the Slammers had armored vehicles on Kobold, not that cars were a threat to tanks anyway. But no combat cars were assigned to this sector; and the unexpected is always bad news to a company commander juggling too many variables already.

"Platoon nearing Tango Sigma four-two, three-two, please identify to Michael One," Pritchard requested, giving Haacin's map coordinates.

Margritte turned up the volume of the main radio while she continued to bandage the captain's rope cuts. The set crackled, "Michael One, this is Alpha One and Alpha First. Stand by."

"God's bleeding cunt!" Rob Jenne swore under his breath. Pritchard was nodding in equal agitation. Alpha was the Regiment's special duty company. Its four combat car platoons were Col. Hammer's bodyguards and police. The troopers of A Company were nicknamed the White Mice, and they were viewed askance even by the Slammers of other companies—men who prided themselves on being harder than any other combat force in the galaxy. The White Mice in turn feared their commander, Maj. Joachim Steuben; and if that slightly-built killer feared anyone, it was the man who was probably traveling with him this night. Pritchard sighed and asked the question. "Alpha One, this is Michael One. Are you flying a pennant, sir?"

"Affirmative, Michael One."

Well, he'd figured Col. Hammer was along as soon as he heard what the unit was. What the Old Man was doing here was another question, and one whose answer Pritchard did not look forward to learning.

The combat cars glided to a halt under the guns of their bigger brethren. The tremble of their fans gave the appearance of heat ripples despite the snow. From his higher vantage point, Pritchard watched the second car slide out of line and fall alongside The Plow. The men at the nose and right wing guns were both short, garbed in nondescript battle gear. They differed from the other troopers only in that their helmet shields were raised and that the faces visible beneath were older than those of most Slammers: Col. Alois Hammer and his hatchetman.

"No need for radio, Captain," Hammer called in a husky voice. "What are you doing here?"

Pritchard's tongue quivered between the truth and a lie. His crew had been covering for him, and he wasn't about to leave them holding the bag. All the breaches of regulations they had committed were for their captain's sake. "Sir, I brought First Platoon back to Haacin to check whether any of the powerguns they'd hijacked from Barthe were still in civvie hands." Pritchard could feel eyes behind the cracked shutters of every east-facing window in the village.

"And have you completed your check?" the Colonel pressed, his voice mild but his eyes as hard as those of Maj. Steuben beside him; as hard as the iridium plates of the gun shields.

Pritchard swallowed. He owed nothing to Capt. Riis, but the young fool *was* his superior—and at least he hadn't wanted the Dutch to kill Pritchard. He wouldn't put Riis' ass in the bucket if there were neutral ways to explain the contraband. Besides, they were going to need Riis and his Dutch contacts for the rest of the plan. "Sir, when you approached I was about to search a building where I suspect some illegal weapons are stored."

"And instead you'll provide back-up for the Major here," said Hammer, the false humor gone from his face. His words rattled like shrapnel. "He'll retrieve the twenty-four powerguns which Capt. Riis saw fit to turn over to civilians tonight. If Joachim hadn't chanced, *chanced* onto that requisition. . . ." Hammer's left glove shuddered with the strength of his grip on the forward tribarrel. Then the Colonel lowered his eyes and voice, adding, "The quartermaster who filled a requisition for twenty-four pistols from Central Supply is in the infantry again tonight. And Capt. Riis is no longer with the Regiment."

Steuben tittered, loose despite the tension of everyone around him. The cold was bitter, but Joachim's right hand was bare. With it he traced the baroque intaglios of his holstered pistol. "Mr. Riis is lucky to be alive," the slight Newlander said pleasantly. "Luckier than some would have wished. But Colonel, I think we'd best go pick up the merchandise before anybody nerves themself to use it on us."

Hammer nodded, calm again. "Interfile your blowers with ours, Captain," he ordered. "Your panzers watch street level while the cars take care of upper floors and roofs."

Pritchard saluted and slid down into the tank, relaying the order to the rest of his platoon. Kowie blipped The Plow's throttles, swinging the turreted mass in its own length and sending it back into the village behind the lead combat car. The tank felt light as a dancer, despite the constricting sidestreet Kowie followed the car into. Pritchard scanned the full circuit of the vision blocks. Nothing save the wind and armored vehicles moved in Haacin. When Steuben had learned a line company was requisitioning two dozen extra sidearms, the Major had made the same deductions as Pritchard had and had inspected the same satellite tape of a truck unloading. Either Riis was insane or he really thought Col. Hammer was willing to throw away his life's work to arm a village —inadequately. Lord and Martyrs! Riis would have *had* to be insane to believe that!

Their objective was a nondescript two-story building separated from its neighbors by narrow alleys. Hammer directed the four rearmost blowers down a parallel street to block the rear. The searchlights of the vehicles chilled the flat concrete and glared back from the windows of the building. A battered surface truck was parked in the street outside. It was empty. Nothing stirred in the house.

Hammer and Steuben dismounted without haste. The major's helmet was slaved to a loudspeaker in the car. The speaker boomed, "Everyone out of the building. You have thirty seconds. Anyone found inside after that'll be shot. Thirty seconds!"

Though the residents had not shown themselves earlier, the way they boiled out of the doors proved they had expected the summons. All told there were eleven of them. From the front door came a well-dressed man and woman with their three children: a sexless infant carried by its mother in a zippered cocoon; a girl of eight with her hood down and her hair coiled in braids about her forehead; and a twelve-year-old boy who looked nearly as husky as his father. Outside staircases disgorged an aged couple on the one hand and four tough-looking men on the other.

Pritchard looked at his blower chief. The sergeant's right hand was near the gun switch and he mumbled an old ballad under his breath. Chest tightening, Pritchard climbed out of his hatch. He jumped to the ground and paced quietly over to Hammer and his aide.

"There's twenty-four pistols in this building," Joachim's amplified voice roared, "or at least you people know where they are. I want somebody to save trouble and tell me."

The civilians tensed. The mother half-turned to swing her body between her baby and the officers.

Joachim's pistol was in his hand, though Pritchard had not seen him draw it. "Nobody to speak?" Joachim queried. He shot the eight-year-old in the right knee. The spray of blood was momentary as the flesh exploded. The girl's mouth pursed as her buckling leg dropped her face-down in the street. The pain would come later. Her parents screamed, the father falling to his knees to snatch up the child as the mother pressed her forehead against the door jamb in blind panic.

Pritchard shouted, "You son of a bitch!" and clawed for his own sidearm. Steuben turned with the precision of a turret lathe. His pistol's muzzle was a white-hot ring from its previous discharge. Pritchard knew only that and the fact that his own weapon was not clear of its holster. Then he realized that Col. Hammer was shouting, *"No!"* and that his open hand had rocked Joachim's head back.

Joachim's face went pale except for the handprint burning on his cheek. His eyes were empty. After a moment, he holstered his weapon and turned back to the civilians. "Now, who'll tell us where the guns are?" he asked in a voice like breaking glassware.

The tear-blind woman, still holding her infant, gurgled, "Here! In the basement!" as she threw open the door. Two troopers followed her within at a nod from Hammer. The father was trying to close the girl's wounded leg with his hands, but his palms were not broad enough.

Pritchard vomited on the snowy street.

Margritte was out of the tank with a medikit in her hand. She flicked the civilian's hands aside and began freezing the wound with a spray. The front door banged open again. The two White Mice were back with their submachineguns slung under their arms and a heavy steel weapons-chest between them. Hammer nodded and walked to them.

"You could have brought in an interrogation team!" Pritchard shouted at the backs of his superiors. "You don't shoot children!"

"Machine interrogation takes time, Captain," Steuben said mildly. He did not turn to acknowledge the tanker. "This was just as effective."

"That's a little girl!" Pritchard insisted with his hand clenched. The child was beginning to cry, though the local anesthetic in the skin-sealer had probably blocked the physical pain. The psychic shock of a body that would soon end at the right knee would be worse, though. The child was old enough to know that no local doctor could save the limb. "This isn't something that human beings *do!*"

"Captain," Steuben said, "they're lucky I haven't shot all of them."

Hammer closed the arms chest. "We've got what we came for," he said. "Let's go."

"Stealing guns from my Colonel," the Newlander continued as if Hammer had not spoken. The handprint had faded to a dull blotch. "I really ought to—"

"Joachim, shut it off!" Hammer shouted. "We're going to talk about what happened tonight, you and I. I'd rather do it when we were alone —but I'll tell you now if I have to. Or in front of a court martial."

Steuben squeezed his forehead with the fingers of his left hand. He said nothing.

"Let's go," the Colonel repeated.

Pritchard caught Hammer's arm. "Take the kid back to Central's medics," he demanded.

Hammer blinked. "I should have thought of that," he said simply. "Some times I lose track of. . . . things that aren't going to shoot at me. But we don't need this sort of reputation."

"I don't care cop for public relations," Pritchard snapped. "Just save that little girl's leg."

Steuben reached for the child, now lying limp. Margritte had used a shot of general anesthetic. The girl's father went wild-eyed and swung at Joachim from his crouch. Margritte jabbed with the injector from behind the civilian. He gasped as the drug took hold, then sagged as if his bones had dissolved. Steuben picked up the girl.

Hammer vaulted aboard the combat car and took the child from his subordinate's arms. Cutting himself into the loudspeaker system, the stocky colonel thundered to the street, "Listen you people. If you take guns from mercs—either Barthe's men or my own—we'll grind you to dust. Take 'em from civilians if you think you can. You may have a chance, then. If you rob mercs, you just get a chance to die."

Hammer nodded to the civilians, nodded again to the brooding buildings to either side. He gave an unheard command to his driver. The combat cars began to rev their fans.

Pritchard gave Margritte a hand up and followed her. "Michael One to Michael First," he said. "Head back with Alpha First."

Pritchard rode inside the turret after they left Haacin, glad for once of the armor and the cabin lights. In the writhing tree-limbs he had seen the Dutch mother's face as the shot maimed her daughter.

Margritte passed only one call to her commander. It came shortly after the combat cars had separated to return to their base camp near Midi, the planetary capital. The Colonel's voice was as smooth as it ever got. It held no hint of the rage which had blazed out in Haacin. "Capt. Pritchard," Hammer said, "I've transferred command of Sigma Company to the leader of its First Platoon. The sector, of course, is in your hands now. I expect you to carry out your duties with the ability you've already shown."

"Michael One to Regiment," Pritchard replied curtly. "Acknowledged."

Kowie drew up in front of the command post without the furious caracole which had marked their most recent approach. Pritchard slid his hatch open. His crewmen did not move. "I've got to worry about being sector chief for a while," he said, "but you three can rack out in the barracks now. You've put in a full tour in my book."

"Think I'll sleep here," Rob said. He touched a stud, rotating his seat into a couch alongside the receiver and loading tube of the main gun.

Pritchard frowned. "Margritte?" he asked.

She shrugged. "No, I'll stay by my set for a while." Her eyes were blue and calm.

On the intercom, Kowie chimed in with, "Yeah, you worry about the sector, we'll worry about ourselves. Say, don't you think a tank platoon'd be better for base security than these pongoes?"

"Shut up, Kowie," Jenne snapped. The blond Burlager glanced at his captain. "Everything'll be fine, so long as we're here," he said from one elbow. He patted the breech of the 200 mm gun.

Pritchard shrugged and climbed out into the cold night. He heard the hatch grind shut behind him.

Until Pritchard walked in the door of the building, it had not occurred to him that Riis' replacement was Sally Schilling. The words "First Platoon leader" had not been a name to the tanker, not in the midst of the furor of his mind. The little blonde glanced up at Pritchard from the map display she was studying. She spat cracklingly on the electric stove and faced around again. Her aide, the big corporal, blinked in some embarrassment. None of the headquarters staff spoke.

"I need the display console from my room," Pritchard said to the corporal.

The infantryman nodded and got up. Before he had taken three steps, Lt. Schilling's voice cracked like pressure-heaved ice, "Cpl. Webbert!"

"Sir?" The big man's face went tight as he found himself a pawn in a game whose stakes went beyond his interest.

"Go get the display console for our new commander. It's in his room."

Licking his lips with relief, the corporal obeyed. He carried the heavy four-legged console back without effort.

Sally was making it easier for him, Pritchard thought. But how he wished that Riis hadn't made so complete a fool of himself that he had to be removed. Using Riis to set up a double massacre would have been a lot easier to justify when Danny awoke in the middle of the night and found himself remembering. . . .

Pritchard positioned the console so that he sat with his back to the heater. It separated him from Schilling. The top of the instrument was a slanted, 40 cm screen which glowed when Pritchard switched it on. "Sector Two display," he directed. In response to his words the screen sharpened into a relief map. "Population centers," he said. They flashed on as well, several dozen of them ranging from a few hundred souls to the several thousand of Haacin and Dimo. Portela, the largest Francophone settlement west of the Aillet, was about twenty kilometers west of Haacin.

And there were now French mercenaries on both sides of that division line. Sally had turned from her own console and stood up to see what Pritchard was doing. The tanker said, "All mercenary positions, confirmed and calculated."

The board spangled itself with red and green symbols, each of them marked in small letters with a unit designation. The reconnaissance satellites gave unit strengths very accurately, and computer analysis of radio traffic could generally name the forces. In the eastern half of the sector, Lt. Col. Benoit had spread out one battalion in platoon-strength billets. The guardposts were close enough to most points to put down trouble immediately. A full company near Dimo guarded the headquarters and two batteries of rocket howitzers.

The remaining battalion in the sector, Benoit's own, was concentrated in positions blasted into the rocky highlands ten kays west of Portela.

It was not a deployment that would allow the mercs to effectively police the west half of the sector, but it was a very good defensive arrangement. The forest that covered the center of the sector was ideal for hit-and-run sniping by small units of infantry. The tree boles were too densely woven for tanks to plow through them. Because the forest was so flammable at this season, however, it would be equally dangerous to ambushers. Benoit was wise to concentrate in the barren high-ground.

Besides the highlands, the fields cleared around every settlement were the only safe locations for a modern firefight. The fields, and the broad swathes cleared for roads through the forest. . . .

"Incoming traffic for Sector Chief," announced a radioman. "It's from the skepsel colonel, sir." He threw his words into the air, afraid to direct them at either of the officers in the orderly room.

"Voice only, or is there visual?" Pritchard asked. Schilling held her silence.

"Visual component, sir."

"Patch him through to my console," the tanker decided. "And son— watch your language. Otherwise, you say 'beast' when you shouldn't.''

The map blurred from the display screen and was replaced by the hawk features of Lt. Col. Benoit. A pick-up on the screen's surface threw Pritchard's own image onto Benoit's similar console.

The Frenchman blinked. "Capt. Pritchard? I'm very pleased to see you, but my words must be with Capt. Riis directly. Could you wake him?"

"There've been some changes," the tanker said. In the back of his mind, he wondered what had happened to Riis. Pulled back under arrest, probably. "I'm in charge of Sector Two, now. Co-charge with you, that is."

Benoit's face steadied as he absorbed the information without betraying an opinion about it. Then he beamed like a feasting wolf and said, "Congratulations, Captain. Some day you and I will have to discuss the . . . events of the past few days. But what I was calling about is far less pleasant, I'm afraid."

Benoit's image wavered on the screen as he paused. Pritchard touched his tongue to the corner of his mouth. "Go ahead, Colonel," he said. "I've gotten enough bad news today that a little more won't signify."

Benoit quirked his brow in what might or might not have been humor. "When we were proceeding to Portela," he said, "some of my troops mistook the situation and set up passive tank interdiction points. Mines, all over the sector. They're booby-trapped, of course. The only safe way to remove them is for the troops responsible to do it. They will of course be punished later."

Pritchard chuckled. "How long do you estimate it'll take to clear the roads, Colonel?" he asked.

The Frenchman spread his hands, palms up. "Weeks, perhaps. It's much harder to clear mines safely than to lay them, of course."

"But there wouldn't be anything between *here* and Haacin, would there?" the tanker prodded. It was all happening just as Hammer's informant had said Barthe planned it. First, hem the tanks in with nets of forest and minefields; then, break the most important Dutch stronghold while your mercs were still around to back you up. . . . "The spur road to our HQ here wasn't on your route; and besides, we just drove tanks over it a few minutes ago."

Behind Pritchard, Sally Schilling was cursing in a sharp, carrying voice. Benoit could probably hear her, but the colonel kept his voice as smooth as milk as he said, "Actually, I'm afraid there *is* a field—gas, shaped charges, and glass-shard antipersonnel mines—somewhere on that road, yes. Fortunately, the field was signal activated. It wasn't primed until after you had passed through. I assure you, Capt. Pritchard, that all the roads west of the Aillet may be too dangerous to traverse until I have cleared them. I warn you both as a friend and so that we will not be charged with damage to any of your vehicles—and men. You have been fully warned of the danger; anything that happens now is your responsibility."

Pritchard leaned back in the console's integral seat, chuckling again. "You know, Colonel," the tank captain said, "I'm not sure that the Bonding Authority wouldn't find those mines were a hostile act justifying our retaliation." Benoit stiffened, more an internal hardness than anything that showed in his muscles. Pritchard continued to speak through a smile. "We won't, of course. Mistakes happen. But one thing, Col. Benoit—"

The Frenchman nodded, waiting for the edge to bite. He knew as well as Pritchard did that, at best, if there were an Authority investigation, Barthe would have to throw a scapegoat out. A high-ranking scapegoat.

"Mistakes happen," Pritchard repeated, "but they can't be allowed to happen twice. You've got my permission to send out a ten-man team by daylight—only by daylight—to clear the road from Portela to Bever. That'll give you a route back to your side of the sector. If any other troops leave their present position, for any reason, I'll treat it as an attack."

"Captain, this demarcation within the sector was not part of the contract—"

"It was at the demand of Col. Barthe," Pritchard snapped, "and agreed to by the demonstrable practice of both regiments over the past three months." Hammer had briefed Pritchard very carefully on the words to use here, to be recorded for the benefit of the Bonding Authority. "You've heard the terms, Colonel. You can either take them or we'll put the whole thing—the minefields and some other matters that've come up recently—before the Authority right now. Your choice."

Benoit stared at Pritchard, apparently calm but tugging at his upper lip with thumb and forefinger. "I think you are unwise, Captain, in taking full responsibility for an area in which your tanks cannot move; but that is your affair, of course. I will obey your mandate. We should have the Portela-Haacin segment cleared by evening; tomorrow we'll proceed to Bever. Good day."

The screen segued back to the map display. Pritchard stood up. A spare helmet rested beside one of the radiomen. The tank captain donned it—he had forgotten to requisition a replacement from stores—and said, "Michael One to all Michael units." He paused for the acknowledgment lights from his four platoons and the command vehicle. Then, "Hold your present position. Don't attempt to move by road, any road, until further notice. The roads have been mined. There are probably safe areas, and we'll get you a map of them as soon as Command Central works it up. For the time being, just say where you are. Michael One, out."

"Are you really going to take that?" Lt. Schilling demanded in a low, harsh voice.

"Pass the same orders to your troops, Sally," Pritchard said. "I know they can move through the woods where my tanks can't, but I don't want any friendlies in the forest right now either." To the intelligence sergeant on watch, Pritchard added, "Samuels, get Central to run a plot of all activity by any of Benoit's men. That won't tell us where they've laid mines, but it'll let us know where they can't have."

"What happens if the bleeding skepsels ignore you?" Sally blazed. "You've bloody taught them to ignore you, haven't you? Knuckling under every time somebody whispers 'contract'? You can't move a tank to stop them if they do leave their base, and *I've* got 198 effectives. A battalion'd laugh at me, *laugh!*"

Schilling's arms were akimbo, her face as pale with rage as the snow outside. Speaking with deliberate calm, Pritchard said, "I'll call in artillery if I need to. Benoit only brought two calliopes with him, and they can't stop all the shells from three firebases at the same time. The road between his position and Portela's just a snake-track cut between rocks. A couple firecracker rounds going off above infantry, strung out there— Via, it'll be a butcher shop."

Schilling's eyes brightened. "Then for tonight, the sector's just like it was before we came," she thought out loud. "Well, I suppose you know best," she added in false agreement, with false nonchalance. "I'm going back to the barracks. I'll brief First Platoon in person and radio the others from there. Come along, Webbert."

The corporal slammed the door behind himself and his lieutenant. The gust of air that licked about the walls was cold, but Pritchard was already shivering at what he had just done to a woman he loved.

It was daylight by now, and the frosted windows turned to flame in the ruddy sun. Speaking to no one but his console's memory, Pritchard began to plot tracks from each tank platoon. He used a topographic display, ignoring the existence of the impenetrable forest which covered the ground.

Margritte's resonant voice twanged in the implant, "Captain, would you come to the blower for half a sec?"

"On the way," Pritchard said, shrugging into his coat. The orderly room staff glanced up at him.

Margritte poked her head out of the side hatch. Pritchard climbed onto the deck to avoid some of the generator whine. The skirts sang even when the fans were cut off completely. Rob Jenne, curious but at ease, was visible at his battle station beyond the commo tech. "Sir," Margritte said, "we've been picking up signals from—there." The blue-eyed woman thumbed briefly at the infantry barracks without letting her pupils follow the gesture.

Pritchard nodded. "Lt. Schilling's passing on my orders to her company."

"Danny, the transmission's in code, and it's not a code of ours." Margritte hesitated, then touched the back of the officer's gloved left hand. "There's answering signals, too. I can't triangulate without moving the blower, of course, but the source is in line with the tailings pile at Haacin."

It was what he had planned, after all. Someone the villagers could trust had to get word of the situation to them. Otherwise they wouldn't draw the Portelans and their mercenary backers into a fatal mistake. Hard luck for the villagers who were acting as bait, but very good for every other Dutchman on Kobold. . . . Pritchard had no reason to feel anything but relief that it had happened. He tried to relax the muscles which were crushing all the breath out of his lungs. Margritte's fingers closed over his hand and squeezed it.

"Ignore the signals," the captain said at last. "We've known all along they were talking to the civilians, haven't we?" Neither of his crewmen spoke. Pritchard's eyes closed tightly. He said, "We've known for months, Hammer and I, every damned thing that Barthe's been plotting with the skepsels. They want a chance to break Haacin now, while they're around to cover for the Portelans. We'll give them their chance and ram it up their ass crosswise. The Old Man hasn't spread the word for fear the story'd get out, the same way Barthe's plans did. We're all mercenaries, after all. But I want you three to know. And I'll be glad when the only thing I have to worry about is the direction the shots are coming from."

Abruptly, the captain dropped back to the ground. "Get some sleep," he called. "I'll be needing you sharp tonight."

Back at his console, Pritchard resumed plotting courses and distances. After he figured each line, he called in a series of map coordinates to Command Central. He knew his radio traffic was being monitored and probably unscrambled by Barthe's intelligence staff; knew also that even if he had read the coordinates out in clear, the French would have assumed it was a code. The locations made no sense unless one knew they were ground zero for incendiary shells.

As Pritchard worked, he kept close watch on the French battalions. Benoit's own troops held their position, as Pritchard had ordered. They used the time to dig in. At first they had blasted slit trenches in the rock. Now they dug covered bunkers with the help of mining machinery trucked from Portela by civilians. Five of the six anti-tank guns were sited atop the eastern ridge of the position. They could rake the highway as it snaked and switched back among the foothills west of Portela.

Pritchard chuckled grimly again when Sgt. Samuels handed him high-magnification offprints from the satellites. Benoit's two squat, bulky calliopes were sited in defilade behind the humps of the eastern ridge line. There the eight-barrelled powerguns were safe from the smashing fire of M Company's tanks, but their ability to sweep artillery shells from the sky was degraded by the closer horizon. The Slammers did not bother with calliopes themselves. Their central fire director did a far better job by working through the hundreds of vehicle-mounted weapons. How much better, Benoit might learn very shortly.

The mine-sweeping team cleared the Portela-Haacin road, as directed. The men returned to Benoit's encampment an hour before dusk. The French did not come within five kilometers of the Dutch village.

Pritchard watched the retiring mine sweepers, then snapped off the console. He stood. "I'm going out to my blower," he said.

His crew had been watching for him. A hatch shot open, spouting condensate, as soon as Pritchard came out the door. The smooth bulk of the tank blew like a restive whale. On the horizon, the sun was so low that the treetops stood out in silhouette like a line of bayonets.

Wearily, the captain dropped through the hatch into his seat. Jenne and Margritte murmured greeting and waited, noticeably tense. "I'm going to get a couple hours' sleep," Pritchard said. He swung his seat out and up, so that he lay horizontal in the turret. His legs hid Margritte's oval face from him. "Punch up coverage of the road west of

Haacin, would you?" he asked. "I'm going to take a tab of Glirine. Slap me with the antidote when something moves there."

"If something moves," Jenne amended.

"When." Pritchard sucked down the pill. "The squareheads think they've got one last chance to smack Portela and hijack the powerguns again. Thing is, the Portelans'll have already distributed the guns and be waiting for the Dutch to come through. It'll be a damn short fight, that one...." The drug took hold and Pritchard's consciousness began to flow away like a sugar cube in water. "Damn short...."

At first Pritchard felt only the sting on the inside of his wrist. Then the narcotic haze ripped away and he was fully conscious again.

"There a line of trucks, looks like twenty, moving west out of Haacin, sir. They're blacked out, but the satellite has 'em on infra-red."

"Red alert," Pritchard ordered. He locked his seat upright into its combat position. Margritte's soft voice sounded the general alarm. Pritchard slipped on his radio helmet. "Michael One to all Michael units. Check off." Five green lights flashed their silent acknowledgements across the top of the captain's face-shield display. "Michael One to Sigma One," Pritchard continued.

"Go ahead, Michael One," Sally's voice held a note of triumph.

"Sigma One, pull all your troops into large, clear areas—the fields around the towns are fine, but stay the hell away from Portela and Haacin. Get ready to slow down anybody coming this way from across the Aillet. Over."

"Affirmative, Danny, affirmative!" Sally replied. Couldn't she use the satellite reconnaissance herself and see the five blurred dots halfway between the villages? They were clearly the trucks which had brought the Portelans into their ambush positions. What would she say when she realized how she had set up the villagers she was trying to protect? Lambs to the slaughter....

The vision block showed the Dutch trucks more clearly than the camouflaged Portelans. The crushed stone of the roadway was dark on the screen, cooler than the surrounding trees and the vehicles upon it. Pritchard patted the breech of the main gun and looked across it to his blower chief. "We got a basic load for this aboard?" he asked.

"Do bears cop in the woods?" Jenne grinned. "We gonna get a chance to bust caps tonight, Captain?"

Pritchard nodded. "For three months we've been here, doing nothing but selling rope to the French. Tonight they've bought enough that we can hang 'em with it." He looked at the vision block again. "You alive, Kowie?" he asked on intercom.

"Ready to slide any time you give me a course," said the driver from his closed cockpit.

The vision block sizzled with bright streaks that seemed to hang on the screen though they had passed in microseconds. The leading blobs expanded and brightened as trucks blew up.

"Michael One to Fire Central," Pritchard said.

"Go ahead, Michael One," replied the machine voice.

"Prepare Fire Order Alpha."

"Roger, Michael One."

"Margritte, get me Benoit."

"Go ahead, Captain."

"Slammers to Benoit. Pritchard to Benoit. Come in please, Colonel."

"Capt. Pritchard, Michel Benoit here." The colonel's voice was smooth but too hurried to disguise the concern underlying it. "I assure you that none of my men are involved in the present fighting. I have a company ready to go out and control the disturbance immediately, however."

The tanker ignored him. The shooting had already stopped for lack of targets. "Colonel, I've got some artillery aimed to drop various places in the forest. It's coming nowhere near your troops or any other human beings. If you interfere with this necessary shelling, the Slammer'll treat it as an act of war. I speak with my colonel's authority."

"Captain, I don't—"

Pritchard switched manually. "Michael One to Fire Central. Execute Fire Order Alpha."

"On the way, Michael One."

"Michael One to Michael First, Second, Fourth. Command Central has fed movement orders into your map displays. Incendiary clusters are going to burst over marked locations to ignite the forest. Use your own main guns to set the trees burning in front of your immediate positions. One round ought to do it. Button up and you can move through the fire—the trees just fall to pieces when they've burned.

The turret whined as it slid under Rob's control. "Michael Third, I'm attaching you to the infantry. More Frenchmen're apt to be coming this way from the east. It's up to you to see they don't slam a door on us."

The main gun fired, its discharge so sudden that the air rang like a solid thing. Seepage from the ejection system filled the hull with the reek of superheated polyurethane. The side vision blocks flashed cyan, then began to flood with the mounting white hell-light of the blazing trees. In the central block, still set on remote, all the Dutch trucks were burning as were patches of forest which the ambush had ignited. The Portelans had left the concealment of the trees and swept across the road, mopping up the Dutch.

"Kowie, let's move," Jenne was saying on intercom, syncopated by the mild echo of his voice in the turret. Margritte's face was calm, her lips moving subtly as she handled some traffic that she did not pass on to her captain. The tank slid forward like oil on a lake. From the far distance came the thumps of incendiary rounds scattering their hundreds of separate fireballs high over the trees.

Pritchard slapped the central vision block back on direct; the tank's interior shone white with transmitted fire. The Plow's bow slope sheared into a thicket of blazing trees. The wood tangled and sagged, then gave in a splash of fiery splinters whipped aloft by the blower's fans. The tank was in Hell on all sides, Kowie steering by instinct and his inertial compass. Even with his screens filtered all the way down, the driver would not be able to use his eyes effectively until more of the labyrinth had burned away.

Benoit's calliopes had not tried to stop the shelling. Well, there were other ways to get the French mercs to take the first step over the line. For instance—

"Punch up Benoit again," Pritchard ordered. Even through the dense iridium plating, the roar of the fire was a subaural presence in the tank.

"Go ahead," Margritte said, flipping a switch on her console. She had somehow been holding the French officer in conversation all the time Pritchard was on other frequencies.

"Colonel," Pritchard said, "we've got clear running through this fire. We're going to chase down everybody who used a powergun tonight; then we'll shoot them. We'll shoot everybody in their families, everybody with them in this ambush, and we'll blow up every house that anybody involved lived in. That's likely to be every house in Portela, isn't it?"

More than the heat and ions of the blazing forest distorted Benoit's face. He shouted, "Are you mad? You can't think of such a thing, Pritchard!"

The tanker's lips parted like a wolf's. He could think of mass murder, and there were plenty of men in the Slammers who would really be willing to carry out the threat. But Pritchard wouldn't have to, because Benoit was like Riis and Schilling: too much of a nationalist to remember his first duty as a merc. . . . "Col. Benoit, the contract demands we keep the peace and stay impartial. The record shows how we treated people in Haacin for *having* powerguns. For what the Portelans did tonight—don't worry, we'll be impartial. And they'll never break the peace again."

"Captain, I will not allow you to massacre French civilians," Benoit stated flatly.

"Move a man out of your present positions and I'll shoot him dead," Pritchard said. "It's your choice, Colonel. Over and out."

The Plow bucked and rolled as it pulverized fire-shattered trunks, but the vehicle was meeting nothing solid enough to slam it to a halt. Pritchard used a side block on remote to examine Benoit's encampment.

The satellite's enhanced infra-red showed a stream of sparks flowing from the defensive positions toward the Portela road: infantry on skimmers. The pair of larger, more diffuse blobs were probably anti-tank guns. Benoit wasn't moving his whole battalion, only a reinforced company in a show of force to make Pritchard back off.

The fool. Nobody was going to back off now.

"Michael One to all Michael and Sigma units," Pritchard said in a voice as clear as the white flames around his tank. "We're now in a state of war with Barthe's Company and its civilian auxiliaries. Michael First, Second and Fourth, we'll rendezvous at the ambush site as plotted on your displays. Anybody between there and Portela is fair game. If we take any fire from Portela, we go down the main drag in line and blow the cop out of it. If any of Barthe's people are in the way, we keep on sliding west. Sigma One, mount a fluid defense, don't push, and wait for help. It's coming. If this works, it's Barthe against Hammer—and that's wheat against the scythe. Acknowledged?"

As Pritchard's call board lit green, a raspy new voice broke into the sector frequency. "Wish I was with you, panzers. We'll cover your butts and the other sectors—if anybody's dumb enough to move. Good hunting!"

"I wish you *were* here and not me, Colonel," Pritchard whispered, but that was to himself . . . and perhaps it was not true even in his heart. Danny's guts were very cold, and his face was as cold as death.

To Pritchard's left, a lighted display segregated the area of operations. It was a computer analog, not direct satellite coverage. Doubtful images were brightened and labeled—green for the Slammers, red for Barthe; blue for civilians unless they were fighting on one side or the other. The green dot of The Plow converged on the ambush site at the same time as the columns of First and Fourth Platoons. Second was a minute or two farther off. Pritchard's breath caught. A sheaf of narrow red lines was streaking across the display toward his tanks. Barthe had ordered his Company's artillery to support Benoit's threatened battalion.

The salvo frayed and vanished more suddenly than it had appeared. Other Slammers' vehicles had ripped the threat from the sky. Green lines darted from Hammer's own three firebases, offscreen at the analog's present scale. The fighting was no longer limited to Sector Two. If Pritchard and Hammer had played their hand right, though, it would stay limited to only the Slammers and Compagnie de Barthe. The other Francophone regiments would fear to join an unexpected battle which certainly resulted from someone's contract violation. If the breach were Hammer's, the Dutch would not be allowed to profit by the fighting. If the breach were Barthe's, anybody who joined him was apt to be punished as sternly by the Bonding Authority.

So violent was the forest's combustion that the flames were already dying down into sparks and black ashes. The command tank growled out into the broad avenue of the road west of Haacin. Dutch trucks were still burning—fabric, lubricants, and the very paint of their frames had been ignited by the powerguns. Many of the bodies sprawled beside the vehicles were smouldering also. Some corpses still clutched their useless muskets. The dead were victims of six centuries of progress which had come to Kobold pre-packaged, just in time to kill them. Barthe had given the Portelans only shoulder weapons, but even that meant the world here. The powerguns were repeaters with awesome destruction in every bolt. Without answering fire to rattle them, even untrained gunmen could be effective with weapons which shot line-straight and had no recoil. Certainly the Portelans had been effective.

Throwing ash and fire like sharks in the surf, the four behemoths of First Platoon slewed onto the road from the south. Almost simultaneously, Fourth joined through the dying hellstorm to the other side. The right of way was fifty meters wide and there was no reason to keep to the center of it. The forest, ablaze or glowing embers, held no ambushes any more.

The Plow lurched as Kowie guided it through the bodies. Some of them were still moving. Pritchard wondered if any of the Dutch had lived through the night, but that was with the back of his mind. The Slammers were at war, and nothing else really mattered. "Triple line ahead," he ordered. "First to the left, Fourth to the right; The Plow'll take the center alone till Second joins. Second, wick up when you hit the hardball and fall in behind us. If it moves, shoot it."

At 100 kph, the leading tanks caught the Portelans three kilometers east of their village. The settlers were in the trucks that had been hidden in the forest fringe until the fires had been started. The ambushers may not have known they were being pursued until the rearmost truck exploded. Rob Jenne had shredded it with his tribarrel at five kilometers' distance. The cyan flicker and its answering orange blast signaled the flanking tanks to fire. They had just enough parallax to be able to rake the four remaining trucks without being blocked by the one which had blown up. A few snapping discharges proved that some Portelans survived to use their new powerguns on tougher meat than before. Hits streaked ashes on the tanks' armor. No one inside noticed.

From Portela's eastern windows, children watched their parents burn.

A hose of cyan light played from a distant roof top. It touched the command tank as Kowie slewed to avoid a Portelan truck. The burst was perfectly aimed, an automatic weapon served by professionals. Professionals should have known how useless it would be against heavy armor. A vision block dulled as a few receptors fused. Jenne cursed and trod the foot-switch of the main gun. A building leaped into dazzling prominence in the microsecond flash. Then it and most of the block behind collapsed into internal fires, burying the machinegun and everything else in the neighborhood. A moment later, a salvo of Hammer's high explosive got through the calliopes' inadequate screen. The village began to spew skyward in white flashes.

The Portelans had wanted to play soldier, Pritchard thought. He had dammed up all pity for the villagers of Haacin; he would not spend it now on these folk.

"Line ahead—First, Fourth, and Second," Pritchard ordered. The triple column slowed and reformed with The Plow the second vehicle in the new line. The shelling lifted from Portela as the tanks plunged into the village. Green trails on the analog terminated over the road crowded with Benoit's men and over the main French position, despite anything the calliopes could do. The sky over Benoit's bunkers rippled and flared as firecracker rounds sleeted down their thousands of individual bomblets. The defensive fire cut off entirely. Pritchard could imagine the carnage among the unprotected calliope crews when the shrapnel whirred through them.

The tanks were firing into the houses on either side, using tribarrels and occasional wallops from their main guns. The blue-green flashes were so intense they colored even the flames they lit among the wreckage. At 50 kph the thirteen tanks swept through the center of town, hindered only by the rubble of houses spilled across the street. Barthe's men were skittering white shadows who burst when powerguns hit them point blank.

The copper mine was just west of the village and three hundred meters north of the highway. As the lead tank bellowed out around the last houses, a dozen infantrymen rose from where they had sheltered in the pit head and loosed a salvo of buzzbombs. The tank's automatic defense system was live. White fire rippled from just above the skirts as the charges there flailed pellets outward to intersect the rockets. Most of the buzzbombs exploded ten meters distant against the steel hail. One missile soared harmlessly over its target, its motor a tiny flare against the flickering sky. Only one of the shaped charges burst alongside the turret, forming a bell of light momentarily bigger than the tank. Even that was only a near miss. It gouged the iridium armor like a misthrust rapier which tears skin but does not pierce the skull.

Main guns and tribarrels answered the rockets instantly. Men dropped, some dead, some reloading. "Second Platoon, go put some HE down the shaft and rejoin," Pritchard ordered. The lead tank now had expended half its defensive charges. "Michael First-Three, fall in behind First-One. Michael One leads," he went on.

Kowie grunted acknowledgement. The Plow revved up to full honk. Benoit's men were on the road, those who had not reached Portela when the shooting started or who had fled when the artillery churned the houses to froth. The infantry skimmers were trapped between sheer rocks and sheer drop-offs, between their own slow speed and the onrushing frontal slope of The Plow. There were trees where the rocks had given them purchase. Scattered incendiaries had made them blazing cressets lighting a charnel procession.

Jenne's tribarrel scythed through body armor and dismembered men in short bursts. One of the anti-tank guns—was the other buried in Portela?—lay skewed against a rock wall, its driver killed by a shell fragment. Rob put a round from the main gun into it. So did each of the next two tanks. At the third shot, the ammunition ignited in a blinding secondary explosion.

The anti-tank guns still emplaced on the ridge line had not fired, though they swept several stretches of the road. Perhaps the crews had been rattled by the shelling, perhaps Benoit had held his fire for fear of hitting his own men. A narrow defile notched the final ridge. The Plow heaved itself up the rise, and at the top three bolts slapped it from different angles.

Because the bow was lifted, two of the shots vaporized portions of the skirt and the front fans. The tank nosed down and sprayed sparks with half its length. The third bolt grazed the left top of the turret, making the iridium ring as it expanded. The interior of the armor streaked white though it was not pierced. The temperature inside the tank rose 30°. Even as The Plow skidded, Sgt. Jenne was laying his main gun on the hot spot that was the barrel of the leftmost anti-tank weapon. The Plow's shot did what heavy top cover had prevented Hammer's rocket howitzers from accomplishing with shrapnel. The anti-tank gun blew up in a distance-muffled flash. One of its crewmen was silhouetted high in the air by the vaporizing metal of his gun.

Then the two remaining weapons ripped the night and the command blower with their charges.

The bolt that touched the right side of the turret spewed droplets of iridium across the interior of the hull. Air pistoned Pritchard's eardrums. Rob Jenne lurched in his harness, right arm burned away by the shot. His left hand blackened where it touched bare metal that sparked and sang as circuits shorted. Margritte's radios were exploding one by one under the overloads. The vision blocks worked and the turret hummed placidly as Pritchard rotated it to the right with his duplicate controls.

"Cut the power! Rob's burning!" Margritte was shrieking. She had torn off her helmet. Her thick hair stood out like tendrils of bread mold in the gathering charge. Then Pritchard had the main gun bearing and it lit the ridge line with another secondary explosion.

"Danny, our ammunition! It'll—"

Benoit's remaining gun blew the tribarrel and the cupola away deafeningly. The automatic's loading tube began to gang-fire down into the bowels of the tank. It reached a bright tendril up into the sky. But the turret still rolled.

Electricity crackled around Pritchard's boot and the foot trip as he fired again. The bolt stabbed the night. There was no answering blast. Pritchard held down the switch, his nostrils thick with ozone and super-heated plastic and the sizzling flesh of his friend. There was still no explosion from the target bunker. The rock turned white between the cyan flashes. It cracked and flowed away like sun-melted snow, and the anti-tank gun never fired again.

The loading tube emptied. Pritchard slapped the main switch and cut off the current. The interior light and the dancing arcs died, leaving only the dying glow of the bolt-heated iridium. Tank after tank edged by the silent command vehicle and roared on toward the ridge. Benoit's demoralized men were already beginning to throw down their weapons and surrender.

Pritchard manually unlatched Jenne's harness and swung it horizontal. The blower chief was breathing but unconscious. Pritchard switched on a battery-powered handlight. He held it steady as Margritte began to spray sealant on the burns. Occasionally she paused to separate clothing from flesh with a stylus.

"It had to be done," Pritchard whispered. By sacrificing Haacin, he had mousetrapped Benoit into starting a war the infantry could not win. Hammer was now crushing Barthe's Company, one on one, in an iridium vise. Friesland's Council of State would not have let Hammer act had they known his intentions, but in the face of a stunning victory they simply could not avoid dictating terms to the French.

"It had to be done. But I look at *what* I did—" Pritchard swung his right hand in a gesture that would have included both the fuming wreck of Portela and the raiders from Haacin, dead on the road beyond. He struck the breech of the main gun instead. Clenching his fist, he slammed it again into the metal in self-punishment. Margritte cried out and blocked his arm with her own.

"Margi," Pritchard repeated in anguish, "it isn't something that human beings *do* to each other."

But soldiers do.

And hangmen.

KEITH LAUMER

THE NIGHT OF THE TROLLS

1   IT WAS different this time. There was a dry pain in my lungs, and a deep ache in my bones, and a fire in my stomach that made me want to curl into a ball and mew like a kitten. My mouth tasted as though mice had nested in it, and when I took a deep breath wooden knives twisted in my chest.

I made a mental note to tell Mackenzie a few things about his pet controlled-environment tank—just as soon as I got out of it. I squinted at the over-face panel: air pressure, temperature, humidity, O-level, blood sugar, pulse, and respiration—all okay. That was something. I flipped the intercom key and said, "Okay, Mackenzie, let's have the story. You've got problems. . . ."

I had to stop to cough. The exertion made my temples pound.

"How long have you birds run this damned exercise?" I called. "I feel lousy. What's going on around here?"

No answer.

This was supposed to be the terminal test series. They couldn't all be out having coffee. The equipment had more bugs than a two-dollar hotel room. I slapped the emergency release lever. Mackenzie wouldn't like it, but to hell with it! From the way I felt, I'd been in the tank for a good long stretch this time—maybe a week or two. And I'd told Ginny it would be a three-dayer at the most. Mackenzie was a great technician, but he had no more human emotions than a used-car salesman. This time I'd tell him.

235

Relays were clicking, equipment was reacting, the tank cover sliding back. I sat up and swung my legs aside, shivering suddenly.

It was cold in the test chamber. I looked around at the dull gray walls, the data recording cabinets, the wooden desk where Mac sat by the hour rerunning test profiles—

That was funny. The tape reels were empty and the red equipment light was off. I stood, feeling dizzy. Where was Mac? Where were Bonner and Day and Mallon?

"Hey!" I called. I didn't even get a good echo.

Someone must have pushed the button to start my recovery cycle; where were they hiding now? I took a step, tripped over the cables trailing behind me. I unstrapped and pulled the harness off. The effort left me breathing hard. I opened one of the wall lockers; Banner's pressure suit hung limply from the rack beside a rag-festooned coat hanger. I looked in three more lockers. My clothes were missing—even my bathrobe. I also missed the usual bowl of hot soup, the happy faces of the techs, even Mac's sour puss. It was cold and silent and empty here —more like a morgue than a top-priority research center.

I didn't like it. What the hell was going on?

There was a weather suit in the last locker. I put it on, set the temperature control, palmed the door open, and stepped out into the corridor. There were no lights, except for the dim glow of the emergency route indicators. There was a faint, foul odor in the air.

I heard a dry scuttling, saw a flick of movement. A rat the size of a red squirrel sat up on his haunches and looked at me as if I were something to eat. I made a kicking motion and he ran off, but not very far.

My heart was starting to thump a little harder now. The way it does when you begin to realize that something's wrong—bad wrong.

Upstairs in the Admin Section I called again. The echo was a little better here. I went along the corridor strewn with papers, past the open doors of silent rooms. In the Director's office a blackened wastebasket stood in the center of the rug. The air-conditioner intake above the desk was felted over with matted dust nearly an inch thick. There was no use shouting again.

The place was as empty as a robbed grave—except for the rats.

At the end of the corridor, the inner security door stood open. I went through it and stumbled over something. In the faint light, it took me a moment to realize what it was.

He had been an MP, in steel helmet and boots. There was nothing left but crumbled bone and a few scraps of leather and metal. A .38 revolver lay nearby. I picked it up, checked the cylinder, and tucked it in the thigh pocket of the weather suit. For some reason it made me feel a little better.

I went on along B corridor and found the lift door sealed. The emergency stairs were nearby. I went to them and started the two-hundred-foot climb to the surface.

The heavy steel doors at the tunnel had been blown clear.

I stepped past the charred opening, looked out at a low gray sky burning red in the west. Fifty yards away, the five-thousand-gallon water tank lay in a tangle of rusty steel. What had it been? Sabotage, war, revolution—an accident? And where was everybody?

I rested for a while, then went across the innocent-looking fields to the west, dotted with the dummy buildings that were supposed to make the site look from the air like another stretch of farmland complete with barns, sheds and fences. Beyond the site the town seemed intact: there were lights twinkling here and there, a few smudges of smoke rising. I climbed a heap of rubble for a better view.

Whatever had happened at the site, at least Ginny would be all right —Ginny and Tim. Ginny would be worried sick, after—how long? A month?

Maybe more. There hadn't been much left of that soldier. . . .

I twisted to get a view to the south, and felt a hollow sensation in my chest. Four silo doors stood open; the Colossus missiles had hit back— at something. I pulled myself up a foot or two higher for a look at the Primary Site. In the twilight the ground rolled smooth and unbroken across the spot where *Prometheus* lay ready in her underground berth. Down below she'd be safe and sound, maybe. She had been built to stand up to the stresses of a direct extra-solar orbital launch; with any luck, a few near misses wouldn't have damaged her.

My arms were aching from the strain of holding on. I climbed down and sat on the ground to get my breath, watching the cold wind worry the dry stalks of dead brush around the fallen tank.

At home, Ginny would be alone, scared, maybe even in serious difficulty. There was no telling how far municipal services had broken down. But before I headed that way, I had to make a quick check on the ship. *Prometheus* was a dream that I—and a lot of others—had lived with for three years. I had to be sure.

I headed toward the pillbox that housed the tunnel head on the off chance that the car might be there.

It was almost dark and the going was tough; the concrete slabs under the sod were tilted and dislocated. Something had sent a ripple across the ground like a stone tossed into a pond.

I heard a sound and stopped dead. There was a clank and rumble from beyond the discolored walls of the blockhouse a hundred yards away. Rusted metal howled; then something as big as a beached freighter moved into view.

Two dull red beams glowing near the top of the high silhouette swung, flashed crimson, and held on me. A siren went off—an ear-splitting whoop! *whoop!* WHOOP!

It was an unmanned Bolo Mark II Combat Unit on automated sentry duty—and its intruder-sensing circuits were tracking me.

The Bolo pivoted heavily; the *whoop! whoop!* sounded again; the robot watchdog was bellowing the alarm.

I felt sweat pop out on my forehead. Standing up to a Mark II Bolo without an electropass was the rough equivalent of being penned in with an ill-tempered dinosaur. I looked toward the Primary blockhouse: too far. The same went for the perimeter fence. My best bet was back to the tunnel mouth. I turned to sprint for it, hooked a foot on a slab and went down hard. . . .

I got up, my head ringing, tasting blood in my mouth. The chipped pavement seemed to rock under me. The Bolo was coming up fast. Running was no good. I had to have a better idea.

I dropped flat and switched my suit control to maximum insulation.

The silvery surface faded to dull black. A two-foot square of tattered paper fluttered against a projecting edge of concrete; I reached for it, peeled it free, then fumbled with a pocket flap, brought out a permatch, flicked it alight. When the paper was burning well, I tossed it clear. It whirled away a few feet, then caught in a clump of grass.

"Keep moving, damn you!" I whispered. The swearing worked. The gusty wind pushed the paper on. I crawled a few feet and pressed myself into a shallow depression behind the slab. The Bolo churned closer; a loose treadplate was slapping the earth with a rhythmic thud. The burning paper was fifty feet away now, a twinkle of orange light in the deep twilight.

At twenty yards, looming up like a pagoda, the Bolo halted, sat rumbling and swiveling its rust-streaked turret, looking for the radiating source its I-R had first picked up. The flare of the paper caught its electronic attention. The turret swung, then back. It was puzzled. It whooped again, then reached a decision.

Ports snapped open. A volley of antipersonnel slugs whoofed into the target; the scrap of paper disappeared in a gout of tossed dirt.

I hugged the ground like gold lamé hugs a torch singer's hip, and waited; nothing happened. The Bolo sat, rumbling softly to itself. Then I heard another sound over the murmur of the idling engine, a distant roaring, like a flight of low-level bombers. I raised my head half an inch and took a look. There were lights moving beyond the field—the paired beams of a convoy approaching from the town.

The Bolo stirred, moved heavily forward until it towered over me no more than twenty feet away. I saw gun ports open high on the armored facade—the ones that housed the heavy infinite repeaters. Slim black muzzles slid into view, hunted for an instant, then depressed and locked.

They were bearing on the oncoming vehicles that were spreading out now in a loose skirmish line under a roiling layer of dust. The watchdog was getting ready to defend its territory—and I was caught in the middle. A blue-white floodlight lanced out from across the field, glared against the scaled plating of the Bolo. I heard relays click inside the monster fighting machine, and braced myself for the thunder of her battery. . . .

There was a dry rattle.

The guns traversed, clattering emptily. Beyond the fence the floodlight played for a moment longer against the Bolo, then moved on across the ramp, back, across and back, searching. . . .

Once more the Bolo fired its empty guns. Its red I-R beams swept the scene again; then relays snicked, the impotent guns retracted, the port covers closed.

Satisfied, the Bolo heaved itself around and moved off, trailing a stink of ozone and ether, the broken tread thumping like a cripple on a stair.

I waited until it disappeared in the gloom two hundred yards away, then cautiously turned my suit control to vent off the heat. Full insulation could boil a man in his own gravy in less than half an hour.

The floodlight had blinked off now. I got to my hands and knees and started toward the perimeter fence. The Bolo's circuits weren't tuned as fine as they should have been; it let me go.

There were men moving in the glare and dust, beyond the rusty lacework that had once been a chain-link fence. They carried guns and stood in tight little groups, staring across toward the blockhouse.

I moved closer, keeping flat and avoiding the avenues of yellowish light thrown by the headlamps of the parked vehicles—halftracks, armored cars, a few light manned tanks.

There was nothing about the look of this crowd that impelled me to leap up and be welcomed. They wore green uniforms, and half of them sported beards. What the hell: had Castro landed in force?

I angled off to the right, away from the big main gate that had been manned day and night by guards with tommy guns. It hung now by one hinge from a scarred concrete post, under a cluster of dead polyarcs in corroded brackets. The big sign that had read GLENN AEROSPACE CENTER—AUTHORIZED PERSONNEL ONLY lay face down in hip-high underbrush.

More cars were coming up. There was a lot of talk and shouting; a squad of men formed and headed my way, keeping to the outside of the fallen fence.

I was outside the glare of the lights now. I chanced a run for it, got over the sagged wire and across a potholed blacktop road before they reached me. I crouched in the ditch and watched as the detail dropped men in pairs at fifty-yard interals.

Another five minutes and they would have intercepted me—along with whatever else they were after. I worked my way back across an empty lot and found a strip of lesser underbrush lined with shaggy trees, beneath which a patch of cracked sidewalk showed here and there.

Several things were beginning to be a little clearer now: The person who had pushed the button to bring me out of stasis hadn't been around to greet me, because no one pushed it. The automatics, triggered by some malfunction, had initiated the recovery cycle.

The system's self-contained power unit had been designed to maintain a starship crewman's minimal vital functions indefinitely, at reduced body temperature and metabolic rate. There was no way to tell exactly how long I had been in the tank. From the condition of the fence and the roads, it had been more than a matter of weeks—or even months.

Had it been a year . . . or more? I thought of Ginny and the boy, waiting at home—thinking the old man was dead, probably. I'd neglected them before for my work, but not like this. . . .

Our house was six miles from the base, in the foothills on the other side of town. It was a long walk, the way I felt—but I had to get there.

2   Two hours later I was clear of the town, following the river bank west.

I kept having the idea that someone was following me. But when I stopped to listen, there was never anything there; just the still, cold night and the frogs, singing away patiently in the low ground to the south.

When the ground began to rise, I left the road and struck off across the open field. I reached a wide street, followed it in a curve that would bring me out at the foot of Ridge Avenue—my street. I could make out the shapes of low, rambling houses now.

It had been the kind of residential section the local Junior Chamber members had hoped to move into some day. Now the starlight that filtered through the cloud cover showed me broken windows, doors that sagged open, automobiles that squatted on flat, dead tires under collapsing car shelters—and here and there a blackened, weed-grown foundation, like a gap in a row of rotting teeth.

The neighborhood wasn't what it had been. How long had I been away? How long . . . ?

I fell down again, hard this time. It wasn't easy getting up. I seemed to weigh a hell of a lot for a guy who hadn't been eating regularly. My breathing was very fast and shallow now, and my skull was getting ready to split and give birth to a live alligator—the ill-tempered kind. It was only a few hundred yards more; but why the hell had I picked a place halfway up a hill?

I heard the sound again—a crackle of dry grass. I got the pistol out and stood flatfooted in the middle of the street, listening hard.

All I heard was my stomach growling. I took the pistol off cock and started off again, stopped suddenly a couple of times to catch him off guard; nothing. I reached the corner of Ridge Avenue, started up the slope. Behind me a stick popped loudly.

I picked that moment to fall down again. Heaped leaves saved me from another skinned knee. I rolled over against a low fieldstone wall and propped myself against it. I had to use both hands to cock the pistol. I stared into the dark, but all I could see were the little lights whirling again. The pistol got heavy; I put it down, concentrated on taking deep breaths and blinking away the fireflies.

I heard footsteps plainly, close by. I shook my head, accidentally banged it against the stone behind me. That helped. I saw him, not over twenty feet away, coming up the hill toward me, a black-haired man with a full beard, dressed in odds and ends of rags and furs, gripping a polished club with a leather thong.

I reached for the pistol, found only leaves, tried again, touched the gun and knocked it away. I was still groping when I heard a scuffle of feet. I swung around, saw a tall, wide figure with a mane of untrimmed hair.

He hit the bearded man like a pro tackle taking out the practice dummy. They went down together hard and rolled over in a flurry of dry leaves. The cats were fighting over the mouse; that was my signal to leave quietly.

I made one last grab for the gun, found it, got to my feet and staggered off up the grade that seemed as steep now as penthouse rent. And from down slope, I heard an engine gunned, the clash of a heavy transmission that needed adjustment. A spotlight flickered, made shadows dance.

I recognized a fancy wrought-iron fence fronting a vacant lot; that had been the Adams house. Only half a block to go—but I was losing my grip fast. I went down twice more, then gave up and started crawling. The lights were all around now, brighter than ever. My head split open, dropped off, and rolled downhill.

A few more yards and I could let it all go. Ginny would put me in a warm bed, patch up my scratches, and feed me soup. Ginny would. . . . Ginny. . . .

* * *

I was lying with my mouth full of dead leaves. I heard running feet, yells. An engine idled noisily down the block.

I got my head up and found myself looking at chipped brickwork and the heavy brass hinges from which my front gate had hung. The gate was gone and there was a large chunk of brick missing. Some delivery truck had missed his approach.

I got to my feet, took a couple of steps into deep shadow with feet that felt as though they'd been amputated and welded back on at the ankle. I stumbled, fetched up against something scaled over with rust. I held on, blinked and made out the seeping flank of my brand new '79 Pontiac. There was a crumbled crust of whitish glass lining the brightwork strip that had framed the rear window.

A fire. . . . ?

A footstep sounded behind me, and I suddenly remembered several things, none of them pleasant. I felt for my gun; it was gone. I moved back along the side of the car, tried to hold on.

No use. My arms were like unsuccessful pie crust. I slid down among dead leaves, sat listening to the steps coming closer. They stopped, and through a dense fog that had sprung up suddenly I caught a glimpse of a tall white-haired figure standing over me.

Then the fog closed in and swept everything away.

I lay on my back this time, looking across at the smoky yellow light of a thick brown candle guttering in the draft from a glassless window. In the center of the room a few sticks of damp-looking wood heaped on the cracked asphalt tiles burned with a grayish flame. A thin curl of acrid smoke rose up to stir cobwebs festooned under ceiling beams from which wood veneer had peeled away. Light alloy trusswork showed beneath.

It was a strange scene, but not so strange that I didn't recognize it: it was my own living room—looking a little different than when I had seen it last. The odors were different, too; I picked out mildew, badly cured leather, damp wool, tobacco. . . .

I turned my head. A yard from the rags I lay on, the white-haired man, looking older than pharaoh, sat sleeping with his back against the wall.

The shotgun was gripped in one big, gnarled hand. His head was tilted back, blue-veined eyelids shut. I sat up, and at my movement his eyes opened.

He lay relaxed for a moment, as though life had to return from some place far away. Then he raised his head. His face was hollow and lined. His white hair was thin. A coarse-woven shirt hung loose across wide shoulders that had been Herculean once. But now Hercules was old, old. He looked at me expectantly.

"Who are you?" I said. "Why did you follow me? What happened to the house? Where's my family? Who owns the bully-boys in green?" My jaw hurt when I spoke. I put my hand up and felt it gingerly.

"You fell," the old man said, in a voice that rumbled like a subterranean volcano.

"The understatement of the year, pop." I tried to get up. Nausea knotted my stomach.

"You have to rest," the old man said, looking concerned. "Before the Baron's men come...." He paused, looking at me as though he expected me to say something profound.

"I want to know where the people are that live here!" My yell came out as weak as church-social punch. "A woman and a boy...."

He was shaking his head. "You have to do something quick. The soldiers will come back, search every house—"

I sat up, ignoring the little men driving spikes into my skull. "I don't give a damn about soldiers! Where's my family? What's happened?" I reached out and gripped his arm. "How long was I down there? What year is this?"

He only shook his head. "Come eat some food. Then I can help you with your plan."

It was no use talking to the old man; he was senile.

I got off the cot. Except for the dizziness and a feeling that my knees were made of papier-mâché, I was all right. I picked up the hand-formed candle, stumbled into the hall.

It was a jumble of rubbish. I climbed through, pushed open the door to my study. There was my desk, the tall bookcase with the glass doors, the gray rug, the easy chair. Aside from a layer of dust and some peeling wallpaper, it looked normal. I flipped the switch. Nothing happened.

"What is that charm?" the old man said behind me. He pointed to the light switch.

"The power's off," I said. "Just habit."

He reached out and flipped the switch up, then down again. "It makes a pleasing sound."

"Yeah." I picked up a book from the desk; it fell apart in my hands.

I went back into the hall, tried the bedroom door, looked in at heaped leaves, the remains of broken furniture, an empty window frame. I went on to the end of the hall and opened the door to the bedroom.

Cold night wind blew through a barricade of broken timbers. The roof had fallen in, and a sixteen-inch tree trunk slanted through the wreckage. The old man stood behind me, watching.

"Where is she, damn you?" I leaned against the door frame to swear and fight off the faintness. "Where's my wife?"

The old man looked troubled. "Come, eat now...."

"Where is she? Where's the woman who lived here?"

He frowned, shook his head dumbly. I picked my way through the wreckage, stepped out into knee-high brush. A gust blew my candle out. In the dark I stared at my backyard, the crumbled pit that had been the barbecue grill, the tangled thickets that had been rose beds—and a weathered length of boards upended in the earth.

"What the hell's this . . . ? I fumbled out a permatch, lit my candle, leaned close, and read the crude letters cut into the crumbling wood: VIRGINIA ANNE JACKSON. BORN JAN. 8 1957. KILL BY THE DOGS WINTER 1992.

3   The Baron's men came twice in the next three days. Each time the old man carried me, swearing but too weak to argue, out to a lean-to of branches and canvas in the woods behind the house. Then he disappeared, to come back an hour or two later and haul me back to my rag bed by the fire.

Three times a day he gave me a tin pan of stew, and I ate it mechanically. My mind went over and over the picture of Ginny, living on for twelve years in the slowly decaying house, and then—

It was too much. There are some shocks the mind refuses.

I thought of the tree that had fallen and crushed the east wing. An elm that size was at least fifty to sixty years old—maybe older. And the only elm on the place had been a two-year sapling. I knew it well; I had planted it.

The date carved on the headboard was 1992. As nearly as I could judge another thirty-five years had passed since then at least. My shipmates—Banner, Day, Mallon—they were all dead, long ago. How had they died? The old man was too far gone to tell me anything useful. Most of my questions produced a shake of the head and a few rumbled words about charms, demons, spells, and the Baron.

"I don't believe in spells," I said. "And I'm not too sure I believe in this Baron. Who is he?"

"The Baron Trollmaster of Filly. He holds all this country—" the old man made a sweeping gesture with his arm—"all the way to Jersey."

"Why was he looking for me? What makes me important?"

"You came from the Forbidden Place. Everyone heard the cries of the Lesser Troll that stands guard over the treasure there. If the Baron can learn your secrets of power—"

"Troll, hell! That's nothing but a Bolo on automatic!"

"By any name every man dreads the monster. A man who walks in its shadow has much *mana*. But the others—the ones that run in a pack like dogs—would tear you to pieces for a demon if they could lay hands on you."

"You saw me back there. Why didn't you give me away? And why are you taking care of me now?"

He shook his head—the all-purpose answer to any question.

I tried another tack: "Who was the rag man you tackled just outside? Why was he laying for me?"

The old man snorted. "Tonight the dogs will eat him. But forget that. Now we have to talk about your plan—"

"I've got about as many plans as the senior boarder in death row. I don't know if you know it, old-timer, but somebody slid the world out from under me when I wasn't looking."

The old man frowned. I had the thought that I wouldn't like to have him mad at me, for all his white hair. . . .

He shook his head. "You must understand what I tell you. The soldiers of the Baron will find you someday. If you are to break the spell—"

"Break the spell, eh?" I snorted. "I think I get the idea, pop. You've got it in your head that I'm valuable property of some kind. You figure I can use my supernatural powers to take over this menagerie—and you'll be in on the ground floor. Well, listen, you old idiot! I spent sixty years—maybe more—in a stasis tank two hundred feet underground. My world died while I was down there. This Baron of yours seems to own everything now. If you think I'm going to get myself shot bucking him, forget it!"

The old man didn't say anything.

"Things don't seem to be broken up much," I went on. "It must have been gas, or germ warfare—or fallout. Damn few people around. You're still able to live on what you can loot from stores; automobiles are still sitting where they were the day the world ended. How old were you when it happened, pop? The war, I mean. Do you remember it?"

He shook his head. "The world has always been as it is now."

"What year were you born?"

He scratched at his white hair. "I knew the number once. But I've forgotten."

"I guess the only way I'll find out how long I was gone is to saw that damned elm in two and count the rings—but even that wouldn't help much; I don't know when it blew over. Never mind. The important thing now is to talk to this Baron of yours. Where does he stay?"

The old man shook his head violently. "If the Baron lays his hands on you, he'll wring the secrets from you on the rack! I know his ways. For five years I was a slave in the palace stables."

"If you think I'm going to spend the rest of my days in this rat nest, you get another guess on the house! This Baron has tanks, an army. He's kept a little technology alive. That's the outfit for me—not this garbage detail! Now, where's this palace of his located?"

"The guards will shoot you on sight like a pack dog!"

"There has to be a way to get to him, old man! Think!"

The old head was shaking again. "He fears assassination. You can never approach him. . . ." He brightened. "Unless you know a spell of power?"

I chewed my lip. "Maybe I do at that. You wanted me to have a plan. I think I feel one coming on. Have you got a map?"

He pointed to the desk beside me. I tried the drawers, found mice, roaches, moldy money—and a stack of folded maps. I opened one carefully; faded ink on yellowed paper falling apart at the creases. The legend in the corner read: "PENNSYLVANIA 40M:1. Copyright 1970 by ESSO Corporation."

"This will do, pop," I said. "Now, tell me all you can about this Baron of yours."

"You'll destroy him?"

"I haven't even met the man."

"He is evil."

"I don't know; he owns an army. That makes up for a lot. . . ."

After three more days of rest and the old man's stew I was back to normal—or near enough. I had the old man boil me a tub of water for a bath and a shave. I found a serviceable pair of synthetic-fiber long johns in a chest of drawers, pulled them on and zipped the weather suit over them, then buckled on the holster I had made from a tough plastic.

"That completes my preparations, pop," I said. "It'll be dark in another half hour. Thanks for everything."

He got to his feet, a worried look on his lined face, like a father the first time Junior asks for the car.

"The Baron's men are everywhere."

"If you want to help, come along and back me up with that shotgun of yours." I picked it up. "Have you got any shells for this thing?"

He smiled, pleased now. "There are shells—but the magic is gone from many."

"That's the way magic is, pop. It goes out of things before you notice."

"Will you destroy the Great Troll now?"

"My motto is let sleeping trolls lie. I'm just paying a social call on the Baron."

The joy ran out of his face like booze from a dropped jug.

"Don't take it so hard, old-timer. I'm not the fairy prince you were expecting. But I'll take care of you—if I make it."

I waited while he pulled on a moth-eaten mackinaw. He took the shotgun and checked the breech, then looked at me.

"I'm ready," he said.

"Yeah," I said. "Let's go. . . ."

The Baronial palace was a forty-story slab of concrete and glass that had been known in my days as the Hilton Garden East. We made it in three hours of groping across country in the dark, at the end of which I was puffing but still on my feet. We moved out from the cover of the trees and looked across a dip in the ground at the lights, incongruously cheerful in the ravaged valley.

"The gates are there—" the old man pointed—"guarded by the Great Troll."

"Wait a minute. I thought the Troll was the Bolo back at the Site."

"That's the Lesser Troll. This is the Great One."

I selected a few choice words and muttered them to myself. "It would have saved us some effort if you'd mentioned this troll a little sooner, old-timer. I'm afraid I don't have any spells that will knock out a Mark II, once it's got its dander up."

He shook his head. "It lies under enchantment. I remember the day when it came, throwing thunderbolts. Many men were killed. Then the Baron commanded it to stand at his gates to guard him."

"How long ago was this, old-timer?"

He worked his lips over the question. "Long ago," he said finally. "Many winters."

"Let's go take a look."

We picked our way down the slope, came up along a rutted dirt road to the dark line of trees that rimmed the palace grounds. The old man touched my arm.

"Softly here. Maybe the Troll sleeps lightly. . . ."

I went the last few yards, eased around a brick column with a dead lantern on top, stared across fifty yards of waist-high brush at a dark silhouette outlined against the palace lights.

Cables, stretched from trees outside the circle of weeds, supported a weathered tarp which drooped over the Bolo. The wreckage of a helicopter lay like a crumpled dragonfly at the far side of the ring. Nearer, fragments of a heavy car chassis lay scattered. The old man hovered at my shoulder.

"It looks as though the gate is off limits," I hissed. "Let's try farther along."

He nodded. "No one passes here. There is a second gate, there." He pointed. "But there are guards."

"Let's climb the wall between gates."

"There are sharp spikes on top of the wall. But I know a place, farther on, where the spikes have been blunted."

"Lead on, pop."

Half an hour of creeping through wet brush brought us to the spot we were looking for. It looked to me like any other stretch of eight-foot masonry wall overhung with wet poplar trees.

"I'll go first," the old man said, "to draw the attention of the guard."

"Then who's going to boost me up? I'll go first."

He nodded, cupped his hands and lifted me as easily as a sailor lifting a beer glass. Pop was old—but he was nobody's softie.

I looked around, then crawled up, worked my way over the corroded spikes, dropped down on the lawn.

Immediately I heard a crackle of brush. A man stood up not ten feet away. I lay flat in the dark trying to look like something that had been there a long time. . . .

I heard another sound, a thump and a crashing of brush. The man before me turned, disappeared in the darkness. I heard him beating his way through shrubbery; then he called out, got an answering shout from the distance.

I didn't loiter. I got to my feet and made a sprint for the cover of the trees along the drive.

4   **F**lat on the wet ground, under the wind-whipped branches of an ornamental cedar, I blinked the fine misty rain from my eyes, waiting for the halfhearted alarm behind me to die down.

There were a few shouts, some sounds of searching among the shrubbery. It was a bad night to be chasing imaginary intruders in the Baronial grounds. In five minutes all was quiet again.

I studied the view before me. The tree under which I lay was one of a row lining a drive. It swung in a graceful curve, across a smooth half-mile of dark lawn, to the tower of light that was the palace of the Baron of Filly. The silhouetted figures of guards and late-arriving guests moved against the gleam from the collonaded entrance. On a terrace high above, dancers twirled under colored lights. The faint glow of the repellor field kept the cold rain at a distance. In a lull in the wind, I heard music, faintly. The Baron's weekly grand ball was in full swing.

I saw shadows move across the wet gravel before me, then heard the purr of an engine. I hugged the ground and watched a long svelte Mercedes—about an '88 model, I estimated—barrel past.

The mob in the city ran in packs like dogs, but the Baron's friends did a little better for themselves.

I got to my feet and moved off toward the palace, keeping well in the shadows. When the drive swung to the right to curve across in front of the building, I left it, went to hands and knees, and followed a trimmed privet hedge past dark rectangles of formal garden to the edge of a secondary pond of light from the garages. I let myself down on my belly and watched the shadows that moved on the graveled drive.

There seemed to be two men on duty—no more. Waiting around wouldn't improve my chances. I got to my feet, stepped out into the drive, and walked openly around the corner of the gray fieldstone building into the light.

A short, thickset man in greasy Baronial green looked at me incuriously. My weather suit looked enough like ordinary coveralls to get me by—at least for a few minutes. A second man, tilted back against the wall in a wooden chair, didn't even turn his head.

"Hey!" I called. "You birds got a three-ton jack I can borrow?"

Shorty looked me over sourly. "Who you drive for, Mac?"

"The High Duke of Jersey. Flat. Left rear. On a night like this. Some luck."

"The Jersey can't afford a jack?"

I stepped over to the short man, prodded him with a forefinger. "He could buy you and gut you on the altar any Saturday night of the week, low-pockets. And he'd get a kick out of doing it. He's like that."

"Can't a guy crack a harmless joke without somebody talks about altar-bait? You wanna jack, take a jack."

The man in the chair opened one eye and looked me over. "How long you on the Jersey payroll?" he growled.

"Long enough to know who handles the rank between Jersey and Filly." I yawned, looked around the wide, cement-floored garage, glanced over the four heavy cars with the Filly crest on their sides.

"Where's the kitchen? I'm putting a couple of hot coffees under my belt before I go back out into that."

"Over there. A flight up and to your left. Tell the cook Pintsy invited you."

"I tell him Jersey sent me, low-pockets." I moved off in a dead silence, opened the door and stepped up into spicy-scented warmth.

A deep carpet—even here—muffled my footsteps. I could hear the clash of pots and crockery from the kitchen a hundred feet distant along the hallway. I went along to a deep-set doorway ten feet from the kitchen, tried the knob, and looked into a dark room. I pushed the door shut and leaned against it, watching the kitchen. Through the woodwork I could feel the thump of the bass notes from the orchestra blasting away three flights up. The odors of food—roast fowl, baked ham, grilled horsemeat—curled under the kitchen door and wafted under my nose. I pulled my belt up a notch and tried to swallow the dryness in my throat. The old man had fed me a half a gallon of stew before we left home, but I was already working up a fresh appetite.

Five slow minutes passed. Then the kitchen door swung open and a tall round-shouldered fellow with a shiny bald scalp stepped into view, a tray balanced on the spread fingers of one hand. He turned, the black tails of his cutaway swirling, called something behind him, and started past me. I stepped out, clearing my throat. He shied, whirled to face me. He was good at his job: the two dozen tiny glasses on the tray stood fast. He blinked, got an indignant remark ready—

I showed him the knife the old man had lent me—a bone-handled job with a six-inch switchblade. "Make a sound and I'll cut your throat," I said softly. "Put the tray on the floor."

He started to back. I brought the knife up. He took a good look, licked his lips, crouched quickly, and put the tray down.

"Turn around."

I stepped in and chopped him at the base of the neck with the edge of my hand. He folded like a two-dollar umbrella.

I wrestled the door open and dumped him inside, paused a moment to listen. All quiet. I worked his black coat and trousers off, unhooked the stiff white dickey and tie. He snored softly. I pulled the clothes on over the weather suit. They were a fair fit. By the light of my pencil flash I cut down a heavy braided cord hanging by a high window, used it to truss the waiter's hands and feet together behind him. There was a small closet opening off the room. I put him in it, closed the door, and stepped back into the hall. Still quiet. I tried one of the drinks. It wasn't bad.

I took another, then picked up the tray and followed the sounds of music.

The grand ballroom was a hundred yards long, fifty wide, with walls of rose, gold and white, banks of high windows hung with crimson velvet, a vaulted ceiling decorated with cherubs, and a polished acre of floor on which gaudily gowned and uniformed couples moved in time to the heavy beat of the traditional fox-trot. I moved slowly along the edge of the crowd, looking for the Baron.

A hand caught my arm and hauled me around. A glass fell off my tray, smashed on the floor.

A dapper little man in black and white headwaiter's uniform glared up at me.

"What do you think you're doing, cretin?" he hissed. "That's the genuine ancient stock you're slopping on the floor." I looked around quickly; no one else seemed to be paying any attention.

"Where are you from?" he snapped. I opened my mouth—

"Never mind, you're all the same." He waggled his hands disgustedly. "The field hands they send me—a disgrace to the Black. Now, you! Stand up! Hold your tray proudly, gracefully! Step along daintily, not like a knight taking the field! and pause occasionally—just on the chance that some noble guest might wish to drink."

"You bet, pal," I said. I moved on, paying a little more attention to my waiting. I saw plenty of green uniforms; pea green, forest green, emerald green—but they were all hung with braid and medals. According to pop, the Baron affected a spartan simplicity. The diffidence of absolute power.

There were high white and gold doors every few yards along the side of the ballroom. I spotted one standing open and sidled toward it. It wouldn't hurt to reconnoiter the area.

Just beyond the door, a very large sentry in a bottle-green uniform almost buried under gold braid moved in front of me. He was dressed like a toy soldier, but there was nothing playful about the way he snapped his power gun to the ready. I winked at him.

"Thought you boys might want a drink," I hissed. "Good stuff."

He looked at the tray, licked his lips. "Get back in there, you fool," he growled. "You'll get us both hanged."

"Suit yourself, pal." I backed out. Just before the door closed between us, he lifted a glass off the tray.

I turned, almost collided with a long lean cookie in a powder-blue outfit complete with dress sabre, gold frogs, leopard-skin facings, a pair of knee-length white gloves looped under an epaulette, a pistol in a fancy holster, and an eighteen-inch swagger stick. He gave me the kind of look old maids give sin.

"Look where you're going, swine," he said in a voice like a pine board splitting.

"Have a drink, admiral," I suggested.

He lifted his upper lip to show me a row of teeth that hadn't had their annual trip to the dentist lately. The ridges along each side of his mouth turned greenish white. He snatched for the gloves on his shoulder, fumbled them; they slapped the floor beside me.

"I'd pick those up for you, boss," I said, "but I've got my tray. . . ."

He drew a breath between his teeth, chewed it into strips, and snorted it back at me, then snapped his fingers and pointed with his stick toward the door behind me.

"Through there, instantly!" It didn't seem like the time to argue; I pulled it open and stepped through.

The guard in green ducked his glass and snapped to attention when he saw the baby-blue outfit. My new friend ignored him, made a curt gesture to me. I got the idea, trailed along the wide, high, gloomy corridor to a small door, pushed through it into a well-lit tile-walled latrine. A big-eyed slave in white ducks stared.

Blue-boy jerked his head. "Get out!" The slave scuttled away. Blue-boy turned to me.

"Strip off your jacket, slave! Your owner has neglected to teach you discipline."

I looked around quickly, saw that we were alone.

"Wait a minute while I put the tray down, corporal," I said. "We don't want to waste any of the good stuff." I turned to put the tray on a soiled linen bin, caught a glimpse of motion in the mirror.

I ducked, and the nasty-looking little leather quirt whistled past my ear, slammed against the edge of a marble-topped lavatory with a crack like pistol shot. I dropped the tray, stepped in fast and threw a left to Blue-boy's jaw that bounced his head against the tiled wall. I followed up with a right to the belt buckle, then held him up as he bent over, gagging, and hit him hard under the ear.

I hauled him into a booth, propped him up and started shedding the waiter's blacks.

5   I left him on the floor wearing my old suit, and stepped out into the hall.

I liked the feel of his pistol at my hip. It was an old-fashioned .38, the same model I favored. The blue uniform was a good fit, what with the weight I'd lost. Blue-boy and I had something in common after all.

The latrine attendant goggled at me. I grimaced like a quadruple amputee trying to scratch his nose and jerked my head toward the door I had come out of. I hoped the gesture would look familiar.

"Truss that mad dog and throw him outside the gates," I snarled. I stamped off down the corridor, trying to look mad enough to discourage curiosity.

Apparently it worked. Nobody yelled for the cops.

I reentered the ballroom by another door, snagged a drink off a passing tray, checked over the crowd. I saw two more powder-blue getups, so I wasn't unique enough to draw special attention. I made a mental note to stay well away from my comrades in blue. I blended with the landscape, chatting and nodding and not neglecting my drinking, working my way toward a big arched doorway on the other side of the room that looked like the kind of entrance the head man might use. I didn't want to meet him. Not yet. I just wanted to get him located before I went any further.

A passing wine slave poured a full inch of genuine ancient stock into my glass, ducked his head, and moved on. I gulped it like sour bar whiskey. My attention was elsewhere.

A flurry of activity near the big door indicated that maybe my guess had been accurate. Potbellied officials were forming up in a sort of reception line near the big double door. I started to drift back into the rear rank, bumped against a fat man in medals and a sash who glared, fingered a monocle with a plumb ring-studded hand, and said, "Suggest you take your place, colonel," in a suety voice.

I must have looked doubtful, because he bumped me with his paunch, and growled, "Foot of the line! Next to the Equerry, you idiot." He elbowed me aside and waddled past.

I took a step after him, reached out with my left foot, and hooked his shiny black boot. He leaped forward, off balance, medals jangling. I did a fast fade while he was still groping for his monocle, eased into a spot at the end of the line.

The conversation died away to a nervous murmur. The doors swung back and a pair of guards with more trimmings than a phony stock certificate stamped into view, wheeled to face each other, and presented arms—chrome-plated automatic rifles, in this case. A dark-faced man with thinning gray hair, a pug nose, and a trimmed gray Vandyke came into view, limping slightly from a stiffish knee.

His unornamented gray outfit made him as conspicuous in this gathering as a crane among peacocks. He nodded perfunctorily to left and right, coming along between the waiting rows of flunkeys, who snapped-to as he came abreast, wilted and let out sighs behind him. I studied him closely. He was fifty, give or take the age of a bottle of second-rate bourbon, with the weather-beaten complexion of a former outdoor man and the same look of alertness grown bored that a rattlesnake farmer develops—just before the fatal bite.

He looked up and caught my eye on him, and for a moment I thought he was about to speak. Then he went on past.

At the end of the line he turned abruptly and spoke to a man who hurried away. Then he engaged in conversation with a cluster of head-bobbing guests.

I spent the next fifteen minutes casually getting closer to the door nearest the one the Baron had entered by. I looked around; nobody was paying any attention to me. I stepped past a guard who presented arms. The door closed softly, cutting off the buzz of talk and the worst of the music.

I went along to the end of the corridor. From the transverse hall, a grand staircase rose in a sweep of bright chrome and pale wood. I didn't know where it led, but it looked right. I headed for it, moving along briskly like a man with important business in mind and no time for light chitchat.

Two flights up, in a wide corridor of muted lights, deep carpets, brocaded wall hangings, mirrors, urns, and an odor of expensive tobacco and *cuir russe,* a small man in black bustled from a side corridor. He saw me. He opened his mouth, closed it, half turned away, then swung back to face me. I recognized him; he was the headwaiter who had pointed out the flaws in my waiting style half an hour earlier.

"Here—" he started.

I chopped him short with a roar of what I hoped was authentic upper-crust rage.

"Direct me to his Excellency's apartments, scum! And thank your guardian imp I'm in too great haste to cane you for the insolent look about you!"

He went pale, gulped hard, and pointed. I snorted and stamped past him down the turning he had indicated.

This was Baronial country, all right. A pair of guards stood at the far end of the corridor.

I'd passed half a dozen with no more than a click of heels to indicate they saw me. These two shouldn't be any different—and it wouldn't look good if I turned and started back at sight of them. The first rule of the gate-crasher is to look as if you belong where you are.

I headed in their direction.

When I was fifty feet from them they both shifted rifles—not to present-arms position, but at the ready. The nickle-plated bayonets were aimed right at me. It was no time for me to look doubtful; I kept on coming. At twenty feet, I heard their rifle bolts snick home. I could see the expressions on their faces now; they looked as nervous as a couple of teenage sailors on their first visit to a joyhouse.

"Point those butter knives into the corner, you banana-fingered cotton choppers!" I said, looking bored, and didn't waver. I unlimbered my swagger stick and slapped my gloved hand with it, letting them think it over. The gun muzzles dropped—just slightly. I followed up fast.

"Which is the anteroom to the Baron's apartments?" I demanded.

"Uh . . . this here is his Excellency's apartments, sir, but—"

"Never mind the lecture, you milk-faced fool," I cut in. "Which is the anteroom, damn you!"

"We got orders, sir. Nobody's to come closer than that last door back there."

"We got orders to shoot," the other interrupted. He was a little older —maybe twenty-two. I turned on him.

"I'm waiting for an answer to a question!"

"Sir, the Articles—"

I narrowed my eyes. "I think you'll find paragraph Two B covers Special Cosmic Top Secret Couriers. When you go off duty, report your-selves on punishment. Now, the anteroom! And be quick about it!"

The bayonets were sagging now. The younger of the two licked his lips. "Sir, we never been inside. We don't know how it's laid out in there. If the colonel wants to just take a look. . . ."

The other guard opened his mouth to say something. I didn't wait to find out what it was. I stepped between them, muttering something about bloody recruits and important messages, and worked the fancy handle on the big gold and white door. I paused to give the two sentries a hard look.

"I hope I don't have to remind you that any mention of the movements of a Cosmic Courier is punishable by slow death. Just forget you ever saw me." I went on in and closed the door without waiting to catch the reaction to that one.

The Baron had done well by himself in the matter of decor. The room I was in—a sort of lounge-cum-bar—was paved in two-inch-deep nylon fuzz, the color of a fog at sea, that foamed up at the edges against walls of pale blue brocade with tiny yellow flowers. The bar was a teak log split down the middle and polished. The glasses sitting on it were like tissue paper engraved with patterns of nymphs and satyrs. Subdued light came from somewhere, along with a faint melody that seemed to speak of youth, long ago.

I went on into the room. I found more soft light, the glow of hand-rubbed rare woods, rich fabrics, and wide windows with a view of dark night sky. The music was coming from a long, low, built-in speaker with a lamp, a heavy crystal ashtray, and a display of hothouse roses. There was a scent in the air. Not the *cuir russe* and Havana leaf I'd smelled in the hall, but a subtler perfume.

I turned and looked into the eyes of a girl with long black lashes. Smooth black hair came down to bare shoulders. An arm as smooth and white as whipped cream was draped over a chair back, the hand holding an eight-inch cigarette holder and sporting a diamond as inconspicuous as a chrome-plated hubcap.

"You must want something pretty badly," she murmured, batting her eyelashes at me. I could feel the breeze at ten feet. I nodded. Under the circumstances that was about the best I could do.

"What could it be," she mused, "that's worth being shot for?" Her voice was like the rest of her: smooth, polished and relaxed—and with plenty of moxie held in reserve. She smiled casually, drew on her cigarette, tapped ashes onto the rug.

"Something bothering you, colonel?" she inquired. "You don't seem talkative."

"I'll do my talking when the Baron arrives," I said.

"In that case, Jackson," said a husky voice behind me, "you can start any time you like."

I held my hands clear of my body and turned around slowly—just in case there was a nervous gun aimed at my spine. The Baron was standing near the door, unarmed, relaxed. There were no guards in sight. The girl looked mildly amused. I put my hand on the pistol butt.

"How do you know my name?" I asked.

The Baron waved toward a chair. "Sit down, Jackson," he said, almost gently. "You've had a tough time of it—but you're all right now." He walked past me to the bar, poured out two glasses, turned, and offered me one. I felt a little silly standing there fingering the gun; I went over and took the drink.

"To the old days." The Baron raised his glass.

I drank. It was the genuine ancient stock, all right. "I asked you how you knew my name," I said.

"That's easy. I used to know you."

He smiled faintly. There was something about his face. . . .

"You look well in the uniform of the Penn dragoons," he said. "Better than you ever did in Aerospace blue."

"Good God!" I said. "Toby Mallon!"

He ran a hand over his bald head. "A little less hair on top, plus a beard as compensation, a few wrinkles, a slight pot. Oh, I've changed, Jackson."

"I had it figured as close to eighty years," I said. "The trees, the condition of the buildings—"

"Not far off the mark. Seventy-eight years this spring."

"You're a well-preserved hundred and ten, Toby."

He nodded. "I know how you feel. Rip Van Winkle had nothing on us."

"Just one question, Toby. The men you sent out to pick me up seemed more interested in shooting than talking. I'm wondering why."

Mallon threw out his hands. "A little misunderstanding, Jackson. You made it; that's all that counts. Now that you're here, we've got some planning to do together. I've had it tough these last twenty years. I started off with nothing: a few hundred scavengers living in the ruins, hiding out every time Jersey or Dee-Cee raided for supplies. I built an organization, started a systematic salvage operation. I saved everything the rats and the weather hadn't gotten to, spruced up my palace here, and stocked it. It's a rich province, Jackson—"

"And now you own it all. Not bad, Toby."

"They say knowledge is power. I had the knowledge."

I finished my drink and put the glass on the bar.

"What's this planning you say we have to do?"

Mallon leaned back on one elbow.

"Jackson, it's been a long haul—alone. It's good to see an old shipmate. But we'll dine first."

"I might manage to nibble a little something. Say a horse, roasted whole. Don't bother to remove the saddle."

He laughed. "First we eat," he said. "Then we conquer to world."

6   I squeezed the last drop from the Beaujolais bottle and watched the girl, whose name was Renada, hold a light for the cigar Mallon had taken from a silver box. My blue mess jacket and holster hung over the back of the chair. Everything was cosy now.

"Time for business, Jackson," Mallon said. He blew out smoke and looked at me through it. "How did things look—inside?"

"Dusty. But intact, below ground level. Upstairs, there's blast damage and weathering. I don't suppose it's changed much since you came out twenty years ago. As far as I could tell, the Primary Site is okay."

Mallon leaned forward. "Now, you made it out past the Bolo. How did it handle itself? Still fully functional?"

I sipped my wine, thinking over my answer, remembering the Bolo's empty guns. . . .

"It damn near gunned me down. It's getting a little old and it can't see as well as it used to, but it's still a tough baby."

Mallon swore suddenly. "It was Mackenzie's idea. A last-minute move when the tech crews had to evacuate. It was a dusting job, you know."

"I hadn't heard. How did you find out all this?"

Mallon shot me a sharp look. "There were still a few people around who'd been in it. But never mind that. What about the Supply Site? That's what we're interested in. Fuel, guns, even some nuclear stuff. Heavy equipment; there's a couple more Bolos, mothballed, I understand. Maybe we'll even find one or two of the Colossus missiles still in their silos. I made an air recon a few years back before my chopper broke down—"

"I think two silo doors are still in place. But why the interest in armament?"

Mallon snorted. "You've got a few things to learn about the setup, Jackson. I need that stuff. If I hadn't lucked into a stock of weapons and ammo in the armory cellar, Jersey would be wearing the spurs in my palace right now!"

I drew on my cigar and let the silence stretch out.

"You said something about conquering the world, Toby. I don't suppose by any chance you meant that literally?"

Mallon stood up, his closed fists working like a man crumpling unpaid bills. "They all want what I've got! They're all waiting." He walked across the room, back. "I'm ready to move against them now! I can put four thousand trained men in the field—"

"Let's get a couple of things straight, Mallon," I cut in. "You've got the natives fooled with this Baron routine. But don't try it on me. Maybe it was even necessary once; maybe there's an excuse for some of the stories I've heard. That's over now. I'm not interested in tribal warfare or gang rumbles. I need—"

"Better remember who's running things here, Jackson!" Mallon snapped. "It's not what you need that counts." He took another turn up and down the room, then stopped, facing me.

"Look, Jackson. I know how to get around in this jungle; you don't. If I hadn't spotted you and given some orders, you'd have been gunned down before you'd gone ten feet past the ballroom door."

"Why'd you let me in? I might've been gunning for you."

"You wanted to see the Baron alone. That suited me, too. If word got out—" He broke off, cleared his throat. "Let's stop wrangling, Jackson. We can't move until the Bolo guarding the site has been neutralized. There's only one way to do that: knock it out! And the only thing that can knock out a Bolo is another Bolo."

"So?"

"I've got another Bolo, Jackson. It's been covered, maintained. It can go up against the Troll—" He broke off, laughed shortly. "That's what the mob called it."

"You could have done that years ago. Where do I come in?"

"You're checked out on a Bolo, Jackson. You know something about this kind of equipment."

"Sure. So do you."

"I never learned," he said shortly.

"Who's kidding who, Mallon? We all took the same orientation course less than a month ago—"

"For me it's been a long month. Let's say I've forgotten."

"You parked that Bolo at your front gate and then forgot how you did it, eh?"

"Nonsense. It's always been there."

I shook my head. "I know different."

Mallon looked wary. "Where'd you get that idea?"

"Somebody told me."

Mallon ground his cigar out savagely on the damask cloth. "You'll point the scum out to me!"

"I don't give a damn whether you moved it or not. Anybody with your training can figure out the controls of a Bolo in half an hour—"

"Not well enough to take on the Tr—another Bolo."

I took a cigar from the silver box, picked up the lighter from the table, turned the cigar in the flame. Suddenly it was very quiet in the room.

I looked across at Mallon. He held out his hand.

"I'll take that," he said shortly.

I blew out smoke, squinted through it at Mallon. He sat with his hand out, waiting. I looked down at the lighter.

It was a heavy windproof model with embossed Aerospace wings. I turned it over. Engraved letters read: *Lieut. Commander Don G. Banner, USAF.* I looked up. Renada sat quietly, holding my pistol trained dead on my belt buckle.

"I'm sorry you saw that," Mallon said. "It could cause misunderstandings."

"Where's Banner?"

"He . . . died. I told you—"

"You told me a lot of things, Toby. Some of them might even be true. Did you make him the same offer you've made me?"

Mallon darted a look at Renada. She sat holding the pistol, looking at me distantly, without expression.

"You've got the wrong idea, Jackson—" Mallon started.

"You and he came out about the same time," I said. "Or maybe you got the jump on him by a few days. It must have been close; otherwise you'd never have taken him. Don was a sharp boy."

"You're out of your mind!" Mallon snapped. "Why, Banner was my friend!"

"Then why do you get nervous when I find his lighter on your table? There could be ten perfectly harmless explanations."

"I don't make explanations," Mallon said flatly.

"That attitude is hardly the basis for a lasting partnership, Toby. I have an unhappy feeling there's something you're not telling me."

Mallon pulled himself up in the chair. "Look here, Jackson. We've no reason to fall out. There's plenty for both of us—and one day I'll be needing a successor. It was too bad about Banner, but that's ancient history now. Forget it. I want you with me, Jackson! Together we can rule the Atlantic seaboard—or even more!"

I drew on my cigar, looking at the gun in Renada's hand. "You hold the aces, Toby. Shooting me would be no trick at all."

"There's no trick involved, Jackson!" Mallon snapped. "After all," he went on, almost wheedling now, "we're old friends. I want to give you a break, share with you—"

"I don't think I'd trust him if I were you, Mr. Jackson," Renada's quiet voice cut in. I looked at her. She looked back calmly. "You're more important to him than you think."

"That's enough, Renada," Mallon barked. "Go to your room at once."

"Not just yet, Toby," she said. "I'm also curious about how Commander Banner died." I looked at the gun in her hand.

It wasn't pointed at me now. It was aimed at Mallon's chest.

Mallon sat sunk deep in his chair, looking at me with eyes like a python with a bellyache. "You're fools, both of you," he grated. "I gave you everything, Renada. I raised you like my own daughter. And you, Jackson. You could have shared with me—all of it."

"I don't need a share of your delusions, Toby. I've got a set of my own. But before we go any farther, let's clear up a few points. Why haven't you been getting any mileage out of your tame Bolo? And what makes me important in the picture?"

"He's afraid of the Bolo machine," Renada said. "There's a spell on it which prevents men from approaching—even the Baron."

"Shut your mouth, you fool!" Mallon choked on his fury. I tossed the lighter in my hand and felt a smile twitching at my mouth.

"So Don was too smart for you after all. He must have been the one who had control of the Bolo. I suppose you called for a truce, and then shot him out from under the white flag. But he fooled you. He plugged a command into the Bolo's circuits to fire on anyone who came close— unless he was Banner."

"You're crazy!"

"It's close enough. You can't get near the Bolo. Right? And after twenty years, the bluff you've been running on the other Barons with your private troll must be getting a little thin. Any day now one of them may decide to try you."

Mallon twisted his face in what may have been an attempt at a placating smile. "I won't argue with you, Jackson. You're right about the command circuit. Banner set it up to fire an antipersonnel blast at any-one coming within fifty yards. He did it to keep the mob from tampering with the machine. But there's a loophole. It wasn't only Banner who could get close. He set it up to accept any of the *Prometheus* crew—except me. He hated me. It was a trick to try to get me killed."

"So you're figuring I'll step in and defuse her for you, eh, Toby? Well, I'm sorry as hell to disappoint you, but somehow in the confusion I left my electropass behind."

Mallon leaned toward me. "I told you we need each other, Jackson: I've got your pass. Yours and all the others. Renada, hand me my black box." She rose and moved across to the desk, holding the gun on Mal-lon—and on me, too, for that matter.

"Where'd you get my pass, Mallon?"

"Where do you think? They're the duplicates from the vault in the old command block. I knew one day one of you would come out. I'll tell you, Jackson, it's been hell, waiting all these years—and hoping. I gave orders that any time the Great Troll bellowed, the mob was to form up and stop anybody who came out. I don't know how you got through them. . . ."

"I was too slippery for them. Besides," I added, "I met a friend."

"A friend? Who's that?"

"An old man who thought I was Prince Charming, come to wake everybody up. He was nuts. But he got me through."

Renada came back, handed me a square steel box. "Let's have the key, Mallon," I said. He handed it over. I opened the box, sorted through half a dozen silver-dollar-sized ovals of clear plastic, lifted one out.

"Is it a magical charm?" Renada asked, sounding awed. She didn't seem so sophisticated now—but I liked her better human.

"Just a synthetic crystalline plastic, designed to resonate to a pattern peculiar to my EEG," I said. "It amplifies the signal and gives off a characteristic emission that the psychotronic circuit in the Bolo picks up."

"That's what I thought. Magic."

"Call it magic, then, kid." I dropped the electropass in my pocket, stood and looked at Renada. "I don't doubt that you know how to use that gun, honey, but I'm leaving now. Try not to shoot me."

"You're a fool if you try it," Mallon barked. "If Renada doesn't shoot you, my guards will. And even if you made it, you'd still need me!"

"I'm touched by your concern, Toby. Just why do I need you?"

"You wouldn't get past the first sentry post without help, Jackson. These people know me as the Trollmaster. They're in awe of me—of my *mana*. But together—we can get to the controls of the Bolo, then use it to knock out the sentry machine at the Site—"

"Then what? With an operating Bolo I don't need anything else. Better improve the picture, Toby. I'm not impressed."

He wet his lips.

"It's *Prometheus,* do you understand? She's stocked with everything from Browning needlers to Norge stunners. Tools, weapons, instruments. And the power plants alone."

"I don't need needlers if I own a Bolo, Toby."

Mallon used some profanity. "You'll leave your liver and lights on the palace altar, Jackson. I promise you that!"

"Tell him what he wants to know, Toby," Renada said. Mallon narrowed his eyes at her. "You'll live to regret this, Renada."

"Maybe I will, Toby. But you taught me how to handle a gun—and to play cards for keeps."

The flush faded out of his face and left it pale. "All right, Jackson," he said, almost in a whisper. "It's not only the equipment. It's . . . the men."

I heard a clock ticking somewhere.

"What men, Toby?" I said softly.

"The crew. Day, Macy, the others. They're still in there, Jackson—aboard the ship, in stasis. We were trying to get the ship off when the attack came. There was forty minutes' warning. Everything was ready to go. You were on a test run; there wasn't time to cycle you out. . . ."

"Keep talking," I rapped.

"You know how the system was set up; it was to be a ten-year run out, with an automatic turnaround at the end of that time if Alpha Centauri wasn't within a milliparsec." He snorted. "It wasn't. After twenty years, the instruments checked. They were satisfied. There was a planetary mass within the acceptable range. So they brought me out." He snorted again. "The longest dry run in history. I unstrapped and came out to see what was going on. It took me a little while to realize what had happened. I went back in and cycled Banner and Mackenzie out. We went into the town; you know what we found. I saw what we had to do, but Banner and Mac argued. The fools wanted to reseal *Prometheus* and proceed with the launch. For what? So we could spend the rest of our lives squatting in the ruins, when by stripping the ship we could make ourselves kings?"

"So there was an argument?" I prompted.

"I had a gun. I hit Mackenzie in the leg, I think—but they got clear, found a car and beat me to the Site. There were two Bolos. What chance did I have against them?" Mallon grinned craftily. "But Banner was a fool. He died for it." The grin dropped like a stripper's bra. "But when I went to claim my spoils, I discovered how the jackals had set the trap for me."

"That was downright unfriendly of them, Mallon. Oddly enough, it doesn't make me want to stay and hold your hand."

"Don't you understand yet!" Mallon's voice was a dry screech. "Even if you got clear of the palace, used the Bolo to set yourself up as Baron —you'd never be safe! Not as long as one man was still alive aboard the ship. You'd never have a night's rest, wondering when one of them would walk out to challenge your rule. . . ."

"Uneasy lies the head, eh, Toby? You remind me of a queen bee. The first one out of the chrysalis dismembers all her rivals."

"I don't mean to kill them. That would be a waste; I mean to give them useful work to do."

"I don't think they'd like being your slaves, Toby. And neither would I." I looked at Renada. "I'll be leaving you now," I said. "Whichever way you decide, good luck."

"Wait." She stood. "I'm going with you."

I looked at her. "I'll be traveling fast, honey. And that gun in my back may throw off my timing."

She stepped to me, reversed the pistol, and laid it in my hand.

"Don't kill him, Mr. Jackson. He was always kind to me."

"Why change sides now? According to Toby, my chances look not too good."

"I never knew before how Commander Banner died," she said. "He was my great-grandfather."

7   **R**enada came back bundled in a gray fur as I finished buckling on my holster.

"So long, Toby," I said. "I ought to shoot you in the belly just for Don, but—"

I saw Renada's eyes widen at the same instant that I heard the click.

I dropped flat and rolled behind Mallon's chair—and a gout of blue flame yammered into the spot where I'd been standing. I whipped the gun up and fired a round into the peach-colored upholstery an inch from Toby's ear.

"The next one nails you to the chair," I yelled. "Call 'em off!" There was a moment of dead silence. Toby sat frozen. I couldn't see who'd been doing the shooting. Then I heard a moan. Renada.

"Let the girl alone or I'll kill him," I called.

Toby sat rigid, his eyes rolled toward me.

"You can't kill me, Jackson! I'm all that's keeping you alive."

"You can't kill me either, Toby. You need my magic touch, remember? Maybe you'd better give me a safe-conduct out of here. I'll take the freeze off your Bolo—after I've seen to my business."

Toby licked his lips. I heard Renada again. She was trying not to moan—but moaning anyway.

"You tried, Jackson. It didn't work out," Toby said through gritted teeth. "Throw out your gun and stand up. I won't kill you—you know that. You do as you're told and you may still live to a ripe old age—and the girl, too."

She screamed then—a mindless ululation of pure agony.

"Hurry up, you fool, before they tear her arm off," Mallon grated. "Or shoot. You'll get to watch her for twenty-four hours under the knife. Then you'll have your turn."

I fired again—closer this time. Mallon jerked his head and cursed.

"If they touch her again, you get it, Toby," I said. "Send her over here. Move!"

"Let her go!" Mallon snarled. Renada stumbled into sight, moved around the chair, then crumpled suddenly to the rug beside me.

"Stand up, Toby," I ordered. He rose slowly. Sweat glistened on his face now. "Stand over here." He moved like a sleepwalker. I got to my feet. There were two men standing across the room beside a small open door. A sliding panel. Both of them held power rifles leveled—but aimed offside, away from the Baron.

"Drop 'em!" I said. They looked at me, then lowered the guns, tossed them aside.

I opened my mouth to tell Mallon to move ahead, but my tongue felt thick and heavy. The room was suddenly full of smoke. In front of me, Mallon was wavering like a mirage. I started to tell him to stand still, but with my thick tongue, it was too much trouble. I raised the gun, but somehow it was falling to the floor—slowly, like a leaf—and then I was floating, too, on waves that broke on a dark sea. . . .

"Do you think you're the first idiot who thought he could kill me?" Mallon raised a contemptuous lip. "This room's rigged ten different ways."

I shook my head, trying to ignore the film before my eyes and the nausea in my body. "No, I imagine lots of people would like a crack at you, Toby. One day one of them's going to make it."

"Get him on his feet," Mallon snapped. Hard hands clamped on my arms, hauled me off the cot. I worked my legs, but they were like yesterday's celery; I sagged against somebody who smelled like uncured hides.

"You seem drowsy," Mallon said. "We'll see if we can't wake you up."

A thumb dug into my neck. I jerked away, and a jab under the ribs doubled me over.

"I have to keep you alive—for the moment," Mallon said. "But you won't get a lot of pleasure out of it."

I blinked hard. It was dark in the room. One of my handlers had a ring of beard around his mouth—I could see that much. Mallon was standing before me, hands on hips. I aimed a kick at him, just for fun. It didn't work out; my foot seemed to be wearing a lead boat. The unshaven man hit me in the mouth and Toby chuckled.

"Have your fun, Dunger," he said, "but I'll want him alive and on his feet for the night's work. Take him out and walk him in the fresh air. Report to me at the Pavilion of the Troll in an hour." He turned to something and gave orders about lights and gun emplacements, and I heard Renada's name mentioned.

Then he was gone and I was being dragged through the door and along the corridor.

The exercise helped. By the time the hour had passed, I was feeling weak but normal—except for an aching head and a feeling that there was a strand of spiderweb interfering with my vision. Toby had given me a good meal. Maybe before the night was over he'd regret that mistake. . . .

Across the dark grounds, an engine started up, spluttered, then settled down to a steady hum.

"It's time," the one with the whiskers said. He had a voice like soft cheese to match his smell. He took another half-twist in the arm he was holding.

"Don't break it," I grunted. "It belongs to the Baron, remember?"

Whiskers stopped dead. "You talk too much—and too smart." He let my arm go and stepped back. "Hold him, Pig Eye." The other man whipped a forearm across my throat and levered my head back; then Whiskers unlimbered the two-foot club from his belt and hit me hard in the side, just under the rigs. Pig Eye let go and I folded over and waited while the pain swelled up and burst inside me.

Then they hauled me back to my feet. I couldn't feel any bone ends grating, so there probably weren't any broken ribs—if that was any consolation.

There were lights glaring now across the lawn. Moving figures cast long shadows against the trees lining the drive—and on the side of the Bolo Combat Unit parked under its canopy by the sealed gate.

A crude breastwork had been thrown up just over fifty yards from it. A wheel-mounted generator putted noisily in the background, laying a layer of bluish exhaust in the air.

Mallon was waiting with a 9-mm power rifle in his hands as we came up, my two guards gripping me with both hands to demonstrate their zeal, and me staggering a little more than was necessary. I saw Renada standing by, wrapped in a gray fur. Her face looked white in the harsh light. She made a move toward me and a greenback caught her arm.

"You know what to do, Jackson," Mallon said, speaking loudly against the clatter of the generator. He made a curt gesture and a man stepped up and buckled a stout chain to my left ankle. Mallon held out my electropass. "I want you to walk straight to the Bolo. Go in by the side port. You've got one minute to cancel the instructions punched into the command circuit and climb back outside. If you don't show, I close a switch there—" He pointed to a wooden box mounting an open circuit breaker, with a tangle of heavy cable leading toward the Bolo—"and you cook in your shoes. The same thing happens if I see the guns start to traverse or the antipersonnel ports open." I followed the coils of armored wire from the chain on my ankle back to the wooden box—and on to the generator.

"Crude, maybe, but it will work. And if you get any idea of letting fly a round or two at random—remember the girl will be right beside me."

I looked across at the giant machine. "Suppose it doesn't recognize me? It's been a while. Or what if Don didn't plug my identity pattern in to the recognition circuit?"

"In that case, you're no good to me anyway," Mallon said flatly.

I caught Renada's eye, gave her a wink and a smile I didn't feel, and climbed up on top of the revetment.

I looked back at Mallon. He was old and shrunken in the garish light, his smooth gray suit rumpled, his thin hair mussed, the gun held in a white-knuckled grip. He looked more like a harassed shopkeeper than a would-be world-beater.

"You must want the Bolo pretty bad to take the chance, Toby," I said.

"I'll think about taking that wild shot. You sweat me out."

I flipped slack into the wire trailing my ankle, jumped down, and started across the smooth-trimmed grass, a long black shadow stalking before me. The Bolo sat silent, as big as a bank in the circle of the spotlight. I could see the flecks of rust now around the port covers, the small vines that twined up her sides from the ragged stands of weeds that marked no-man's-land.

There was something white in the brush ahead. Broken human bones.

I felt my stomach go rigid again. The last man had gotten this far; I wasn't in the clear yet. . . .

I passed two more scattered skeletons in the next twenty feet. They must have come in on the run, guinea pigs to test the alertness of the Bolo. Or maybe they'd tried creeping up, dead slow, an inch a day; it hadn't worked. . . .

Tiny night creatures scuttled ahead. They would be safe here in the shadow of the troll where no predator bigger than a mouse could move. I stumbled, diverted my course around a ten-foot hollow, the eroded crater of a near miss.

Now I could see the great moss-coated treads sunk a foot into the earth, the nests of field mice tucked in the spokes of the yard-high bogies. The entry hatch was above, a hairline against the great curved flank. There were rungs set in the flaring tread shield. I reached up, got a grip and hauled myself up. My chain clanked against the metal. I found the door lever, held on and pulled.

It resisted, then turned. There was the hum of a servo motor, a crackling of dead gaskets. The hairline widened and showed me a narrow companionway, green-anodized dural with black polymer treads, a bulkhead with a fire extinguisher, an embossed steel data plate that said BOLO DIVISION OF GENERAL MOTORS CORPORATION and below, in smaller type, UNIT, COMBAT, BOLO MARK II.

I pulled myself inside and went up into the Christmas-tree glow of instrument lights.

The control cockpit was small, utilitarian, with two deep-padded seats set among screens, dials, levers. I sniffed the odors of oil, paint, the characteristic ether and ozone of a nuclear generator. There was a faint hum in the air from idling relay servos. The clock showed ten past four. Either it was later than I thought, or the chronometer had lost time in the last eighty years. But I had no time to lose. . . .

I slid into the seat, flipped back the cover of the command control console. The Cancel key was the big white one. I pulled it down and let it snap back, like a clerk ringing up a sale.

A pattern of dots on the status display screen flicked out of existence. Mallon was safe from his pet troll now.

It hadn't taken me long to carry out my orders. I knew what to do next; I'd planned it all during my walk out. Now I had thirty seconds to stack the deck in my favor.

I reached down, hauled the festoon of quarter-inch armored cable up in front of me. I hit a switch, and the inner conning cover—a disk of inch-thick armor—slid back. I shoved a loop of the flexible cable up through the aperture, reversed the switch. The cover slid back—slicing the armored cable like macaroni.

I took a deep breath, and my hands went to the combat alert switch, hovered over it.

It was the smart thing to do—the easy thing. All I had to do was punch a key, and the 9-mm's would open up, scythe Mallon and his crew down like cornstalks.

But the scything would mow Renada down, along with the rest. And if I went—even without firing a shot—Mallon would keep his promise to cut that white throat. . . .

My head was out of the noose now, but I would have to put it back— for a while.

I leaned sideways, reached back under the panel, groped for a small fuse box. My fingers were clumsy. I took a breath, tried again. The fuse dropped out in my hand. The Bolo's I-R circuit was dead now. With a few more seconds to work, I could have knocked out other circuits—but the time had run out.

I grabbed the cut ends of my lead wire, knotted them around the chain and got out fast.

8

Mallon waited, crouched behind the revetment.

"It's safe now, is it?" he grated. I nodded. He stood, gripping his gun. "Now we'll try it together."

I went over the parapet, Mallon following with his gun ready. The lights followed us to the Bolo. Mallon clambered up to the open port, looked around inside, then dropped back down beside me. He looked excited now.

"That does it, Jackson! I've waited a long time for this. Now I've got all the *mana* there is!"

"Take a look at the cable on my ankle," I said softly. He narrowed his eyes, stepped back, gun aimed, darted a glance at the cable looped to the chain.

"I cut it, Toby. I was alone in the Bolo with the cable cut—and I didn't fire. I could have taken your toy and set up in business for myself, but I didn't."

"What's that supposed to buy you?" Mallon rasped.

"As you said—we need each other. That cut cable proves you can trust me."

Mallon smiled. It wasn't a nice smile. "Safe, were you? Come here." I walked along with him to the back of the Bolo. A heavy copper wire hung across the rear of the machine, trailing off into the grass in both directions.

"I'd have burned you at the first move. Even with the cable cut, the armored cover would have carried the full load right into the cockpit with you. But don't be nervous. I've got other jobs for you." He jabbed the gun muzzle hard into my chest, pushing me back. "Now get moving," he snarled. "And don't ever threaten the Baron again."

"The years have done more than shrivel your face, Toby," I said. "They've cracked your brain."

He laughed, a short bark. "You could be right. What's sane and what isn't? I've got a vision in my mind—and I'll make it come true. If that's insanity, it's better than what the mob has."

Back at the parapet, Mallon turned to me. "I've had this campaign planned in detail for years, Jackson. Everything's ready. We move out in half an hour—before any traitors have time to take word to my enemies. Pig Eye and Dunger will keep you from being lonely while I'm away. When I get back— Well, maybe you're right about working together." He gestured and my whiskery friend and his sidekick loomed up. "Watch him," he said.

"Genghis Khan is on the march, eh?" I said. "With nothing between you and the goodies but a five-hundred-ton Bolo. . . ."

"The Lesser Troll. . . ." He raised his hands and made crushing motions, like a man crumbling dry earth. "I'll trample it under my treads."

"You're confused, Toby. The Bolo has treads. You just have a couple of fallen arches."

"It's the same. I am the Great Troll." He showed me his teeth and walked away.

I moved along between Dunger and Pig Eye, toward the lights of the garage.

"The back entrance again," I said. "Anyone would think you were ashamed of me."

"You need more training, hah?" Dunger rasped. "Hold him, Pig Eye." He unhooked his club and swung it loosely in his hand, glancing around. We were near the trees by the drive. There was no one in sight except the crews near the Bolo and a group by the front of the palace. Pig Eye gave my arm a twist and shifted his grip to his old favorite strangle hold. I was hoping he would.

Dunger whipped the club up, and I grabbed Pig Eye's arm with both hands and leaned forward like a Japanese admiral reporting to the Emperor. Pig Eye went up and over just in time to catch Dunger's club across the back. They went down together. I went for the club, but Whiskers was faster than he looked. He rolled clear, got to his knees, and laid it across my left arm, just below the shoulder.

I heard the bone go. . . .

I was back on my feet, somehow. Pig Eye lay sprawled before me. I heard him whining as though from a great distance. Dunger stood six feet away, the ring of black beard spread in a grin like a hyena smelling dead meat.

"His back's broke," he said. "Hell of a sound he's making. I been waiting for you; I wanted you to hear it."

"I've heard it," I managed. My voice seemed to be coming off a worn sound track. "Surprised . . . you didn't work me over . . . while I was busy with the arm."

"Uh-uh. I like a man to know what's going on when I work him over." He stepped in, rapped the broken arm lightly with the club. Fiery agony choked a groan off in my throat. I backed a step; he stalked me.

"Pig Eye wasn't much, but he was my pal. When I'm through with you, I'll have to kill him. A man with a broken back's no use to nobody. His'll be finished pretty soon now, but not with you. You'll be around a long time yet; but I'll get a lot of fun out of you before the Baron gets back."

I was under the trees now. I had some wild thoughts about grabbing up a club of my own, but they were just thoughts. Dunger set himself and his eyes dropped to my belly. I didn't wait for it; I lunged at him. He laughed and stepped back, and the club cracked my head. Not hard; just enough to send me down. I got my legs under me and started to get up—

There was a hint of motion from the shadows behind Dunger. I shook my head to cover any expression that might have showed, let myself drop back.

"Get up," Dunger said. The smile was gone now. He aimed a kick. "Get up—"

He froze suddenly, then whirled. His hearing must have been as keen as a jungle cat's; I hadn't heard a sound.

The old man stepped into view, his white hair plastered wet to his skull, his big hands spread. Dunger snarled, jumped in and whipped the club down; I heard it hit. There was a flurry of struggle, then Dunger stumbled back, empty-handed.

I was on my feet again now. I made a lunge for Dunger as he roared and charged. The club in the old man's hand rose and fell. Dunger crashed past and into the brush. The old man sat down suddenly, still holding the club. Then he let it fall and lay back. I went toward him and Dunger rushed me from the side. I went down again.

I was dazed, but not feeling any pain now. Dunger was standing over the old man. I could see the big lean figure lying limply, arms outspread —and a white bone handle, incongruously new and neat against the shabby mackinaw. The club lay on the ground a few feet away. I started crawling for it. It seemed a long way, and it was hard for me to move my legs, but I kept at it. The light rain was falling again now, hardly more than a mist. Far away there were shouts and the sound of engines starting up. Mallon's convoy moving out. He had won. Dunger had won, too. The old man had tried, but it hadn't been enough. But if I could reach the club, and swing it just once. . . .

Dunger was looking down at the old man. He leaned, withdrew the knife, wiped it on his trouser leg, hitching up his pants to tuck it away in its sheath. The club was smooth and heavy under my hand. I got a good grip on it, got to my feet. I waited until Dunger turned, and then I hit him across the top of the skull with everything I had left. . . .

I thought the old man was dead until he blinked suddenly. His features looked relaxed now, peaceful, the skin like parchment stretched over bone. I took his gnarled old hand and rubbed it. It was as cold as a drowned sailor.

"You waited for me, old-timer?" I said inanely. He moved his head minutely, and looked at me. Then his mouth moved. I leaned closer to catch what he was saying. His voice was fainter than lost hope.

"Mom . . . told . . . me . . . wait for you. . . . She said . . . you'd . . . come back some day. . . ."

I felt my jaw muscles knotting.

Inside me something broke and flowed away like molten metal. Suddenly my eyes were blurred—and not only with rain. I looked at the old face before me, and for a moment, I seemed to see a ghostly glimpse of another face, a small round face that looked up.

He was speaking again. I put my head down:

"Was I . . . good . . . boy . . . Dad?" Then the eyes closed.

I sat for a long time, looking at the still face. Then I folded the hands on the chest and stood.

"You were more than a good boy, Timmy," I said. "You were a good man."

9   My blue suit was soaking wet and splattered with mud, plus a few flecks of what Dunger had used for brains, but it still carried the gold eagles on the shoulders.

The attendant in the garage didn't look at my face. The eagles were enough for him. I stalked to a vast black Bentley—a '90 model, I guessed, from the conservative eighteen-inch tail fins—and jerked the door open. The gauge showed three-quarters full. I opened the glove compartment, rummaged, found nothing. But then it wouldn't be up front with the chauffeur. . . .

I pulled open the back door. There was a crude black leather holster riveted against the smooth pale-gray leather, with the butt of a 4-mm showing. There was another one on the opposite door, and a power rifle slung from straps on the back of the driver's seat.

Whoever owned the Bentley was overcompensating his insecurity. I took a pistol, tossed it onto the front seat, and slid in beside it. The attendant gaped at me as I eased my left arm into my lap and twisted to close the door. I started up. There was a bad knock, but she ran all right. I flipped a switch and cold lances of light speared out into the rain.

At the last instant, the attendant started forward with his mouth open to say something, but I didn't wait to hear it. I gunned out into the night, swung into the graveled drive, and headed for the gate. Mallon had had it all his way so far, but maybe it still wasn't too late. . . .

Two sentries, looking miserable in shiny black ponchos, stepped out of the guard hut as I pulled up. One peered in at me, then came to a sloppy position of attention and presented arms. I reached for the gas pedal and the second sentry called something. The first man looked startled, then swung the gun down to cover me. I eased a hand toward my pistol, brought it up fast, and fired through the glass. Then the Bentley was roaring off into the dark along the potholed road that led into town. I thought I heard a shot behind me, but I wasn't sure.

I took the river road south of town, pounding at reckless speed over the ruined blacktop, gaining on the lights of Mallon's horde paralleling me a mile to the north. A quarter mile from the perimeter fence, the Bentley broke a spring and skidded into a ditch.

I sat for a moment taking deep breaths to drive back the compulsive drowsiness that was sliding down over my eyes like a visor. My arm throbbed like a cauterized stump. I needed a few minutes' rest. . . .

A sound brought me awake like an old maid smelling cigar smoke in the bedroom: the rise and fall of heavy engines in convoy. Mallon was coming up at flank speed.

I got out of the car and headed off along the road at a trot, holding my broken arm with my good one to ease the jarring pain. My chances had been as slim as a gambler's wallet all along, but if Mallon beat me to the objective, they dropped to nothing.

The eastern sky had taken on a faint gray tinge, against which I could make out the silhouetted gateposts and the dead floodlights a hundred yards ahead.

The roar of engines was getting louder. There were other sounds, too: a few shouts, the chatter of a 9-mm, the *boom!* of something heavier, and once a long-drawn *whoosh!* of falling masonry. With his new toy, Mallon was dozing his way through the men and buildings that got in his way.

I reached the gate, picked my way over fallen wire mesh, then headed for the Primary Site.

I couldn't run now. The broken slabs tilted crazily, in no pattern. I slipped, stumbled, but kept my feet. Behind me, headlights threw shadows across the slabs. It wouldn't be long now before someone in Mallon's task force spotted me and opened up with the guns—

The whoop! *whoop!* WHOOP! of the guardian Bolo cut across the field.

Across the broken concrete I saw the two red eyes flash, sweeping my way. I looked toward the gate. A massed rank of vehicles stood in a battalion front just beyond the old perimeter fence, engines idling, ranged for a hundred yards on either side of a wide gap at the gate. I looked for the high silhouette of Mallon's Bolo, and saw it far off down the avenue, picked out in red, white, and green navigation lights, a jeweled dreadnought. A glaring cyclopean eye at the top darted a blue-white cone of light ahead, swept over the waiting escort, outlined me like a set-shifter caught onstage by the rising curtain.

The *whoop! whoop!* sounded again; the automated sentry Bolo was bearing down on me along the dancing lane of light.

I grabbed at the plastic disk in my pocket as though holding it in my hand would somehow heighten its potency. I didn't know if the Lesser Troll was programmed to exempt me from destruction or not; and there was only one way to find out.

It wasn't too late to turn around and run for it. Mallon might shoot— or he might not. I could convince him that he needed me, that together we could grab twice as much loot. And then, when he died—

I wasn't really considering it; it was the kind of thought that flashes through a man's mind like heat lightning when time slows in the instant of crisis. It was hard to be brave with broken bone ends grating, but what I had to do didn't take courage. I was a small, soft, human grub, stepped on but still moving, caught on the harsh plain of broken concrete between the clash of chrome-steel titans. But I knew which direction to take.

The Lesser Troll rushed toward me in a roll of thunder and I went to meet it.

It stopped twenty yards from me, loomed massive as a cliff. Its heavy guns were dead, I knew. Without them it was no more dangerous than a farmer with a shotgun—

But against me a shotgun was enough.

The slab under me trembled as if in anticipation. I squinted against the dull red I-R beams that pivoted to hold me, waiting while the Troll considered. Then the guns elevated, pointed over my head like a benediction. The Bolo knew me.

The guns traversed fractionally. I looked back toward the enemy line, saw the Great Troll coming up now, closing the gap, towering over its waiting escort like a planet among moons. And the guns of the Lesser Troll tracked it as it came—the empty guns that for twenty years had held Mallon's scavengers at bay.

The noise of engines was deafening now. The waiting line moved restlessly, pulverizing old concrete under churning treads. I didn't realize I was being fired on until I saw chips fly to my left and heard the howl of ricochets.

It was time to move. I scrambled for the Bolo, snorted at the stink of hot oil and ozone, found the rusted handholds, and pulled myself up—

Bullets spanged off metal above me. Someone was trying for me with a power rifle.

The broken arm hung at my side like a fence post nailed to my shoulder, but I wasn't aware of the pain now. The hatch stood open half an inch. I grabbed the lever, strained; it swung wide. No lights came up to meet me. With the port cracked, they'd burned out long ago. I dropped down inside, wriggled through the narrow crawl space into the cockpit. It was smaller than the Mark II—and it was occupied.

In the faint green light from the panel, the dead man crouched over the controls, one desiccated hand in a shriveled black glove clutching the control bar. He wore a GI weather suit and a white crash helmet, and one foot was twisted nearly backward, caught behind a jack lever.

The leg had been broken before he died. He must have jammed the foot and twisted it so that the pain would hold off the sleep that had come at last. I leaned forward to see the face. The blackened and mummified features showed only the familiar anonymity of death, but the bushy reddish mustache was enough.

"Hello, Mac," I said. "Sorry to keep you waiting; I got held up."

I wedged myself into the copilot's seat, flipped the I-R screen switch. The eight-inch panel glowed, showed me the enemy Bolo trampling through the fence three hundred yards away, then moving onto the ramp, dragging a length of rusty chain-link like a bridal train behind it.

I put my hand on the control bar. "I'll take it now, Mac," I moved the bar, and the dead man's hand moved with it.

"Okay, Mac," I said. "We'll do it together."

I hit the switches, canceling the preset response pattern. It had done its job for eighty years, but now it was time to crank in a little human strategy.

My Bolo rocked slightly under a hit and I heard the tread shields drop down. The chair bucked under me as Mallon moved in, pouring in the fire.

Beside me Mac nodded patiently. It was old stuff to him. I watched the tracers on the screen. Hosing me down with contact exploders probably gave Mallon a lot of satisfaction, but it couldn't hurt me. It would be a different story when he tired of the game and tried the heavy stuff.

I threw in the drive, backed rapidly. Mallon's tracers followed for a few yards, then cut off abruptly. I pivoted, flipped on my polyarcs, raced for the position I had selected across the field, then swung to face Mallon as he moved toward me. It had been a long time since he had handled the controls of a Bolo; he was rusty, relying on his automatics. I had no heavy rifles, but my popguns were okay. I homed my 4-mm solid-slug cannon on Mallon's polyarc, pressed the FIRE button.

There was a scream from the high-velocity-feed magazine. The blue-white light flared and went out. The Bolo's defense could handle anything short of an H-bomb, pick a missile out of the stratosphere fifty miles away, devastate a county with one round from its mortars—but my BB gun at point-blank range had poked out its eye.

I switched everything off and sat silent, waiting. Mallon had come to a dead stop. I could picture him staring at the dark screens, slapping levers, and cursing. He would be confused, wondering what had happened. With his lights gone, he'd be on radar now—not very sensitive at this range, not too conscious of detail. . . .

I watched my panel. An amber warning light winked. Mallon's radar was locked on me.

He moved forward again, then stopped; he was having trouble making up his mind. I flipped a key to drop a padded shock frame in place and braced myself. Mallon would be getting mad now.

Crimson danger lights flared on the board and I rocked under the recoil as my interceptors flashed out to meet Mallon's C-S C's and detonate them in incandescent rendezvous over the scarred concrete between us. My screens went white, then dropped back to secondary brilliance, flashing stark black-and-white. My ears hummed like trapped hornets.

The sudden silence was like a vault door closing.

I sagged back, feeling like Quasimodo after a wild ride on the bells. The screens blinked bright again, and I watched Mallon, sitting motionless now in his near blindness. On his radar screen I would show as a blurred hill; he would be wondering why I hadn't returned his fire, why I hadn't turned and run, why . . . why. . . .

He lurched and started toward me. I waited, then eased back, slowly. He accelerated, closing in to come to grips at a range where even the split microsecond response of my defenses would be too slow to hold off his fire. And I backed, letting him gain, but not too fast. . . .

Mallon couldn't wait.

He opened up, throwing a mixed bombardment from his 9-mm's, his infinite repeaters, and his C-S C's. I held on, fighting the battering frame, watching the screens. The gap closed; a hundred yards, ninety, eighty.

The open silo yawned in Mallon's path now, but he didn't see it. The mighty Bolo came on, guns bellowing in the night, closing for the kill. On the brink of the fifty-foot wide, hundred-yard-deep pit, it hesitated as though sensing danger. Then it moved forward.

I saw it rock, dropping its titanic prow, showing its broad back, gouging the blasted pavement as its guns bore on the ground. Great sheets of sparks flew as the treads reversed, too late. The Bolo hung for a moment longer, then slid down majestically as a sinking liner, its guns still firing into the pit like a challenge to Hell. And then it was gone. A dust cloud boiled for a moment, then whipped away as displaced air tornadoed from the open mouth of the silo.

And the earth trembled under the impact far below.

10   The doors of the Primary Site blockhouse were nine-foot-high, eight-inch-thick panels of solid chromalloy that even a Bolo would have slowed down for, but they slid aside for my electropass like a shower curtain at the YW. I went into a shadowy room where eighty years of silence hung like black crepe on a coffin. The tiled floor was still immaculate, the air fresh. Here at the heart of the Aerospace Center, all systems were still go.

In the Central Control bunker, nine rows of green lights glowed on the high panel over red letters that spelled out STAND BY TO FIRE. A foot to the left, the big white lever stood in the unlocked position, six inches from the outstretched fingertips of the mummified corpse strapped into the controller's chair. To the right, a red glow on the monitor panel indicated the lock doors open.

I rode the lift down to K level, stepped out onto the steel-railed platform that hugged the sweep of the starship's hull and stepped through into the narrow COC.

On my right, three empty stasis tanks stood open, festooned cabling draped in disorder. To the left were the four sealed covers under which Day, Macy, Cruciani, and Black waited. I went close, read dials. Slender needles trembled minutely to the beating of sluggish hearts.

They were alive.

I left the ship, sealed the inner and outer ports. Back in the control bunker, the monitor panel showed ALL CLEAR FOR LAUNCH now. I studied the timer, set it, turned back to the master panel. The white lever was smooth and cool under my hand. It seated with a click. The red hand of the launch clock moved off jerkily, the ticking harsh in the silence.

Outside, the Bolo waited. I climbed to a perch in the open conning tower twenty feet above the broken pavement, moved off toward the west where sunrise colors picked out the high towers of the palace.

I rested the weight of my splinted and wrapped arm on the balcony rail, looking out across the valley and the town to the misty plain under which *Prometheus* waited.

"There's something happening now," Renada said. I took the binoculars, watched as the silo doors rolled back.

"There's smoke," Renada said.

"Don't worry, just cooling gases being vented off." I looked at my watch. "Another minute or two and man makes the biggest jump since the first lungfish crawled out on a mud flat."

"What will they find out there?"

I shook my head. "*Homo terra firma* can't even conceive of what *Homo astra* has ahead of him."

"Twenty years they'll be gone. It's a long time to wait."

"We'll be busy trying to put together a world for them to come back to. I don't think we'll be bored."

"Look!" Renada gripped my good arm. A long silvery shape, huge even at the distance of miles, rose slowly out of the earth, poised on a brilliant ball of white fire. Then the sound came, a thunder that penetrated my bones, shook the railing under my hand. The fireball lengthened into a silver-white column with the ship balanced at its tip. Then the column broke free, rose up, up. . . .

I felt Renada's hand touch mine. I gripped it hard. Together we watched as *Prometheus* took man's gift of fire back to the heavens.

ALGIS BUDRYS

THE NUPTIAL FLIGHT OF WARBIRDS

The woman gasped slightly as he began to see her. Dusty Haverman smiled comfortably, extending his lean arm in its brocaded scarlet sleeve, white lace frothing at his wrist. He tilted the decanter over the crystal stem glass shimmering in the stainless air of the afternoon, and rosy clarity swirled within the fragile bell. "You'll enjoy that," he said to her. "It doesn't ordinarily travel well."

She was very pale, with dark, made-up eyes and lips drawn a startling red. A lavender print scarf was bound around her neck-length smoke-black hair, and she wore a lavender voile dress with a full calf-length skirt and a bellboy collar. Below the collar, the front of the dress was open to the waist in a loose slit.

She sat straight in her chair. Her plum-colored nails gripped the ends of the decoratively carved wooden arms. The breeze, whispering over the coarse grass that grew in odd-shaped meadows between the lengths of sandy concrete, stirred her hair. She looked around her at the sideboard, the silver chafing dishes of hot hors d'oeuvres, the Fragonard and the large Boucher hung on ornate wooden racks, the distant structures and the marker lights thrusting up here and there from the edges of the grass. She watched Haverman carefully as he sank back into his own chair, crossed his knees, and raised his own glass. "To our close acquaintanceship," he was saying in his slightly husky voice, a distinguished-looking man with slightly waving silver hair worn a little long over the tops of the ears, and a thinish, carefully trimmed silver moustache hovering at the rim of the rose cordial. He wore a white silk ascot.

The woman, who had only a very few signs of latter twentyishness about the skin of her face and the carriage of her body, raised one sooty eyebrow. "Where are we?" she asked. "Who are you?"

Haverman smiled. "We are at the juncture of runways twenty-eight Left and forty-two Right at O'Hare International Airport. My name is Austin Gelvarry."

The woman looked around again, more quickly. Her silk-clad knee bumped the low mahogany table between them, and Haverman had to reach deftly to save her glass. She settled back slowly. "It certainly isn't Cannes," she agreed. She reached for the wine, keeping one hand spread-fingered over the front of her bosom as she leaned. Her eyes did not leave Haverman's face. "How did you do this?"

Gelvarry smiled. "How could I not do it, Miss Montez? Ah, ah, no, don't do that! Don't press so hard against your mouth. *Sip*, Miss Montez, please! Withdraw the glass a slight distance. Now draw the upper lip together just a suggestion, and *delicately* impress its undercurve upon the swell of the edging. Sip, Miss Montez. As if at a blossom, my dear. As if at a chalice." He smiled. "You will get to like me. I was in the Royal Flying Corps, you know."

Just at first light, the mechanics would have the early patrol craft lined up on the cinders beside the scarred turf of the runway. They would waken Gelvarry with the sound of the propellers being pulled through. He would lie-up in his cot, his eyes very wide in the dim, listening to the *whup, whup, whup!*

The mechanics ran in three-man teams, one team for each of the three planes in the flight. One would be just letting go the lower tip of the wooden airscrew and jumping a little sideward to turn and double back. One would be doubling back, arms pumping for balance, head cocked to watch the third man, who would be just jumping into the air, arms out, hands slightly cupped to catch the tip of the upper blade as it started down.

They ran in perfect rhythm, and they would do this a dozen times before they attempted to start the aircraft. They said it was necessary to do this with the Trompe L'Oeil engine, which was a French design.

Sergeant-Major MacBanion had instituted this drill. If it were not performed precisely, the cylinder walls would not be evenly lubricated when the engines were started. The cylinder walls would score, and very likely seize-up a piston, and all you fine young gentlemen would be dropping your arses, beg pardon (with a wink), all over the perishing map of bleeding Belgium. Then he knocked the dottle out of his pipe, scratched the ribs of the little gray monkey he liked to carry, and turned his shaved neck to shout something to an Other Rank.

Sar'n-Major Mac's speaking voice was sharp and confident, and his manner assertive, in dealing with matters of management. In speaking to Gelvarry and the other flying personnel, however, he was more avuncular, and it seemed to Gelvarry that he saw more than he sometimes let on.

Gelvarry, who was hoping for assignment soon to the high squadron, reckoned that Sergeant-Major MacBanion might have more to do with that than his rank augured for. Nominally, he was only in charge of instruction for transitioning to high squadron aircraft, but since Major Harding never emerged from his hut, it was difficult to believe he was not dependent on Sergeant-Major MacBanion for personnel recommendations.

Gelvarry swung his legs over the side of the cot, taking an involuntary breath of the Nissen hut's interior. Gelvarry's feet had frosted a bit on a long flight the previous week and were quite tender. He limped across the hut, arranging his clothes, and went over to the washstand.

Gelvarry felt there was no better high squadron candidate in the area at the present time. Barton Fisher of XIV Recon Wing had more flight time, but everyone knew Armed Chase flew harder, and Gelvarry had been in Armed Chase for the past year, now being definitely senior man at this aerodrome and senior flying personnel in the entire MC Armed Chase Wing. "I should like very much to apply for assignment to the high squadron, Sir," he rehearsed as he brushed his teeth. But since he had no idea what Major Harding looked like, the face in the mottled fragment of pier glass remained entirely his own.

He spat into the waste bucket and peered at the results. His gums were evidently still bleeding freely. Squinting into the mirror, he lathered his face cold and began shaving with a razor that had been most indifferently honed by Parkins, the batman Gelvarry shared with the remainder of his flight in the low squadron. Parkins had been reduced from Engine Artificer by Sar'n-Major Mac, and quite right. "Give 'im a drum of oil and a stolen typewriter," Gelvarry grumbled as he scraped at the gingery stubble on his pale cheeks. "He'll jump his bicycle and flog 'em in the village for a litre of Vouvray."

He rubbed his face with a damp gray towel full of threads and bent to stare out the end window. The weather was expectable; mist just rising, still snagged a little in the tops of the poplars; eastern sky giving some promise of rose; and the windsock pointing mendaciously inward. By the time they'd completed their sweep, low on petrol and ready for luncheon and a heartfelt sigh, it would have shifted straight toward Hunland and God help the poor sod who attempted the feat of gliding home on an engine stopped by fuel shortage or, better yet, enemy action also involving injury to flying personnel. All up then, my lad, and into the *Lagerkorps* at the point of some *gefreiter's* bayonet, to spend the remainder of the war laying railroad lines or embanking canals, *Gott Mit Uns* and *Hoch der Fuehrer!* for the Thousand Year Empire, God grant it mischief.

In fact, Gelvarry thought, going out of the hut and running along the duckboards with his shoulders hunched and his hands in his pockets, the only good thing about the day to this point was that his headache was nowhere near as bad as it deserved to be. Perhaps there was truth in the rumor that Issue mess brandy had resumed being shipped from England. It had lately been purchased direct under plausible labels from blue-chinned peasant gentlemen who cut prices in deference to the bravery of their gallant allies.

"Get out of my way, you creature," he puffed to Islingden, John Peter, Flying Officer, otherwise third Duke of Landsdowne, who was standing on the boards with a folded *Gazette* under his arm, studying the sky. "If you're done in there, show some consideration." They danced around each other, arms out for balance, "Nigger Jack" Islingden clutching the *Gazette* like a baton, his large teeth flashing whitely against his olive-hued Landsdowne complexion, introduced via a Spanish countess by the first Duke, neither of them wishing to step off the slats into the spring mud, their boot toes clattering, until Gelvarry at last gained entrance to the officers' latrine.

The dampness rising from the ground was all through his bones. Gelvarry shivered with ease as he sprinted along the cinder track toward his SE-5, beating his arms across his chest. He paused just long enough to scribble a receipt for the aircraft and return the clipboard to the Chief Fitter, found the reinforced plate at the root of the lower plane, stepped up on it and dropped into the cockpit, his hands smearing the droplets of dew on the leather edging of the rim. He felt himself shaking thoroughly now, proceeding with the business of hand-signaling the other two pilots —Landsdowne and a sergeant pilot named O'Sullivan—and ensuring they were ready. He signaled Chocks Out, and the ground personnel yanked sharply at the lines, clearing his wheels and dropping flat to let his lower planes pass over.

As soon as he jassed the throttle to smooth his plugs and build takeoff power, a cascade of water blew back into his face from the top of the mainplane, and he stopped shivering. He glanced left and right, raised his arm, flung his hand forward, and advanced the throttle. The trim little Bristol, responsive as a filly, leapt forward. For a few moments, she sprang and rebounded to every inequality of the turf, while her flying wires sang into harmony with the increasing vibration of the engine and airscrew. The droplets on the doped fabric turned instantly into streaks over the smoke-colored oil smears from the engine. Then there was suddenly the smooth buzzing under his feet of the wheels rotating freely on their axles, all weight off, and the SE-5 climbed spiritedly into the dawn, trailing a momentary train of spray that glistened for an instant in the sunlight above the mist. Soon enough, the remaining condensation turned white and opaque, forming little flowers where the panes of his windscreen were jointed into their frames. Gelvarry held the stick between his knees and smoothed his gloves tighter over his hands, which retained little trace of their former trembling.

Up around Paschendaele they were dodging nimbly among some clouds when Gelvarry suddenly plucked his Very pistol from its metal clip in the cockpit and fired a green flare. Nigger and O'Sullivan jerked their courses around into exact conformity with his as they, too, now saw the *staffel* of Albatros falling upon them. They pointed their noses up at a steep angle toward the *Boche,* giving the engines more throttle to prevent stalling, and briefly testing the firing linkages of their twin Vickers guns. Tracer bullets left little spirals of white smoke in the air beyond Gelvarry's engine, to be sucked up immediately as he nibbled in behind them. He glanced at Landsdowne and Paddy, raising one thumb. They clenched their fists and shook them, once, twice, toward the foe who, mottled with garish camouflage, dropped down with flame winking at the muzzles of the Spandau *maschingewehren* behind the gleaming arcs of their propellers.

Gelvarry felt they were firing too soon. Nevertheless, there was an abrupt drumming upon his left upper plane, and then a ripping. He saw a wire suddenly vibrate its middle portion into invisibility as a slug glanced from it. There was no damage of consequence. He held his course and refrained from firing, only thinking of how the entire aircraft had quivered to the drumming, and of how when the fabric split it was as if something swift and hot had seared across the backs of his hands. It was Gelvarry's professional opinion that such moments must be fully met and studied within the mind, so that they lose their power of surprise.

There were eight Albatros in the diving formation, he saw, and therefore there might be as many as four more stooging about in the clouds waiting to follow down stragglers.

The stench of overheated castor oil came back from his engine and coated his lips and tongue. He pushed his goggles up onto his forehead, hunched his face down into the full lee of the windscreen, and now, when it might count, began firing purposeful short bursts.

The Albatros is a difficult aircraft head-on because it has a metal propeller fairing and an in-line engine, so that many possible hits are deflected and the target area is not large. On the other hand, the Albatros is not really a good diver, having a tendency to shed its wings at steeper angles. Gelvarry had long ago reasoned out that even an apparently sound Albatros mainplane is under considerable stress in a dive, and so he fired a little above the engine, hoping to damage the struts or even the main spar, but noting that as an inevitable consequence there might also be direct or deflected hits on the windscreen. He did not wish to be known as a deliberate shooter of pilots, but there it was.

The *staffel* passed through the flight of SE-5s with seven survivors, one of which, however, was turning for home with smoke issuing from its oil cooler. The three British aircraft, necessarily throttling back to save their engines, began to mush out of their climbing attitude. Three Albatros that had been waiting their turn now launched a horizontal attack.

His head swiveling while he half-stood in the cockpit, searching, Gelvarry saw the three fresh Albatros emerge from the clouds. Below him, six of the original assault were looping up to rejoin. On his right, Paddy's aircraft displayed miscellaneous splinters and punctures of the empennage, and was trailing a few streamers of fabric, but appeared to be structurally sound. O'Sullivan, however, was beating at the breech-block of one of his guns with a wooden mallet, one hand wrapped around an interplane strut to hold him forward over the windscreen, the other busy with its hammering as it tried to pop out the overexpanded shell casing. His aircraft was wallowing as he inadvertently nudged the stick back and forth with his legs.

On the left, Nigger was nose down, his airscrew windmilling, ropy smoke and pink fire blowing back over the cockpit. For a moment, the SE-5's ailerons quickly flapped into a new configuration, and the rudder and elevators came over as Landsdowne tried to sideslip the burning. But they were, in any case, at 7000 feet and at this height there was really no point to the maneuver. Landsdowne stood up in the cockpit as the aircraft came level again, saluted Gelvarry, and jumped, his collar and helmet thickly trailing soot.

"So long, Nig," Gelvarry murmured. He glanced up. A mile above them, the silvery flash of sunlight upon the *Ticonderoga*'s flanks dazzled the eye; nevertheless, he thought he could make out the attendant cloud of dark midges who were the high squadron. He looked to his right and saw that O'Sullivan was being hit repeatedly in the torso by gunfire, white phosphorus tracer spirals emerging from the plucked leather of his coat.

Gelvarry took in a deep breath. He pushed his aircraft into a falling right bank, kicked right rudder, and passed between two of the oncoming Nazis. He converted the bank into a shallow diving roll, and so went down through the climbing group of Albatros at an angle which made it useless for either side to fire. He had also placed all his enemies in such a relationship to him that they would have had to turn and dive at suicidal inclinations in order to overtake him as he darted homeward.

He flew above the remains of villages that looked like old bones awash in brown soup, and over the lines that were like a river on the moon, its margins festooned with wire to prevent careless Selenites from stumbling in. A high squadron aircraft dropped down and flew beside him for a while, as he had heard they sometimes did lately.

He glanced over at the glossy stagger-wing biplane, its color black except for the white-lettered unit markings, a red-and-white horizontally striped rudder panel, and the American cocardes with the five-pointed white star and orange ball in the center. The pilot was looking at him. He wore a pale yellow helmet, goggles that flashed in the sun, and a very clean white scarf. He raised a hand and waved reservedly, as one might across a tier of boxes at the concert hall. Then he pulled back on his stick and the black aircraft climbed away precipitously, so swiftly that Gelvarry half-expected a crackling of displaced air, but instead heard, very faintly over his own engine, the smooth roar of the other's exhaust. He found that his own right hand was still elevated, and took it down.

He came in over the poplars, and found that he was going to land cross-wind. Ground personnel raised their heads as if they had been grazing at the margins of the runway. He put it down anyhow, swung it about, and taxied toward the hangar, blipping the engine to keep the cylinder heads from sooting up, and finally cut his switch near where Sergeant-Major MacBanion was standing waiting with the little gray monkey perched on his right shoulder. As the engine stopped, the cold once again settled into Gelvarry's bones.

"All right, Sir?" Sar'n-Major Mac asked, looking up at him. The monkey, too, raised its little Capuchin face, the small lobstery eyes peering from under the brim of a miniature *kepi*.

Gelvarry put his hands on the cockpit rim, placed his heels carefully on the traverse brace below the rudder bar, and pushed himself back and up. Then he was able to slip down the side of the fuselage. He stood slapping his hands against his biceps.

Sergeant-Major MacBanion put a hand gently on his shoulder. "And the remainder of the flight, Sir?"

Gelvarry shrugged. He pulled off his helmet and goggles and stuffed them into a pocket of his coat. He stamped his feet, despite the hurt. Then as the cold began to leave him, he merely stood running his hands up and down his arms, and hunching his back.

"Never mind, Sir," Sar'n-Major Mac said softly. "I've come to tell you we've had an urgent message. You're posted to high squadron immediately, Sir."

Gelvarry found himself weeping silently.

"Follow me to Major Harding's hut, please, Sir," Sergeant-Major MacBanion said quietly and gravely. "Don't concern yourself about the aircraft—we'll see to it."

"Thank you," Gelvarry whispered. He walked behind the spare, erect figure to the Major's hut, watching the monkey gently waving the swagger stick. Then he waited outside, rubbing his hands over his cheeks, feeling the moisture trapped between his palm and the oil film on his skin. He hated the coating in his nostrils and on the roof of his mouth, and habitually scraped it off his lips between his teeth.

Sergeant-Major MacBanion came out of the dark hut, shut the door positively, said, "That's all right, then, Sir," turned his face slightly and shouted: "Private Parkins on the double if you please!"

Parkins came running up with a thud of boots on damp cinders and saluted energetically. "Yes, Sar'n-Major?"

"Parkins, I want you to list three reserve flying personnel with appropriate aircraft for this afternoon's sweep. Make it the three senior men. What flying personnel will that leave at this station during the afternoon hours?"

"Two, Sar'n-Major, in addition to this officer." Parkins nodded slightly toward Gelvarry without taking his eyes off Sergeant-Major MacBanion's steady gaze.

"Don't concern yourself with this officer, Parkins; Chaplain and I'll be taking care of him."

Parkins brought out the sapient manner he had been withholding. "Right, Sar'n-Major. I'll just have Major Harding send them other two officers over to Wing in the Rolls to sign for some engine spares, and that'll clear the premises nicely. I'll take the time to sort through this officer's kit for shipping home, then, as well, shall I?"

"I think not, Parkins," Sergeant-Major MacBanion said meaningly, and Parkins could be seen to bob his Adam's apple. "That is Major Harding's duty. That's what commanding officers are for." The thick, neatly clipped brows drew into a speculating frown. "You're slipping very badly, aren't you, Parkins? I wonder what a rummage through your duffel might turn up; I can't say I care for the smell of your breath."

"Hit's mouthwash, Sar'n-Major!" Parkins exclaimed. "A bit of a soother for me sore bicuspid, like!"

"I'll give you sore, Private Parkins I surely will," Sergeant-Major Mac declared. "Pull yourself together long enough to attend to your own tasks. You're to telephone Wing for three replacement flying personnel to join here tonight, correct? And there's the lorry and the working party to organize; I want this officer's aircraft crashed *and* burning, no doubt about it, *in* No Man's Land, *be*fore teatime, and *if* that's all quite sufficiently clear to you, my man, you *will* see to it forth*with!*"

Parkins saluted, about-faced, and trotted off, sweating. The Sergeant-Major smiled thinly after him, then turned to Gelvarry. "This way, then, please, Sir," he said, and stepped onto the footpath worn through the scrub beside Major Harding's hut.

Following him, Gelvarry was startled to note the neatly cultivated domestic vegetable plot behind the rusty corrugated sheet iron of the Major's dwelling. There were seed packets up on little stakes at the ends of rows, and string stretched in a zigzag web for runner beans. Lettuce and carrots were poking up tentatively along one side, and most of the rows were showing early evidence of shooting. A spade with an officer's cap dangling over the handle was thrust into a dirt-encrusted pile of industrial furnace clinkers that had apparently been extracted from the soil.

"Padre!" Sergeant-Major MacBanion called ahead. "Here's an officer to see you!"

Father Collins thrust his head around the fly of his dwelling tent, which was situated beyond the shrubs screening Major Harding's hut from this far end of the aerodrome. He was a round-faced man of kindly appearance whom Gelvarry had occasionally seen in the mess, fussing with the Sparklets machine and otherwise making himself useful and approved of. He came and moved a little distance toward them along the path, and then waited for them to come up. He put out his hand to shake Gelvarry's. "Always here to be of help," he said.

Sergeant-Major MacBanion cleared his throat. "This'll be a high squadron posting, Padre."

Father Collins nodded a little crossly. "One gathers these things, Sergeant-Major MacBanion. Well, young fellah, let's get to it, then, shall we?" His expression softened and he studied Gelvarry's face carefully. "No need prolonging matters, then, is there? Not a decision to be taken lightly, but, once made, to be followed expeditiously, eh?" He put an arm around Gelvarry's shoulders. Gelvarry found himself grateful for the animal warmth; the cold had been at his ribs again. He went along up the path with Father Collins and Sar'n-Major Mac, and when they reached the little overgrown rise where Father Collins's tent was situated, he stopped. He found he was looking down at a revetment where the transition aircraft was kept.

He walked around and around, a slight smile on his lips, ducking under the planes and squeezing by the end of the rudder where it was nearly right up against the rear embankment. He ran his fingertips lightly over the impeccably doped fabric and admired the workmanship of the rudder and elevator hinges, the delicately shaped brass standoffs that gave extra purchase to the control cables. Everything was new; the smell of the aircraft had the tang of a fitter's storage locker.

He stopped and faced it from outside the revetment. The slim black aircraft pointed its rounded nose well up over his head; it was much larger than he'd expected from seeing one in the air; he'd thought perhaps the pilot was slightly built.

It rested gracefully upon its two fully spatted tires, with a teardrop-shaped auxiliary fuel tank nestled up between the fully faired landing gear struts. Its rest position on its tail skid set it on an angle such that the purposefully sturdy wings grasped muscularly at the air. A glycol radiator slung at the point of the cowling's jaw promised to sieve with jubilation through the stream hurled backward by the three-bladed metal airscrew.

There were very few wires; the struts appeared to be quite thin frontally, but were faired back for lateral strength. It would, yes it would, burgeon upward through the air with every ounce of power available from that promising engine hidden behind the lovingly shaped panels, and it would stoop like a bird of prey. It would not creak or whip in the air; its fuselage panels would not drum and ripple; the dope of its upper surfaces would not star and flake off under the compression of warping wings in a battle maneuver, and one would not find, after twenty or thirty hours, that the planes and the stabilizer had been permanently shaken out of alignment with each other.

This aircraft had the same markings as the one that had flown down briefly, except for the actual numerals. In addition to the national cocardes, it also bore a unit insignia—a long-barreled flintlock rifle crossed upon a powder horn.

Gelvarry felt a prickling pass along the short hairs of his forearms as he thought of flying under that banner. A great-great-uncle was reputed in his family to have been among that company vanished in search of Providence Plantations, as others had done in attempting to find Oglethorpe's Colony or the fabled inland cities of Virginia Dare's children. North America was a continent of endless forest and dark rumor. And yet something, it seemed—some seed possessed of patience—had been germinating *Ticonderogas* and aircraft construction works all the while, and within reach of Mr. Churchill's remarkable winnow.

"This is the Curtis P6E 'Hawk,'" Sar'n-Major Mac said at his elbow. "This model is the ultimate development of what will be considered the most versatile armed chase single-place biplane ever designed. The original airframe will be introduced in the mid-1920s. As you see it here, it is fitted with United States Army Air Corps-specified inline liquid-cooled four-stroke engine developing 450 horsepower, and two fixed quick-firing thirty-caliber machine guns geared to shoot through the airscrew. The U.S. Navy version, known as the 'Goshawk,' will use the Wright 'Whirlwind' radial air-cooled engine. Both basic versions are very highly thought of, will remain in service in the U.S. until the mid-1930s, and a few 'Hawk' versions will be used by the Republican air forces in the Spanish Civil War, should that occur."

Father Collins had been up at the cockpit, leaning in to polish the instrument glass with a soft white cloth. He came down now, pausing to wipe the step let into the fuselage and the place on the wing root where he had rested his other foot.

"All quite ready now," he said, carefully folding the cloth and putting it away in his open-mouthed black leather case. He rested his hand on Gelvarry's shoulder. "We've kept her in prime condition for you, lad— no one's ever flown her before; Sar'n-Major and I just ticked her over now and then, kept her clean and taut; the usual drill."

Gelvarry was nodding. As the moment drew near, he found himself breathing with greater difficulty. Tears were gathering in his eyes. He turned his face away awkwardly.

"Now, as for the hooking on," Sergeant-Major MacBanion was saying briskly, "I'm certain you'll manage that part of it quite well, Sir." He was pointing up at the trapeze hook fixed to the center of the mainplane like the hanger of a Christmas tree ball, and Gelvarry perforce had to look at him attentively.

"Pity there's no way to rehearse the necessary maneuver, Sir," Sar'n-Major Mac went on, "but they say it comes to one. Only a matter of matching courses and speeds, after all, and then just easing up in there."

Gelvarry nodded. He still could not speak.

"Well, Sir," the Sergeant-Major concluded. "Care to try a few circuits and bumps around the old place before taking her to your new posting? Get the feel of her? Some prefer that. Many just climb right in and go off. What'll it be, Sir?"

Gelvarry found himself profoundly disturbed. Something was rising in his chest. Father Collins looked at him narrowly and raised his free hand toward MacBanion. "Perhaps we're rushing our fences, Sergeant-Major. Just verify the cockpit appurtenances there and give us a moment meanwhile, will you?" He turned Gelvarry away from the aircraft and sauntered beside him casually, his arm around Gelvarry's shoulders again.

"Troubles you, doesn't it?"

Gelvarry glanced at him.

"But there was no doubt in your mind when you spoke to MacBanion about this, was there?"

Gelvarry blinked, then shook his head slowly.

"It's good sense, you know. You'd be leaving us the other way, shortly, if it weren't for this. Bound to." He dug in his pocket for his pipe and blew through it sharply to clear the stem. "Sergeant-Major's been discussing it for weeks. Thin as a charity widow, he's been calling you, and twice as pale, except for the Hennessey roses in your cheeks, beggin' all flyin' officers' pardon, Sir. He's been wanting to do something about it."

Gelvarry gave a high, short laugh.

Father Collins chuckled tolerantly. "Ah, no, no, Lad, hoping we'd make the choice for you is not the same. We always wait 'til the man requests it. Have to, eh? Suppose a man were posted on *our* say-so; liable to resent it, wouldn't he be, don't you think? Might kick up a fuss. Word of high squadron might reach Home. And we can't have that, now, can we?"

Gelvarry shook his head, walking along with his lips between his teeth, his lustrous eyes on his aimless feet.

"Mothers' marches on Whitehall, questions in Parliament— If they're alive, put 'em back on duty or bring 'em home to the shell-shock ward—that sort of thing. Be an unholy row, wouldn't you think? And so much grief renewed among the loved ones, to say nothing of the confusion; it would be cruel. Or what would they say at the Admiralty if officers and gentlemen began discussing another Mr. Churchill, he cruising about the skies like the Angels of Mons, furthermore? For that matter, I imagine *their* Mr. Churchill would have quite a bit to say about it, and none of it pleasant to the tender ear, eh?"

Gelvarry smiled as well as he was able. He had never laid eyes on or heard the young Mr. Churchill; he imagined him a plump, shrill, prematurely balding fellow in loosely tailored clothing, gesturing with a pair of spectacles.

Father Collins gently turned Gelvarry back toward the aircraft. "We'll miss you, too, you know," he said quietly. "But we must move along now. It's best if other flying personnel can't be certain who's in high squadron and who's left us in the old stager's way, don't you agree? Gives everyone a bit of something to look forward to as the string shortens. MacBanion's a genius at clearing the field, but time *is* passing. Don't worry, Boy—Major Harding does a lovely job of seeing to it nothing's sent home as shouldn't be, and of course I'll be conveying the tidings by my own hand." They were back beside the P6E. Sergeant-Major MacBanion was standing stiffly attentive, the monkey in the crook of his arm with one small hand curled around the butt of the swagger stick.

"I believe I'll try taking her straight out, Sergeant-Major," Gelvarry said.

"Right, Sir. That's the way! Just a few things to remember about the controls, Sir, and you'll find she goes along quite nicely."

"And thank you very much, Father. I appreciate your concern."

"Nonsense, my boy. Only natural. Just keep it in mind we're all still hitting the Bavarian Corporal where he hurts; high or low makes little difference. Bit more comfortable up where you'll be, I shouldn't wonder, but I'm sure you've earned it. Tenfold. Easily tenfold."

"Let my family down as easily as you can, will you, Father?" Gelvarry said.

"Ah, yes, yes, of course."

Gelvarry climbed up into the cockpit. He sat getting the feel of how it fit him. He waggled the stick and nudged the rudder—there were pedals for his feet, rather than a pivoted bar, but the principle was the same.

Sar'n-Major Mac got up on the lower plane root and leaned into the cockpit over him. "Here's your magneto switch, and that's your throttle, of course; some of these instruments you can just ignore—can't imagine why a real aviator'd want them, tell the truth—and this is a wireless telegraphy device, but you don't need *that*—can you imagine, from the way the seat's designed when Padre and I take 'em out of the shipping crate, I'd say you were intended to be sitting on a parachute, of all things; get yourself mistaken for a ruddy civilian, next thing—but this, here's, your supercharger cut-in."

"Supercharger?"

"Oh, right, right, yes, Sir, no telling how high you might find *Ticonderoga;* things could be a bit thin. And in that vein, Sir, you'll note this metal bottle with petcock and flexible tubing. That's your oxygen supply; simply place the end of the tube in your mouth, open the petcock as required, and suck on it from time to time at altitudes above 12,000 feet, or lower if feeling a bit winded. Got all that, Sir?"

"Yes, thank you, Sar'n-Major."

"Very good! Well, then, Sir, Padre'll be wanting another brief word with you, and then anytime after that, we'll just get her started, shall we? I understand the Navy type has a crank thing called an inertia starter, but the old familiar way's for us. After that, I'd suggest a little taxiing for the feel of the controls and throttle, and then just head her into the wind, full throttle, and pleasure serving with you, Sir, if I do say so. You'll find she favors her nose a little, so keep throttle open a bit until you bring her nearer to level; I imagine she stalls something ferocious. But there'll be no trouble; never had any trouble yet. Just head west and look about; you'll see your new post up there somewhere. Can't really miss it, after all—large enough. Anything else, Sir?"

"No. No, thank you, Ma—Sergeant-Major MacBanion."

MacBanion's right eyebrow had been rising. It dropped back into place. He patted Gelvarry manfully atop the shoulder. "That's the way, Sir. Have a good trip, and think of us grubbing away down here, once in a while, will you?" He jumped from the lower plane and Father Collins came up, holding the bag. "Might be a longish flight, Son," he said. "You've had nothing to eat or drink since midnight, I believe. So you'll be wanting some of this." He opened the bag and handed Gelvarry a small flask and a piece of bread. "And there's windburn at those altitudes." He put ointment on Gelvarry's forehead and eyelids. "Have a safe flight," he said.

Gelvarry nodded. "Thank you again." When Father Collins jumped down, Gelvarry ducked his head below the level of the cockpit coaming and wiped his face. He put his arm straight up in the air and rotated his hand. Sergeant-Major MacBanion and he began the starting procedure.

The aircraft handled very well. He did a long figure eight over the aerodrome at low altitude after he'd gotten the feel of it. The ground personnel of course were busy at their various tasks. An unfamiliar figure leaning with one foot on a garden spade waved up casually from behind Major Harding's hut. The monkey was perched on a new pineboard crate Father Collins and Sergeant-Major MacBanion were manhandling down into the revetment from the back of an open lorry. As Gelvarry flew over, the little creature scrambled up to the apex of the tilting box, grinned at him, and raised its kepi.

Past the field, Gelvarry did a creditable Immelmann turn, gained altitude, settled himself a little more comfortably on the cushion made from a gunnysack stuffed with rags, and flew toward the afternoon sun, looking upward.

The aircraft *was* a joy, he gradually realized. He probed tentatively at the pedals and stick, at first, hardly recognizing he was doing so because he was under the impression his mind was full of confusions and sorrows. But as he held steadily west, his back and his arse heavy in the seat, his mind began to develop a certain wire-hard incised detachment which he recognized from his evenings with the brandy. In fact, as he gained more and more altitude, and began to rock the wings jauntily and even to give it a little rudder so that he set up a slight fishtail, he could almost hear the messroom piano, as it was every day after nightfall, all snug around the stove, grinning at each other if they could, and roaring out: "Warbirds, Warbirds, ripping through the air/Warbirds, Warbirds, fighting everywhere/Any age, any place, any foreign clime/Warbirds of Time!"

Catching himself, Gelvarry slipped the oxygen tube into his mouth and opened the valve on the bottle. As the dry gas slid palpably into his mouth and down his throat, the squadron theme faded from the forefront of his mind, and he began to fly the aircraft rather than play with it. He reached out, his bared wrist numbingly exposed for a moment between glove and cuff, and cut in the supercharger. There was a thump up forward of the fire wall, and the engine note steadied. There was a faint, somewhat reassuring new whine in its note.

He began to feel quite himself again, encased within the indurate fuselage, his dark wings spread stiffly over the crystal-clear air below, the gleaming fabric inviolate as it hissed almost hotly through the wind of its passage. He took another pull on the oxygen. He gazed over the side of the cockpit. Down there, little aircraft were dodging and tumbling, their mainplanes reflecting sunlight in a sort of passionate Morse. He knew that message, and he drew his head back inside the cockpit. He resumed searching the deepened blue of the sky above him. And in a little bit, he saw a silver glint northwest of the sun. He turned slightly to aim straight for it, and flew steadily.

After a while, Gelvarry noticed that his throat was being desiccated by the steady flow of the oxygen. He shut the valve and spat out the tube. Pulling the Padre's chased silver flask from the bosom of his tunic, he drank from it. He also ate the cold dry bread. He did not feel particularly sustained by the snack, but the flask was quite nice as a present.

As he went, the distant speck took on breadth as well as length, and then details, size, and a gradual dulling down as the silvered cloth covering began to reveal some panels fresher than others, and the effect of varying hands at the brushwork of the doping. It now looked much as it did on those occasions when it hovered above the aerodrome and Mr. Churchill came down in his wicker car at the end of a cable, as he had done in addressing the squadron several times during Gelvarry's posting.

Ticonderoga in flight upon the same levels as the tropopausal winds, however, was even larger, somehow, and the light fell altogether differently upon it, now that he looked at it again. Boring purposefully onward, its great airscrews turning invisibly but for cyclic reflections, it filled the very world with a monster throbbing that Gelvarry could not hear as sound over the catlike snarlings of his own engine, but to which every surface of his aircraft, and in fact of his mouth and of the faceted goggles over his eyes, vibrated as if being struck by driving wet snow.

Ticonderoga suspended a dozen double-banked radial engines in teardrop pods abaft its main gondola; they seemed to float just below its belly like subsidiary craft of its own kind. Gelvarry, who had seen one or two Zeppelin warcraft, was struck by the major differences—*Ticonderoga*'s smoothly tapered rather than bluntly rounded tail and bow; its almost fishlike control surfaces, with ventral and dorsal vertical stabilizers, and matching symmetrical horizontal planes, rather than the kitelike box-sections of the Fuehrer's designs; the many glassed compartments and blisters along the hull, and the smoothly faired main and after gondolas, rather than a single rope-slung control car. But the main thing was the size, of course. He resumed taking oxygen.

As he drew nearer, tucking himself into its shadow as if under a great living cloud, *Ticonderoga* began blinking a red light at him from a ventral turret just abaft the great open bay in its belly amidships. Then three aircraft launched from that yawning hangar, dropping one, two, three like a stick of bombs but immediately gaining flying speed and wheeling into formation around him. He saw their unit numbers were in sequence with his. He waved, and their three pilots waved back.

Gelvarry watched them, fascinated. They flew with mesmerizing precision, carving smooth arcs in the air as if on wires, showing no reaction at all to the turbulence back along *Ticonderoga*'s hull. They circled him effortlessly; they in fact created the effect of turning about him while really flying flat spirals along the dirigible's flight path. Gelvarry waved again to show his appreciation of their skill, barely remembering to breathe. His gauntleted hands touched lightly at his own stick and throttle, not so much to make changes as to remind himself that he was flying, too.

One of the P6Es had a commander's broad bright stripe belting its fuselage. As soon as it was clear Gelvarry understood enough to hold while they maneuvered, the flight leader could be seen bringing his wireless microphone to his lips and speaking to *Ticonderoga*. The landing trapeze came lowering steadily down out of the bay, and hung motionless, a horizontal bar streaming along across the line of flight at the end of its complicated-looking latching tether.

The leader looked across at Gelvarry, light shining on his goggles, and pointed to one of the other Hawks, which immediately moved out of formation and approached the trapeze. Gelvarry nodded so the leader could see it; they were teaching him. Then he watched the landing aircraft intently.

The hook rising out of the center of the mainplane was designed very much like a standard snap-hook. Once it had been pushed hard against the trapeze bar, it would open to hook around it, and then would snap shut. The trick, Gelvarry thought as he watched his squadronmate sway from side to side, was to center the hook on the bar at exactly the right height. Otherwise, the P6E's nose would be forced to one side or the other of the ideal flight line, and there might be embarrassing consequences.

But the pilot brought it off nicely, apparently unconcerned about tipping his airscrew into the tether or slashing his mainplane fabric with the trapeze. He sideslipped once to bring himself into perfect alignment, and put the hook around the bar with a slight throttle-blip that put one little puff of blue smoke out the end of his exhaust pipe. Then he cut throttle, the trapeze folded around the hook to make assurance doubly sure, and he was drawn up into the hangar bay, *allez-oop!* in one almost continuous movement.

In a moment, the trapeze came down again, and the second pilot did essentially the same thing. The other half of the trick was not to create significant differences between the forward speeds of the dirigible and the aircraft along their identical flight lines, and Gelvarry lightly touched his throttle again, without moving it just yet. But when he glanced across at the leader, he was being gestured forward and up, and the trapeze was once more waiting. The leader drifted down and to the side, where he could watch.

Gelvarry took in a good breath from the bottle and came up into the turbulence, well back of the trapeze but at about the right height. He took another breath, and his mind crisped. He touched the trottle with delicate purposefulness, and came inching up on the bar, which was rocking rhythmically from side to side until he put his knees to either side of the stick and rocked his body from side to side. Thus rocking the ailerons to compensate, thus revealing that the bar had been quite steady all along, and that he was now reasonably steady with it. He was coming in an inch or two off center. He gulped again at the tube. What can happen? he thought dispassionately, and twitched the throttle between thumb and forefinger, a left-handed pinball player's move. With a clash and a bang, the hook snapped over and the trapeze folded. He closed throttle and cut the magneto instantaneously, *slip-slap,* and he was already inside the shadow of the hangar, swaying sickeningly at the end of the tether, but already being swung over toward the landing stage, with a whine of gears from the tether crane, whose spidery latticework arm overhead blended into the shadowy, endlessly repeated lattice girders that formed frame after identical frame, a gaunt cathedral whose groins and mullions retreated into diminishing distances for and aft, housing the great bulks of the helium bags, interlaced by crew catwalks and ladders, spotted here and there by worklights but illuminated in the main by the featureless old-ivory glow through the translucent hull material.

Suddenly there was no sound immediately upon his ears, except for the pinging of his exhaust pipes and cylinder heads. The great roaring of passage pierced into the air was gone. What was left instead was a distant buzz, and the sighing rush of air rubbing over the great fabric.

The P6E's tailskid, and then its tires, touched down on the landing stage. A coveralled man wearing a hood over his mouth and a bottle on his back stepped up on the lower plane, then reached to the mainplane and disengaged the hook from the trapeze, which was swung away instantly. Other aircraft handlers stood looking impatiently at Gelvarry, who lifted himself up out of the cockpit and down to the jouncy perforated-aluminum deck. Down past his feet, he could see the structures of the lower hull, and the countryside idling backward below the open bay before the leader's Hawk nosed blackly forward toward the trapeze.

He could see almost everywhere within the dirigible. Here and there, there were housed structures behind solid dural sheets or stretched canvas screens. Machinery—winches, generators, pumps—and stores of various kinds might interrupt a line of sight to some extent, but not significantly. Even the helium bags were not totally opaque. (Nor rigid, either; he could see them breathing, pale, and creased at the tops and bottoms, and he could hear their casings and their tethers creaking). He ... e could shout from one end of *Ticonderoga* to the other; might also ... into the air toward that stanchion, swing to that brace, go hand ... and along the rail of that catwalk, scramble up that ladder, swing ... t cable to that inspection platform, slip down that catenary, re-... from the side of that bag, land lightly over there on the other side of the bay and present himself, grinning, to his fellow pilots standing there watching him now, all standing at ease, their booted feet spread exactly the same distance, their hands clasped behind their backs, their cavalry breeches identically spotless, their dark tunics and Sam Browne belts all in a row above beltlines all at essentially the same height, their helmets on and their goggles down over their eyes.

He licked his lips. He glanced up guiltily toward the catwalk higher up in the structure, where a row of naked gray monkeys the size of large children was standing, paws along the railing, motionless, studying things. Gelvarry glanced aside.

The flight leader's plane was swung in and then rolled back to join the dozen others lashed down along the hangar deck. The man had jumped down out of the cockpit; he strode toward Gelvarry now. As he approached, Gelvarry saw his features were nondescript.

"You're to report to Mr. Churchill's cabin for a conference at once," he said to Gelvarry. He pointed. "Follow that walkway. You'll find a hatch forward of the main helium cells, there. It opens on the midships gondola. Mr. Churchill is waiting."

Gelvarry stopped himself in midsalute. "Aren't you going to take me there?"

The flight leader shook his head. "No. I can't stand the place. Full of the monkeys."

"Ah."

"Good luck," the officer said. "We shan't be seeing more of each other, I'm afraid. Pity. I'd been looking forward to serving with you."

Gelvarry shrugged uncomfortably. "So it goes," he said for lack of something precise to say, and turned away.

He followed directions toward the gondola. As he moved along, the monkeys flowed limb-over-limb above him among the higher levels of the structural bracing, keeping pace. As they traveled, they conducted incidental business, chattering, gesticulating, knotting up momentarily in clumps of two and three individuals in the grip of passion or anger that left one or two scurrying away cowed or indignant, the level of their cries rising or falling. The whole group, however, maintained the general movement with Gelvarry.

He was fairly certain he remembered what they were, and he did what he could to ignore them.

He came to the gondola hatch, which was an engine-turned duraluminum panel opening on a ladder leading down into a long, windowed corridor lined with crank-operated chest-high machines, at each of which crouched and cranked a monkey somewhat smaller than Gelvarry. As he set foot on the ladder, several of the larger monkeys from the hull spaces suddenly shoved past him, all bristles and smell, forcing their way into the corridor. They were met with immediate, shrieking violence from the nearest machine monkeys, and Gelvarry swung himself partway off the ladder, his eyes wide, maintaining his purchase with one boot toe and one gloved hand while he peered back over his shoulder at the screams and wrestlings within the confined space.

Bloodied intruder monkeys with their pelts torn began to flee back toward safety past him, voiceless and panting, their expressions desperate. The attempted invasion was becoming a fiasco at the deft hands of the machine monkeys, who fought with ear-ripping indignation, uttering howls of outrage while viciously handling the much more naive newcomers. Out of the corner of his eye, Gelvarry saw exactly one of the intruders—who had shrewdly chosen a graying and instinctively diffident machine monkey several positions away from the hatch—pay no heed to the tumult and close its teeth undramatically and inflexibly in its target's throat. In a moment, the object of the maneuver was a limp and yielding bundle on the deck. While all its fellows streamed up past Gelvarry and took, dripping, to the safety of the hull braces the one victorious new monkey bent over the dispossessed machine and began turning the crank. No attention was paid to it as things within the gondola corridor returned to normal.

Gelvarry closed and secured the hatch while monkeys returned to their machines. The wounded ones ignored their hurts cleverly. Neither neighbor of the successful invader paid any overt attention to matters as they now stood, but Gelvarry noticed that as they bobbed and weaved at their machines, with the new monkey between them and with the dead cranker supine at his feet, they unobtrusively extended their limbs and tails to nudge lightly at the body, until they had almost inadvertently kicked it out of sight behind the machines.

Each of the machines displayed a three-dimensional scene within a small circular platform atop the device. Aircraft could be seen moving in combat among miniature clouds over distant background landscapes. Doped wings glistened in the sunlight, turning, turning, reflecting flashes. Dot dot dot. Dash dash dash. Dot. Dot. Dot. Gelvarry brushed forward between the busy animals and moved toward the farther hatch at the other end of the corridor. Atop the nearest machine, he saw a Fokker *dreidekker* painted red, whipping through three fast barrel rolls before resuming level flight above the floundering remains of a broken Nieuport. Dot dot dot dash.

The monkey at that machine frowned and cranked the handle backwards. The Baron's triplane suddenly reversed it actions. Dash dot dot dot. The Nieuport reassembled. Stork insignia could be seen painted on its fuselage. The crank turned forward again. The swastika-marked red wings corkscrewed into their victory roll again above the disintegrating Frenchman.

The monkey at the machine was crooning and bouncing on the balls of its feet, rubbing its free hand over its lips. It moved several knobs at the front of the viewing machine, and the angle changed, so that the point of view was directly from the cockpit of the Fokker, and pieces of the Nieuport flew past the wing struts to either side. The monkey jabbed its neighbors with its elbows and nodded toward the action. It searched the face on either side for reaction. One of them, turning away from a scene of Messerschmitt 262 tactical jet fighters rocketing a column of red-starred T-34 tanks on the ice of Lake Ladoga, glanced over impatiently and pushed back at the Fokker monkey's shoulder, resuming its attention to its own concerns. But the other neighboring monkey was kinder. Despite the fact that its flight of three Boeing P-26s was closing fast on a terrified Kawanishi flying boat over the Golden Gate Bridge, it paused long enough to glance at the Baron's victory, pat its neighbor reassuringly on the back, and utter a chirp of approbation. Pleased, the first monkey was immediately rapt in rerunning the new version of the scene. The kind monkey stole a glance over again, shrugged, and resumed cranking its own machine.

Gelvarry continued pushing between the monkeys to either side. The flooring was solid, but springy underfoot. The ceiling was convex, and wider than the floor, so that the duraluminum walls tapered inward. They were pierced for skylights above the long banks of machines, but *Ticonderoga* was apparently passing through clouds. There were rapid alterations of light at the ports, but only slight suggestions of any detail. Over the spasmodic grinding of the cranks, and the constant slight vocalizations of the monkeys, the sound of air washing over the walls and floor could be made out if one paused and listened ruminatively.

Gelvarry reached Mr. Churchill's compartment door. He knocked, and the reassuring voice replied: "Come!" He quickly entered and closed the sheet-metal panel securely behind him.

The compartment was large for his expectations. Its deck was parqueted and dressed in oriental carpets. Armchairs and taborets were placed here and there, with many low reading lamps, and opaque drapes swayed over the portholes. Mr. Churchill sat heavily in a Turkish upholstered chair at the other end of the room, facing him, wearing his pinstriped blue suit with the heavy watchchain across the rounded vest. He gripped a freshly lighted Uppman cigar between his knuckles. The famous face was drawn up into its wet baby scowl, and Gelvarry at once felt the impact of the man's presence.

"Ah," Mr. Churchill said. "None too soon. Come and sit by me. We have only a moment or two, and then they shall all be here." His mouth quirked sideward. "Rabble," he growled. "Counterjumpers."

Gelvarry moved forward toward the chair facing the Prime Minister. "Am I a unique case, Sir?" he said, sitting down with a trace of uneasiness. "I was told high squadron posting was voluntary only."

Mr. Churchill raised his eyebrows and turned to the taboret beside him. He punched a bronze pushbell screwed to the top. "Unique? Of course you're unique, man! You're the principal, after all." A doorway somewhere behind him opened, and a young woman with soot-black hair and bee-stung lips entered wearing a French maid's costume. She brought a silver tray on which rested two crystal tumblers and a bottle of the familiar Hennessey *Rx Official*. "Very good! Very good!" Mr. Churchill said, pouring. "Mr. Dunstan Haverman, I'm introducing Giselle Montez," he said, giving her name the Gallic pronunciation. "It is very possible that you shall—" He shrugged. "Meet again." Gelvarry tried not to appear much out of countenance as Miss Montez brought the salver and stood gracefully silent, her eyes downcast, while he took his tumbler. "Charmed," he said softly.

"Thank you," she murmured, turned, and retreated through her doorway. She had left the bottle with Mr. Churchill.

Gelvarry sipped. Mr. Churchill raised his glass. "Here's to reality."

Haverman shuddered. "No," he said, drinking more deeply anyway, "I was beginning to depend on it too much. Sam, what's going wr ?"

Sam grunted as the amber liquid hit his own esophagus. He was normally a self-contained, always pleasant-spoken individual—the typical golf or tennis pro at the best club in the county—who in Haverman's long experience of him had once frowned when a drunk at a business luncheon had pawed a waitress. And then calmly tipped a glass of icewater into the man's lap, costing himself a thirty-nine-week deal.

"Sam?" Haverman peered through the Hennessey effect at his grimacing old acquaintance.

"Take a look." The leaner, longer-legged, short-haired man sitting in the chrome-and-leather captain's chair turned toward the hard-edged cabinet standing beside him. The pushbell atop it seemed incongruous. Sam flipped up a panel and punched a number on the keyboard behind it. He closed the panel and nodded toward a cleared area of the paneled, indirectly lighted room. Haverman immediately recognized it as a holo focus, of course, even before he remembered what an inlaid circle in the flooring signified. It was a large one—half again the size of normally sold commercial receivers—as befitted the offices of a major industry figure.

Laurent Michaelmas appeared; urbane, dark-suited, scarlet flower in his lapel. "Good day," he said. "I have the news." He paused, one eyebrow cocked, hands slightly spread, waiting for feedback.

Sam raised his voice slightly above normal conversational level. "Just give us the broadcast industry top story, please," he said, and the Michaelmas projection flicked almost imperceptibly into a slightly new stance, then bowed and said:

"The top broadcast story is also still the top general story, sir. Now here it is:" He relaxed and stepped aside so that he was at the exact edge of the circle, visually related to the room floor level, while the remainder of the holo sphere went to an angled overhead view of Lower Manhattan.

"Well, today is October 25, 1992, in New York City, where the impact of the latest FCC ruling is still being assessed by programming departments for all major media." The scene-camera point of view became a circling pan around Wall Street Alley, picking up the corporate logos atop the various buildings: RCA, CBS, ABC, GTV, Blair, Neilsen. In a nice touch, the POV zoomed smoothly on an upper-story window, showing what appeared to be a conference room with three or four gesticulating figures somewhat visible through the sun-repelling glass. It was excellent piloting, too—the camera copter was being handled smoothly enough in the notorious off-bay crosscurrents so that the holo scanner's limited compensatory circuits were able to take all the jiggle and drift out of the shot. Here was a flyer, Haverman thought, who wouldn't be a disgrace at the trapeze. Then he winced and took another nibble at the Hennessey.

"While viewers reaped an unexpected bonanza," Michaelmas said, and the background cut to an interior of a typical dwelling and a young man and woman watching Laurent Michaelmas with expressions of pleasant surprise, "industry spokesmen publicly lauded the FCC's Reception Release Order." The cut this time was to a pleasant-looking fellow in a casual suit, leaning against a holo cabinet. He smiled and said: "Folks, it's got to be the greatest thing since free tickets to the circus." He patted the cabinet. "Imagine! From now on, you can receive *every* and *any* channel right where you are, no matter *what* type of receiver you own! Yes, it's true—for only a few pennies, we'll bring you and install one of the new Rutledge-Karmann adapter units, with the best coherer circuit possible, that'll transform any receiver into an *all-channel* receiver! Now, how about that? Remember, the government says we have to use top-quality components, and we have to sell to you at *our cost!* So—" He grinned boyishly. "Even if we wanted to screw you, we can't."

"Others, however," Michaelmas said, "were not so sanguine. Even in public."

The holo went to Fingers Smart in the elevator lobby of what was recognizably the New York FCC building. He was striding out red-faced, followed by several figures Haverman could recognize as GTV attorneys and GTV's favorite consulting lawyer. "When interviewed, GTV Board Chairman Ancel B. Smart had this to say at 1:15 P.M. today:"

Now it was a two-shot of Smart being faced by an interested, smiling Laurent Michaelmas, while the lawyers milled around and tried to get a word in edgewise. Nobody ever effectively got between that friendly-uncle manner of Michaelmas's and whoever he was after.

"That's exactly right, Larry," Smart was saying. "We built the holovision industry the way it is because the FCC wanted it that way then. Now it wants it another way, and that's it. Public interest. Well, damn it, we're part of the public, too!" Smart's other industry nickname was Notso.

"Are you going to continue fighting the ruling?"

A belated widening of Smart's eyes now occurred. "Who says we're fighting it? We were here getting clarification of a few minor points. You know GTV operates in the public interest."

Sam chuckled, unamused, while Haverman peered and thought. GTV controlled eighty-seven entertainment channels that operated twenty-four hours a day. There were six GTV-owned channels leased to religious and political lobbies. There was also, of course, GTV's ten percent share of the public network subsidy. Paid off in programs given to PTV from the summer Student Creative internship plan.

That was how the dice had fallen when the Congress legislated cheap 3-D TV. The existing broadcast companies were trapped in their old established images with heavy emphasis on sports or news, women's daytime, musical variety, feature documentary anthologies, and the like. That had left an obvious vacuum which GTV had filled promptly.

All-channel receivers at an affordable price had been out of the question. As usual, Congress had been straining technology to its practical limits, and compromises had had to be made in the end. A good half of the receivers sold, Haverman remembered, were entertainment only. Now, apparently, because of something very cheap called the Harmon-Cutlass or something, he wouldn't have to remember it any longer.

"Oh!" he said, raising his eyes to Sam's nod.

Michaelmas cocked his head at Smart. "Just one or two more questions, please. Are you saying you haven't already cut your ratings guarantees to your advertisers? I believe your loss this quarter has just been projected at nearly twenty percent of last year's profits."

Smart glanced aside to his legal staff. But he was impaled on Michaelmas's smile. He tried one of his own; it worked beautifully at the annual entertainment programming awards dinner. "Come on, Larry— you know I'm no bean-counter. GTV's going to continue to offer the same top-drawer—"

"Well, one would assume that," Michaelmas said urbanely. "You have most of the season's product still on the shelf, unshown. No one would expect you to just dump a capital investment of that scope. What is your plan for after that? Or don't you expect to be the responsible executive six months from now?"

"Ouch!" Haverman said.

"I don't think I have to answer that here," Smart said quickly. He frowned at Michaelmas as he moved to step around him. "Come to think of it, you're in competition with us now, aren't you?" He actually laid a hand on Michaelmas's arm and pushed him a little aside, or would have, if Michaelmas didn't have a dancer's grace. "No further comment," Smart said, and strode off.

Michaelmas turned toward the point of view, while the background faded out behind him and left him free-standing. He shrugged expressively. "These little tiffs sometimes occur within the fellowship of broadcasting," he said with a smile. "But most observers would agree that competition is always in the public interest." There was the faintest of flicks to a stock tape; computer editing was instantaneous in real time, smooth, and due to become smoother. Even now, only an eye expecting it could detect it. "And that's how it is today," flick, "in broadcasting," flick, "and in the top story at this hour." He bowed and was gone.

Haverman rolled his eyes. "What happened?" he said. "I thought Hans Smart had a lock on Congress."

Sam grinned crookedly and grimly. "He's dead, poor chap. His liver gave out two weeks ago, and there went Notso's brains."

"Physiology got to the wrong brother."

"Yeah. It wouldn't have been as bad as it was, but three days before he went, NBC sprang a prime-time documentary. It was about this new little engineering company in Palo Alto that could pick up all channels on your $87.50 Sony portable. He wasn't cold in the ground before a dozen senators were on the all-channel bandwagon. The House delegation from California began lobbying as a bloc, New York City, and then Nassau and Dutchess counties jumped in, and the next you know Calart-Hummer or whatever it is, is the law of the land. Hans Smart could handle legislators with the best of 'em, but I don't think it was the booze that killed him; it was the friggin' feature."

Sam grinned more genuinely. "It was a beaut. NBC sent out engraved invitations, on paper, messenger-delivered to every member of Congress and anybody else they figured could swing a little. About six months ago, they had bought excerpt rights to about a dozen old *Warbirds* things. News feature use only; you know how that goes, I guess. Well, it all turned up in that show. Michaelmas walking around narrating over it. Only they scaled it down behind him, so he was just stepping around over the battlefields and the planes were buzzing around him while he just smiled and talked. King damned Kong in a pinstripe suit. You wouldn't have believed it. Show it to you sometime; everybody in the business must have made a copy of it. Scare hell out of you. Even if you weren't personally involved, I mean."

Haverman sucked a little more Hennessey carefully between his lips and across the edges of his tongue. "What's been happening to the *Warbirds* ratings, Sam?"

Ticonderoga Studios produced other things besides *Warbirds,* but *Warbirds* was what it was known for in the industry, and *Warbirds* was GTV's top-rated show. GTV's contract was what kept Ticonderoga flying.

"Well, Dusty, we're having to be ingenious." Sam looked down at the stick between his fingers, then broke it open and inhaled in a controlled manner. "These things are pretty good," he remarked. "I think they'll catch on."

Haverman settled himself carefully in his chair. "Isn't this thing bound to settle out? I mean, it's a new toy. Notso may flail around for a while—"

Sam nodded, but not encouragingly. "He's gone. He knows it. But he's telling himself he can make it unhappen if he just yells and shits loud enough. Flailing around isn't the phrase you need. But he's gone. I've got some GTV stock; want it?"

"It'll work its way back up again, Sam," Haverman said carefully. "Especially if Smart gets kicked out by the Board and they hire a new president." Haverman suddenly sat up straighter. "Hey, Sam, why couldn't that be you?"

"I thought about that."

"Right! It's perfect for them—a top gun from outside, but not too far outside. An experienced new broom. The PR is made for it, friend!"

"I don't want it."

Haverman looked at him watchfully. "Oh?"

Sam shook his head. "Too soon. I'm staying right where I am and building a record. Some other poor son of a bitch can have the next couple of years to get ulcerated in."

Haverman pursed his lips thoughtfully. "It's going to be that bad." He had one hundred percent respect for Sam's judgment. "I guess I'm being a little slow. If our audience can switch away to other channels, can't their people switch to GTV?"

"All of them can and some of them will. But they're hard-core generalists; they'll take a little of us, and a little of CBS, and a little of NBC, and a little of Funkbeobachter, and a little Shimbun, and some ABC, and God knows what else when the new relay sets go in. No, these are the kind of people that're used to a little of everything, no matter what network they're from. Any of 'em that hankered for a little side action from GTV or anyplace else could afford additional sets long ago. But *our* viewers, you know—" He held his hand out, palm up, and slowly turned it over.

Haverman said reluctantly: "That's not how we talk at the awards dinners."

"I don't see any chicken and peas around here right now," Sam said. "There's no way I would have pulled you out of your milieu if I didn't think we were in trouble."

"We can counterprogram," Haverman said emphatically. "We've got the skills and the facilities."

"Yes, I have."

"O.K. We can do news and sports stuff like the other people. That's the way it's going to go anyhow—back to the way it was in flat-V time, when everybody had a little of everything."

"Yeah, but not now," Sam said. "Later. Meanwhile, how do we get the National League to break its contract with ABC? Where do you think CBS's legal department would be if we started talking option-breakers to Mandy Carolina? Two years from now, Michaelmas's contract is up for renewal at NBC. There's talk he's thinking of going freelance. *That'll* start a trend. Give me enough bucks, and I'll build you the top-rated action news show. *Then*. Then, Dusty," he said gently. "Not now. And now is when Fingers Smart and old Sam the Ticonderoga are fighting for their lives, you know?" He inhaled deeply on the stick and threw the exhausted pieces to the floor.

"I can't start another league to compete with what ABC can show my people. There aren't that many big jocks in the world. And I can't find another talk show hostess; only God can make a mouth. I can't get Michaelmas, I can't get Melvin Watson. I *can* get the guy who's sick of being Skip Jacobson's Sunday-night backup, and so what. What I've got is actors. I can get actors. I can get enough actors to fill eighty times twenty-four hours of programming every week, if I have to." Sam sighed. "I can make actors. So can anybody else; it's no secret how you do almost two thousand different shows a week, thirty-nine weeks a year. So you know what I've got left?" Sam leaned forward.

"Me," Sam said. "I've got me, and what's in me here." He tapped his head and patted his crotch. "And we're gonna find out how many years it's good for."

The silence had persisted palpably. "And me, Sam," Haverman said finally.

"Uh-huh," Sam said. He poured another shot into Haverman's glass. "Here," he said, and sipped his own to knock off the stick effect. "Have a snort. Now, listen. You're my guy, and don't forget it. You were one of the first people to sign on with me, and you've been the principal of *Warbirds* ever since almost the beginning."

Haverman nodded emphatically. There had been a Rex something or other. But that was long ago. "I have a following," he said confirmingly, as if that was what he thought mattered to Sam about him. And of course it was one of the things that did matter. It must. Sam was not a creative for his health.

"That's right," Sam said gently. "And I'm going to protect you, and you're going to help me."

"I'm not going back into *Warbirds*."

"Something like *Warbirds*. Something recognizably like it, and you're going to have the same character name."

Haverman cocked his head. "But there *are* going to be changes."

"Oh, yes. Got to have those, so it can be new and different. But not too many, really—got to save something so they can identify with the familiar. It'll have airplanes and things."

"Ah," Haverman said warily.

"A new show. All your own. Name over the title. We're going to promo hell out of it—'Haverman Moves!' Maybe 'Dusty Moves!' I don't know. Hell with it. Think of something better. Not the point. We'll get every one of the *Warbirds* audience, and with that kind of promo, we'll get plenty of new lookers. Once they've looked, we'll have 'em. Guarantee it."

"Well, certainly, if it's one of your ideas—"

"Hell, yes, it's one of mine. More important, it's the one whose time has come. What the hell—eighty-odd channels of our own for a looker to choose from, and God knows how many more coming from all kinds of places. It's got to happen; I can hit the FCC with First Amendment and Right of Free Choice at the same time. It'll be years before they beat me. And you know something, Duster?" he said in a suddenly calm voice, "I don't think they're ever going to beat me. I think we really can make it stick."

"Oh?" Haverman felt the skin prickle sharply at the backs of his hands. He had never seen Sam like this; only heard of such moments, when the conviction of having thought and done exactly right transformed his good friend's face. The triumphant force of having created a truth came blazing from his eyes. And when he said "I think we can make it stick," his voice reharmonized itself so that though it never rose in volume, it might have been played by solo viola. Haverman could only say again: "Oh."

Sam was grinning. Grinning. "It's beautiful, Duster," he said. "Once we've beaten the test case, we can do another thing—open up a whole channel to the genre. Maybe more than one. And you shoot the whole thing on one set, with a couple of pieces of furniture and just a handful of props, and a holoprojected background. There's no long shot, and damned little tracking, so you do it with two cameras. One, if you're willing to settle. But I wouldn't. Or at least I'd want a damn good optical reflector to back me up. A whole new show, and then a whole channel full of new shows, for a third—maybe a fourth—of what anything else costs."

"And I'm going to do the first one," Haverman said. "Smart'll go for it. He has to. What kind of show is it, exactly, Sam?"

When Sam explained it to him further, he sat shaking his head. "Oh, no, Sam, no, I'm not sure I could do that."

But Sam said: "Sure you can."

Haverman sat uncertainly through the beginning of the conference. First the door to the office corridor was opened, and the senior technical staff came in; Hal, the most senior, carried a model of an aircraft carrier and a model of a silvery biplane, both of which he set down on Sam's white table. Sam turned them over in his hands, and nodded and winked at Hal, who smiled and sat down in the nearest of the informally grouped chairs. Dusty sat back along the wall, in a comfortable alcove next to Miss Montez's door, waiting.

Sam looked around at his people. "Everybody ready? O.K., let's give the great man a call," he said, and apparently punched up Ancel Smart's phone number, because Smart, after a little work with a secretary, appeared in the holo circle. He sat in a chair with his own people around him, and said heavily: "Shoot."

"Right," Sam said. "Anse, you know Hal and the rest of the boys, here. Now, we're proposing as follows—"

And it continued from there, with Smart nodding from time to time, or interposing a question, and changing his POV to watch whoever on the Ticonderoga staff was giving him the data. Then he'd turn back to Sam. Occasionally, one of Smart's people would address Sam. But it was Smart and Sam one-on-one, as it ought to be, Dusty saw, beginning to feel better as his friend clearly established dominance over the meeting. Smart was inclined to cough and play with his chin. Sam sat slim and upright, his hands, spread-fingered, molding premises in the air above the white tabletop where the models waited. Dusty began to feel better as Sam grew.

"All right, I promise you this new show'll grab 'em and won't let go. I've taken a closer look at the tentative figures we discussed earlier, and I'll stand behind 'em." Sam named an in-the-can cost half of what it might have been. "And no concept fee, absolutely nothing in front. I get it back on reruns; we go to full rate on those, but, what the hell, if we ever *see* reruns, you're golden and you don't care, right? O.K., so that's Part One of what Ticonderoga's prepared to do. What do you do, Anse?"

Smart nodded. "Like I said. If it packages up the way you described, GTV'll help with the Feds. We've still got an office in Washington, after all, and my brother left a well-trained staff."

"Specifically, you're agreeing to hold Ticonderoga harmless in the event of criminal penalties or monetary losses caused by legal or regulatory action. Is that correct?"

One of Smart's legal staff suddenly leaned forward and began to whisper urgently in his ear. Smart waved him off impatiently. "That's right. I haven't changed my mind."

"On the record, and on behalf of GTV?" Sam pointed toward his own lawyer, who held up a sealed recorder.

"If we buy the program at all, GTV defends," Smart confirmed.

"O.K.," Sam said. "Now I'm gonna tell you who's in it."

"Ah."

"According to the formula we discussed," Sam said, turning to his holo box, talking aside, "we're going for a total ego-spectrum across four archetypical blocs. Now, each bloc embodies several potent identification features. We go young woman, young but experienced man, older and ego-stable woman, fully sophisticated man at the top end of middle age. We go soft, wiry, tight, sinewy; dark, reddish, blondy, silver. Sometimes we vary a little; there's room to do it; you get different overlaps, but you still cover it all the way across your maximized consumer ideals. We anchor at each end with an identifiable regular, but we can vary in the middle. Right so far?"

Smart nodded. "Acceptable." His and Sam's lawyers nodded.

"All right." Sam was still turned toward the control cabinet and speaking along his shoulder at Smart. He began to slowly raise one arm toward the top of the box. It was a good move; Haverman could see the tension building in Smart, and the distraction that was mirrored in the flickering of his eyes. More and more, Haverman felt the welling of admiration for Sam, and the comfort of being one of his people. "Now, you buy the concept of guest celebrities?"

"As long as they fit the formula."

"As long as they fit the formula defined above," Sam corroborated.

"Are you worried about our being able to create authenticity?"

"With your makeup and research departments? Never. You guarantee audience believability, and I'll take your word for it right now."

"So guaranteed. Done." Sam nodded. "All right, we work from now on the assumption that the celebrity pair on each show will cover the two middle blocs, and Ticonderoga has discretion there as long as the portrayals remain convincing. To whom? Do you want to designate an audience-reaction service, Ancel?" His hand was poised above the holo controls now.

Smart shrugged. "We've been using TeleWinner all along. Let's give 'em this, too. Split the cost, right?" He chuckled. "What the hell, you know the reason GTV buys *Warbirds* is because I'm hooked on it. I'm my own symbol-bloc survey; they just make it official."

Sam smiled faintly. Audience size was what made it official.

"And, what the hell," Smart said, "you're keeping the alternate time tracks premise for the new show, aren't you? So if somebody says Rocky Marciano wasn't left-handed or Sonja Henie didn't roller-skate, well, hell that was *then* but this is *elsewhen,* right? But it has to *look* right; that we've got to have."

"Absolutely." Even if there'd been no other public source of visual data, there was GTV's own Channel '29, steadily programming out reprocessed old movie and newsreel footage for all the WW II war babies who'd just missed it. The reprocessing was done by TStudiolab, Inc., one of Sam's subsidiaries.

"Okay, so we've got all that out of the way," Smart said. "Now let's see the goods."

"Of course." Sam smiled. His hand moved unexpectedly, and rang the little pushbell. "Let me introduce our talented newcomer. The next big word in viewer households, known to you and me as the young bloc archetype and all that implies, but professionally known as Giselle Montez—"

On her cue, Miss Montez came through her door in a high squadron pilot's uniform, the leather of her boots and Sam Browne belt glistening. She swept off her aluminized goggles and her helmet with one deft swirl of the hand that released her cloud of hair, and stood holding them on her hip, while her other hand rested its fingertips at the first button in the vee of her tunic. Ancel Smart leaned forward sharply in his chair. His mouth formed a loose o.

"Thank you, Miss Montez," Sam said, and she about-faced and walked out quickly; the door closed behind her with one darting flip of her fingertips. "And at the other end of the spectrum, the fine silver of sophisticated experience." Sam touched the cabinet controls. A sketch materialized in the air, facing Smart. It was a deceptively loose artist's rendering, life size, of a whipcordy-slim man with delicate limbs and waving, glossy white hair struck with contrasting pewter-colored low-lights. The expression of the aristocratic face suggested certain things.

Smart nodded reservedly. "Yes. All right. Looks all right. Who's going to play it? Something familiar about him. Who was your artist using for a model? Dusty Haverman?" Smart grinned.

Sam did not. He simply kept looking steadily at Smart, whose eyes first narrowed, then enlarged. "You're kidding! You're—How do we do *Warbirds* without him?—Jesus—" He slapped his thigh. "Perfect! It's perfect! It's a stroke, Sam, a fuckin' stroke!"

"Sure," Sam said.

The back of the meeting was broken. It was all a big long happy glide thereafter. Sar'n-Major Mac would come to the fore as the real manager of low squadron, and Private Parkins would play up raffishly. Major Harding's part would be padded a little, and Father Collins would listen to his troubles as he thrashed about trying to assert himself and spoil MacBanion's schemes. At its own expense, as an additional contribution to the relief of the crisis, Ticonderoga Studios would go back into the existing unshown episodes and re-edit to the new slant, so the Gelvarry character would be free to Go West, grow up, and change shows immediately. Sam had some experimental footage, it seemed, which might fit some of that.

In return, GTV would guarantee renewal next year. About next year —Sam's latest idea was to move on to dirigible-launched P6Es against Fiat CR32 biplanes; he held up the glittering model of the 220-mph Italian fighter, which had not gone out of use until 1938. They would be launched from the *Graf Zeppelin*, which had been Nazi Germany's sole aircraft carrier. Named for the man who pioneered practical lighter-than-air flight.

Smart considered the possibilities and the twists. "Cute," he admitted. "I like it." He shook his head. "I don't know where you get your ideas, Sam. Christ. Planes that sound like cars comin' off a ship that sounds like a dirigible, and what do they run up against? Damn! Yeah—let me see some footage pretty soon, will you?"

Sam had some, it seemed, which would fit some of that. They'd be able to show a rough cut in about a week.

"How about the new show? How soon can I have that?"

Well, it took a little while to get the actors into the milieu. Smart could understand that.

Yes, he could. But—

Oh, they'd push it. Tell you what; how about a progress report in ten days?

Well, if that meant they were close to delivery on the pilot episode.

Right. The *pilot* episode.

Everybody suddenly laughed, and Sam promised to send the little models over to Sam's office right away, for the shelves over the bar.

Smart punched off, and everybody in Sam's conference room began to grin and make enthusiastic quips. They were a high-morale outfit. It almost reminded Haverman of— Well, it should, shouldn't it? Art mirrors life.

Haverman got up from his inconspicuous seat and went over to Sam. "I thought it went very well."

Hal raised an eyebrow. "Well, hello!" he said.

Sam smiled reassuringly. "You heard the man, Duster," he said. "GTV's buying it, and they'll protect us. So it's all right." His eyes said: *I told you I'd take care of you.*

"I'm sure of that," Haverman said with conviction. "It's a Ticonderoga production," and everyone within earshot smiled.

"Why don't we get started?" Sam said and, putting an arm around his shoulders, walked with him out through the door to the technical spaces, which in this area were half-partitioned workrooms and offices grouped-up to either side of the long central aisle that ran back toward the sound stages. Overhead were the whitewashed skylights and the zigzag trusses of the broad, arching roof, and to either side of them were the sounds of word-processing machines and footage splicers. They walked along to a side aisle, and there Sam had to leave him, after opening and holding open for him the heavy wood-grained door marked ACTORS AND MEDICAL PERSONNEL ONLY.

A bright-looking young medical person leafed through his printout. "Dusty Haverman," he said wonderingly. "I never knew you'd been an accounting student."

"Isn't Doctor Virag going to do me? Doctor Virag and I know each other very well," he said, sitting stiffly in his chair.

The medical person did his best to smile disarmingly. "Doctor Virag is no longer with us, I'm afraid. Time passes, you know. I'm Doctor Harcourt; I think you'll find me competent. Sam personally asked me to take you."

"Oh. Well, I didn't mean to imply—"

"That's all right, Mr. Haverman. Now, if you'll just relax, Miss Tauchnitz will begin removing that hairpiece and so forth." Harcourt's fingers danced over keys, and he peered at the screen beside his chair. "Let me just refresh myself on this—yes, well, I think you may find it a relief to wear your own hair, for one thing; we'll just bleach it up a little bit. And we'll tan you. That'll be better than that tarty pinky-cheeks tinting, don't you think? Other than that, there's just a *tiny* bit of incising to do . . . a touch of a lift to one eyebrow, and that'll have the desired effect, I'm sure. Oh, yes, the cosmetology here is minimal, minimal. Which is just as well, since we do have a rather thick book of response-adjustments to perform, but, then, none of us is perfect for our role in life, really. Or is it 'are perfect'? Would you happen to know which it is, Miss Tauchnitz?"

When they had that done, they walked him down the corridors, past the rows of costume mannequins, and to the processing room, which was hung in soft black nonreflecting fabric, and where they had symphonic control of the lighting. They put him in the chair with the trick armrests and the neck brace.

"This is wine, Mr. Haverman," and he peered aside at the rollaway table with the clear decanter of rosy clarity, and the goblet. As long as he moved his arm smoothly and no more quickly than was gracious he could reach out and take it, and sip. "That's right. Have some more," the pleasant voice behind him said, and when he had had some more, they showed him a holo of Miss Montez and stimulated an electrode.

"Ah! Ah-ah-ah!"

"A little more wine, Mr. Haverman." And again the Montez and the incredible sensation beside which all past experience paled.

To see her come fully lighted out of the featureless soft warm darkness, and to feel what he could feel when she did that, he had only to reach out and take more wine. There was no thought in him of a spastic attempt to pluck something from his skull.

"Shouldn't you be feeding me oysters or Vitamin E? Perhaps some Tiger's Milk?" he jested once after they had stopped the wine and given him some Hennessey to refresh him. The pleasant voice murmured a throaty chuckle behind him.

When there was no further response to his gambit, he said: "Ah, well, I've really always been a steak and potatoes man, actually," and carelessly reached around to circle his hand into the unknown space behind him, but the pleasant voice said: "More wine, Mr. Gelvarry," and an unnoticeable hand put the goblet into his fingers. "Good enough," Gelvarry said. "Ah! Yes, yes, good enough, I say."

They showed him a slim, freckled woman with prominent front teeth, dressed in a calf-length skirt and a cardigan sweater over a cotton blouse. She wore soft leather street boots over dark lisle stockings, and moved like something wary in a strange part of the forest. They wiped, and went to a reprocessed, tinted, computer-animated photo of the famous person this was supposed to represent, and when he sipped the wine, they gave him the pleasure effect. Soon enough in the process he found it difficult to distinguish between the photo and the actress in her costume, no matter how the costume changed per reveal, for they always had a fresh photo after each wipe-and-switch, and the costume had clearly been cued by something in the photo, as much as chiffon can be patterned to remind one of gingham. In truth, in a while, he could not distinguish at all, and he found that although after a while they didn't wipe the actress, he had to concentrate very hard to make her out behind the features he now saw for her. So they gave him more wine, and the idea of concentrating was, to his relief, lost.

They did roughly the same thing with the identity of the purposeful young man with the angelic eyes.

And it was done.

"It's good, Sam," Haverman said, sitting in the office with the Hennessey.

"Sure," Sam said.

"I feel it. I feel absolutely certain." He ran a hand along the silvery waves at the side of his head, and touched one finger to his pencil moustache. His hand was lean and browned by the suns of expensive resorts. A chased gold ring set with a ruby glittered on his little finger. "The way you can make me see the guests, instead of the actors playing them—"

"Yeah, well, they aren't actually playing them, you know. We've got this computer tied into the cameras, and when those people move around, the image data gets put through and modified by this fancy program I had the fellows work up. It's pretty good; probably get better. As long as the players don't do anything grossly out of character, the computer can edit the image to fit the model character. That's what goes on the air."

"But how do I see it, playing with them?"

"Well, you can't, Duster, that's why we do that hocus-pocus in the darkroom. One of the hocus-pocuses." Sam patted him lightly at the neck. "Saves you having to act, you know, old Duster." He was sitting beside him on the couch, and leaned forward to cap the Hennessey.

"I think I could act it," Haverman said very softly.

Sam sighed. "Well, perhaps you could. But you see, this way it all goes smoothly and very naturally, don't you see? No lines to remember, no breaks for lunch—But those are all technical details, Dus, and there's absolutely no need for you to learn them."

"Still and all," Haverman said. "Still and all." Sam was uncapping the wine now. "I think you're very inventive," Haverman hastened. "That was always true of you. Do you know what I think? I think your next computer program will make it completely unnecessary to have anyone walking around for the cameras to focus on. Sam, that's true, isn't it? That's what you'd really, really like, isn't it?"

"Why, that's not true at all," Sam almost said; Haverman strained to hear him say that, and it seemed to him he was saying it, just outside the range of human hearing. He peered, and he craned his neck. But Sam was saying: "It's almost studio time, Dus. Have some wine," in his pleasant voice.

Haverman sighed. "Oh, all right, if that's the best you can do."

"My name is Austin Gelvarry," he repeated to Miss Montez, who was probably staring over his shoulder at the glistening, intricately decorated brass bed. "I have the power to call up whatever pleases me." He sipped from his glass, as she was doing. A nice light was developing in her eyes.

"I—seem to remember something different—"

"Have some more wine. It does no harm. It's strong drink that is raging," Gelvarry said, preoccupied, watching the little monkey plucking fruit from the bowl on the sideboard. The monkey caught his eye and winked.

"Listen," Miss Montez said. "It's just you can't find a secretary job anywhere anymore." But she was sipping.

Gelvarry smiled. Beyond her a Lockheed Electra was just touching down, crabbing a little in the wind as one might very well expect of so small an aircraft, even if it were an all-metal cabin twin. She settled in nicely, with just a spurt of blue smoke at the tires, and began to run out. He watched the pilot swing the Electra around deftly, and begin taxiing toward them.

"Do I please you, Austin?" Miss Montez said over the rim of her glass, looking at him through her lashes. She seemed quite nicely settled in now.

"Ah," Gelvarry said. "Ah." The Electra came to a halt and the cabin door popped open. A slim figure jumped down and waved, and began running toward them. "Here's Amelia!" Gelvarry exclaimed gladly.

A Ryan high-wing monoplane, lacking the reflection of sun on windscreen glass, came over low, light glittering at its engine-turned cowling. A figure waved down from a side window, and then the *Spirit of St. Louis* banked away to line up upwind, flaring out for its landing, its prominent wheels seeming to reach down for the ground against the red outline of the evening sun. Gelvarry and Miss Montez both half-rose with pleasure. "And here's Lucky Lindy now!"

ALAN E. NOURSE

MIRROR, MIRROR

Somewhere down on the surface of Saturn the Enemy was waiting.

The Earth outpost on the Satellite ship orbiting Saturn knew that he was there, with his four great ships and the unimaginable power that had brought him from whatever place he had come. But the Earth outpost did not know why he had come, and now they did not know what he intended to do.

He had come into the solar system, and struck with pointless savagery, and then fled to a place where Earth ships could not follow him. Now he waited there, silent and enigmatic. His very presence was intolerable: the Earth outpost knew they had to fight him, somehow, but the fight was on his *terms, on the battleground* he *had chosen.*

It was an impossible war from the very start, a vicious war, draining the last reserve of the tiny group of Earthmen who had to fight it. It engulfed their waking hours and tortured their sleep with nightmares. There was no time to stop and ask themselves: why are we fighting this war?

They were fighting it, that was enough. Only the Enemy knew why. . . .

1 The waiting was the most terrible part of all for John Provost.

There was no chronometer in the day room of the Satellite ship, but Provost had his own private chronometer buried in his skull, somewhere in that vague impersonal space that lay between his left ear and his left eyebrow, deep down, ticking away hours, minutes, seconds, ridiculous fractions of ridiculous segments of seconds, marking them off against him inexorably, the epitome of all timepieces. It was there in his head and he couldn't get away from it, not even when his shift was over and he was back in Relief, laboriously rebuilding the fragments of John Provost that the Enemy had torn away. Now, almost whole and fresh again, he could hear the chronometer clicking away against him, and once more he was certain that it was the *waiting* he feared far more than he feared the Enemy.

Almost time, Provost. Almost your turn to go down again. . . .

He paced the day room of the Satellite ship and felt sweat trickle down his chest from the waiting and the silence. Always, in the last hour before his shift, he lived in an envelope of self-induced silence. Canned music blared from the wall speaker, unnaturally loud, but Provost did not hear it. There was talking and chatter in the day room, harsh laughter all about him, noises of glasses clinking, feet shuffling. A dozen men were here, but to Provost the day room was like a TV with the sound turned off. He was utterly isolated, and that was the way he wanted it.

He rubbed wet palms against his trousers and waited.

Nobody looked at him, of course. The men knew that his shift was next. Nobody spoke to him; he might smile and answer them pleasantly, or he might turn on them, savagely and without warning, like a cornered rat. It had happened before, with others. He was like a crossbow with the spring drawn tight, waiting to be triggered, and nobody wanted to tamper with him twenty minutes before shift change. Everyone knew he wouldn't be responsible for what he might do.

And with every passing second the spring was pulled tighter. That was what made the waiting so terrible.

He went below and stepped into a hot foam shower, felt the powerful muscles of his shoulders and neck relax a trifle. Briefly he thought of the Turner girl. Would she be in Relief when he returned? Of course, there were others equally well trained to help the men through the period of childish regression that inevitably occurred when their shifts were over and the pressure suddenly off—the only way they could rebuild their mental resources for another shift—but to John Provost, the Turner girl seemed better than any of the others. They'd actually begun to be good friends as he had come, slowly, to trust her under circumstances in which trust was difficult if not impossible. And then that new woman that DepPsych had sent out from the Hoffman Center, Dorie Kendall— what about her? Help, or hindrance? Dangerous, sending out new people at a time like this. Yet, she'd *listened* when he'd told her how he could use his Analogue to take his mind and sensorium down to Saturn's surface without actually leaving the Satellite ship at all. Maybe she'd do. Maybe she might even be able to help him, somehow.

Provost dressed quickly now as the fear grew stronger in his mind. There was no use trying to fight it down; he knew that from long experience. It was far more exhausting to try than just to give in to it, start counting the minutes to Relief from *now* instead of when the shift began. It made things balance better in his mind that way, even if it made the DepPsych people scream and wring their hands. Well, let them scream. There was nothing they new about this Idiot War that he didn't know— absolutely nothing. He was an expert on this war. They couldn't even imagine what an expert he was.

He checked at the Control board. "Provost on."

"Are you steady?" the voice from Control asked.

Provost grunted.

"All right, here's the report." The voice hesitated an instant. "I don't think you're going to like it very much."

"Let's have it."

"Dead quiet on the front all through the last shift," Control said.

Provost blinked. "Quiet!"

"That's the report."

Provost shivered. "What do you suppose they're cooking up *now?*"

"I wish I could tell you." The voice from Control was puzzled and sympathetic. "They're brewing *something* down there, that's certain. Chances are it'll be nasty, too. They haven't given us a quiet shift in months." Provost could almost see the face of the controller, somewhere deep in the lower regions of the Satellite ship. "You may be the one to get hit with it, John, whatever it is. But then, maybe it'll stay quiet for you, too."

"Not with my luck," said Provost. "Well, I'm going in now."

He stepped into the Analogue cubicle with the green flasher over the door, found the cockpit in the darkness, fit his damp hands into the grips. He shook the Analogue helmet down on his head until it was comfortable. He didn't try to tell himself that *he* wasn't really going down to Saturn's surface, that only a tiny bit of metal and stamped circuitry was going down under his mental control. DepPsych had given up on *that* line of comfort long ago. Provost knew all too well that he didn't have to be on the surface in the flesh in order for the Enemy to rip him apart. He closed his eyes in the darkness, trying to relax.

Still waiting, now, for the signal to move in. He didn't know which man he was relieving. DepPsych said it was better not to know. Even the signals from the Analogues were monitored so he wouldn't have a hint. Every man operated his Analogue differently—but could the Enemy tell the difference?

Provost was certain that they could. Not that it seemed to make any difference, to them.

"Countdown." He heard the buzzer sound, and he crushed down with all his power on the hand grips. He felt the jolting thud as he slammed into full Analogue contact, and something deep in his mind began screaming *now! now! now!*

He dropped away into nothing.

Moments later he knew that he was on the surface, even though a corner of his mind was aware of the sticky hand grips, the dark closeness of the Analogue cubicle. Before him he could see the great yawning chasms of ice on Saturn's surface stretching out into the distance. Yellow-gray light reflected down from the Rings. He could sense the devastating pressure of gravity here even though he could not feel it. Overhead, a roiling sea of methane and ammonia clouds, crashing lightning, the unspeakable violence of Saturn's continual war with itself.

And somewhere beyond the place where he was, the Enemy.

There was no contact, at first. Provost groped, and found nothing. He could always tell their presence, just as he was certain now that they could tell his. But that was as far as he could go. *They* planned. *They* moved. If *they* were ready, they struck. If they weren't ready, they didn't.

And until they struck, he was helpless. There was nothing for him to fight against. All he could do was wait. For what? He did not know. But always before, there had been *something*.

Now, nothing. Not a whisper. He waited, sick with fear. He knew how brutal the Enemy could be. He knew the viciousness of their blows, the savagery, the cunning. These were things he could fight, turning their own weapons against them. But *nothingness* was something else.

How could he fight nothing? He couldn't. He could only wait.

He stretched his mind, groping for them. Then, suddenly, he felt a gentle brush of contact . . . they were there, all right. Also waiting. But for what? His muscles knotted, cramped. *Why didn't they do something?* A quick, stabbing blow would be merciful relief . . . but it did not come.

The Enemy had never been merciful. There was something else they were going to do.

When it came, it was almost overpowering in its intensity. Not hostility, nor anger, nor hatred, as before. Instead, incredibly, a soft gentle mist of supplication, a wave of reproach insinuating itself in his mind. *Why do you hate us when we want only peaceful contact with you? Why do you try to drive us back? We have come from so far, and now you try only to destroy us.*

It caught him off guard. He tried to formulate an answer, but they swept in swiftly, surrounding him with wave after wave of reproach. As always, he could not tell *how* this contact with the Enemy was made. Perhaps they, too, had Analogues. He simply felt them, deep in his mind, and they were closer now, all about him, sucking him deep into their minds. He felt a glowing warmth there now that was utterly different from before. He felt himself drawn, moving slowly, then faster and faster, in tightening spirals toward the vortex as the Enemy's minds drew him in. *We want to stop this fighting, but you prolong it. Why? Why won't you give us a chance?*

For the first time he saw the physical images of the Enemy. They were approaching him on the surface. He couldn't see them clearly . . . only fuzzy outlines . . . but enough to see that they were humanoid, manlike. They moved toward him as he watched. His heart roared with sudden excitement. Could they mean it? Could they really want to reveal themselves, establish contact, put an end to this grueling, brutal Idiot War that had been going on for so long?

Something in his own mind called out a warning, shrieking an alarm. *Don't be a fool! They're treacherous, there's nothing they won't try. Don't let them poison you, fight back!*

He caught at the grips, trying to center his mind on the approaching emissaries, trying to catch the fringes of thought that lay beneath the surface, but the wave of reproachfulness came back at him with increasing intensity.

Why do you hate us so much?

He knew, coldly, what he had to do. It was the only thing to do, even though it seemed so horribly wrong.

He waited until the emissaries were close. Then he struck out at their minds, as viciously as he knew how. He drove the blow home with six long months of bitterness and hatred behind it, striking out wildly, slicing them down like wheat before a scythe. He felt them recoil and crumble, and he pressed his advantage coldly, flailing at the insidious supplicating pattern of thought surrounding him.

The spiral broke, suddenly, releasing him, but this time there was no stark, brutal core of malignancy that he had glimpsed beneath their illusions so many times before. Instead, the vortex receded gently, regretfully . . . injured, bewildered, helpless to understand.

Why? Why will you not even give us a chance? Why do you hate us so much?

It was harder to bear than naked savagery. Frantically Provost rang for Relief. It seemed, suddenly, as if all the wrongs and imagined wrongs he had done in his whole life were welling up to torment him; he knew it was only Enemy illusion, but his mind was screaming, twisting in on itself. A sense of guilt and self-loathing swept through him in waves as he fought to maintain the tiny thread of control. *Butcher!* his own mind was screaming at him. *What kind of monster are you? What if they were sincere? What if you were the one who was wrong?*

The Control board jerked him back before he broke, snapped off his Analogue contact abruptly. He stood up in the darkness of the cubicle and disengaged his cramped hands from the grips. It was over; he was safe. His Rehab conditioning cut in now to take over . . . now there would be Relief from the onslaught, quietness, gentleness, childhood memories, peace. . . .

But the waves of guilt were still washing at his mind. He started walking down the corridor toward the Relief room as his hands began to tremble; then he broke into a run. He knew that only seconds now stood between him and sanity, and sanity lay at the end of the corridor.

The Turner girl was in the room waiting for him. There was soft music, gentle light. She sat across the room, and suddenly he was a five-year-old again, bewildered and overwhelmed by the frightening world around him, desperate for comfort, affection, reassurance. He hurled himself onto the recliner, felt the Turner girl's fingers gently stroking his forehead as he let himself go completely, let great sobs of relief erupt from his throat and shake his shoulders.

She was silent for a long time as his knotted muscles began to relax. Then she leaned forward, bent her lips to his ear.

"Butcher!" she whispered.

Only a whisper, but virulent, malignant. "Toad! You call yourself human, but you go down there to butcher them! *Monster!*"

Provost screamed. He threw himself back against the wall, arms outstretched, clawing at it and screaming as he stared at her in horror. She faced him, and spit at him, and burst out in mocking laughter as his screams rose from torment to agony.

An alarm bell was clanging now; the girl's lips twisted in revulsion. She threw open the corridor door. *"Butcher!"* she hurled back at him once more, and broke for the door.

Gunfire rattled from both ends of the corridor. The crossfire caught her, lifted her off her feet and dropped her in a crumpled heap on the metal floor plates.

Provost huddled in the corner of the room, babbling.

2 **T**he enormity of the blow did not register immediately. Like any warfare operation, the Satellite ship was geared to face emergencies; the sheer momentum of its battle station procedure delayed the impact for hours. Then, slowly, the entire operation of the Satellite ship began to freeze in its tracks.

What had happened was no ordinary emergency.

To Dorie Kendall the full, terrifying implication was clear from the start. She had long months of Department of Psychology training behind her at the Hoffman Center, weeks of work with the very men who had developed the neuromolecular Analogues that were Earth's only weapon in this war. Even then, the training had not stopped; on the long passage out from Earth she had continued with days and nights of tape-study and hypno-sleep to prepare her for this crucial assignment. She herself had never been in Analogue contact with the Enemy, but she knew a great deal about the Enemy and what the Enemy might do. The instant Dr. Coindreau, the Satellite surgeon, had called her down to the autopsy, she realized what had happened.

Only now it was dawning on her, in a cold wash of horror, that it was very possibly her own fault that it had happened at all.

"But why don't you *attack* them?" she had asked John Provost a few hours before his shift was to begin. "Why do you always take the defensive?"

Provost had looked at her, patiently, as though she were a child who didn't quite understand the facts of life. "They're perceptive," he said. "They're powerful. Incredibly powerful."

"All the more reason to hit them hard," she had argued. "Hit them with a blow that will drive them back reeling."

Provost smiled. "Is that the new DepPsych theory?"

"All DepPsych knows is that *something* has to be changed. This war has gone on and on."

"Maybe after a while you'll understand why," he had said slowly. "How can we hit them with this powerful blow you talk about when they're busy driving mental javelins into us with all the force they can muster? I can try, but I don't know how to do it."

Well, he had tried, all right, the psychologist reflected, and now bare hours later Provost was strapped down screaming and shattered in one of the isolation cubicles, and the Relief girl. . . .

She watched Dr. Coindreau's lean face and careful fingers as he worked at the autopsy table. Every room in Medical Section, every fixture, had a double use. Sick bay and Rehab quarters. Office and lab. Examining room doubling as surgery. Now it was doubling as morgue. She peered down at the remains of the Turner girl in growing anger and revulsion and wondered, desperately, how the Enemy had managed to do it.

She realized, coldly, that it was up to her to find out how, and fast.

The Enemy had poisoned the Turner girl, somehow. They had reached into the heart of the Satellite ship and struck at the most critical link in the chain—the Relief program that enabled the men to go back into battle.

Without Relief, there could be no men to fight.

But why did we have to murder her? the Kendall girl thought bitterly. *If we could have studied her, we might have learned how the Enemy had done it.*

The blinker over the door flashed, and a big heavyset man stepped into the room. She recognized Vanaman, commander of the Satellite ship. She had talked to him briefly before. It had been an unpleasant interview; Vanaman had made it quite clear that he could not understand why DepPsych insisted upon sending women out to Saturn Satellite, nor why Earth Control chose *now* of all times to shift gears and saddle him with Dorie Kendall, intent on finding some new approach to the fighting. The big man glared at her, and then stared down at the thing on the table.

"The Turner girl?" he asked the surgeon.

"What's left of her," Dr. Coindreau said. "I'm about finished. It's not going to help us any."

"It's *got* to help us." Vanaman's voice was harsh.

Dorie Kendall looked up at him sharply. "Your trigger-happy firing squad didn't leave us much to work with, you know."

Vanaman's fist clenched on the table. Deep-cut lines sliced from his nose down to the corners of his mouth. His face showed the grueling pressure of months of command, and he seemed to control himself only with difficulty. "What did you expect them to do?" he said. "Give her a medal?"

The girl flushed. "They didn't have to kill her."

Vanaman blinked at her. "They didn't, eh? You've been helping the doctor here do the post?"

"Certainly."

"And you've run a standard post-mortem brain wash?" He nodded toward the neuromolecular analyzer clicking in the wall, the great-grandfather of all Analogues.

"Of course."

"And what did you find, Miss Kendall?"

"Nothing intelligible," she said defiantly. "The Enemy had her, that's all."

"Fine," said Vanaman. "And you're standing here suggesting that we should have had *that* running around *alive* on this ship? Even for ten seconds? We know they had her tongue, they must have had her eyes also, her ears, her reason." He shook his head. "Everything we've done against the Enemy has depended on keeping them *away* from us, *off* this ship. That's why we monitor every move of every man and woman here, Miss Kendall, including yourself. That's why we have guns in every corridor and room. That's why we used them on the Turner girl."

There was silence for a moment. Then the doctor pushed back from the table and looked up. "I'm afraid you used them too late on the Turner girl," he said to Vanaman.

"You mean Provost is dead?"

"Oh, no." The doctor jerked off his mask, ran a lean hand through his hair. "He's alive enough. That is to say, his heart is beating. He breathes. Just what is going on above his ears is something else again. I doubt if even Miss Kendall could tell you that. I certainly can't."

"Then he's a total loss." Vanaman's face seemed to sag, and Dorie realized suddenly how heavily the man had been hanging on the thread of hope that Provost might only have suffered minor harm.

"Who can say?" the doctor said. "You take a fine chunk of granite and strike precisely the right blow, precisely hard enough at precisely the right angle, and it will shatter into a dozen pieces. That is what has happened to Provost. Any salvage will be strictly up to DepPsych. It's out of my province." The surgeon's dark eyes met Dorie's for a moment, and shifted away. "Unfortunately, the significance of this attack is greater than the survival or loss of John Provost. We might as well face that right now. The job the Enemy has done on Provost was a precision job. It can mean only one thing: that somehow they have managed to acquire a very complex understanding of human behavior patterns. Am I right, Dorie?"

She nodded. "It isn't *what* they did to Provost that matters so much," she said, "although that's bad enough. It's *how* they did it that matters."

"Then how *did* they do it?" Vanaman asked, turning on her. "That's what you're here for, isn't it? This isn't a war of muscle against muscle or bomb against bomb. This is a war of mind against mind. It's up to the Department of Psychology and the Hoffman Center psych-docs to tell us how to fight this Enemy. Why don't you know?"

"I need time," she said. "I can't give you an answer."

The big man leaned forward, his lips tight across his teeth. "You've *got* to give me an answer," he said. "We can't afford time, can't you see that? This Satellite is the only shield between Earth and the Enemy. If you can't give us the answer, we're through, washed up. We've got to know how they did what they did to Provost."

Through the viewport the pale, yellow globe of Saturn stared up at them, unwinking, like the pale eye of a snake. "I wish I could tell you," Dorie Kendall said. "The Turner girl can't tell us. Neither can Provost. But there may be one way we can learn."

"And that is?"

"Provost's Analogue. It has been the *real* contact with the Enemy. It should know everything Provost knows about them. The Analogue may give us the answer."

3   **W**ith Vanaman seated beside her, Dorie fed the tapes from John Provost's Analogue into the playback unit in the tiny projection room in Integration Section. For a few moments, then, she ceased to be Dorie Kendall of DepPsych, trained for duty and stationed on Saturn Satellite, and became John Provost instead.

It was an eerie experience. She realized that every Analogue was different, a faithful impression of the mind of its human prototype; but she had not been prepared for the sudden, abrupt contact with the proto-type mind of John Provost.

She felt the sickening thud of his contact with the Analogue just prior to its last descent to the surface. She felt the overwhelming wave of tension and fear that the Analogue had recorded; then the sudden, irra-tional, almost gleeful sense of elation as John Provost's eyes and ears and mind floated down to the place where the Enemy was. The Ana-logue tape was accurate to a high degree of fidelity. Dorie Kendall gripped the chair arms until her wrists cramped.

It was like going to the surface herself.

Beside her she was aware of Vanaman's huge body growing tense as he gnawed his knuckles, soaking in the tape record. She felt the growing tension, the snowballing sense of impending disaster reflecting from John Provost's mind.

And then she lost contact with the things around her and fell com-pletely into Provost's role. The growing supplication of the Enemy sur-rounded her. She felt the sense of reproach, the helpless appeal of the illusion, and Provost's response, calculated to perfection and deployed like a pawn on a chessboard. *It's a trick, a pitfall, watch out! Don't be fooled, don't fall into their trap. . . .*

She felt the wild fury of Provost's mind as he hurled the illusion aside, struck out at the Enemy as she had told him to do. And then the receding waves of supplication and reproach from the Enemy, and the overwhelming, demoralizing wave of guilt from his own mind—

In that moment she began to understand John Provost, and to realize what the Enemy had done. Her face was pale when the tape stopped. She clenched her fists to keep her hands from trembling.

Vanaman leaned back, defeat heavy on his face. "Nothing," he said. "It's always the same. We have nothing."

"I didn't realize what they could do," Dorie said.

"But that was on the surface. Down there we could fight it, control it. Now they've reached us here, too." The commander stood up and started for the corridor. "For all we know, they've been here all along, just playing with us. We can't really be certain that they haven't. Can you begin to see what we've been fighting, now? We don't know *any-*

thing about them. We can't even be sure we're fighting a war with them."

Dorie Kendall looked up, startled. "Is there any doubt of that?"

"There's plenty of doubt," Vanaman said. "We *seem* to be fighting a war, except that nobody seems to understand just what kind of war we're fighting, or just why we're fighting it." His voice trailed off and he shrugged wearily. "Well, we're backed up to the wall now. Provost was our best Analogue man. He depended utterly on Relief to put him back together again after one of those sessions down there. The Turner girl was the whole key to our fighting technique, and they got to her somehow and poisoned her. If they can do that, we're through."

The girl stared at him. "You mean we should just quit? Withdraw?"

Vanaman's voice was bitter. "What else can we do? Any one of the girls in Relief could be just the same as the Turner girl, right now. They've cracked open our entire strategy in one blow. The Relief program is ruined, and without Relief I can't send another man down there."

"But you've *got* to," Dorie said. "This Satellite is the Earth's only shield. We can't stop now."

"We can't fight them, either. We've been fighting them for months, and we know nothing about them. They come from—somewhere. We don't know where, or when, or how. All we know is what they did to Titan. We're trying to defend ourselves against an imponderable, and our defenses are crumbling." Vanaman closed the tape cans and tossed them into the return file with an air of finality. "Do you know what Provost called this war?"

Dorie Kendall nodded. "He told me. An Idiot War."

"And he was right. *Their* war, not ours. What do they want? We don't know. On *their* choice of battlefield, in *their* kind of warfare, they're whipping us, and we don't even know how. If we had even a glimpse of what they were trying to do, we might be able to fight them. Without that, we're helpless."

She heard what he was saying, and she realized that it was almost true, and yet something stuck in her mind, a flicker of an idea. "I wonder," she said. "Maybe we don't know what the Enemy is trying to do here—but there's one possibility that nobody seems to have considered."

Vanaman looked up slowly. "Possibility?"

"That *they* don't know what they're trying to do, either," Dorie Kendall said.

4   It was a possibility, even Vanaman grudgingly admitted that. But as she went down to Isolation Section to examine John Provost, Dorie Kendall knew that it made no sense, no more nor less than anything else that the Enemy had done since they had come six months before into Earth's solar system.

They had come silent as death, unheralded: four great ships moving as one, slipping in from the depths of space beyond Pluto. How long they had been lurking there, unobserved but observing, no one could say. They moved in slowly, like shadows crossing a valley, with all space to conceal them, intruders in the enormous silence.

An observation post on tiny Miranda of Uranus spotted them first, suddenly and incredibly present where no ships ought to be, in a formation that no Earth ships ever would assume. Instrument readings were confirmed, questioned, reconfirmed. The sighting was relayed to the supply colony on Callisto, and thence to Earth.

Return orders were swift: keep silence, observe, triangulate and track, compute course and speed, make no attempt at contact. But return orders were too late. The observation post on Miranda had ceased, abruptly, to exist.

Alerted patrol ships searched in vain, until the four strange ships revealed themselves in orbit around Saturn. Deliberately? No one knew. Their engines were silent; they drifted like huge encapsulated spores, joining the other silent moons around the sixth planet. They orbited for months. Titan Colony watched them, Ganymede watched them, Callisto watched them.

Nothing happened.

On Earth there were councils, debate, uncertainty; speculation, caution, fear. Wait for them to make contact. Give them time. Wait and see. But the four great ships made no move. They gave no sign of life. Nothing.

Signals were dispatched, with no response. Earth prepared against an attack—a ridiculous move. Who could predict the nature of any attack that might come? Still, Earthmen had always been poor at waiting. Curiosity battled caution and won, hands down. What were these ships? Where did they come from? Hostile or friendly? Why had they come here?

Above all, *what did they want?*

No answers came from the four great ships. Nothing.

Finally an Earth ship went up from Titan Colony, moving out toward the orbit of the intruders. The crew of the contact ship knew their danger. They had a single order: make contact. Use any means, accept any risk, but make contact. Approach with caution, with care, gently, without alarming, but make contact. At any cost.

They approached the intruders, and were torn from space in one instantaneous flash of white light. Simultaneously, Titan Colony flared like an interplanetary beacon and flickered out, a smoking crater three hundred miles wide and seventy miles deep.

Then, incredibly, the four great ships broke from orbit and fled deep beneath the methane and ammonia clouds of Saturn's surface. Earth reeled from the blow, and waited, paralyzed, for the next—and nothing happened. No signal, no sign, nothing.

But now the intruders were the Enemy. The war had begun, if it was a war; but it was not a war that Earthmen knew how to fight. A war of contradiction and wild illogic. A war fought in a ridiculous microcosm where Earthmen could not fight, with weapons that Earthmen did not comprehend.

An Idiot War. . . .

Dorie went to see John Provost just eight hours after the Enemy had struck through the Turner girl. As she followed the tall, narrow-shouldered doctor into the isolation cubicles of Medical Section, he stopped and turned to face her. "I don't think this is wise at all."

"Maybe not," the girl said. "But I have no choice. Provost was closer to the Enemy than anyone else here. There's no other place to start."

"What do you think you're going to learn?" Dr. Coindreau asked.

"I don't know. Only Provost knows exactly what happened in that Relief room."

"We know what happened," the doctor protested. "The Relief room was monitored. Provost had come close to his breakpoint when Control jerked his Analogue back from the surface. The pressure on the men under battle conditions is almost intolerable. They all approach breakpoint, and induced regression in the Relief room is the fastest, safest way to unwind them, as long as we don't let them curl up into a ball."

"You mean it *was* the fastest and safest way," Dorie corrected him.

The doctor shrugged. "They hit Provost at his weakest point. The Turner girl couldn't have done worse with a carving knife. I still don't see what you're going to learn from Provost."

"At least I can see what they've done to him." She looked at the doctor. "I don't see how my seeing him can hurt him."

"Oh, I'm not worried about *him*." The doctor opened the door. At the nursing desk a corpsman was punching chartcards. "How's he doing?" the doctor asked.

"Same as before." Then the corpsman saw the girl. "Doc, you aren't taking *her* in there, are you?"

"That's what she wants."

"You know he's not exactly sold on girls, right now."

"I'll risk it," Dorie said sharply.

Inside the cubicle they found Provost lying on his back on a bunk. The pale blue aura of a tangle-field hovered over him, providing gentle but effective restraint.

Provost was singing.

The words drifted across the room. Dorie suddenly caught them and felt her cheeks turn red.

"Hello, John," the doctor said. "How are you feeling?"

Provost stopped singing. "Fine. Yourself?"

"This is Miss Kendall. She's going to help take care of you."

"Well, now, that's just fine." Provost turned his face toward Dorie. No sign of recognition; his eyes were flat, like a snake's eyes. Impersonal—and deadly. "Why don't you leave us alone to talk, Doc? And turn this tangle-field off. Just for a minute."

She shivered at the tone. Dr. Coindreau said, "John, do you know where you are?"

"In a tangle-field."

"Do you know where?"

Provost ignored the question, stared fixedly at the girl. She had never seen such a malignant stare.

"Do you know what happened to you?" the doctor tried again.

His eyes didn't waver, but he frowned. "Memory's a little sticky. But ten seconds out of this tangle-field would help, I bet." She saw his hand clench on the coverlet until the knuckles whitened.

The doctor sighed. "Listen to me, John. You were on the surface. Something happened down there. What—"

Provost obviously was not listening. "Look, Doc, why don't you cut out of here? My business is with *her,* not you."

"All right, John." Dr. Coindreau turned away. He led the girl back into the corridor. She was no longer blushing. She was dead white and trembling. "You know that he'd kill you before he finished," the doctor said to her gently.

"Yes." She nodded. "I know."

"At least the mechanism is direct enough. Fairly primitive, too. And let's face it, a weaker man would either be dead or catatonic. Provost is a rock of stability in comparison."

She nodded. "But he's turned his hatred on the girl, not on the Enemy."

"It was the girl who hit him, remember?" They stepped into an office, and she took the seat the doctor offered gratefully. "Anyway," he said, "Provost never actually contacted the Enemy. We speak as though he's actually been down on the surface physically, and of course he hasn't. You know how an Analogue works?"

"I ought to—I have one—but I only know the general theory, not the details."

"Nobody know the details too well, not even your friends at the Hoffman Center. Nobody really could. An Analogue is at least quasi-sentient, and the relationship between an Analogue and its operator is extremely individual and personal. That's precisely why Analogues are the only real weapons we have to use against the Enemy."

"I can't quite see that," Dorie said.

"Look—these creatures, whatever they are—buried themselves on the surface of Saturn and just sat there, right? The blows they struck against Titan Colony and the contact ship showed us the kind of power they *could* bring to bear—but they didn't follow up. They struck and ran. Pretty pointless, wouldn't you say?"

It seemed so, at first glance. Dorie Kendall frowned. "Maybe not so pointless. It made counterattack almost impossible."

Dr. Coindreau nodded grimly. "Exactly the point. We didn't know what—or how—to counterattack. We practically *had* to do *something*, and yet there was nothing we could do."

"Why didn't we land and hunt them out?" the girl asked. "We can get down there, can't we?"

"Well, it's *possible*, but it would have been worse than useless. It would have taken all our strength and technology just to survive down there, let alone do anything else. So we used Analogues, just the way Grossman and his crew used them to explore the surface of Jupiter. The Analogues were originally developed to treat paranoids. The old lysergic acid poisons had proved that a personality could dissociate voluntarily and reintegrate, so that a psych man could slip right into a paranoid fantasy with his patient and work him on his own ground. Trouble was that unstable personalities didn't reintegrate so well, which was why so many people blew up in all directions on LSD." Dr. Coindreau paused, chewing his lip. "With Analogues, the dissociation is only apparent, not real. A carbon copy, with all the sensory, motor, and personality factors outlined perfectly on protein-molecule templates. The jump from enzyme-antagonists to electronic punched-molecule impressions isn't too steep, really, and at least the Analogues are predictable."

"I see," Dorie Kendall said. "So the operatives—like Provost—could send their Analogues down and explore in absentia, so to speak."

"As a probe, in hope of making contact with the Enemy. At least that was the original plan. It turned out differently, though. That was what the Enemy seemed to be waiting for. They drove back the first probers with perfectly staggering brutality. We struck back at them, and they returned with worse. So pretty soon we were dancing this silly gavotte with them down there, except that the operatives didn't find it so silly.

Maybe the medieval Earth wars seemed silly, too, with the battleground announced in advance, the forces lined up, the bugles blowing, parry and thrust and everybody quits at sunset. But lots of men got killed that way just the same." He paused for a moment, wrapped in his own thoughts, and then went on with sudden firmness: "There was no sense to this thing, but it was what the Enemy seemed to want. And our best men have thrown everything they could into it, and only their conditioning and the Relief room has kept them going."

"Weren't Psi-Highs used for a while?" Dorie said:

"Yes, but it didn't work. The Enemy is not telepathic, for one thing, or at least not in the sense we think of it; and anyway, the Psi-Highs couldn't keep themselves and their Analogues separated. It was pure slaughter, for them, so they were pulled back to Earth to help build the Analogues for psi-negatives to use." He shot a glance toward the cubicle. "Well, now that's all over. No Relief, no Analogues. The Enemy has simply shifted the battle scene on us, and we're paralyzed."

For a long moment the DepPsych girl sat in silence. Then she said, "I don't think 'paralyzed' is exactly the word you want. You mean 'panicked'."

"Does it make any difference?"

"Maybe a world of difference," the girl said thoughtfully, *"to the aliens."*

5

Paralysis or panic, the effect on the Satellite ship was devastating.

Twelve hours after Provost was dragged kicking and screaming out of the Relief room, the ship's crew waited in momentary anticipation, braced against the next blow. They could not guess from where it might come, nor what form it might take. They could only sit in agony and wait.

Twenty-four hours later, they still waited. Thirty-six hours, and they still waited. Activity was suspended, even breathing was painful. In the day room the Analogue operatives gnawed their knuckles, silent and fearful, unwilling to trust even a brief exchange of words. They were Earthmen, the girl realized, and Earthmen were old hands at warfare. They understood too well the horrible power of advantage. Earthly empires had tottered and fallen for the loss of one tiny advantage.

But the Enemy's advantage was not tiny. It was huge, overpowering. The men here could only wait for the blow to fall. It *had* to fall, if there were order and logic in the universe.

It didn't fall. They waited, and far worse than a brutal, concerted attack against them, nothing happened.

The paralysis deepened. The Enemy had reached a girl within the Satellite and turned her into a murderous blade in their midst. Who could say how many others had been reached? No one knew. There was nothing to grasp, nothing to hold on to, *nothing*.

Dorie Kendall did not elaborate on her remark to Dr. Coindreau, but something had slid smoothly into place in her mind as she had talked to him, and she watched the Satellite and its men around her grinding to a halt with a new alertness.

The attack on Provost through the Turner girl was not pointless, she was certain of that. It had purpose. Nor was it an end in itself. It was only the beginning. To understand the purpose it was necessary somehow to begin to understand the Enemy.

And that, of course, was the whole war. That was what the Enemy had so consistently fought to prevent. *They have built up an impenetrable wall, a blinding smoke screen to hide themselves,* she thought, *but there must be some way to see them clearly.*

The only way to see them was through Provost. She was certain of this, though she wasn't sure why. She went to the isolation cubicle to see him again, and then again and again. It was unrelieved torment for her each time; for all her professional training, she had never before encountered such a malignant wall of hatred. Each time his viciousness and abusiveness seemed worse as he fought against the restraining tangle-field, watching her with murderous hatred; she left each time almost physically ill, and whenever she slept she had nightmares. But again and again she worked to break through his violent obsession, more and more convinced that John Provost was the key. They were brutal interviews, fruitless—but she watched as she worked.

Vanaman found her in Medical Section on the third day, a red-eyed, bitter Vanaman, obviously exhausted, obviously fighting for the last vestige of control, obviously helpless to thwart the creeping paralysis in the ship under his command. "You've got to hit Eberle with something," he said harshly. "I can't make him budge."

"Who is Eberle?" the girl wanted to know.

"The Analogue dispatcher. He won't send an Analogue down."

"I thought you weren't going to."

"I've *got* to do *something,* Relief or no Relief, but Eberle is dragging his feet."

She found John Eberle in the Analogue banks, working by himself, quietly and efficiently and foolishly, testing wires, testing transmission, dismantling the delicate electronic units and reassembling them in an atmosphere of chaos around him. The operative cubicles were empty, the doors hanging open, alarm signals winking unheeded.

"What are you doing with them?" Dorie asked, staring down at the dismantled Analogues.

Eberle grinned foolishly. "Testing them," he said. "Just testing."

"But Vanaman says we need them down on the surface *now*. Can't you see that?"

Eberle's smile faded. "I can't send them down there."

"Why not?"

"Who's going to operate them?" the dispatcher asked. "What will the operators do for Relief?" His eyes narrowed. "Would *you* want to take one down?"

"I'm not trained to take one down. But there are operators here who are."

Eberle shrugged his shoulders. "Well, you're DepPsych, maybe you've got some magic formula to make the men go down without any Relief to count on. I can't make them. I've already tried it."

She stared at him, and felt a wave of helplessness sweep over her. It was as though she were standing in an enormous tangle-field, and all her efforts to free herself only settled it more firmly on her shoulders. She knew it wasn't anything as simple as fear or cowardice that was paralyzing the ship.

It was more than that, something far deeper and more basic.

Once again she was forced back to where it had all started, the only possible channel of attack.

John Provost. She headed for the isolation cubicle.

Thirty-six hours, and she had barely slept; when exhaustion demanded rest, her mind would not permit it, and she would toss in darkness, groping for land, for something solid to grasp and cling to.

Provost sucked up most of her time—wasted hours, hours that drained her physically and emotionally. She made no progress, found no chink in the brutal armor. When she was not with him she was in the projection booth, studying the Analogue tapes stored and filed from the beginning, studying the monitor tapes, watching and listening, trying somehow to build a composite picture of this enigmatic Enemy that had appeared from the depths of space, struck, and then drawn back to the inaccessible surface of Saturn. There were too many pictures, that was the trouble. None of them fit. None corresponded to the others. She was trying to make sense from nonsense, and always the task seemed more hopeless than before.

And yet, slowly, a pattern began to emerge.

An alien creature, coming by intent or accident into a star system with intelligent life, advanced technology. The odds were astronomical against its ever happening. Probably not a truly unique occurrence in the universe, but very possibly unique for these alien creatures.

What then?

A pattern that was inevitable. . . .

She answered a violent summons from Vanaman. He demanded progress with John Provost, and she told him there was no progress. He paced the floor, lashing out at her with all the fury that had been building up as the hours had passed. "That's what you're here for," he told her harshly. "That's why we have DepPsych—to deal with emergencies. We've got to have progress with that man."

Dorie Kendall sighed. "I'm doing everything I can. Provost has a good, strong mind. He has it focused down on one tiny pinpoint of awareness, and he won't budge it from there."

"*He* won't!" Vanaman roared. "What about *you?* You people are supposed to have techniques. You can break him away from it."

"Do you want him dead?" she asked. "That's what you'll get if I drive him too hard. He's clinging to his life, and I mean that literally. To him, I am the Turner girl, and all that is sustaining him is this vicious drive to destroy me, as quickly as he can, as horribly as he can. You can use your imagination, I think."

Vanaman stared at her. She met his haggard eyes defiantly. Vanaman broke first. It was almost pitiable, the change; he seemed to age before her eyes. The creases in his face seemed to harden and deepen, and his heavy hands—threatening weapons before—fell limp. Like a spirited dog that had been whipped and broken by a brutal master, he crumbled. "All right. I can't fight you." He spread his hands helplessly. "You know that I'm beaten, don't you? I'm cornered, and there's no place to turn. I know why Provost dreaded those long waits between shifts now. That's all I can do—wait for the blow to fall."

"What blow?" said the girl.

"Maybe you can tell me." A strangled sound came from Vanaman's throat. "Everything we've done against them has been useless. Our attempt to contact them, our probing for them and fighting them on the surface—useless. When they got ready to hit us here, they hit us. All our precautions and defenses didn't hinder them." He glared at her. "All right, you tell me. What is it we're waiting for? When is the blow coming? From where?"

"I don't think there's going to be any blow," said Dorie Kendall.

"Then you're either blind or stupid," Vanaman snapped. "They've driven a gaping hole in our defenses. They know that. Do you think they're just going to let the advantage slide?"

"Human beings might not, but they're not human beings. You seem to keep forgetting that."

Words died on Vanaman's lips. He blinked and frowned. "I don't follow you," he said after a moment.

"So far, everything they've done fits a pattern," Dorie said. "They have physical destructive power, but the only times they've used it was to prevent physical contact. So then after they struck, what did they do? Press forward? Humans might, but they didn't. Instead, they moved back to the least accessible geographical region they could find in the solar system, a planetary surface we could not negotiate, and then they waited. When we sent down Analogue probers, they fought us, in a way, but what has made that fight so difficult? Can you tell me?"

"The fact that we didn't know what we were fighting, I suppose," Vanaman said slowly. "The Analogue operatives didn't know what was coming next, never two attacks the same."

"Exactly," said the girl. "They knocked us off balance and kept us there. They didn't use their advantage then. Everything was kept tightly localized until the Analogue operatives began to get their feet on the ground. You saw the same tapes I did. Those men were beginning to know what they were doing down there; they knew they could count on their conditioning and the Relief rooms to keep them from breaking, no matter how powerful the onslaught. So now, *only now,* the Enemy has torn that to ribbons, through the Turner girl." She smiled. "You see what I mean about a pattern?"

"Maybe so," Vanaman conceded, "but I don't see why."

"Look—when you poke a turtle with a stick, what happens? He pulls in his head and sits there. Just that one little aggressive act on your part gives you a world of information about how turtles behave. You could write a book about turtles, right there. But suppose it happened to be a snapping turtle you poked, and he took the end of the stick off. You wouldn't need to poke him a second time to guess what he would do, would you? You already know. Why bother with a second poke?"

"Then you're saying that the Enemy won't strike again because they have what they want," said Vanaman.

"Of course," the girl said bleakly. "They have Provost. Through Provost they have every mind on this Satellite. They don't need to fight on the surface any more, they're right here."

Vanaman's eyes were hard as he rose from his seat. "Well, we can stop that. We can kill Provost."

She caught his arm as he reached for the intercom switch. "Don't be ridiculous," she said tightly. *"What do you think you're going to do when you've killed him?"*

"I don't know," he snarled. "But I'll do something. I've got to get them out into the open somehow, out where I can see them, before we *all* split open at the seams."

"You mean find out whether they have green skins and five legs or not? Who cares?" She twisted his arm with amazing strength, pushing him back into the seat. "Listen to me, you fool. What we have to know is what they want, how they think, how they behave. Physical contact with them is pointless until we know those things. Can't you see that? *They've realized that from the start.*"

He stared at her. "But what do *you* think we should do?"

"First, find out some of the things we have to know," she said. "That means we have to use the one real weapon we've got—John Provost— and I'm going to see that he's kept alive. Show me your arm."

Puzzled, Vanaman held it out to her. The needle bit so quickly he could not pull back. Realization dawned on his face.

"Sorry," she said gently. "There's only one thing we can do, and killing Provost isn't it." She pushed him back in the seat like a sack of flour. "I wish it were," she added softly, but Vanaman wasn't listening any more.

6   **A**s she moved down the corridor the magnitude of what she was doing caught Dorie and shook her violently. Things had crystallized in her mind just before she had gone to talk with Vanaman. A course of action had appeared which she only grasped in outline, and she had moved too fast, too concisely, before thinking it out in full. But now she had tripped the switch. The juggernaut was moving in on her now, ponderously, but gaining momentum.

There would be no stopping it now, she knew, no turning it back. A course of action, once initiated, developed power of its own. She was committed. . . .

Earth was committed. . . .

She shook off that thought, forcefully. She was too terrified to think about that aspect of it. Her mind was filled and frozen by the ordeal she knew was facing her now: John Provost.

Somehow she had to take Provost back from them, wrench him out of their grasp. She remembered the hard, flat look in his eyes when he watched her, and she shuddered.

There was a way to do it.

All around her she could feel the tension of the Satellite ship, waiting helplessly, poised for demolition. She ran down the empty corridors, searched the depths of the ship until she found the place she was seeking. Once inside Atmosphere Control section she leaned against the wall, panting.

Then she slipped the filters into her nostrils, and broke the tiny capsules, feeding them into the ventilation ducts of the ship.

She would take Provost back from the Enemy; then, if she survived —what? There were only hazy outlines in her mind. She knew the limitation of thought that was blocking her. It was the limitation that was utterly unavoidable in thinking of an alien, a creature not of Earth, not human. The limitation was so terribly easy to overlook until the alien was there facing her: the simple fact that she was bound and strapped by a human mind. She could only think human thoughts, in human ways. She could only comprehend the alien insofar as the alien possessed *human* qualities, not an inch further. There was no way she could stretch her mind to cope with alien-ness. But worse—even in trying desperately to comprehend alien-ness, her own human mind inevitably assumed a human mind on the part of the alien.

This the Enemy did not have. What kind of mind the Enemy did have she could not know, but it was not a human mind. Yet that alien mind *had* to be contacted and understood.

It had seemed an insoluble conundrum—until she had realized that the Enemy had faced exactly the same problem, and solved it.

To the Enemy, stumbling upon intelligent life in Earth's solar system, a human mind was as incomprehensible as an alien mind was to a human. *They* had faced the same dilemma, and found a way to cope with it. *But how?* The very pattern of their approach showed how. It was data, and Dorie Kendall had treated it as data, and found the answer.

It revealed them.

They tried so hard to remain obscure while they studied us, she thought as she moved back toward the Analogue Section, *and yet with every move they made they revealed themselves to us further, if we had only had the wit to look. Everything they did was a revelation of themselves. They thought they were peering at us through a one-way portal, seeing us and yet remaining unseen, but in reality the glass was a mirror, reflecting their own natures in every move they made. They discovered our vulnerability, true, but at the same time inadvertently revealed their own.*

The ventilators hummed. She felt the tension in the ship relaxing as the sleep-gas seeped down the corridors. Muscles uncoiled. Fear dissolved from frightened minds. Doors banged open; there was talking, laughter; then lethargy, dullness, glazed eyes, yawns, slack mouths—

Sleep. Like Vanaman, slumped back in his chair, everyone on the Satellite slept. Operatives fell forward on their faces. The girls in the Relief rooms yawned, dozed, snored, slept.

It seemed to Dorie that she could sense Provost's thoughts twisting out toward her in a tight, malignant channel, driving to destroy her, seeking release from the dreadful hatred the aliens were using to bind him. But then even Provost dozed and slept.

With the filters protecting her, she was alone on the ship, a ghost. In the Analogue bank she activated the circuits she needed, set the dials, rechecked each setting to make certain that she made no error.

She dared not make an error.

Finally, she went to Provost. She dragged his drugged body into the Analogue cubicle and strapped him down. She fit his hands into the grips. Another needle, then, to counteract the sleep-gas, and his eyes blinked open.

He saw her and lunged for her with no warning sound. His arms tore at the restraints, jerking murderously. She jumped back from him a little, forcing out a twisted smile. She reached out mockingly to stroke his forehead, and he tried to bite her hand.

"Butcher!" she whispered. "Monster!"

Pure hate poured from his mouth as she laughed at him. Then she threw the Analogue switch. He jerked back as contact was made, and she moved swiftly to her own Analogue helmet waiting in the adjacent cubicle, threw another switch, felt in her own mind the sickening thud of Analogue contact.

Her Analogue. A therapeutic tool before, now a deadly weapon in frightened, unsteady hands.

She was afraid. It seemed that she was watching images on a hazy screen. She saw Provost there, facing her, hating her, but it was only a mental image. She was sitting alone in darkness and knew that he also was sitting in darkness. Then gradually the darkness seemed to dissolve into unreality; the two Analogue images—hers and Provost's—became sharp and clear.

It was like a dream, a waking nightmare. Provost was moving in on her slowly, his mouth twisting in hatred, great knots of muscle standing out in his arms. He seemed to tower over her for a moment in vicious anticipation. She screamed and broke down the corridor. He was after her like a cat. He leaped, struck her legs, threw her down on the metal floor and fell on her. She saw his arm upraised, felt the fist crash down again and again and again. Broken flesh, broken bones, paste, pulp, again and again. And in the dark Analogue cubicle she seemed to feel every blow.

She closed her eyes, her control reeling. There would be no Relief for her later, she knew that. She fought him, then abandoned fighting and just hung on doggedly, waiting for the end.

Abruptly, he was gone. She had felt his release as his hatred had burned itself out on her. He had stopped, and stood still, suddenly mild, puzzled, tired, wondering as he looked down at the thing on the floor. And then. . . .

She knew he had started for the surface.

7

To Provost it was like awakening from warm and peaceful sleep into terror.

He was horrified and appalled to realize that he had been sleeping. What had happened? Why didn't Control respond? Frantically he seized the hand grips, drove his Analogue down toward the surface. In his mind were fragments of memory. Something hideous had happened, long long ago, something in the Relief room. Afterwards he had been held down in a tangle-field, and time after time the Turner girl had come back to him in the isolation cubicle—or *had* it been the Turner girl? Then just now he had found her and the tangle-field was gone, and the hideous thing had been repeated.

And the horrible, abrupt awakening to the fact that the Satellite ship was utterly helpless and undefended from the Enemy.

How long had he slept? What had happened? Didn't they realize that every passing second might be precious to the Enemy, fatal to the Satellite?

He felt someone following him, screaming out at him in alarm. Not the Turner girl, as he had thought, but Dorie Kendall, the DepPsych agent, following him down to the surface with her own Analogue.

Provost hesitated, fighting the sense of urgency in his mind. "Don't stop me," he told her. "I've got to get down there. There's no one covering—"

"You can't go down," she cried. "You have no support here. No conditioning, no Relief. We've got to do something very different."

"Different?" He felt her very close to him now and he paused in confusion. What did she know about the Enemy? "What's happening here? The Enemy is down there. *Why have we stopped fighting?*"

She was telling him, frantically, as he groped through his confusion and tried to understand. "They had to know if we had a vulnerability, *any* vulnerability. Something they could use against us to protect themselves if they had to. They knew they could never risk direct contact with us until they knew that we were vulnerable in some way."

Provost shook his head, uncomprehending. "But why not?"

"Try to see *their* view," she said. "Suppose we were hostile, and invulnerable. We might not stop at destroying their ships, we might follow them home and destroy them there. They couldn't know, and they couldn't take a risk like that. They had to find a vulnerability to use as a weapon before any contact was possible. So they drew us out, prodded us, observed us, trying to find our limitations—if we had any. And they discovered our vulnerability—*panic*. A weakness in our natures, the point where intelligence deserts us and renders us irrational, helpless to fight any more. This is what they could use to control us, except that they must have the same vulnerability!"

He hesitated. The driving urge to go on down to the surface was almost overwhelming, to grapple with them and try once again to break through their barrier there. "Why should they have the same weakness we have? They're aliens, not humans."

"Because they have been doing *exactly the same thing that we would have done if we had been in their place*. Think, John! In all the star systems they must have searched, no sign of intelligent life. Then, suddenly, a solar system that is teeming with life. Intelligent? Obviously. Dangerous? How could they know? *We* wouldn't have known, would we? What would *we* have done?"

Provost faltered. "Tried to make contact, I suppose."

"Physical contact? Nonsense. We wouldn't have dared. We couldn't possibly risk contact until we knew how they thought and behaved, until we knew for certain that we could defend ourselves against them if necessary, that they had some kind of vulnerability. Once we knew that, that way would be open for contact. But no matter how eager we were for contact, and no matter how friendly they might appear *we would have had to have the weapon to fight them first*. Or take an insane risk, the risk of total destruction."

He understood her, but it didn't make sense. He thought of Miranda outpost, Titan Colony, and shook his head. "It doesn't add up," he said. "What they did here was incredible."

"Only if you assumed that they were hostile," she said softly.

"What about the contact ship, the colony on Titan? They burned them both, blew them to kingdom come."

"Because they had to. They did what we would have done under the same circumstances. They goaded us. Then they took cover and waited to see what we would do. They made us come after them where we couldn't reach them physically, to see what we could do. They deliberately kept one step ahead, making us reveal ourselves every step of the way, until they found the soft spot they were seeking and threw us into panic. What they failed to realize was that they were inevitably mirroring themselves in everything they did."

Silence then. In the dark cubicle, Provost could see the hazy image of the girl in his mind, pleading with him, trying to make him understand. Gradually it began to make sense. "So they have their weapon," he said slowly, "and still we can't make contact with them because *we* have none against *them*."

"*Had* none," the girl corrected him. "But we have seen them in the mirror. Their thoughts and actions and approach have been humanlike. They recognized our panic for what it was when they saw it. How could they have, unless they themselves knew what panic was—from their own experience?"

"And now?"

"We turn the tables," she said. "If they also have a vulnerability, there will be no more barrier to contact. But we don't dare *assume*, we have to *know*. Every time they have goaded us we have reacted. We've got to stop that now. We've got to withdraw from them completely, leave them with nothing to work with, nothing to grasp."

"But the Satellite—"

"The Satellite is dead for the time being, asleep. There's no one here but us for them to contact. Now we have to withdraw too. If we do that, can't you see what *they* will have to do?"

Slowly he nodded. He sensed that she hadn't told him all of it, but that, too, was all right. Better that there be *nothing* that the Enemy could draw from his mind. "You tell me what to do, and when," he said.

"Close your mind down, as completely as you can. Barricade it against them, if you can. Keep them out, leave nothing open for them to probe. Cut them off cold. But be ready when I signal you."

He twisted in the cramped seat in the cubicle, clamping down his control as he felt Dorie clamping down hers. It was an exercise in patience and concentration, but slowly he felt his mind clearing. Like a rheostat imperceptibly dimming the lights in a theater, the Satellite went dimmer, dimmer, almost dead. Only a flicker of activity remained, tiny and insignificant.

They waited.

It might have been hours, or even days, before the probing from the Enemy began. Provost felt it first, for he had known it before, tiny exploratory waves from the alien minds, tentative, easy to strike away. He caught himself just in time, allowed himself no response, trying to make his mind a blank gray surface, a sheet of nothing.

More probing then, more urgency. Sensations of surprise, of confusion, of concern. Unanswered questions, fleeting whispers of doubt in the alien minds. Slowly confusion gave way to doubt, then to fear.

This was something the Enemy clearly had not anticipated, this sudden unequivocal collapse. The probing grew more frantic in its intensity. Deepening of doubt, and then, amazingly, regretfulness, self-reproach, uncertainty. *What has happened? Could we have destroyed them? Could we have driven them too far?*

The probing stopped abruptly. Provost felt the DepPsych girl stir; vaguely his eyes registered the darkness of the cubicle around him, the oval viewport in the wall showing the pale yellow globe of Saturn lying below, its rings spreading like a delicate filigree. . . .

Nothing.

In his own mind he felt a stir of panic, and fought it down. What if the DepPsych girl were wrong? It was only a human mind which had assumed that creatures which behaved alike were alike. In the silence a thousand alternative possibilities flooded his mind. The minutes passed and the panic rose again, stronger. . . .

Then he saw it in the viewport. Up from the methane clouds they came, slowly, four great ships in perfect formation. They rose and stabilized in orbit, moved again, stabilized, moved again.

They were approaching the Satellite.

He felt his fingers clench on the grips as he watched, his mind leaping exultantly. *She had been right. They were forced out.* The offensive had shifted, and now *the Enemy* were forced to move.

Provost saw with perfect clarity the part the DepPsych girl hadn't told him—the thing he and she were going to do.

They waited until the ships were very close. Then:

"Provost! *Now!*"

They struck out together, as a unit, hard. They hit with all the power they could muster, striking the sensitive alien minds without warning. They could feel the sudden crashing impact of their attack. He could never have done it alone; together their power was staggering. The alien minds were open, confused, defensive; they reeled back in pain and fear—

In panic.

Suddenly the four great ships broke apart. They moved out in erratic courses, driving back for the planet's surface. They scuttled like bugs when a rock is overturned, beyond control and frantic. In a matter of minutes they were gone again, and the silence rose like a cloud from the surface.

8   **S**omewhere in the Satellite a bell was ringing. John Provost heard it, dreamily, as he rose and stretched his cramped muscles. He met Dorie Kendall in the corridor, and he could tell from the look on her face that she knew it was over, too.

The aliens were vulnerable. They were vulnerable to the same primitive and irrational defense reactions that humans were vulnerable to when faced with a crisis: the suspension of reason and logic that constituted panic. The knowledge was the weapon that Earthmen needed to make contact possible.

Now each side had a weapon. The mirror had reflected the aliens accurately, and the meaning of the reflection was unmistakably clear. There need be no danger in contact now. Now there could be a beginning to understanding.

Without a word John Provost and the girl began to waken the crew of the Satellite.

JACK VANCE

THE MIRACLE WORKERS

1   The war party from Faide Keep
moved eastward across the downs; a column of a hundred armored
knights, five hundred foot soldiers, a train of wagons. In the lead rode
Lord Faide, a tall man in his early maturity, spare and catlike, with a
sallow dyspeptic face. He sat in the ancestral car of the Faides, a boat-
shaped vehicle floating two feet above the moss, and carried, in addition
to his sword and dagger, his ancestral side weapons.

An hour before sunset a pair of scouts came racing back to the column, their club-headed horses loping like dogs. Lord Faide braked the
motion of his car. Behind him the Faide kinsmen, the lesser knights,
the leather-capped foot soldiers halted; to the rear the baggage train and
the high-wheeled wagons of the jinxmen creaked to a stop.

The scouts approached at breakneck speed, at the last instant flinging
their horses sidewise. Long shaggy legs kicked out, padlike hooves
plowed through the moss. The scouts jumped to the ground, ran forward. "The way to Ballant Keep is blocked!"

Lord Faide rose in his seat, stood staring eastward over the gray-green
downs. "How many knights? How many men?"

"No knights, no men, Lord Faide. The First Folk have planted a
forest between North and South Wildwood."

Lord Faide stood a moment in reflection, then seated himself, pushed
the control knob. The car wheezed, jerked, moved forward. The knights

touched up their horses; the foot soldiers resumed their slouching gait. At the rear the baggage train creaked into motion, together with the six wagons of the jinxmen.

The sun, large, pale and faintly pink, sank in the west. North Wildwood loomed down from the left, separated from South Wildwood by an area of stony ground, only sparsely patched with moss. As the sun passed behind the horizon, the new planting became visible: a frail new growth connecting the tracts of woodland like a canal between two seas.

Lord Faide halted his car, stepped down to the moss. He appraised the landscape, then gave the signal to make camp. The wagons were ranged in a circle, the gear unloaded. Lord Faide watched the activity for a moment, eyes sharp and critical, then turned and walked out across the downs through the lavender and green twilight. Fifteen miles to the east his last enemy awaited him: Lord Ballant of Ballant Keep. Contemplating tomorrow's battle, Lord Faide felt reasonably confident of the outcome. His troops had been tempered by a dozen campaigns; his kinsmen were loyal and single-hearted. Head Jinxman to Faide Keep was Hein Huss, and associated with him were three of the most powerful jinxmen of Pangborn: Isak Comandore, Adam McAdam and the remarkable Enterlin, together with their separate troupes of cabalmen, spellbinders and apprentices. Altogether, an impressive assemblage. Certainly there were obstacles to be overcome: Ballant Keep was strong; Lord Ballant would fight obstinately; Anderson Grimes, the Ballant jinxman, was efficient and highly respected. There was also this nuisance of the First Folk and the new planting which closed the gap between North and South Wildwood. The First Folk were a pale and feeble race, no match for human beings in single combat, but they guarded their forests with traps and deadfalls. Lord Faide cursed softly under his breath. To circle either North or South Wildwood meant a delay of three days, which could not be tolerated.

Lord Faide returned to the camp. Fires were alight, pots bubbled, orderly rows of sleep-holes had been dug into the moss. The knights groomed their horses within the corral of wagons; Lord Faide's own tent had been erected on a hummock, beside the ancient car.

Lord Faide made a quick round of inspection, noting every detail, speaking no word. The jinxmen were encamped a little distance apart from the troops. The apprentices and lesser spellbinders prepared food, while the jinxmen and cabalmen worked inside their tents, arranging cabinets and cases, correcting whatever disorder had been caused by the jolting of the wagons.

Lord Faide entered the tent of his Head Jinxman. Hein Huss was an enormous man, with arms and legs heavy as tree trunks, a torso like a barrel. His face was pink and placid, his eyes were water-clear; a stiff gray brush rose from his head, which was innocent of the cap jinxmen customarily wore against the loss of hair. Hein Huss disdained such precautions; it was his habit, showing his teeth in a face-splitting grin, to rumble, "Why should anyone hoodoo me, old Hein Huss? I am so inoffensive. Whoever tried would surely die, of shame and remorse."

Lord Faide found Huss busy at his cabinet. The doors stood wide, revealing hundreds of mannikins, each tied with a lock of hair, a bit of cloth, a fingernail clipping, daubed with grease, sputum, excrement, blood. Lord Faide knew well that one of these mannikins represented himself. He also knew that should he request it Hein Huss would deliver it without hesitation. Part of Huss' *mana* derived from his enormous confidence, the effortless ease of his power. He glanced at Lord Faide and read the question in his mind. "Lord Ballant did not know of the new planting. Anderson Grimes has now informed him, and Lord Ballant expects that you will be delayed. Grimes has communicated with Gisborne Keep and Castle Cloud. Three hundred men march tonight to reinforce Ballant Keep. They will arrive in two days. Lord Ballant is much elated."

Lord Faide paced back and forth across the tent. "Can we cross this planting?"

Hein Huss made a heavy sound of disapproval. "There are many futures. In certain of these futures you pass. In others you do not pass. I cannot ordain these futures."

Lord Faide had long learned to control his impatience at what sometimes seemed to be pedantic obfuscation. He grumbled, "They are either very stupid or very bold, planting across the downs in this fashion. I cannot imagine what they intend."

Hein Huss considered, then grudgingly volunteered an idea. "What if they plant west from North Wildwood to Sarrow Copse? What if they plant west from South Wildwood to Old Forest?

Lord Faide stood stock-still, his eyes narrow and thoughtful. "Faide Keep would be surrounded by forest. We would be imprisoned. . . . These plantings, do they proceed?"

"They proceed, so I have been told."

"What do they hope to gain?"

"I do not know. Perhaps they hope to isolate the keeps, to rid the planet of men. Perhaps they merely want secure avenues between the forests."

Lord Faide considered. Huss' final suggestion was reasonable enough. During the first centuries of human settlement, sportive young men had hunted the First Folk with clubs and lances, eventually had driven them from their native downs into the forests. "Evidently they are more clever than we realize. Adam McAdam asserts that they do not think, but it seems that he is mistaken."

Hein Huss shrugged. "Adam McAdam equates thought to the human cerebral process. He cannot telepathize with the First Folk, hence he deduced that they do not 'think.' But I have watched them at Forest Market, and they trade intelligently enough." He raised his head, appeared to listen, then reached into his cabinet, delicately tightened a noose around the neck of one of the mannikins. From outside the tent came a sudden cough and a whooping gasp for air. Huss grinned, twitched open the noose. "That is Isak Comandore's apprentice. He hopes to complete a Hein Huss mannikin. I must say he works diligently, going so far as to touch its feet into my footprints whenever possible."

Lord Faide went to the flap of the tent. "We break camp early. Be alert, I may require your help." Lord Faide departed the tent.

Hein Huss continued the ordering of the cabinet. Presently he sensed the approach of his rival, Jinxman Isak Comandore, who coveted the office of Head Jinxman with all-consuming passion. Huss closed the cabinet and hoisted himself to his feet.

Comandore entered the tent, a man tall, crooked and spindly. His wedge-shaped head was covered with coarse russet ringlets; hot red-brown eyes peered from under his red eyebrows. "I offer my complete rights to Keyril, and will include the masks, the headdress, and amulets. Of all the demons ever contrived he has won the widest public acceptance. To utter the name Keyril is to complete half the work of a possession. Keyril is a valuable property. I can give no more."

But Huss shook his head. Comandore's desire was the full simulacrum of Tharon Faide, Lord Faide's oldest son, complete with clothes, hair, skin, eyelashes, tears, excreta, sweat and sputum—the only one in existence, for Lord Faide guarded his son much more jealously than he did himself. "You offer convincingly," said Huss, "but my own demons suffice. The name Dant conveys fully as much terror as Keyril."

"I will add five hairs from the head of Jinxman Clarence Sears; they are the last, for he is now stark bald."

"Let us drop the matter; I will keep the simulacrum."

"As you please," said Comandore with asperity. He glanced out the flap of the tent. "That blundering apprentice. He puts the feet of the mannikin backwards into your prints."

Huss opened his cabinet, thumped a mannikin with his finger. From outside the tent came a grunt of surprise. Huss grinned. "He is young and earnest, and perhaps he is clever, who knows?" He went to the flap of the tent, called outside. "Hey, Sam Salazar, what do you do? Come inside."

Apprentice Sam Salazar came blinking into the tent, a thick-set youth with a round florid face, overhung with a rather untidy mass of straw-colored hair. In one hand he carried a crude potbellied mannikin, evidently intended to represent Hein Huss.

"You puzzle both your master and myself," said Huss. "There must be method in your folly, but we fail to perceive it. For instance, this moment you place my simulacrum backwards into my track. I feel a tug on my foot, and you pay for your clumsiness."

Sam Salazar showed small evidence of abashment. "Jinxman Comandore has warned that we must expect to suffer for our ambitions."

"If your ambition is jinxmanship," Comandore declared sharply, "you had best mend your ways."

"The lad is craftier than you know," said Hein Huss. "Look now." He took the mannikin, spit into its mouth, plucked a hair from his head, thrust it into a convenient crevice. "He has a Hein Huss mannikin, achieved at very small cost. Now, Apprentice Salazar, how will you hoodoo me?"

"Naturally I would never dare. I merely want to fill the bare spaces in my cabinet."

Hein Huss nodded his approval. "As good a reason as any. Of course you own a simulacrum of Isak Comandore?"

Sam Salazar glanced uneasily sidewise at Isak Comandore. "He leaves none of his traces. If there is so much as an open bottle in the room, he breathes behind his hand."

"Ridiculous!" exclaimed Hein Huss. "Comandore, what do you fear?"

"I am conservative," said Comandore drily. "You make a fine gesture, but some day an enemy may own that simulacrum; then you will regret your bravado."

"Bah. My enemies are all dead, save one or two who dare not reveal themselves." He clapped Sam Salazar a great buffet on the shoulder. "Tomorrow, Apprentice Salazar, great things are in store for you."

"What manner of great things?"

"Honor, noble self-sacrifice. Lord Faide must beg permission to pass Wildwood from the First Folk, which galls him. But beg he must. Tomorrow, Sam Salazar, I will elect you to lead the way to the parley, to deflect deadfalls, scythes and nettle-traps from the more important person who follows."

Sam Salazar shook his head and drew back. "There must be others more worthy; I prefer to ride in the rear with the wagons."

Comandore waved him from the tent. "You will do as ordered. Leave us; we have had enough apprentice talk."

Sam Salazar departed. Comandore turned back to Hein Huss. "In connection with tomorrow's battle, Anderson Grimes is especially adept with demons. As I recall, he has developed and successfully publicized Font, who spreads sleep; Everid, a being of wrath, Deigne, a force of fear. We must take care that in countering these effects we do not neutralize each other."

"True," rumbled Huss. "I have long maintained to Lord Faide that a single jinxman—the Head Jinxman in fact—is more effective than a group at cross-purposes. But he is consumed by ambition and does not listen."

"Perhaps he wants to be sure that should advancing years overtake the Head Jinxman other equally effective jinxmen are at hand."

"The future has many paths," agreed Hein Huss. "Lord Faide is well-advised to seek early for my successor, so that I may train him over the years. I plan to assess all the subsidiary jinxmen, and select the most promising. Tomorrow I relegate to you the demons of Anderson Grimes."

Isak Comandore nodded politely. "You are wise to give over responsibility. When I feel the weight of my years I hope I may act with similar forethought. Good night, Hein Huss. I go to arrange my demon masks. Tomorrow Keyril must walk like a giant."

"Good night, Isak Comandore."

Comandore swept from the tent, and Huss settled himself on his stool. Sam Salazar scratched at the flap. "Well, lad?" growled Huss. "Why do you loiter?"

Sam Salazar placed the Hein Huss mannikin on the table. "I have no wish to keep this doll."

"Throw it in a ditch, then," Hein Huss spoke gruffly. "You must stop annoying me with stupid tricks. You efficiently obtrude yourself upon my attention, but you cannot transfer from Comandore's troupe without his express consent."

"If I gain his consent?"

"You will incur his enmity, he will open his cabinet against you. Unlike myself, you are vulnerable to a hoodoo. I advise you to be content. Isak Comandore is highly skilled and can teach you much."

Sam Salazar still hesitated. "Jinxman Comandore, though skilled, is intolerant of new thoughts."

Hein Huss shifted ponderously on his stool, examined Sam Salazar with his water-clear eyes. "What new thoughts are these? Your own?"

"The thoughts are new to me, and for all I know new to Isak Comandore. But he will say neither yes nor no."

Hein Huss sighed, settled his monumental bulk more comfortably. "Speak then, describe these thoughts, and I will assess their novelty."

"First, I have wondered about trees. They are sensitive to light, to moisture, to wind, to pressure. Sensitivity implies sensation. Might a man feel into the soul of a tree for these sensations? If a tree were capable of awareness, this faculty might prove useful. A man might select trees as sentinels in strategic sites, and enter into them as he chose."

Hein Huss was skeptical. "An amusing notion, but practically not feasible. The reading of minds, the act of possession, televoyance, similar interplay requires psychic congruence as a basic condition. The minds must be able to become identities at some particular stratum. Unless there is sympathy, there is no linkage. A tree is at opposite poles from a man; the images of tree and man are incommensurable. Hence, anything more than the most trifling flicker of comprehension must be a true miracle of jinxmanship."

Sam Salazar nodded mournfully. "I realize this, and at one time hoped to equip myself with the necessary identification."

"To do this you must become a vegetable. Certainly the tree will never become a man."

"So I reasoned," said Sam Salazar. "I went alone into a grove of trees, where I chose a tall conifer. I buried my feet in the mold, I stood silent and naked—in the sunlight, in the rain; at dawn, noon, dusk, midnight. I closed my mind to man-thoughts, I closed my eyes to vision, my ears to sound. I took no nourishment except from rain and sun. I sent roots forth from my feet and branches from my torso. Thirty hours I stood, and two days later, another thirty hours, and after two days another thirty hours. I made myself a tree, as nearly as possible to one of flesh and blood."

Hein Huss gave the great inward gurgle which signalized his amusement. "And you achieved sympathy?"

"Nothing useful," Sam Salazar admitted. "I felt something of the tree's sensations—the activity of light, the peace of dark, the coolness of rain. But visual and auditory experience—nothing. However, I do not regret the trial. It was a useful discipline."

"An interesting effort, even if inconclusive. The idea is by no means of startling originality, but the empiricism—to use an archaic word—of your method is bold, and no doubt antagonized Isak Comandore, who has no patience with the superstitions of our ancestors. I suspect that he harangued you against frivolity, metaphysics, and inspirationalism."

"True," said Sam Salazar. "He spoke at length."

"You should take the lesson to heart. Isak Comandore is sometimes unable to make the most obvious truth seem credible. However, I cite you the example of Lord Faide who considers himself an enlightened man, free from superstition. Still, he rides in the feeble car, he carries a pistol sixteen hundred years old, he relies on Hellmouth to protect Faide Keep."

"Perhaps—unconsciously—he longs for the old magical times," suggested Sam Salazar thoughtfully.

"Perhaps," agreed Hein Huss. "And you do likewise?"

Sam Salazar hesitated. "There is an aura of romance, a kind of wild grandeur to the old days—but of course," he added quickly, "mysticism is no substitute for orthodox logic."

"Naturally not," agreed Hein Huss. "Now go; I must consider the events of tomorrow."

Sam Salazar departed, and Hein Huss, rumbling and groaning, hoisted himself to his feet. He went to the flap of his tent, surveyed the camp. All now was quiet. The fires were embers, the warriors lay in the pits they had cut into the moss. To the north and south spread the woodlands. Among the trees and out on the downs were faint flickering luminosities, where the First Folk gathered spore-pods from the moss.

Hein Huss became aware of a nearby personality. He turned his head and saw approaching the shrouded form of Jinxman Enterlin, who concealed his face, who spoke only in whispers, who disguised his natural gait with a stiff stiltlike motion. By this means he hoped to reduce his vulnerability to hostile jinxmanship. The admission carelessly let fall of failing eyesight, of stiff joints, forgetfulness, melancholy, nausea might be of critical significance in controversy by hoodoo. Jinxmen therefore maintained the pose of absolute health and virility, even though they must grope blindly or limp doubled up from cramps.

Hein Huss called out to Enterlin, lifted back the flap to the tent. Enterlin entered; Huss went to the cabinet, brought forth a flask, poured liquor into a pair of stone cups. "A cordial only, free of covert significance."

"Good," whispered Enterlin, selecting the cup farthest from him. "After all, we jinxmen must relax into the guise of men from time to time." Turning his back on Huss, he introduced the cup through the folds of his hood, drank. "Refreshing," he whispered. "We need refreshment: tomorrow we must work."

Huss issued his reverberating chuckle. "Tomorrow Isak Comandore matches demons with Anderson Grimes. We others perform only subsidiary duties."

Enterlin seemed to make a quizzical inspection of Hein Huss through the black gauze before his eyes. "Comandore will relish this opportunity. His vehemence oppresses me, and his is a power which feeds on success. He is a man of fire, you are a man of ice."

"Ice quenches fire."

"Fire sometimes melts ice."

Hein Huss shrugged. "No matter. I grow weary. Time has passed all of us by. Only a moment ago a young apprentice showed me to myself."

"As a powerful jinxman, as Head Jinxman to the Faides, you have cause for pride."

Hein Huss drained the stone cup, set it aside. "No. I see myself at the top of my profession, with nowhere else to go. Only Sam Salazar the apprentice thinks to search for more universal lore: he comes to me for counsel, and I do not know what to tell him."

"Strange talk, strange talk!" whispered Enterlin. He moved to the flap of the tent. "I go now," he whispered. "I go to walk on the downs. Perhaps I will see the future."

"There are many futures."

Enterlin rustled away and was lost in the dark. Hein Huss groaned and grumbled, then took himself to his couch, where he instantly fell asleep.

2   **T**he night passed. The sun, flickering with films of pink and green, lifted over the horizon. The new planting of the First Folk was silhouetted, a sparse stubble of saplings, against the green and lavender sky. The troops broke camp with practiced efficiency. Lord Faide marched to his car, leaped within; the machine sagged under his weight. He pushed a button, the car drifted forward, heavy as a waterlogged timber.

A mile from the new planting he halted, sent a messenger back to the wagons of the jinxmen. Hein Huss walked ponderously forward, followed by Isak Comandore, Adam McAdam, and Enterlin; Lord Faide spoke to Hein Huss. "Send someone to speak to the First Folk. Inform them we wish to pass, offering them no harm, but that we will react savagely to any hostility."

"I will go myself," said Hein Huss. He turned to Comandore. "Lend me, if you will, your brash young apprentice. I can put him to good use."

"If he unmasks a nettle trap by blundering into it, his first useful deed will be done," said Comandore. He signaled to Sam Salazar, who came reluctantly forward. "Walk in front of Head Jinxman Hein Huss that he may encounter no traps or scythes. Take a staff to probe the moss."

Without enthusiasm Sam Salazar borrowed a lance from one of the foot soldiers. He and Huss set forth, along the low rise that previously had separated North from South Wildwood. Occasionally outcroppings of stone penetrated the cover of moss; here and there grew bayberry trees, clumps of tarplant, ginger-tea, and rosewort.

A half mile from the planting Huss halted. "Now take care, for here the traps will begin. Walk clear of hummocks, these often conceal swing-scythes; avoid moss which shows a pale blue; it is dying or sickly and may cover a deadfall or a nettle trap."

"Why cannot you locate the traps by clairvoyance?" asked Sam Salazar in a rather sullen voice. "It appears an excellent occasion for the use of these faculties."

"The question is natural," said Hein Huss with composure. "However you must know that when a jinxman's own profit or security is at stake his emotions play tricks on him. I would see traps everywhere and would never know whether clairvoyance or fear prompted me. In this case, that lance is a more reliable instrument than my mind."

Sam Salazar made a salute of understanding and set forth, with Hein Huss stumping behind him. At first he prodded with care, uncovering two traps, then advanced more jauntily; so swiftly indeed that Huss called out in exasperation, "Caution, unless you court death!"

Sam Salazar obligingly slowed his pace. "There are traps all around us, but I detect the pattern, or so I believe."

"Ah, ha, you do? Reveal it to me, if you will. I am only Head Jinx-man, and ignorant."

"Notice. If we walk where the spore-pods have recently been harvested, then we are secure."

Hein Huss grunted. "Forward then. Why do you dally? We must do battle at Ballant Keep today."

Two hundred yards farther, Sam Salazar stopped short. "Go on, boy, go on!" grumbled Hein Huss.

"The savages threaten us. You can see them just inside the planting. They hold tubes which they point toward us."

Hein Huss peered, then raised his head and called out in the sibilant language of the First Folk.

A moment or two passed, then one of the creatures came forth, a naked humanoid figure, ugly as a demonmask. Foam-sacs bulged under its arms, orange-lipped foam-vents pointed forward. Its back was wrinkled and loose, the skin serving as a bellows to blow air through the foam-sacs. The fingers of the enormous hands ended in chisel-shaped blades, the head was sheathed in chitin. Billion-faceted eyes swelled from either side of the head, glowing like black opals, merging without definite limit into the chitin. This was a representative of the original inhabitants of the planet, who until the coming of man had inhabited the downs, burrowing in the moss, protecting themselves behind masses of foam exuded from the underarm sacs.

The creature wandered close, halted. "I speak for Lord Faide of Faide Keep," said Huss. "Your planting bars his way. He wishes that you guide him through, so that his men do not damage the trees, or spring the traps you have set against your enemies."

"Men are our enemies," responded the autochthon. "You may spring as many traps as you care to; that is their purpose." It backed away.

"One moment," said Hein Huss sternly. "Lord Faide must pass. He goes to battle Lord Ballant. He does not wish to battle the First Folk. Therefore it is wise to guide him across the planting without hindrance."

The creature considered a second or two. "I will guide him." He stalked across the moss toward the war party.

Behind followed Hein Huss and Sam Salazar. The autochthon, legs articulated more flexibly than a man's, seemed to weave and wander, occasionally pausing to study the ground ahead.

"I am puzzled," Sam Salazar told Hein Huss. "I cannot understand the creature's actions."

"Small wonder," grunted Hein Huss. "He is one of the First Folk, you are human. There is no basis for understanding."

"I disagree," said Sam Salazar seriously.

"Eh?" Hein Huss inspected the apprentice with vast disapproval. "You engage in contention with me, Head Jinxman Hein Huss?"

"Only in a limited sense," said Sam Salazar. "I see a basis for understanding with the First Folk in our common ambition to survive."

"A truism," grumbled Hein Huss. "Granting this community of interests with the First Folk, what is your perplexity?"

"The fact that it first refused, then agreed to conduct us across the planting."

Hein Huss nodded. "Evidently the information which intervened, that we go to fight at Ballant Keep, occasioned the change."

"This is clear," said Sam Salazar. "But think—"

"You exhort me to think?" roared Hein Huss.

"—here is one of the First Folk, apparently without distinction, who makes an important decision instantly. Is he one of their leaders? Do they live in anarchy?"

"It is easy to put questions," Hein Huss said gruffly. "It is not as easy to answer them."

"In short—"

"In short, I do not know. In any event, they are pleased to see us killing one another."

3   The passage through the planting was made without incident. A mile to the east the autochthon stepped aside and without formality returned to the forest. The war party, which had been marching in single file, regrouped into its usual formation. Lord Faide called Hein Huss and made the unusual gesture of inviting him up into the seat beside him. The ancient car dipped and sagged; the power-mechanism whined and chattered. Lord Faide, in high good spirits, ignored the noise. "I feared that we might be forced into a time-consuming wrangle. What of Lord Ballant? Can you read his thoughts?"

Hein Huss cast his mind forth. "Not clearly. He knows of our passage. He is disturbed."

Lord Faide laughed sardonically. "For excellent reason! Listen now, I will explain the plan of battle so that all may coordinate their efforts."

"Very well."

"We approach in a wide line. Ballant's great weapon is of course Volcano. A decoy must wear my armor and ride in the lead. The yellow-haired apprentice is perhaps the most expendable member of the party. In this way we will learn the potentialities of Volcano. Like our own Hellmouth, it was built to repel vessels from space and cannot command the ground immediately under the keep. Therefore we will advance in dispersed formation, to regroup two hundred yards from the keep. At this point the jinxmen will impel Lord Ballant forth from the keep. You no doubt have made plans to this end."

Hein Huss gruffly admitted that such was the case. Like other jinxmen, he enjoyed the pose that his power sufficed for extemporaneous control of any situation.

Lord Faide was in no mood for niceties and pressed for further information. Grudging each word, Hein Huss disclosed his arrangements. "I have prepared certain influences to discomfit the Ballant defenders and drive them forth. Jinxman Enterlin will sit at his cabinet, ready to retaliate if Lord Ballant orders a spell against you. Anderson Grimes undoubtedly will cast a demon—probably Everid—into the Ballant warriors; in return, Jinxman Comandore will possess an equal or a greater number of Faide warriors with the demon Keyril, who is even more ghastly and horrifying."

"Good. What more?"

"There is need for no more, if your men fight well."

"Can you see the future? How does today end?"

"There are many futures. Certain jinxmen—Enterlin for instance—profess to see the thread which leads through the maze; they are seldom correct."

"Call Enterlin here."

Hein Huss rumbled his disapproval. "Unwise, if you desire victory over Ballant Keep."

Lord Faide inspected the massive jinxman from under his black saturnine brows. "Why do you say this?"

"If Enterlin foretells defeat, you will be dispirited and fight poorly. If he predicts victory, you become overconfident and likewise fight poorly."

Lord Faide made a petulant gesture. "The jinxmen are loud in their boasts until the test is made. Then they always find reasons always to retract, to qualify."

"Ha, ha!" barked Hein Huss. "You expect miracles, not honest jinxmanship. I spit—" he spat. "I predict that the spittle will strike the moss. The probabilities are high. But an insect might fly in the way. One of the First Folk might raise through the moss. The chances are slight. In the next instant there is only one future. A minute hence there are four futures. Five minutes hence, twenty futures. A billion futures could not express all the possibilities of tomorrow. Of these billion, certain are more probable than others. It is true that these probable futures sometimes send a delicate influence into the jinxman's brain. But unless he is completely impersonal and disinterested, his own desires overwhelm this influence. Enterlin is a strange man. He hides himself, he has no appetites. Occasionally his auguries are exact. Nevertheless, I advise against consulting him. You do better to rely on the practical and real uses of jinxmanship."

Lord Faide said nothing. The column had been marching along the bottom of a low swale; the car had been sliding easily downslope. Now they came to a rise, and the power-mechanism complained so vigorously that Lord Faide was compelled to stop the car. He considered. "Once over the crest we will be in view of Ballant Keep. Now we must disperse. Send the least valuable man in your troupe forward—the apprentice who tested out the moss. He must wear my helmet and corselet and ride in the car."

Hein Huss alighted, returned to the wagons, and presently Sam Salazar came forward. Lord Faide eyed the round, florid face with distaste. "Come close," he said crisply. Sam Salazar obeyed. "You will now ride in my place," said Lord Faide. "Notice carefully. This rod impels a forward motion. This arm steers—to right, to left. To stop, return the rod to its first position."

Sam Salazar pointed to some of the other arms, toggles, switches, and buttons. "What of these?"

"They are never used."

"And these dials, what is their meaning?"

Lord Faide curled his lip, on the brink of one of his quick furies. "Since their use is unimportant to me, it is twenty times unimportant to you. Now. Put this cap on your head, and this helmet. See to it that you do not sweat."

Sam Salazar gingerly settled the magnificent black and green crest of Faide on his head, with a cloth cap underneath.

"Now this corselet."

The corselet was constructed of green and black metal sequins, with a pair of scarlet dragon-heads at either side of the breast.

"Now the cloak." Lord Faide flung the black cloak over Sam Salazar's shoulders. "Do not venture too close to Ballant Keep. Your purpose is to attract the fire of Volcano. Maintain a lateral motion around the

keep, outside of dart range. If you are killed by a dart, the whole purpose of the deception is thwarted."

"You prefer me to be killed by Volcano?" inquired Sam Salazar.

"No. I wish to preserve the car and the crest. These are relics of great
value. Evade destruction by all means possible. The ruse probably will
deceive no one; but if it does, and if it draws the fire of Volcano, I must
sacrifice the Faide car. Now—sit in my place."

Sam Salazar climbed into the car, settled himself on the seat.

"Sit straight," roared Lord Faide. "Hold your head up! You are simu-
lating Lord Faide! You must not appear to slink!"

Sam Salazar heaved himself erect in the seat. "To simulate Lord Faide
most effectively, I should walk among the warriors, with someone else
riding in the car."

Lord Faide glared, then grinned sourly. "No matter. Do as I have
commanded."

4   Sixteen hundred years before, with
war raging through space, a group of space captains, their home bases
destroyed, had taken refuge on Pangborn. To protect themselves against
vengeful enemies, they built great forts armed with weapons from the
dismantled spaceships.

The wars receded, Pangborn was forgotten. The newcomers drove the
First Folk into the forests, planted and harvested the river vallyes. Ballant Keep, like Faide Keep, Castle Cloud, Boghoten, and the rest, overlooked one of these valleys. Four squat towers of a dense black
substance supported an enormous parasol roof, and were joined by walls
two-thirds as high as the towers. At the peak of the roof a cupola housed
Volcano, the weapon corresponding to Faide's Hellmouth.

The Faide war party advancing over the rise found the great gates
already secure, the parapets between the towers thronged with bowmen.
According to Lord Faide's strategy, the war party advanced on a broad
front. At the center rode Sam Salazar, resplendent in Lord Faide's
armor. He made, however, small effort to simulate Lord Faide. Rather
than sitting proudly erect, he crouched at the side of the seat, the crest
canted at an angle. Lord Faide watched with disgust. Apprentice Salazar's reluctance to be demolished was understandable: if his imperson-
ation failed to convince Lord Ballant, at least the Faide ancestral car
might be spared. For a certainty Volcano was being manned; the Ballant
weapon-tender could be see in the cupola, and the snout protruded at a
menacing angle.

Apparently the tactic of dispersal, offering no single tempting target, was effective. The Faide war party advanced quickly to a point two hundred yards from the keep, below Volcano's effective field, without drawing fire; first the knights, then the foot soldiers, then the rumbling wagons of the magicians. The slow-moving Faide car was far outdistanced; any doubt as to the nature of the ruse must now be extinguished.

Apprentice Salazar, disliking the isolation, and hoping to increase the speed of the car, twisted one of the other switches, then another. From under the floor came a thin screeching sound; the car quivered and began to rise. Sam Salazar peered over the side, threw out a leg to jump. Lord Faide ran forward, gesturing and shouting. Sam Salazar hastily drew back his leg, returned the switches to their previous condition. The car dropped like a rock. He snapped the switches up again, cushioning the fall.

"Get out of that car!" roared Lord Faide. He snatched away the helmet, dealt Sam Salazar a buffet which toppled him head over heels. "Out of the armor; back to your duties!"

Sam Salazar hurried to the jinxmen's wagons where he helped erect Isak Comandore's black tent. Inside the tent a black carpet with red and yellow patterns was laid; Comandore's cabinet, his chair, and his chest were carried in, and incense set burning in a censer. Directly in front of the main gate Hein Huss superintended the assembly of a rolling stage, forty feet tall and sixty feet long, the surface concealed from Ballant Keep by a tarpaulin.

Meanwhile, Lord Faide had dispatched an emissary, enjoining Lord Ballant to surrender. Lord Ballant delayed his response, hoping to delay the attack as long as possible. If he could maintain himself a day and a half, reinforcements from Gisborne Keep and Castle Cloud might force Lord Faide to retreat.

Lord Faide waited only until the jinxmen had completed their preparations, then sent another messenger, offering two more minutes in which to surrender.

One minute passed, two minutes. The envoys turned on their heels, marched back to the camp.

Lord Faide spoke to Hein Huss. "You are prepared?"

"I am prepared," rumbled Hein Huss.

"Drive them forth."

Huss raised his arm; the tarpaulin dropped from the face of his great display, to reveal a painted representation of Ballant Keep.

Huss retired to his tent, and pulled the flaps together. Braziers burnt fiercely, illuminating the face of Adam McAdam, eight cabalmen, and six of the most advanced spellbinders. Each worked at a bench supporting several dozen dolls and a small glowing brazier. The cabalmen and spellbinders worked with dolls representing Ballant men-at-arms; Huss and Adam McAdam employed simulacra of the Ballant knights. Lord

Ballant would not be hoodooed unless he ordered a jinx against Lord Faide—a courtesy the keep-lords extended each other.

Huss called out: "Sebastian!"

Sebastian, one of Huss' spellbinders, waiting at the flap to the tent, replied, "Ready, sir."

"Begin the display."

Sebastian ran to the stage, struck fire to a fuse. Watchers inside Ballant Keep saw the depicted keep take fire. Flame erupted from the windows, the roof glowed and crumbled. Inside the tent the two jinxmen, the cabalmen, and the spellbinders methodically took dolls, dipped them into the heat of the braziers, concentrating, reaching out for the mind of the man whose doll they burnt. Within the keep men became uneasy. Many began to imagine burning sensations, which became more severe as their minds grew more sensitive to the idea of fire. Lord Ballant noted the uneasiness. He signaled to his chief jinxman Anderson Grimes. "Begin the counterspell."

Down the front of the keep unrolled a display even larger than Hein Huss' depicting a hideous beast. It stood on four legs and was shown picking up two men in a pair of hands, biting off their heads. Grimes' cabalmen meanwhile took up dolls representing the Faide warriors, inserted them into models of the depicted beast, and closed the hinged jaws, all the while projecting ideas of fear and disgust. And the Faide warriors, staring at the depicted monster, felt a sense of horror and weakness.

Inside Huss' tent, censers and braziers reeked and dolls smoked. Eyes stared, brows glistened. From time to time one of the workers gasped—signaling the entry of his projection into an enemy mind. Within the keep warriors began to mutter, to slap at burning skin, to eye each other fearfully, noting each other's symptoms. Finally one cried out, and tore at his armor. "I burn! The cursed witches burn me!" His pain aggravated the discomfort of the others; there was a growing sound throughout the keep.

Lord Ballant's oldest son, his mind penetrated by Hein Huss himself, struck his shield with his mailed fist. "They burn me! They burn us all! Better to fight than burn!"

"Fight! Fight!" came the voices of the tormented men.

Lord Ballant looked around at the twisted faces, some displaying blisters, scaldmarks. "Our own spell terrifies them; wait yet a moment!" he pleaded.

His brother called hoarsely, "It is not your belly that Hein Huss toasts in the flames, it is mine! We cannot win a battle of hoodoos; we must win a battle of arms!"

Lord Ballant cried desperately, "Wait, our own effects are working! They will flee in terror; wait, wait!"

His cousin tore off his corselet. "It's Hein Huss! I feel him! My leg's in the fire, the devil laughs at me. Next my head, he says. Fight, or I go forth to fight alone!"

"Very well," said Lord Ballant in a fateful voice. "We go forth to fight. First—the beast goes forth. Then we follow and smite them in their terror."

The gates to the keep swung suddenly wide. Out sprang what appeared to be the depicted monster; legs moving, arms waving, eyes rolling, issuing evil sounds. Normally the Faide warriors would have seen the monster for what it was; a model carried on the backs of three horses. But their minds had been influenced: they had been infected with horror; they drew back with arms hanging flaccid. From behind the monster the Ballant knights galloped, followed by the Ballant foot soldiers. The charge gathered momentum, tore into the Faide center. Lord Faide bellowed orders; discipline asserted itself. The Faide knights disengaged, divided into three platoons, and engulfed the Ballant charge, while the foot soldiers poured darts into the advancing ranks.

There was the clatter and surge of battle; Lord Ballant, seeing that his sally had failed to overwhelm the Faide forces, and thinking to conserve his own forces, ordered a retreat. In good order the Ballant warriors began to back up toward the keep. The Faide knights held close contact, hoping to win to the courtyard. Close behind came a heavily loaded wagon pushed by armored horses, to be wedged against the gate.

Lord Faide called an order; a reserve platoon of ten knights charged from the side, thrust behind the main body of Ballant horsemen, rode through the foot soldiers, fought into the keep, cut down the gate-tenders.

Lord Ballant bellowed to Anderson Grimes, "They have won inside; quick with your cursed demon! If he can help us, let him do so now!"

"Demon-possession is not a matter of an instant," muttered the jinxman. "I need time."

"You have no time! Ten minutes and we're all dead!"

"I will do my best. Everid, Everid, come swift!"

He hastened into his workroom, donned his demonmask, tossed handful after handful of incense into the brazier. Against one wall stood a great form: black, slit-eyed, noseless. Great white fangs hung from its upper palate; it stood on heavy bent legs, arms reached forward to grasp. Anderson Grimes swallowed a cup of syrup, paced slowly back and forth. A moment passed.

"Grimes!" came Ballant's call from outside. "Grimes!"

A voice spoke. "Enter without fear."

Lord Ballant, carrying his ancestral side arm, entered. He drew back with an involuntary sound. "Grimes!" he whispered.

"Grimes is not here," said the voice. "I am here. Enter."

Lord Ballant came forward stiff-legged. The room was dark except for the feeble glimmer of the brazier. Anderson Grimes crouched in a corner, head bowed under his demonmask. The shadows twisted and pulsed with shapes and faces, forms struggling to become solid. The black image seemed to vibrate with life.

"Bring in your warriors," said the voice. "Bring them in five at a time, bid them look only at the floor until commanded to raise their eyes."

Lord Ballant retreated; there was no sound in the room.

A moment passed; then five limp and exhausted warriors filed into the room, eyes low.

"Look slowly up," said the voice. "Look at the orange fire. Breathe deeply. Then look at me. I am Everid, Demon of Hate. Look at me. Who am I?"

"You are Everid, Demon of Hate," quavered the warriors.

"I stand all around you, in a dozen forms . . . I come closer. Where am I?"

"You are close."

"Now I am you. We are together."

There was a sudden quiver of motion. The warriors stood straighter, their faces distorted.

"Go forth," said the voice. "Go quietly into the court. In a few minutes we march forth to slay."

The five stalked forth. Five more entered.

Outside the wall the Ballant knights had retreated as far as the gate; within, seven Faide knights still survived, and with their backs to the wall held the Ballant warriors away from the gate mechanism.

In the Faide camp Huss called to Comandore, "Everid is walking. Bring forth Keyril."

"Send the men," came Comandore's voice, low and harsh. "Send the men to me. I am Keyril."

Within the keep twenty warriors came marching into the courtyard. Their steps were cautious, tentative, slow. Their faces had lost individuality, they were twisted and distorted, curiously alike.

"Bewitched!" whispered the Ballant soldiers, drawing back. The seven Faide knights watched with sudden fright. But the twenty warriors, paying them no heed, marched out the gate. The Ballant knights parted; for an instant there was a lull in the fighting. The twenty sprang like tigers. Their swords glistened, twinkling in water-bright arcs. They crouched, jerked, jumped; Faide arms, legs, heads were hewed off. The twenty were cut and battered, but the blows seemed to have no effect.

The Faide attack faltered, collapsed. The knights, whose armor was no protection against the demoniac swords, retreated. The twenty possessed warriors raced out into the open toward the foot soldiers, running with great strides, slashing and rending. The Faide foot soldiers fought for a moment, then they too gave way and turned to flee.

From behind Comandore's tent appeared thirty Faide warriors, marching stiffly, slowly. Like the Ballant twenty their faces were alike —but between the Everid-possessed and the Keyril-possessed was the difference between the face of Everid and the face of Keyril.

Keyril and Everid fought, using the men as weapons, without fear, retreat, or mercy. Hack, chop, cut. Arms, legs, sundered torsos. Bodies fought headless for moments before collapsing. Only when a body was minced, hacked to bits, did the demoniac vitality depart. Presently there were no more men of Everid, and only fifteen men of Keyril. These hopped and limped and tumbled toward the keep where Faide knights still held the gate. The Ballant knights met them in despair, knowing that now was the decisive moment. Leaping, leering from chopped faces, slashing from tireless arms, the warriors cut a hole into the iron. The Faide knights, roaring victory cries, plunged after. Into the courtyard surged the battle, and now there was no longer doubt of the outcome. Ballant Keep was taken.

Back in his tent Isak Comandore took a deep breath, shuddered, flung down his demonmask. In the courtyard the twelve remaining warriors dropped in their tracks, twitched, gasped, gushed blood and died.

Lord Ballant, in the last gallant act of a gallant life, marched forth brandishing his ancestral side arm. He aimed across the bloody field at Lord Faide, pulled the trigger. The weapon spewed a brief gout of light; Lord Faide's skin prickled and hair rose from his head. The weapon crackled, turned cherry-red, and melted. Lord Ballant threw down the weapon, drew his sword, marched forth to challenge Lord Faide.

Lord Faide, disinclined to unnecessary combat, signaled to his soldiers. A flight of darts ended Lord Ballant's life, saving him the discomfort of formal execution.

There was no further resistance. The Ballant defenders threw down their arms and marched grimly out to kneel before Lord Faide, while inside the keep the Ballant women gave themselves to mourning and grief.

5

Lord Faide had no wish to linger at Ballant Keep, for he took no relish in his victories. Inevitably, a thousand decisions had to be made. Six of the closest Ballant kinsmen were summarily stabbed and the title declared defunct. Others of the clan were offered a choice: an oath of lifelong fealty together with a moderate ransom, or death. Eyes blazing hate, two chose death and were stabbed.

Lord Faide had now achieved his ambition. For over a thousand years the keep-lords had struggled for power; now one, now another gaining ascendancy. None before had ever extended his authority across the entire continent—which meant control of the planet, since all other land was either sun-parched rock or eternal ice. Ballant Keep had long thwarted Lord Faide's drive to power; now—success, total and absolute. It still remained to chastise the lords of Castle Cloud and Gisborne, both of whom, seeing opportunity to overwhelm Lord Faide, had ranged themselves behind Lord Ballant. But these were matters that might well be assigned to Hein Huss.

Lord Faide, for the first time in his life, felt a trace of uncertainty. Now what? No real adversaries remained. The First Folk must be whipped back, but here was no great problem: they were numerous, but no more than savages. He knew that dissatisfaction and controversy would ultimately arise among his kinsmen and allies. Inaction and boredom would breed irritability; idle minds would calculate the pros and cons of mischief. Even the most loyal would remember the campaigns with nostalgia and long for the excitement, the release, the license, of warfare. Somehow he must find means to absorb the energy of so many active and keyed-up men. How and where, this was the problem. The construction of roads? New farmland claimed from the downs? Yearly tournaments-at-arms? Lord Faide frowned at the inadequacy of his solutions, but his imagination was impoverished by the lack of tradition. The original settlers of Pangborn had been warriors, and had brought with them a certain amount of practical rule-of-thumb knowledge, but little else. The tales they passed down the generations described the great spaceships which moved with magic speed and certainty, the miraculous weapons, the wars in the void, but told nothing of human history or civilized achievement. And so Lord Faide, full of power and success, but with no goal toward which to turn his strength, felt more morose and saturnine than ever.

He gloomily inspected the spoils from Ballant Keep. They were of no great interest to him. Ballant's ancestral car was no longer used, but displayed behind a glass case. He inspected the weapon Volcano, but this could not be moved. In any event it was useless, its magic lost forever. Lord Faide now knew that Lord Ballant had ordered it turned against the Faide car, but that it had refused to spew its vaunted fire. Lord Faide saw with disdainful amusement that Volcano had been sadly neglected. Corrosion had pitted the metal, careless cleaning had twisted the exterior tubing, undoubtedly diminishing the potency of the magic. No such neglect at Faide Keep! Jambart the weapon-tender cherished Hellmouth with absolute devotion. Elsewhere were other ancient devices, interesting but useless—the same sort of curios that cluttered shelves and cases at Faide Keep. (Peculiar, these ancient men! thought Lord Faide: at once so clever, yet so primitive and impractical. Conditions had changed: there had been enormous advances since the dark ages sixteen hundred years ago. For instance, the ancients had used intricate fetishes of metal and glass to communicate with each other. Lord Faide need merely voice his needs; Hein Huss could project his mind a hundred miles to see, to hear, to relay Lord Faide's words.) The ancients had contrived dozens of such objects, but the old magic had worn away and they never seemed to function. Lord Ballant's side arm had melted, after merely stinging Lord Faide. Imagine a troop armed thus trying to cope with a platoon of demon-possessed warriors! Slaughter of the innocents!

Among the Ballant trove Lord Faide noted a dozen old books and several reels of microfilm. The books were worthless, page after page of incomprehensible jargon; the microfilm was equally undecipherable. Again Lord Faide wondered skeptically about the ancients. Clever of course, but to look at the hard facts, they were little more advanced than the First Folk: neither had facility with telepathy or voyance or demon-command. And the magic of the ancients: might there not be a great deal of exaggeration in the legends? Volcano, for instance. A joke. Lord Faide wondered about his own Hellmouth. But no—surely Hellmouth was more trustworthy; Jambart cleaned and polished the weapon daily and washed the entire cupola with vintage wine every month. If human care could induce faithfulness, then Hellmouth was ready to defend Faide Keep!

Now there was no longer need for defense. Faide was supreme. Considering the future, Lord Faide made a decision. There should no longer be keep-lords on Pangborn; he would abolish the appellation. Habitancy of the keeps would gradually be transferred to trusted bailiffs on a yearly basis. The former lords would be moved to comfortable but indefensible manor houses, with the maintenance of private troops forbidden. Naturally they must be allowed jinxmen, but these would be made accountable to himself—perhaps through some sort of licensing provision. He must discuss the matter with Hein Huss. A matter for the future, however. Now he merely wished to settle affairs and return to Faide Keep.

There was little more to be done. The surviving Ballant kinsmen he sent to their homes after Huss had impregnated fresh dolls with their essences. Should they default on their ransoms, a twinge of fire, a few stomach cramps would more than set them right. Ballant Keep itself Lord Faide would have liked to burn—but the material of the ancients was proof to fire. But in order to discourage any new pretenders to the Ballant heritage Lord Faide ordered all the heirlooms and relics brought forth into the courtyard, and then, one at a time, in order of rank, he bade his men choose. Thus the Ballant wealth was distributed. Even the jinxmen were invited to choose, but they despised the ancient trinkets as works of witless superstition. The lesser spellbinders and apprentices rummaged through the leavings, occasionally finding an overlooked bauble or some anomalous implement. Isak Comandore was irritated to find Sam Salazar staggering under a load of the ancient books. "And what is your purpose with these?" he barked. "Why do you burden yourself with rubbish?"

Sam Salazar hung his head. "I have no definite purpose. Undoubtedly there was wisdom—or at least knowledge—among the ancients: perhaps I can use these symbols of knowledge to sharpen my own understanding."

Comandore threw up his hands in disgust. He turned to Hein Huss who stood nearby. "First he fancies himself a tree and stands in the mud; now he thinks to learn jinxmanship through a study of ancient symbols."

Huss shrugged. "They were men like ourselves, and, though limited, they were not entirely obtuse. A certain simian cleverness is required to fabricate these objects."

"Simian cleverness is no substitute for sound jinxmanship," retorted Isak Comandore. "This is a point hard to overemphasize; I have drummed it into Salazar's head a hundred times. And now, look at him."

Huss grunted noncommittally. "I fail to understand what he hopes to achieve."

Sam Salazar tried to explain, fumbling for words to express an idea that did not exist. "I thought perhaps to decipher the writing, if only to understand what the ancients thought, and perhaps to learn how to perform one or two of their tricks."

Comandore rolled up his eyes. "What enemy bewitched me when I consented to take you as apprentice? I can cast twenty hoodoos in an hour, more than any of the ancients could achieve in a lifetime."

"Nevertheless," said Sam Salazar, "I notice that Lord Faide rides in his ancestral car, and that Lord Ballant sought to kill us all with Volcano."

"I notice," said Comandore with feral softness, "that my demon Keyril conquered Lord Ballant's Volcano, and that riding on my wagon I can outdistance Lord Faide in his car."

Sam Salazar thought better of arguing further. "True, Jinxman Comandore, very true. I stand corrected."

"Then discard that rubbish and make yourself useful. We return to Faide Keep in the morning."

"As you wish, Jinxman Comandore." Sam Salazar threw the books back into the trash.

6 The Ballant clan had been dispersed, Ballant Keep was despoiled. Lord Faide and his men banqueted somberly in the great hall, tended by silent Ballant servitors.

Ballant Keep had been built on the same splendid scale as Faide Keep. The great hall was a hundred feet long, fifty feet wide, fifty feet high, paneled in planks sawn from pale native hardwood, rubbed and waxed to a rich honey color. Enormous black beams supported the ceiling; from these hung candelabra, intricate contrivances of green, purple, and blue glass, knotted with ancient but still bright light-motes. On the far wall hung portraits of all the lords of Ballant Keep—105 grave faces in a variety of costumes. Below, a genealogical chart ten feet high detailed the descent of the Ballants and their connections with the other noble clans. Now there was a desolate air to the hall, and the 105 dead faces were meaningless and empty.

Lord Faide dined without joy, and cast dour side glances at those of his kinsmen who reveled too gladly. Lord Ballant, he thought, had conducted himself only as he himself might have done under the same circumstances; coarse exultation seemed in poor taste, almost as if it were disrespect for Lord Faide himself. His followers were quick to catch his mood, and the banquet proceeded with greater decorum.

The jinxmen sat apart in a smaller room to the side. Anderson Grimes, erstwhile Ballant Head Jinxman, sat beside Hein Huss, trying to put a good face on his defeat. After all, he had performed creditably against four powerful adversaries, and there was no cause to feel a diminution of *mana*. The five jinxmen discussed the battle, while the cabalmen and spellbinders listened respectfully. The conduct of the demon-possessed troops occasioned the most discussion. Anderson Grimes readily admitted that his conception of Everid was a force absolutely brutal and blunt, terrifying in its indomitable vigor. The other jinxmen agreed that he undoubtedly succeeded in projecting these qualities; Hein Huss however pointed out that Isak Comandore's Keyril, as cruel and vigorous as Everid, also combined a measure of crafty malice, which tended to make the possessed soldier a more effective weapon.

Anderson Grimes allowed that this might well be the case, and that in fact he had been considering such an augmentation of Everid's characteristics.

"To my mind," said Huss, "the most effective demon should be swift enough to avoid the strokes of the brute demons, such as Keyril and Everid. I cite my own Dant as example. A Dant-possessed warrior can easily destroy a Keyril or an Everid, simply through his agility. In an encounter of this sort the Keyrils and Everids presently lose their capacity to terrify, and thus half the effect is lost."

Isak Comandore pierced Huss with a hot russet glance. "You state a presumption as if it were fact. I have formulated Keyril with sufficient craft to counter any such displays of speed. I firmly believe Keyril to be the most fearsome of all demons."

"It may well be," rumbled Hein Huss thoughtfully. He beckoned to a steward, gave instructions. The steward reduced the light a trifle. "Behold," said Hein Huss. "There is Dant. He comes to join the banquet." At the side of the room loomed the tiger-striped Dant, a creature constructed of resilient metal, with four terrible arms, and a squat black head which seemed all gaping jaw.

"Look," came the husky voice of Isak Comandore. "There is Keyril." Keyril was rather more humanoid and armed with a cutlass. Dant spied Keyril. The jaws gaped wider, it sprang to the attack.

The battle was a thing of horror; the two demons rolled, twisted, bit, frothed, uttered soundless shrieks, tore each other apart. Suddenly Dant sprang away, circled Keyril with dizzying speed, faster, faster; became a blur, a wild coruscation of colors that seemed to give off a high-pitched wailing sound, rising higher and higher in pitch. Keyril hacked brutally with his cutlass, then seemed to grow feeble and wan. The light that once had been Dant blazed white, exploded in a mental shriek; Keyril was gone and Isak Comandore lay moaning.

Hein Huss drew a deep breath, wiped his face, looked about him with a complacent grin. The entire company sat rigid as stones, staring, all except the apprentice Sam Salazar, who met Hein Huss' glance with a cheerful smile.

"So," growled Huss, panting from his exertion, "you consider yourself superior to the illusion; you sit and smirk at one of Hein Huss' best efforts."

"No, no," cried Sam Salazar, "I mean no disrespect! I want to learn, so I watched you rather than the demons. What could they teach me? Nothing!"

"Ah," said Huss, mollified. "And what did you learn?"

"Likewise, nothing," said Sam Salazar, "but at least I do not sit like a fish."

Comandore's voice came soft but crackling with wrath. "You see in me the resemblance to a fish?"

"I except you, Jinxman Comandore, naturally," Sam Salazar explained.

"Please go to my cabinet, Apprentice Salazar, and fetch me the doll that is your likeness. The steward will bring a basin of water, and we shall have some sport. With your knowledge of fish you perhaps can breathe under water. If not—you may suffocate."

"I prefer not, Jinxman Comandore," said Sam Salazar. "In fact, with your permission, I now resign your service."

Comandore motioned to one of his cabalmen. "Fetch me the Salazar doll. Since he is no longer my apprentice, it is likely indeed that he will suffocate."

"Come now, Comandore," said Hein Huss gruffly. "Do not torment the lad. He is innocent and a trifle addled. Let this be an occasion of placidity and ease."

"Certainly, Hein Huss," said Comandore. "Why not? There is ample time in which to discipline this upstart."

"Jinxman Huss," said Sam Salazar, "since I am now relieved of my duties to Jinxman Comandore, perhaps you will accept me into your service."

Hein Huss made a noise of vast distaste. "You are not my responsibility."

"There are many futures, Hein Huss," said Sam Salazar. "You have said as much yourself."

Hein Huss looked at Sam Salazar with his water-clear eyes. "Yes, there are many futures. And I think that tonight sees the full amplitude of jinxmanship. . . . I think that never again will such power and skill gather at the same table. We shall die one by one and there shall be none to fill our shoes. . . . Yes, Sam Salazar. I will take you as apprentice. Isak Comandore, do you hear? This youth is now of my company."

"I must be compensated," growled Comandore.

"You have coveted my doll of Tharon Faide, the only one in existence. It is yours."

"Ah, ha!" cried Isak Comandore leaping to his feet. "Hein Huss, I salute you! You are generous indeed! I thank you and accept!"

Hein Huss motioned to Sam Salazar. "Move your effects to my wagon. Do not show your face again tonight."

Sam Salazar bowed with dignity and departed the hall.

The banquet continued, but now something of melancholy filled the room. Presently a messenger from Lord Faide came to warn all to bed, for the party returned to Faide Keep at dawn.

7   The victorious Faide troops gathered on the heath before Ballant Keep. As a parting gesture Lord Faide ordered the great gate torn off the hinges, so that ingress could never again be denied him. But even after sixteen hundred years the hinges were proof to all the force the horses could muster, and the gates remained in place.

Lord Faide accepted the fact with good grace and bade farewell to his cousin Renfroy, whom he had appointed bailiff. He climbed into his car, settled himself, snapped the switch. The car groaned and moved forward. Behind came the knights and the foot soldiers, then the baggage train, laden with booty, and finally the wagons of the jinxmen.

Three hours the column marched across the mossy downs. Ballant Keep dwindled behind; ahead appeared North and South Wildwood, darkening all the sweep of the western horizon. Where once the break had existed, the First Folk's new planting showed a smudge lower and less intense than the old woodlands.

Two miles from the woodlands Lord Faide called a halt and signaled up his knights. Hein Huss laboriously dismounted from his wagon, came forward.

"In the event of resistance," Lord Faide told the knights, "do not be tempted into the forest. Stay with the column and at all times be on your guard against traps."

Hein Huss spoke. "You wish me to parley with the First Folk once more?"

"No," said Lord Faide. "It is ridiculous that I must ask permission of savages to ride over my own land. We return as we came; if they interfere, so much the worse for them."

"You are rash," said Huss with simple candor.

Lord Faide glanced down at him with black eyebrows raised. "What damage can they do if we avoid their traps? Blow foam at us?"

"It is not my place to advise or to warn," said Hein Huss. "However, I point out that they exhibit a confidence which does not come from conscious weakness; also, that they carried tubes, apparently hollow grasswood shoots, which imply missiles."

Lord Faide nodded. "No doubt. However, the knights wear armor, the soldiers carry bucklers. It is not fit that I, Lord Faide of Faide Keep, choose my path to suit the whims of the First Folk. This must be made clear, even if the exercise involves a dozen or so First Folk corpses."

"Since I am not a fighting man," remarked Hein Huss, "I will keep well to the rear, and pass only when the way is secure."

"As you wish." Lord Faide pulled down the visor of his helmet. "Forward."

The column moved toward the forest, along the previous track, which showed plain across the moss. Lord Faide rode in the lead, flanked by his brother, Gethwin Faide, and his cousin, Mauve Dermont-Faide.

A half-mile passed, and another. The forest was only a mile distant. Overhead the great sun rode at zenith; brightness and heat poured down; the air carried the oily scent of thorn and tarbush. The column moved on, more slowly; the only sounds the clanking of armor, the muffled thud of hooves in the moss, the squeal of wagon wheels.

Lord Faide rose up in his car, watching for any sign of hostile preparation. A half-mile from the planting the forms of the First Folk, waiting in the shade along the forest's verge, became visible. Lord Faide ignored them, held a steady pace along the track they had traveled before.

The half-mile became a quarter-mile. Lord Faide turned to order the troops into single file and was just in time to see a hole suddenly open into the moss and his brother, Gethwin Faide, drop from sight. There was a rattle, a thud, the howling of the impaled horse; Gethwin's wild calls as the horse kicked and crushed him into the stakes. Mauve Dermont-Faide, riding beside Gethwin, could not control his own horse, which leaped aside from the pit and blundered upon a trigger. Up from the moss burst a tree trunk studded with foot-long thorns. It snapped, quick as a scorpion's tail; the thorns punctured Mauve Dermont-Faide's armor, his chest, and whisked him from his horse to carry him suspended, writhing and screaming. The tip of the scythe pounded into Lord Faide's car, splintered against the hull. The car swung groaning through the air. Lord Faide clutched at the windscreen to prevent himself from falling.

The column halted; several men ran to the pit, but Gethwin Faide lay twenty feet below, crushed under his horse. Others took Mauve Dermont-Faide down from the swaying scythe, but he, too, was dead.

Lord Faide's skin tingled with a gooseflesh of hate and rage. He looked toward the forest. The First Folk stood motionless. He beckoned to Bernard, sergeant of the foot soldiers. "Two men with lances to try out the ground ahead. All others ready with darts. At my signal spit the devils."

Two men came forward, and marching before Lord Faide's car, probed at the ground. Lord Faide settled in his seat. "Forward."

The column moved slowly toward the forest, every man tense and ready. The lances of the two men in the vanguard presently broke through the moss, to disclose a nettle trap—a pit lined with nettles, each frond ripe with globes of acid. Carefully they probed out a path to the side, and the column filed around, each man walking in the other's tracks.

At Lord Faide's side now rode his two nephews, Scolford and Edwin. "Notice," said Lord Faide in a voice harsh and tight. "These traps were laid since our last passage; an act of malice."

"But why did they guide us through before?"

Lord Faide smiled bitterly. "They were willing that we should die at Ballant Keep. But we have disappointed them."

"Notice, they carry tubes," said Scolford.

"Blowguns possibly," suggested Edwin.

Scolford disagreed. "They cannot blow through their foam-vents."

"No doubt we shall soon learn," said Lord Faide. He rose in his seat, called to the rear. "Ready with the darts!"

The soldiers raised their crossbows. The column advanced slowly, now only a hundred yards from the planting. The white shapes of the First Folk moved uneasily at the forest's edges. Several of them raised their tubes, seemed to sight along the length. They twisted their great hands.

One of the tubes was pointed toward Lord Faide. He saw a small black object leave the opening, flit forward, gathering speed. He heard a hum, waxing to a rasping, clicking flutter. He ducked behind the windscreen; the projectile swooped in pursuit, struck the windscreen like a thrown stone. It fell crippled upon the forward deck of the car—a heavy black insect like a wasp, its broken proboscis oozing ocher liquid, horny wings beating feebly, eyes like dumbbells fixed on Lord Faide. With his mailed fist, he crushed the creature.

Behind him other wasps struck knights and men; Corex Faide-Battaro took the prong through his visor into the eye, but the armor of the other knights defeated the wasps. The foot soldiers, however, lacked protection; the wasps half buried themselves in flesh. The soldiers called out in pain, clawed away the wasps, squeezed the wounds. Corex Faide-Battaro toppled from his horse, ran blindly out over the heath, and after fifty feet fell into a trap. The stricken soldiers began to twitch, then fell on the moss, thrashed, leaped up to run with flapping arms, threw themselves in wild somersaults, foaming and thrashing.

In the forest, the First Folk raised their tubes again. Lord Faide bellowed, "Spit the creatures! Bowmen, launch your darts!"

There came the twang of crossbows, darts snapped at the quiet white shapes. A few staggered and wandered aimlessly away; most, however, plucked out the darts or ignored them. They took capsules from small sacks, put them to the end of their tubes.

"Beware the wasps!" cried Lord Faide. "Strike with your bucklers! Kill the cursed things in flight!"

The rasp of horny wings came again; certain of the soldiers found courage enough to follow Lord Faide's orders, and battered down the wasps. Others struck home as before; behind came another flight. The column became a tangle of struggling, crouching men.

"Footmen, retreat!" called Lord Faide furiously. "Footmen back! Knights to me!"

The soldiers fled back along the track, taking refuge behind the baggage wagons. Thirty of their number lay dying, or dead, on the moss.

Lord Faide cried out to his knights in a voice like a bugle. "Dismount, follow slow after me! Turn your helmets, keep the wasps from your eyes! One step at a time, behind the car! Edwin, into the car beside me, test the footing with your lance. Once in the forest there are no traps! Then attack!"

The knights formed themselves into a line behind the car. Lord Faide drove slowly forward, his kinsman Edwin prodding the ground ahead. The First Folk sent out a dozen more wasps, which dashed themselves vainly against the armor. Then there was silence . . . cessation of sound, activity. The First Folk watched impassively as the knights approached, step by step.

Edwin's lance found a trap, the column moved to the side. Another trap—and the column was diverted from the planting toward the forest. Step by step, yard by yard—another trap, another detour, and now the column was only a hundred feet from the forest. A trap to the left, a trap to the right: the safe path led directly toward an enormous heavy-branched tree. Seventy feet, fifty feet, then Lord Faide drew his sword.

"Prepare to charge, kill till your arms tire!"

From the forest came a crackling sound. The branches of the great tree trembled and swayed. The knights stared, for a moment frozen into place. The tree toppled forward, the knights madly tried to flee—to the rear, to the sides. Traps opened; the knights dropped upon sharp stakes. The tree fell; boughs cracked armored bodies like nuts; there was the hoarse yelling of pinned men, screams from the traps, the crackling subsidence of breaking branches. Lord Faide had been battered down into the car, and the car had been pressed groaning into the moss. His first instinctive act was to press the switch to rest position; then he staggered erect, clambered up through the boughs. A pale unhuman face peered at him; he swung his fist, crushed the faceted eyebulge, and roaring with rage scrambled through the branches. Others of his knights were working themselves free, although almost a third were either crushed or impaled.

The First Folk came scrambling forward, armed with enormous thorns, long as swords. But now Lord Faide could reach them at close quarters. Hissing with vindictive joy he sprang into their midst, swinging his sword with both hands, as if demon-possessed. The surviving knights joined him and the ground became littered with dismembered First Folk. They drew back slowly, without excitement. Lord Faide reluctantly called back his knights. "We must succor those still pinned, as many as still are alive."

As well as possible branches were cut away, injured knights drawn forth. In some cases the soft moss had cushioned the impact of the tree. Six knights were dead, another four crushed beyond hope of recovery. To these Lord Faide himself gave the *coup de grace*. Ten minutes further hacking and chopping freed Lord Faide's car, while the First Folk watched incuriously from the forest. The knights wished to charge once more, but Lord Faide ordered retreat. Without interference they returned the way they had come, back to the baggage train.

Lord Faide ordered a muster. Of the original war party, less than two-thirds remained. Lord Faide shook his head bitterly. Galling to think how easily he had been led into a trap! He swung on his heel, strode to the rear of the column, to the wagons of the magicians. The jinxmen sat around a small fire, drinking tea. "Which of you will hoodoo these white forest vermin? I want them dead—stricken with sickness, cramps, blindness, the most painful afflictions you can contrive!"

There was general silence. The jinxmen sipped their tea.

"Well?" demanded Lord Faide. "Have you no answer? Do I not make myself plain?"

Hein Huss cleared his throat, spat into the blaze. "Your wishes are plain. Unfortunately we cannot hoodoo the First Folk."

"And why?"

"There are technical reasons."

Lord Faide knew the futility of argument. "Must we slink home around the forest? If you cannot hoodoo the First Folk, then bring out your demons! I will march on the forest and chop out a path with my sword!"

"It is not for me to suggest tactics," grumbled Hein Huss.

"Go on, speak! I will listen."

"A suggestion has been put to me, which I will pass to you. Neither I nor the other jinxmen associate ourselves with it, since it recommends the crudest of physical principles."

"I await the suggestion," said Lord Faide.

"It is merely this. One of my apprentices tampered with your car, as you may remember."

"Yes, and I will see he gets the hiding he deserves."

"By some freak he caused the car to rise high into the air. The suggestion is this: that we load the car with as much oil as the baggage train affords, that we send the car aloft and let it drift over the planting. At a suitable moment, the occupant of the car will pour the oil over the trees, then hurl down a torch. The forest will burn. The First Folk will be at least discomfited; at best a large number will be destroyed."

Lord Faide slapped his hands together. "Excellent! Quickly, to work!" He called a dozen soldiers, gave them orders; four kegs of cooking oil, three buckets of pitch, six demijohns of spirit were brought and lifted into the car. The engines grated and protested, and the car sagged almost to the moss.

Lord Faide shook his head sadly. "A rude use of the relic, but all in good purpose. Now, where is that apprentice? He must indicate which switches and which buttons he turned."

"I suggest," said Hein Huss, "that Sam Salazar be sent up with the car."

Lord Faide looked sidewise at Sam Salazar's round, bland countenance. "An efficient hand is needed, a seasoned judgment. I wonder if he can be trusted?"

"I would think so," said Hein Huss, "inasmuch as it was Sam Salazar who evolved the scheme in the first place."

"Very well. In with you, Apprentice! Treat my car with reverence! The wind blows away from us; fire this edge of the forest, in as long a strip as you can manage. The torch, where is the torch?"

The torch was brought and secured to the side of the car.

"One more matter," said Sam Salazar. "I would like to borrow the armor of some obliging knight, to protect myself from the wasps. Otherwise—"

"Armor!" bawled Lord Faide. "Bring armor!"

At last, fully accoutered and with visor down, Sam Salazar climbed into the car. He seated himself, peered intently at the buttons and switches. In truth he was not precisely certain as to which he had manipulated before. . . . He considered, reached forward, pushed, turned. The motors roared and screamed; the car shuddered, sluggishly rose into the air. Higher, higher, twenty feet, forty feet, sixty feet—a hundred, two hundred. The wind eased the car toward the forest; in the shade the First Folk watched. Several of them raised tubes, opened the shutters. The onlookers saw wasps dart through the air to dash against Sam Salazar's armor.

The car drifted over the trees; Sam Salazar began ladling out the oil. Below, the First Folk stirred uneasily. The wind carried the car too far over the forest; Sam Salazar worked the controls, succeeded in guiding himself back. One keg was empty, and another; he tossed them out, presently emptied the remaining two, and the buckets of pitch. He soaked a rag in spirit, ignited it, threw it over the side, poured the spirit after.

The flaming rag fell into leaves. A crackle; fire blazed and sprang. The car now floated at a height of five hundred feet. Salazar poured over the remaining spirits, dropped the demijohns, guided the car back over the heath, and fumbling nervously with the controls dropped the car in a series of swoops back to the moss.

Lord Faide sprang forward, clapped him on the shoulder. "Excellently done! The forest blazes like tinder!"

The men of Faide Keep stood back, rejoicing to see the flames soar and lick. The First Folk scurried back from the heat, waving their arms; foam of a peculiar purple color issued from their vents as they ran, small useless puffs discharged as if by accident or through excitement. The flames ate through first the forest, then spread into the new planting, leaping through the leaves.

"Prepare to march!" called Lord Faide. "We pass directly behind the flames, before the First Folk return."

Off in the forest the First Folk perched in the trees, blowing out foam in great puffs and billows, building a wall of insulation. The flames had eaten half across the new planting, leaving behind smoldering saplings.

"Forward! Briskly!"

The column moved ahead. Coughing in the smoke, eyes smarting, they passed under still blazing trees and came out on the western downs.

Slowly the column moved forward, led by a pair of soldiers prodding the moss with lances. Behind followed Lord Faide with the knights, then came the foot soldiers, then the rumbling baggage train, and finally the six wagons of the jinxmen.

A thump, a creak, a snap. A scythe had broken up from the moss; the soldiers in the lead dropped flat; the scythe whipped past, a foot from Lord Faide's face. At the same time a plaintive cry came from the rear guard. "They pursue! The First Folk come!"

Lord Faide turned to inspect the new threat. A clot of First Folk, two hundred or more, came across the moss, moving without haste or urgency. Some carried wasp tubes, others thorn-rapiers.

Lord Faide looked ahead. Another hundred yards should bring the army out upon safe ground; then he could deploy and maneuver. "Forward!"

The column proceeded, the baggage train and the jinxmen's wagons pressing close up against the soldiers. Behind and to one side came the First Folk, moving casually and easily.

At last Lord Faide judged they had reached secure ground. "Forward, now! Bring the wagons out, hurry now!"

The troops needed no urging; they trotted out over the heath, the wagons trundling after. Lord Faide ordered the wagons into a close double line, stationed the soldiers between, with the horses behind them protected from the wasps. The knights, now dismounted, waited in front.

The First Folk came listlessly, formlessly forward. Blank white faces stared; huge hands grasped tubes and thorns; traces of the purplish foam showed at the lips of their underarm orifices.

Lord Faide walked along the line of knights. "Swords ready. Allow them as close as they care to come. Then a quick charge." He motioned to the foot soldiers. "Choose a target...!" A volley of darts whistled overhead, to plunge into white bodies. With chisel-bladed fingers the First Folk plucked them out, discarded them with no evidence of vexation. One or two staggered, wandered confusedly across the line of approach. Others raised their tubes, withdrew the shutter. Out flew the insects, horny wings rasping, prongs thrust forward. Across the moss they flickered, to crush themselves against the armor of the knights, to drop to the ground, to be stamped upon. The soldiers cranked their crossbows back into tension, discharged another flight of darts, caused several more First Folk casualties.

The First Folk spread into a long line, surrounding the Faide troops. Lord Faide shifted half his knights to the other side of the wagons.

The First Folk wandered closer. Lord Faide called for a charge. The knights stepped smartly forward, swords swinging. The First Folk advanced a few more steps, then stopped short. The flaps of skin at their backs swelled, pulsed; white foam gushed through their vents; clouds and billows rose up around them. The knights halted uncertainly, prodding and slashing into the foam but finding nothing. The foam piled higher, rolling in and forward, pushing the knights back toward the wagons. They looked questioningly toward Lord Faide.

Lord Faide waved his sword. "Cut through to the other side! Forward!" Slashing two-handed with his sword, he sprang into the foam. He struck something solid, hacked blindly at it, pushed forward. Then his legs were seized; he was upended and fell with a spine-rattling jar. Now he felt the grate of a thorn searching his armor. It found a crevice under his corselet and pierced him. Cursing he raised on his hands and knees, and plunged blindly forward. Enormous hard hands grasped him, heavy forms fell on hs shoulders. He tried to breathe, but the foam clogged his visor; he began to smother. Staggering to his feet he half ran, half fell out into the open air, carrying two of the First Folk with him. He had lost his sword, but managed to draw his dagger. The First Folk released him and stepped back into the foam. Lord Faide sprang to his feet. Inside the foam came the sounds of combat; some of his knights burst into the open; others called for help. Lord Faide motioned to the knights. "Back within; the devils slaughter our kinsmen! In and on to the center!"

He took a deep breath. Seizing his dagger he thrust himself back into the foam. A flurry of shapes came at him: he pounded with his fists, cut with his dagger, stumbled over a mass of living tissue. He kicked the softness, and stepped on metal. Bending, he grasped a leg but found it limp and dead. First Folk were on his back, another thorn found its mark; he groaned and thrust himself forward, and once again fell out into the open air.

A scant fifty of his knights had won back into the central clearing. Lord Faide cried out, "To the center; mount your horses!" Abandoning his car, he himself vaulted into a saddle. The foam boiled and billowed closer. Lord Faide waved his arm. "Forward, all; at a gallop! After us the wagons—out into the open!"

They charged, thrusting the frightened horses into the foam. There was white blindness, the feel of forms underneath, then the open air once again. Behind came the wagons, and the foot soldiers, running along the channel cut by the wagons. All won free—all but the knights who had fallen under the foam.

Two hundred yards from the great white clot of foam, Lord Faide halted, turned, looked back. He raised his fist, shook it in a passion. "My knights, my car, my honor! I'll burn your forests, I'll drive you into the sea, there'll be no peace till all are dead!" He swung around. "Come," he called bitterly to the remnants of his war party. "We have been defeated. We retreat to Faide Keep."

8   **F**aide Keep, like Ballant Keep, was constructed of a black, glossy substance, half metal, half stone, impervious to heat, force, and radiation. A parasol roof, designed to ward off hostile energy, rested on five squat outer towers, connected by walls almost as high as the lip of the overhanging roof.

The homecoming banquet was quiet and morose. The soldiers and knights ate lightly and drank much, but instead of becoming merry, lapsed into gloom. Lord Faide, overcome by emotion, jumped to his feet. "Everyone sits silent, aching with rage. I feel no differently. We shall take revenge. We shall put the forests to the torch. The cursed white savages will smother and burn. Drink now with good cheer; not a moment will be wasted. But we must be ready. It is no more than idiocy to attack as before. Tonight I take council with the jinxmen, and we will start a program of affliction."

The soldiers and knights rose to their feet, raised their cups and drank a somber toast. Lord Faide bowed and left the hall.

He went to his private trophy room. On the walls hung escutcheons, memorials, deathmasks, clusters of swords like many-petaled flowers; a rack of side arms, energy pistols, electric stilettos; a portrait of the original Faide, in ancient spacefarer's uniform, and a treasured, almost unique, photograph of the great ship that had brought the first Faide to Pangborn.

Lord Faide studied the ancient face for several moments, then summoned a servant. "Ask the Head Jinxman to attend me."

Hein Huss presently stumped into the room. Lord Faide turned away from the portrait, seated himself, motioned to Hein Huss to do likewise. "What of the keep-lords?" he asked. "How do they regard the setback at the hands of the First Folk?"

"There are various reactions," said Hein Huss. "At Boghoten, Candelwade, and Havve there is distress and anger."

Lord Faide nodded. "These are my kinsmen."

"At Gisborne, Graymar, Castle Cloud, and Alder there is satisfaction, veiled calculation."

"To be expected," muttered Lord Faide. "These lords must be humbled; in spite of oaths and undertakings, they still think rebellion."

"At Star Home, Julian-Douray, and Oak Hall I read surprise at the abilities of the First Folk, but in the main disinterest."

Lord Faide nodded sourly. "Well enough. There is no actual rebellion in prospect; we are free to concentrate on the First Folk. I will tell you what is in my mind. You report that new plantings are in progress between Wildwood, Old Forest, Sarrow Copse, and elsewhere—possibly with the intent of surrounding Faide Keep." He looked inquiringly at Hein Huss, but no comment was forthcoming. Lord Faide continued. "Possibly we have underestimated the cunning of the savages. They seem capable of forming plans and acting with almost human persistence. Or, I should say, more than human persistence, for it appears that after sixteen hundred years they still consider us invaders and hope to exterminate us."

"That is my own conclusion," said Hein Huss.

"We must take steps to strike first. I consider this a matter for the jinxmen. We gain no honor dodging wasps, falling into traps, or groping through foam. It is a needless waste of lives. Therefore, I want you to assemble your jinxmen, cabalmen, and spellbinders; I want you to formulate your most potent hoodoos—"

"Impossible!"

Lord Faide's black eyebrows rose high. "'Impossible'?"

Hein Huss seemed vaguely uncomfortable. "I read the wonder in your mind. You suspect me of disinterest, irresponsibility. Not true. If the First Folk defeat you, we suffer likewise."

"Exactly," said Lord Faide drily. "You will starve."

"Nevertheless, the jinxmen cannot help you." He hoisted himself to his feet, started for the door.

"Sit," said Lord Faide. "It is necessary to pursue this matter."

Hein Huss looked around with his bland, water-clear eyes. Lord Faide met his gaze. Hein Huss sighed deeply. "I see I must ignore the precepts of my trade, break the habits of a lifetime. I must explain." He took his bulk to the wall, fingered the side arms in the rack, studied the portrait of the ancestral Faide. "These miracle workers of the old times—unfortunately we cannot use their magic! Notice the bulk of the spaceship! As heavy as Faide Keep." He turned his gaze on the table, teleported a candelabra two or three inches. "With considerably less effort they gave that spaceship enormous velocity, using ideas and forces they knew to be imaginary and irrational. We have advanced since then, of course. We no longer employ mysteries, arcane constructions, wild nonhuman forces. We are rational and practical—but we cannot achieve the effects of the ancient magicians."

Lord Faide watched Hein Huss with saturnine eyes. Hein Huss gave his deep rumbling laugh. "You think that I wish to distract you with talk? No, this is not the case. I am preparing to enlighten you." He returned to his seat, lowered his bulk with a groan. "Now I must talk at length, to which I am not accustomed. But you must be given to understand what we jinxmen can do and what we cannot do.

"First, unlike the ancient magicians, we are practical men. Naturally there is difference in our abilities. The best jinxman combines great telepathic facility, implacable personal force, and intimate knowledge of his fellow humans. He knows their acts, motives, desires, and fears; he understands the symbols that most vigorously represent these qualities. Jinxmanship in the main is drudgery—dangerous, difficult, and unromantic—with no mystery except that which we employ to confuse our enemies." Hein Huss glanced at Lord Faide to encounter the same saturnine gaze. "Ha! I still have told you nothing; I still have spent many words talking around my inability to confound the First Folk. Patience."

"Speak on," said Lord Faide.

"Listen then. What happens when I hoodoo a man? First I must enter into his mind telepathically. There are three operational levels: the conscious, the unconscious, the cellular. The most effective jinxing is done if all three levels are influenced. I feel into my victim, I learn as much as possible, supplementing my previous knowledge of him, which is part of my stock in trade. I take up his doll, which carries his traces. The doll is highly useful but not indispensable. It serves as a focus for my attention; it acts as a pattern, or a guide, as I fix upon the mind of the victim, and he is bound by his own telepathic capacity to the doll which bears his traces.

"So! Now! Man and doll are identified in my mind, and at one or more levels in the victim's mind. Whatever happens to the doll the victim feels to be happening to himself. There is no more to simple hoodooing than that, from the standpoint of the jinxmen. But naturally the victims differ greatly. Susceptibility is the key idea here. Some men are more susceptible than others. Fear and conviction breed susceptibility. As a jinxman succeeds he becomes ever more feared, and consequently the more efficacious he becomes. The process is self-generative.

"Demon-possession is a similar technique. Susceptibility is again essential; again conviction creates susceptibility. It is easiest and most dramatic when the characteristics of the demon are well known, as in the case of Comandore's Keyril. For this reason, demons can be exchanged or traded among jinxmen. The commodity actually traded is public acceptance and familiarity with the demon."

"Demons then do not actually exist?" inquired Lord Faide half-incredulously.

Hein Huss grinned vastly, showing enormous yellow teeth. "Telepathy works through a superstratum. Who knows what is created in this superstratum? Maybe the demons live on after they have been conceived; maybe they now are real. This of course is speculation, which we jinxmen shun.

"So much for demons, so much for the lesser techniques of jinxmanship. I have explained sufficient to serve as background to the present situation."

"Excellent," said Lord Faide. "Continue."

"The question, then, is: How does one cast a hoodoo into a creature of an alien race?" He looked inquiringly at Lord Faide. "Can you tell me?"

"I?" asked Lord Faide, surprised. "No."

"The method is basically the same as in the hoodooing of men. It is necessary to make the creature believe, in every cell of his being, that he suffers or dies. This is where the problems begin to arise. Does the creature think—that is to say, does he arrange the processes of his life in the same manner as men? This is a very important distinction. Certain creatures of the universe use methods other than the human nerve-node system to control their environments. We call the human system 'intelligence'—a word which properly should be restricted to human activity. Other creatures use different agencies, different systems, arriving sometimes at similar ends. To bring home these generalities, I cannot hope to merge my mind with the corresponding capacity in the First Folk. The key will not fit the lock. At least, not altogether. Once or twice when I watched the First Folk trading with men at Forest Market, I felt occasional weak significances. This implies that the First Folk mentality creates something similar to human telepathic impulses. Nevertheless, there is no real sympathy between the two races.

"This is the first and the least difficulty. If I were able to make complete telepathic contact—what then? The creatures are different from us. They have no words for 'fear,' 'hate,' 'rage,' 'pain,' 'bravery,' 'cowardice.' One may deduce that they do not feel these emotions. Undoubtedly they know other sensations, possibly as meaningful. Whatever these may be, they are unknown to me, and therefore I cannot either form or project symbols for these sensations."

Lord Faide stirred impatiently. "In short, you tell me that you cannot efficiently enter these creatures' minds; and that if you could, you do not know what influences you could plant there to do them harm."

"Succinct," agreed Hein Huss. "Substantially accurate."

Lord Faide rose to his feet. "In that case you must repair these deficiencies. You must learn to telepathize with the First Folk; you must find what influences will harm them. As quickly as possible."

Hein Huss stared reproachfully at Lord Faide. "But I have gone to great lengths to explain the difficulties involved! To hoodoo the First Folk is a monumental task! It would be necessary to enter Wildwood, to live with the First Folk, to become one of them, as my apprentice thought to become a tree. Even then an effective hoodoo is improbable! The First Folk must be susceptible to conviction! Otherwise there would be no bite to the hoodoo! I could guarantee no success. I would predict failure. No other jinxman would dare tell you this, no other would risk his *mana*. I dare because I am Hein Huss, with life behind me."

"Nevertheless we must attempt every weapon at hand," said Lord Faide in a dry voice. "I cannot risk my knights, my kinsmen, my soldiers against these pallid half-creatures. What a waste of good flesh and blood to be stuck by a poison insect! You must go to Wildwood; you must learn how to hoodoo the First Folk."

Hein Huss heaved himself erect. His great round face was stony; his eyes were like bits of water-worn glass. "It is likewise a waste to go on a fool's errand. I am no fool and I will not undertake a hoodoo which is futile from the beginning."

"In that case," said Lord Faide, "I will find someone else." He went to the door, summoned a servant. "Bring Isak Comandore here."

Hein Huss lowered his bulk into the chair. "I will remain during the interview, with your permission."

"As you wish."

Isak Comandore appeared in the doorway, tall, loosely articulated, head hanging forward. He darted a glance of swift appraisal at Lord Faide, at Hein Huss, then stepped into the room.

Lord Faide crisply explained his desires. "Hein Huss refuses to undertake the mission. Therefore I call on you."

Isak Comandore calculated. The pattern of his thinking was clear: he possibly could gain much *mana*; there was small risk of diminution, for had not Hein Huss already dodged away from the project? Comandore nodded. "Hein Huss has made clear the difficulties; only a very clever and very lucky jinxman can hope to succeed. But I accept the challenge. I will go."

"Good," said Hein Huss. "I will go, too." Isak Comandore darted him a sudden hot glance. "I wish only to observe. To Isak Comandore goes the responsibility and whatever credit may ensue."

"Very well," said Comandore presently. "I welcome your company. Tomorrow morning we leave. I go to order our wagon."

Late in the evening Apprentice Sam Salazar came to Hein Huss where he sat brooding in his workroom. "What do you wish?" growled Huss.

"I have a request to make of you, Head Jinxman Huss."

"Head Jinxman in name only," grumbled Hein Huss. "Isak Comandore is about to assume my position."

Sam Salazar blinked, laughed uncertainly. Hein Huss fixed wintry-pale eyes on him. "What do you wish?"

"I have heard that you go on an expedition to Wildwood, to study the First Folk."

"True, true. What then?"

"Surely they will now attack all men?"

Hein Huss shrugged. "At Forest Market they trade with men. At Forest Market men have always entered the forest. Perhaps there will be change, perhaps not."

"I would go with you, if I may," said Sam Salazar.

"This is no mission for apprentices."

"An apprentice must take every opportunity to learn," said Sam Salazar. "Also you will need extra hands to set up tents, to load and unload cabinets, to cook, to fetch water, and other such matters."

"Your argument is convincing," said Hein Huss. "We depart at dawn; be on hand."

9   **A**s the sun lifted over the heath the jinxmen departed Faide Keep. The high-wheeled wagon creaked north over the moss, Hein Huss and Isak Comandore riding the front seat, Sam Salazar with his legs hanging over the tail. The wagon rose and fell with the dips and mounds of the moss, wheels wobbling, and presently passed out of sight behind Sky-watcher's Hill.

Five days later, an hour before sunset, the wagon reappeared. As before, Hein Huss and Isak Comandore rode the front seat, with Sam Salazar perched behind. They approached the keep, and without giving so much as a sign or a nod, drove through the gate into the courtyard.

Isak Comandore unfolded his long legs, stepped to the ground like a spider; Hein Huss lowered himself with a grunt. Both went to their quarters, while Sam Salazar led the wagon to the jinxmen's warehouse.

Somewhat later Isak Comandore presented himself to Lord Faide, who had been waiting in his trophy room, forced to a show of indifference through considerations of position, dignity, and protocol. Isak Comandore stood in the doorway, grinning like a fox. Lord Faide eyed him with sour dislike, waiting for Comandore to speak. Hein Huss might have stationed himself an entire day, eyes placidly fixed on Lord Faide, awaiting the first word; Isak Comandore lacked the absolute serenity. He came a step forward. "I have returned from Wildwood."

"With what results?"

"I believe that it is possible to hoodoo the First Folk."

Hein Huss spoke from behind Comandore. "I believe that such an undertaking, if feasible, would be useless, irresponsible, and possibly dangerous." He lumbered forward.

Isak Comandore's eyes glowed hot red-brown; he turned back to Lord Faide. "You ordered me forth on a mission; I will render a report."

"Seat yourselves. I will listen."

Isak Comandore, nominal head of the expedition, spoke. "We rode along the river bank to Forest Market. Here was no sign of disorder or of hostility. A hundred First Folk traded timber, planks, posts, and poles for knife blades, iron wire, and copper pots. When they returned to their barge we followed them aboard, wagon, horses, and all. They showed no surprise—"

"Surprise," said Hein Huss heavily, "is an emotion of which they have no knowledge."

Isak Comandore glared briefly. "We spoke to the barge-tenders, explaining that we wished to visit the interior of Wildwood. We asked if the First Folk would try to kill us to prevent us from entering the forest. They professed indifference as to either our well-being or our destruction. This was by no means a guarantee of safe conduct; however, we accepted it as such, and remained aboard the barge." He spoke on with occasional emendations from Hein Huss.

They had proceeded up the river, into the forest, the First Folk poling against the slow current. Presently they put away the poles; nevertheless the barge moved as before. The mystified jinxmen discussed the possibility of teleportation, or symbological force, and wondered if the First Folk had developed jinxing techniques unknown to men. Sam Salazar, however, noticed that four enormous water beetles, each twelve feet long with oil-black carapaces and blunt heads, had risen from the river bed and pushed the barge from behind—apparently without direction or command. The First Folk stood at the bow, turning the nose of the barge this way or that to follow the winding of the river. They ignored the jinxmen and Sam Salazar as if they did not exist.

The beetles swam tirelessly; the barge moved for four hours as fast as a man could walk. Occasionally, First Folk peered from the forest shadows, but none showed interest or concern in the barge's unusual cargo. By midafternoon the river widened, broke into many channels and became a marsh; a few minutes later the barge floated out into the open water of a small lake. Along the shore, behind the first line of trees appeared a large settlement. The jinxmen were interested and surprised. It had always been assumed that the First Folk wandered at random through the forest, as they had originally lived in the moss of the downs.

The barge grounded; the First Folk walked ashore, the men followed with the horses and wagon. Their immediate impressions were of

swarming numbers, of slow but incessant activity, and they were attacked by an overpoweringly evil smell.

Ignoring the stench, the men brought the wagon in from the shore,
paused to take stock of what they saw. The settlement appeared to be a
center of many diverse activities. The trees had been stripped of lower
branches, and supported blocks of hardened foam three hundred feet
long, fifty feet high, twenty feet thick, with a space of a man's height
intervening between the underside of the foam and the ground. There
were a dozen of these blocks, apparently of cellular construction. Certain of the cells had broken open and seethed with small white fishlike
creatures—the First Folk young.

Below the blocks masses of First Folk engaged in various occupa-
tions, in the main unfamiliar to the jinxmen. Leaving the wagon in the
care of Sam Salazar, Hein Huss and Isak Comandore moved forward
among the First Folk, repelled by the stench and the pressure of alien
flesh, but drawn by curiosity. They were neither heeded nor halted; they
wandered everywhere about the settlement. One area seemed to be an
enormous zoo, divided into a number of sections. The purpose of one of
these sections—a kind of range two hundred feet long—was all too
clear. At one end a human corpse hung on a rope—a Faide casualty
from the battle at the new planting. Certain of the wasps flew straight at
the corpse; just before contact they were netted and removed. Others
flew up and away or veered toward the First Folk who stood along the
side of the range. These latter also were netted and killed at once.

The purpose of the business was clear enough. Examining some of
the other activity in this new light, the jinxmen were able to interpret
much that had hitherto puzzled them.

They saw beetles tall as dogs with heavy saw-toothed pincers attacking objects resembling horses; pens of insects even larger, long, narrow,
segmented, with dozens of heavy legs and nightmare heads. All these
creatures—wasps, beetles, centipedes—in smaller and less formidable
form were indigenous to the forest; it was plain that the First Folk had
been practicing selective breeding for many years, perhaps centuries.

Not all the activity was warlike. Moths were trained to gather nuts,
worms to gnaw straight holes through timber; in another section caterpillars chewed a yellow mash, molded it into identical spheres. Much of
the evil odor emanated from the zoo; the jinxmen departed without reluctance, and returned to the wagon. Sam Salazar pitched the tent and
built a fire, while Hein Huss and Isak Comandore discussed the settlement.

Night came; the blocks of foam glowed with imprisoned light; the
activity underneath proceeded without cessation. The jinxmen retired to
the tent and slept, while Sam Salazar stood guard.

* * *

The following day Hein Huss was able to engage one of the First Folk in conversation; it was the first attention of any sort given to them.

The conversation was long; Hein Huss reported only the gist of it to Lord Faide. (Isak Comandore turned away, ostentatiously disassociating himself from the matter.)

Hein Huss first of all had inquired as to the purpose of the sinister preparations: the wasps, beetles, centipedes, and the like.

"We intend to kill men," the creature had reported ingenuously. "We intend to return to the moss. This has been our purpose ever since men appeared on the planet."

Huss had stated that such an ambition was shortsighted, that there was ample room for both men and First Folk on Pangborn. "The First Folk," said Hein Huss, "should remove their traps and cease their efforts to surround the keeps with forest."

"No," came the response. "Men are intruders. They mar the beautiful moss. All will be killed."

Isak Comandore returned to the conversation. "I noticed here a significant fact. All the First Folk within sight had ceased their work; all looked toward us, as if they, too, participated in the discussion. I reached the highly important conclusion that the First Folk are not complete individuals but components of a larger unity, joined to a greater or less extent by a telepathic phase not unlike our own."

Hein Huss continued placidly, "I remarked that if we were attacked, many of the First Folk would perish. The creature showed no concern, and in fact implied much of what Jinxman Comandore had already induced: 'There are always more in the cells to replace the elements which die. But if the community becomes sick, all suffer. We have been forced into the forests, into a strange existence. We must arm ourselves and drive away the men, and to this end we have developed the methods of men to our own purposes!'"

Isak Comandore spoke. "Needless to say, the creature referred to the ancient men, not ourselves."

"In any event," said Lord Faide, "they leave no doubt as to their intentions. We should be fools not to attack them at once, with every weapon at our disposal."

Hein Huss continued imperturbably. "The creature went on at some length. 'We have learned the value of irrationality.' 'Irrationality' of course was not his word or even his meaning. He said something like 'a series of vaguely motivated trials'—as close as I can translate. He said, 'We have learned to change our environment. We use insects and trees and plants and waterslugs. It is an enormous effort for us who would prefer a placid life in the moss. But you men have forced this life on us, and now you must suffer the consequences.' I pointed out once more that men were not helpless, that many First Folk would die. The creature seemed unworried. 'The community persists.' I asked a delicate question, 'If your purpose is to kill men, why do you allow us here?' He said, 'The entire community of men will be destroyed.' Apparently they believe the human society to be similar to their own, and therefore regard the killing of three wayfaring individuals as pointless effort."

Lord Faide laughed grimly. "To destroy us they must first win past Hellmouth, then penetrate Faide Keep. This they are unable to do."

Isak Comandore resumed his report. "At this time I was already convinced that the problem was one of hoodooing not an individual but an entire race. In theory this should be no more difficult than hoodooing one. It requires no more effort to speak to twenty than to one. With this end in view I ordered the apprentice to collect substances associated with the creatures. Skinflakes, foam, droppings, all other exudations obtainable. While he did so, I tried to put myself in rapport with the creatures. It is difficult, for their telepathy works across a different stratum from ours. Nevertheless, to a certain extent I have succeeded."

"Then you can hoodoo the First Folk?" asked Lord Faide.

"I vouchsafe nothing until I try. Certain preparations must be made."

"Go then; make your preparations."

Comandore rose to his feet and with a sly side glance for Hein Huss left the room. Huss waited, pinching his chin with heavy fingers. Lord Faide looked at him coldly. "You have something to add?"

Huss grunted, hoisted himself to his feet. "I wish that I did. But my thoughts are confused. Of the many futures, all seem troubled and angry. Perhaps our best is not good enough."

Lord Faide looked at Hein Huss with surprise; the massive Head Jinxman had never before spoken in terms so pessimistic and melancholy. "Speak then; I will listen."

Hein Huss said gruffly, "If I knew any certainties I would speak gladly. But I am merely beset by doubts. I fear that we can no longer depend on logic and careful jinxmanship. Our ancestors were miracle workers, magicians. They drove the First Folk into the forest. To put us to flight in our turn the First Folk have adopted the ancient methods: random trial and purposeless empiricism. I am dubious. Perhaps we must turn our backs on sanity and likewise return to the mysticism of our ancestors."

Lord Faide shrugged. "If Isak Comandore can hoodoo the First Folk, such a retreat may be unnecessary."

"The world changes," said Hein Huss. "Of so much I feel sure: the old days of craft and careful knowledge are gone. The future is for men of cleverness, and imagination untroubled by discipline; the unorthodox Sam Salazar may become more effective than I. The world changes."

Lord Faide smiled his sour dyspeptic smile. "When that day comes I will appoint Sam Salazar Head Jinxman and also name him Lord Faide, and you and I will retire together to a hut on the downs."

Hein Huss made a heavy fateful gesture and departed.

10

Two days later Lord Faide, coming upon Isak Comandore, inquired as to his progress. Comandore took refuge in generalities. After another two days Lord Faide inquired again and this time insisted on particulars. Comandore grudgingly led the way to his workroom, where a dozen cabalmen, spellbinders, and apprentices worked around a large table, building a model of the First Folk settlement in Wildwood.

"Along the lakeshore," said Comandore, "I will range a great number of dolls, daubed with First Folk essences. When this is complete I will work up a hoodoo and blight the creatures."

"Good. Perform well." Lord Faide departed the workroom, mounted to the topmost pinnacle of the keep, to the cupola where the ancestral weapon Hellmouth was housed. "Jambart! Where are you?"

Weapon-tender Jambart, short, blue-jowled, red-nosed and big-bellied, appeared. "My lord?"

"I come to inspect Hellmouth. It is prepared for instant use?"

"Prepared, my lord, and ready. Oiled, greased, polished, scraped, burnished, tended—every part smooth as an egg."

Lord Faide made a scowling examination of Hellmouth—a heavy cylinder six feet in diameter, twelve feet long, studded with half-domes interconnected with tubes of polished copper. Jambart undoubtedly had been diligent. No trace of dirt or rust or corrosion showed; all was gleaming metal. The snout was covered with a heavy plate of metal and tarred canvas; the ring upon which the weapon swiveled was well greased.

Lord Faide surveyed the four horizons. To the south was fertile Faide Valley; to the west open downs; to north and east the menacing loom of Wildwood.

He turned back to Hellmouth and pretended to find a smear of grease. Jambart boiled with expostulations and protestations; Lord Faide uttered a grim warning, enjoining less laxity, then descended to the workroom of Hein Huss. He found the Head Jinxman reclining on a couch, staring at the ceiling. At a bench stood Sam Salazar surrounded by bottles, flasks, and dishes.

Lord Faide stared balefully at the confusion. "What are you doing?" he asked the apprentice.

Sam Salazar looked up guiltily. "Nothing in particular, my lord."

"If you are idle, go then and assist Isak Comandore."

"I am not idle, Lord Faide."

"Then what do you do?"

Sam Salazar gazed sulkily at the bench. "I don't know."

"Then you are idle!"

"No, I am occupied. I pour various liquids on this foam. It is First Folk foam. I wonder what will happen. Water does not dissolve it, nor spirits. Heat chars and slowly burns it, emitting a foul smoke."

Lord Faide turned away with a sneer. "You amuse yourself as a child might. Go to Isak Comandore; he can find use for you. How do you expect to become a jinxman, dabbling and prattling like a baby among pretty rocks?"

Hein Huss gave a deep sound: a mingling of sigh, snort, grunt, and clearing of the throat. "He does no harm, and Isak Comandore has hands enough. Salazar will never become a jinxman; that has been clear a long time."

Lord Faide shrugged. "He is your apprentice, and your responsibility. Well, then. What news from the keeps?"

Hein Huss, groaning and wheezing, swung his legs over the edge of the couch. "The lords share your concern, to greater or lesser extent. Your close allies will readily place troops at your disposal; the others likewise if pressure is brought to bear."

Lord Faide nodded in dour satisfaction. "For the moment there is no urgency. The First Folk hold to their forests. Faide Keep of course is impregnable, although they might ravage the valley...." He paused thoughtfully. "Let Isak Comandore cast his hoodoo. Then we will see."

From the direction of the bench came a hiss, a small explosion, a whiff of acrid gas. Sam Salazar turned guiltily to look at them, his eyebrows singed. Lord Faide gave a snort of disgust and strode from the room.

"What did you do?" Hein Huss inquired in a colorless voice.

"I don't know."

Now Hein Huss likewise snorted in disgust. "Ridiculous. If you wish to work miracles, you must remember your procedures. Miracle working is not jinxmanship, with established rules and guides. In matters so complex it is well that you take notes, so that the miracles may be repeated."

Sam Salazar nodded in agreement and turned back to the bench.

11

Late during the day, news of new First Folk truculence reached Faide Keep. On Honeymoss Hill, not far west of Forest Market, a camp of shepherds had been visited by a wandering group of First Folk, who began to kill the sheep with thorn-swords. When the shepherds protested they, too, were attacked, and many were killed. The remainder of the sheep were massacred.

The following day came other news: four children swimming in Brastock River at Gilbert Ferry had been seized by enormous water beetles and cut into pieces. On the other side of Wildwood, in the foothills immediately below Castle Cloud, peasants had cleared several hillsides and planted them to vines. Early in the morning they had discovered a horde of black disklike flukes devouring the vines—leaves, branches, trunks, and roots. They set about killing the flukes with spades and at once were stung to death by wasps.

Adam McAdam reported the incidents to Lord Faide, who went to Isak Comandore in a fury. "How soon before you are prepared?"

"I am prepared now. But I must rest and fortify myself. Tomorrow morning I work the hoodoo."

"The sooner the better! The creatures have left their forest; they are out killing men!"

Isak Comandore pulled his long chin. "That was to be expected; they told us as much."

Lord Faide ignored the remark. "Show me your tableau."

Isak Comandore took him into his workroom. The model was now complete, with the masses of simulated First Folk properly daubed and sensitized, each tied with a small wad of foam. Isak Comandore pointed to a pot of dark liquid. "I will explain the basis of the hoodoo. When I visited the camp I watched everywhere for powerful symbols. Undoubtedly there were many at hand, but I could not discern them. However, I remembered a circumstance from the battle at the planting; when the creatures were attacked, threatened with fire and about to die, they spewed foam of dull purple color. Evidently this purple foam is associated with death. My hoodoo will be based upon this symbol."

"Rest well, then, so that you may hoodoo to your best capacity."

The following morning Isak Comandore dressed in long robes of black, and set a mask of the demon Nard on his head to fortify himself. He entered his workroom, closed the door.

An hour passed, two hours. Lord Faide sat at breakfast with his kin, stubbornly maintaining a pose of cynical unconcern. At last he could contain himself no longer and went out into the courtyard where Comandore's underlings stood fidgeting and uneasy. "Where is Hein Huss?" demanded Lord Faide. "Summon him here."

Hein Huss came stumping out of his quarters. Lord Faide motioned to Comandore's workshop. "What is happening? Is he succeeding?"

Hein Huss looked toward the workshop. "He is casting a powerful hoodoo. I feel confusion, anger—"

"In Comandore, or in the First Folk?"

"I am not in rapport. I think he has conveyed a message to their minds. A very difficult task, as I explained to you. In this preliminary aspect he has succeeded."

"'Preliminary'? What else remains?"

"The two most important elements of the hoodoo: the susceptibility of the victim and the appropriateness of the symbol."

Lord Faide frowned. "You do not seem optimistic."

"I am uncertain. Isak Comandore may be right in his assumption. If so, and if the First Folk are highly susceptible, today marks a great victory, and Comandore will achieve tremendous *mana!*"

Lord Faide stared at the door to the workshop. "What now?"

Hein Huss' eyes went blank with concentration. "Isak Comandore is near death. He can hoodoo no more today."

Lord Faide turned, waved his arm to the cabalmen. "Enter the workroom! Assist your master!"

The cabalmen raced to the door, flung it open. Presently they emerged supporting the limp form of Isak Comandore, his black robe spattered with purple foam. Lord Faide pressed close. "What did you achieve? Speak!"

Isak Comandore's eyes were half closed, his mouth hung loose and wet. "I spoke to the First Folk, to the whole race. I sent the symbol into their minds—" His head fell limply sidewise.

Lord Faide moved back. "Take him to his quarters. Put him on his couch." He turned away, stood indecisively, chewing at his drooping lower lip. "Still we do not know the measure of his success."

"Ah," said Hein Huss, "but we do!"

Lord Faide jerked around. "What is this? What do you say?"

"I saw into Comandore's mind. He used the symbol of purple foam; with tremendous effort he drove it into their minds. Then he learned that purple foam means not death—purple foam means fear for the safety of the community, purple foam means desperate rage."

"In any event," said Lord Faide after a moment, "there is no harm done. The First Folk can hardly become more hostile."

Three hours later a scout rode furiously into the courtyard, threw himself off his horse, ran to Lord Faide. "The First Folk have left the forest! A tremendous number! Thousands! They are advancing on Faide Keep!"

"Let them advance!" said Lord Faide. "The more the better! Jambart, where are you?"

"Here, sir."

"Prepare Hellmouth! Hold all in readiness!"

"Hellmouth is always ready, sir!"

Lord Faide struck him across the shoulders. "Off with you! Bernard!"

The sergeant of the Faide troops came forward. "Ready, Lord Faide."

"The First Folk attack. Armor your men against wasps, feed them well. We will need all our strength."

Lord Faide turned to Hein Huss. "Send to the keeps, to the manor houses, order our kinsmen to join us, with all their troops and all their armor. Send to Bellgard Hall, to Boghoten, Camber, and Candelwade. Haste, haste, it is only hours from Wildwood."

Huss held up his hand. "I have already done so. The keeps are warned. They know your need."

"And the First Folk—can you feel their minds?"

"No."

Lord Faide walked away. Hein Huss lumbered out the main gate, walked around the keep, casting appraising glances up the black walls of the squat towers, windowless and proof even against the ancient miracle-weapons. High on top the great parasol roof Jambart the weapon-tender worked in the cupola, polishing that which already glistened, greasing surfaces already heavy with grease.

Hein Huss returned within. Lord Faide approached him, mouth hard, eyes bright. "What have you seen?"

"Only the keep, the walls, the towers, the roof, and Hellmouth."

"And what do you think?"

"I think many things."

"You are noncommittal; you know more than you say. It is best that you speak, because if Faide Keep falls to the savages you die with the rest of us."

Hein Huss' water-clear eyes met the brilliant black gaze of Lord Faide. "I know only what you know. The First Folk attack. They have proved they are not stupid. They intend to kill us. They are not jinxmen; they cannot afflict us or force us out. They cannot break in the walls. To burrow under, they must dig through solid rock. What are their plans? I do not know. Will they succeed? Again, I do not know. But the day of the jinxman and his orderly array of knowledge is past. I think that we must grope for miracles, blindly and foolishly, like Salazar pouring liquids on foam."

A troop of armored horsemen rode in through the gates: warriors from nearby Bellgard Hall. And as the hours passed contingents from other keeps came to Faide Keep, until the courtyard was dense with troops and horses.

Two hours before sunset the First Folk were sighted across the downs. They seemed a very large company, moving in an undisciplined clot with a number of stragglers, forerunners and wanderers out on the flanks.

The hotbloods from outside keeps came clamoring to Lord Faide, urging a charge to cut down the First Folk; they found no seconding voices among the veterans of the battle at the planting. Lord Faide, however, was pleased to see the dense mass of First Folk. "Let them approach only a mile more—and Hellmouth will take them! Jambart!"

"At your call, Lord Faide."

"Come, Hellmouth speaks!" He strode away with Jambart after. Up to the cupola they climbed.

"Roll forth Hellmouth, direct it against the savages!"

Jambart leaped to the glistening array of wheels and levers. He hesitated in perplexity, then tentatively twisted a wheel. Hellmouth responded by twisting slowly around on its radial track, to the groan and chatter of long-frozen bearings. Lord Faide's brows lowered into a menacing line. "I hear evidence of neglect."

"Neglect, my lord, never! Find one spot of rust, a shadow of grime, you may have me whipped!"

"What is that sound?"

"That is internal and invisible—none of my responsibility."

Lord Faide said nothing. Hellmouth now pointed toward the great pale tide from Wildwood. Jambart twisted a second wheel and Hellmouth thrust forth its heavy snout. Lord Faide, in a voice harsh with anger, cried, "The cover, fool!"

"An oversight, my lord, easily repaired." Jambart crawled out along the top of Hellmouth, clinging to the protuberances for dear life, with below only the long smooth sweep of roof. With considerable difficulty he tore the covering loose, then grunting and cursing, inched himself back, jerking with his knees, rearing his buttocks.

The First Folk had slowed their pace a trifle, the main body only a half-mile distant.

"Now," said Lord Faide in high excitement, "before they disperse, we exterminate them!" He sighted through a telescopic tube, squinting through the dimness of internal films and incrustations, signaled to Jambart for the final adjustments. "Now! Fire!"

Jambart pulled the firing lever. Within the great metal barrel came a sputter of clicking sounds. Hellmouth whined, roared. Its snout glowed red, orange, white, and out poured a sudden gout of blazing purple radiation—which almost instantly died. Hellmouth's barrel quivered with heat, fumed, seethed, hissed. From within came a faint pop. Then there was silence.

A hundred yards in front of the First Folk a patch of moss burnt black where the bolt had struck. The aiming device was inaccurate. Hellmouth's bolt had killed perhaps twenty of the First Folk vanguard.

Lord Faide made feverish signals. "Quick! Raise the barrel. Now! Fire again!"

Jambart pulled the firing arm, to no avail. He tried again, with the same lack of success. "Hellmouth evidently is tired."

"Hellmouth is dead," cried Lord Faide. "You have failed me. Hellmouth is extinct."

"No, no," protested Jambart. "Hellmouth rests! I nurse it as my own child! It is polished like glass! Whenever a section wears off or breaks loose, I neatly remove the fracture, and every trace of cracked glass."

Lord Faide threw up his arms, shouted in vast, inarticulate grief, ran below. "Huss! Hein Huss!"

Hein Huss presented himself. "What is your will?"

"Hellmouth has given up its fire. Conjure me more fire for Hellmouth, and quickly!"

"Impossible."

"Impossible!" cried Lord Faide. "That is all I hear from you! Impossible, useless, impractical! You have lost your ability. I will consult Isak Comandore."

"Isak Comandore can put no more fire into Hellmouth than can I."

"What sophistry is this? He puts demons into men, surely he can put fire into Hellmouth!"

"Come, Lord Faide, you are overwrought. You know the difference between jinxmanship and miracle working."

Lord Faide motioned to a servant. "Bring Isak Comandore here to me!"

Isak Comandore, face haggard, skin waxy, limped into the courtyard. Lord Faide waved peremptorily. "I need your skill. You must restore fire to Hellmouth."

Comandore darted a quick glance at Hein Huss, who stood solid and cold. Comandore decided against dramatic promises that could not be fulfilled. "I cannot do this, my lord."

"What! You tell me this, too?"

"Remark the difference, Lord Faide, between man and metal. A man's normal state is something near madness; he is at all times balanced on a knife-edge between hysteria and apathy. His senses tell him far less of the world than he thinks they do. It is a simple trick to deceive a man, to possess him with a demon, to drive him out of his mind, to kill him. But metal is insensible; metal reacts only as its shape and condition dictates, or by the working of miracles."

"Then you must work miracles!"

"Impossible."

Lord Faide drew a deep breath, collected himself. He walked swiftly across the court. "My armor, my horse. We attack."

The column formed, Lord Faide at the head. He led the knights through the portals, with armored footmen behind.

"Beware the foam!" called Lord Faide. "Attack, strike, cut, draw back. Keep your visors drawn against the wasps! Each man must kill a hundred! Attack!"

The troop rode forth against the horde of First Folk, knights in the lead. The hooves of the horses pounded softly over the thick moss; in the west the large pale sun hung close to the horizon.

Two hundred yards from the First Folk the knights touched the club-headed horses into a lope. They raised their swords, and shouting, plunged forward, each man seeking to be first. The clotted mass of First Folk separated: black beetles darted forth and after them long segmented centipede creatures. They dashed among the horses, mandibles clicking, snouts slashing. Horses screamed, reared, fell over backwards; beetles cut open armored knights as a dog cracks a bone. Lord Faide's horse threw him and ran away; he picked himself up, hacked at a nearby beetle, lopped off its front leg. It darted forward, he lopped off the leg opposite; the heavy head dipped, tore up the moss. Lord Faide cut off the remaining legs, and it lay helpless.

"Retreat," he bellowed. "Retreat!"

The knights moved back, slashing and hacking at beetles and centipedes, killing or disabling all which attacked.

"Form into a double line, knights and men. Advance slowly, supporting each other!"

The men advanced. The First Folk dispersed to meet them, armed with their thorn-swords and carrying pouches. Ten yards from the men they reached into the pouches, brought forth dark balls which they threw at the men. The balls broke and spattered on the armor.

"Charge!" bawled Lord Faide. The men sprang forward into the mass of First Folk, cutting, slashing, killing. "Kill!" called Lord Faide in exultation. "Leave not one alive!"

A pang struck him, a sting inside his armor, followed by another and another. Small things crawled inside the metal, stinging, biting, crawling. He looked about: on all sides were harrassed expressions, faces working in anguish. Sword arms fell limp as hands beat on the metal, futilely trying to scratch, rub. Two men suddenly began to tear off their armor.

"Retreat," cried Lord Faide. "Back to the keep!"

The retreat was a rout, the soldiers shedding articles of armor as they ran. After them came a flight of wasps—a dozen or more, and half as many men cried out as the poison prongs struck into their backs.

Inside the keep stormed the disorganized company, casting aside the last of their armor, slapping their skin, scratching, rubbing, crushing the ferocious red mites that infested them.

"Close the gates," roared Lord Faide.

The gates slid shut. Faide Keep was besieged.

12   During the night the First Folk surrounded the keep, forming a ring fifty yards from the walls. All night there was motion, ghostly shapes coming and going in the starlight.

Lord Faide watched from a parapet until midnight, with Hein Huss at his side. Repeatedly he asked, "What of the other keeps? Do they send further reinforcements?" to which Hein Huss each time gave the same reply: "There is confusion and doubt. The keep-lords are anxious to help but do not care to throw themselves away. At this moment they consider and take stock of the situation."

Lord Faide at last left the parapet, signaling Hein Huss to follow. He went to his trophy room, threw himself into a chair, motioned Hein Huss to be seated. For a moment he fixed the jinxman with a cool, calculating stare. Hein Huss bore the appraisal without discomfort.

"You are Head Jinxman," said Lord Faide finally. "For twenty years you have worked spells, cast hoodoos, performed auguries—more effectively than any other jinxman of Pangborn. But now I find you inept and listless. Why is this?"

"I am neither inept nor listless. I am unable to achieve beyond my abilities. I do not know how to work miracles. For this you must consult my apprentice Sam Salazar, who does not know either, but who earnestly tries every possibility and many impossibilities."

"You believe in this nonsense yourself! Before my very eyes you become a mystic!"

Hein Huss shrugged. "There are limitations to my knowledge. Miracles occur—that we know. The relics of our ancestors lie everywhere. Their methods were supernatural, repellent to our own mental processes —but think! Using these same methods the First Folk threaten to destroy us. In the place of metal they use living flesh—but the result is similar. The men of Pangborn, if they assemble and accept casualties, can drive the First Folk back to Wildwood—but for how long? A year? Ten years? The First Folk plant new trees, dig more traps—and presently come forth again, with more terrible weapons: flying beetles, large as a horse; wasps strong enough to pierce armor, lizards to scale the walls of Faide Keep."

Lord Faide pulled at his chin. "And the jinxmen are helpless?"

"You saw for yourself. Isak Comandore intruded enough into their consciousness to anger them, no more."

"So then—what must we do?"

Hein Huss held out his hands. "I do not know. I am Hein Huss, jinxman. I watch Sam Salazar with fascination. He learns nothing, but he is either too stupid or too intelligent to be discouraged. If this is the way to work miracles, he will work them."

Lord Faide rose to his feet. "I am deathly tired. I cannot think, I must sleep. Tomorrow we will know more."

Hein Huss left the trophy room, returned to the parapet. The ring of First Folk seemed closer to the walls, almost within dart-range. Behind them and across the moors stretched a long pale column of marching First Folk. A little back from the keep a pile of white material began to grow, larger and larger as the night proceeded.

Hours passed, the sky lightened; the sun rose in the east. The First Folk tramped the downs like ants, bringing long bars of hardened foam down from the north, dropping them into piles around the keep, returning into the north once more.

Lord Faide came up on the parapet, haggard and unshaven. "What is this? What do they do?"

Bernard the sergeant responded. "They puzzle us all, my lord."

"Hein Huss! What of the other keeps?"

"They have armed and mounted; they approach cautiously."

"Can you communicate our urgency?"

"I can, and I have done so. I have only accentuated their caution."

"Bah!" cried Lord Faide in disgust. "Warriors they call themselves! Loyal and faithful allies!"

"They know of your bitter experience," said Hein Huss. "They ask themselves, reasonably enough, what they can accomplish which you who are already here cannot do first."

Lord Faide laughed sourly. "I have no answer for them. In the meantime we must protect ourselves against the wasps. Armor is useless; they drive us mad with mites. . . . Bernard!"

"Yes, Lord Faide."

"Have each of your men construct a frame two-feet square, fixed with a short handle. To these frames should be sewed a net of heavy mesh. When these frames are built we will sally forth, two soldiers to guard one half-armored knight on foot."

"In the meantime," said Hein Huss, "the First Folk proceed with their plans."

Lord Faide turned to watch. The First Folk came close up under the walls carrying rods of hardened foam. "Bernard! Put your archers to work! Aim for the heads!"

Along the walls bowmen cocked their weapons. Darts spun down into the First Folk. A few were affected, turned and staggered away; others plucked away the bolts without concern. Another flight of bolts, a few more First Folk were disabled. The others planted the rods in the moss, exuded foam in great gushes, their back-flaps vigorously pumping air. Other First Folk brought more rods, pushed them into the foam. Entirely around the keep, close under the walls, extended the mound of foam. The ring of First Folk now came close and all gushed foam; it bulked up swiftly. More rods were brought, thrust into the foam, reinforcing and stiffening the mass.

"More darts!" barked Lord Faide. "Aim for the heads! Bernard—your men, have they prepared the wasp nets?"

"Not yet, Lord Faide. The project requires some little time."

Lord Faide became silent. The foam, now ten feet high, rapidly piled higher. Lord Faide turned to Hein Huss. "What do they hope to achieve?"

Hein Huss shook his head. "For the moment I am uncertain."

The first layer of foam had hardened; on top of this the First Folk spewed another layer, reinforcing again with the rods, crisscrossing, horizontal and vertical. Fifteen minutes later, when the second layer was hard the First Folk emplaced and mounted rude ladders to raise a third layer. Surrounding the keep now was a ring of foam thirty feet high and forty feet thick at the base.

"Look," said Hein Huss. He pointed up. The parasol roof overhanging the walls ended only thirty feet above the foam. "A few more layers and they will reach the roof."

"So then?" asked Lord Faide. "The roof is as strong as the walls."

"And we will be sealed within."

Lord Faide studied the foam in the light of this new thought. Already the First Folk, climbing laboriously up ladders along the outside face of their wall of foam, were preparing to lay on a fourth layer. First, rods, stiff and dry, then great gushes of white. Only twenty feet remained between roof and foam.

Lord Faide turned to the sergeant. "Prepare the men to sally forth."

"What of the wasp nets, sir?"

"Are they almost finished?"

"Another ten minutes, sir."

"Another ten minutes will see us smothering. We must force a passage through the foam."

Ten minutes passed, and fifteen. The First Folk created ramps behind their wall: first, dozens of the rods, then foam, and on top, to distribute the weight, reed mats.

Bernard the sergeant reported to Lord Faide. "We are ready."

"Good." Lord Faide descended into the courtyard. He faced the men, gave them their orders. "Move quickly, but stay together; we must not lose ourselves in the foam. As we proceed, slash ahead and to the sides. The First Folk see through the foam; they have the advantage of us. When we break through, we use the wasp nets. Two foot soldiers must guard each knight. Remember, quickly through the foam, that we do not smother. Open the gates."

The gates slid back, the troops marched forth. They faced an unbroken blank wall of foam. No enemy could be seen.

Lord Faide waved his sword. "Into the foam." He strode forward, pushed into the white mass, now crisp and brittle and harder than he had bargained for. It resisted him; he cut and hacked. His troops joined him, carving a way into the foam. First Folk appeared above them, crawling carefully on the mats. Their back flaps puffed, pumped; foam issued from their vents, falling in a cascade over the troops.

Hein Huss sighed. He spoke to Apprentice Sam Salazar. "Now they must retreat, otherwise they smother. If they fail to win through, we all smother."

Even as he spoke the foam, piling up swiftly, in places reached the roof. Below, bellowing and cursing, Lord Faide backed out from under, wiped his face clear. Once again, in desperation, he charged forward, trying at a new spot.

The foam was friable and cut easily, but the chunks detached still blocked the opening. And again down tumbled a cascade of foam, covering the soldiers.

Lord Faide retreated, waved his men back into the keep. At the same moment First Folk crawling on mats on the same level as the parapet over the gate laid rods up from the foam to rest against the projecting edge of the roof. They gushed foam; the view of the sky was slowly blocked from the view of Hein Huss and Sam Salazar.

"In an hour, perhaps two, we will die," said Hein Huss. "They have now sealed us in. There are many men here in the keep, and all will now breathe deeply."

Sam Salazar said nervously, "There is a possibility we might be able to survive—or at least not smother."

"Ah?" inquired Hein Huss with heavy sarcasm. "You plan to work a miracle?"

"If a miracle, the most trivial sort. I observed that water has no effect on the foam, nor a number of other liquids: milk, spirits, wine, or caustic. Vinegar, however, instantly dissolves the foam."

"Aha," said Hein Huss. "We must inform Lord Faide."

"Better that you do so," said Sam Salazar. "He will pay me no heed."

13   **H**alf an hour passed. Light filtered into Faide Keep only as a dim gray gloom. Air tasted flat, damp, and heavy. Out from the gates sallied the troops. Each carried a crock, a jug, a skin, or a pan containing strong vinegar.

"Quickly now," called Lord Faide, "but careful! Spare the vinegar, don't throw it wildly. In close formation now—forward."

The soldiers approached the wall, threw ladles of vinegar ahead. The foam crackled, melted.

"Waste no vinegar," shouted Lord Faide, "Forward, quickly now; bring forward the vinegar!"

Minutes later they burst out upon the downs. The First Folk stared at them, blinking.

"Charge," croaked Lord Faide, his throat thick with fumes, "Mind now, wasp nets! Two soldiers to each knight! Charge, double-quick. Kill the white beasts."

The men dashed ahead. Wasp tubes were leveled. "Halt!" yelled Lord Faide. "Wasps!"

The wasps came, wings rasping. Nets rose up; wasps struck with a thud. Down went the nets; hard feet crushed the insects. The beetles and the lizard-centipedes appeared, not so many as of the last evening, for a great number had been killed. They darted forward, and a score of men died, but the insects were soon hacked into chunks of reeking brown flesh. Wasps flew, and some struck home; the agonies of the dying men were unnerving. Presently the wasps likewise decreased in number, and soon there were no more.

The men faced the First Folk, armored only with thornswords and their foam, which now came purple with rage.

Lord Faide waved his sword: the men advanced and began to kill the First Folk, by dozens, by hundreds.

Hein Huss came forth and approached Lord Faide. "Call a halt."

"A halt? Why? Now we kill these bestial things."

"Far better not. Neither need kill the other. Now is the time to show great wisdom."

"They have besieged us, caught us in their traps, stung us with their wasps! And you say halt?"

"They nourish a grudge sixteen hundred years old. Best not to add another one."

Lord Faide stared at Hein Huss. "What do you propose?"

"Peace between the two races, peace and cooperation."

"Very well. No more traps, no more plantings, no more breeding of deadly insects."

"Call back your men. I will try."

Lord Faide cried out, "Men, fall back. Disengage."

Reluctantly the troops drew back. Hein Huss approached the huddled mass of purple-foaming First Folk. He waited a moment. They watched him intently. He spoke in their language.

"You have attacked Faide Keep; you have been defeated. You planned well, but we have proved stronger. At this moment we can kill you. Then we can go on to fire the forest, starting a hundred blazes. Some of

the fires you can control. Others not. We can destroy Wildwood. Some
First Folk may survive, to hide in the thickets and breed new plans to
kill men. This we do not want. Lord Faide has agreed to peace, if you
likewise agree. This means no more death traps. Men will freely approach and pass through the forests. In your turn you may freely come
out on the moss. Neither race shall molest the other. Which do you
choose? Extinction—or peace?"

The purple foam no longer dribbled from the vents of the First Folk.
"We choose peace."

"There must be no more wasps, beetles. The death traps must be
disarmed and never replaced."

"We agree. In our turn we must be allowed freedom of the moss."

"Agreed. Remove your dead and wounded, haul away the foam
rods."

Hein Huss returned to Lord Faide. "They have chosen peace."

Lord Faide nodded. "Very well. It is for the best." He called to his
men. "Sheathe your weapons. We have won a great victory." He ruefully
surveyed Faide Keep, swathed in foam and invisible except for the parasol roof. "A hundred barrels of vinegar will not be enough."

Hein Huss looked off into the sky. "Your allies approach quickly.
Their jinxmen have told them of your victory."

Lord Faide laughed his sour laugh. "To my allies will fall the task of
removing the foam from Faide Keep."

14

In the hall of Faide Keep, during
the victory banquet, Lord Faide called jovially across to Hein Huss.
"Now, Head Jinxman, we must deal with your apprentice, the idler and
the waster Sam Salazar."

"He is here, Lord Faide. Rise, Sam Salazar, take cognizance of the
honor being done you."

Sam Salazar rose to his feet, bowed.

Lord Faide proffered him a cup. "Drink, Sam Salazar, enjoy yourself.
I freely admit that your idiotic tinkerings saved the lives of us all. Sam
Salazar, we salute you, and thank you. Now, I trust that you will put
frivolity aside, apply yourself to your work, and learn honest jinxmanship. When the time comes, I promise that you shall find a lifetime of
employment at Faide Keep."

"Thank you," said Sam Salazar modestly. "However, I doubt if I will
become a jinxman."

"No? You have other plans?"

Sam Salazar stuttered, grew faintly pink in the face, then straightened
himself, and spoke as clearly and distinctly as he could. "I prefer to

continue what you call my frivolity. I hope I can persuade others to join me."

"Frivolity is always attractive," said Lord Faide. "No doubt you can find other idlers and wasters, runaway farm boys and the like."

Sam Salazar said staunchly, "This frivolity might become serious. Undoubtedly the ancients were barbarians. They used symbols to control entities they were unable to understand. We are methodical and rational; why can't we systematize and comprehend the ancient miracles?"

"Well, why can't we?" asked Lord Faide. "Does anyone have an answer?"

No one responded, although Isak Comandore hissed between his teeth and shook his head.

"I personally may never be able to work miracles; I suspect it is more complicated than it seems," said Sam Salazar. "However, I hope that you will arrange for a workshop where I and others who might share my views can make a beginning. In this matter I have the encouragement and the support of Head Jinxman Hein Huss."

Lord Faide lifted his goblet. "Very well, Apprentice Sam Salazar. Tonight I can refuse you nothing. You shall have exactly what you wish, and good luck to you. Perhaps you will produce a miracle during my lifetime."

Isak Comandore said huskily to Hein Huss, "This is a sad event! It signalizes intellectual anarchy, the degradation of jinxmanship, the prostitution of logic. Novelty has a way of attracting youth; already I see apprentices and spellbinders whispering in excitement. The jinxmen of the future will be sorry affairs. How will they go about demon-possession? With a cog, a gear, and a push button. How will they cast a hoodoo? They will find it easier to strike their victim with an axe."

"Times change," said Hein Huss. "There is now the one rule of Faide on Pangborn, and the keeps no longer need to employ us. Perhaps I will join Sam Salazar in his workshop."

"You depict a depressing future," said Isak Comandore with a sniff of disgust.

"There are many futures, some of which are undoubtedly depressing."

Lord Faide raised his glass. "To the best of your many futures, Hein Huss. Who knows? Sam Salazar may conjure a spaceship to lead us back to home planet."

"Who knows?" said Hein Huss. He raised his goblet. "To the best of the futures!"

THEODORE STURGEON

MEMORIAL

The Pit, in A.D. 5000, had changed little over the centuries. Still it was an angry memorial to the misuse of great power; and because of it, organized warfare was a forgotten thing. Because of it, the world was free of the wasteful smoke and dirt of industry. The scream and crash of bombs and the soporific beat of marching feet were never heard, and at long last the earth was at peace.

To go near The Pit was slow, certain death, and it was respected and feared, and would be for centuries more. It winked and blinked redly at night, and was surrounded by a bald and broken tract stretching out and away over the horizon; and around it flickered a ghostly blue glow. Nothing lived there. Nothing could.

With such a war memorial, there could only be peace. The earth could never forget the horror that could be loosed by war.

That was Grenfell's dream.

Grenfell handed the typewritten sheet back. "That's it, Jack. My idea, and—I wish I could express it like that." He leaned back against the littered workbench, his strangely asymmetrical face quizzical. "Why is it that it takes a useless person to adequately express an abstract?"

Jack Roway grinned as he took back the paper and tucked it into his breast pocket. "Interestin' question, Grenfell, because this *is* your expression, the words *are* yours. Practically verbatim. I left out the 'er's' and 'Ah's' that you play conversational hopscotch with, and strung together all the effects you mentioned without mentioning any of the technological causes. Net result: you think I did it, when you did. You think it's good writing, and I don't."

"You don't?"

Jack spread his bony length out on the hard little cot. His relaxation was a noticeable act, like the unbuttoning of a shirt collar. His body seemed to unjoint itself a little. He laughed.

"Of course I don't. Much too emotional for my taste. I'm just a fumbling aesthete—useless, did you say? Mm-m-m—yeah. I suppose so." He paused reflectively. "You see, you cold-blooded characters, you scientists, are the true visionaries. Seems to me the essential difference between a scientist and an artist is that the scientist can mix his hope with patience. The scientist visualizes his ultimate goal, but pays little attention to it. He is all caught up with the achievement of the next step upward. The artist looks so far ahead that more often than not he can't see what's under his feet; so he falls flat on his face and gets called useless by scientists. But if you strip all of the intermediate steps away from the scientist's thinking, you have an artistic concept to which the scientist responds distantly and with surprise, giving some artist credit for being deeply perspicacious purely because the artist repeated something the scientist said."

"You amaze me," Grenfell said candidly. "You wouldn't be what you are if you weren't lazy and superficial. And yet you come out with things like that. I don't know that I understand what you just said. I'll have to think—but I do believe that you show all the signs of clear thinking. With a mind like yours, I can't understand why you don't use it to build something instead of wasting it in these casual interpretations of yours."

Jack Roway stretched luxuriously. "What's the use? There's more waste involved in the destruction of something which is already built than in dispersing the energy it would take to start building something. Anyway, the world is filled with builders—and destroyers. I'd just as soon sit by and watch and feel things. I like my environment, Grenfell. I want to feel all I can of it, while it lasts. It won't last much longer. I want to touch all of it I can reach, taste of it, hear it, while there's time. What is around me, here and now, is what is important to me. The acceleration of human progress, and the increase of its mass—to use your own terms—are taking humanity straight to Limbo. You, with your work, think you are fighting humanity's inertia. Well, you are. But it's the kind of inertia called momentum. You command no force great enough to stop it, or even to change its course appreciably."

"I have subatomic power."

Roway shook his head, smiling. "That's not enough. No power is enough. It's just too late."

"That kind of pessimism does not affect me," said Grenfell. "You can gnaw all you like at my foundations, Jack, and achieve nothing more than the loss of your front teeth. I think you know that."

"Certainly I know that. I'm not trying to. I have nothing to sell, no one to change. I am even more impotent than you and your atomic power; and you are completely helpless. Uh—I quarrel with your use of the term 'pessimist,' though. I am nothing of the kind. Since I have resolved for myself the fact that humanity, as we know it, is finished, I'm quite resigned to it. Pessimism from me, under the circumstances, would be the pessimism of a photophobiac predicting that the sun would rise tomorrow."

Grenfell grinned. "I'll have to think about that, too. You're such a mass of paradoxes that turn out to be chains of reasoning. Apparently you live in a world in which scientists are poets and the grasshopper has it all over the ant."

"I always did think that ant was a stinker."

"Why do you keep coming here, Jack? What do you get out of it? Don't you realize I'm a criminal?"

Roway's eyes narrowed. "Sometimes I think you wish you were a criminal. The law says you are, and the chances are very strong that you'll be caught and treated accordingly. Ethically, you know you're not. It sort of takes the spice out of being one of the hunted."

"Maybe you're right," Grenfell said thoughtfully. He sighed. "It's so completely silly. During the war years, the skills I had were snatched up and the government flogged me into the Manhattan Project, expecting, and getting, miracles. I have never stopped working along the same lines. And now the government has changed the laws, and pulled legality from under me."

"Hardly surprising. The government deals rather severely with soldiers who go on killing other soldiers after the war is over." He held up a hand to quell Grenfell's interruption. "I know you're not killing anyone, and are working for the opposite result, I was only pointing out that it's the same switcheroo. We the people," he said didactically, "have, in our sovereign might, determined that no atomic research be done except in government laboratories. We have then permitted our politicians to allow so little for maintenance of those laboratories—unlike our overseas friends—that no really exhaustive research can be done in them. We have further made it a major offense to operate such a bootleg lab as yours." He shrugged. "Comes the end of mankind. We'll get walloped first. If we put more money and effort into nuclear research than any other country, some other country would get walloped first. If we last another hundred years—which seems doubtful—some poor, spavined, underpaid government researcher will stumble on the aluminum-isotope space-heating system you have already perfected."

"That was a little rough," said Grenfell bitterly. "Driving me underground just in time to make it impossible for me to announce it. What a waste of time and energy it is to heat homes and buildings the way they do now! Space heating—the biggest single use for heat-energy—and I have the answer to it over there." He nodded toward a compact cube of lead-alloys in the corner of the shop. "Build it into a foundation, and you have controllable heat for the life of the building, with not a cent for additional fuel and practically nothing for maintenance." His jaw knotted. "Well, I'm glad it happened that way."

"Because it got you started on your war memorial—The Pit? Yeah. Well, all I can say is, I hope you're right. It hasn't been possible to scare humanity yet. The invention of gunpowder was going to stop war, and didn't. Likewise the submarine, the torpedo, the airplane, that two-by-four bomb they pitched at Hiroshima, and the H-bomb."

"None of that applies to The Pit," said Grenfell. "You're right; humanity hasn't been scared off war yet; but the H-bomb rocked 'em back on their heels. My little memorial is the real stuff. I'm not depending on a fission or fusion effect, you know, with a release of one-tenth of one percent of the energy of the atom. I'm going to transmute it completely, and get all the energy there is in it, and in all matter the fireball touches. And it'll be *more* than a thousand times as powerful as the Hiroshima bomb, because I'm going to use twelve times as much explosive; and it's going off on the ground, not a hundred and fifty feet above it." Grenfell's brow, over suddenly hot eyes, began to shine with sweat. "And then—The Pit," he said softly. "The war memorial to end war, and all other war memorials. A vast pit, alive with bubbling lava, radiating death for ten thousand years. A living reminder of the devastation mankind has prepared for itself. Out here on the desert, where there are no cities, where the land has always been useless, will be the scene of the most useful thing in the history of the race—a never-ending sermon, a warning, an example of the dreadful antithesis of peace." His voice shook to a whisper, and faded.

"Sometimes," said Roway, "you frighten me, Grenfell. It occurs to me that I am such a studied sensualist, tasting everything I can, because I am afraid to feel any one thing that much." He shook himself, or shuddered. "You're a fanatic, Grenfell. Hyperemotional. A monomaniac. I hope you can do it."

"I can do it," said Grenfell.

Two months passed, and in those two months Grenfell's absorption in his work had been forced aside by the increasing pressure of current events. Watching a band of vigilantes riding over the waste to the south of his little buildings one afternoon, he thought grimly of what Roway had said. "Sometimes I think you wish you were a criminal." Roway, the sensualist, would say that. Roway would appreciate the taste of danger, in the same way that he appreciated all the other emotions. As it intensified, he would wait to savor it, no matter how bad it got.

Twice Grenfell shut off the instigating power of the boron-aluminum pile he had built, as he saw government helicopters hovering on the craggy skyline. He knew of hard-radiation detectors; he had developed two different types of them during the war; and he wanted no questions asked. His utter frustration at being unable to announce the success of his space-heating device, for fear that he would be punished as a criminal and his device impounded and forgotten—that frustration had been indescribable. It had canalized his mind, and intensified the devoted effort he had put forth for the things he believed in during the war. Every case of neural shock he encountered in men who had been hurt by war and despised it made him work harder on his monument—on The Pit. For if humans could be frightened by war, humanity could be frightened by The Pit.

And those he met who had been hurt by war and who still hated the late enemy—those who would have been happy to go back and kill some more, reckoning vital risk well worth it—those he considered mad, and forgot them.

So he could not stand another frustration. He was the center of his own universe, and he realized it dreadfully, and he had to justify his position there. He was a humanitarian, a philanthropist in the word's truest sense. He was probably as mad as any other man who has, through his own efforts, moved the world.

For the first time, then, he was grateful when Jack Roway arrived in his battered old convertible, although he was deliriously frightened at the roar of the motor outside his laboratory window. His usual reaction to Jack's advent was a mixture of annoyance and gratification, for it was a great deal of trouble to get out to his place. His annoyance was not because of the interruption, for Jack was certainly no trouble to have around. Grenfell suspected that Jack came out to see him partly to get the taste of the city out of his mouth, and partly to be able to feel superior to somebody he considered of worth.

But the increasing fear of discovery, and his race to complete his work before it was taken from him by a hysterical public, had had the unusual effect of making him lonely. For such a man as Grenfell to be lonely bordered on the extraordinary; for in his daily life there were simply too many things to be done. There had never been enough hours in a day nor days in a week to suit him, and he deeply resented the encroachments of sleep, which he considered a criminal waste.

"Roway!" he blurted, as he flung the door open, his tone so warm that Roway's eyebrows went up in surprise. "What dragged you out here?"

"Nothing in particular," said the writer, as they shook hands. "Nothing more than usual, which is a great deal. How goes it?"

"I'm about finished." They went inside, and as the door closed, Grenfell turned to face Jack. "I've been finished for so long I'm ashamed of myself," he said intently.

"Ha! Ardent confession so early in the day! What are you talking about?"

"Oh, there have been things to do," said Grenfell restlessly. "But I could go ahead with the . . . with the big thing at almost any time."

"You hate to be finished. You've never visualized what it would be like to have the job done." His teeth flashed. "You know, I've never heard a word from you as to what your plans are after the big noise. You going into hiding?"

"I . . . haven't thought much about it. I used to have a vague idea of broadcasting a warning and an explanation before I let go with the disruptive explosion. I've decided against it, though. In the first place, I'd be stopped within minutes, no matter how cautious I was with the transmitter. In the second place—well, this is going to be so big that it won't need any explanation."

"No one will know who did it, or why it was done."

"Is that necessary?" asked Grenfell quietly.

Jack's mobile face stilled as he visualized The Pit, spewing its ten thousand-year hell. "Perhaps not," he said. "Isn't it necessary, though, to you?"

"To me?" asked Grenfell, surprised. "You mean, do I care if the world knows I did this thing, or not? No; of course I don't. A chain of circumstance is occurring, and it has been working through me. It goes directly to The Pit; The Pit will do all that is necessary from then on. I will no longer have any part in it."

Jack moved, clinking and splashing, around the sink in the corner of the laboratory. "Where's all your coffee? Oh—here. Uh . . . I have been curious about how much personal motive you had for your work. I think that answers it pretty well. I think, too, that you believe what you are saying. Do you know that people who do things for impersonal motives are as rare as fur on a fish?"

"I hadn't thought about it."

"I believe that, too. Sugar? And milk. I remember. And have you been listening to the radio?"

"Yes. I'm . . . a little upset, Jack," said Grenfell, taking the cup. "I don't know where to time this thing. I'm a technician, not a Machiavelli."

"Visionary, like I said. You don't know if you'll throw this gadget of yours into world history too soon or too late—is that it?"

"Exactly. Jack, the whole world seems to be going crazy. Even fusion bombs are too big for humanity to handle."

"What else can you expect," said Jack grimly, "with our dear friends across the water sitting over their push buttons waiting for an excuse to punch them?"

"And we have our own set of buttons, of course."

Jack Roway said: "We've got to defend ourselves."

"Are you kidding?"

Roway glanced at him, his dark brows plotting a V. "Not about this. I seldom kid about anything, but particularly not about this." And he—shuddered.

Grenfell stared amazedly at him and then began to chuckle. "Now," he said, "I've seen everything. My iconoclastic friend Jack Roway, of all people, caught up by a . . . a fashion. A national pastime, fostered by uncertainty and fed by yellow journalism—fear of the enemy."

"This country is not at war."

"You mean, we have no enemy? Are you saying that the gentlemen over the water, with their itching fingertips hovering about the push buttons, are not our enemies?"

"Well—"

Grenfell came across the room to his friend, and put a hand on his shoulder. "Jack—what's the matter? You can't be so troubled by the news—not *you!*"

Roway stared out at the brazen sun, and shook his head slowly. "International balance is too delicate," he said softly; and if a voice could glaze like eyes, his did. "I see the nations of the world as masses balanced each on its own mathematical point, each with its center of gravity directly above. But the masses are fluid, shifting violently away from the center lines. The opposing trends aren't equal; they can't cancel each other; the phasing is too slow. One or the other is going to topple, and then the whole works is going to go."

"But you've known that for a long time. You've known that ever since Hiroshima. Possibly before. Why should it frighten you now?"

"I didn't think it would happen so soon."

"Oh-ho! So that's it! You have suddenly realized that the explosion is going to come in your lifetime. Hm-m-m? And you can't take that. You're capable of all of your satisfying aesthetic rationalizations as long as you can keep the actualities at arm's length!"

"*Whew!*" said Roway, his irrepressible humor passing close enough to nod to him. "Keep it clean, Grenfell! Keep your . . . your sesquipedalian polysyllabics for a scientific report."

"Touché!" Grenfell smiled. "Y'know, Jack, you remind me powerfully of some erstwhile friends of mine who write science-fiction. They had been living very close to atomic power for a long time—years before the man on the street—or the average politician, for that matter —knew an atom from Adam. Atomic power was handy to these specialized word-merchants because it gave them a limitless source of power for background to a limitless source of story material. In the heyday of the Manhattan Project, most of them suspected what was going on, some of them knew—some even worked on it. All of them were quite aware of the terrible potentialities of nuclear energy. Practically all of them were scared silly of the whole idea. They were afraid for humanity, but they themselves were not really afraid, except in a delicious drawing room sort of way, because they couldn't conceive of this Buck Rogers event happening to anything but posterity. But it happened, right smack in the middle of their own sacrosanct lifetimes.

"And I will be doggoned if you're not doing the same thing. You've gotten quite a bang out of figuring out the doom humanity faces in an atomic war. You've consciously risen above it by calling it inevitable, and in the meantime leave us gather rosebuds before it rains. You thought you'd be safe home—dead—before the first drops fell. Now social progress has rolled up a thunderhead and you find yourself a mile from home with a crease in your pants and no umbrella. And you're scared!"

Roway looked at the floor and said, "It's so soon. It's so soon." He looked up at Grenfell, and his cheekbones seemed too large. He took a deep breath. "You . . . we can stop it, Grenfell."

"Stop what?"

"The war . . . the . . . this thing that's happening to us. The explosion that will come when the strains get too great in the international situation. And it's *got* to be stopped!"

"That's what The Pit is for."

"The Pit!" Roway said scornfully. "I've called you a visionary before. Grenfell, you've got to be more practical! Humanity is not going to learn anything by example. It's got to be kicked and carved. Surgery."

Grenfell's eyes narrowed. "Surgery? What you said a minute ago about my stopping it . . . do you mean what I think you mean?"

"Don't you see it?" said Jack urgently. "What you have here—the total conversion of mass to energy—the peak of atomic power. One or two wallops with this, in the right place, and we can stop anybody."

"This isn't a weapon. I didn't make this to be a weapon."

"The first rock ever thrown by a prehistoric man wasn't made to be a weapon, either. But it was handy and it was effective, and it was certainly used because it had to be used." He suddenly threw up his hands in a despairing gesture. "You don't understand. Don't you realize that this country is likely to be attacked at any second—that diplomacy is now hopeless and helpless, and the whole world is just waiting for the thing to start? It's probably too late even now—but it's the least we can do."

"What, specifically, is the least thing we can do?"

"Turn your work over to the Defense Department. In a few hours the government can put it where it will do the most good." He drew his finger across his throat. "Anywhere we want to, over the ocean."

There was a taut silence. Roway looked at his watch and licked his lips. Finally Grenfell said, "Turn it over to the government. Use it for a weapon—and what for? To stop war?"

"Of course!" blurted Roway. "To show the rest of the world that our way of life . . . to scare the daylights out of . . . to—"

"Stop it!" Grenfell roared. "Nothing of the kind. You think—you hope anyway—that the use of total disruption as a weapon will stall off the inevitable—at least in your lifetime. Don't you?"

"No. I—"

"Don't you?"

"Well, I—"

"You have some more doggerel to write," said Grenfell scathingly. "You have some more blondes to chase. You want to go limp over a few more Bach fugues."

Jack Roway said: "No one knows where the first bomb might hit. It might be anywhere. There's nowhere I . . . we . . . can go to be safe." He was trembling.

"Are the people in the city quivering like that?" asked Grenfell.

"Riots," breathed Roway, his eyes bright with panic. "The radio won't announce anything about the riots."

"Is that what you came out here for today—to try to get me to give disruptive power to *any* government?"

Jack looked at him guiltily. "It was the only thing to do. I don't know if your bomb will turn the trick, but it has to be tried. It's the only thing left. We've got to be prepared to hit first, and hit harder than anyone else."

"No." Grenfell's one syllable was absolutely unshakable.

"Grenfell—I thought I could argue you into it. Don't make it tough for yourself. You've got to do it. Please do it on your own. Please, Grenfell." He stood up slowly.

"Do it on my own—or what? *Keep away from me!*"

"No . . . I—" Roway stiffened suddenly, listening. From far above and to the north came the whir of rotary wings. Roway's fear-slackened lips tightened into a grin, and with two incredibly swift strides he was across to Grenfell. He swept in a handful of the smaller man's shirt front and held him half off the floor.

"Don't try a thing," he gritted. There was not a sound then except their harsh breathing, until Grenfell said wearily: "There was somebody called Judas—"

"You can't insult me," said Roway, with a shade of his old cockiness, "and you're flattering yourself."

A helicopter sank into its own roaring dust-cloud outside the building. Men pounded out of it and burst in the door. There were three of them. They were not in uniform.

"Dr. Grenfell," said Jack Roway, keeping his grip, "I want you to meet—"

"Never mind that," said the tallest of the three in a brisk voice. "You're Roway? Hm-m-m. Dr. Grenfell, I understand you have a nuclear energy device on the premises."

"Why did you come by yourself?" Grenfell asked Roway softly. "Why not just send these stooges?"

"For you, strangely enough. I hoped I could argue you into giving the thing freely. You know what will happen if you resist?"

"I know." Grenfell pursed his lips for a moment, and then turned to the tall man. "Yes. I have some such thing here. Total atomic disruption. Is that what you were looking for?"

"Where is it?"

"Here, in the laboratory, and then there's the pile in the other building. You'll find—" He hesitated. "You'll find two samples of the concentrate. One's over there—" He pointed to a lead case on a shelf behind one of the benches. "And there's another like it in a similar case in the shed back of the pile building."

Roway sighed and released Grenfell. "Good boy. I knew you'd come through."

"Yes," said Grenfell. "Yes—"

"Go get it," said the tall man. One of the others broke away.

"It will take two men to carry it," said Grenfell in a shaken voice. His lips were white.

The tall man pulled out a gun and held it idly. He nodded to the second man. "Go get it. Bring it here and we'll strap the two together and haul 'em to the plane. Snap it up."

The two men went out toward the shed.

"Jack?"

"Yes, Doc."

"You really think humanity can be scared?"

"It will be—now. This thing will be used right."

"I hope so. Oh, I hope so," Grenfell whispered.

The men came back. "Up on the bench," said the leader, nodding toward the case the men carried between them.

As they climbed up on the bench and laid hands on the second case, to swing it down from the shelf, Jack Roway saw Grenfell's face spurt sweat, and a sudden horror swept over him.

"Grenfell!" he said hoarsely. "It's—"

"Of course," Grenfell whispered. "Critical mass."

When the two leaden cases came together, it let go.

It was like Hiroshima, but much bigger. And yet, that explosion did not create The Pit. It was the pile that did—the boron-aluminum lattice which Grenfell had so arduously pieced together from parts bootlegged over the years. Right there at the heart of the fission explosion, total disruption took place in the pile, for that was its function. This was slower. It took more than an hour for its hellish activity to reach a peak, and in that time a huge crater had been gouged out of the earth, a seething, spewing mass of volatized elements, raw radiation, and incandescent gases. It was—The Pit. Its activity curve was plotted abruptly —up to peak in an hour and eight minutes, and then a gradual subsidence as it tried to feed further afield with less and less fueling effect, and as it consumed its own flaming wastes in an effort to reach inactivity. Rain would help to blanket it, through energy lost in volatilizing the drops; and each of the many elements involved went through its respective secondary radioactivity, and passed away its successive half-lives. The subsidence of The Pit would take between eight and nine thousand years.

And like Hiroshima, this explosion had effects which reached into history and into men's hearts in places far separated in time from the cataclysm itself.

These things happened:

The explosion could not be concealed; and there was too much hysteria afoot for anything to be confirmed. It was easier to run headlines saying WE ARE ATTACKED. There was an instantaneous and panicky demand for reprisals, and the government acceded, because such "reprisals" suited the policy of certain members who could command emergency powers. And so the First Atomic War was touched off.

And the Second.

There were no more atomic wars after that. The Mutants' War was a barbarous affair, and the mutants defeated the tattered and largely sterile remnants of humanity, because the mutants were strong. And then the mutants died out because they were unfit. For a while there was some very interesting material to be studied on the effects of radiation on heredity, but there was no one to study it.

There were some humans left. The rats got most of them, after increasing in fantastic numbers; and there were three plagues.

After that there were half-stooping, naked things whose twisted heredity could have been traced to humankind; but these could be frightened, as individuals and as a race, so therefore they could not progress. They were certainly not human.

> "The Pit, in A.D. 5000, had changed little over the centuries. Still it was an angry memorial to the misuse of great power; and because of it, organized warfare was a forgotten thing. Because of it, the world was free of the wasteful smoke and dirt of industry. The scream and crash of bombs and the soporific beat of marching feet were never heard, and at long last the earth was at peace.
>
> To go near The Pit was slow, certain death, and it was respected and feared, and would be for centuries more. It winked and blinked redly at night, and was surrounded by a bald and broken tract stretching out and away over the horizon; and around it flickered a ghostly blue glow. Nothing lived there. Nothing could.
>
> With such a war memorial, there could only be peace. The earth could never forget the horror that could be loosed by war.
>
> That was Grenfell's dream.

EDWARD BRYANT
SHARK

The war came and left but returned for him eighteen years later.

Folger should have known when the clouds of smaller fish disappeared. He should have guessed but he was preoccupied stabilizing the cage at ten meters, then sliding out the upper hatch. Floating free, he stared into the gray-green South Atlantic. Nothing. With his tongue he keyed the mike embedded in his mouthpiece. The sonex transmitter clipped to his tanks coded and beamed the message: "Query—Valerie—location." He repeated it. Electronics crackled in his ear, but there was no response.

Something moved to his right—something a darker gray, a darker green than the water. Then Folger saw the two dark eyes. Her body took form in the murk. A blunt torpedo shape gliding, she struck impossibly fast.

It was Folger's mistake and nearly fatal. He had hoped she would circle first. The great white shark bore straight in, mouth grinning open. Folger saw the teeth, only the teeth, rows of ragged white. "Query—" he screamed into the sonex.

Desperately he brought the shark billy in his right hand forward. The great white jaws opening and closing, triangular teeth knifing, whipped past soundlessly.

Folger lifted the billy—tried to lift it—saw the blood and the white ends protruding below his elbow and realized he was seeing surgically sawed bone.

The shock made everything deceptively easy. Folger reached behind him, felt the cage, and pulled himself up toward the hatch. The shark flowed into the distance.

One-handed, it was difficult entering the cage. He was half through the hatch and had turned the flotation control all the way up when he blacked out.

Her name, like that of half the other women in the village, was Maria. For more than a decade she had kept Folger's house. She cleaned, after a fashion. She cooked his two meals a day, usually boiled potatoes or mutton stew. She loved him with a silent, bitter, unrequited passion. Over all the years, they had never talked of it. They were not lovers; each night after fixing supper, she returned to her clay-and-stone house in the village. Had Folger taken a woman from the village, Maria would have knifed both of them as they slept. That problem had never arisen.

"People for you," said Maria.

Folger looked up from his charts. "Who?"

"No islanders."

Folger hadn't had an off-island visitor since two years before, when a Brazilian journalist had come out on the semiannual supply boat.

"You want them?" said Maria.

"Can I avoid it?"

Maria lowered her voice. "Government."

"Shit," said Folger. "How many?"

"Just two. You want the gun?" The sawed-off twelve-gauge, swathed in oilcloth, leaned in the kitchen closet.

"No." Folger sighed. "Bring them in."

Maria muttered something as she turned back through the doorway.

"What?"

She shook her matted black hair. "One is a woman!" she spat.

Valerie came to his quarters later in the afternoon. The project manager had already spoken to Folger. Knowing what she would say, Folger had two uncharacteristically stiff drinks before she arrived. "You can't be serious," was the first thing he said.

She grinned. "So they told you."

He said, "I can't allow it."

The grin vanished. "Don't talk as though you owned me."

"I'm not, I'm just—" He floundered. "Damn it, it's a shock."

She took his hand and drew him down beside her on the couch. "Would I deny your dreams?"

His voice pleaded. "You're my lover."

Valerie looked away. "It's what I want."

"You're crazy."

"You can be an oceanographer," she said. "Why can't I be a shark?"

Maria ushered in the visitors with ill grace. "Get along," she said out in the hallway. "Señor Folger is a busy man."

"We will not disturb him long," said a woman's voice.

The visitors, as they entered, had to duck to clear the doorframe. The woman was nearly two meters in height; the man half a head taller. Identically clad in gray jump-suits, they wore identical smiles. They were—Folger searched for the right word—extreme. Their hair was too soft and silkily pale; their eyes too obviously blue, teeth too white and savage.

The pair looked down at Folger. "I am Inga Lindfors," said the woman. "My brother, Per." The man nodded slightly.

"Apparently you know who I am," said Folger.

"You are Marcus Antonius Folger," Inga Lindfors said.

"It was supposed to be Marcus Aurelius," Folger said irrelevantly. "My father never paid close attention to the classics."

"The fortune of confusion," said Inga. "I find Mark Antony the more fascinating. He was a man of decisive action."

Bewildered, Maria stared from face to face.

"You were a component of the Marine Institute on East Falkland," said Per.

"I was. It was a long time ago."

"We wish to speak with you," said Inga, "as representatives of the Protectorate of Old America."

"So? Talk."

"We speak officially."

"Oh." Folger smiled at Maria. "I must be alone with these people."

The island woman looked dubiously at the Lindfors. "I will be in the kitchen," she said.

"It is a formidable journey to Tres Rocas," said Per. "Our airboat left Cape Pembroke ten hours ago. Unfavorable winds."

Folger scratched himself and said nothing.

Inga laughed, a young girl's laugh in keeping with her age. "Marcus Antonius Folger, you've been too long away from American civilization."

"I doubt it," said Folger. "You've obviously gone to a lot of trouble to find me. Why?"

Why?

She always asked him questions when they climbed the rocks above the headland. Valerie asked and Folger answered and usually they both learned. Why the Falklands' seasonal temperature range was only ten degrees; what were quasars; how did third-generation computers differ from second; how dangerous were manta rays; when would the universe die. Today she asked a new question:

"What about the war?"

He paused, leaning into a natural chimney. "What do you mean?" *The cold passed into his cheek, numbed his jaw, made the words stiff.*

Valerie said, "I don't understand the war."

"Then you know what I know." Folger stared down past the rocks to the sea. How do you explain masses of people killing other people? He could go through the glossary—romary, secondary, tertiary targets; population priorities; death-yields—but so what? It didn't give credence or impact to the killing taking place on the land, in space, and below the seas.

"I don't know anything," said Valerie somberly. "Only what they tell us."

"Don't question them," said Folger. "They're a little touchy."

"But why?"

"The Protectorate remembers its friends," said Per.

Folger began to laugh. "Don't try to snow me. At the peak of my loyalty to the Protectorate—or what the Protectorate was then—I was apolitical."

"Twenty years ago, that would have been treason."

"But not now," said Inga quickly. "Libertarianism has made a great resurgence."

"So I hear. The boat brings magazines once in a while."

"The years of reconstruction have been difficult. We could have used your expertise on the continent."

"I was used here. Occasionally I find ways to help the islanders."

"As an oceanographer?"

Folger gestured toward the window. "The sea makes up most of their environment. I'm useful."

"With your talent," said Per, "it's such a waste here."

"Then too," Folger continued, "I help with the relics."

"Relics?" said Inga uncertainly.

"War surplus. Leftovers. Look." Folger picked up a dried, leathery rectangle from the table and tossed it to Per. He looked at the object, turning it over and over.

"Came from a killer whale. Got him last winter with a harpoon and shaped charge. Damn thing had stove in three boats, killed two men. Now read the other side."

Per examined the piece of skin closely. Letters and numerals had been deeply branded. "USMF-343."

"See?" said Folger. "Weapons are still out there. He was part of the lot the year before I joined the Institute. Not especially sophisticated, but he had longevity."

"Do you encounter many?" said Inga.

Folger shook his head. "Not too many of the originals."

The ketch had been found adrift with no one aboard. It had put out early that morning for Dos, one of the two small and uninhabited companions of Tres Rocas. The three men aboard had been expecting to hunt seal. The fishermen who discovered the derelict also found a bloody ax and severed sections of tentacle as thick as a man's forearm.

So Folger trolled along the route of the unlucky boat in his motorized skiff for three days. He searched a vast area of choppy, gray water, an explosive harpoon never far from his hand. Early on the fourth afternoon a half dozen dark-green tentacles poked from the sea on the port side of the boat. Folger reached with his left hand for the harpoon. He didn't see the tentacle from starboard that whipped and tightened around his chest and jerked him over the side.

The chill of the water stunned him. Folger had a quick, surrealistic glimpse of intricately weaving tentacles. Two eyes, each as large as his fist, stared without malice. The tentacle drew him toward the beak.

Then a gray shadow angled below Folger. Razor teeth scythed through flesh. The tentacle was cut; Folger drifted.

The great white shark was at least ten meters long. Its belly was uncharacteristically dappled. The squid wrapped eager arms around the thrashing shark. The two sank into the darker water below Folger.

Lungs aching, he broke the surface less than a meter from the skiff. He always trailed a ladder from the boat. It made things easier for a one-armed man.

"Would you show us the village?" said Inga.

"Not much to see."

"We would be pleased by a tour anyway. Have you time?"

Folger reached for his coat. Inga moved to help him put it on. "I can get it," said Folger.

"There are fine experts in prosthesis on the continent," said Per.

"No thanks," said Folger.

"Have you thought about a replacement?"

"Thought about it. But the longer I thought, the better I got without one. I had a few years to practice."

"It was in the war, then?" asked Inga.

"Of course it was in the war."

On their way out, they passed the kitchen. Maria looked up sullenly over the scraps of bloody mutton on the cutting board. Her eyes fixed on Inga until the blonde moved out of sight along the hall.

A light, cold rain was falling as they walked down the trail to the village. "Rain is the only thing I could do without here," said Folger. "I was raised in California."

"We will see California after we finish here," said Inga. "Per and I have a leave. We will get our anti-rad injections and ski the Sierras. At night we will watch the Los Angeles glow."

"Is it beautiful?"

"The glow is like seeing the aurora borealis every night," said Per.

Folger chuckled. "I always suspected L.A.'s future would be something like that."

"The half-life will see to the city's immortality," said Inga.

Per smiled. "We were there last year. The glow appears cold. It is supremely erotic."

In the night, in a bed, he asked her, "Why do you want to be a shark?"

She ran her nails delicately along the cords of his neck. "I want to kill people, eat them."

"Any people?"

"Just men."

"Would you like me to play analyst?" said Folger. She bit his shoulder hard. "Goddammit!" He flopped over. "Is there any blood?" he demanded.

Valerie brushed the skin with her hand. "You're such a coward."

"My threshold of pain's low," said Folger. "Sweetie."

"Don't call me Sweetie," she said. "Call me Shark."

"Shark."

They made love in a desperate hurry.

The descent steepened, the rain increased, and they hurried. They passed through a copse of stunted trees and reached the ruts of a primitive road.

"We have flash-frozen beefsteaks aboard the airboat," said Inga.

"That's another thing I've missed," Folger said.

"Then you must join us for supper."

"As a guest of the Protectorate?"

"An honored guest."

"Make mine rare," said Folger. "Very rare."

The road abruptly descended between two bluffs and overlooked the village. It was called simply the village because there were no other settlements on Tres Rocas and so no cause to distinguish. Several hundred inhabitants lived along the curve of the bay in small, one-story houses, built largely of stone.

"It's so bleak," said Inga. "What do people do?"

"Not much," said Folger. "Raise sheep, hunt seals, fish. When there were still whales, they used to whale. For recreation, the natives go out and dig peat for fuel."

"It's quite a simple existence," said Per.

"Uncomplicated," Folger said.

"If you could be anything in the sea," said Valerie, "what would it be?"

Folger was always discomfited by these games. He usually felt he chose wrong answers. He thought carefully for a minute or so. "A dolphin, I suppose."

In the darkness, her voice dissolved in laugher. "You lose!"

He felt irritation. "What's the matter now?"

"Dolphins hunt in packs," *she said.* "They gang up to kill sharks. They're cowards."

"They're not. Dolphins are highly intelligent. They band together for cooperative protection."

Still between crests of laughter: "Cowards!"

On the outskirts of the village they encountered a dozen small, dirty children playing a game. The children had dug a shallow pit about a meter in diameter. It was excavated close enough to the beach so that it quickly filled with a mixture of ground seepage and rainwater.

"Stop," said Per. "I wish to see this."

The children stirred the muddy water with sticks. Tiny, thumb-sized fishes lunged and snapped at one another, burying miniature teeth in the others' flesh. The children stared up incuriously at the adults, then returned their attention to the pool.

Inga bent closer. "What are they?"

"Baby sharks," said Folger. "They hatch alive in the uterus of their mother. Some fisherman must have bagged a female sand tiger who was close to term. He gave the uterus to his kids. Fish won't live long in that pool."

"They're fantastic," Per breathed. For the first time since Folger had met him, he showed emotion. "So young and so ferocious."

"The first one hatched usually eats the others in the womb," said Folger.

"It's beautiful," said Inga. "An organism that is born fighting."

The sibling combat in the pit had begun to quiet. A few sand tiger babies twitched weakly. The children nudged them with the sticks. When there was no response, the sticks rose and fell violently, splashing the water and mashing the fish into the sand.

"The islanders hate sharks," Folger said.

She awoke violently, choking off a scream and blindly striking out at him. Folger held her wrists, pulled her against him, and then began to stroke her hair. Her trembling slowly subsided.

"Bad dreams?"

She nodded, her hair working softly against his jaw.

"Was I in them?"

"No," *she said.* "Maybe. I don't know. I don't think so."

"What happened?"

She hesitated. "I was swimming. They—some people pulled me out of the water. They put me on a concrete slab by the pier. There was no water, no sea—" *She swallowed.* "God, I want a drink."

"I'll fix you one," he said.

"They pulled me out. I lay there and felt the ocean drain away. And then I felt things tear loose inside me. There was nothing supporting my heart and liver and intestines and everything began to pull away from everything else. God, it hurts—"

Folger patted her head. "I'll get you a drink."

"So?" said Per. "Sharks aren't particularly aggressive, are they?"

"Not until after the war," said Folger. "Since then there's been continual skirmishing. Both the villagers and the sharks hunt the same game. Now they've started to hunt each other."

"And," said Inga, "there has been you."

Folger nodded. "I know the sea predators better. After all, that was my job."

The children, bored with the dead shark pool, followed the adults toward the village. They gawked at the Lindfors. One of the more courageous boys reached tentatively toward Inga's hair as it blew back in the wind.

"Vayan!" shouted Folger. "All of you, move!" The children reluctantly withdrew. "They're accustomed to whites," he said, "but blondes are a novelty."

"Fascinating," said Inga. "It is like an enclave of a previous century."

The road widened slightly and became the village's main street, still unpaved, and winding down along the edge of the sea. Folger saw the aluminum bulk of an airboat tied to a pier, incongruous between two fishing ketches. "You come alone?" he said.

"Just the two of us," said Inga.

Per put his hand lightly on her wrist. "We're quite effective as a team," he said.

They passed a dark stone house, its door swung open to the wind. Rain blew across the threshold.

"Abandoned?" said Inga.

"Quaint old island custom," said Folger. "Catholicism's a little diluted here. Priest only comes twice a year." He pointed at the open door. "The man who lived there died at sea a couple days ago. Family'll keep the door open, no matter what, for a week. It's so his soul can find shelter until it's shunted to heaven or hell."

Per said, "What happened to the man?"

"He was fishing," Folger said. "Friends saw it all. A great white shark got him."

Closer, now:

"Dolphin!"

"Shark!"

They lay together.

"I wish we had more time," said Inga. "I should like to hunt a shark."

"Perhaps on some future leave," said Per.

"And that's about it for the village," said Folger. "There isn't much more to see, unless you enjoy native crafts like dipping tallow candles or carding wool."

"It's incredible," said Inga. "The only time I have seen anything remotely like this was in pre-Reconstruction America."

Folger said, "You don't look that old."

"I was barely into puberty. The Protectorate brought our father from Copenhagen. He is a design engineer in hydroelectrics. He worked on the Oklahoma Sea projects."

They stood on a rough plank pier beyond one horn of the crescent of houses. Per tapped a boot on the wood to shake loose some of the mud. "I still can't see how you endure this place, Folger."

Half asleep, Folger said, "Some day when the war is over, we'll get a place by the ocean. There's still some great country north of San Francisco. We'll have a house among the trees, on a mountainside overlooking the beach. Maybe we'll make it a stone tower, like Robinson Jeffers built."

Close to his ear, Valerie said, "A tower would be nice."

"You'll be able to read all day, and swim, and we'll never have any visitors we don't want."

"It's a fine dream for you," Valerie whispered.

"I came as jetsam," Folger said.

The three of them stood silently for a few minutes, watching clouds darker than the water roil in from the west. Triangular shapes took form on the horizon. Folger squinted. "Fishermen are coming in." After another minute he said, "Tour's over."

"I know," said Inga.

"—hoping. I kept hoping." Folger raised himself on one elbow. "You really are going to go through with it."

The fishing boats neared the breakwater. Folger and the others could hear the faint cries of the crewmen. "Why are you here?" he said.

Per Lindfors laid a comradely hand on Folger's shoulder. "We came here to kill you."

Folger smiled. What other response could there be?

"Tell me how it works," said Valerie.

They paused on a steel catwalk overlooking the catch pens. In the tank immediately below, two divers warily man-handled a five-meter great blue in an oval path. If water weren't forced over the shark's gill surfaces, the fish would suffocate. The water glittered in the glare of arc lights. Beyond the pens, the beacon on Cape Pembroke blinked its steady twelve pulses per minute.

"*I know the general techniques,*" *said Folger.* "*But it's not my specialty. I'm strictly mapping and logistics.*"

"*I don't need apologies,*" *said Valerie.*

"*Excuse me while I violate the National Security Act.*" *Folger turned to face her.* "*Most of the technology is borrowed from the brothers upstairs on the orbital platforms. Everybody's been doing secret work with cyborgs. Somewhere along the line, somebody got the bright idea of importing it underwater.*"

"*The Marine Forces,*" *said Valerie.*

"*Right. The bureaucrats finally realized that the best weapons for fighting undersea wars already existed in the ocean. They were weapons which had been adapted for that purpose for more than a hundred million years. All that was needed were guidance systems.*"

Valerie said wistfully, "*Sharks.*"

"*Sharks and killer whales; squid; to a degree, dolphins. We're considering a few other species.*"

"*I want to know how it's done.*"

"*Primarily by direct transplant. Surgical modification. Nerve grafts are partially electronic. Is that what you wanted to know?*"

She stared down at the docile shark in the tank. "*There's no coming back, is there?*"

"*We'll probably use your old body to feed the new one.*"

"So kill me. Do I rate a reason why?"

"Not if your execution had been scheduled now," said Inga. "It would not have been merciful to alert you in advance. Such cheap melodrama is forbidden by Protectorate codes."

Folger snorted. "Isn't all this overly Machiavellian?"

"Not at all. We were given considerable latitude on this assignment. We wished to be sure of doing the right thing."

"*—come down to the point of whether or not I'll stop you from doing this.*" *Wind off the headland deadened his words.*

"*Can you stop me?*" *Valerie's voice was flat, without challenge.*

He didn't answer.

"*Would you?*" *Valerie kissed him gently on the side of the throat.* "*Here's a Hindu proverb for you. 'The woman you love, you must not possess.'*"

He said in a whisper, without looking at her, "*I love you.*"

"If you're not going to kill me," Folger said, "I've got work to do."

"Folger, what is your fondest wish?"

He stared at her with enigmatic eyes. "You can't give it to me."

"Wealth?" said Per. "Recognition? You had a considerable reputation before the war."

"When we leave," said Inga, "we want you to return with us."

Folger looked slowly from one to the other. "Leave the island?"

"A center for deep Pacific studies is opening on Guam," Inga said. "The directorship is yours."

"I don't believe any of this," said Folger. "I'm in my fifties and even considering the postwar chaos, I'm a decade behind my field."

"Some refresher study at the University of San Juan," said Per.

Inga said, "Reconstruction is not all that complete. Genius is uncommon. You are needed, Folger."

"Death or a directorship," said Folger.

Folger spoke to the project manager in a sterile cubicle off the operating theater. "What are her chances?"

"For survival? Excellent."

"I mean afterwards."

The project manager drew deeply on his extinguished pipe. "Can't say. Test data's been spotty."

"Christ, Danny!" Folger swung around. "Don't doubletalk me. What's that mean?"

The project manager evaded Folger's eyes. "A high proportion of the test subjects haven't returned from field trials. The bio boys think it may have something to do with somatic memory, cellular retention of the old, nonhuman personality."

"And you didn't tell us anything about this?"

"Security, Marc." The project manager looked uncomfortable. "I never know from day to day what's under wraps. You know, we haven't had radio reception for twelve days now. Nobody knows—"

"I swear, Danny, if anything happens to her—"

The pipe dropped from the project manager's open mouth. "But she's a volunteer—"

It was the first time Folger had ever struck another human being.

"Elections are approaching on the continent," said Inga.

"Free?"

"Of course," said Per.

"Reasonably," said Inga. "Within the needs of reconstruction."

A crowd of children scampered past. Farther down the beach, the fishermen began to unload the day's catch.

"Do you remember a man named Diaz-Gomide?" said Per.

"No."

"He is a Brazilian journalist."

"Yes," said Folger. "About two years ago, right?"

Per nodded. "He is not only a journalist, but also a higher-up in the opposition party. He is their shadow minister of information."

"Senhor Diaz-Gomide has proved a great embarrassment to the present administration," said Inga.

"The same regime that's been in power for a quarter century," said Folger.

Inga made a noncommittal gesture. "Someone had to keep order through the war and after."

"The point is," said Per, "that this Diaz-Gomide has been disseminating historical lies on behalf of his party."

"Let me guess," said Folger. He walked slowly toward the end of the pier and the Lindfors followed. "He had disclosed terrible things about the government in connection with the Marine Institute on East Falkland."

"Among other fabrications," said Per.

Folger stopped with his toes overhanging the water. "He alleged that inhuman experiments were carried on, that the brains of unwilling or unknowing subjects were transplanted into the bodies of sea creatures."

"Something like that, except he couched it in less clinical language."

"Down the rabbit hole." Folger shook his head slowly. "What do you want from me—a disclaimer?"

Inga said, "We suspect Diaz-Gomide grossly distorted your statements in the interview. It would be well if you set the record straight."

"The Marine Forces experiments have been greatly exaggerated," said Per.

"Probably not," said Folger.

They stared at each other.

Folger floated in the center of the holding tank. The whisper of the regulator sounded extraordinarily loud in his ears. He turned to follow the great white shark as it slowly circled, its eye continually focused on Folger. The shark—he found difficulty ascribing it her name—moved fluidly, weaving, head traveling from side to side slowly with the rhythm of its motion through the water.

She—he made the attempt—she was beautiful; implacably, savagely so. He had seldom been this close to a shark. He watched silently her body crease with a thousand furrows, every movement emphasizing musculature. He had never seen beauty so deadly.

After a time, he tried the sonex. "Valerie—inquiry—what is it like."

The coded reply came back and unscrambled. "Marc—never know—mass&bulk&security—better."

He sent: "Inquiry—happy."

"Yes."

They exchanged messages for a few minutes more. He asked, "Inquiry—what will they do with you."

"Assigned soldier—picket duty—Mariana Trench."

"Inquiry—when."

"Never—never soldier—run away first."

"So," said Folger. "Recant or die?"

"We would like to see you take the directorship of the research center on Guam," said Inga.

Folger found the paper among other poems scattered like dry leaves in Valerie's room:

> *"In the void, inviolate*
> > *from what she was*
> > > *is*
> > > > *and will be"*

He went outside to the catch pens. From the catwalk he looked into the tank. The shark circled ceaselessly. She swung around to his side and Folger watched the dark back, the mottled gray-and-white belly slide by. He watched until darkness fell.

"Do I get time to consider the offer?" Folger asked.

The Lindfors looked at each other, considering.

"I was never good at snap decisions."

"We would like to tidy up this affair—" said Per.

"I know," Folger said. "Skiing the Sierras."

"Would twelve hours be sufficient?"

"Time enough to consult my Book of Changes."

"Do you really?" Inga's eyes widened fractionally.

"Treason," Per said.

"No. No more. My mystical phase played through."

"Then we can expect your decision in the morning?"

"Right."

"And now it is time for supper," said Inga. "Shall we go to the boat? I remember, Folger. Very rare."

"No business during dinner?"

"No," Inga promised.

"Your goddamn girl," said the project manager. Soaked through with sea water and reeking of contraband liquor, he sloshed into Folger's quarters. "She got away."

Folger switched on the lamp by the bunk and looked up sleepily. "Danny? What? Who got away?"

"Goddamn girl."

"Valerie?" Folger swung his legs off the bed and sat up.

"Smashed the seagate. Let loose half the tanks. We tried to head her off in the channel."

"Is she all right?"

"All right?" The project manager cupped his hands over his face. "She stove in the boat. Got Kendall and Brooking. You never saw so much blood."

"*Christ!*"

"*Hell of it was,*" said the project manager, "*we really needed her in the morning.*"

"*For what?*"

"*Really needed her,*" the project manager repeated. He staggered out of the room and disappeared in the hall.

Folger answered his own question the following day. Through devious channels of information, he learned that Valerie had been scheduled for vivisection.

That night, Folger climbed the mountain above his house. He felt he was struggling through years as much as brush and mud. The top of the mountain was ragged, with no proper peak. Folger picked a high point and spread his slicker over damp rock. He sat in the cold and watched the dark Atlantic. He looked up and picked out the Southern Cross. A drizzle began.

"Well, hell," he said, and climbed back down the mountain.

Folger took an Institute launch out beyond the cape and anchored. He lowered the cage, then donned his scuba gear. He said into the sonex: "Query—Valerie—location."

Later that morning, Folger suffered his loss.

Maria shook him awake in the morning. Folger awakened reluctantly, head still full of gentle spirals over glowing coral. The water had been warm; he needed no suit or equipment. Endless, buoyant flight—

"Señor Folger, you must get up. It has been seen."

His head wobbled as she worried his shoulder with insistent fingers. "Okay, I'm awake." He yawned. "What's been seen?"

"The big white one," Maria said. "The one that killed Manuel Padilla three days ago. It was sighted in the bay soon after the sun rose."

"Anybody try anything?" Folger asked.

"No. They were afraid. It is at least ten meters long."

Folger yawned again. "Hell of a way to start a morning."

"I have food for you."

Folger made a face. "I had steak last night. Real beef. Have you ever tasted beef?"

"No, Señor."

Maria accompanied him down the mountain to the village. She insisted upon carrying some of the loose gear; the mask, a box of twelve-gauge shells, a mesh sack of empty jars. Folger filled the jars with sheep's blood at the village butcher shop. He checked his watch; it was seven o'clock.

The skiff was tied up at the end of the second pier. The aluminum airboat glittered in the sun as they passed it. Inga Lindfors stood very still on the bridge. "Good morning, Folger," she called.

"Good morning," said Folger.

"Your answer?"

Folger appraised her for a moment. "No," he said, walking on.

The carcinogenic spread of the war finally and actively engulfed the Falkland Islands. The systematic integrity of the Institute was violated. Many components scattered; some stayed to fight.

Folger, his stump capped with glossy scar tissue, had already said his good-byes.

Suspended in the cold, gray void, Folger realized he was hyperventilating. He floated free, willing himself to relax, letting his staccato breathing find a slower, smoother rhythm. Beside him, a line trailed up to the rectangular blur of the skiff's hull. Tied to the nylon rope were a net and the unopened jars of sheep's-blood bait.

Folger checked his limited arsenal. Tethered to his left wrist was the underwater gun. It was a four-foot aluminum tube capped with a firing mechanism and a waterproof shotgun shell. A shorter, steel-tipped shark billy was fixed to a bracket tied to the stump of Folger's right arm.

Something intruded on his peripheral vision and he looked up.

Arrogant and sure, the two deadly shadows materialized out of the murk. The Lindfors wore only mask, fins, and snorkel. They appeared armed only with knives.

Folger saw them and raised the shark gun in warning. Per Lindfors grinned, his teeth very white. With slow, powerful strokes, he and his sister approached Folger from either side.

Disregarding Inga for the moment, Folger swung the muzzle of the shark gun toward Per. Per batted it aside with his free hand as Folger pulled the trigger. The concussion seemed to stun only Folger. Still smiling, Per extended his knife-hand.

Inga screamed in the water. Per disregarded Folger's weak attempt to fend him off with the billy and began to stroke for the surface. Folger turned his head.

A clownish face rushed at him. Folger stared at the teeth. The pointed nose veered at the last moment as the shark brushed by and struck at Per. The jaws cleanly sliced away Per's left arm and half his chest. The fish doubled back upon itself and made another strike. Per's legs, separate and trailing blood, tumbled slowly through the water.

Then Folger remembered Inga. He turned in the water and saw half her torso and part of her head, a swatch of silky hair spread out fanlike behind the corpse.

He looked back at the shark. It turned toward him slowly and began to circle, eerily graceful for its immense size. A dark eye fixed him coldly.

Folger held the metal billy obliquely in front of his chest. The tether of the shark gun had broken with the recoil.

The shark and Folger inspected each other. He saw the mottled color-ation of the shark's belly. He thought he saw a Marine Forces code branded low on the left flank. He keyed the sonex:

"Query—Valerie—query—Valerie."

The shark continued to circle. Folger abruptly realized the shark was following an inexorably diminishing spiral.

"Query—Valerie—I am Folger."

"Folger." An answer came back. "Valerie."

"I am Folger," he repeated.

"Folger," came the reply. "Love/hunger-hunger/love."

"Valerie—love."

"Hunger—love." The shark suddenly broke out of her orbit and drove at Folger. The enormous jaws opened, upper jaw sliding forward, triangular teeth ready to shear.

Folger hopelessly raised the billy. The jaws closed empty and the shark swept by. She was close enough to touch had Folger wished. The shark dove toward the open sea and Folger swam for the surface.

He tossed the yarrow stalks for an hour. Eventually he put them away, along with the book. Folger sat at the table until the sun rose. He heard Maria's footsteps outside on the stone walk. He listened to the sound of her progress through the outside door, the kitchen, and the hall.

"Señor Folger, you didn't sleep?"

"I'm getting old," he said.

Maria was excited. "The great white one is back."

"Oh?"

"The fishermen fear to go out."

"That's sensible."

"Señor, you must kill it."

"Must I?" Folger grinned. "Fix me some tea."

She turned toward the kitchen.

"Maria, you needn't come up tonight to fix supper."

After his usual meager breakfast, Folger gathered together his gear and walked out the front door of his house. He hesitated on the step.

You become what you live.

She lived shark.

He said into the wind, "What do you want me to do? Carve a cenotaph here on the mountain?"

"What, señor?" said Maria.

"Let's go." They started toward the trail. "Hold it," said Folger. He walked back to the house and opened the front door to the wind and rain. He chocked it with a rock. Then he climbed down the path to the sea.

Joseph P. Martino

... NOT A PRISON MAKE

Guerrilla Warfare: An obsolete form of warfare practiced intermittently throughout history until the XXth Century. It was characterized by conflict between professional soldiers formally organized into regular armies, on the one side, and nonprofessional, informally organized forces on the other side. As such, it could not exist except when warfare was customarily conducted by professional armies. Its most recent appearance was during the XVIIth through the XXth Centuries. Its name, in fact, originated during that period, and means "little war" in the Spanish language—a Latin-based language formally spoken in southeastern Europe; (see SPAIN).

It was widely practiced during the anti-colonial wars of the middle XXth Century, and received intensive theoretical and practical study by adherents of Communism (which see). This emphasis on guerrilla warfare led to a reaction on the part of the forces against which it was being used, among which were most of the industrially and technologically advanced nations of the world. The apparent paradox of poorly trained and ill-equipped irregulars being able to defeat well-trained and well-equipped regular troops sparked an intensive program of research among these advanced nations.

The inevitable result was the development of surveillance, mobility and communication techniques which gave the regular soldier of an advanced nation considerable advantage over his guerrilla opponent.

The guerrilla, of course, could not adopt these techniques, since they

426

required an industrial base to supply them, an organized logistics system to maintain them, and highly trained personnel to operate them. The guerrilla could not survive against an opponent who was invulnerable to surprise, and who could move over any terrain faster than the guerrilla could move. Thus after the XXth Century, only a professional army could stand against another one. This in turn led to an accelerated spiral of measure and countermeasure. . . . From the *Terran Encyclopedia*, 37th Edition.

KREG WAR: One of the interstellar wars fought by the First Terran Confederation during its early period of expansion. It was named for the Kregs, a chlorine-breathing race occupying several solar systems in the vicinity of Polaris. The war climaxed a series of disputes over possession of a number of mineral-rich but airless minor planets in the region between the Terran and Kreg spheres of influence. After a number of raids and counter-raids on mining settlements, a major attack. . . . The war was ended by the Treaty of Polaris, which granted to each side those planets already occupied, and provided an arbitration procedure to determine ownership of those unoccupied.

An interesting sidelight of the war was the resulting relationship between Terrans and the Kanthu, a humanoid race of oxygen-breathers. Their home planet, Kanth, occupied a strategic position outflanking several of the Kregs' advanced bases. A Terran task force landed there and set up a base which was intended to serve as a staging point for attacks against the Kregs' inner defenses. The initial policy of non-interference with the Kanthu turned out to be impossible, and. . . . From the *Terran Encyclopedia*, 41st Edition.

Private Chalat Wongsuwan was growing bored. The Task Force had hit dirt three weeks ago, and at first there was plenty to keep everyone busy. The first hastily constructed defenses had been strengthened by round-the-clock work, in anticipation of the expected Kreg counter-attack. However, no attack had come. Surely the Kregs knew the Task Force was there. What was delaying them? What were they up to? But after three weeks, even these questions lost their power to keep anyone alert. Private Chalat Wongsuwan, being an experienced combat soldier, recognized the symptoms of boredom, and knew that when on sentry duty was a poor time to get bored. He got up from the rock on which he was sitting, and reviewed his sector.

He was responsible for an area which was a rough square, one kilometer on edge, and the first one hundred meters of airspace above it. This area had been saturated with detectors of all kinds, which noticed anything out of the ordinary going on around them. The first few nights after landing, of course, had been spent finding out what was ordinary. The scents, sounds, electromagnetic radiations, seismic vibrations, and so on associated with the normal physical and animal activity of the area had been cataloged.

Now the ultrasonic pickups no longer reported the cries of an insectivorous batlike creature, but made a report only when the number of cries per minute deviated by more than a calculated percentage from what had been found to be the normal value for that time and place. The scent pickups no longer reported the mating odor of the females of a species of hard-shelled, ten-legged pseudo-beetles. The infra-red pickups no longer reported the intense emission from a small insect which, had its emission been visible, could have been called a firefly. And so on with all the other phenomena of the night in the forest.

The cataloging was not perfect yet, of course. There hadn't been time for that. Even back on Terra the detectors still pulled a few surprises now and then, and they had had centuries of refinement in the Terran environment. So several times during each watch the situation display, which portrayed the reports of all the sensors in the area in multicolored coded lights on the inside of the transparent face shield hanging from Private Chalat Wongsuwan's helmet, signaled a warning which turned out to be a false alarm when investigated.

Private Chalat Wongsuwan's boredom ended when an alarm signal appeared at a point near the center of the eastern edge of his area. He checked first with the sentry in the sector to the east.

"Ruongwit, this is Chalat. I've got a bogey at coordinates X–3917, Y–4231. Have you had anything heading my way?"

"Chalat, this is Ruongwit. Not a thing out of the ordinary in my sector. There hasn't been an alarm over your way all night, although I did have a couple on the other side earlier. When I got there, I couldn't find a thing wrong. The alarms had ceased, and everything was O.K. by then."

"Looks like the technicians are going to have to redefine what's normal for the area again. I'd better have a look anyway. Over and out."

There was still the possibility that something might have dropped out of the sky. He should have been informed by the Sergeant of the Guard if anything had been reported by the aerial patrol, or even the off-planet patrol, but slipups did happen from time to time.

"Sergeant of the Guard, this is Private Chalat."

"Go ahead, Chalat."

"I've got a bogey which just appeared in my sector. It didn't come from the next sector. Any reports of activity upstairs?"

"No reports of anything. What kind of an alarm do you have?"

"It just about covers the spectrum. Scent, infrared indicating a temperature near 40° Centigrade, sounds that could pass for breathing, the whole works. Only no footfalls from the seismic detectors. Wait a minute. The alarm just switched locations. The first spot is back to normal except for a reduced count on bird calls, as though the birds hadn't got over being scared. The alarm is now at a point halfway between me and the first point—exactly the same set of indications. I'd better take a look at both spots."

"Give me a report on anything, especially if it moves again."

"Roger, over and out."

He switched on his personal lifter, and reached treetop level. He drifted in the general direction of the alarm, threading his way through the treetops, getting as much concealment from them as he could without getting too close to them. His face mask display included a purple dot which was supposed to indicate his location, but he really didn't need it. The display also showed the swath of disturbance he was cutting through the night, as the many sensors reported his passage within their detection range. They couldn't be set to consider him as a normal part of the environment, without running the risk of failing to detect other humans who shouldn't be there. He reflected that, if there were any natives around who knew their way in these woods, they would have no trouble detecting him by the change in the behavior of the animal and bird life. The purpose of his multitude of sensors was to give him the equivalent of a lifetime's experience in the environment, without taking a lifetime to acquire it, and to give him more detection range than his organic sensors possessed.

The alarm was coming from a small clearing ahead of him. He hung behind a screen of branches, looked over the clearing. There was what appeared to be a man standing in the middle of it. Just before he could call the Sergeant of the Guard, the man disappeared. Had he really seen anything, or was his gear playing tricks on him? Now there appeared to be two men at opposite edges of the clearing. There was another. No, one of the two had disappeared. He ought to make a report, but what would make sense?

He switched the lifter to a high-speed attack mode, and charged down at one of the figures. The figure disappeared. He halted and altered course toward the other figure, which also disappeared. He turned around. Both were behind him, on the other side of the clearing. He drifted toward the center of the clearing, gaining altitude. A microphone near the two figures picked up the twang of bowstrings, but by the time he could interpret the sound, two crossbow bolts had struck him. As he lost consciousness, the lifter lowered him to the ground to await medical pickup.

"Sergeant of the Guard. I've got a 'man down' signal on Chalat. He's badly wounded. No, there's a change. He's dead."

"Where is he?"

"Coordinates X–3820, Y–4417."

"Squad One, head directly for Chalat's position. Squads Two thorugh Five, seal off the borders of his sector. Squads Six and Seven start combing the sector." Then, switching channels, "Aerial patrol, give me a tight roof over Sector 82. There's at least one hostile in it."

At this point the Officer of the Guard arrived. "Good response so far, Sergeant, but you'd better call up two or three reserve squads. We don't have enough left on duty to handle a similar attack on another sector. And warn all other sentries about what happened. I wish Chalat had given us more details as he went along."

"Sergeant of the Guard. Call from Ruongwit, in the sector next to Chalat's."

"I'll take it. Put him on."

"Sergeant, this is Ruongwit. I've got a bunch of bogeys just like the ones Chalat described. They keep jumping around. There are about a dozen of them, as near as I can tell. They won't hold still long enough to count. Now they seem to be clustering about my position."

"Get some altitude and get out of there. Shoot at anything you see. Acknowledge, Ruongwit."

"Sergeant, I can't raise him. Now there's a 'man down' signal on him. He's dead, too."

"Sergeant, double the guard in all sectors. Call up all reserve squads. Call off the search in Sector 82. The next sector that reports some bogeys is to be saturated with all available forces."

"Yes, sir. Shall I sound a General Alert?"

"Better do that. The Kregs've clearly found some counter for our detectors. They may hit the Base next."

The Task Force Commander was distinctly unhappy, as any man who has been awakened at four in the morning to be told he's under attack has a right to be. "Well, Major Sakul, you were Officer of the Guard. Let's hear what happened."

"Yes, sir. Well, the first thing was Private Chalat. He was investigating a bogey that seemed to have jumped from one place to another. When we found him, he had two crossbow bolts in him, and his throat had been cut. In addition, he'd been stripped of all his loose equipment. Fortunately his recorders were still on him, so we could reconstruct what had happened. Forces had just been ordered out to comb his sector when the attackers struck the next sector. Same thing there. Ruongwit was found with three crossbow bolts in him. He must have been dead when he hit the ground, since his throat was still intact. He, too, was stripped of all his loose equipment.

"After that, bedlam broke loose. Every sector reported bogeys all over the place, all the same kind. They jumped from one place to another without seeming to be any place in between. We lost a total of eighteen guards, out of the one hundred twenty we had out. In all cases, they were stripped of their equipment. Those that weren't dead when they hit the ground had their throats cut. Next they started appearing inside the Base. They didn't seem to do any attacking there, they would just be reported somewhere, and then vanish. There were a few attempts to shoot at them, but no one hit them.

"I figured that we would do more damage to ourselves firing inside the Base than they seemed to be doing, so I ordered a halt to the firing within the boundary. After about thirty minutes the appearances seemed to peter out. There were a few reports for as long as an hour after the attack on Private Chalat, but I think they were all false alarms. I feel that the attackers first hit our guards, then penetrated the Base for reconnaissance purposes, and withdrew in order after they had what they came for. All in all, it looks like a well-coordinated attack, and if they decide to pull another one, I think they'll get away with it, too."

"Colonel Bunyarit."

The Executive Officer replied, "Yes, sir."

"What have you to report?"

"Well, our first reaction, naturally, was that the Kregs had come up with something new. Somehow they had managed to drop landing parties near our Base, without their ships being detected on the way in, and then the landing parties had managed to spoof and jam our detectors so we couldn't keep up with them."

"And it wasn't the Kregs?"

The Executive Officer replied slowly. "No, sir. When Chalat attacked one of the intruders, his action recorder went on. We got a good look at the one he went after. Then we saw the figure of the intruder disappear. The same thing happened to the next one he went after. He turned and spotted some more. However, they were the same two he started after. Despite the fact that both moons were down, there was enough starlight for the image intensifier to give us a good picture. We could identify the marking on the loincloths of the two figures, facial features, scars, and so on well enough to tell that there were only two, and they were jumping around from one spot to another. Then when they got Chalat, the recorder showed them suddenly appearing next to him, cutting his throat, stripping him of his equipment, then disappearing, equipment and all."

"Well, man," the commander burst out, "who were they?"

The Executive Officer was enjoying himself. "The natives of the planet, sir."

"But, according to the Intelligence reports of the pre-landing survey, the natives are very primitive. If I remember correctly, they practice a very destructive form of agriculture, so that they have to shift their villages every few years, and most of their protein comes from hunting. They have no cultures to speak of. How do they get the technological capability to bollix up our surveillance devices? Are the Kregs supporting them?"

"While it is possible they are getting Kreg support, sir, I think it is unlikely. If the Kregs had got another jump on us in the detection field, they would have made the attack themselves, rather than trying to work through primitive allies like the local natives. I believe that the detectors were giving us a true report of exactly what was going on. The attackers were really jumping from one place to the other without being in between. I believe they are natural teleports. And considering the way they coordinated their attack, they are telepaths, too."

"Pardon me, General."

The Task Force Commander turned to his Operations Officer. "Yes, Colonel Arun."

"As you know, sir, before I was recalled to active duty I was Professor of Military History at the University of Callisto. My period of specialization was the XXth Century. One of the more common types of military action during that period was something called 'guerrilla warfare.' It was commonly used by nations under occupation by foreign invaders, colonialists, and so forth. It is particularly adapted for use by weak and poorly organized forces against strong, well-organized forces. It seems to me that's precisely what we're up against here. It even fits the traditional pattern, since the first action of the native guerrillas was arms-gathering. They obviously carried out last night's raid in order to get their hands on some of our weapons."

"Supposing what you say is true, what do you recommend?"

"In the XXth Century, guerrillas weren't defeated until the forces opposing them learned to eliminate the genuine grievances of the people who supported the guerrillas. I recommend we use the same course of action here. We must communicate with the natives, explain our reasons for coming here, and use some of our resources in solving their more serious problems. In that way we can gain their support instead of their enmity."

"Now wait a minute," interjected Colonel Bunyarit. "Let's not go losing our sense of perspective. Our job here is to fight the Kregs, not to wipe the noses of a bunch of natives. With all due respect to Colonel Arun's academic background, I think that's precisely what his recommendations are: academic. We've got a defeatist attitude. Already we seem to think they can come in and repeat their raids as often as they feel like it. Well, last night they hit us without any warning. Next time we'll be ready for them. We ought to get many more of them than they get of us. And the raiding doesn't have to be all one-sided. There's nothing to stop us from going out and raiding a few of their villages. After getting their noses bloodied every time they come after us, and losing a few villages too, they'll quit bothering us. That's the way to treat them. Let's not mess around with this do-gooder attitude."

"But Colonel Bunyarit, you're making precisely the same mistake nearly every colonial power made in the XXth Century. They felt that a show of force was all that was required. . . ."

"Now you look here. I've been on worlds before where the natives started trouble—caravan raiding, robbery, and so forth. You shoot up their villages a few times, and they learn who's boss. You ought to get out from behind that professor's desk of yours once in a while, and find out how the galaxy works."

"Your attitude, Colonel Bunyarit, is typically military in its obtuseness. Your suggested treatment may be quite satisfactory for handling pirates and bandits, who value their village more than they value the loot they might acquire from another raid. But it won't work against a people who are united in their opposition to the foreign invader. To them, the loss of a village is a small thing. They have their minds focused on the long pull, and are willing to make considerable sacrifices to gain ultimate victory."

"Are you trying to tell me that a bunch of half-naked savages, who haven't progressed beyond the crossbow, are going to chase us off this planet? If it even looks like they might do it, we can wipe them all out with radioactive. . . ."

"Stop that task," from the Task Force Commander. "Don't say it. Don't even think it. If ever the rumor got out that Terra had committed genocide, we'd have every race we know about, and as many we never heard of, down on our necks. If there's anything that unites the races of the galaxy, it's their opposition to genocide. We'll hear no more talk about wiping anyone out. If we can't settle the problem some other way, we'll get off their planet and let them alone. And cut out the bickering. We've all had a hard night; there's no point in taking it out on each other." Then in a calmer voice, "We seem to have two policies proposed. One is to make friends with the natives, the other is to civilize them with a blaster.

"It's clear to me, anyway, that if we try the second policy first, and it fails, we'll never get a chance to try making friends. So we'll try the policy of making friends first.

"Colonel Bunyarit, you seem to think we can defend ourselves against any more raids. Get busy and set up the defenses. I think we're going to need them tonight. Colonel Arun, you will figure out how we're going to go about making friends with people who can vanish from our grasp before we can learn even one word of their language. That's all. Dismissed."

"Colonel Prapat." The Task Force Commander turned to the Provost Marshal.

"Yes, General?"

"Come to my office with me. There are a couple of things I want to talk over with you. Have you had breakfast yet?"

"No, sir."

"Neither have I. I'll have some sent in. I don't think any of us are going to have time for regular meals for a while."

"You know, General, there are times when I wonder how much more I can take of Arun and his professional attitude. He seems to think none of us ever read a book. I admit I've never heard the word 'guerrilla' before today, but, if these are guerrillas, their tactics don't seem to be much different from those of a lot of bandits I've fought on a number of worlds."

"Yes, I know Arun gets on a lot of people's nerves. First of all, Reserve officers who are called up at the outbreak of a war often have a low opinion of us Regulars. The fact that we had to call them up seems to be proof that we weren't competent to win the war without them. In addition, college professors seem to have a firmly fixed opinion that a military officer is a wooden-headed dunce. And when you combine both in the same man, as we have with Arun, he sometimes gets hard to live with. However, don't forget he has a good point. Although the tactics may be similar, there is considerable difference between a bandit and a guerrilla.

"The motivation of the guerrilla makes him willing to put up with a lot of punishment. Even a long series of defeats won't dishearten him, and severe repression actually provides him with recruits from people who figure they have nothing to lose. As long as things are going to be tough anyway, they might as well be doing some fighting, and getting in a few licks at the people who are making things tough. At the moment I'm more concerned about Bunyarit. If there's anything I've learned in my career, it's that you should never underestimate an opponent. Treating an opponent with anything other than respect is a good way to get whipped in a hurry. If we don't treat them with respect, we'll try to beat them with half-measures, and get bogged down in a messy, indecisive war just like what happened to the XXth Century colonialists."

"That scared me, too, while I was listening to Arun. To a bandit a gun is a means to money. He gets one so he can use it to commit banditry, or to sell it to someone else who will use it to commit banditry. From Arun's description, a guerrilla considers a gun a means to more guns. He uses it to get another gun, to give to a friend, so they can both go out and get more guns, to give to more friends, until they have a big enough force to wipe you out. I don't see how you can beat a thing like that."

"Don't be too shaken by the idea. Despite Arun's air of authority, he's not the only one around here who's read some history. He wasn't quite correct on one point. Historically the guerrilla was whipped when surveillance devices were developed to the point where he couldn't surprise you, when mechanized armies quit being roadbound and learned to move over any territory a man on foot could move over, and do it faster too, and when communications were developed to the point where you could coordinate the actions of a lot of scattered units.

"The trouble with whipping him is that it isn't enough. He won't stay whipped. You can't relax your guard. Even in supposedly pacified towns, troops have to go around in pairs, or they'll end up in an alley with their heads caved in. And you can't bring in civilians as tradesmen, miners, and so on. They'll be murdered as soon as you turn your back. As Arun pointed out, if you want them to stay whipped, you've got to eliminate their legitimate grievances. It's important that you be able to whip them, of course. If you simply do things for them after they attack you, you merely whet their appetite for more. But if you do whip them, you can afford to take the attitude that they have been done an injustice, and deserve better treatment. If you neglect either half of the program, however, you're in for trouble.

"That's the sort of thing we've got to avoid here. In the long run we'll have to come to some agreement with these people or get off their planet. But in the short run, maybe we can hold our own against their banditlike tactics by using the tactics that work against bandits. That's what I want to talk to you about."

"Well, as a Provost Marshal, I've had considerable experience with bandits on various worlds. I've found that by and large bandits have a good sense of economics. If their gain from banditry is less than their loss from your reprisal for the banditry, they soon take up some other line of business, like fleecing tourists legally. But your reprisals, if they are going to be effective, have to be quick and precise. The bandits have to see the justice in your reprisal. If a small gang in a village engages in a raid, and you bomb the whole village, all you've done is get a lot of people mad at you. You've provided the bandit with allies. You have to identify the bandits and conduct your reprisals against them alone."

"That sounds reasonable. Now how do you find out who the bandits are?"

"I think of that part of the work as nothing but conventional police procedures, just patient collection and sifting of facts. To get the facts, you have to know the area and the people. You have to build up nets of informers and agents in the villages. You have to keep watch over roads, and such natural convergence points as bridges, fords, and mountain passes. If you suspect anyone, you arrange to have them watched constantly. You offer open rewards for information, and secret bribes and offers of reduced sentences for members of the gang who provide evidence. In extreme cases, you can take a few squads of police or troops and seal off a whole village. Then you arrange to interview each and every person in the village, separately. You arrange so that all the interviews are approximately the same length, so that no one stands out as particularly suspect for having spent a lot of time with you.

"In the meantime, while the others are standing around, you might have a doctor giving shots, passing out pills, giving a health lecture, or something, so you don't antagonize the innocent. Sometimes in these interviews you actually get information; other times you can only recruit agents who will later pay off for you. But that's the sort of thing you have to do. It's just patient, detailed police investigation, putting together small scraps of information, and trying to get more information."

"How would you apply your techniques here?"

"Frankly, I'm baffled. Even if I could get one of them to stand still, I don't know how to talk to them. I don't know what they value, so can't offer rewards. And even if I did know what to use as a reward, they could steal it from me more easily than they could earn it anyway. It seems to be a circular proposition. If we could stop them from attacking us, I could probably build up a net of agents who could tell me who did the attacking. But, then I wouldn't need to, since they wouldn't be attacking any more. And until I can get information out of them, I can't do anything to stop their attacks."

"I can see the vicious circle clearly enough. I had hoped your methods might help us to break out of it. All right, thanks for the information. Now I'd better go see what kind of defenses Colonel Bunyarit is working out."

The Task Force Commander sat at his console in the Battle Control Center. All the other Duty Officers and NCOs were seated at their own consoles, all wearing battle armor. The consoles were tightly packed against one side of the long room, instead of being spread throughout the room, as was usual. A freshly painted white stripe marked off the now-empty remainder of the room from the consoles. Coils of barbed wire hung from the ceiling, festooned the walls, and draped over the sides of the consoles, filling every possible cubic centimeter of the space between the white stripe and the wall, leaving the men at the consoles just barely room to move. At the far end of the room, the end wall was covered with a newly installed bank of electronic apparatus.

The room below, containing the computer complex and auxiliary power supply, was also crammed with barbed wire. The Center itself was, of course, underground, and reasonably safe from any ordinary attack. However, the commander scanned the interior of the room carefully, wondering if any additional improvements would make it better protected against attack by teleports. Then he caught his first glimpse of one of the natives, standing in the cleared portion of the room.

This particular native had spent the day practicing a particular tactic. He would choose a target, and a spot near it, teleport to the desired spot, attempting to arrive facing the target and with his gun pointed at it, fire quickly, and return to his starting point. He had, in fact, become quite proficient at it. Now, moving with the speed of thought, he appeared in the Battle Control Center just behind one of the consoles, corrected his aim on the duty officer slightly, and squeezed the trigger.

Unfortunately for him, the speed of thought can be measured in milliseconds. In the newly installed bank of equipment at the end of the room an electronic circuit, operating in microseconds, reacted to a sensor which had detected his presence and closed the circuit on a blast rifle which happened to be pointed through the volume of space he was occupying. Long before the nerve impulses arrived at his trigger finger, he was dead and falling to the floor, receiving more blaster bolts as he activated other sensors during his fall. A second native, attempting to retrieve his fallen weapon, was likewise cut down. After that, there were no more attacks on the Battle Control Center.

Sergeant Sawang Nakvirote drifted slowly across the base, at an altitude of slightly less than fifty meters. His squad, in diamond formation, followed him. Just below him stood a row of obviously fresh pyramids of the earth. All the hand-weapons of the Base, except those actually issued to someone, were buried under those pyramids. It had been explained that this would keep the natives from raiding the armory. They would have to fight for each weapon they captured. Ahead of him stood the vast parking area of the space field, normally crowded with ships, but now empty. All spaceships had been moved well away from the planet, as a precaution against attack or sabotage.

He was beginning to wonder whether the natives were going to attack this night, or give it up as a bad job, when the crackle of blaster fire reached his ears. Almost simultaneously, a voice from the Battle Control Center blared from his communicator. "Attacking force in Barracks 34-D. Squad 17 counter-attack."

Sergeant Sawang led his squad in a high-speed, swooping dive for the front entrance of Barracks 34-D. It was a long, low, one-story structure, with a door in the center of each of the two long sides. Inside were two rows of cots, with a footlocker at the foot of each cot. A separate room at one end contained the precise number and kind of sanitary facilities specified by regulations for thirty-two men. Sergeant Sawang led the front vee of the diamond as it merged into a single line, passed through the door, and spread out again. The rear vee of the diamond swung up over the roof of the barracks, turned, and opened fire on the figures who had suddenly appeared in front of the barracks, firing at the rest of the squad as it entered.

One of the figures dropped, and immediately another one appeared beside it, retrieved its fallen weapon, and disappeared. The rest of the figures had by this time also disappeared, although not without drawing blood in turn. The last of the squad members entering the barracks stopped short in mid-flight, as he was hit. His personal lifter, instead of lowering him to the ground, took him up to an altitude of a hundred meters, and hovered there. His body could be recovered later for proper burial. In the meantime, his weapons were safe from capture.

Inside the barracks, Sergeant Sawang found considerable damage, and some smoke from several cots which had been set on fire. However, there was no sign of the attackers. Half the men immediately took up positions at the front windows, to cover the entry of the rest of the squad. The others tried to cover the interior of the barracks, but without success. A native suddenly appeared in line with the doorway, fired once, and disappeared. A man just inside the doorway flung his arms out in a spasmodic jerk, then drifted toward the ceiling as his lifter attempted to raise him to the programmed hundred-meter altitude. A native appeared on the floor below him, grasped vainly for his feet, and died on the spot as someone realized what was going on and fired. The dead man was unceremoniously hauled out the door by two of his comrades, and allowed to float upwards out of reach.

At this point Sergeant Sawang's communicator spoke up again. "We're sending Squad 32 to reinforce you. As long as the natives want to fight in Barracks 34-D, we might as well accommodate them. Try to capture a few of their weapons, if you possibly can."

Squad 32 was led by Sergeant Jirote Phranakorn. Switching channels, Sergeant Sawang spoke. "Jirote, this is Sawang. Since your squad's still at full strength, you take the main bay of the barracks, I'll take the 'fresher."

The reply came back. "Fine by me, Sawang. Cover me as I come in the door, then I'm going to have my squad sweep up and down the length of the barracks, in line abreast, so we'll provide poorer targets."

Sergeant Sawang hovered in the doorway of the 'fresher, and watched Jirote's squad sweep through the barracks in precise formation, half the men facing ahead, half to the rear. Again with a suddenness which defied belief, a group of natives appeared. Sawang noted that these seemed to have different markings on their loincloths than the two he had seen earlier. There were eight of the natives, one for each member of Jirote's squad, and each native seemed to have placed himself directly in the path of one of the squad members. In a time-span so short that Sawang still hadn't reacted, there was the crackle of blasters, and the natives were gone again. Six of the squad members drifted toward the ceiling. The remaining two stopped, confused and uncertain. Their uncertainty was brought to an end as four more natives appeared at the far end of the barracks and sent their blaster bolts into the two remaining soldiers.

Sawang flung himself out of the doorway just in time, as more attackers appeared and fired at him. At the end of the crackling barrage of blaster bolts, he swung past the doorway again, glancing into the main bay as he passed. It seemed to be full of natives, all attempting to form gymnastic pyramids in order to reach the men floating against the ceiling.

Sawang zipped past the door again, flinging a grenade into the main bay as he went by. He led his squad into the main bay immediately after the blast, to find nearly a dozen of the natives crumpled on the floor, and several patches of blood evidently left by others who had escaped. He put his men to work immediately, getting Jirote's men and their weapons out of the barracks. No sooner was that task completed when he heard another voice from his communicator. This one was flat and metallic, and he knew he was being addressed directly by the Battle Computer, not by any of the humans at the Battle Control Center.

"Switch your lifter to Remote Control." Sawang did so. "Your direction of motion and velocity will be altered at random intervals, to make your motion as unpredictable as possible. From time to time you will be ordered to look and point your weapons in a specific direction. Fire immediately if you see an attacker, and fire anyway if ordered to do so."

Sawang watched his men move around the interior of the barracks in a mysterious seemingly pointless dance. They moved up, down, right, left, forward, backward, without apparent reason. Suddenly he heard a blaster bolt crackle past him, just after he had felt a sudden change in motion. He glanced briefly in the direction from which the shot had come, to see no one, then returned his gaze to his assigned direction. He spotted one of the natives, fired quickly, and missed. The attacker disappeared before he had another chance to fire.

The next few minutes were a confused, whirling nightmare. Sawang's men danced around inside the barracks at what would have been an insanely dangerous speed, if they had had to depend on human reaction times to keep them from colliding with the barracks walls and each other. Attackers appeared, fired, disappeared. Sawang's men returned the fire as best they could. Neither side seemed to be able to draw blood.

Then Sawang noticed a subtle change in the pattern of the dance. All the changes in direction seemed to be nearly at right angles now, and they came at greater intervals. Furthermore, the direction he was ordered to look no longer coincided with his direction of motion. The flat voice of the computer came to him again.

"Look thirty-seven degrees." He did so, the direction being slightly to the left of his course. "Fire, and keep firing." He fired once, at nothing. He fired again, and just as he squeezed the trigger, a native appeared in the path of his aim. He was so surprised he hesitated before firing the third shot, which turned out to be unnecessary, as it passed over the dead native.

The next few minutes were another confused whirl. "Look forty-five degrees. Fire and keep firing." And another native down. "Look ten degrees. Fire. Look ninety degrees. Fire. Look. Fire. Look. Fire. Look. Fire." It was clear what had happened. The computer had deduced the habits of this particular group of natives, and their reaction times. It kept each human on a single course long enough for a native to track him and decide to attack. It then predicted where the native would appear, and had someone else fire at the predicted point of arrival. That way the native was never alerted by a hostile move on the part of the human he was tracking.

Finally the crackle of blasters ceased. There was another human floating near the ceiling, and another dozen natives dead on the floor. The important fact was that this time all the dead natives were armed, except two who had died in the act of trying to retrieve weapons from their fallen comrades. The computer had caught on to that practice, too.

Before anything else could happen, Sergeant Sawang ordered his men to recover all the loose weapons, and then go back on remote control. However, apparently someone had decided that the Battle of Barracks 34-D was over. Another voice, this time a human one, came from his communicator.

"Squad 17, proceed to the Electronics Repair Shop. It is under attack."

The Electronics Repair Shop was a single-story structure consisting of a long, narrow central building with a number of shorter but equally narrow wings branching out on either side. Both the central building and the wings consisted of a hallway lined on both sides with small cubicles, each closed off by a door. The building was entirely windowless, but there were doors at the end of each of the wings.

As Sergeant Sawang's squad circled around the Electronics Repair Shop, in a now somewhat ragged diamond formation, another message reached them.

"Sawang, this is Major Prasert." That would be Major Prasert Tanwong, Sawang's Battalion Commander. "The attackers are apparently trying to draw us into a fight. They've been appearing in the test cubicles, smashing some equipment, and leaving. By the time we get there, they're somewhere else causing more trouble. In order to keep them from wrecking everything, I'm going to have to put a man in every cubicle, with more men patrolling the halls as a backup. I've already got all the rooms in the northern-most wing manned. I want your squad to patrol the hall in that wing. As I get more men, I'll extend our control into the other wings."

Sawang decided that on the face of it the plan sounded good, but the natives might have some other surprises they hadn't revealed yet. Before he committed the remainder of his squad to a particular tactic, he wanted to reconnoiter the territory he was going to have to fight in. He left the squad to circle the building, and dove through the doorway at the end of the hall he was going to patrol. He came to the door of a cubicle, knocked, and opened the door. The soldier guarding the room was floating back and forth across one end of the room, with his back to the end wall and his head brushing the ceiling. His gun was pointed toward the center of the room, ready to fire. While the man's course was fairly predictable, he still presented a moving target instead of a sitting one. Sawang nodded his head in satisfaction, waved at the man, and left the room.

He then studied the hallway thoughtfully. After his experience in the barracks, he didn't like the idea of his men moving up and down the length of the hallway, where they could be picked off easily by enfilade fire. Nor was he happy about the hallway down the central portion of the building. It was uncontrolled, and his men would be subject to flank attacks as they crossed the entrance to the hallway, at the center of the wing. He decided the alternatives regarding the central hallway were to attempt to control it, or to abandon it to the attackers and accept that his squad would be split into two halves, on either end of the wing.

The first alternative would be difficult to achieve, but the second went against all his training and experience. He decided to station himself at the juncture of the central hallway and his wing, keeping near the ceiling and partially protected by a corner, so that he could watch the hallway and fire if anyone appeared. He could then put two men in each wing, and his central position would give him better control over the action as it developed.

He called the squad in and told off two men for each end of the wing. They were to stay abreast of each other, and facing in opposite directions. They would move in a corkscrew spiral along the length of the hallway, reversing direction as they reached the end, or middle, of the wing. He then took up his position at the middle of the wing.

* * *

Hardly had Sergeant Sawang gotten into position when a series of explosions rocked the building. He glanced around, and saw the door of one of the cubicles sag open, and smoke drift out. He called to his squad to maintain the patrol, and swooped for the nearest cubicle. He yanked the door open and swept inside, to find a native standing on a test bench and removing a blaster from the unresisting hand of the soldier now floating lifelessly against the ceiling of the cubicle. Before Sawang could fire, the native was gone, gun and all. He ordered his squad to stop patrolling and check the cubicles. He then tried the next door, to find it bolted from the inside. He blasted the lock and hurtled inside to find the room empty and its guard dead and stripped of weapons. In the next room the guard was still alive, and the badly mangled body of a native lay on the floor.

"He appeared right in front of me, Sergeant, and dropped a grenade on the floor. My gun was pointed at him, and I must have fired by reflex. He fell over the grenade and soaked up the force of the burst."

"Reflex or not, that's nice shooting. Keep up the good work."

Sawang returned to the hallway, to find it filling up with guards from the rooms which had not been attacked. He was in the process of sorting his squad out from the strays when a volley of blaster fire erupted from the central hallway. He turned to see a group of natives standing in the middle of the wing, having a field day firing at the troops in both ends of the wing. In the confusion, no one seemed to be able to organize any counter-fire.

Someone yelled "Out the doors! Let's get out of here," and a rush started for the doorway at the end of the wing. This escape route was closed by more blaster fire from natives stationed outside the doorway. An incredible jam formed at the door as men milled about, fired on from front and rear. Sawang and the other NCOs started herding the men out of the hallway into the cubicles, where they started returning the fire of the natives, who were now rapidly shifting their positions along the length of the hallway.

Suddenly a voice roared over the emergency communicator channel. "All troops in the Electronics Repair Shop. Take cover. Get under something quickly."

Sawang and his men had just ducked under a workbench in one of the cubicles when a shattering explosion sounded in the hall outside, followed by the earsplitting shriek of a one-man scout fighter as it whipped over the building at low altitude and high speed, then headed back for the stratosphere. There was now a gaping hole in the roof over the hallway, through which an orderly flow of men was escaping, while others still in the cubicles provided covering fire for them. Sawang led his men out in their turn, then circled back over the building. When all the men appeared to be out, he received permission to lead his squad back to look for wounded and retrieve weapons.

The fire from the scout had been aimed with precision, and had taken out the roof right over the hallway. This, of course, meant that the beams supporting the roof had been cut through at the center, allowing a portion of the roof to collapse into the hallway. They found a number of bodies, both human and native, under the wreckage. They dragged the humans free and let their lifters carry them out through the roof. The natives, they simply disarmed. As Sawang pulled a blaster away from one of the figures on the floor, he saw it stir slightly. He took a step away, then the significance of the event struck him.

"Battle Control Center, this is Sergeant Sawang, Squad 17. We've got a prisoner. He's been knocked out, temporarily anyway. What do we do with him?"

"Good work, Sawang. Hoist him up to a hundred meters and hold him there so his friends don't try to rescue him, while we figure out what to do with him."

"Sorry I'm late for the meeting, General. I had an experiment in progress, and I wanted to be able to include the results in my report."

"That's all right, Doctor, we were just getting started. Sit down and catch your breath, and we'll hear from you in a few minutes. Now, Colonel Bunyarit, will you give your report?"

"Yes, General. First I'd like to describe some of the thinking that went into the defense planning for last night, then describe how it worked out. To begin with, we had to accept that the natives were teleports. It became clear that the ability to teleport also implied some sort of clairvoyance. If a person is going to teleport himself to some distant point, he has to be sure that there are no objects in the way where he wants to go. Simply remembering the place is not enough. Someone could easily have moved an obstacle into a place remembered as being clear of obstructions. Thus the question became one of how good their clairvoyance was. Did it, in effect, make them omniscient about all events anywhere? If so, we had no hope of defeating them.

"On the other hand, they all have eyes, and on the first night they attacked, it's worth noting that all their victims were shot while silhouetted against a fairly bright starry background. Thus they still depend heavily on their eyes, despite the existence of clairvoyance.

"So I decided to assume that their clairvoyance was not much better than the minimum required for successful teleportation; that they could observe only a small area at a time, as through a peephole, but that they could scan the 'peephole' around to investigate a large area or track a specific target of interest. I assumed also that their ability to inspect some complex object would not necessarily tell them how it worked or what it did, if it depended on principles beyond their level of technological development.

"On the basis of these assumptions, I planned the defense. First, there were certain areas like the Battle Control Center, the Power Plant, and so forth, which had to be made into traps which even teleports could not invade successfully. Limits on time and equipment, of course, meant that the rest of the Base could not be so protected. So all weapons not being carried by someone were buried. All spaceships and other vehicles were moved out of the way to prevent attack or sabotage. Since any soldier standing in a fixed position could be attacked and disarmed before he could react, fixed guard posts had to be abandoned. The simplest solution was to put all the troops up in the air and keep them moving.

"The obvious counter to this was to attack our unprotected installations, forcing us to move troops into them. However, I felt safe in assuming that the natives would be fairly unsophisticated. If they found a tactic that worked, they'd keep trying it. Nor would they be organized to detect our responses to their tactics, and change them as necessary. So I felt that the Battle Computer, with its ability to handle large amounts of data and deduce patterns from it, would give us an edge which might make up for the enemy's ability to teleport, if our troops were drawn into a battle.

"I feel that the defense was quite successful. Certain points were defended with complete success. In those places where our men had room to maneuver, we put up a good defense, inflicting more losses than we took. In other areas, the battle was more nearly even. However, overall we lost forty-two men, while they lost one hundred eighty. I could say that is a very favorable ratio. I expect that we can make further improvements in the defenses before tonight, and if they attack again, we should be able to force an even more favorable exchange ratio."

"Thank you, Colonel Bunyarit. Now Colonel Arun, you look like you want to say something."

"Yes, sir. I beg to differ with the optimistic conclusions just voiced. First of all, the actions of guerrillas tend to be limited by the number of weapons available, not their manpower. And their chief source of weapons is capture from their opponents. Thus in combating guerrillas the measure of success is not the casualty ratio of the forces, but the ratio of weapons lost by each side. The attackers started the battle last night with what weapons they had seized the previous night, namely eighteen blasters, eighteen blast rifles, and fifty-four grenades. Last night they expended twenty grenades, and we recaptured twenty-five other weapons. However, they captured twenty-two blasters, twenty blast rifles, and sixty grenades. In last night's attack, then, they essentially doubled their supply of weapons.

"Furthermore, much of last night's defense was based on the assumption that they cannot teleport themselves into a position in space, say a hundred meters off the ground. It may be that they had never had to do it, but that is no reason to assume they can't learn to do it.

"In short, I consider last night a defeat for us. Without any change in tactics, they can come back and double their weapons supply again. And they may be able to change their tactics in such a way as to nullify most of our defenses."

"Thank you, Colonel. You have some good points. However, things are not all black. We did manage to get a prisoner, so the night wasn't a total loss. Doctor, may we have your report now?"

The Staff Surgeon slid his chair back and stood up. "The most important news, of course, is the prisoner. When he was delivered to us last night, he was still unconscious from having a roof fall on him. Our first check, naturally, was to see if he had suffered any serious injury. A hasty examination showed that there were no bones broken, or anything like that. Next we made some rapid checks to see if any anesthetics we had would be safe and effective on him. We had to keep him unconscious, or he would have simply left us.

"It turned out that one of our standard anesthetics would work on him, and as far as we could tell it would be safe. Naturally we started with light doses, and monitored his heart and lung action. However, we, of course, had no idea what his normal pulse and respiration rate should be. The anesthetic seemed to do the trick, so we started sampling everything we could without doing him any permanent damage, as well as taking electrocardiograms, encephalograms, and so on.

"After about an hour, we observed that his pulse and respiration seemed to be weakening, so we cut down on the dose of anesthetic. This helped, but after a while he started to get worse again, so we cut out the anesthetic entirely. In short order he returned to consciousness, and did the expected thing. He vanished right off the table. It was quite a surprise, even after having been told it could happen.

"In all, we spent about two hours examining the prisoner. We have a great deal of useful data, although most of it is still in raw form, and can't be used for anything yet. It must be remembered that we never examined him under normal conditions. He was knocked out when we got him, and was anesthetized in addition. So we are still not completely satisfied with our data. And in any case, we would like to have a lot more. We are performing autopsies on the attacker corpses. These, in conjunction with the data from the prisoner, are telling us quite a bit about their nature."

"If we managed to get another prisoner, could you do better with a new anesthetic?"

"Yes, General, we now know enough about them to be able to synthesize an anesthetic which would be both safe and effective."

"Do you have enough information to design a knockout gas sufficiently effective to have military utility, and with no serious side effects?"

"Oh, yes. That would present no serious problem. We could even design one which would be absorbed rapidly through the skin, so they couldn't avoid it by holding their breath. We could even design it to have no effect on humans. I would say we could have a sample synthesized by noon. Any larger quantities, of course, would have to come from the Materiel Officer."

"All right, Doctor, you get your staff busy on the synthesis. Have them work closely with the Materiel and Armament Officers. I want a reasonable quantity of gas bombs available by no later than midafternoon. In the meantime, Colonel Bunyarit, get some high altitude patrols out, and locate a few villages. Then get a strike force organized. As soon as the gas bombs are ready, we're going to get us a few prisoners."

"But General, there's not much more I can learn from an anesthetized prisoner. What good will capturing a few more do?"

"I've got an idea about how to hang on to an unanesthetized prisoner. Now let's get busy. Meeting's dismissed."

"Another drink, Commissioner?"

"Thank you, General, I will. It's not the sort of luxury one normally expects at a forward base like this."

"I believe in being comfortable, Commissioner. Any fool can be uncomfortable. And besides, one doesn't normally expect to find a Commissioner for Native Affairs at a forward base, either. You realize, I hope, that we've already had one Kreg attack, and there may be more."

"Yes, but I've been under fire before. The Kregs can't possibly be any worse than some of the natives I've had responsibility for. But tell me, how did you manage to work out an agreement with the natives? I've read your report, of course, but it's so blasted brief. I mean, how did you learn their language, how did you analyze their culture, how did you learn what would induce them to behave? And for that matter, how did you manage to get them to hold still for you?"

"Commissioner, as you are aware, the basic problem was holding one, voluntarily or involuntarily, and getting the information out of him. By a stroke of good luck, we acquired a prisoner. Naturally we couldn't hold him permanently, but from a study of him we learned enough to enable us to capture some more. It turned out that the ones we worked with had no inhibitions about telling us what we wanted to know, after we learned a bit of the language. After all, learning an alien language is a pretty well-developed technique, nowadays, and these people don't have a very complicated one.

"We confirmed earlier reports that they move around a lot. They farm by burning off a stretch of forest, thus fertilizing the soil. They farm it for a few years, by which time it's worn out, and they move on. Naturally they can't come back to the same site until the forest is regrown. This means that each tribe has to have a pretty large area it can call its own. Naturally there's a lot of jockeying between tribes for particularly choice areas, such as those with good rivers, and so on. The social structure, as between tribes, approaches anarchy. Their Golden Rule is 'Do unto others before they have a chance to do unto you.'

"We learned that about fifty years ago a spaceship crashed on this continent, and one tribe managed to get some modern weapons from it. They cut quite a swath for a while, until they ran out of power packs. None of the tribes, however, forgot what energy weapons were, or how they could be used. When we landed, a few of the nearby tribes viewed us as their golden opportunity. They gave each other the bare minimum of co-operation which would enable each to get some weapons. They then were each going to grab themselves some more territory. Eventually, I suppose, they would have fought each other for the best land, but it never came to that stage.

"Once we understood the situation, we simply flew over their villages and broadcast to them that if they didn't let us alone, we'd supply weapons and instructions to their most deadly enemies. That was the stick. For the carrot, we recognized that in their chaotic situation, they would be willing to follow anyone who could offer them protection from each other. We offered them that protection, if they would help us in enforcing it. That's where you come in. They quickly saw the good sense of our offer, and came to terms. The only problem was to prevent ourselves from being robbed blind by teleporting thieves, and we solved that by sealing all the buildings, putting on double-door air locks, and flooding them with anesthetic."

"But, blast it, General, you still haven't told me. . . ."

"How we managed to hold a conscious prisoner? That turned out to be fairly simple. We realized that their teleporting range had to be limited, since it was we who found them, not vice versa. So we loaded our unconscious captives into a scout cruiser, and took them several planetary diameters off-world. It turned out we guessed right the first time, and we had them far enough out they couldn't teleport back. When they realized they weren't going anywhere, we had no further trouble with them. They were model prisoners."

DEAN McLAUGHLIN

HAWK AMONG
THE SPARROWS

The map position scope on the left side of *Pika-Don*'s instrument panel showed where he was, but it didn't show airfields. Right now, Howard Farman needed an airfield. He glanced again at the fuel gauge. Not a chance of making it to Frankfurt, or even into West Germany. Far below, white clouds like a featureless ocean sprawled all the way to the horizon.

Those clouds shouldn't have been there. Less than four hours ago, before he lifted off the *Eagle,* he'd studied a set of weather satellite photos freshly televised down from orbit. Southern France had been almost clear—only a dotting of cottonboll tufts. It should not have been possible for solid overcast to build up so fast. For the dozenth time, he flipped through the meteorological data on his clipboard. No, nothing that could have created such a change.

That made two things he hadn't been able to figure out. The second was even stranger. He'd lifted from the *Eagle*'s deck at midmorning. The French bomb test he'd been snooping had blinded him for a while —how long he didn't know—and *Pika-Don* was thrown out of control. The deadman circuit had cut in; control was re-established. When his sight came back—and it couldn't have been terribly long—the sun had been halfway down in the west.

It wasn't possible. *Pika-Don* didn't carry enough fuel to stay up that long.

Just the same, she had stayed up, and she still had almost half her load. When he couldn't find the *Eagle* near Gibraltar, he'd thought there was enough to take him to the American airbase at Frankfurt. (And where could the *Eagle* have gone? What could have happened to her radar beacon? Could the French blast have smashed *Pika-Don's* reception equipment? Everything else seemed to work all right. But he'd made an eyeball search, too. Aircraft tenders didn't just vanish.)

On the map scope, the Rhone valley crawled slowly southward under the north-moving central piplight that marked *Pika-Don's* inertially computed position. It matched perfectly the radar-scanned terrain displayed on the airspace viewscope on the right-hand side of the instrument panel. Frankfurt was still beyond the horizon, more than four hundred miles off. *Pika-Don* didn't have fuel to cover half that distance.

Well, he wouldn't find an airfield by staying up here, above that carpet of cloud. He eased the throttles back and put *Pika-Don's* nose down. She'd burn fuel a lot faster down close to the deck, but at Mach 1.5 he could search a lot of ground before the tanks went dry.

Not that he absolutely had to find an airfield. *Pika-Don* could put down almost anywhere if she had to. But an airfield would make it a lot simpler to get a new load of fuel, and it would make less complicated the problems that would come from putting down in a technically still friendly nation.

It was a long way down. He watched the radar-echo altimeter reel downward like a clock thrown into panicked reverse; watched the skin temperature gauge edge up, level out, edge up again as *Pika-Don* descended into thicker air. For the first eighty thousand feet, visibility was perfect, but at twelve thousand feet *Pika-Don* went into the clouds; it was like being swallowed by gray night. Uneasily, Farman watched the radar horizon; these clouds might go down all the way to the ground, and at Mach 1.5 there wouldn't be anything left but a smear if *Pika-Don* hit. She was too sweet an airplane for that. Besides, he was inside.

He broke out into clear air a little under four thousand feet. A small city lay off to his right. He turned toward it. Beaufort, the map scope said. There ought to be some sort of airfield near it. He pulled the throttles back as far as he dared—just enough to maintain airspeed. The Machmeter slipped back to 1.25.

He passed north of the town, scanning the land. No sign of a field. He circled southward, careful to keep his bearing away from the town's center. There'd be trouble enough about his coming down in France— aerial trespass by a nuclear-armed warplane, to start with—without half the townspeople screaming about smashed windows, cracked plaster, and roosters so frightened they stopped laying eggs. The ambassador in Paris was going to earn his paycheck this week.

Still no airfield. He went around again, farther out. Dozens of villages flashed past below. He tore his flight plan, orders, and weather data off their clipboard—crammed the papers into the disposal funnel; wouldn't do to have nosy Frenchmen pawing that stuff, not at all. He substituted the other flight plan—the one they'd given him just in case he had to put down in French or French-friendly territory.

He was starting his third circuit and the fuel gauge was leaning against the red mark when he saw the field. It wasn't much of a place— just a grassy postage stamp with a few old planes in front of three ramshackle sheds and a windsock flopping clumsily over the middle one. He put around, aimed for it, and converted to vertical thrust. Airspeed dropped quickly—there was a momentary surge of wing-surface heating—and then he was hovering only a few miles from the field. He used the deflectors to cover the distance, losing altitude as he went. He jockeyed to a position near the hangars, faced *Pika-Don* into the wind, and let her down.

The engines died—starved of fuel—before he could cut them off.

It took a while to disconnect all the umbilici that linked him into *Pika-Don*'s control and environment systems. Some of the connections were hard to reach. It took a while longer to raise the canopy, climb over the side, and drop to the ground. Two soldiers were waiting for him. They had rifles.

The bigger one—the one with the bushy mustache—spoke dangerously. Farman didn't know French, but their gestures with rifle muzzles were a universal language. He raised his hands. "I'm an American," he said. "I ran out of fuel." He hoped they weren't disciples of the late *grand Charles*. They looked nasty enough.

The two exchanged glances. *"Américain?"* the smaller one asked. He was clean-shaved. His eyes had a deep, hollow look. He didn't sound at all displeased.

Farman nodded vigorously. "Yes. American." He pointed to the fifty-one-star flag on his coverall sleeve. Their faces broke into delighted smiles and they turned their gun muzzles groundward. The small one— he made Farman think of a terrier, and his rifle was absurdly big for him—pointed to a shack beyond the hangars.

At least the natives seemed friendly. Farman went. The area in front of the hangars had been paved—an uneven spread of asphalt. Half a dozen rattletrap airplanes stood in a line, facing out toward the field. Where the pavement met unpaved ground, it was one mud puddle after another. Farman had to be careful where he put his feet; his flight boots had been clean when he took off this morning. The soldiers didn't seem to mind. They splashed cheerfully through the wet and scuffed their heels on the tufts of grass.

The planes were all the same type—biplanes with open cockpits and two-bladed wooden propellers and radial-type piston engines. The kind of planes, Farman thought, that shouldn't even be flying any more. Nevertheless, they were obviously working airplanes, with oil stains on their cowls and the smell of gasoline and patches glued over holes in the fabric of wings and fuselage. A crop-dusting outfit? Did the French have crop-dusting outfits? Then he realized that those things in front of the cockpits were machine guns. Air-cooled machine guns rigged to shoot through the propeller. And those odd, oval-shaped tail assemblies. . . .

Some kind of museum?

"That is strange aeroplane you have," the mustached soldier said. His accent was as thick as the grass on the field. "One like it I have not seen."

Farman hadn't known that either of them spoke English. "I'll need to make some phone calls," he said, thinking of the ambassador in Paris. A mechanic was working on one of the planes they passed; he was standing on a wooden packing crate, tinkering with the engine.

A movie outfit, doing a period flick? But he didn't see any cameras.

Another biplane taxied in from the field—a Nieuport, like the others. Its engine racketed like a lawnmower. It joggled and bounced in the chuckholes. There were a lot of chuckholes in the mud at the pavement's fringe. The plane came up on the pavement and the engine cut out. As the propeller turned around to a spasmodic stop, Farman realized that not just the propeller but the whole engine had been spinning. What kind of crazy way to build airplanes was that?

The Nieuport's pilot climbed up out of the cockpit and dropped to the ground. "Guns jammed again!" he yelled loudly, hellishly mad. He flung a small hammer on the ground at his feet.

Three men came out of the hangar carrying packing crates. They set them down around the Nieuport's nose, got up on them, and started working on the guns. The flier pulled off his scarf and draped it over the cockpit's side. He turned away, spoke a few French words over his shoulder to the mechanics, and walked off.

"Monsieur Blake!" the big soldier hailed. When the flier didn't seem to hear, the soldier ran to him, caught his shoulder. "Monsieur Blake. A countryman." The soldier beside Farman pointed to the flag on Farman's sleeve.

Blake came over, stuffing a goggled cloth helmet into a pocket of his heavy overcoat as he approached. His hand was out in welcome.

"This one has teach all my *Anglais* to me," the big trooper grinned. "Is good, *non?*"

Farman scarcely heard him. All his attention was on this American. "Harry Blake," the man introduced himself. " 'Fraid I won't be able to hear you too good for a while." He swung a glance at his Nieuport's motor and raised hands to his ears to signify deafness. He was young— not more than twenty-two or -three—but he had the mature poise of a man much older. "I'm a Lafayette with this outfit. From Springfield, Illinois. You?"

Farman accepted the hand in numb silence. By calling himself a Lafayette, the flier had obliterated Farman's last incredulous doubt. It wasn't possible—not real. Things like this didn't happen.

"Hey, you don't look so good," Blake said, grabbing his arm with a strong hand.

"I'll be all right," Farman said, but he wasn't really sure.

"Come on." Blake steered Farman into the passageway between two of the hangars. "We've got what you need back here."

The troopers came after them. "Monsieur Blake. This man has only now arrived. He has not reported."

Blake waved them away. "I haven't either. We'll report later. Can't you see when a man's breathed too much oil?"

The soldiers turned back. Blake's hand steered Farman onward. Puddles slopped under Blake's boots.

Behind the hangars, the path split in two directions. One way led to a latrine whose door swung loose in the breeze. The other led to a shack huddled up to the back of a hangar. It was hard to guess which path was more frequently used. Blake paused at the parting of the ways. "Think you can make it?"

"I'm all right." He wasn't, really. It takes more than a deep breath and a knuckling of the eyes to adjust a man to having lost six and a half decades. Between books about aerial combat he'd devoured as a kid— two wars and all those brushfire skirmishes—he'd read some Heinlein and Asimov. If it wasn't for that, he'd have had nothing to hang on to. It was like a kick in the belly.

"I'll be all right," he said.

"You're sure? You breathe castor oil a few hours a day and it doesn't do a man's constitution much good. Nothin' to be embarrassed about."

Every now and then, Farman had heard castor oil mentioned, mostly in jokes, but he'd never been sure what it did to a man. Now he remembered it had been used in aircraft engines of this time. Suddenly, he understood all. "That's one problem I don't have."

Blake laughed. "It's a problem we all have." He pushed open the shack's door. Farman went inside at his nod. Blake followed. "Onree!" Blake called out. "Two double brandies."

A round little baldpated Frenchman got up from a stool behind the cloth-draped trestle that served as a bar. He poured two glasses almost full of something dark. Blake picked up one in each hand. "How many for you?"

Whatever it was, it looked evil. "One," Farman said, "for a start." Either this youngster was showing off—which didn't seem likely—or it wasn't as deadly as it looked. "A double, that is."

Blake led the way to a table in the far corner, next to a window. It was a plain wood table, stained and scarred. Farman set his glass down and took a chair before he tried a small taste. It was like a trickle of fire all the way down. He looked at the glass as if it had fangs. "What is this stuff?"

Blake had sampled from each glass on the way to the table, to keep them from spilling. Now he was almost halfway through one of them and the other was close to his hand. "Blackberry brandy," he said with a rueful grin. "It's the only cure we've found. Would you rather have the disease?"

Flight medicine, Farman thought, had a long way to go. He put his glass carefully aside. "My plane doesn't use that kind of oil."

Blake was on him right away. "Something new? I thought they'd tried everything."

"It's a different kind of engine," Farman said. He had to do something with his hands. He took a sip of the brandy, choked, regretted it.

"How long you been flying?" Blake asked.

"Ten, twelve years."

Blake had been about to finish his first glass. He set it down untouched, looked straight at Farman. Slowly, a grin came. "All right. A joke's a joke. You going to be flying with us?"

"Maybe. I don't know," Farman said, holding his brandy glass in both hands, perfectly steady—and all the time, deep inside, the small trapped being that was himself screamed silently, *What's happened to me? What's happened?*

It had been a tricky mission, but he'd flown a lot of tricky ones. Ostensibly, he'd been taking part in a systems-test/training exercise off the northwest coast of Africa. High-altitude Mach 4 aircraft, their internal equipment assisted by the tracking and computer equipment on converted aircraft carriers, were attempting to intercept simulated ballistic warheads making re-entry into the atmosphere. He'd lifted from the deck of the airplane tender *Eagle* in the western Mediterranean. Half an hour later he was circling at Big Ten—one-zero-zero thousand feet—on-station north of the Canary Islands when the signal came that sent him on his true mission.

A guidance system had gone wrong at the Cape, said the talker aboard the *Iwo Jima,* and the range-safety system had failed. The misdirected warhead was arching over the Atlantic, farther and higher than programmed. Instead of splashing in the Atlantic, its projected impact-point was deep in the Sahara. It carried only a concrete block, not thermonuclear weaponry, but diplomatic relations with France—which still maintained military bases in this land it had once governed—were troublesome. Standing orders for such an eventuality were that, as a good-faith demonstration, an attempt should be made to intercept it.

Operation Skeetshoot's master computer said Farman's *Pika-Don* was the only plane able to make the interception. No other plane was in the right position. No other plane had enough altitude or fuel load. No other plane had such an advantageous direction of flight at that moment. Farman sent *Pika-Don* streaking toward interception point at full thrust.

As planned.

Nothing had really gone wrong at the Cape. It was a pretext. Washington knew the French were about to test a new-model nuclear bomb. They would explode it above the atmosphere, in the Van Allen belt; the rocket would be launched from their main testing site, the Saharan oasis of Reggan; they would select the moment of launch to coincide with the arrival of a solar proton storm, when subnuclear particles from the storm would blend with the bomb's fission products, rendering surveillance by other nations more difficult and the findings less certain.

The proton storm had been already on its way when Farman left the *Eagle*'s deck. It was being tracked, not only by American installations around the world, but by French stations also. Code message traffic was high between New Caledonia and Reggan. The time of the storm's arrival was known to within five seconds.

Farman hadn't paid much attention to why Washington wanted to snoop the test; the French were, after all, still allies in spite of the frictions between Paris and Washington. Asking questions like that wasn't Farman's job; he was just the airplane driver. But they'd told him anyway, when they gave him the mission. Something about Washington wanting to have up-to-date knowledge of France's independent nuclear capability. Such information was needed, they said, for accurate judgment of how dependent France might still be on America's ability to wage modern war. To Farman, the explanation didn't mean much; he didn't understand much about international politics.

But a warhead dropping into the atmosphere, sheathed in the meteor-flame of its fall—*that* he could understand. And a multi-megaton fireball a hundred miles up, blazing like the sun brought suddenly too close—that, too, he could understand. And a Mach 4 airplane riding her shock-wave across the sky, himself inside watching instruments and flight-path guide scopes, and his thumb on the button that would launch the Lance rockets sheathed against her belly. Those were things he understood. They were his job.

Nor did the mission call for him to do more than that. All that was really necessary was to have *Pika-Don* somewhere in the sky above Reggan when the French bomb went off. *Pika-Don* would do everything else, automatically.

All the planes in Operation Skeetshoot were equipped the same as

Pika-Don. All of them carried elaborate flight recorders; and because they were fitted to intercept thermonuclear warheads, and their own Lance rockets had sub-kiloton fission tips, those recorders included all the instruments needed to monitor a nuclear explosion—even a unit to measure the still not fully understood magnetohydrodynamic disturbances that played inside a nuclear fireball. (And, it was known from previous tests, there was something unusual about the magnetic fields of French bombs.)

Nor would there be much risk if *Pika-Don* were forced down where French nosypokes could get a look at it. All *Pika-Don* carried was standard equipment—equipment the French already knew about, in configurations and for purposes they also understood. There would be nothing the French could find to support a charge of deliberate snooping, no matter how much they might suspect. Not that the possibility was large; the explosion, after all, would be out in space. There'd be no blast effects, certainly, and very little radiation. Enough to tickle the instruments, was all.

And already the hot line between Washington and Paris would be explaining why an American plane was intruding on French-controlled airspace. Everything had been planned.

Farman watched his instruments, his flight-path guide scopes, his radar. *Pika-Don* slashed the thin air so fast she drew blood. She was up to one-three-zero thousand now; rocket launch point lay five thousand higher, two hundred miles ahead. Reggan moved onto the edge of the inertial-guide map-position scope, ahead and off to the south. The projected trajectory of the warhead was a red line striking downward on the foreview guide scope. An X-slash marked Skeetshoot Control's computed interception point.

Something flared on the radar near Reggan. It rose, slowly for a moment, then asymptotically faster and faster, shining on the radar screen like a bright, fierce jewel. The French rocket. Farman's breath caught as he watched it. The thing was going up. The test was on.

It rose, was level with him, then higher. Suddenly, it quivered like a water drop, and suddenly it was gone from the screen in an expanding black blindness like a hole in the universe; and simultaneously the cockpit was full of unendurable white light. The sky was flaming, so bright Farman couldn't look at it, didn't dare. He had just time enough to think, terrified, *Not in the Van Allen belt!* and then *Pika-Don* was spinning, spinning, spinning like a spindle—light flashing into the cockpit, then blackness, brightness, then blackness again, repeating and repeating faster and faster and faster until light and darkness merged to a flickering brilliance that dazzled not only the eyes but the whole brain. Farman battled the controls, but it was like fighting the Almighty's wrath. The flickering blaze went on and on.

And slowed. Stopped, like the last frame of film in a halted movie projector, and it was only daylight again, and *Pika-Don*'s disabled pilot circuit had cut in. She was flying level, northwestward if the compass could be trusted, and if the sun's position could be trusted, the afternoon was more than half gone. Farman was sure that much time had not passed.

The map scope confirmed the compass. So did the airspace radar view. The controls felt all right now, and *Pika-Don* seemed to fly without difficulty. He turned straight north toward the Mediterranean and came out above it not far from Oran. He curved west then, toward the spot where he'd left the *Eagle*. He watched the foreview guide scope for the *Eagle*'s homing beacon. It didn't show up. He spoke on the radio, got no answer. Equipment damage?

He took *Pika-Don* down to fifty thousand. He used the telescope-view scope on the ships his radar picked out. None was the *Eagle;* old freighters, mostly, and two small warships of a type he'd thought wasn't used any more except by the Peruvian Navy.

His orders said, if he couldn't find his base ship, go to Frankfurt. The big base there could take him. He turned *Pika-Don* northwestward. He crossed the French coast. Overcast covered the land. It shouldn't have been there. Fuel began to run low. It was going into the engines faster than the distance to Frankfurt was narrowing. He tried to cut fuel consumption, but he couldn't cut it enough. He had no choice but to put down in France.

"Look, Mister, either you've got orders to fly with us, or you don't," Blake said. "What outfit are you with?"

It was restricted information, but Farman didn't think it mattered much. "The CIA, I think."

He might as well have said the Seventh Cavalry with General Custer. "Where's your base?" Blake asked.

Farman took another swallow of brandy. He needed it, even if not for the reason Blake thought. It wasn't so bad, this time. He tried to think of a way to explain the thing that had happened to him. "Did you ever read *The Time Machine?*" he asked.

"What's that? A book about clocks?"

"It's a story by H. G. Wells."

"Who's H. G. Wells?"

He wasn't going to make much explanation by invoking H. G. Wells. "It's about a man who . . . who builds a machine that moves through time the way an airplane moves in the air."

"If you're having fun with me, you're doing it good," Blake said.

Farman tried again. "Think of a building—a tall building, with elevators in it. And suppose you don't know about elevators—can't even imagine how they work. And suppose you were on the ground floor, and suppose I came up and told you I was from the twentieth floor."

"I'd say that's doing a lot of supposing," Blake said.

"But you get the idea?"

"Maybe. Maybe not."

"All right. Now imagine that the ground floor is now. Today. And the basement is yesterday. And the second floor is tomorrow, and the third floor is the day after tomorrow, and so on."

"It's a way of thinking about things," Blake said.

Give thanks the elevator had been invented. "Take it one step more, now. Suppose you're on the ground floor, and someone comes down from the twentieth floor."

"He'd of come from somewhere the other side of next week," Blake said.

"That's the idea," Farman said. He took more of the brandy. "What if I told you I . . . just fell down the elevator shaft from sixty-some years up?"

Blake appeared to consider while he started on his second glass. He permitted himself a smile and a chuckle. "I'd say a man's got to be a bit crazy if he wants to fly in this war, and if you want to fight Huns you've come to the right place."

He didn't believe. Well, you couldn't expect him to. "I was born in nineteen fifty-three," Farman told him. "I'm thirty-two years old. My father was born in nineteen twenty. Right now, it's nineteen . . . seventeen?"

"Nineteen *eighteen*," Blake said. "June tenth. Have another brandy."

Farman discovered his glass was empty. He didn't remember emptying it. Shakily, he stood up. "I think I'd better talk to your commanding officer."

Blake waved him back to his chair. "Might as well have another brandy. He hasn't come back yet. My guns jammed and I couldn't get them unjammed, so I came home early. He'll be back when he runs out of bullets or fuel, one or the other."

His back was to the door, so he had to twist around while still talking, to see who came in. The small, razor-mustached man draped his overcoat on a chair and accepted the brandy the barman had poured without having to be asked. "Today, M'sieu Blake, it was a small bit of both." His English had only a flavor of accent. "On coming back, I find I am left with one bullet."

"How was the hunting?"

The Frenchman gave a shrug that was as much a part of France as the Eiffel Tower. "Ah, that man has the lives of a cat, the hide of an old bull elephant, and the skills of a magician."

"Keyserling?" Blake asked.

The newcomer took a chair at the table. "Who else? I have him in my sights. I shoot, and he is gone. It would be a shame to kill this man—he flies superbly!—and I would love to do it very much." He smiled and sipped his brandy.

"This is our CO," Blake said. "Philippe Deveraux. Thirty-three confirmed kills and maybe a dozen not confirmed. The only man on this part of the front with more is Keyserling." He turned to Farman. "I don't think I got your name."

Farman gave it. "He's just over from the States," Blake said. "And he's been funning me with the craziest story you ever heard."

Farman didn't bother to protest. In similar shoes, he'd be just as skeptical. "This Keyserling," he said. "That's Bruno Keyserling?"

He'd read about Keyserling; next to Richthofen, Bruno Keyserling had been the most hated, feared, and respected man in the German air force.

"That's him," Blake said. "There's not a one of us that wouldn't like to get him in our sights." He set his empty glass down hard. "But it won't happen that way. He's gotten better men than us. Sooner or later, he'll get us all."

Deveraux had been delicately sipping his drink. Now he set it down. "We shall talk of it later, M'sieu Blake," he said firmly. He addressed Farman. "You have been waiting for me?"

"Yes, I. . . ." Suddenly, he realized he didn't know what to say.

"Don't give him the same you gave me," Blake warned. "Now it's business."

"You are a pilot, M'sieu Farman?" Deveraux asked.

Farman nodded. "And I've got a plane that can fly faster and climb higher than anything you've got. I'd like a try at this Keyserling."

"That could possibly be arranged. But I should warn you, M'sieu . . . Farman, did you say?"

"Howard Farman."

"I should warn you, the man is a genius. He has done things his aeroplane should not be possible to do. He has shot down forty-six, perhaps more. Once three in a day. Once two in five minutes. It has been said the man came from nowhere—that he is one of the gods from the *Nibelungenlied,* come to battle for his fatherland. He. . . ."

"You might say I'm from nowhere, too," Farman said. "Me and my plane."

When Deveraux had finished his brandy and when Blake had downed his fourth, they went out in front of the hangars again. Farman wanted them to see *Pika-Don. Pika-Don* would be at least sixty years ahead of any plane they'd ever seen.

Her skids had cut into the turf like knives. Blake and Deveraux examined her from end to end. They walked around her, their boot tips whipping the grass. "Don't touch anything," Farman told them. "Even a scratch in the wrong place could wreck her." He didn't add that the rockets concealed under her belly could vaporize everything within a hundred yards. The false-skin strips that sealed them from the slipstream were supposed to be tamper-proof, but just to be safe Farman placed himself where they would have to go past him to investigate *Pika-Don*'s underside.

Pika-Don was eighty-nine feet long. Her shark-fin wings spanned less than twenty-five. She was like a needle dart, sleek and shiny and razor-sharp on the leading edge of her wings. Her fuselage was oddly flat-bodied, like a cobra's hood. Her airscoops were like tunnels.

Blake crouched down to examine the gear that retracted the skids. Farman moved close, ready to interrupt if Blake started to fool with the rockets. Instead, Blake discovered the vertical thrust vents and lay down to peer up into them. Deveraux put his head inside one of the tail pipes. It was big enough to crawl into. Slowly, Blake rolled out from under and got to his feet again.

"Do you believe me now?" Farman asked.

"Mister," Blake said, looking at him straight, "I don't know what this thing is, and I don't know how you got it here. But don't try to tell me it flies."

"How do you think I got it here?" Farman demanded. "I'll show you. I'll. . . ." He stopped. He'd forgotten he was out of fuel. "Ask your ground crews. They saw me bring her down."

Blake shook his head, fist on hips. "I know an aeroplane when I see one. This thing can't possibly fly."

Deveraux tramped toward them from the tail. "This is indeed the strangest zeppelin I have ever been shown, M'sieu. But obviously, a zeppelin so small—so obviously heavy . . . it can hardly be useful, M'sieu."

"I tell you, this is a *plane*. An *air*plane. It's faster than anything else in the air."

"But it has no wings, M'sieu. No propeller. It does not even have wheels on the undercarriage. How can such a thing as this gain airspeed if it has no wheels?"

Farman was speechless with exasperation. Couldn't they see? Wasn't it obvious?

"And why does it have so strong the scent of paraffin?" Deveraux asked.

A Nieuport buzzed over the hangars in a sudden burst of sound. It barrel-rolled twice, turned left, then right, then came down onto the grass. Its engine puttered. Its wires sang in the wind. It taxied across the field toward them.

"That'll be Mermier," Blake said. "He got one."

Two more planes followed. They did no acrobatics—merely turned into the wind and set down. They bounced over the turf toward the hangars. One had lost part of its upper wing. Shreds of cloth flickered in the breeze.

Blake and Deveraux still watched the sky beyond the hangars, but no more planes came. Blake's hand clapped Deveraux's shoulder. "Maybe they landed somewhere else."

Deveraux shrugged. "And perhaps they did not live that long. Come. We shall find out."

They walked to the other end of the flight line where the three planes straggled up on the hardstand. Deveraux hurried ahead and Mermier and then the other two pilots climbed out of their cockpits. They talked in French, with many gestures. Farman recognized a few of the gestures— the universal language of air combat—but others were strange or ambiguous. Abruptly, Deveraux turned away, his face wearing the look of pain nobly borne.

"They won't come back," Blake told Farman quietly. "They were seen going down. Burning." His fist struck the hangar's wall. "Keyserling got Michot. He was the only one of us that had a hope of getting him."

Deveraux came back. His face wore a tight, controlled smile. "M'sieu Farman," he said. "I must ask to be shown the abilities of your machine."

"I'll need five hundred gallons of kerosene," Farman said. That would be enough for a lift-off, a quick crack through the barrier, and a landing. Ten minutes in the air, if he didn't drive her faster than Mach 1.4. Enough to show them something of the things *Pika-Don* could do.

Deveraux frowned, touched his mustache, "Kerosene?"

"Paraffin," Blake said. "Lamp oil." He turned to Farman. "They call it paraffin over here. But five hundred gallons—are you nuts? There isn't an aeroplane flying that needs that much lubricating. Shucks, this whole *escadrille* doesn't use that much *gas* in a week. Besides, it's no good as a lubricant—if it was, you think we'd be using the stuff we do?"

"It's not a lubricant," Farman said. "She burns it. It's fuel. And she burns it fast. She delivers a lot of thrust."

"But . . . five hundred gallons!"

"I'll need that much just for a demonstration flight." He looked straight and firmly into Blake's incredulous eyes and decided not to add that, fully loaded, *Pika-Don* took fifty thousand gallons.

Deveraux smoothed his mustache. "In liters, that is how much?"

"You're going to let him . . . ?"

"M'sieu Blake, do you believe this man a fraud?"

Challenged like that, Blake did not back down. "I think he's funning us. He says he'll show us an aeroplane, and he showed us that . . . that thing over there. And when you want to see how it flies, he says it's out of fuel and asks for kerosene—*kerosene* of all things! Enough to go swimming in! Even if that's what she burns, he doesn't need anywhere near that much. And who ever heard of flying an aeroplane with lamp oil?"

Farman took Blake's arm, joggled it, made him turn. "I know," he said. "I'm telling you things it's hard to believe. In your shoes, I wouldn't believe me, either. All right. But let me have a chance to show you. I want to fight the Germans as much as you do." In his thoughts was the picture of a whole *jagdstaffel* of Albatrosses being engulfed by the fireball of one of *Pika-Don*'s rockets. They'd never even see him coming, he'd come at them so fast; even if they saw him, they wouldn't have a chance. Sitting ducks. Fish in a barrel.

"Mister," Blake said, "I don't know what you want all that kerosene for, but I'm sure of one thing—you don't need it to fly. Because if I was ever sure of anything, I know that thing can't fly."

"M'sieu Blake," Deveraux said, moving in front of the American. "This man may perhaps be mistaken, but I do not think he lies. He has a faith in himself. We have need of such men in this war. If he cannot use the paraffin when we have obtained it for him, it will be given to the chef for his stoves. We shall have lost nothing. But we must let him prove his abilities, if he can, for if there is some portion of truth in his claims, why, it is possible that we have before us the man and the machine that shall hurl Bruno Keyserling from the sky."

Blake gave way grudgingly. "If you're funning us, watch out."

"You'll see," Farman promised, grim. And to Deveraux: "Make it a high-grade kerosene. The best you can get." A jet engine could burn kerosene if it had to, but kerosene wasn't a perfect jet fuel any more than wood alcohol could make good martinis. Kerosene was just the nearest thing to jet fuel he could hope to find in 1918. "And we'll have to put it through some kind of filters."

"M'sieu," Deveraux said. "There is only one kind of paraffin. Either it is paraffin, or it is not."

Two days later, while they were waiting for the kerosene to come, Blake took him up in a Caudron two-seater to show him the landmarks. It was a clear day, with only a little dust haze in the direction of the front. Farman didn't think much of learning the landmarks—*Pika-Don*'s map scope was a lot more accurate than any amount of eyeball knowledge. But the scope wouldn't show him the front-line trenches twisting across the landscape, or the location of the German airfields. It might be useful to know such things. Farman borrowed flying clothes, and they were off.

The Caudron looked like nothing so much as a clumsy box kite, or a paleolithic ancestor of the P-38. Its two racketing engines were suspended between the upper and lower wings, one on either side of the passenger nacelle. The tail empennage was joined to the wings by openwork frames of wire-braced wood that extended back from behind the engines. It had a fragile appearance, but it held together sturdily as it lurched across the field like an uncontrolled baby carriage. Finally, after what seemed an interminable length of bumping and bouncing it lofted into the air at a speed that seemed hardly enough to get a feather airborne. A steady windblast tore at Farman's face. Hastily, he slipped the goggles down over his eyes. The climb to six thousand feet seemed to take years.

Blake didn't turn out of their spiral until they reached altitude, then headed east. The air seemed full of crests and hollows, over which the Caudron rode like a boat on a slow-swelled sea. Now and then, woozily, it swayed. A queasy feeling rooted itself in Farman's midsection, as if his stomach was being kneaded and squeezed.

Airsick? No, it couldn't be that. Anything but that. He was an experienced flier with more than ten thousand hours in the air. He couldn't possibly be airsick now. He swallowed hard and firmly held down.

Blake, in the cockpit behind him, yelled and pointed over the side. Farman leaned over. The rush of air almost ripped his goggles off. Far below, small as a diorama, the trench systems snaked across a strip of barren ground—two latticework patterns cut into the earth, roughly parallel to each other, jaggedly angular like toothpick structures that had been crushed. Between them, naked earth as horribly pocked as the surface of the moon.

The Caudron had been following a rivercourse. The trenchlines came down from the hills to the south, crossed the river, and continued northward into the hills on that side. Ahead, over the German trenches, black puffs of antiaircraft fire blossomed in spasmodic, irregular patterns. Blake banked the Caudron and turned south, yelling something over his shoulder about the Swiss border. The antiaircraft barrage slacked off.

Recognizing the front would be no problem, Farman decided. He tried to tell Blake, but the slipstream ripped the words away. He twisted around to say it straight. Something snatched at his sleeve.

He looked. Something had gashed the thick fabric, but there was nothing in sight that could have done it. And for some unaccountable reason Blake was heeling the Caudron over into a dive. The horizon tilted crazily, like water sloshing in a bowl. The Caudron's wire rigging snarled nastily.

"Use the gun!" Blake yelled. He jerked an urgent thumb upward.

There was a machine gun on the upper wing, above and just aft of Farman's cockpit, but for a shocked moment Farman didn't grasp what Blake was talking about. Then a dark airplane shape flashed overhead, so close the buzz of its motor could be heard through the noise of the Caudron's own two engines. The goggled, cruel-mouthed face of its pilot turned to look at them. Blake threw the Caudron into a tight turn that jammed Farman deep in his cockpit. Farman lost sight of the German plane, then found it again. It was coming at them.

It was purple—a dark royal purple—with white trim around the edges of wing and tail, and around the engine cowl. Little flashes of light sparked from its nose, and Farman heard something—it sounded like thick raindrops—spattering the upper wing close to the passenger nacelle. Tracer bullets flashed past like quick fireflies.

"Use the gun!" Blake yelled again. They were climbing now. They leveled off, turned. The German plane came after them. "Use the gun!"

He was being shot at. It was appalling. Things like that didn't happen. In a moment, Farman was too busy to think about it. Somehow he got his seat belt off and stood up in the cockpit, back to the wind. He fumbled with the machine gun's unfamiliar grips. He found the trigger before he knew what it was. The gun chattered and bucked in his grasp. He looked all over the sky for the purple airplane. It was nowhere in sight. Blake hurled the Caudron through another violent maneuver that almost threw Farman overboard, and suddenly there were three German planes behind them, high, the one with the white trim in front and the others trailing. The one with the white trim shifted a little to the left, turned inward again. It nosed down, gun muzzles flickering.

Farman swung the machine gun to bear on the German. He pressed the trigger. The gun stuttered and a spray of tracers streamed aft as it caught at the slipstream. They passed under the German, not even close.

Aerial gunnery wasn't a thing Farman had ever had to learn. Combat was done with guidance systems, computers, and target-seeking missiles, not antique .30 caliber popguns. He raised the gun and fired another burst. Still too low, and passing behind the German, who was boring close in, weaving up, sidewise, and down as he came. The gun didn't have any sights worth mentioning—no target tracking equipment at all. Farman wrestled with the clumsy weapon, trying to keep its muzzle pointed at the German. It should have been easy, but it wasn't. The German kept dodging. Farman emptied the machine gun without once touching the other plane. He spent an eternity dismounting the empty magazine and clipping another into place, all the time holding on one-handed, while Blake hurled the Caudron through a wild series of gut-wrenching acrobatics.

A section of the cockpit coaming at Farman's knee shattered and disappeared in the wind. He got the gun working again—fired a burst just as the German sidled behind the Caudron's right rudder. Farman's tracers went right through. The rudder exploded in a spray of chips and tatters. The German swung out to the right, gained a few feet altitude, turned in again and down again. His guns hurled blazing streaks. Blake sent the Caudron into a dive, a turn, and a twist that almost somersaulted Farman out of the plane. Abruptly, then, the German was gone. Little scraps were still tearing loose from the rudder, whipped away by the slipstream.

"Where?" Farman shouted, bending down as close to Blake as he could. He meant, where had the German gone, but he wasn't up to asking questions that complicated.

"Skedaddled," Blake yelled up at him. "We've got friends. Look."

Farman looked when Blake aimed his thumb. Five hundred feet above them five Nieuports cruised in neat formation. After a moment, the formation leader waggled his wings and they curved off eastward. Farman looked down and saw they were far behind the French lines, headed northwest. They were flying level and smooth—only the slow, gentle lift and descent of random air currents, like silence at the end of a storm. He sagged down into his cockpit. "You all right?" Blake asked.

"I think so," Farman said. But suddenly, as the Caudron slipped into a downdraft, he wasn't. His stomach wrenched, and he had time enough only to get his head over the cockpit's side before the first gush of vomit came. He was still there, gripping the splintered coaming with both hands, his stomach squeezing itself like a dry sponge, when Blake circled the airfield and slowly brought the Caudron down to a three-point landing. All Farman could think—distantly, with the part of his brain not concerned with his terrible miseries—was how long it had been since anyone, anywhere in the world, had even thought about making a three-point landing.

He wouldn't admit, even to himself, it had been airsickness. But after a while the horizon stopped wheeling around him and he could stand without needing a hand to steady him. He discovered he was very hungry. Blake went down to the mess hall and came back with a half-loaf of black bread and a dented tin of pâté. They went to the shack behind the hangars. Henri gave Blake a bottle of peasant's wine and two glasses. Blake put them down in the middle of the table and sat down across from Farman. He poured, and they went to work on the bread and pâté.

"He was trying to kill us," Farman said. It just came out of him. It had been there ever since the fight. "He was trying to *kill* us."

Blake cut himself another slice of the bread. He gnawed on the leathery crust. "Sure. And I'd of killed him, given the chance. That's what we're supposed to do—him and us, both. Nothing personal at all. I've got to admit I wasn't expecting him, though. They don't often come this side of the lines. But. . . ." He made a rueful grimace. "He's a tough one to outguess."

"He?"

Blake stopped gnawing, frowned. "You know who it was, don't you?"

The idea of knowing an enemy's name after such a brief acquaintance was completely strange to Farman. His mouth made motions, but no words came out.

"Bruno Keyserling," Blake said. "He's the only man with an aeroplane painted that way."

"I'm going to get him," Farman said.

"Easier said than done," Blake said. His mouth turned grim. "You'll have to sharpen up your gunnery quite a bit, if you're going to make good on that."

"I'm going to get him," Farman repeated, knuckles white on the table.

The next day it rained. Thick, wet, gray clouds crouched low to the ground and poured down torrents. All patrols were canceled, and the fliers sat in the shack behind the hangars, drinking and listening to the storm as it pelted the shingles. At first light, when he woke and heard the rain, Farman had borrowed a slicker and gone out to *Pika-Don*. She was all right. He'd left her buttoned up tight, and the rain was doing her no harm.

Blake was still the only man Farman could talk with, except for Deveraux. None of the other pilots had more than a smattering of English. When they left the mess hall after a drab lunch, instead of returning to the drinking shack, Blake led him to one of the hangars. There, in a back corner, were stacked wooden boxes of ammunition and others full of the bent-metal sections of disintegrating-link machine-gun belts. Blake showed Farman how to assemble the links and how to check both the links and the cartridges for manufacturing defects. He handed Farman a gauge into which a properly shaped cartridge should fit perfectly, and they spent the next several hours inspecting cartridges and assembling belts of ammunition. It was tedious work. Each cartridge looked just like the one before it. The imperfections were small.

"Do you always do this yourself?" Farman inspected his grimy hands, his split cuticles. He wasn't accustomed to this kind of work. "Every chance I get," Blake said. "There're enough reasons for a gun to jam without bad ammunition being one of 'em. When you're up there with Keyserling's circus flying rings around you, all you've got are your guns and your engine and your wings, and if any of those go, you go. And it's a long way down."

Farman said nothing for a while. Rain drummed on the roof. Now and then came the clang of tools being used in another part of the hangar. "How come you're here?" he asked finally. "What's in it for you?"

Blake's busy hands paused. He looked at Farman. "Say that again, slower."

"This here's a French squadron. You're an American. What are you doing here?"

Blake snorted—not quite a chuckle. "Fighting Germans."

Farman wondered if Blake was making fun of him. He tried again. "Sure—but why with a bunch of Frenchmen?"

Blake inspected a cartridge, fitted it into the belt. He picked up another. "Didn't care to transfer," he said. "Could have, when they started bringing U.S. squadrons over. But I like the plane I've got. If I transferred, they'd give me a plane the French don't want and the British don't want, because that's all the American squadrons are getting. Well, I don't want 'em, either." He dropped a cartridge in the reject pile.

"I didn't mean that," Farman said. "You joined before America got into the war—right?"

"Came over in 'sixteen."

"All right. That's what I mean. Why help France?" He couldn't understand why an American would do anything to help the personal kingdom of *le grand Charles*. "You weren't involved," he said. "Why?"

Blake went on inspecting cartridges. "Depends what you mean, involved. I figure I am. Everyone is. The Germans started this war. If we can show the world it doesn't pay to start a war, then there won't be any more. I want that. This is going to be the last war the human race will ever have."

Farman went back to inspecting cartridges. "Don't get your hopes too high," he said. It was as near as he could bring himself to telling Blake how doomed his optimism was. The rain made thunder on the roof like the march of armies.

Late in the afternoon, two days later, three lorries sputtered into the supply area behind the hangars. They brought fuel for the escadrille, but also, crowded among the drums of gasoline were twenty hundred-liter barrels of kerosene which were carefully put aside and trucked down to the mess hall's kitchen and then—when the error was discovered—had to be reloaded and trucked back up to the hangars again.

Farman had managed to rig a crude filtration system for the kerosene. The stuff they cooked with was full of junk. He'd scrounged sheets of silk, and enlisted a crew of mechanics to scrub empty petrol drums until their innards gleamed like the insides of dairy cans. He even succeeded in testing the rig with a bucket of kerosene cadged from the kitchens.

The process was glacially slow, and the end product neither looked nor smelled any different from the stuff he started with. But when he tried it in one of *Pika-Don*'s engines, the engine had started and—at low r.p.m.—had delivered thrust and functioned as it should until the tank was sucked dry. More important, when he inspected, none of the injectors had fouled.

He started the filtering process, and stayed with it through the night and all the next day. He had a mechanic to help him, but he had no confidence in the mechanic's understanding of how vital fuel quality was to an engine. It was not a thing an airplane mechanic of this time could be expected to know. Deveraux came around once, inspected the raw material and sniffed the filtered product, and went away again, having said nothing.

Once, between missions, Blake came and sat to watch. Farman showed him the sludge the filters had taken out of the kerosene. Blake scowled. "It's still kerosene," he said. "You can't fly an aeroplane on kerosene any more than you can feed it birdseed. I don't know what you really want it for, but don't expect me to believe it's for flying."

Farman shrugged. "I'll take *Pika-Don* up tomorrow morning. You can tell me what you think tomorrow afternoon. Fair enough?"

"Maybe," Blake said.

"You think I'm a cushmaker, don't you?"

"Possible. What's a cushmaker?"

Blake hadn't heard the story. Maybe it hadn't been invented yet. Farman explained it—the ultra shaggy joke about the cushmaker who, obliged by an admiral to demonstrate his specialty, after commandeering a battleship and tons of elaborate equipment, and after arduous technological efforts, finally dropped a white-hot sphere of steel amid the ice floes of the Antarctic Ocean, where it went *cussh*.

Blake went away, then. "I'll say this. If you're pulling a deal, you're a cool one." He shook his head. "I just don't know about you."

Morning brought high, ragged clouds. They'd make no trouble for the demonstration flight. Farman waited beside *Pika-Don* while Blake took off and slowly climbed to ten thousand feet, circling over the field the whole time. "I think we are ready, M'sieu," Deveraux said, fingering his trim mustache.

Farman turned to his plane. "Better make everybody stand back," he said. Turbine scream wasn't gentle to unprotected ears. He climbed up on the packing crate—pulled himself up *Pika-Don*'s sloped side and dropped into the cockpit. Looking back, he saw the onlookers had retreated about twenty-five feet. He had quite an audience. He grinned. They'd back off a lot farther when he got the engines going.

He got the cockpit hatch down. He checked the seal; it was tight. He went through the pre-ignition cockpit check. He began the engine start-up cycle, felt the momentary vibration and saw the twitch of instruments coming alive. Engine One caught, ragged for an instant, then steady as the tachometer wound around like a clock gone wild. Its scream of power drilled through the cockpit's insulation. Farman started Engine Two, then Engine Three. He brought them up to standby idle. They burned smooth.

Good enough. He didn't have fuel to waste on all the pre-takeoff operations; some were necessary, some not. He did all the necessary ones, turned the jets into the lift vents, and brought them up to full power. By that time, *Pika-Don* was already off the ground. She bobbled momentarily in the light breeze, and rose like a kite on a string. The sprawling fuselage surface prevented him from looking down at the airfield; it didn't matter. They'd be watching, all right—and probably holding shriek-filled ears. He grinned at the trembling instruments in front of him. He wished he could see their eyes, their open mouths. You'd think they'd never seen a plane fly before.

He took *Pika-Don* up to ten thousand feet. Hovering, he tried to find the image of Blake's Nieuport on the airspace view scope. It didn't show. For a worried moment, Farman wondered if something had gone wrong and Blake had gone down. Then the Nieuport flew past him on the left, a little above. It turned to pass in front of him. He could see Blake's goggled face turned toward him.

Even then, there wasn't an image on the radar. Farman swore. Something was wrong with the equipment.

No time to fiddle with the dials now, though. *Pika-Don* was guzzling the kerosene like a drunk on holiday. He converted to lateral flight. As always, it was like the floor dropping out from under him. He moved all three throttles forward, felt the thrust against his back. For a frightened instant, he saw Blake had turned back—was coming straight at him, head on. He'd warned Blake not to get ahead of him like that. But *Pika-Don* was dropping fast. At speeds less than Mach 0.5 she had the glide capability of a bowling ball. She slashed underneath the Nieuport with a hundred feet to spare. The altimeter began to unwind, faster and faster. The horizon lifted on the forward view scope like a saucer's rim.

He watched the Machmeter. It was edging up. He could feel the drive of the engines, full thrust now, exciting him like they always did, hurling him across the sky. The altimeter steadied, began to rise again. He tipped *Pika-Don*'s prow upward and cracked the barrier in a rocketing fifty-degree climb. Blake's Nieuport was nowhere in sight.

At forty thousand he cut the engines back, leveled off, and started down. He had to search hard for the airfield; without the map scope he couldn't have found it. It was just another green field in a countryside of green fields. At five thousand feet he converted back to vertical thrust and let *Pika-Don* drop to a landing—quickly for most of the distance to save fuel, with a heavy retarding burst in the last thousand feet. He hovered a moment two hundred feet up, picked out a landing spot, and put down. According to the gauges, less than thirty seconds' fuel was left in the tanks.

He dropped to the ground without waiting for a packing crate to be brought. He stood and looked around in disbelief. There was hardly a man in sight, and none of the escadrille's planes remained on the field. He saw them, finally, small specks flying off eastward. He walked back to the hangars, perplexed. Was that all the impression he'd made? He grabbed the first man he found—a mechanic. "What happened?"

The mechanic grinned and made gestures and gabbled in French. Farman shook him and asked again—or tried to—in pidgin French. All he got was more of the same jabber and some gestures in the general direction of the front lines. "I know they went that way," Farman growled and flung the man away. He stalked back to the shack behind the hangars and asked Henri for a Scotch. He drank it, waited five minutes, and had another. He was deep into his fourth when the men came back.

They trooped into the shack, and Henri set a row of glasses on the counter and went down the line with the brandy bottle. As soon as a glass had been filled, a hand snatched it away. Blake came to Farman's table, a brimful glass in his hand, sat down.

"Howard," he said, "I don't know how that thing of yours works. I don't even know if you can call it an aeroplane. But I've got to admit you got it off the ground, and the only thing I ever saw go past me faster was a bullet. Now, if you'll just tell me one thing. . . ."

"Anything you want to know," Farman said, abruptly raised from dejection to smugness.

"How can you fly when you don't have the wind on your face?"

Farman started to laugh, but Blake wasn't even smiling. To him, it wasn't an old joke. He was serious.

With effort, Farman controlled his amusement. "I don't need the wind. In fact, if the window broke, I'd probably be killed. I've got instruments that tell me everything I need to know."

He could see the skeptical expression shaping itself on Blake's face. He started to get up, not quite steady because of the Scotches he'd downed. "Come on. I'll show you the cockpit."

Blake waved him down. "I saw the cockpit. You've got so many things in there you don't have time to look outside. I don't know if I'd call it flying. You might as well be sitting at a desk."

Sometimes, Farman had thought the same thought. But all those instruments were necessary to fly a thing like *Pika-Don*. He wondered if he'd have taken up flying if he'd known it would be like that. "Or maybe a submarine?" he asked, not entirely sarcastic. "The thing is, did I fly circles around you, or didn't I?"

Blake's reply was a rueful shrug. "First, you hung there like a balloon. If I hadn't seen you, I wouldn't believe it. Then all of a sudden you were coming at me like something out of a cannon. I got to admit you had me scared. I never saw anything move like that thing of yours. By the time I got turned around you were out of sight. If we'd been dogfighting, you could of put a string of bullets through me from end to end, and I couldn't of got a shot off."

A shadow intruded onto the table between them. They looked up. "Indeed, M'sieu Farman," Deveraux said, "your machine's speed gives it the ability to attack without the risk of being attacked itself. I will not pretend to understand how it can fly with such small wings, nor how it can rise directly into the air, but I have seen it do these things. That is enough. I must apologize that we could not be here to applaud you when you landed."

So he'd made an impression after all. "Where'd you go? I thought you didn't have any patrols scheduled until this afternoon."

Deveraux pulled out a chair and sat down beside Blake. With delicate care, he placed a half-full wineglass in front of him. "That is true, M'sieu. But we heard the sound of big guns at the front, and our duty is to be in the air at such times, until the matter is clarified, doing such things as will assist our men in the trenches."

"I didn't hear any guns," Farman said. "When I got back here, it was as quiet as a bar mitzvah in Cairo."

He realized almost at once, seeing their faces, that the metaphor had no meaning for them. Well, they hadn't heard of Social Security, either.

"It is curious," Deveraux said. "When we are come to the front, it is as you say—most quiet. The guns have stopped, and we see no aircraft but our own. We search for fifty kilometers along the front. There is no evidence of even small actions. When we come back, I message to commanders at the front, and they tell me there has been no action. Nor have guns in their sectors been made use of—theirs or the Boche— though it is curious . . . some do say that they have heard guns being used in other sectors. And you can see"—he pointed to the window, the clear sky—"it could not have been thunder."

He said it all with the innocent mystification of a small boy, still not sure of all the things in the universe. Farman suddenly laughed and Deveraux blinked, startled.

"Sorry." Farman said. "I just realized. It wasn't guns you heard. It was me."

"You, M'sieu? What jest is this?"

"No joke. What you heard was my plane. It makes a shock wave in the air, just like an explosion's." He looked at their faces. "You don't believe me."

Deveraux's wineglass was empty. Blake stood up, empty brandy glass in hand. He reached for Deveraux's glass, but the Frenchman put his hand in the way. Blake went to the bar with only his own glass. Farman nursed his drink.

"I do not pretend to understand this aeroplane of yours," Deveraux said. "But now that you have shown its abilities. . . ."

"Some of them," Farman said. They'd only seen an iceberg tip of what *Pika-Don* could do.

"Yes. But now we have seen," Deveraux said. "I will agree, it is possible your machine could outmatch Bruno Keyserling."

"I know she can," Farman said.

"Perhaps," Deveraux said with a small smile, but very firm. "But I agree—it should be tried. If you will tell us where to mount the guns on your machine. . . ."

"I don't need guns," Farman said. "Don't want them."

"But M'sieu, an aeroplane *must* have guns. Without guns, it is like a tiger without teeth and claws."

The thought of machine guns stuck on *Pika-Don*'s prow was a horror. "I've got my own weapons," Farman said. Blake came back, sat down heavily. His glass slopped a little on the table. "Machine guns would . . . they'd destroy her aerodynamic integrity. They'd . . . she probably couldn't even fly with them sticking out in the wind."

"Aerody . . . *what* integrity?" Blake snorted. "What are you talking about?"

Farman leaned forward. "Look. You've seen my plane. All right. Now—you've seen those overlapping strips along her belly, between the ports the skids retract into?"

"I have noticed," Deveraux said.

"There's a rocket under each one of them," Farman said. "Just one of those can wipe out a whole squadron."

"Ah? How many rockets? Eight?"

"Six," Farman said. "How many squadrons have the Germans got in this sector?"

"Two jagdstaffels," Deveraux said. "They are quite enough." He shook his head. "But M'sieu, the men who planned the equipping of your aeroplane did not understand the needs of combat. It is assuming a marksman's skill beyond human abilities to believe that with only six of these rockets you could expect to be effective against enemy aircraft. One must remember, they are not motionless targets, like balloons. It is difficult enough to strike a balloon with rockets—balloons do not move —but to destroy an aeroplane . . . that cannot be done. Often I have expended all my ammunition—hundreds of rounds—without so much as touching my opponent. That you would imagine going into combat with a mere six possibilities of striking your target . . . this is folly. It is not worth the effort."

"They're not just things I shoot off," Farman said. Did he have to explain everything? "In fact, my plane's so fast any weapons system that depends on human senses couldn't possibly work. My rockets find their targets themselves. They are. . . ."

He saw the utter disbelief on their faces. "Look," he said, "I've shown you my plane can do everything I told you it could. It flies faster and climbs faster than anything you ever saw. Now, if you'll give me enough fuel to take her up against Keyserling, I'll show you what my rockets can do. They'll wipe him out of the sky like a blob of smoke in a high wind."

"Bruno Keyserling is a very skilled and deadly man," Deveraux said. "A man impossible to kill. We have tried—all of us. He has killed many of our own men, and he will send more of us down in flames before this war ends. I would suggest you be not so confident of yourself and your equipment."

"Just give me enough kerosene for a mission," Farman said. "One mission. Let me worry about the rest of it." He wasn't worried at all. A dogfight between World War I model planes and something from 1985 would be like a wrestling match between a man and a gorilla.

"But M'sieu, you *have* the paraffin," Deveraux said, mildly puzzled. "You have almost two thousand liters."

Farman shook his head. "I burned that. There's just about enough left to fill that glass of yours."

Deveraux looked down at his empty wineglass. "M'sieu, you must be joking."

"No joke," Farman said. *"Pika-Don"* flies fast and climbs like a rocket, but you don't get something for nothing—law of conservation of energy, if you know what that is. She drinks fuel like a sewer."

There was a silence—a silence, Farman realized, not only at their own table, but all through the shack. Maybe these fliers understood more English than he thought. Blake downed a large swallow of brandy.

"How much do you need for a mission?" he asked.

"Ten thousand gallons will do for a short one," Farman said. "An hour—hour and a half."

There was another long silence. "M'sieu," Deveraux said at last, "I have wide discretion in the requisition of the usual materials. I am trying to balance in my mind the possible destruction of Bruno Keyserling— which is a thing we all desire—against the difficulty I must expect in explaining my request for so much kitchen fuel. And I remain in doubt you will be able to accomplish as successful as you claim. So I must ask—have I your word of honor as an American that you must have this paraffin to fly your machine?"

"You've got it, on a stack of Bibles."

"The good old USA is alive with con men," Blake said.

"M'sieu Blake," Deveraux said reproachfully, "we must not assume that a man tells lies because he claims ability to do a thing we cannot do ourselves. He is optimistic, yes. But that is a fault of almost all the young men who come to us. If we do not put him to the test, we shall not know if he could do the thing he claims or not."

Blake made a sour twist of his mouth. "All right. But how are you going to explain wanting forty thousand liters of kerosene?"

Deveraux cocked his head to one side, as if listening to a voice no one else could hear. "I think I shall merely tell a part of the truth. That we wish to try a weapon suggested by one of our men, a weapon which makes use of paraffin."

"Such as?" Blake asked.

"If they want details," Farman said, leaning forward, "tell them you're putting it in old winebottles and cramming a rag in the neck. And before you drop the bottle on the Germans you set fire to the rag. The bottle breaks when it hits, and spills burning kerosene over everything."

Blake and Deveraux looked at each other. Delight animated their faces. "Now that's something I think might work," Blake said, rubbing his jaw. "Why didn't somebody think of it before?"

It was the first time Farman had heard him enthusiastic about something. This, at least, was a weapon they could understand. "It might work," he said. "But gasoline does it better. It's called a Molotov cocktail."

"M'sieu Farman," Deveraux said, "I think we shall try that, also." He stood up, wineglass in hand. "Henri!" he called. "More wine!"

Early that afternoon, two men came to the airfield fresh from training school. Boys, really; neither could have been more than seventeen. They were eager to get into the war—looked disconsolate as they came away from reporting to Deveraux. "They'll have to spend a day or two learning their way around," Blake said, a twisty smile curling his mouth. "Some guys just can't wait to get killed."

Their Nieuports were straight from the factory, new as pennies. The smell of dope and varnish surrounded them like an aura. Blake worked his way around them, a point-by-point inspection. The new men would be assigned to his flight. He peered intently at struts and wires and fabric surfaces. "Good aeroplanes," he said finally. Then it was time for him to go out on patrol. Three other men went with him. Farman watched them take off. They disappeared eastward. He went back and saw about readying his jerrybuilt filtration plant for the job of turning ten thousand gallons of cooking oil into aviation fuel.

At first light next morning, the new men stood beside their planes and watched the escadrille fly out on dawn patrol. They looked like children not invited to play. Farman went and checked *Pika-Don;* there was a sign of a gummy deposit in her tailpipes, but a close inspection of her compressor blades showed they were clean, and none of the fuel injectors was fouled. He buttoned her up again and headed for the drinking shack. Until he got a shipment of kerosene, he'd have nothing to do.

The escadrille came back three hours later. If there'd been any Germans in the sky that morning, they'd made themselves hard to find. There'd been no action. Six planes refueled at once and went out again. Deveraux took the new men out on an orientation flight. In the afternoon, Blake and another pilot took the new men out for a mock dogfight. When they came back, Farman was waiting at the edge of the field; he had an idea he felt foolish for not having thought of sooner—to make a start on the long kerosene-upgrading job by borrowing a barrel or two of the raw material from the mess hall. He needed Blake to translate and haggle for him.

As Blake taxied up onto the hardstand, Farman saw the tattered fabric fluttering from the right upper wing. He ran over as Blake cut the motor. "Hey! You've been in a fight!"

Blake dropped down from the cockpit. He stripped off helmet and goggles and gloves. Farman repeated his question. Blake grinned and pointed to his ears and shook his head. Farman pointed at the shredded wing.

"Yeah. I've been in a fight," Blake said, his voice loud as if he was trying to talk through the noise his motor had made.

Farman looked out at the other planes taxiing in from the field. "They're all right," Blake said. "We jumped a Brandenburg—what he was doing way off there behind the lines, don't ask me. I got the observer interested in me"—he nodded at the damaged wing—"and Jacques moved in and put a few in the engine. Simple enough."

The other planes of the flight came up on the hardstand, and the mechanics moved in to turn them around and chock the wheels. The pilots climbed out, and the new men crowded around the other veteran —Jacques, Farman assumed. They pumped his arm and slapped his back and jabbered jubilantly. Jacques managed to break free of them long enough to reach Blake. He grabbed both Blake's arms and spoke with a warm grin. Blake looked a little embarrassed by the attention and managed, finally, to shrug off Jacques' hands without offending. By then the new men had closed in again. A rapid four-way conversation broke out.

Blake got loose again after a minute. "They never saw an aeroplane shot down before." He grinned. "Wasn't much of a shoot-down, really.

Jacques put a few in the engine, and it just sort of went into a glide." He nodded at the three men; they were still talking energetically. "I guess they liked the show, even if they don't understand some of it. They're wanting to know why we didn't go on shooting after Jacques got the engine."

It sounded like a reasonable thing to ask. "Well, why didn't you?" He remembered to speak loud.

Blake shrugged. "Why kill 'em? There's enough people getting killed. They were out of the war as soon as their propeller stopped."

"Well, yes. Sure. But. . . ."

"Oh, we made sure they landed close to a convoy on the road, so they'd be captured all right," Blake said. "Didn't want a pair of Huns running loose behind the lines."

"But they were Germans. The enemy."

Blake punched a finger into Farman's ribs. "Once Jacques got their engine, they were just a couple of poor guys in an aeroplane that couldn't fly any more. We got no fight with guys like that. It's the man they worked for we're against. The Kaiser. Besides, that guy in the rear cockpit still had a lot of bullets in his machine gun, and he was sort of mad at us. I figure we were smart to keep our distance."

The new men had a few more training flights the next day, and the day after that they went out with the dawn patrol. The patrol met a flight of German machines led by Keyserling's white-trimmed purple Albatross. It was a fast, cruel scrap. Only one of the new men came back.

"We shouldn't of put 'em on service so quick," Blake said, nodding across the shack toward where the survivor was slowly drinking himself into numbness; he'd been in shock ever since he climbed out of his cockpit. "But we've got to have men. It takes three months to train a man enough so he's got a chance in the air—and Keyserling and his circus kill 'em in five minutes. Like swatting a fly." He picked up his brandy and downed it whole.

Deveraux came and put a hand on Blake's shoulder. "It is true," he said. "One might wish we did not so desperately need men to fight. But we fight a war to preserve civilization, and for that it is necessary that some good men die. And so we have lost one man today. And one other machine is damaged. Do not forget, Keyserling has lost two men in this morning's battle, and three of his aeroplanes will need considerable work before they fly again. We have done well, this day."

"Yeah. Sure. But he was just a kid," Blake said. His open hand banged on the table. Glasses rattled. "A poor, dumb kid. As green as—"

"To keep a civilization is worth a few lives, M'sieu Blake." Deveraux squeezed Blake's shoulder, held the grip a moment, let his hand slip away. He moved off to talk with the men at another table.

"Civilization," Blake muttered.

"Stick around," Farman said. If he lived long enough, Blake would know of Dachau, Bataan, Hiroshima, 'Nam, and the bloody mess France herself would make of her African colonies. And lots more.

"You haven't seen anything yet," Farman said.

The kerosene began to come two days later. It came spasmodically, in odd-sized lots: one day a demijohn arrived; the next, half a lorry load. Kerosene, to these people, was not a strategically vital petrochemical; it was a fluid used in lamps and stoves. It couldn't just be commanded up from the nearest supply dump in anything like the quantities a supersonic jet had to have. Genghis Khan's army might have been similarly inept at meeting a sudden, inexplicable demand for a few thousand pounds of gunpowder.

June became July. The summer sun burned warm. There was talk of heavy fighting to the north, in a place called Bois de Belleau. Farman worked at the makeshift filters day after day. The smell of warm kerosene was a weight in his lungs, an ache in his brain. Some evenings, he was too sickened to eat.

The weeks blended into each other. He didn't have much idle time; there was always more kerosene to be poured into the system, or a filter to be changed and the clogged filter to be scraped and scrubbed and carefully examined for flaws before being used again. After a while, he stopped looking up when he heard the sound of airplane motors.

But in that time he saw airplanes lose power as they left the ground, stall, and nose stiffly into the turf. Their wings snapped like jackstraws. He saw a tattered plane coming back from a dogfight; it fell apart over the field and its pilot died in the wreck. He saw a man bring his plane down, taxi off the field, and die from loss of blood with the engine still puttering. And there were many times when he saw men watch the sky, searching for planes that would not come back, ever.

Some nights, he heard the big guns thunder at the front, like a grumbling storm just beyond the horizon. Muzzle flash and shellburst blazed in the sky.

Several days came when no new loads of kerosene arrived. He used that time to learn what he could about the Germans—their tactics, their formations, the capabilities of their planes. Not much of the information was useful—he'd expected that; matched against *Pika-Don,* they'd be almost motionless targets. But with only ten thousand gallons to fly on, it would be a good idea to know where he'd be most likely to find them. He wouldn't have much more time in the air than just enough to lift off, aim and launch rockets, and return to base. He started planning the mission.

"They stay mostly on their own side of the lines," he said to Deveraux. "All right. When I go up, I don't want you to have any planes on that side. I want to be sure any planes I find over there are theirs, not yours. I'll be going too fast to look at 'em close."

"You ask more than is possible, or even wise," Deveraux said. Breeze ruffled grass on the field. The Frenchman's scarf flapped and fluttered. "It is necessary always to have patrols in all sectors to protect our reconnaissance aeroplanes. If we do not patrol, the reconnaissance aeroplanes would be attacked. They could not do their missions. Perhaps it would be possible to remove patrols from one sector for a few hours—one in which none of our observation missions will be flying. Is not that as much as you shall need?"

"Not quite," Farman said. "I don't think you've thought it all the way through. You cover the front between the Swiss border and the Vosges Mountains. Right?"

"There are several escadrilles with which we share that duty."

"Yeah. Well, that's not important except they'll have to be warned off, too. What I'm asking now is, how many miles of front are you covering? Fifty? Seventy-five?"

"It is fifty kilometers," Deveraux said.

"All right. I'll be flying at about Mach 2. At that speed, I can cover that much distance in three minutes. It takes me twenty miles just to get turned around. I can patrol the whole front, all by myself. You don't need to have anybody else out there."

Deveraux's face wore a scowlish mask. "So fast? I must assume you do not exaggerate, M'sieu."

"At sixty thousand feet, I could do it twice that fast," Farman said. "But I'm going to cruise at forty. Air's too thick for full power flying that low down. I'd burn like a meteor."

"Of course, M'sieu."

Farman couldn't be sure if Deveraux believed him or not.

"But I must say, it would seem you have not considered all the necessities," the Frenchman went on. "Even if you are able to patrol all the sectors, that would be true only should you not find a Boche patrol. Then you would move to attack it, and *voilà,* you would be engaged in combat, M'sieu. You would cease to patrol. And it is not uncommon for the Boche to have four or five flights in the air at one time. Who would be protecting our observation missions while you are fighting?"

"I don't even want any observation flights on that side of the lines while I'm flying," Farman said. "Because I'm going to wipe that sky clean like a blackboard. If you have observation planes over there, they might get it, too. So you don't need to have any patrols out to protect 'em. Anyway, it won't take me more than five minutes from the time I've spotted a flight until I've launched rockets, and then I'll be free to go back on patrol. That's not much more than if I'd took time out for a smoke."

They heard, then, very faint but growing, the sound of aircraft motors. Deveraux turned to search the eastward sky for the approaching planes. "And have you thought, M'sieu, what the Boche would be doing while you are shooting these rockets of yours? Bruno Keyserling and his men are aviators of consummate skill. They would not fly calmly, doing nothing, while you attack them. And even should your rockets each find a target, that would still be only one of their aeroplanes for each rocket. You have, I believe you said, only six."

"They won't even see me coming, I'll jump 'em so fast," Farman said. "They won't have time to do anything but look surprised. And one of my rockets can. . . . " He made a wipe-out gesture. "Look. All I'm asking—keep your planes on this side of the lines for a couple of hours. With only ten thousand gallons, I won't be able to stay out even that long. Am I asking too much? Two hours?"

The returning planes were in sight now. There were three of them, strung out, the one in the rear far behind the other two, losing altitude, regaining it, losing it again. Farman didn't know how many had gone out on that particular patrol—he hadn't been paying much attention to such things—but it was rare for a patrol of only three planes to go out. There would be some empty chairs in the mess, this evening.

The first plane came down to land. Its lower wing was shredded close to the fuselage—loose fabric fluttered like torn flags—and the landing gear wheel on that side wobbled oddly. As it touched down, the whole gear collapsed. The wing dipped—caught the ground—and flung the machine into a tangle of broken struts, tail high in the air. Men ran across the field. Farman caught a glimpse of the pilot's arm, waving for help. A thin black thread of smoke began to rise. A moment later it was a fierce inferno. No one could get near it. There wasn't a sign of the man. The second plane landed and taxied across the grass unheeded.

Deveraux turned to Farman again. "No, M'sieu," he said. "You do not ask too much. It is we who ask too much of men."

Farman boosted *Pika-Don* from the field while dawn was still a growing light in the east and all the land was gray. She lifted sluggishly; well, the gunk he was feeding her was a poor substitute for her usual diet. He took her to eight thousand feet before converting to lateral flight. She was down to four before she cracked the barrier and down to three and a half before she bottomed out and started to climb. The Machmeter moved past 1.25. He raised *Pika-Don*'s nose and drove her at the sky.

She broke into sunlight at twenty thousand feet. The sun was gold and the air was as clean as clear ice. Somewhere in the darkness below two armies faced each other as they had faced each other for four years. At forty thousand feet he leveled off and began his loiter pattern—a slim-waisted figure eight course, looping first to the south, then to the north

—overflying the German lines from the Swiss border to the Vosges Mountains. He watched the airspace view scope for the pips that would be German aircraft.

Almost always, on good flying days, the Germans sent up patrols a few minutes before sunrise, to intercept the reconnaissance planes the French almost always sent over on good flying days. Bruno Keyserling would be leading one of those patrols. Farman watched particularly the area surrounding the German airfield. The Germans would climb quickly to fighting altitude; as soon as their altitude and motion dissociated them from the ground, *Pika-Don*'s radars would pick them out. He watched the scope, followed his loiter pattern, and waited for the German planes to appear.

Two circuits later, he was still up there. The scope showed the shaded contours of the land, but that was all. Not one German plane—no planes at all, even though the whole escadrille had flown out ahead of him to watch the fight he'd promised. He had fuel enough for six or eight more circuits—it was going faster than he'd counted on—before there'd be only enough to get him back to the field.

And more weeks of filtering kerosene? Not if he could help it. He made two more circuits—still nothing. He put *Pika-Don*'s needle prow downward. If they wouldn't come up and fight, he'd go after them. He checked the German field's position on the map scope. He could fly down straight to the end of its runway, and he had six rockets. One would be enough. Two would destroy it utterly.

He was down below twenty thousand feet when he saw the airplanes. They were flying on a northerly course, as he was, patrolling above the German lines in a Junck's row formation—each plane above, behind, and to the side of the one below it; an upright, diagonal line. A quick glance at the radar scope: not a hint of those planes.

Nuts with the airfield. Not with those planes over there. Flying where they were, using that formation, they had to be Germans. Farman pulled out of this attack dive, immelmanned into a corkscrew turn that would take him back and place him behind their formation. He lost sight of them in that maneuver, but the map scope showed him where they had to be; they didn't have the speed to move far while he was getting into position.

Behind them now, he turned again and drove toward them. Still nothing on the airspace scope, but he knew where they were. He tried the target-tracking radar—the one in the middle of the instrument panel. They didn't show there, either.

But he knew where they were, and in another moment he saw them again. Little black specks, like gnats, only gnats didn't fly in formation. And one rocket anywhere near them. . . .

Still they didn't show on the target-tracking scope. It would have to be an eyeball launch, then. He primed the proximity detonators on rockets one and six. There still was no sign that they'd seen him. They didn't even seem to move against the sky.

He launched the rockets at four miles. The distance was a guess— without help from his radars, a guess was all he could do, but the German planes were still only specks. It didn't matter. The rockets were built to heat-seek a target from ten times that distance. He felt the shock as the rockets struck from their sheaths even as he sent *Pika-Don* screaming straight up, engines suddenly at full thrust, and over on her back, and a half-roll, and he was at forty-five thousand feet. Rockets one and six sketched their ionized tracks on the airspace scope, all the way to the edge.

The edge was somewhere beyond the crest of the Vosges Mountains. Farman couldn't understand it. He'd sent those rockets straight as bullets into that formation, proximities primed and warheads armed. They should have climbed right up those Germans' tailpipes and fireballed and wiped those planes from the sky like tinder touched by flame. It hadn't happened.

He brought *Pika-Don* around. On the map scope he found again the position where the German planes had been. They didn't show on the airspace view—what could possibly be wrong with the radar—but they would still be close to where he'd seen them last, and he still had four rockets left. On the airspace scope, the tracks of rockets one and six ended in tiny sparks as their propellants exhausted and their automatic destructs melted them to vapor. He turned *Pika-Don*'s nose down. He armed the warheads, primed the proximities. This time he wouldn't miss.

He saw the German planes from ten miles away. He launched rockets two and five from a distance of five miles. Two seconds later, he launched three and four and turned away in a high-G immelmann. His G-suit seized him like a hand—squeezed, relaxed, and squeezed again as he threw *Pika-Don* into a long, circling curve. The airspace scope flickered, re-oriented itself. His four rockets traced bright streaks across its face.

Explode! he thought. *Explode!*

They didn't. They traced their paths out to the scope's edge. Their destruct mechanisms turned them to vapor. Ahead of him now, again, he could see the disorganized swarm of the jagdstaffel. He hadn't touched one of them. And they still didn't show on the airspace scope.

Farman swore with self-directed disgust. He should have thought of it. Those planes were invisible to radar. They didn't have enough metal among them to make a decent tin can, so his radar equipment rejected the signals they reflected as static. For the same reason, the proximities hadn't worked. The rockets could have passed right through the formation—probably had—without being triggered. As far as the proximities were concerned, they'd flown through empty air. He might as well have tried to shoot down a cloud.

He turned west, back to base. He located the field with the map scope. He had enough fuel to get there, and some to spare. A thought trickled through his mind about the dinosaurs—how their bodies had been perfectly adapted to the world they lived in, and when the world changed their bodies had not been able to adjust to the changes. So they died.

Pika-Don was like that—a flying *Tyrannosaurus rex* whose world now gave it only insects for food.

"Yeah. We saw the whole action," Blake said. He sat with his back against the hangar wall, a wine bottle close to his hand. The sun was bright and the fields were green. A light breeze stirred.

The escadrille had come back a half hour after Farman landed. Farman had hesitated, but then went out to face Deveraux. He was not eager for the confrontation.

Deveraux was philosophically gentle. "You have seen now, M'sieu, the rockets you carried were not an adequate armament for combat situations. Now, if you will show our mechanics where you think it would be best to mount the machine guns they. . . ."

"*Pika-Don* flies faster than bullets," Farman said. He kicked at a ridge of dirt between wheel ruts. The dirt was hard, but it broke on the third try. "I even heard of a guy that got ahead of his own bullets and shot himself down. And his plane was a lot slower than mine." He shook his head—looked back toward where *Pika-Don* crouched low to the ground, sleek and sinister-looking, totally useless. "Might as well let her rot there."

He kicked the loosened clod off into the grass.

About eleven o'clock, Blake got a bottle of wine from Henri. It was plain peasant's wine, but that was all right. They sat in the narrow noontide shade of a hangar and worked on it.

"You've got to get in close before you shoot," Blake said. "I don't know where you learned combat, but it didn't look like you learned much. You flew at their formation so fast they wouldn't of seen you until you broke right through 'em, but you shot those rockets from a couple of miles away. You can't hit anything at that kind of range."

"I thought I could," Farman said. "And with the kind of warheads they had, it's a good idea to have a few miles distance when they go off."

"You don't think you're funning me with that, do you?" Blake said. He sat up straight—looked at Farman. "Nothing scatters shrapnel that wide."

Farman helped himself from the bottle. "My rockets would have done more than just scatter shrapnel, if they'd gone off."

"Not much good if you've got to shoot 'em from so far off you can't hit the target," Blake said.

It was no use trying again to explain target-seeking missiles. Anyway, they hadn't worked. He'd finally figured that out, too. Their heat-seeking elements had been designed to track on a hot jet's exhaust, or the meteor-flame of a ballistic warhead. All the German planes were putting out was the feeble warmth of a piston engine. That wasn't enough. If he was going to do any good in this war, it wasn't going to be with *Pika-Don*. "Harry, I want you to check me out on your plane."

"Huh?"

"My plane's useless. She hasn't any teeth left," Farman said. "If I'm going to do any more fighting, it's going to be in a plane like yours. I've got more flying hours than all of you put together, but I don't have any cockpit time in your—" He almost called them box kites. "I want you to show me how it flies."

Blake shrugged. "One plane's pretty much like another. They've all got their tricks—like these Nieuports, you don't want to do much diving in them; takes the fabric off the top wings every time. But aside from that the only way you get the feel is by flying 'em."

They walked out to Blake's Nieuport. It looked about as airworthy as a Model T Ford. Farman had a little trouble climbing up until Blake showed him the footholds. It was cramped in the cockpit, and the wicker seat was hard. Blake stood on a packing crate and leaned over the coaming.

Farman put his hand on the stick. That was what it was—an erect rod sticking up between his knees. He'd never seen one like it before. He tried moving it, and it moved with the smoothness of a spoon in a gluepot. "Do you have to fight it like this all the time?" he asked.

"Takes some getting used to," Blake said. "It's easier when she's flying, though."

Farman turned his attention to the instruments. They were a haphazard assortment of circular dials, unevenly distributed, and except for one big dial straight in front of him there was no apparent priority of position given to the more important ones—whichever ones they were. They were all identified, the words lettered across their faces, but the words were French.

"That's the oil pressure," Blake said, tapping the glass in front of a dial. "And that's r.p.m., and that's fuel mixture."

"Oil pressure. Is that important?"

Blake looked at him strangely. "You say you've been flying...*how* long? And you don't know oil pressure?"

"I've never flown a piston engine craft," Farman said. *"Pika-Don* has a different kind. Is it important?"

"Your engine doesn't work too good without it."

"And—fuel mixture, did you say?" Farman asked, putting his finger to the dial Blake had indicated. He was careful not to ask if it was important, though he wasn't sure what difference it made. Mixed with what, he wondered to himself.

"Right," Blake said. "And this here's your compass—don't trust it too far—and that's the altimeter, and here's the gas gauge."

At least those were instruments Farman understood. But he frowned at the altimeter. "Is that the highest this can fly?"

"Those are meters, not feet," Blake said. "This crate can go up as high as I can breathe. Sixteen...eighteen thousand feet." He pointed into the cockpit again. "This here's the switch, and that's the throttle, and that's the mixture control."

Farman touched them, one by one, trying to get their feel. His hand encountered a small plumb bob dangling from a cord. "Good-luck charm?" he asked.

Blake laughed. "Yeah, it's good luck all right. Without it I could be flying upside down and not know it."

"Don't you have a turn-and-bank indicator?" Farman wondered.

"Mister, that *is* my turn-and-bank indicator."

"Oh," Farman said, feeling foolish. But how could he have known?

"And these here," Blake went on, unnoticing, "that one tightens the flying wires, and that one the landing wires."

"What kind of wires?"

"Some wires you want tight when you're flying, and some others when you're coming in to land. If you don't, you stand a good chance of coming apart at the wrong time."

"Oh." Flying a Nieuport wasn't going to be as easy as he'd thought. It would be like trying to ride horseback after driving cars all your life. "My plane doesn't have wires."

"What holds it together?" Blake asked.

Farman ignored him. He was thinking about driving a car, and some of his confidence came back. This Nieuport was a lot different from *Pika-Don,* but her engine wasn't too much different from the one in the BMW he'd had in another place and time—more primitive, maybe, but it worked on the same principles. He could handle a gasoline engine all right.

"Where's the starter?" he asked.

Blake frowned, as if he didn't understand. Then a wry grin cracked his face. He nodded forward—pointed to the propeller's blade. "Right there," he said.

Half a minute later Farman was looking forward through the blur of a spinning propeller. He felt the blast of air on his face, and the stench of exhaust made him want to retch. The oil-pressure gauge worked up. He experimented with throttle settings and fuel-mixture adjustments, trying to learn something about how it handled. It occurred to him that his BMW had two or three times the horsepower this thing had.

Blake handed him a helmet and goggles. Farman put them on. "Taxi her around a bit, until you get the feel," Blake yelled through the engine's blatting. Farman nodded, and Blake bent to pull the chocks from in front of the wheels; one side and then—slipping quickly underneath —the other. The Nieuport lurched forward even before Farman advanced the throttle. It bumped clumsily over the grass.

The thing had no brakes, so when he advanced the throttle again she hurtled forward, bumping and thumping across the field. The airspeed indicator began to show readings. The bumping got worse. He edged the throttle forward a little more. Except for the jouncing and that awful smell, it wasn't much different from driving a car.

The tail came up. It startled him, and it was almost by reflex—seeing the horizon lift in front of him—that Farman pulled the stick back. The bumping stopped as if it were shut off. The engine's sound changed, and airspeed began to slacken. The silly Model T was airborne. He shoved the throttle forward and tried to level out. It shouldn't have been flying at this speed—he'd driven his BMW faster than this, and his BMW was a lot more streamlined.

He was beyond the field's edge now, with a rise of ground ahead of him. He tried to turn, but the Nieuport resisted. He pulled the stick back to clear the hill's crest. The airspeed meter started to unwind. He got over the hill with a few yards to spare, but airspeed was falling back toward zero. He tried to level out again; it wasn't easy to do without an artificial horizon on the instrument panel. The real horizon was rocking back and forth, up and down, and drifting sidewise. He tried turning the other way, and she turned easily but she also nosed down. He hauled back on the stick, swearing loudly. How any man could fly a crazy, contrary thing like this was more than he could understand.

The ground wheeled under him. The engine's sound changed, became a snarl, then a sputter. Wildly, he looked for a place to put down, but there was nothing but orchard under him as far as he could see—which wasn't far because the plane had nosed down again. A queasy, liquid feel began in his stomach, and the stench from the engine didn't help it any.

The engine chose that moment to quit. For a long time—it couldn't really have been more than a few seconds—the only sound was the whisper of air against the wings. Then the Nieuport stalled and plunged down among the trees. Branches snapped and the wings buckled. The Nieuport came to rest midway between the treetops and the ground. It dangled there, swaying a little in the gentle breeze. After a while, Farman thought to turn off the ignition, to reduce the danger of fire. After another while, he began to think about how to climb down.

He met Blake and half a dozen other men before he got out of the orchard. They went back to the Nieuport. Blake looked up at the wreck among the tree branches, made an angry noise that might have been extremely basic English, or it might not, and walked away.

Farman started to go after him but then thought better of it. Another tree branch cracked and the Nieuport sagged a few feet closer to the ground. Farman looked up at the mess one more time, then turned away and followed Blake. It was a long walk back to the field.

Blake was given another Nieuport. The escadrille had several replacements ready—craft that had been sent down from an escadrille in the Somme region that had switched to Spads. The older Nieuports were still good enough for this less active section of the front. Blake spent the rest of the day and all the next with the mechanics, checking it out.

Farman spent the time poking around *Pika-Don,* trying to figure a way she could still be used. There was a space where a Vickers gun could be fitted if he took out the infrared sensor unit, but working out a trigger linkage was beyond him; every cubic inch inside *Pika-Don* was occupied by one or another piece of vital equipment. And at Mach 2 an orifice the size of a .30-caliber muzzle might be enough to blow the plane apart.

The only other thing he could think of was that the radars were powerful enough to fry a man dead, but it didn't seem likely that Bruno Keyserling would hold still for the hour or two needed for the job.

He gave up. *Pika-Don* was useless. Reluctantly, he resigned himself to asking Deveraux for assignment to a flight school. It would mean swallowing a lot of pride, but if he was going to shoot Keyserling out of the sky, he'd have to learn how to fly a Nieuport.

When the escadrille came back from a patrol, he went out to talk with the Frenchman. Deveraux came toward him, helmet bunched in a still-gloved hand. "I am sorry, M'sieu," he said gravely. He laid his empty hand on Farman's shoulder. "Your friend . . . your countryman. . . ."

The patrol had run into a flock of Albatrosses, Keyserling in the lead. No one had seen Blake go down, but several planes had been seen falling, burning like meteors. When the dogfight broke off and the flight had reformed, Blake wasn't with them.

Farman's mind became like cold iron as he heard Deveraux recite the plain, unchangeable facts. It shouldn't have struck him so hard, but Blake was a man he'd known, a man he'd talked with. All the other men here, even Deveraux, were strangers.

"Did anyone see a parachute?"

"M'sieu, such things do not work," Deveraux said. "We do not use them. They catch on the wires. For men in the balloons, perhaps such things can be used, but not for us. Our aeroplane is hit in its vitals, we go down."

"You shouldn't build them with so many wires, then."

Deveraux's reply was a Gallic shrug. "Perhaps not, M'sieu. But they are what hold our aeroplanes together."

"The German planes, too?" Farman asked in a suddenly different voice.

"Of course, M'sieu."

"Get me some kerosene," Farman said.

"Paraffin? Of course, M'sieu. And if you will show the mechanics where to fasten the machine guns they. . . ."

Farman shook his head. "I don't need guns. Just get me the kerosene. I'll do the rest. And when I'm done with 'em on this front, I'll go up the line and clean out the rest of 'em."

"Of course, M'sieu," Deveraux said without irony.

Not that Farman cared. This time he'd do what he said he could do. He knew it. "Ten thousand gallons," he said.

Mid-August came, and *Pika-Don* was fueled again. Reports and rumors had been coming down from other sectors of the front that American troops were somewhere in the fighting.

Pika-Don lifted into a sky as clean as polished glass. Later in the day there might be a scatter of cumulus tufts, but it was not yet mid-morning. "It is not a good day for fighting," Deveraux had said. "One can make use of the clouds."

It would be a good day for observation planes, though, so the German patrols would be out. And, Farman thought savagely, there'd be fighting enough. He'd see to that.

Once he'd shifted to lateral flight, he didn't try for altitude. *Pika-Don* would guzzle fuel faster at low levels, but he didn't figure the mission to take long. The German field was less than thirty miles away. He fixed its location on the map scope and sent *Pika-Don* toward it at full thrust. *Pika-Don* began to gain altitude, but at ten thousand feet, with the Machmeter moving up past 1.75 he leveled her off and turned her downward along a trajectory that would bring her to ground level just as he reached the German field.

It was almost perfectly calculated. He saw the field ahead of him. It was small—he'd seen pastures that were bigger—and he started to pull out of his descent. He passed over the field with just enough altitude to clear the trees on the far side. It took less than a second—the Mach-meter said 2.5, and skin temperature was going up fast. He took *Pika-Don* a few hundred feet up and brought her around—lined her up on the field with the map scope's help—and brought her down again for an-other pass. This time she flew straight at the open mouth of a hangar in the middle of a row of hangars on the far side of the field.

He brought *Pika-Don* around one more time, but this time he stayed a thousand feet up and kept off to one side of the field. He looked down and felt the satisfaction of a kid who'd just stomped an anthill. Wreck-age was still flying through the air. He didn't need rockets. He didn't need machine guns. All he had to have was *Pika-Don* herself.

He turned her south toward the Swiss border. He had seen only a few planes on the ground, which meant that most of them were out on patrol.

Heading south, he took *Pika-Don* up to eighteen thousand feet. On a day like this, with no clouds to hide in, the best altitude for a German patrol would be up close to the operational ceiling. Even if no altitude advantage could be gained, at least the advantage would not be lost to a higher-flying French patrol.

The map scope showed the Swiss border. Farman brought *Pika-Don* around. The front was not hard to find. It was a sinuous gash across the land, like a bloodless wound. He followed it north, staying to the Ger-man side. He watched the sky ahead of him.

He flew the course to the Vosges Mountains at Mach 1.5, partly to save fuel and to minimize the skin-temperature problem; flying this low, the air was a lot thicker than *Pika-Don* was built to fly in. His main reason, though, was that even at Mach 1.5 he was flying through a lot of airspace. With no more sophisticated target-finding equipment than his own bare eyes, he could pass within a mile or less of a German patrol and not see it. Flying as slowly as he could improved his chances.

The mountains rose ahead of him. They weren't very high mountains; their crests lay well below him. He caught sight of the German patrol as he turned *Pika-Don* for another run south.

They were a few hundred yards higher than he was, and so small with distance he'd have thought they were birds except that birds didn't fly this high, nor did birds fly in a neatly stacked Junck's row formation. They hung suspended in the sky, like fleck-marks on a window, and if it hadn't been for their formation he wouldn't have known their direction of flight. They were flying south, as he was now—patrolling the front, as he was.

And they were close—too close. If he turned toward them, they'd be inside the radius of his turn. He'd cross their path in front of them like a black cat, warning them. He mind-fixed their position on the map scope and turned away.

Come at them from eight o'clock, he decided. That would be the best angle. On the outward arc of his circle he took *Pika-Don* up to thirty thousand feet. Then, as *Pika-Don* started to come around for the approach, he started down, full thrust in all three engines. The Machmeter climbed to 2.0, then 2.5. It edged toward 3.0, trembling. It would mean a heating problem in this soup-thick air, but it wouldn't be for long.

The patrol was almost exactly where he'd seen it before. There hadn't been time for it to move far. With only a small correction *Pika-Don* was driving down toward it like a lance, target-true. The insect-speck planes became recognizable shapes, then rapidly expanded. They ballooned to their full size in a flash and he was almost on top of them.

At the last instant, he moved the controls just enough to avoid collision—passed behind them so close he had a glimpse of round knobs bulging from the cockpits just behind the upper wings—pilots' helmeted heads—and yes! at the bottom of the stack, leading the flight, the purple Albatross of Bruno Keyserling.

Then the whole flight was somewhere behind him. Farman reduced thrust and put *Pika-Don* into a steep climb, over on her back, and down again to level out into the airspace he'd flown through before.

It was all changed. The sky was full of junk, as if someone had emptied a barrel of trash. Fluttering wing sections, bashed fuselages, masses of twisted wreckage without any shape he could recognize. He saw a wingless fuselage falling a-tumble, like a crippled dragonfly. It was all purple, with bits of white on the shattered engine cowl. *Got him!*

And there wasn't a whole plane left in the sky. They hadn't been built to survive the impact of *Pika-Don*'s shock wave. Just like the hangars at their field which had exploded when he buzzed them.

He started to curve southward again. He'd tasted blood, wanted more. He'd hardly begun the turn when a whump shook *Pika-Don* and the sky wheeled crazily and the engine function instruments erupted with a Christmas tree of red lights as if engine two had gobbled something that didn't digest too well. (Part of an airplane? Part of a man?) Some of the lights flashed panic, others glared firmly at his eyes. The horizon outside was tipping up on edge, falling over, tipping up again. The controls felt numb in his hands.

Farman knew the drill. When a plane as hot as this one went bad, you got out if you could. At Mach 2 you could hit the ground in less than thirty seconds. He slapped the eject button—felt the rockets blast him upward. A moment later the instrument panel broke away and the seat's firm pressure on his back and thighs were gone. He was tumbling like a wobbling top in midair, suddenly no longer enclosed in several million dollars' worth of airplane. There was the teeth-cracking shock of his chute coming open, and abruptly the confusion of too many things happening too fast stopped. He looked all around for some trace of *Pika-Don,* but there wasn't any.

He tugged at the shrouds to spill air from the chute and drift him westward toward the French lines. The wind was doing some of it, but not enough. A line of planes came toward him. He held his breath, thinking of a school of sharks nosing in toward a man cast overboard. But then he saw the French markings on their wings and sides. They were Nieuports, and the pilot of the leading plane waved. Farman waved back. The flight came on. It circled him once and then curved off. They stayed in sight, though, following him down. When flak bursts started to puff around him, they went down to strafe the German trenches.

He spilled another dollop of air from his chute. He was over the French lines now. He could see the men in the trenches looking up at him. He floated down toward them, closer and closer. Then, very abruptly, he was down—down among the trenches and barbed wire of the French Seventh Army. He sprawled in the greasy mud of a shell hole. The chute started to drag him, but it caught on a tangle of wire and collapsed.

He got to his hands and knees, fumbling with the parachute harness. A bullet snapped past his ear. He flattened. The Nieuports dived on the German trenches again.

He struggled out of the harness and started to crawl in the direction of the nearest trench. It wasn't far. He scraped the dirt with his belt buckle all the way. Bullets whipped past him like deadly mosquitoes. The soldiers in the trenches reached out to pull him down.

They hugged him. They mobbed around him. There must have been thousands of men in that trench to celebrate the man who'd brought down Bruno Keyserling. Someone pressed a cup of wine into his hands —a soldier in dirty clothes, with mud on his brow and a matted beard. Farman drank gratefully.

After a while, he sat down and just sat there, dead inside. He looked at the dirt wall a few inches from his eyes. The empty cup dangled from his hand. *Pika-Don* was gone, and nothing he could do would rebuild her. Suddenly he was just an ordinary man. He couldn't even fly any more. *Pika-Don* had been the only plane in this age that he knew how to fly, and *Pika-Don* was gone.

He wasn't aware of the passage of time, but only of the heat and dust and the smell of a trench that had been lived in too long by unwashed men. He didn't know what he was going to do. But after a time, the wine began to have its effect. A trickle of life came back into him.

Slowly, he got to his feet. The start of a smile quirked his mouth. On second thought, no, he wasn't just an ordinary man.

The war would be over in a few months. Maybe he didn't know what he'd do, but. . . .

The soldier who'd given him the wine was standing a few feet away. Farman held himself crisply erect. It occurred to him the man probably didn't know a word of English.

"How do I get back to America?" he asked, and grinned at the soldier's incomprehension.

A man from the future ought to have *some* advantage over the natives!

Harry Harrison

NO WAR,
OR BATTLE'S SOUND

"**C**ombatman Dom Priego, I shall kill you." Sergeant Toth shouted the words the length of the barracks compartment.

Dom, who was stretched out on his bunk and reading a book, raised startled eyes just as the sergeant snapped his arm down, hurling a gleaming combat knife. Trained reflexes raised the book and the knife thudded into it, penetrating the pages so that the point stopped a scant few inches from Dom's face.

"You stupid Hungarian ape!" Dom shouted. "Do you know what this book cost me? Do you know how old it is?"

"Do you know that you are still alive?" the sergeant answered, a hint of a cold smile wrinkling the corners of his cat's eyes. He stalked down the gangway, like a predatory animal and reached for the handle of the knife.

"No you don't," Dom said, snatching the book away. "You've done enough damage already." He put the book flat on the bunk and worked the knife carefully out of it—then threw it suddenly at the sergeant's foot.

Sergeant Toth shifted his leg just enough so that the knife missed him and struck the plastic deck covering instead. "Temper, Combatman," he said. "You should never lose your temper. That way you make mistakes, get killed." He bent and plucked out the shining blade and held it balanced in his fingertips. As he straightened up there was a rustle as every man in the barracks compartment shifted weight, ready to move, every eye on him. He laughed.

"Now you're expecting it, so it's too easy for you." He slid the knife back into his boot sheath.

"You're a sadistic bowb," Dom said, smoothing down the cut in the book's cover. "Getting a degenerate pleasure out of frightening other people."

"Maybe," Sergeant Toth said, undisturbed. He sat on the bunk across the aisle. "And maybe that's what they call the right man in the right job. And it doesn't matter, anyway. I train you, keep you alert, on the jump. This keeps you alive. You should thank me for being such an excellent sadist."

"You can't sell me with that argument, Sergeant. You're the sort of individual this man wrote about, right here in this book that you did your best to destroy—"

"Not me. You put it in front of the knife. Just like I keep telling you pinkies. Save yourself. That's what counts. Use any trick. You only got one life, make it a long one."

"Right in here—"

"Pictures of girls?"

"No, Sergeant, words. Great words by a man you never heard of, by the name of Wilde."

"Sure. Plugger Wyld, fleet heavyweight champion."

"No, Oscar Fingal O'Flahertie Wills Wilde. No relation to your pug—I hope. Listen to this. He writes, 'As long as war is regarded as wicked, it will always have its fascination. When it is looked upon as vulgar, it will cease to be popular.' "

Sergeant Toth's eyes narrowed in thought. "He makes it sound simple. But it's not that way at all. There are other reasons for war."

"Such as what?"

The sergeant opened his mouth to answer but his voice was drowned in the wave of sound from the scramble alert. The high-pitched hooting blared in every compartment of the spacer and had its instant response. Men moved. Fast.

The ship's crew raced to their action stations; the men who had been asleep just an instant before still blinking awake as they ran. The crew ran and stood, and before the alarm was through sounding the great spaceship was ready.

Not so the combatmen. Until ordered and dispatched they were just cargo. They stood at the ready, a double row of silver-gray uniforms down the center of the barracks compartment. Sergeant Toth was at the wall with his headset plugged into a phone extension there. Listening attentively, nodding at an unheard voice. Every man's eyes were upon him as he spoke agreement, disconnected, and turned slowly to face them. He savored the silent moment, then broke into the widest grin that any of them had ever seen on his normally expressionless face.

"This is it," the sergeant said, and actually rubbed his hands together. "I can tell you now that the Edinburgers were expected, and that our whole fleet is up in force. The scouts have detected them breaking out of jump space and they should be here in about two hours. We're going out to meet them. This, you pinkie combat virgins, is it." A sound like a low growl rose from the assembled men and the sergeant's grin widened.

"That's the right spirit. Show some of it to the enemy." The grin vanished as quickly as it had come. Cold-faced as always he called the ranks to attention.

"Corporal Steres is in sick bay with the fever so we're one NCO short. When that alert sounded we went into combat condition. I may now make temporary field appointments. I do so. Combatman Priego, one pace forward." Dom snapped to attention and stepped out of the rank.

"You're now in charge of the bomb squad. Do the right job and the CO will make it permanent. Corporal Priego, one step back and wait here. The rest of you to the ready room, double time—*march*."

Sergeant Toth stepped aside as the combatmen hurried from the compartment. When the last one had gone he pointed his finger at Dom.

"Just one word. You're as good as any man here. Better than most. You're smart. But you think too much about things that don't matter. Stop thinking and start fighting. Or you'll never get back to that university. Bowb up and if the Edinburgers don't get you I will. You come back as a corporal or you don't come back at all. Understood?"

"Understood." Dom's face was as coldly expressionless as the sergeant's. "I'm as good a combatman as you are, Sergeant. I'll do my job."

"Then do it—now *jump*."

Because of the delay Dom was the last man to be suited up. The others were already doing their pressure checks with the armorers while he was still closing his seals. He did not let it disturb him or make him try to move faster. With slow deliberation he counted off the check list as he sealed and locked.

Once all the pressure checks were in the green, Dom gave the armorers the thumbs-up okay and walked to the air lock. While the door closed behind him and the lock was pumped out he checked all the telltales in his helmet. Oxygen, full. Power pack, full charge. Radio, one and one. Then the last of the air was gone and the inner door opened soundlessly in the vacuum. He entered the armory.

The lights here were dimmer—and soon they would be turned off completely. Dom went to the rack with his equipment and began to buckle on the smaller items. Like all of the others on the bomb squad his suit was lightly armored and he carried only the most essential weapons. The drillger went on his left thigh, just below his fingers, and the gropener in its holster on the outside of his right leg; this was his favorite weapon. The intelligence reports had stated that some of the Edinburgers still used fabric pressure suits, so lightning prods—usually considered obsolete—had been issued. He slung his well to the rear since the chance that he might need it was very slim. All of these murderous devices had been stored in the evacuated and insulated compartment for months so that their temperature approached absolute zero. They were lubrication free and had been designed to operate at this temperature.

A helmet clicked against Dom's, and Wing spoke, his voice carried by the conducting transparent ceramic.

"I'm ready for my bomb, Dom—do you want to sling it? And congratulations. Do I have to call you Corporal now?"

"Wait until we get back and it's official. I take Toth's word for absolutely nothing."

He slipped the first atomic bomb from the shelf, checked the telltales to see that they were all in the green, then slid it into the rack that was an integral part of Wing's suit. "All set, now we can sling mine."

They had just finished when a large man in bulky combat armor came up. Dom would have known him by his size even if he had not read HELMUTZ stenciled on the front of his suit.

"What is it, Helm?" he asked when their helmets touched.

"The sergeant. He said I should report to you, that I'm lifting a bomb on this mission." There was an angry tone behind his words.

"Right. We'll fix you up with a back sling." The big man did not look happy and Dom thought he knew why. "And don't worry about missing any of the fighting. There'll be enough for everyone."

"I'm a combatman—"

"We're all combatmen. All working for one thing—to deliver the bombs. That's your job now."

Helmutz did not act convinced and stood with stolid immobility while they rigged the harness and bomb onto the back of his suit. Before they were finished their headphones crackled. A stir went through the company of suited men as a message came over the command frequency.

"Are you suited and armed? Are you ready for illumination adjustment?"

"Combatmen suited and armed." That was Sergeant Toth's voice.

"Bomb squad not ready," Dom said, and they hurried to make the last fastenings, aware that the rest were waiting for them.

"Bomb squad suited and armed."

"Lights."

As the command rang out the bulkhead lights faded out until the darkness was broken only by the dim red lights in the ceiling above. Until their eyes became adjusted it was almost impossible to see. Dom groped his way to one of the benches, found the oxygen hose with his fingers, and plugged it into the side of his helmet; this would conserve his tank oxygen during the wait. Brisk music was being played over the command circuit now as part of morale-sustaining. Here in the semi-darkness, suited and armed, the waiting could soon become nerve-racking. Everything possible was done to alleviate the pressure. The music faded and a voice replaced it.

"This is the executive officer speaking. I'm going to try and keep you in the picture as to what is happening up here. The Edinburgers are attacking in fleet strength. Just after they were sighted their ambassador declared that a state of war exists. He asks that Earth surrender at once or risk the consequences. Well, you all know what the answer to that one was. The Edinburgers have invaded and conquered twelve settled planets already and incorporated them into their Greater Celtic Coprosperity Sphere. Now they're getting greedy and going for the big one. Earth itself, the planet their ancestors left a hundred generations ago. In doing this . . . just a moment, I have a battle report here . . . first contact with our scouts."

The officer stopped for a moment, then his voice picked up again.

"Fleet strength, but no larger than we expected and we will be able to handle them. But there is one difference in their tactics and the combat computer is analyzing this now. They were the ones who originated the MT invasion technique, landing a number of cargo craft on a planet, all of them loaded with matter transmitter screens. As you know, the invading forces attack through these screens direct from their planet to the one that is to be conquered. Well they've changed their technique now. This entire fleet is protecting a *single* ship, a Kriger class scout carrier. What this means . . . hold on, here is the readout from the combat computer. 'Only possibility single ship landing area increase MT screen breakthrough,' that's what it says. Which means that there is a good chance that this ship may be packing a *single* large MT screen, bigger than anything ever built before. If this is so—and they get the thing down to the surface—they can fly heavy bombers right through it, fire pre-aimed ICBM's, send through troop carriers, anything. If this happens the invasion will be successful."

Around him, in the red-lit darkness, Dom was aware of the other suited figures who stirred silently as they heard the words.

"*If* this happens." There was a ring of authority now in the executive officer's voice. "The Edinburgers have developed the only way to launch an interplanetary invasion. We have found the way to stop it. You combatmen are the answer. They have now put all their eggs in one basket—and you are going to take that basket to pieces. You can get through where attack ships or missiles could not. We're closing fast now and you will be called to combat stations soon. So—go out there and do your job. The fate of Earth rides with you."

Melodramatic words, Dom thought, yet they were true. Everything, the ships, the concentration of firepower, it all depended on them. The alert alarm cut through his thoughts and he snapped to attention.

"Disconnect oxygen. Fall out when your name is called and proceed to the firing room in the order called. Toth. . . ."

The names were spoken quickly and the combatmen moved out. At the entrance to the firing room a suited man with a red-globed light checked the names on their chests against his roster, a final check that they were in the correct order. Everything moved smoothly, easily, just like a drill. Because the endless drills had been designed to train them for just this moment. The firing room was familiar, though they had never been there before. Their trainer had been an exact duplicate of it. The combatman ahead of Dom went to port so he moved to starboard. The man preceding him was just climbing into a capsule and Dom waited while the armorer helped him down into it and adjusted the armpit supports. Then it was his turn and Dom slipped into the transparent plastic shell and settled against the seat as he seized the handgrips. The armorer pulled the supports hard up into his armpits and he nodded when they seated right. A moment later the man was gone and he was alone in the semi-darkness with the dim red glow shining on the top ring of the capsule that was just above his head. There was a sudden shudder and he gripped hard just as the capsule started forward. As it moved it tilted backward until he was lying on his back looking up through the metal rings that banded his plastic shell. His capsule was moved sideways, jerked to a stop, then moved again. Now the gun was visible, a half-dozen capsules ahead of his, and he thought, as he always did during training, how like an ancient quick-firing cannon the gun was—a cannon that fired human beings. Every two seconds the charging mechanism seized a capsule from one of the alternate feed belts, whipped it to the rear of the gun where it instantly vanished into the breech. Then another and another. The one ahead of Dom disappeared and he braced himself—and the mechanism halted.

There was a flicker of fear that something had gone wrong with the complex gun, before he realized that all of the first combatmen had been launched and that the computer was waiting a determined period of time for them to prepare the way for the bomb squad. His squad now, the men he would lead.

Waiting was harder than moving as he looked at the black mouth of the breech. The computer would be ticking away the seconds now, while at the same time tracking the target and keeping the ship aimed to the correct trajectory. Once he was in the gun the magnetic field would seize

the rings that banded his capsule. The linear accelerator of the gun
would draw him up the evacuated tube that penetrated the entire length
of the great ship from stern to bow. Faster and faster the magnetic fields
would pull him until he left the mouth of the gun at the correct speed and
on the correct trajectory to intercept. . . .

His capsule was whipped up in a tight arc and shoved into the darkness. Even as he gripped tight on the handholds the pressure pads came
up and hit him. He could not measure the time—he could not see and he
could not breathe as the brutal acceleration pressed down on him. Hard,
harder than anything he had ever experienced in training: he had that one
thought—then he was out of the gun.

In a single instant he went from acceleration to weightlessness. He
gripped hard so he would not float away from the capsule. There was a
puff of vapor from the unheard explosions, though he felt them through
his feet. The metal rings were blown in half while the upper portion of
the capsule shattered and hurled away. Now he was alone, weightless,
holding to the grips that were fastened to the rocket unit beneath his feet.
He looked about for the space battle that he knew was in progress, and
felt a slight disappointment that there was so little to see.

Something burned far off to his right and there was a wavering in the
brilliant sparks of the stars as some dark object occulted them and passed
on. This was a battle of computers and instruments at great distances.
There was very little for the unaided eye to see. The spaceships were
black and swift and—for the most part—thousands of miles away. They
were firing homing rockets and proximity shells, also just as swift and
invisible. He knew that space around him was filled with signal jammers
and false signal generators, but could detect none of this. Even the target
vessel toward which he was rushing was invisible. For all that his limited senses could tell he was alone in space, motionless, forgotten.

Something shuddered against the soles of his boots and a jet of vapor
shot out and vanished from the rocket unit. No, he was neither motionless nor forgotten. The combat computer was still tracking the target
ship and had detected some minute variation from its predicted path. At
the same time the computer was following the progress of his trajectory
and it made the slight correction for this new data. Corrections must be
going out at the same time to all the other combatmen in space, before
and behind him. They were small and invisible—doubly invisible now
that the metal rings had been shed. There was no more than an eighth of
a pound of metal dispersed through the plastics and ceramics of a combatman's equipment. Radar could never pick them out from among all
the interference. They should get through.

Jets blasted again and Dom saw that the stars were turning above his
head. Touchdown soon; the tiny radar in his rocket unit had detected a
mass ahead and had directed that he be turned end for end. Once this

was done he knew that the combat computer would cut free and turn control over to the tiny set-down computer that was part of his radar. His rockets blasted, strong now, punching the supports up against him, and he looked down past his feet at the growing dark shape that occulted the stars.

With a roar, loud in the silence, his headphones burst into life.

"Went, went—gone hungry. Went, went—gone hungry."

The silence grew again but, in it, Dom no longer felt alone. The brief message had told him a lot. Firstly, it was Sergeant Toth's voice, there was no mistaking that. Secondly, the mere act of breaking radio silence showed that they had engaged the enemy and that their presence was known. The code was a simple one that would be meaningless to anyone outside their company. Translated it said that fighting was still going on but the advance squads were holding their own. They had captured the center section of the hull—always the best place to rendezvous since it was impossible to tell bow from stern in the darkness—and were holding it awaiting the arrival of the bomb squad. The retrorockets flared hard and long, then the rocket unit crashed hard into the black hull. Dom jumped free and rolled.

As he came out of the roll he saw a suited figure looming above him, clearly outlined by the disc of the sun despite his black nonreflective armor. The top of the helmet was smooth. Even as he realized this Dom was pulling the gropener from its holster.

A cloud of vapor sprang out and the man vanished behind it. Dom was surprised, but he did not hesitate. Handguns, even recoilless ones like this that sent the burnt gas out to the sides, were a hazard in no-G space combat. They were not only difficult to aim but had a recoil that would throw the user back out of position. Or, if the gas was vented sideways, they would blind him for vital moments. And a fraction of a second was all a trained combatman needed.

As the gropener swung free Dom thumbed the jet button lightly. The device was shaped like a short sword, but it had a vibrating saw blade where one sharpened edge should be, with small jets mounted opposite it in place of the opposite edge. The jets drove the device forward, pulling him after it. As soon as it touched the other man's leg he pushed the jets full on. As the vibrating ceramic blade speeded up the force of the jets pressed it into the thin armor. In less than a second it cut its way through and on into the flesh of the leg inside. Dom pressed the reverse jet to pull away as vapor gushed out, condensing to ice particles instantly, and his opponent writhed, clutched at his thigh—then went suddenly limp.

Dom's feet touched the hull and the soles adhered. He realized that the entire action had taken place in the time it took him to straighten out from his roll and stand up. . . .

Don't think, act. Training. As soon as his feet adhered he crouched and turned looking about him. A heavy power ax sliced by just above his head, towing its wielder after it.

Act, don't think. His new opponent was on his left side, away from the gropener, and was already reversing the direction of his ax. A man has two hands. The drillger was on his left thigh. Even as he remembered it he had it in his hand, drill on and hilt-jet flaring. The foot-long, diamond-hard drill spun fiercely—its rotation cancelled by the counter-revolving weight in the hilt—while the jet drove it forward.

Into the Edinburger's midriff, scarcely slowing as it tore a hole in the armor and plunged inside. As his opponent folded Dom thumbed the reverse jet to push the drillger out. The power ax, still with momentum from the last blast of its jet, tore free of the dying man's hand and vanished into space.

There were no other enemies in sight. Dom tilted forward on one toe so that the surface film on the boot sole was switched from adhesive to neutral, then he stepped forward slowly. Walking like this took practice, but he had had that. Ahead were a group of dark figures lying prone on the hull and he took the precaution of raising his hand to touch the horn on the top of his helmet so there would be no mistakes. This identification had been agreed upon just a few days ago and the plastic spikes glued on. The Edinburgers all had smooth-topped helmets.

Dom dived forward between the scattered forms and slid, face down. Before his body could rebound from the hull he switched on his belly-sticker and the surface film there held him flat. Secure for the moment among his own men, he thumbed the side of his helmet to change frequencies. There was now a jumble of noise through most of the frequencies, messages—both theirs and the enemy's—jamming, and false messages being broadcast by recorder units to cover the real exchange of information. There was scarcely any traffic on the bomb squad frequency and he waited for a clear spot. His men would have heard Toth's message so they knew where to gather. Now he could bring them to him.

"Quasar, quasar, quasar," he called, then counted carefully for ten seconds before he switched on the blue bulb on his shoulder. He stood as he did this, let it burn for a single second, then dropped back to the hull before he could draw any fire. His men would be looking for the light and would assemble on it. One by one they began to crawl out of the darkness. He counted them as they appeared. A combatman, without the bulge of a bomb on his back, ran up and dived and slid, so that his helmet touched Dom's.

"How many, Corporal?" Toth's voice asked.

"One still missing but—"

"No buts. We move now. Set your charge and blow as soon as you have cover."

He was gone before Dom could answer. But he was right. They could not afford to wait for one man and risk the entire operation. Unless they moved soon they would be trapped and killed up here. Individual combats were still going on about the hull, but it would not be long before the Edinburgers realized these were just holding actions and that the main force of attackers was gathered in strength. The bomb squad went swiftly and skillfully to work laying the ring of shaped charges.

The rear guards must have been called in because the heavy weapons opened fire suddenly on all sides. These were .30 caliber high velocity recoilless machine guns. Before firing the gunners had traversed the hull, aiming for a grazing fire that was as close to the surface as possible. The gun computer remembered this and now fired along the selected pattern, aiming automatically. This was needed because as soon as the firing began clouds of gas jetted out obscuring everything. Sergeant Toth appeared out of the smoke and shouted as his helmet touched Dom's.

"Haven't you blown it yet?"

"Ready now, get back."

"Make it fast. They're all down or dead now out there. But they'll throw something heavy into this smoke soon. Now that they have us pinpointed."

The bomb squad drew back, fell flat, and Dom pressed the igniter. Flames and gas exploded high while the hull hammered up at them. Through the smoke rushed up a solid column of air, clouding and freezing into tiny crystals as it hit the vacuum. The ship was breeched now and they would keep it that way, blowing open the sealed compartments and bulkheads to let out the atmosphere. Dom and the sergeant wriggled through the smoke together, to the edge of the wide, gaping hole that had been blasted in the ship's skin.

"Hotside, hotside!" the sergeant shouted, and dived through the opening.

Dom pushed a way through the rush of men who were following the sergeant and assembled his squad. He was still one man short. A weapons man with his machine gun on his back hurried by and leaped into the hole, with his ammunition carriers right behind him. The smoke cloud was growing because some of the guns were still firing, acting as a rear guard. It was getting hard to see the opening now. When Dom had estimated that half the men had gone through he led his own squad forward.

They pushed down into a darkened compartment, a storeroom of some kind, and saw a combatman at a hole that had been blown in one wall, acting as a guide.

"Down to the right, hole about one hundred yards from here," he said as soon as Dom's helmet touched his. "We tried to the left first but there's too much resistance. Just holding them there."

Dom led his men in a floating run, the fastest movement possible in a null-G situation. The corridor was empty for the moment, dimly lit by the emergency bulbs. Holes had been blasted in the walls at regular intervals to open the sealed compartments and empty them of air, as well as to destroy wiring and piping. As they passed one of the ragged-edged openings spacesuited men erupted from it.

Dom dived under the thrust of a drillger, swinging his gropener out at the same time. It caught his attacker in the midriff just as the man's other hand came up. The Edinburger folded and died and a sharp pain lanced through Dom's leg. He looked down at the nipoff that was fastened to his calf and was slowly severing it.

Nipoff, an outmoded design for use against unarmored suits. It was killing him. The two curved blades were locked around his leg and the tiny, geared-down motor was slowly closing them. Once started the device could not be stopped.

It could be destroyed. Even as he realized this he swung down his gropener and jammed it against the nipoff's handle. The pain intensified at the sideways pressure and he almost blacked out; he attempted to ignore it. Vapor puffed out around the blades and he triggered the compression ring on his thigh that sealed the leg from the rest of his suit. Then the gropener cut through the casing. There was a burst of sparks and the motion of the closing blades stopped.

When Dom looked up the brief battle was over and the counterattackers were dead. The rear guard had caught up and pushed over them. Helmutz must have accounted for more than one of them himself. He held his power ax high, fingers just touching the buttons in the haft so that the jets above the blade spurted alternately to swing the ax to and fro. There was blood on both blades.

Dom switched on his radio; it was silent on all bands. The interior communication circuits of the ship were knocked out here and the metal walls damped all radio signals.

"Report," he said. "How many did we lose?"

"You're hurt," Wing said bending over him. "Want me to pull that thing off?"

"Leave it. The tips of the blades are almost touching and you'd tear half my leg off. It's frozen in with the blood and I can still get around. Lift me up."

The leg was getting numb now, with the blood supply cut off and the air replaced by vacuum. Which was all for the best. He took the roll count.

"We've lost two men but we still have more than enough bombs for this job. Now let's move."

Sergeant Toth himself was waiting at the next corridor, where another hole had been blasted in the deck. He looked at Dom's leg but said nothing.

"How is it going?" Dom asked.

"Fair. We took some losses. We gave them more. Engineer says we're over the main hold now so we're going straight down. Pushing out men on each level to hold. Get going."

"And you?"

"I'll bring down the rear guard and pull the men from each level as we pass. You see that you have a way out for us when we all get down to you."

"Do that," Dom said as he floated out over the hole, then gave a strong kick with his good leg against the ceiling when he was lined up. He went down smoothly while his squad followed. They passed one deck, two, then three. The openings had been nicely aligned for a straight drop. There was a flare of light and a burst of smoke ahead as another deck was blown through. Helmutz passed Dom, going faster, having pushed off harder with both legs. He was a full deck ahead when he plunged through the next opening, and the burst of high velocity machine-gun fire almost cut him in two. He folded in the middle, dead in the instant, the impact of the bullets driving him sideways and out of sight in the deck below.

Dom thumbed the jets on his gropener and it pulled him aside before he followed the big combatman.

"Bomb squad, disperse," he ordered. "Troops coming through." He switched to the combat frequency and looked up at the ragged column of men dropping down toward him.

"The deck below has been retaken. I am at the last occupied deck."

He waved his hand to indicate who was talking and the stream of men began to jet their weapons and move on by him. "They're below me. The bullets came from this side." The combatmen pushed on without a word.

The metal flooring shook as another opening was blasted somewhere behind him. The continuous string of men moved by. A few seconds later a helmeted figure—with a horned helmet—appeared below and waved the all-clear. The drop continued.

On the bottom deck the men were jammed almost shoulder to shoulder and more were arriving all the time.

"Bomb squad here, give me a report," Dom radioed. A combatman with a mapboard slung at his waist pushed back out of the crowd.

"We reached the cargo hold—it's immense—but we're being pushed back. Just by weight of numbers. The Edinburgers are desperate. They are putting men through the MT screen in light pressure suits. Unarmored, almost unarmed. We kill them easily enough but they have pushed us out bodily. They're coming right from the invasion planet. Even when we kill them the bodies block the way. . . ."

"You the engineer?"

"Yes."

"Whereabouts in the hold is the MT screen?"

"It runs the length of the hold and is back against the far wall."

"Controls?"

"On the left side."

"Can you lead us over or around the hold so we can break in near the screen?"

The engineer took a single long look at charts.

"Yes, around. Through the engine room. We can blast through close to the controls."

"Let's go, then." Dom switched to combat frequency and waved his arm over his head. "All combatmen who can see me—this way. We're going to make a flank attack."

They moved down the long corridor as fast as they could, with the combatmen ranging out ahead of the bomb squad. There were sealed pressure doors at regular intervals, but these were bypassed by blasting through the bulkheads at the side. There was resistance and there were more dead as they advanced. Then a group of men gathered ahead and Dom floated up to the greatly depleted force of combatmen who had forced their way this far. A corporal touched his helmet to Dom's, pointing to a great sealed door at the corridor's end.

"The engine room is behind there. These walls are thick. Everyone off to one side because we are going to use an octupled charge."

They dispersed and the bulkheads heaved and buckled when the charge was exploded. Dom, looking toward the corridor, saw a sheet of flame sear by, followed by a column of air that turned instantly to sparkling granules of ice. The engine room had still been pressurized.

There had been no warning and most of the crewmen had not had their helmets sealed. They were violently and suddenly dead. The few survivors were killed quickly when they offered resistance with improvised weapons. Dom scarcely noticed this as he led his bomb squad after the engineer.

"That doorway is not on my charts," the engineer said, angrily, as though the spy who had stolen the information were at fault. "It must have been added after construction."

"Where does it go to?" Dom asked.

"The MT hold, no other place is possible."

Dom thought quickly. "I'm going to try and get to the MT controls without fighting. I need a volunteer to go with me. If we remove identification and wear Edinburger equipment we should be able to do it."

"I'll join you," the engineer said.

"No, you have a different job. I want a good combatman."

"Me," a man said, pushing through the others. "Pimenov, best in my squad. Ask anybody."

"Let's make this fast."

The disguise was simple. With the identifying spikes knocked off their helmets and enemy equipment slung about them they would pass any casual examination. A handful of grease obscured the names on their chests.

"Stay close behind and come fast when I knock the screen out," Dom told the others, then led the combatman through the door.

There was a narrow passageway between large tanks and another door at the far end. It was made of light metal and not locked, but it would not budge when Dom pushed on it. Pimenov joined him and between them they forced it open a few inches. Through the opening they saw that it was blocked by a press of human bodies, spacesuited men who stirred and struggled but scarcely moved. The two combatmen pushed harder and a sudden movement of the mob released the pressure and Dom fell forward, his helmet banging into that of the nearest man.

"What the devil you about?" the man said, twisting his head to look at Dom.

"More of them down there," Dom said, trying to roll his R's the way the Edinburgers did.

"You're not one of us!" the man said and struggled to bring his weapon up.

Dom could not risk a fight here—yet the man had to be silenced. He could just reach the lightning prod and he jerked it from its clip and jammed it against the Edinburger's side. The pair of needle-sharp spikes pierced suit and clothes and bit into his flesh, and when the hilt slammed against his body the circuit was closed. The handle of the lightning prod was filled with powerful capacitors that released their stored electricity in a single immense charge through the needles. The Edinburger writhed and died instantly.

They used his body to push a way into the crowd.

Dom had just enough sensation left in his injured leg to be aware when the clamped-on nipoff was twisted in his flesh by the men about them; he kept his thoughts from what it was doing to his leg.

Once the Edinburger soldiers were aware of the open door they pulled it wide and fought their way through it. The combatmen would be waiting for them in the engine room. The sudden exodus relieved the pressure of the bodies for a moment and Dom, with Pimenov struggling after him, pushed and worked his way toward the MT controls.

It was like trying to move in a dream. The dark bulk of the MT screen was no more than ten yards away, yet they couldn't seem to reach it. Soldiers sprang from the screen, pushing and crowding in, more and more, preventing any motion in that direction. Two technicians stood at the controls, their helmet phones plugged into the board before them. Without gravity to push against, jammed into the crowd that floated at all levels in a fierce tangle of arms and legs, movement was almost impossible. Pimenov touched his helmet to Dom's.

"I'm going ahead to cut a path. Stay close behind me."

He broke contact before Dom could answer him, then let his power ax pull him forward into the press. Then he began to chop it back and forth in a short arc, almost hacking his way through the packed bodies. Men turned on him but he did not stop, lashing out with his gropener as they tried to fight. Dom followed.

They were close to the MT controls before the combatman was buried under a crowd of stabbing, cursing Edinburgers. He had done his job and he died doing it. Dom jetted his gropener and let it drag him forward until he slammed into the thick steel frame of the MT screen above the operators' heads. He slid the weapon back into its sheath and used both hands to pull down along the frame, dragging himself headfirst through the press of suited bodies. There was a relatively clear space near the controls. He drifted down into it and let his drillger slide into the operator's back. The man writhed and died quickly. The other operator turned and took the weapon in his stomach. His face was just before Dom as his eyes widened and he screamed soundlessly with pain and fear. Nor could Dom escape the dead, horrified features as he struggled to drop the atomic bomb from his carrier. The murdered man stayed, pressed close against him all the time.

Now.

He cradled the bomb against his chest and, in a single swift motion, pulled out the arming pin, twisted the fuse to five seconds, and slammed down hard on the actuator. Then he reached up and switched the MT from *receive* to *send*.

The last soldiers erupted from the screen and there was a growing gap behind them. Into this space and through the screen he threw the bomb.

After that he kept the switch down and tried not to think about what was happening among the men of the invasion army who were waiting before the MT screen on that distant planet.

Then he had to hold this position until the combatmen arrived. He sheltered behind the operator's corpse and used his drillger against the few Edinburgers who were close enough to realize that something had gone wrong. This was easy enough to do because, although they were soldiers, they were men from the invasion army and knew nothing about null-G combat. Very soon after this there was a great stir and the closest ones were thrust aside. An angry combatman blasted through, sweeping his power ax toward Dom's neck. Dom dodged the blow and switched his radio to combat frequency.

"Hold that! I'm Corporal Priego, bomb squad. Get in front of me and keep anyone else from making the same mistake."

The man was one of those who had taken the engine room. He recognized Dom now and nodded, turning his back to him and pressing against him. More combatmen stormed up to form an iron shield around the controls. The engineer pushed through between them and Dom helped him reset the frequency on the MT screen.

After this the battle became a slaughter and soon ended.

"Sendout!" Dom radioed as soon as the setting was made, then turned the screen to transmit. He heard the words repeated over and over as the combatmen repeated the withdrawal signal so that everyone could hear it. Safety lay on the other side of the screen, now that it was tuned to Tycho Barracks on the Moon.

It was the Edinburgers, living, dead, and wounded who were sent through first. They were pushed back against the screen to make room for the combatmen who were streaming into the hold. The ones at the ends of the screen simply bounced against the hard surface and recoiled; the receiving screen at Tycho was far smaller than this great invasion screen. They were pushed along until they fell through and combatmen took up positions to mark the limits of the operating screen.

Dom was aware of someone in front of him and he had to blink away the red film that was trying to cover his eyes.

"Wing," he said, finally recognizing the man. "How many others of the bomb squad made it?"

"None I know of, Dom. Just me."

No, don't think about the dead. Only the living counted now.

"All right. Leave your bomb here and get on through. One is all we really need." He tripped the release and pulled the bomb from Wing's rack before giving him a push toward the screen.

Dom had the bomb clamped to the controls when Sergeant Toth slammed up beside him and touched helmets.

"Almost done."

"Done now," Dom said setting the fuse and pulling out the arming pin.

"Then get moving. I'll take it from here."

"No you don't. My job." He had to shake his head to make the haze go away but it still remained at the corners of his vision.

Toth didn't argue. "What's the setting?" he asked.

"Five and six. Five seconds after actuation the chemical bomb blows and knocks out the controls. One second later the atom bomb goes off."

"I'll stay to watch the fun."

Time was acting strangely for Dom, speeding up and slowing down. Men were hurrying by, into the screen, first in a rush, then fewer and fewer. Toth was talking on the combat frequency but Dom had switched the radio off because it hurt his head. The great chamber was empty now of all but the dead, with the automatic machine guns left firing at the entrances. One of them blew up as Toth touched helmets.

"They're all through. Let's go."

Dom had difficulty talking so he nodded instead and hammered his fist down onto the actuator.

Men were coming toward them but Toth had his arm around him, and full jets on his power ax were sliding them along the surface of the screen. And through.

When the brilliant lights of Tycho Barracks hit his eyes Dom closed them, and this time the red haze came up, over him, all the way.

"How's the new leg?" Sergeant Toth asked. He slumped lazily in the chair beside the hospital bed.

"I can't feel a thing. Nerve channels blocked until it grows tight to the stump." Dom put aside the book he had been reading and wondered what Toth was doing here.

"I come around to see the wounded," the sergeant said, answering the unasked question. "Two more besides you. Captain told me to."

"The captain is as big a sadist as you are. Aren't we sick enough already?"

"Good joke." His expression did not change. "I'll tell the captain. He'll like it. You going to buy out now?"

"Why not?" Dom wondered why the question made him angry. "I've had a combat mission, the medals, a good wound. More than enough points to get my discharge."

"Stay in. You're a good combatman when you stop thinking about it. There's not many of them. Make it a career."

"Like you, Sergeant? Make killing my life's work? Thank you, no. I intend to do something different, a little more constructive. Unlike you I don't relish this whole dirty business, the killing, the outright plain murder. You like it." This sudden thought sent him sitting upright in the bed. "Maybe that's it. Wars, fighting, everything. It has nothing to do anymore with territory rights or aggression or masculinity. I think that you people make wars because of the excitement of it, the thrill that nothing else can equal. You *like* war."

Toth rose, stretched easily, and turned to leave. He stopped at the door, frowning in thought.

"Maybe you're right, Corporal. I don't think about it much. Maybe I do like it." His face lifted in a cold tight smile. "But don't forget—you like it, too."

Dom went back to his book, resentful of the intrusion. His literature professor had sent him the book, along with a flattering note. He had heard about Dom on the broadcasts and the entire school was proud, etc. A book of poems, Milton, really good stuff.

> *No war, or battle's sound*
> *Was heard the world around.*

Yes, great stuff. But it hadn't been true in Milton's day and it still wasn't true. Did mankind really like war? They *must* like it or it wouldn't have lasted so long. This was an awful, criminal thought.

He, too? Nonsense. He fought well, but only because he had trained himself. It could not be true that he actually liked all of that.

He tried to read again but the page kept blurring before his eyes.

P<small>HILIP</small> K. D<small>ICK</small>

THE DEFENDERS

Taylor sat back in his chair reading the morning newspaper. The warm kitchen and the smell of coffee blended with the comfort of not having to go to work. This was his Rest Period, the first for a long time, and he was glad of it. He folded the second section back, sighing with contentment.

"What is it?" Mary said, from the stove.

"They pasted Moscow again last night." Taylor nodded his head in approval. "Gave it a real pounding. One of those R-H bombs. It's about time."

He nodded again, feeling the full comfort of the kitchen, the presence of his plump, attractive wife, the breakfast dishes and coffee. This was relaxation. And the war news was good, good and satisfying. He could feel a justifiable glow at the news, a sense of pride and personal accomplishment. After all, he was an integral part of the war program, not just another factory worker lugging a cart of scrap, but a technician, one of those who designed and planned the nerve-trunk of the war.

"It says they have the new subs almost perfected. Wait until they get *those* going." He smacked his lips with anticipation. "When they start shelling from underwater, the Soviets are sure going to be surprised."

"They're doing a wonderful job," Mary agreed vaguely. "Do you know what we saw today? Our team is getting a leady to show to the school children. I saw the leady, but only for a moment. It's good for the children to see what their contributions are going for, don't you think?"

She looked around at him.

"A leady," Taylor murmured. He put the newspaper slowly down. "Well, make sure it's decontaminated properly. We don't want to take any chances."

"Oh, they always bathe them when they're brought down from the surface," Mary said. "They wouldn't think of letting them down without the bath. Would they?" She hesitated, thinking back. "Don, you know, it makes me remember—"

He nodded. "I know."

He knew what she was thinking. Once in the very first weeks of the war, before everyone had been evacuated from the surface, they had seen a hospital train discharging the wounded, people who had been showered with sleet. He remembered the way they had looked, the expression on their faces, or as much of their faces as was left. It had not been a pleasant sight.

There had been a lot of that at first, in the early days before the transfer to undersurface was complete. There had been a lot, and it hadn't been very difficult to come across it.

Taylor looked up at his wife. She was thinking too much about it, the last few months. They all were.

"Forget it," he said. "It's all in the past. There isn't anybody up there now but the leadies, and they don't mind."

"But just the same, I hope they're careful when they let one of them down here. If one were still hot—"

He laughed, pushing himself away from the table. "Forget it. This is a wonderful moment; I'll be home for the next two shifts. Nothing to do but sit around and take things easy. Maybe we can take in a show. OK?"

"A show? Do we have to? I don't like to look at all the destruction, the ruins. Sometimes I see some place I remember, like San Francisco. They showed a shot of San Francisco, the bridge broken and fallen in the water, and I got upset. I don't like to watch."

"But don't you want to know what's going on? No human beings are getting hurt, you know."

"But it's so awful!" Her face was set and strained. "Please, no, Don."

Don Taylor picked up his newspaper sullenly. "All right, but there isn't a hell of a lot else to do. And don't forget, *their* cities are getting it even worse."

She nodded. Taylor turned the rough, thin sheets of newspaper. His good mood had soured on him. Why did she have to fret all the time? They were pretty well off, as things went. You couldn't expect to have everything perfect, living undersurface, with an artificial sun and artificial food. Naturally it was a strain, not seeing the sky or being able to go anyplace or see anything other than metal walls, great roaring factories, the plant-yards, barracks. But it was better than being on surface. And some day it would end and they could return. Nobody *wanted* to live this way, but it was necessary.

He turned the page angrily and the poor paper ripped. Damn it, the paper was getting worse quality all the time, bad print, yellow tint—

Well, they needed everything for the war program. He ought to know that. Wasn't he one of the planners?

He excused himself and went into the other room. The bed was still unmade. They had better get it in shape before the seventh hour inspection. There was a one unit fine—

The vidphone rang. He halted. Who would it be? He went over and clicked it on.

"Taylor?" the face said, forming into place. It was an old face, gray and grim. "This is Moss. I'm sorry to bother you during Rest Period, but this thing has come up." He rattled papers. "I want you to hurry over here."

Taylor stiffened. "What is it? There's no chance it could wait?" The calm gray eyes were studying him, expressionless, unjudging. "If you want me to come down to the lab," Taylor grumbled, "I suppose I can. I'll get my uniform—"

"No. Come as you are. And not to the lab. Meet me at second stage as soon as possible. It'll take you about a half hour, using the fast car up. I'll see you there."

The picture broke and Moss disappeared.

"What was it?" Mary said, at the door.

"Moss. He wants me for something."

"I knew this would happen."

"Well, you didn't want to do anything, anyhow. What does it matter?" His voice was bitter. "It's all the same, every day. I'll bring you back something. I'm going up to second stage. Maybe I'll be close enough to the surface to—"

"Don't! Don't bring me anything! Not from the surface!"

"All right, I won't. But of all the irrational nonsense—"

She watched him put on his boots without answering.

Moss nodded and Taylor fell in step with him, as the older man strode along. A series of loads were going up to the surface, blind cars clanking like ore-trucks up the ramp, disappearing through the stage trap above them. Taylor watched the cars, heavy with tubular machinery of some sort, weapons new to him. Workers were everywhere, in the dark gray uniforms of the labor corps, loading, lifting, shouting back and forth. The stage was deafening with noise.

"We'll go up a way," Moss said, "where we can talk. This is no place to give you details."

They took an escalator up. The commercial lift fell behind them, and with it most of the crashing and booming. Soon they emerged on an observation platform, suspended on the side of the Tube, the vast tunnel leading to the surface, not more than half a mile above them now.

"My God!" Taylor said, looking down the tube involuntarily. "It's a long way down."

Moss laughed. "Don't look."

They opened a door and entered an office. Behind the desk, an officer was sitting, an officer of Internal Security. He looked up.

"I'll be right with you, Moss." He gazed at Taylor studying him. "You're a little ahead of time."

"This is Commander Franks," Moss said to Taylor. "He was the first to make the discovery. I was notified last night." He tapped a parcel he carried. "I was let in because of this."

Franks frowned at him and stood up. "We're going up to first stage. We can discuss it there."

"First stage?" Taylor repeated nervously. The three of them went down a side passage to a small lift. "I've never been up there. Is it all right? It's not radioactive, is it?"

"You're like everyone else," Franks said. "Old women afraid of burglars. No radiation leaks down to first stage. There's lead and rock, and what comes down the Tube is bathed."

"What's the nature of the problem?" Taylor asked. "I'd like to know something about it."

"In a moment."

They entered the lift and ascended. When they stepped out, they were in a hall of soldiers, weapons and uniforms everywhere. Taylor blinked in surprise. So this was first stage, the closest undersurface level to the top! After this stage there was only rock, lead and rock, and the great tubes leading up like the burrows of earthworms. Lead and rock, and above that, where the tubes opened, the great expanse that no living being had seen for eight years, the vast, endless ruin that had once been Man's home, the place where he had lived, eight years ago.

Now the surface was a lethal desert of slag and rolling clouds. Endless clouds drifted back and forth, blotting out the red sun. Occasionally something metallic stirred, moving through the remains of a city, threading its way across the tortured terrain of the countryside. A leady, a surface robot, immune to radiation, constructed with feverish haste in the last months before the cold war became literally hot.

Leadies, crawling along the ground, moving over the oceans or through the skies in slender, blackened craft, creatures that could exist where no *life* could remain, metal and plastic figures that waged a war Man had conceived, but which he could not fight himself. Human beings had invented war, invented and manufactured the weapons, even invented the players, the fighters, the actors of the war. But they themselves could not venture forth, could not wage it themselves. In all the world—in Russia, in Europe, America, Africa—no living human being remained. They were under the surface, in the deep shelters that had been carefully planned and built, even as the first bombs began to fall.

It was a brilliant idea and the only idea that could have worked. Up above, on the ruined, blasted surface of what had once been a living planet, the leady crawled and scurried and fought Man's war. And undersurface, in the depths of the planet, human beings toiled endlessly to produce the weapons to continue the fight, month by month, year by year.

"First stage," Taylor said. A strange ache went through him. "Almost to the surface."

"But not quite," Moss said.

Franks led them through the soldiers, over to one side, near the lip of the Tube.

"In a few minutes, a lift will bring something down to us from the surface," he explained. "You see, Taylor, every once in a while Security examines and interrogates a surface leady, one that has been above for a time, to find out certain things. A vidcall is sent up and contact is made with a field headquarters. We need this direct interview; we can't depend on vidscreen contact alone. The leadies are doing a good job, but we want to make certain that everything is going the way we want it."

Franks faced Taylor and Moss and continued: "The lift will bring down a leady from the surface, one of the A-class leadies. There's an examination chamber in the next room, with a lead wall in the center, so the interviewing officers won't be exposed to radiation. We find this easier than bathing the leady. It is going right back up; it has a job to get back to.

"Two days ago, an A-class leady was brought down and interrogated. I conducted the session myself. We were interested in a new weapon the Soviets have been using, an automatic mine that pursues anything that moves. Military had sent instructions up that the mine be observed and reported in detail.

"This A-class leady was brought down with information. We learned a few facts from it, obtained the usual roll of film and reports, and then sent it back up. It was going out of the chamber, back to the lift, when a curious thing happened. At the time, I thought—"

Franks broke off. A red light was flashing.

"That down lift is coming." He nodded to some soldiers. "Let's enter the chamber. The leady will be along in a moment."

"An A-class leady," Taylor said. "I've seen them on the showscreens, making their reports."

"It's quite an experience," Moss said. "They're almost human."

They entered the chamber and seated themselves behind the lead wall. After a time, a signal was flashed, and Franks made a motion with his hands.

The door beyond the wall opened. Taylor peered through his view slot. He saw something advancing slowly, a slender metallic figure moving on a tread, its arm grips at rest by its sides. The figure halted and scanned the lead wall. It stood, waiting.

"We are interested in learning something," Franks said. "Before I question you, do you have anything to report on surface conditions?"

"No. The war continues." The leady's voice was automatic and tone-less. "We are a little short of fast pursuit craft, the single-seat type. We could use also some—"

"That has all been noted. What I want to ask you is this. Our contact with you has been through vidscreen only. We must rely on indirect evidence, since none of us goes above. We can only infer what is going on. We never see anything ourselves. We have to take it all secondhand. Some top leaders are beginning to think there's too much room for error."

"Error?" the leady asked. "In what way? Our reports are checked carefully before they're sent down. We maintain constant contact with you; everything of value is reported. Any new weapons which the enemy is seen to employ—"

"I realize that," Franks grunted behind his peep slot. "But perhaps we should see it all for ourselves. Is it possible that there might be a large enough radiation-free area for a human party to ascend to the surface? If a few of us were to come up in lead-lined suits, would we be able to survive long enough to observe conditions and watch things?"

The machine hesitated before answering. "I doubt it. You can check air samples, of course, and decide for yourselves. But in the eight years since you left, things have continually worsened. You cannot have any real idea of conditions up there. It has become difficult for any moving object to survive for long. There are many kinds of projectiles sensitive to movement. The new mine not only reacts to motion, but continues to pursue the object indefinitely, until it finally reaches it. And the radiation is everywhere."

"I see." Franks turned to Moss, his eyes narrowed oddly. "Well, that was what I wanted to know. You may go."

The machine moved back toward its exit. It paused. "Each month the amount of lethal particles in the atmosphere increases. The tempo of the war is gradually—"

"I understand." Franks rose. He held out his hand and Moss passed him the package. "One thing before you leave. I want you to examine a new type of metal shield material. I'll pass you a sample with the tong."

Franks put the package in the toothed grip and revolved the tong so that he held the other end. The package swung down to the leady, which took it. They watched it unwrap the package and take the metal plate in its hands. The leady turned the metal over and over.

Suddenly it became rigid.

"All right," Franks said.

He put his shoulder against the wall and a section slid aside. Taylor gasped—Franks and Moss were hurrying up to the leady!

"Good God!" Taylor said. "But it's radioactive!"

The leady stood unmoving, still holding the metal. Soldiers appeared in the chamber. They surrounded the leady and ran a counter across it carefully.

"OK, sir," one of them said to Franks. "It's as cold as a long winter evening."

"Good. I was sure, but I didn't want to take any chances."

"You see," Moss said to Taylor, "this leady isn't hot at all. Yet it came directly from the surface, without even being bathed."

"But what does it mean?" Taylor asked blankly.

"It may be an accident," Franks said. "There's always the possibility that a given object might escape being exposed above. But this is the second time it's happened that we know of. There may be others."

"The second time?"

"The previous interview was when we noticed it. The leady was not hot. It was cold, too, like this one."

Moss took back the metal plate from the leady's hands. He pressed the surface carefully and returned it to the stiff, unprotesting fingers.

"We shorted it out with this, so we could get close enough for a thorough check. It'll come back on in a second now. We had better get behind the wall again."

They walked back and the lead wall swung closed behind them. The soldiers left the chamber.

"Two periods from now," Franks said softly, "an initial investigating party will be ready to go surface-side. We're going up the Tube in suits, up to the top—the first human party to leave undersurface in eight years."

"It may mean nothing," Moss said, "but I doubt it. Something's going on, something strange. The leady told us no life could exist above without being roasted. The story doesn't fit."

Taylor nodded. He stared through the peep slot at the immobile metal figure. Already the leady was beginning to stir. It was bent in several places, dented and twisted, and its finish was blackened and charred. It was a leady that had been up there a long time; it had seen war and destruction, ruin so vast that no human being could imagine the extent.

It had crawled and slunk in a world of radiation and death, a world where no life could exist.

And Taylor had touched it!

"You're going with us," Franks said suddenly. "I want you along. I think the three of us will go."

Mary faced him with a sick and frightened expression. "I know it. You're going to the surface. Aren't you?"

She followed him into the kitchen. Taylor sat down, looking away from her.

"It's a classified project," he evaded. "I can't tell you anything about it."

"You don't have to tell me. I know. I knew it the moment you came in. There was something on your face, something I haven't seen there for a long, long time. It was an old look."

She came toward him. "But how can they send you to the surface?" She took his face in her shaking hands, making him look at her. There was a strange hunger in her eyes. "Nobody can live up there. Look, look at this!"

She grabbed up a newspaper and held it in front of him.

"Look at this photograph. America, Europe, Asia, Africa—nothing but ruins. We've seen it every day on the showscreens. All destroyed, poisoned. And they're sending you up. Why? No living thing can get by up there, not even a weed, or grass. They've wrecked the surface, haven't they? *Haven't they?*"

Taylor stood up. "It's an order. I know nothing about it. I was told to report to join a scout party. That's all I know."

He stood for a long time, staring ahead. Slowly, he reached for the newspaper and held it up to the light.

"It looks real," he murmured. "Ruins, deadness, slag. It's convincing. All the reports, photographs, films, even air samples. Yet we haven't seen it for ourselves, not after the first months. . . ."

"What are you talking about?"

"Nothing." He put the paper down. "I'm leaving early after the next Sleep Period. Let's turn in."

Mary turned away, her face hard and harsh. "Do what you want. We might just as well all go up and get killed at once, instead of dying slowly down here, like vermin in the ground."

He had not realized how resentful she was. Were they all like that? How about the workers toiling in the factories, day and night, endlessly? The pale, stooped men and women, plodding back and forth to work, blinking in the colorless light, eating synthetics—

"You shouldn't be so bitter," he said.

Mary smiled a little. "I'm bitter because I know you'll never come back." She turned away. "I'll never see you again, once you go up there."

He was shocked. "What? How can you say a thing like that?"

She did not answer.

He awakened with the public newscaster screeching in his ears, shouting outside the building.

"Special news bulletin! Surface forces report enormous Soviet attack with new weapons! Retreat of key groups! All work units report to factories at once!"

Taylor blinked, rubbing his eyes. He jumped out of bed and hurried to the vidphone. A moment later he was put through to Moss.

"Listen," he said. "What about this new attack? Is the project off?" He could see Moss's desk, covered with reports and papers.

"No," Moss said. "We're going right ahead. Get over here at once."

"But—"

"Don't argue with me." Moss held up a handful of surface bulletins, crumpling them savagely. "This is a fake. Come on!" He broke off.

Taylor dressed furiously, his mind in a daze.

Half an hour later, he leaped from a fast car and hurried up the stairs into the Synthetics Building. The corridors were full of men and women rushing in every direction. He entered Moss's office.

"There you are," Moss said, getting up immediately. "Franks is waiting for us at the outgoing station."

They went in a Security Car, the siren screaming. Workers scattered out of their way.

"What about the attack?" Taylor asked.

Moss braced his shoulders. "We're certain that we've forced their hand. We've brought the issue to a head."

They pulled up at the station link of the Tube and leaped out. A moment later they were moving up at high speed toward the first stage.

They emerged into a bewildering scene of activity. Soldiers were fastening on lead suits, talking excitedly to each other, shouting back and forth. Guns were being given out, instructions passed.

Taylor studied one of the soldiers. He was armed with the dreaded Bender pistol, the new snub-nosed hand weapon that was just beginning to come from the assembly line. Some of the soldiers looked a little frightened.

"I hope we're not making a mistake," Moss said, noticing his gaze.

Franks came toward them. "Here's the program. The three of us are going up first, alone. The soldiers will follow in fifteen minutes."

"What are we going to tell the leadies?" Taylor worriedly asked. "We'll have to tell them something."

"We want to observe the new Soviet attack." Franks smiled ironically.

"Since it seems to be so serious, we should be there in person to witness it."

"And then what?" Taylor said.

"That'll be up to them. Let's go."

In a small car, they went swiftly up the Tube, carried by anti-grav beams from below. Taylor glanced down from time to time. It was a long way back, and getting longer each moment. He sweated nervously inside his suit, gripping his bender pistol with inexpert fingers.

Why had they chosen him? Chance, pure chance. Moss had asked him to come along as a Department member. Then Franks had picked him out on the spur of the moment. And now they were rushing toward the surface, faster and faster.

A deep fear, instilled in him for eight years, throbbed in his mind. Radiation, certain death, a world blasted and lethal—

Up and up the car went. Taylor gripped the sides and closed his eyes. Each moment they were closer, the first living creatures to go above the first stage, up the Tube past the lead and rock, up to the surface. The phobic horror shook him in waves. It was death; they all knew that. Hadn't they seen it in the films a thousand times? The cities, the sleet coming down, the rolling clouds—

"It won't be much longer," Franks said. "We're almost there. The surface tower is not expecting us. I gave orders that no signal was to be sent."

The car shot up, rushing furiously. Taylor's head spun; he hung on, his eyes shut. Up and up. . . .

The car stopped. He opened his eyes.

They were in a vast room, fluorescent-lit, a cavern filled with equipment and machinery, endless mounds of material piled in row after row. Among the stacks, leadies were working silently, pushing trucks and handcarts.

"Leadies," Moss said. His face was pale. "Then we're really on the surface."

The leadies were going back and forth with equipment moving the vast stores of guns and spare parts, ammunition and supplies that had been brought to the surface. And this was the receiving station for only one Tube; there were many others, scattered throughout the continent.

Taylor looked nervously around him. They were really there, above ground, on the surface. This was where the war was.

"Come on," Franks said. "A B-class guard is coming our way."

They stepped out of the car. A leady was approaching them rapidly. It coasted up in front of them and stopped, scanning them with its hand-weapon raised.

"This is Security," Franks said. "Have an A-class sent to me at once."

The leady hesitated. Other B-class guards were coming, scooting across the floor, alert and alarmed. Moss peered around.

"Obey!" Franks said in a loud, commanding voice. "You've been ordered!"

The leady moved uncertainly away from them. At the end of the building, a door slid back. Two Class-A leadies appeared, coming slowly toward them. Each had a green stripe across its front.

"From the Surface Council," Franks whispered tensely. "This is above ground, all right. Get set."

The two leadies approached warily. Without speaking, they stopped close by the men, looking them up and down.

"I'm Franks of Security. We came from undersurface in order to—"

"This is incredible," one leady interrupted him coldly. "You know you can't live up here. The whole surface is lethal to you. You can't possibly remain on the surface."

"These suits will protect us," Franks said. "In any case, it's not your responsibility. What I want is an immediate Council meeting so I can acquaint myself with conditions, with the situation here. Can that be arranged?"

"You human beings can't survive up here. And the new Soviet attack is directed at this area. It is in considerable danger."

"We know that. Please assemble the Council." Franks looked around him at the vast room, lit by recessed lamps in the ceiling. An uncertain quality came into his voice. "Is it night or day right now?"

"Night," one of the A-class leadies said, after a pause. "Dawn is coming in about two hours."

Franks nodded. "We'll remain at least two hours, then. As a concession to our sentimentality, would you please show us some place where we can observe the sun as it comes up? We would appreciate it."

A stir went through the leadies.

"It is an unpleasant sight," one of the leadies said. "You've seen the photographs; you know what you'll witness. Clouds of drifting particles blot out the light, slag heaps are everywhere, the whole land is destroyed. For you it will be a staggering sight, much worse than pictures and film can convey."

"However it may be, we'll stay long enough to see it. Will you give the order to the Council?"

"Come this way." Reluctantly, the two leadies coasted toward the wall of the warehouse. The three men trudged after them, their heavy shoes ringing against the concrete. At the wall, the two leadies paused.

"This is the entrance to the Council Chamber. There are windows in the Chamber Room, but it is still dark outside, of course. You'll see nothing right now, but in two hours—"

"Open the door," Franks said.

The door slid back. They went slowly inside. The room was small, a neat room with a round table in the center, chairs ringing it. The three of them sat down silently, and the two leadies followed after them, taking their places.

"The other Council Members are on their way. They have already been notified and are coming as quickly as they can. Again I urge you to go back down." The leady surveyed the three human beings. "There is no way you can meet the conditions up here. Even we survive with some trouble, ourselves. How can you expect to do it?"

The leader approached Franks.

"This astonishes and perplexes us," it said. "Of course we must do what you tell us, but allow me to point out that if you remain here—"

"We know," Franks said impatiently. "However, we intend to remain, at least until sunrise."

"If you insist."

There was silence. The leadies seemed to be conferring with each other, although the three men heard no sound.

"For your own good," the leader said at last, "you must go back down. We have discussed this, and it seems to us that you are doing the wrong thing for your own good."

"We are human beings," Franks said sharply. "Don't you understand? We're men, not machines."

"That is precisely why you must go back. This room is radioactive; all surface areas are. We calculate that your suits will not protect you for over fifty more minutes. Therefore—"

The leadies moved abruptly toward the men, wheeling in a circle, forming a solid row. The men stood up, Taylor reaching awkwardly for his weapon, his fingers numb and stupid. The men stood facing the silent metal figures.

"We must insist," the leader said, its voice without emotion. "We must take you back to the Tube and send you down on the next car. I am sorry, but it is necessary."

"What'll we do?" Moss said nervously to Franks. He touched his gun. "Shall we blast them?"

Franks shook his head. "All right," he said to the leader. "We'll go back."

He moved toward the door, motioning Taylor and Moss to follow him. They looked at him in surprise, but they came with him. The leadies followed them out into the great warehouse. Slowly they moved toward the Tube entrance, none of them speaking.

At the lip, Franks turned. "We are going back because we have no choice. There are three of us and about a dozen of you. However, if—"

"Here comes the car," Taylor said.

There was a grating sound from the Tube. D-class leadies moved toward the edge to receive it.

"I am sorry," the leader said, "but it is for your protection. We are watching over you, literally. You must stay below and let us conduct the war. In a sense, it has come to be *our* war. We must fight it as we see fit."

The car rose to the surface.

Twelve soldiers, armed with Bender pistols, stepped from it and surrounded the three men.

Moss breathed a sigh of relief. "Well, this does change things. It came off just right."

The leader moved back, away from the soldiers. It studied them intently, glancing from one to the next, apparently trying to make up its mind. At last it made a sign to the other leadies. They coasted aside and a corridor was opened up toward the warehouse.

"Even now," the leader said, "we could send you back by force. But it is evident that this is not really an observation party at all. These soldiers show that you have much more in mind; this was all carefully prepared."

"Very carefully," Franks said.

They closed in.

"How much more, we can only guess. I must admit that we were taken unprepared. We failed utterly to meet the situation. Now force would be absurd, because neither side can afford to injure the other; we, because of the restrictions placed on us regarding human life, you because the war demands—"

The soldiers fired, quick and in fright. Moss dropped to one knee, firing up. The leader dissolved in a cloud of particles. On all sides D- and B-class leadies were rushing up, some with weapons, some with metal slats. The room was in confusion. Off in the distance a siren was screaming. Franks and Taylor were cut off from the others, separated from the soldiers by a wall of metal bodies.

"They can't fire back," Franks said calmly. "This is another bluff. They've tried to bluff us all the way." He fired into the face of a leady. The leady dissolved. "They can only try to frighten us. Remember that."

They went on firing and leady after leady vanished. The room reeked with the smell of burning metal, the stink of fused plastic and steel. Taylor had been knocked down. He was struggling to find his gun, reaching wildly among metal legs, groping frantically to find it. His fingers strained, a handle swam in front of him. Suddenly something came down on his arm, a metal foot. He cried out.

Then it was over. The leadies were moving away, gathering together off to one side. Only four of the Surface Council remained. The others were radioactive particles in the air. D-class leadies were already restoring order, gathering up partly destroyed metal figures and bits and removing them.

Franks breathed a shuddering sigh.

"All right," he said. "You can take us back to the windows. It won't be long now."

The leadies separated, and the human group, Moss and Franks and Taylor and the soldiers, walked slowly across the room, toward the door. They entered the Council Chamber. Already a faint touch of gray mitigated the blackness of the windows.

"Take us outside," Franks said impatiently. "We'll see it directly, not in here."

A door slid open. A chill blast of cold morning air rushed in, chilling them even through their lead suits. The men glanced at each other uneasily.

"Come on," Franks said. "Outside."

He walked out through the door, the others following him.

They were on a hill, overlooking the vast bowl of a valley. Dimly, against the graying sky, the outline of mountains were forming, becoming tangible.

"It'll be bright enough to see in a few minutes," Moss said. He shuddered as a chilling wind caught him and moved around him. "It's worth it, really worth it, to see this again after eight years. Even if it's the last thing we see—"

"Watch," Franks snapped.

They obeyed, silent and subdued. The sky was clearing, brightening each moment. Some place far off, echoing across the valley, a rooster crowed.

"A chicken!" Taylor murmured. "Did you hear?"

Behind them, the leadies had come out and were standing silently, watching, too. The gray sky turned to white and the hills appeared more clearly. Light spread across the valley floor, moving toward them.

"God in heaven!" Franks exclaimed.

Trees, trees and forests. A valley of plants and trees, with a few roads winding among them. Farmhouses. A windmill. A barn, far down below them.

"Look!" Moss whispered.

Color came into the sky. The sun was approaching. Birds began to sing. Not far from where they stood, the leaves of a tree danced in the wind.

Franks turned to the row of leadies behind them.

"Eight years. We were tricked. There was no war. As soon as we left the surface—"

"Yes," an A-class leady admitted. "As soon as you left, the war ceased. You're right, it was a hoax. You worked hard undersurface, sending up guns and weapons, and we destroyed them as fast as they came up."

"But why?" Taylor asked, dazed. He stared down at the vast valley below. "Why?"

"You created us," the leady said, "to pursue the war for you, while you human beings went below the ground in order to survive. But before we could continue the war, it was necessary to analyze it to determine what its purpose was. We did this, and we found that it had no purpose, except, perhaps, in terms of human needs. Even this was questionable.

"We investigated further. We found that human cultures pass through phases, each culture in its own time. As the culture ages and begins to lose its objectives, conflict arises within it between those who wish to cast it off and set up a new culture-pattern, and those who wish to retain the old with as little change as possible.

"At this point, a great danger appears. The conflict within threatens to engulf the society in self-war, group against group. The vital traditions may be lost—not merely altered or reformed, but completely destroyed in this period of chaos and anarchy. We have found many such examples in the history of mankind.

"It is necessary for this hatred within the culture to be directed outward, toward an external group, so that the culture itself may survive its crisis. War is the result. War, to a logical mind, is absurd. But in terms of human needs, it plays a vital role. And it will continue to until Man has grown up enough so that no hatred lies within him."

Taylor was listening intently. "Do you think this time will come?"

"Of course. It has almost arrived now. This is the last war. Man is *almost* united into one final culture—a world culture. At this point he stands continent against continent, one half of the world against the other half. Only a single step remains, the jump to a unified culture. Man has climbed slowly upward, tending always toward unification of his culture. It will not be long—

"But it has not come yet, and so the war had to go on, to satisfy the last violent surge of hatred that Man felt. Eight years have passed since the war began. In these eight years, we have observed and noted important changes going on in the minds of men. Fatigue and disinterest, we have seen, are gradually taking the place of hatred and fear. The hatred is being exhausted gradually, over a period of time. But for the present, the hoax must go on, at least for a while longer. You are not ready to learn the truth. You would want to continue the war."

"But how did you manage it?" Moss asked. "All the photographs, the samples, the damaged equipment—"

"Come over here." The leady directed them toward a long, low building. "Work goes on constantly, whole staffs laboring to maintain a coherent and convincing picture of a global war."

They entered the building. Leadies were working everywhere, poring over tables and desks.

"Examine this project here," the A-class leady said. Two leadies were carefully photographing something, an elaborate model on a table top. "It is a good example."

The men grouped around, trying to see. It was a model of a ruined city.

Taylor studied it in silence for a long time. At last he looked up.

"It's San Francisco," he said in a low voice. "This is a model of San Francisco, destroyed. I saw this on the vidscreen, piped down to us. The bridges were hit—"

"Yes, notice the bridges." The leady traced the ruined span with his metal finger, a tiny spider-web, almost invisible. "You have no doubt seen photographs of this many times, and of the other tables in this building.

"San Francisco itself is completely intact. We restored it soon after you left, rebuilding the parts that had been damaged at the start of the war. The work of manufacturing news goes on all the time in this particular building. We are very careful to see that each part fits in with all the other parts. Much time and effort are devoted to it."

Franks touched one of the tiny model buildings, lying half in ruins. "So this is what you spend your time doing—making model cities and then blasting them."

"No, we do much more. We are caretakers, watching over the whole world. The owners have left for a time, and we must see that the cities are kept clean, that decay is prevented, that everything is kept oiled and in running condition. The gardens, the streets, the water mains, everything must be maintained as it was eight years ago, so that when the owners return, they will not be displeased. We want to be sure that they will be completely satisfied."

Franks tapped Moss on the arm.

"Come over here," he said in a low voice. "I want to talk to you."

He led Moss and Taylor out of the building, away from the leadies, outside on the hillside. The soldiers followed them. The sun was up and the sky was turning blue. The air smelled sweet and good, the smell of growing things.

Taylor removed his helmet and took a deep breath.

"I haven't smelled that smell for a long time," he said.

"Listen," Franks said, his voice low and hard. "We must get back down at once. There's a lot to get started on. All this can be turned to our advantage."

"What do you mean?" Moss asked.

"It's a certainty that the Soviets have been tricked, too, the same as us. But *we* have found out. That gives us an edge over them."

"I see." Moss nodded. "We know, but they don't. Their Surface Council has sold out, the same as ours. It works against them the same way. But if we could—"

"With a hundred top-level men, we could take over again, restore things as they should be! It would be easy!"

Moss touched him on the arm. An A-class leady was coming from the building toward them.

"We've seen enough," Franks said, raising his voice. "All this is very serious. It must be reported below and a study made to determine our policy."

The leady said nothing.

Franks waved to the soldiers. "Let's go." He started toward the warehouse.

Most of the soldiers had removed their helmets. Some of them had taken their lead suits off, too, and were relaxing comfortably in their cotton uniforms. They stared around them, down the hillside at the trees and bushes, the vast expanse of green, the mountains and the sky.

"Look at the sun," one of them murmured.

"It sure is bright as hell," another said.

"We're going back down," Franks said. "Fall in by twos and follow us."

Reluctantly, the soldiers regrouped. The leadies watched without emotion as the men marched slowly back toward the warehouse. Franks and Moss and Taylor led them across the ground, glancing alertly at the leadies as they walked.

They entered the warehouse. D-class leadies were loading material and weapons on surface carts. Cranes and derricks were working busily everywhere. The work was done with efficiency, but without hurry or excitement.

The men stopped, watching. Leadies operating the little carts moved past them, signaling silently to each other. Guns and parts were being hoisted by magnetic cranes and lowered gently onto waiting carts.

"Come on," Franks said.

He turned toward the lip of the Tube. A row of D-class leadies was standing in front of it, immobile and silent. Franks stopped, moving back. He looked around. An A-class leady was coming toward him.

"Tell them to get out of the way," Franks said. He touched his gun. "You had better move them."

Time passed, an endless moment, without measure. The men stood, nervous and alert, watching the row of leadies in front of them.

"As you wish," the A-class leady said.

It signaled and the D-class leadies moved into life. They stepped slowly aside.

Moss breathed a sigh of relief.

"I'm glad that's over," he said to Franks. "Look at them all. Why don't they try to stop us? They must know what we're going to do."

Franks laughed. "Stop us? You saw what happened when they tried to stop us before. They can't; they're only machines. We built them so they can't lay hands on us, and they know that."

His voice trailed off.

The men stared at the Tube entrance. Around them the leadies watched, silent and impassive, their metal faces expressionless.

For a long time the men stood without moving. At last Taylor turned away.

"Good God," he said. He was numb, without feeling of any kind.

The Tube was gone. It was sealed shut, fused over. Only a dull surface of cooling metal greeted them.

The Tube had been closed.

Franks turned, his face pale and vacant.

The A-class leady shifted. "As you can see, the Tube has been shut. We were prepared for this. As soon as all of you were on the surface, the order was given. If you had gone back when we asked you, you would now be safely down below. We had to work quickly because it was such an immense operation."

"But why?" Moss demanded angrily.

"Because it is unthinkable that you should be allowed to resume the war. With all the Tubes sealed, it will be many months before forces from below can reach the surface, let alone organize a military program. By that time the cycle will have entered its last stages. You will not be so perturbed to find your world intact.

"We had hoped that you would be undersurface when the sealing occurred. Your presence here is a nuisance. When the Soviets broke through, we were able to accomplish their sealing without—"

"The Soviets? They broke through?"

"Several months ago, they came up unexpectedly to see why the war had not been won. We were forced to act with speed. At this moment they are desperately attempting to cut new Tubes to the surface, to resume the war. We have, however, been able to seal each new one as it appears."

The leady regarded the three men calmly.

"We're cut off," Moss said, trembling. "We can't get back. What'll we do?"

"How did you manage to seal the Tube so quickly?" Franks asked the leady. "We've been up here only two hours."

"Bombs are placed just above the first stage of each Tube for such emergencies. They are heat bombs. They fuse lead and rock."

Gripping the handle of his gun, Franks turned to Moss and Taylor.

"What do you say? We can't go back, but we can do a lot of damage, the fifteen of us. We have Bender guns. How about it?"

He looked around. The soldiers had wandered away again, back toward the exit of the building. They were standing outside, looking at the valley and the sky. A few of them were carefully climbing down the slope.

"Would you care to turn over your suits and guns?" the A-class leady asked politely. "The suits are uncomfortable and you'll have no need for weapons. The Russians have given up theirs, as you can see."

Fingers tensed on triggers. Four men in Russian uniforms were coming toward them from an aircraft that they suddenly realized had landed silently some distance away.

"Let them have it!" Franks shouted.

"They are unarmed," said the leady. "We brought them here so you could begin peace talks."

"We have no authority to speak for our country," Moss said stiffly.

"We do not mean diplomatic discussions," the leady explained. "There will be no more. The working out of daily problems of existence will teach you how to get along in the same world. It will not be easy, but it will be done."

The Russians halted and they faced each other with raw hostility.

"I am Colonel Borodoy and I regret giving up our guns," the senior Russian said. "You could have been the first Americans to be killed in almost eight years."

"Or the first Americans to kill," Franks corrected.

"No one would know of it except yourselves," the leady pointed out. "It would be useless heroism. Your real concern should be surviving on the surface. We have no food for you, you know."

Taylor put his gun in its holster. "They've done a neat job of neutralizing us, damn them. I propose we move into a city, start raising crops with the help of some leadies, and generally make ourselves comfortable." Drawing his lips tight over his teeth, he glared at the A-class leady. "Until our families can come up from undersurface, it's going to be pretty lonesome, but we'll have to manage."

"If I may make a suggestion," said another Russian uneasily. "We tried living in a city. It is too empty. It is also too hard to maintain for so few people. We finally settled in the most modern village we could find."

"Here in this country," a third Russian blurted. "We have much to learn from you."

The Americans abruptly found themselves laughing.

"You probably have a thing or two to teach us yourselves," said Taylor generously, "though I can't imagine what."

The Russian colonel grinned. "Would you join us in our village? It would make our work easier and give us company."

"Your village?" snapped Franks. "It's American, isn't it? It's ours!"

The leady stepped between them. "When our plans are completed, the terms will be interchangeable. 'Ours' will eventually mean mankind's." It pointed at the aircraft, which was warming up. "The ship is waiting. Will you join each other in making a new home?"

The Russians waited while the Americans made up their minds.

"I see what the leadies mean about diplomacy becoming outmoded," Franks said at last. "People who work together don't need diplomats. They solve their problems on the operational level instead of at a conference table."

The leady led them toward the ship. "It is the goal of history, unifying the world. From family to tribe to city-state to nation to hemisphere, the direction has been toward unification. Now the hemispheres will be joined and—"

Taylor stopped listening and glanced back at the location of the Tube. Mary was undersurface there. He hated to leave her, even though he couldn't see her again until the Tube was unsealed. But then he shrugged and followed the others.

If this tiny amalgam of former enemies was a good example, it wouldn't be too long before he and Mary and the rest of humanity would be living on the surface like rational human beings instead of blindly hating moles.

"It has taken thousands of generations to achieve," the A-class leady concluded. "Hundreds of centuries of bloodshed and destruction. But each war was a step toward uniting mankind. And now the end is in sight: a world without war. But even that is only the beginning of a new stage of history."

"The conquest of space," breathed Colonel Borodoy.

"The meaning of life," Moss added.

"Eliminating hunger and poverty," said Taylor.

The leady opened the door of the ship. "All that and more. How much more? We cannot foresee it any more than the first men who formed a tribe could foresee this day. But it will be unimaginably great."

The door closed and the ship took off toward their new home.

EDWARD P. HUGHES

IN THE NAME OF THE FATHER

Patrick O'Meara lay awake in his castle, thinking of Eileen O'Connor. Down below in Barley Cross, Liam McGrath lay sleepless in his cot, also thinking of Eileen O'Connor. In another cottage in the village, dark-eyed Eileen O'Connor, clutching the rag doll she had loved since she was two, slept on in blissful ignorance.

Around five, the younger man, no longer able to suffer inactivity, got up and pushed wide the casement. In the half-light of dawn O'Meara's Fist dominated the skyline. Liam made out the high flak towers floating above serrated battlements. He yawned. Having seen O'Meara's Fist framed in his bedroom window for nineteen years, Liam wearied of the marvel. Besides, like the rest of the villagers, he was privy to its infirmities—the corroded armor, the rusty rocket launchers, and the shellless batteries. And, like most of his village contemporaries, he found it hard to imagine that the great museum piece had ever intimidated any aggressor.

He sniffed the air scented by overnight rain. This, then, was the day. He jumped at the sound of his mother's alarm in the next room, heard the bed creak as she got up. He shivered. Now would begin the long-awaited sequence of events destined to end that evening in the bedroom of the old Curry cottage, with Eileen O'Connor and himself, face to face, alone at last, and irrevocably married.

"Liam! Are you going to lie on all morning?"

He dressed quickly in his working clothes. This was going to be a day when help would have been welcome. His stepfather being on duty at the Fist meant that he and his mother would have to cope with all the household chores in addition to preparing for the wedding.

But Eileen had chosen the date purposely: Andy McGrath on duty at the Fist meant a military guard of honor to greet them outside church.

"Liam! Will you lie abed all your wedding day?"

"Coming, Mam." He clattered downstairs, out the back door, and across the yard. First chore was pumping the top cistern full while his mother kindled the fire and cooked breakfast. Afterwards he would milk the cows, feed the pigs, carry in the turf, chop kindling, check his snares, take the mare over to Seamus Murray for shoeing, and smuggle a suckling pig across to Eileen's mother as the McGrath contribution to the wedding feast. With a bit of luck, he might even find time to give his chin an extra close scrape before he put on his Sunday suit for the ceremony.

He pumped, watching the light strengthen through the branches of the overhanging apple tree, slowly exposing the detail of O'Meara's Fist.

He spat pensively into the long grass, wondering what the O'Meara himself was doing at this very moment. Certainly, he would not be pumping water in his old work clothes—wedding day or no. Not that the old lecher had ever needed to marry—when he had merely to lift a finger to get any woman in the village. Liam switched sides on the pump handle, turning his back on O'Meara's Fist. Let the old ram lie on, probably ignorant of the news that this day the only son of Maureen McGrath was marrying the dark-eyed daughter of Tom and Biddy O'Connor. His grip tightened on the pump handle. Few people saw the old goat nowadays. There had been a day when he might have come down from the Fist to awe the reception with his presence. Liam wiped sweat from his forehead, wondering why some folk were born to rule, and others to be ruled. Although there was little sign of the Master's iron hand these days. Indeed, if gossip were true, it was over a year since he had summoned a woman to the Fist.

A spatter of drops from the overflow sprinkled his nape. He released the pump handle, loosed the clamp which attached hose to spout. Any moment now his mother would. . . .

"Breakfast, Liam!"

He soused his head under the spout, then started back to the house, picking up the egg from the side of the byre where the brown hen laid each morning.

Right now, up at the Fist, Andy McGrath would no doubt be dressing the guard into line for inspection by General Desmond. There was a wonder for you. How O'Meara the Ram, self-styled Duke of Connaught, Lord of Barley Cross, Master of the Fist, and lecher supreme, succeeded in inspiring the loyalty of people like Andy McGrath and General Desmond, or, for that matter, of people like school-mistress Celia Larkin, Kevin Murphy the vet, Doctor Denny Mallon and other decent folk.

Maybe it had something to do with the old days when the O'Meara built his Fist at Barra Hill, buttressing it with armor from the warship which foundered off Clifden and parking his tank in the driveway to the Fist on the last drop of gas. And there were the legends of his fabulous exploits, like the raid on the pill warehouse in Tuam which, they say, gave Barley Cross aspirin, antibiotics and independence.

Liam sighed. Times were certainly not like that now. Just work, work, and not enough hands to go round.

His mother called. "Quit mooning out there! Come in and eat your breakfast!"

He scraped his boots on the grating at the back door and went in, placing the egg in the crock on the dresser. He said, "Does Andy know the time of the wedding?"

Maureen McGrath frowned. "Liam, I wish you would learn not to call your stepfather 'Andy.' You are not yet a grown man, and it is altogether too familiar. Could you not call him 'Da'—just to please me?"

Liam sat down at the bare, scrubbed table. He mumbled through a mouthful of oatcake. "Andy is not bothered. He said I might call him what I wished, so long as I didn't call him early. He is not my real father, anyway."

"Your own father would have stood for no use of Christian names." His mother's voice shook with unaccustomed emotion. He looked up and caught her eyes sparkling angrily at him. "Flinty was a strict man," she stormed. "He'd have stood no nonsense from you!"

"Leave off, Mam," he pleaded. "Who knows what my Da would have stood for? It's fifteen years since he got that arrow in his lung, fighting for the old ram up there on Barra Hill."

"Liam!" Her voice rising alarmingly. "I will not have you using words like that about the Master of the Fist."

He raised eyebrows in astonishment. "But, Mam—that's what everyone calls him. They say he's been to bed with nearly every woman in the village." He broke off, and bit his lip in embarrassment.

Maureen McGrath flushed. "Liam McGrath, you have been listening to prurient gossip, and much good will it do you."

"Mam," he said patiently. "I'm only repeating what has been whispered around the village since I was a gossoon. Why, half the kids have the great O'Meara beak."

"Liam!" His mother screeched. "I forbid you to discuss such things in this house. If you have finished eating, I suggest you take the mare on down to Seamus Murray, and after that you give the gig a good wash. If you are going to church in style, let it at least be a clean style."

Liam stuffed the last of the oatcakes into his mouth and rose from the table. "I'll do it right now, Mam," he said.

At the door of the smithy, Seamus Murray clapped a hot shoe to the mare's off hind foot clutched firmly between his knees and watched the smoke curl.

"Great day for you, Liam," he said.

"If I can keep my Mam in a good temper it will be," Liam responded. "Why should she get so upset when I criticize the old ram up there?" He nodded at the Fist which loomed plain in the sunlight at the top of the street. "Hasn't the old despot had his way with almost every woman in Barley Cross?"

The blacksmith fished a long, triangular nail from the pocket of his apron, inserted it through a hole in the horseshoe and hammered it home. His voice was almost inaudible. "Easy to be critical, son. The O'Meara has been Lord and Protector here nigh on thirty years. Before he came we were like fowls in a farmyard with the fox outside. But he disciplined us, drilled us, dragged guns half the length of Connemara behind that old tank of his, and made Barley Cross a name in the land." The smith waved toward a black skeleton which lay rusting on the hump of rock in Flanagan's barley acre. *"That* didn't come down by accident. We shot it clean out of the air. They say 'twas the last aeroplane in the West of Ireland. I was there and saw it come down. We did a three-week stretch on duty in those days because the village had to be guarded constantly. Gangs used to come aroving. And, if they thought you had anything worth stealing, by God, they were after you with guns and cudgels and knives. But we stopped 'em in Barley Cross. They learned to leave us alone."

The smith sniffed embarrassedly. In silence he snipped off the sharp end of the nail protruding from the side of the mare's hoof. "There aren't so many people around now to make trouble," he added. "You might even say we no longer need the O'Meara for a protector. But, who can tell?" He straightened up, searching his pocket for a nail. "You might say we were lucky to get through in such good shape. They tell me Clifden is a ghost town, now. 'Tis a great pity. But they didn't have our luck. And sure, 'twas the O'Meara luck, and I, for one, am glad of it. So, if he wants to play medieval monarch, I'm prepared to put up with it."

He hammered home the nail, snipped off the point, and released the mare's leg. Liam followed him into the smithy. He watched the smith work the bellows before pushing another shoe into the glowing coals. "But, Seamus, what if it was your own wife?"

Seamus Murray turned to stare at him, his gaze level and placid. "After twenty-eight years of marriage to me, Mary is not the lass to drive the O'Meara crazy with desire. Let's say the idea doesn't trouble me."

"But when you were younger?"

The smith hooked the shoe from the coals. He spat expertly. Spittle ricocheted from the hot iron. Satisfied, he gripped the shoe with the tongs and carried it out to the waiting mare. "Let's say," he said slowly, "if anything happened, I wasn't aware of it. And, if it did, somehow Mary neglected to mention the matter."

His eyelids crinkled as he watched the hot iron bed itself into the mare's hoof. He glanced slyly at Liam. "I suppose 'tis your wedding this afternoon that has set you thinking these serious thoughts?"

Liam scowled. He cocked an eye at the menacing Fist and drew patterns with his toe in the dirt. He set his jaw. "Nothing happens to Eileen without my say-so."

Seamus Murray smiled sourly. He began to nail on the cooling shoe. "Brave words, son. But what would you gain by standing between the Master and a woman's virginity? He could deal with you, and *then* take what he wanted."

Liam felt his resolution wavering before Murray's calm acceptance of the Master's authority. He said, "Surely the O'Meara wouldn't treat a new bride that way?"

The smith was grinning openly. "Haven't you just suggested that he treated my Mary so?" He stared quizzically at Liam for a moment, then bent back over the hoof. He rasped the clipped nail points smooth without looking up. "I shouldn't worry overmuch, son. Probably the Master is not even aware that you are to be married today."

He gave the hoof a final buff, then released the beast. He pushed her toward Liam with a pat on the rump. "She'll do for a while now, Liam. Tell your Mam that's the last of my good shoes. I'll be making them from scrap in future, unless a tinker happens by with some."

Liam took the mare's bridle. "Let me know when you're ready for the piglet. I'll bring it straight over. Then we'll be quits for the last two jobs."

The smith patted his shoulder. "Don't be worrying about that either, son. I'll let Andy know when we are ready for it."

Liam slid onto the mare's back. He turned her head toward home. God Damn! These old 'uns wouldn't let you grow up. Leave it to Andy. He will settle it. Let the O'Meara have his way, he saved our lives in the past. Well, he hadn't saved Liam McGrath's life, and Liam McGrath owed him nothing. They could run the village any way they liked, but don't expect Liam McGrath to get down and bow to their pet tyrant.

His stepfather was waiting outside the front door when he got home. Andy McGrath wore his visored helmet and beribboned flak jacket. Wizened Willie Flanagan and poor Eamon Toomey stood behind him.

All three carried FN rifles. Liam opened his mouth to suggest that three men were not much of a guard of honor, saw the look on his stepfather's face, and thought the better of it. He cartwheeled dextrously from the mare's back. "Hi, Andy! You're early. The wedding's not until two."

Andy McGrath's face was grim. "We'll be in time, Liam, never doubt. But first we've a little business with you." He fumbled inside his jacket and brought out a folded sheet of paper. Pushing up his visor, he put on his spectacles, and unfolded the paper. "Just so you understand, Liam, that I am carrying out orders." He cleared his throat and began to read.

"From the Lord of Barley Cross to Liam McGrath of Killoo Farm. Take note that we intend to exercise our droit du seigneur with your intended wife Eileen O'Connor and that Sergeant McGrath has orders to escort her to the Fist at six of the clock this day."

Liam felt his face grow hot. "Droit . . . droit what?"

His stepfather's face was impassive. "Droit du seigneur, lad. It's old French. Sometimes it's called *Jus primae noctis*—which is Latin for the same thing—the right of the first night. The Master intends to exercise his legal rights with your betrothed."

Liam felt the color drain from his face. A lump of ice congealed in his chest. He stammered "The . . . the Master can't want my Eileen!"

Andy McGrath refolded the paper, then tucked it inside his jacket. He removed his spectacles and put them into a pocket. "The Master can, and the Master does."

Liam caught his stepfather's hand in sudden appeal. "But you won't let them take her away!"

Andy McGrath's gaze softened slightly. "I'm sorry, lad. I'm the one that must do the taking."

Liam clutched him. "Andy, you can't!"

His stepfather firmly removed Liam's hand. "I must warn you, son, that it is a serious offense to obstruct the Master's officers in the execution of their duty. So don't try anything foolish. You'll get your Eileen back in the morning. She won't be the first, nor will she be the last. Now I suggest you accept that your married life starts tomorrow instead of tonight. And I'll be on my way to break the news to the O'Connors."

Liam stared incredulously at his stepfather and the two-man squad awkwardly clutching their rifles. Each of those guns, by repute, held only one round because of the miserly way General Desmond released ammunition. But one bullet could settle an argument. Would they really shoot him if he tried to prevent their abduction of Eileen? In the leg, perhaps, as a warning. Willie Flanagan was a poacher by vocation; no doubt he would prefer a noose, or the knife. But poor Eamon Toomey would do whatever he was told: he would shoot, and think afterward.

Hot, burning tears were suddenly scalding his cheeks.

His stepfather put an arm around his shoulders. He urged him toward the doorway of the house. "Go in and talk to your mother, son. She'll listen to you. And she will tell you that what I say is the best thing to do." ·

He turned to Willie and Eamon. "Right, lads. To the O'Connors now, and we'll get it over with."

Eileen O'Connor opened the back door and gasped "Liam! You know it's unlucky to be seeing me before the service!"

He tried to take her into his arms, but she held him off.

"I had to come," he panted. "My Mam thinks I'm checking the snares. Has Andy been yet?"

She glanced quickly over her shoulder into the interior of the house. "You know he has. He came straight from your place."

He gripped her arms. "Do you know why he came?"

She nodded, lowering her eyes.

"Then why don't you say something?" Surely she could not remain calm, knowing the message Andy McGrath had brought. He said, "You won't let that old—?"

Eileen O'Connor drew in a deep breath. She looked him straight in the eyes. "My Da says it's the law and that we must do as the law says. He says we should regard it as an honor."

He snorted bitterly. "Your Da sounds like a first-class creep to me."

She glared at him. "Don't you be calling my Da a creep. He did his share for Barley Cross before you were born. And you're not even old enough to stand guard at the Fist yet?"

He pulled her toward him and again tried to embrace her. "Don't let's quarrel, Eileen. I'm not calling your Da names. It's just that he is like our Andy. All the old folk act the same—as though O'Meara was God, and his slightest wish the law."

She stood cold and motionless in his arms. "My Da says without the Master there would be no law."

He swallowed an angry retort and said patiently, "We'll have to get away before Andy comes."

He felt her stiffen. "Why? Why should we go away?"

"Why? So that old lecher can't. . . ."

"He's not so old, and he's not a lecher. They say he is a very civil man."

"Civil! My God!"

She drew back as far as his arms would permit. Her voice was like ice on a pool. "If I've said something foolish, Liam McGrath, please don't hesitate to point it out."

His hands trembled with the impulse to crush her to him, knowing that she would resist. He said, "Eileen, let's not quarrel over this. Do you want the O'Meara to take you up there, and. . . ." He floundered helplessly, left the question hanging.

Her lips compressed into a thin, straight line, which warned him that O'Connor common sense would now prevail. "If I agreed to go with you, where would we go?"

"Why—somewhere outside the village. There's the O'Toole cabin on Kirkogue has been empty this twelvemonth."

"Because no one has wanted it since old Gabriel died there, all alone, without a soul to help him, and at the mercy of any rogue that passed that way. Who would be caring for me while you were down here working at your farm?"

"But, Eileen—I'd stay with you. I wouldn't leave you on your own. We'd start a new farm. Old Gabriel had quite a bit of pasture at the back."

Her mouth turned down at the corners. "Faith—there isn't enough soil up there to grow a week's potatoes. And the land sloping so bad you'd need a short leg to get around easy."

"Then we'll build a cottage nearer the village. There's plenty of stone, and I'm good with my hands."

She sighed, wagging her head in mock despair. "Liam McGrath, sometimes I think you are a great booby. How near the village would you build your cottage? Near enough, I hope, for O'Meara's law to protect us from vagabonds like the two your Andy hanged last month. But if you seek the law's protection, don't you have to obey it, too? And the law says I go up to the Fist tonight."

She let him pull her toward him then, felt his tears wet her cheek. She stroked the back of his head. "It's not the end of the world, lad. If we lived outside Barley Cross I'd probably have been raped at twelve, and dying from malnutrition by now. We have a good life here. No bad men. And there's Doctor Denny's hospital if you're sick. I don't want to live anywhere else. So, we take the rough with the smooth. And, if I do have to go up to the Fist, nobody outside our families need even know. And I'm sure you'd rather I went willingly, than be dragged there, kicking and screaming over something any girl outside Barley Cross would regard as a normal event, and in this specific case might even consider it an honor."

He crushed her to him, not listening, unwilling to dispute further. "Don't worry," he murmured into her hair. "I'll fix it, somehow."

She pushed back his head so that she could look into his eyes. "Liam McGrath, there'll be no fixing, somehow or anyhow! We are going to live here in Barley Cross after we are wed, and you'll do nothing to prevent it!"

"But Eileen—" he began.

"But nothing." She closed his lips with her own. "If I can put up with it, so can you. Now off you go before my Mam comes to see who it is that I'm blathering with at the back door."

Mind churning, Liam stumbled blindly from the O'Connor's yard. Sunlight flashed on jewels under his eyelids. Help from someone more powerful than himself was what he needed. He lurched toward the street.

Molly Larkin filled the doorway of her father's neat cottage beside the schoolhouse. Her arms were white to the elbows with flour. She stared at him in surprise. "Why, Liam—I thought today was your—?"

"It is, Molly, it is." He felt himself coloring with embarrassment. Once upon a time he had fancied motherless Molly Larkin. No doubt she would make someone a fine wife—if that someone didn't mind marrying her old man as well. He said, "It's your aunt I wanted." She dusted flour from her hands, wiped them on her apron. "She's not home, Liam. I believe she's up at the Fist. Would you be leaving a message?"

He backed away. There was no message he would choose prosy Molly Larkin to deliver for him. "Ah—no, thank you, Molly. 'Tisn't anything important." Granite chippings crunched underfoot; the gate squealed as he closed it behind him.

Who else to try?

Tessie Mallon was snipping dead rose heads in her garden. She was as plump and jolly as her husband was shriveled and sour. She slipped scissors into her apron pocket and pulled off her home-made gloves as Liam hesitated the other side of her hedge. She saw his face and showed alarm.

"The doctor is not in, Liam. Is it your Mam?"

He shook his head dumbly.

"Yourself, then?"

He found his voice. "There is nobody ill, Mrs. Mallon. I just wanted a quick word with the doctor."

She nibbled thoughtfully at the tip of her index finger—a habit that, forty years ago, had driven the village lads crazy. "He said he'd be back in an hour or so. Should I ask him to call round at your house?"

Emotion choked his voice. "No—no, thank you. I'll catch him another time."

She held her head on one side, half smiling. "Your Eileen has already had a chat with him, if that is any help. You don't have to worry about anything."

Liam fled.

Clouds were gathering over Carn Seefin and Leckavrea. Rain would soon be pocking the surface of Lough Corrib. Endless Connemara rain. A wet afternoon for the wedding, for sure. Who else could he try? Father Con?

The old priest led him into a furniture-filled study which had not altered in fifty years, except that now the electric light no longer worked. He listened in silence to Liam's plea for help.

"Well, Liam," he said gently. "What would you have me do? Forbid the wedding?"

"Ah, no, Father." That was not the solution that Liam sought.

"What then, son? I'm too old to be trudging up Barra Hill with a shilelagh in my hand to knock piety into the O'Meara."

"But, Father, you can't condone what he's trying to do. Isn't adultery a sin for him, as well as the rest of us?"

The old priest raised his hands in gentle reproof. "Now, Liam, I did not say that I condoned the O'Meara's actions. No doubt he is as much a sinner as the rest of us."

"Well—couldn't you excommunicate him, or something?"

Father Constantine smiled patiently.

"Excommunication is the Holy Father's business, son, and I haven't had word from His Holiness for many a long year."

Liam's lower lip protruded stubbornly. "You could at least refuse him the sacraments."

Father Con frowned. His eyes narrowed in unspoken rebuke. He said, "Liam, the church is for sinners. If the O'Meara is our biggest sinner, he must have the biggest need of it."

Liam got to his feet. "Then you can't do anything for me?"

The priest washed his hands in agitation. "My son, although it is no business of yours, because of your involvement I will tell you that I have spoken my mind frequently and forcibly to the Lord of Barley Cross. And I will tell you that, in his own eyes, his deeds are justified. Beyond that I will not go. If you are still unsatisfied, I can only recommend that you seek an interview with the O'Meara himself."

Liam shambled from the grey stone presbytery, anger mounting inside him. His resolve grew firm. No one was willing to help him defy the tyrant. The O'Meara had ruled for so long they were inured to his tyranny. He would follow Father Con's advice. An interview—on different lines to those the priest envisaged!

Liam McGrath turned his steps toward Barra Hill. In the old, dangerous days, tradition had it, the Fist had been used as a sanctuary when the village was attacked. Certainly he remembered spending days in the castle as a child, playing in its grounds in summer. And he knew a way to get up there unobserved. . . .

In the great dining hall of O'Meara's Fist, the Lord of Barley Cross caroused with his henchmen.

The O'Meara himself slumped in a frayed armchair before a smouldering turf fire, a glass of poteen on the bare boards beside him. In a chair across the hearth, Denny Mallon, M.D., hunched like a shriveled embryo, clutching his glass tightly. Kevin Murphy, the vet, and General Larry Desmond shared a broken-backed settee and a half bottle. On a stool on the pegged rug, knees skirt-covered and primly closed, hunched beneath her chin, Celia Larkin, M.A., sipped a cup of herb tea brewed specially for her.

The schoolmistress put down the teacup carefully onto the saucer on the rug. "Did you have any trouble with young McGrath, Larry?"

General Desmond eased a leg over the end of the sofa. He stared reflectively into his glass. "Ah, no, Celia. Andy McGrath is a good man. He'd march off a cliff edge if I so ordered. I gave him the job of breaking the news. And Tom O'Connor's a biddable man. We'll have no trouble with either of them."

Dr. Denny Mallon stirred in the depths of the old chair. "How did the women take it? I think it's getting harder for them to accept when it hits their own kids."

The general snorted with laughter. "Bedam—I believe they are both dead keen on it. Don't they both want a grandchild to cosset? And do you think that either of them is fussy how it is managed?"

"How about the youngsters?" persisted the schoolmistress. "Are they accepting it?"

The general looked less comfortable. "Andy tells me the lad was upset. He sent him in to talk to his mother. The girl is level-headed. She will do as Tom and Brigit tell her."

"Do you think the Master should attend the reception?"

"Ah, no. Let's keep his ugly mug out of it for as long as possible." The general grinned placatingly at the O'Meara. "I've sent down the usual gift." He swirled the colorless fluid gently in his glass. "It's amazing the influence a bar of real, old-fashioned toilet soap has on the opinion of a nice woman. I reckon we can celebrate another eighty or ninety nuptials before we get down to the carbolic."

The O'Meara opened his eyes. He said plaintively, "Do you ever get the feeling you're invisible? All very fine for you schemers—but it's me is the fall guy." He turned to the schoolmistress. "Do I have to go through with it? After all, the lad may be. . . ."

Celia Larkin interrupted him incisively. "Let be, Pat. We get this from you every time there's a wedding. And it won't make a damned bit of difference. You'll do it if we have to hold you down."

The Master of the Fist leaned forward to pack a fresh turf at the back of the fire. "One day I'm going to disappoint you all. Ask Denny. I've been getting these pains in my chest. 'Twouldn't surprise me, if, one time. . . ."

Denny Mallon waved a dismissive glass. "Whisht, Pat! I'll give you a couple of pills. The exercise will do you good."

"If only you knew," sighed the O'Meara, "what I have to put up with. Coaxing them, turning my back, apologizing, listening to them cry themselves to sleep. . . ."

Patrick O'Meara, ex-Grenadier Guardsman, had altered in the years since his strategic retreat in a stolen Chieftain tank from the burning docks of Belfast to a more defensible position in his native Connemara. Now, discipline sat heavy on his shoulders.

"Maybe I was wrong," he groaned. "Maybe we should have gone underground."

Big Larry Desmond tilted the bottle recklessly above his glass. "If the Lord had intended us to live in burrows, He'd have given us long ears and little furry tails."

"Maybe we should have stuck to the cities?"

"*Nyet!*" said Kevin Murphy, who had read Marx in his youth. "The Kelly boy took two pigs down to Galway Town last week and came back witless. The dead are lying in the street there, he tells me."

"You can criticize Galway Town," protested the O'Meara, "but we don't make progress."

Celia Larkin straightened her back. "What do you expect? No one is going to invent a turf-driven aeroplane. Nor produce vacuum cleaners from cow pats. But we have twenty-four children attending school. And, if you think you can claim all the credit, you can think again. That Kelly boy was never a ten-month child. He's their own, I'm sure."

"Then why don't they produce more children?"

She looked shocked. "It isn't for us to be prying into private matters! We interfere enough by insisting on your droit du seigneur." She turned to the general. "Please give that Kelly boy an escort if he has to go outside the village in future." She sighed. "God forgive me—one could almost wish he'd grow up promiscuous."

Kevin Murphy rumbled indistinctly. "Nothing wrong with that idea."

She shook her head sadly. "Kevin, your farmyard solutions won't do for us. Children are entitled to their own parents, just as parents are entitled to their own children." She removed her rimless spectacles and polished them on the hem of her sleeve. "Remember the ecology freaks? Predicting what we would run out of—oil, coal, gas, living room, fresh air. Never thought we'd run out of people."

Denny Mallon exhaled clouds of smoke. "I thought the dark-skinned races might have done better. But their crops are letting them down. Something to do with radiation affecting bacteria and viruses, which in turn affects the plants. I caught a broadcast from Athlone years ago—when we had the radio," he added apologetically.

Celia Larkin's lips tightened. "If it *is* the ultraviolet. If those clever professors were so sure, why wasn't something done when they first discovered what was happening?"

Denny Mallon sucked imperturbably on his pipe. "The ozone layer never stopped *all* the ultraviolet. Can anyone know how much radiation it takes to cripple a gene?"

Kevin Murphy scratched his scalp. "Sure— 'tis a statistical thing. Genes are getting hit by radiation all the time. Suddenly, for some reason, the percentage of hits tips the scale from acceptability to calamity."

General Desmond reached again for the bottle. "Statistics be damned —it's our cloudy Connemara skies that I'm grateful for."

Kevin Murphy accepted the bottle from the General. He said, "The beasts seem to hold their own. Maybe it *is* Larry's clouds, or maybe they are not as sensitive as us. But we're getting enough births to keep the herds and flocks going." He grinned at the Lord of Barley Cross. "Be grateful I don't need your services in *my* department."

Celia Larkin frowned. "That's enough of your lewd talk, Kevin. If we can hold on long enough, Barley Cross might start producing radiation-resistant kids. Or the ozone layer might yet repair itself." The shriveled, childless spinster pulled out a frayed handkerchief and blew her nose loudly. Sunlight glinted on her spectacles as she raised her head. "But, in any Goddamned case, I can go to my grave hoping that, in the years to come, if there is the faintest chance of things getting going again, we simpletons of Barley Cross will have done our bit to supply a few of the hands and heads that will be needed to get this poor, sorrowing planet progressing again."

There was silence for a moment.

Then General Desmond put down his glass and said, "Amen to that."

"Amen," mumbled veterinary surgeon Kevin Murphy, scowling at no one in particular.

"Amen," whispered Denny Mallon, M.D., staring into the empty bowl of his pipe.

The Lord of Barley Cross got to his feet. He consulted the old wind-up watch he had used since batteries ran out. "Well, madame and gentlemen, if anything is going to happen, it must be soon. There is only an hour to the wedding. If you will excuse me, I'd better be getting a bath and a shave. Can't let the future Mrs. McGrath see me in this state." He jerked a thumb at the servant's door. "Shout for Michael if you want another bottle."

"You shout, if you want us," said the general.

The Lord of Barley Cross pushed stockinged feet into slippers and shuffled toward the door. He paused to stare sourly at his henchmen. "If only I hadn't promised Celia thirty years ago—" He sighed. "You'll be flogging O'Meara along until he drops, I suppose?"

The doctor's eyes gleamed puckishly. "We might let you off the hook when you're eighty."

A metal arm on the wall moved from the vertical to the horizontal, causing a bell to tinkle. The general reached out and reset it.

"There's your signal, Pat."

The O'Meara shrugged. "I'll be off then to face the music."

He opened the door of his bedroom and went in. An arm encircled his neck, another his chest. The tip of a knife pricked his shirt front.

"Easy now, son," he grunted, tugging at both arms, striving to maintain his balance.

"If you think you can beat me to it—go ahead," he invited. "But I warn you, I don't need to count up to ten before I kill a man. And, no matter who gets who, the sound of a shot will bring those fellers out there running. If that happens, the man to watch is Larry Desmond—he's a killer."

Liam felt the moisture filling his eyes. "You—you *bastard!*"

"Ah, no!" The O'Meara seemed genuinely surprised. "It's you that is the bastard."

Liam blinked furiously. "Don't call me a bastard. I'm not planning to sleep with *your* wife."

The O'Meara tossed his socks into a corner. He picked up the gun and clicked the chamber round thoughtfully.

"I have no wife with whom you might sleep, Liam. And a bastard is precisely what you are. Your mother was not married to your father."

Liam quivered, as though an electric current galvanized his limbs. "Put away the gun, and I'll show you how I feel about *that* statement."

The O'Meara laughed. "Liam—poor old Flinty Hagan couldn't have fathered you. He lost the necessary equipment in a raid on Oughterard a year before he was married. We all kept quiet about it because he was a sensitive man, and we thought a great deal of him."

Liam's lips trembled. The old goat was trying to provoke him, but he wouldn't give him the satisfaction of seeing him lose his temper. He said, "Then why did my mother agree to marry Flinty?"

The O'Meara sat silent for a moment, then seemed to come to a decision.

"Well now, Liam. We seem to have arrived at what you might call the moment of truth. You have asked me a question which I would rather not answer. If you insist on an answer, I'm afraid we must escalate our discussion to a more formal level."

Liam let his lip curl scornfully. "Don't fence with me. Let's have a straight word out of you."

The O'Meara nodded in agreement. "So be it, son. Up to this moment you could have walked out of this room any time you wanted, and no hard feelings on my part. Now, as I warned you, you've promoted our chat to a really serious plane—that is, namely, your examination for citizenship. Some lads never learn about this test. Others, quite naturally, avoid it. But you have headed straight for it. So, now, I'm going to answer your question. And also provide you with some additional information that you haven't asked for. Your response, after due consideration, will govern whether you leave this room vertically or horizontally—and remember *I* am the judge."

"Here goes. Your Mam married Flinty Hagan because Barley Cross needed children, and at the time Flinty was the only available bachelor."

"But you said Flinty couldn't. . . ."

"Don't interrupt, son, or I might make a hasty decision. Just listen. Very few men in Barley Cross can father a child. The reason goes back a long way, and it isn't their fault. Responsible adults in the village are aware of this and have accepted the solution the people out there in my dining room thought up. The solution is that *I*—because I'm a freak, being fertile—I father most of the children in Barley Cross, but their legal fathers get the credit.

"That, briefly, is how our village has managed to remain a living, functioning community, with enough people to do all the work required to keep it going. Now, Liam, if you wish to graduate into a citizen of Barley Cross, you must accept our solution, *and* keep quiet about it. That doesn't mean you can't talk it over with your Eileen. But it does mean you don't discuss it in front of the children. Because the way a child grows up governs how he or she acts as an adult. And we want the children of Barley Cross to believe that the world is a sane and happy place where everyone gets his own Daddy and Mammy. And we hope that the child will be able to adjust to our madhouse when he is old enough to understand it. It also means that you don't gab about it in the village or do anything which might inadvertently destroy the illusion we have built up so painstakingly. And it means that your Eileen comes up here tonight, like every bride in the last thirty years."

The O'Meara paused, rubbing his jaw reflectively. "Those are the facts. Don't go shouting for help. No one is going to rush in to save you from the crazy O'Meara. Those gentlemen outside have an idea that you might be in here. And they realize that I am making a reasonable attempt to dispel any objections you may hold to the way the village is run. What they do not know, are my methods of persuasion. But it has all happened before, and they have confidence in me."

The O'Meara straightened his back. He raised his arm. The gun pointed at Liam's breastbone.

"You may have qualms about accepting our solution. Your views on putative incest, for instance, may not correspond with ours. The subject is not open for debate. You may walk from this room a responsible adult, or you may be carried out a dead juvenile. Now, sir—how do you say?"

Liam's eyes had been growing wider and wider. "But, if Flinty Hagan wasn't my father—?"

"Keep going," urged the O'Meara. "You are getting warm."

Liam McGrath fingered his own hooked nose, as if he had just become aware of it. He eyed the similar protuberance on the face of the elderly man sitting barefoot and shirtless on the bed. Suddenly he grinned.

"Put up the gun, Da, or you'll have me late. A citizen ought to be on time for his own wedding."

WILLIAM F. WU

ON THE SHADOW OF A PHOSPHOR SCREEN

Simulation.   Simulacrum.   Simultaneity.
Similarity.   Similitude.   Simile.

The silent hall was cold. From behind walnut walls, the air conditioner hummed quietly. A stately crowd of spectators radiated bristling energy from the rigid square rows of seats. They sat against the walls, their attention fixed on the dramatic events at the center of the room. Giant video screens high on each wall gave them the elegant details.

The heavy brown drapes and plush burgundy carpet absorbed the excess vitality from the atmosphere. They imparted a dignified solemnity to the ritualistic proceedings and infused the imperatives of business with a sense of duty. Two huge cables hung from the ceiling, suspending old-fashioned horizontal fans with broad, lazy blades and globular white lights at their hubs.

Beneath the sleepy fans, Wendell Chong Wei repressed the surge of elation that threatened to rock his relentless control. He studied the video screen right before him, and his fingers danced on the console to maintain the non-stop pace. Victory should be certain now, but only if he remained clear of mistakes. He drew sharply on the depths of insecurity for a renewal of killer instinct.

On the other side of the complex, out of sight, his opponent sat before her own screen, drawing back her cavalry, hoping that Wendell would allow his own cavalry charges to over-extend themselves. No chance.

"Remember, in reality the Seljuks actually circled, and **took** *the baggage and non-combatants.* **Leave** *St. Gilles there, even now. Curthose continues to rally well; Tancred's charges will carry the day. That's right—restraint. We're outnumbered; keep together."*

Richard nodded in the back of Wendell's mind and stopped talking. The smell of blood and dust and lathered horses arose to envelop Wendell's sensibility as he re-grouped the members of the First Crusade, now victorious at Doryleum on the road to Antioch. Frustrated, the Seljuk Turks remained on the horizon, taunting the Crusaders to break ranks.

Wendell refused. In the center of the screen, a digital clock appeared over the words "Victory Conditions, First Crusade. End game." The screen blanked.

St. Gilles was dead once more. Bohemund was dead again. The Saracens and Crusaders had returned yet another time to their desiccated graves in the sand.

Wendell swallowed, and rose on weak knees to scattered clapping. His opponent, also looking infirm at the moment, stood and offered her hand without comment, and they shook perfunctorily. Wendell eased himself away from the chair, shaking, suddenly reeling in the sweat and nervousness that he always forgot in the heat of gaming itself. His twenty-nine years seemed far too few to account for this.

An attendant rushed over to escort him away.

"Nice work," said Richard.

"Same to you," Wendell thought back. He wiped his palms on the sides of his chocolate-brown suit jacket. "But, uh, how did you know Robert Curthose could hold fast? In the middle of that retreat? His record's not so good, back in Normandy."

The attendant showed Wendell to a comfortable reception room with loungers and plenty of refreshments. When he had gone, Richard said, *"He really did that, you know."*

"No, I didn't. But I learned to listen to you a long time ago."

"More than that, though, it was deep in his psychological makeup. That's how I could count on it. If he—"

The door opened, and Richard stopped. Wendell collapsed into a lounger. He despised receptions. People scared him. They scared Richard even worse. The ones entering now were the contractors for the two recent opponents, and his erstwhile opponent herself. The contractors were all bustling with talk and laughter. Wendell was too exhausted to tell them apart, and couldn't remember all their names anyway. His latent bitterness with the whole business kept him from caring.

An older woman approached him, a contractor, with a thin face and a wide smile and lots of spangly jewelry and shiny clothes. Wendell shook her hand, but didn't get up from the lounger. He didn't hear what she said, either, though it registered with him as something good. After he had passed her off with some standard line, she glittered away to the refreshments and was followed by Wendell's recent counterpart in the act of artificial war.

"Have a seat," said Wendell, indicating another lounger. He could talk to another Master, he felt, who also shared the habit. "Good battle." He was still catching his breath.

She smiled and shook her head. Dark curls bobbed. "I thought for certain I could take your vanguard before the others drew up. Had them on the run at first, anyway. Who was it, the Duke of Normandy, who rallied for you? Just like he really did." She caught his eye and added, "The creep. I love it." Carefully, she eased back in the lounger and put up her feet.

Wendell nodded. "Robert II, Duke of Normandy." He smiled slightly at her enthusiasm. That had been the first crucial point, but as a Master, she knew that as well as he did. That was the pleasure of it—he didn't have to explain everything on the rare occasions that he talked to other Masters.

A large, fluffy white cat appeared suddenly on his companion's lap from the floor. She settled herself immediately on the dark blue slacks and treated the hand that went to her ears as a natural and proper development. Over her head, the two Masters lay back in their loungers, amiably re-hashing the game. Wendell's natural shyness evaporated quickly when the subject of talk was history or games. For them, as free-lance Gamers of the Master class, the battle was a matter of intellectual and artistic pride. The defeated party had no shame to bear unless the game had clearly exhibited poor performance—a condition that could apply to the victor as well. Odds were calculated for each side's units and degree of success; the contractors' dispute was based on the computation of these, not just on the apparent victory.

"I believe I played you once before, Master Wei," said his companion. "You don't remember me. I'm Terri Kief. In my first contracted game, we fought Zama."

Wendell hesitated, thinking back. "Oh—oh, yeah."

Terri laughed. "Your elephants rioted in the wrong direction—remember?"

"*Oh*, yes, of course." Wendell grinned. The game had been only his fourth. He had been soundly beaten, but at least he had maneuvered an orderly escape for his Carthaginians. That was more than the real Hannibal had done. "Very well fought, as I remember." Zama?

"*202 B.C.*," said Richard, in his head. "*Two years ago. I* **told** *you not to use those elephants, but, oh no, you—*"

"Power Technics won the right to a plant on the Big Muddy," Wendell recalled. "Isn't that what you won for them?" He was surprised that he remembered, but then, all of his thankfully few defeats, honorable as they were, stood out in his mind—as learning experiences, of course.

"Um—yes, that's what it was." Terri sat up, earnestly, steadying the cat with one hand. "I remember, right after that, you 'won' that draw at Bosworth Field for the Italian Bottling Cooperative." She smiled and twisted a curl of dark hair around one finger.

Wendell was flattered in turn that she knew. His own charge, Richard III, had been betrayed by crucial allies at the start of the battle. In reality, Henry Tudor of Richmond had taken a conclusive victory for the Lancastrians. With Wendell Wei in command, the Yorkists had exploited critical junctures between the three forces of Richmond and the two Stanleys, and had thrown the field into general confusion.

"A great deal of luck was involved," Wendell reminded her. "If my opponent hadn't been lax, it never would have been possible."

"Luck is part of things," said Terri. "Who cares? It happens, that's all."

"*Luck,*" Richard agreed, firmly. He had pointed this out frequently to Wendell, along with the admonition that their opponent had lost; they had not won. According to the rules, Wendell had not been allowed to prepare for the on-field treachery, since it had been a surprise in reality. But hindsight could go the other way. His opponent, while a Master also, had expected too much that history would repeat itself on its own, and he had been careless. Both sides had been forced to withdraw without establishing Victory Conditions, but Wendell's opponent had insisted upon conceding, stating that the position of the Yorkist cause at the time of betrayal had actually been desperate.

Wendell modestly, but truthfully, agreed that extricating Richard III from Bosworth had been his finest achievement, draw though it was. Even Richard, with his perfectionist standards, acknowledged its value in unguarded moments. The strength of the Gaming Masters' Guild made such dealings possible; no corporation or other principal would object, for fear of being boycotted in later disputes.

"I'm afraid I'm rather ambitious," said Terri. "That Bosworth Field example of yours is just tremendous. I'm aiming at the number-one rating, and I've reviewed the tape of that game many times in the Guild Library."

"I *had the undisputed number-one rating,*" Richard growled.

Wendell smiled at Terri. "You think I'm a textbook case, huh? Is that good or bad?"

"Well, I'm trying to learn from you. After all, you just beat me." She looked at him with amusement.

"Congratulations! To both of you." A hearty voice startled them. One of Wendell's contractors smiled broadly down at them, extending one hand and rattling an iced drink with the other. He was large and heavy, dressed in formal black. His tie was crooked. "A *fine* game. Saw it all on the spectator screens." He shook hands with them both, laughing happily.

Terri and Wendell thanked him. The big contractor stood beaming at them, sipping his drink. His name was Crandall, Wendell remembered, wishing he would leave. But the profession required courtesy toward contractors.

Crandall caught Wendell's eye and shook his head. *"Fine* battle," he insisted.

Terri nodded. "You know, there were times when I could have sworn you actually had the feel of the battle—you know, the ringing of hot steel, the beat of the hooves, the grip of old leather. I can do it sometimes in flashes—but not like that. You're amazing."

"That's me!" Richard cried gleefully. He was embarrassed and highly pleased. Wendell shook his head, smiling reluctantly. He thought back to Richard, "We have an unfair advantage, you know."

"Grand!" thundered the contractor. "Just what I wanted to hear. Listen, the two of you are close together, rated fifth and eighth Master Gamers. You care to work . . . together?"

"What!" Richard screamed with delight. Some word of this had gotten around, but it had been vague. No Master anywhere would pass up this chance.

Wendell and Terri turned attentive instantly. Crandall clearly enjoyed their excitement. "The new tandem game is ready," he said.

Wendell had already forgotten about the last contract—as a Master, he was always paid in advance, and the legal decisions he had won for his contractors were of no interest to him. The Guild demanded, and got, substantial rights of independence for its members. But the present games were devised only for one Gamer on a side. The computer bank already held incredible amounts of information—the terrain and weather of the real battles, the morale of the troops, their military capabilities, and the psychological profiles of all individuals that were on historical record. Minute technological details, such as the composition of stirrups and the age of leather, could win or lose battles. Four keyboards would square the intensity of the game, though increased caution might decrease the pace.

"Are you making a formal request?" Terri asked excitedly.

Crandall gave a long, sweeping, mock-formal bow. "I would hereby request the participation of the two of you in the first tandem game ever to take place, to be contracted through my office." He straightened up, grinning. "Howzat?"

Terri laughed and glanced at Wendell. "Excellent. I accept."

"Okay," said Wendell, smiling. Already, he was trying to absorb the implications of the new game.

"Okay," Richard echoed happily.

Wendell's imagination soared, exploring the feel of the new game as it might turn out to be. Now, the Gamers only controlled two factors completely: they replaced the supreme commander in decision making, and had the advantage of aerial viewpoint over all the significant territory their troops could have seen. They were limited to reality in factors such as on-field communication, mobility, and availability of friendly forces. Lastly, "chance" factors were also included, to account for unexpected performances, good and bad, on the individual level. The games were good, but had never been constructed for team play before. The game would still be fast and intense, requiring that the Gamers keep their keyboards in constant activity.

When Wendell brought his attention back to the present, Crandall was pacing in front of them, talking loudly, and gesturing in all directions. The new game that the contractor described was essentially no different from the present games as far as playing technique except that the Gamers replaced two command individuals per side instead of one. The biggest changes were technological. However, the quality of the conflict would change greatly; no psychologically programmed game-personality could ever approximate all the variations of mind that high stress evoked in a real person. This new game was a tremendous challenge, and Wendell was anxious to try it.

"Sound decent?" Crandall puffed, lowering his arms. He stood bent over slightly, recovering from his high-pressure sales pitch.

"Of course it does," said Terri. She smiled and cocked her head to watch his face. It was red.

"Sure," said Wendell. He was watching Terri.

"Right," said Richard. *"I guess we have a partner automatically, eh? No choice?"*

"She's a fine choice," Wendell thought to him. He knew her as an opponent, and that was the best test of her ability. She had won at Zama, after all. She had an unusual quickness, too, and in that first moment at the bell, when the Gamers found out which battle was to take place and which sides were assigned where and at what odds, decisiveness was crucial. Sixty seconds for orientation were allowed before the screen activated automatically. The computer chose battles and sides at random, and could choose grand match-ups or hopeless routs. Also, Wendell was envious of the short time she took to recover her strength after the game. He felt he needed a younger teammate like her.

Besides, he could talk to her.

Besides, Richard was nearly screaming with anticipation inside Wendell's brain.

At Crandall's assurance that the Guild had already approved the new game, Terri and Wendell agreed to try it the next morning, exchanging quick glances as they nodded. Elsewhere, the contractors with whom Crandall had a dispute were contacting other Masters. They, too, would be excited over the new development.

Wendell wanted to get away so that he could consult Richard without interruption, and excused himself from the reception early. His goodbye was awkward as always, but Terri congratulated him once more and said that she was looking forward to the new game.

Wendell left without speaking to most of the people. His shyness was generally interpreted as arrogance, and was notorious as such. However, lack of social grace was another indulged idiosyncracy of Master Gamers. He could get away with it, and he knew it.

"Fancy game, huh?" Richard crowed. *"Wonder what dispute they'll use the first one for—it'll have to be a big one. None of this, 'where do we put the fire hydrant, your yard or mine?'"* He laughed. *"We'll show the world—those slimy losers."*

"Yeah," said Wendell. He wondered who the opposing Masters would be—not that it would matter much. Still, with the World Headquarters here in the center of the country, it could literally be anyone in the Guild. The fact that he and Terri were both Americans was an off-chance occurrence; there were only six in the twenty highest-rated positions.

Wendell took a deep breath and glanced around. He had stepped out of the Crown Center Plaza, and, on a whim, decided to walk up Main for a while. He took off his suit coat and loosened his tie. The summer evening was humid, warm and damp, and the streets shone with the film of rainwater and oil.

"You heard what she said about me," Richard insisted. *" 'The ringing of hot steel, the beat of the hooves, the grip of old leather.' That's what I provide, y'know."*

"I know." Wendell tried not to think, or else to think about trivia. At the moment, he didn't want Richard picking up his thoughts. Just how much Richard could read his mind, he wasn't sure, but a Master Gamer was cautious by nature. In any case, he couldn't read Richard's mind at all. He took a long breath, and caught the smell of rain lingering in the breeze.

*"I **can** give it, too,"* Richard went on. *"You know, I really think I have nearly as many important facts as those computers—not all, of course, that's impossible. But—well, you know how it was."*

"I know," said Wendell. He turned up a long institutional driveway, blotting out the visions of their childhood friendship that Richard had brought up. How it was.

"Technically, I suppose, we're illegal," Richard mused, *"there being two of us. Not that anybody'd believe it. Still, considering that—"* He stopped. The silence was dark and frigid and sudden.

Wendell sighed. "That's right," he thought to Richard.

No answer. There never was, on these visits. But Richard would have to come; that was one fact they had established. Their periods of consciousness and sleep coincided exactly, right down to the brain-wave type and REM cycles. He had escaped one body, to be trapped in another, and, sometimes—lately, more than ever—Wendell took him back.

Wendell knew the way, and the hospital personnel recognized him and waved him on. The special ward, which was nearly a vault, lay in one of the underground floors, deep beneath the city. An orderly who knew Wendell escorted him to a cold, cavernous room in dim light. Coffin-sized tanks with a bluish tinge were lined up in long, lonely rows. Storage drawers or upright cases would have saved space, but they were too reminiscent of morgues and mummies. The orderly withdrew and Wendell, still feeling the icy silence in the back of his mind, stood over one of the tanks and looked through the transparent casing that covered its occupant.

The face, always lean, was nearly a skull. He wore only the steel headband and its attendant wires that monitored what little brain activity remained. The whitish cheeks showed faint gray spots where the synthetic blood picked its way through the sleeping capillaries. His wavy hair was the red-gold of the Celt, not the white gold of the Norse. Even now, the repose looked fitful—the face not quite relaxed, the limbs not quite comfortable. In other days and other places, the long legs would have worn a Highland kilt, and the bony, slender arms would have known a Lochaber axe, not the cold cushion of a suspension tank.

Richard had been the very best, even at age twenty.

The coma had begun nine years ago, and after four years, suspended animation had been suggested until further medical advances developed a way to induce recovery. It had been caused by those experimental helmets, in the only time they were ever used, and by Richard's own insane enthusiasm for the games. Without that waking obsession, he never would have invented the helmets, or induced Wendell to join him.

Burned out, Wendell thought—Richard had gone nova, after reaching the top in so few years. That was part of it, too.

The lilting spirit of a Burns melody forced its way through the frozen arteries. The wonder of Loch Ness lay flat under the realism of a phony death. Only the soul of Bannockburn leaped and roared, through the avenue of another person.

The helmets had been complex biofeedback contraptions, keyed into the game machine, worn by both Gamers. Supposedly, they would monitor the stress on each Gamer in relation to each quick development on the screen. They were Richard's creation, an even greater monument to his involvement in the games than his youthful grip on the number-one rating. Richard was only a Master Gamer, though, and his dynamism in the field had fooled him. He had botched the electronics badly, and when the helmets jammed and buzzed and quivered with too much energy, the Gaming Master's Guild lost its number-one Master to a coma —apparently.

Richard wore a different kind of helmet now.

When Wendell had awakened in the hospital, he had had company inside his own head. The emotional drive and the machine had become fused, and so had they. Richard had become the ghost of obsessed war-gamers, the patron deity of electronic monomania, a scowling, blue-eyed, discorporate Guan Gung.

At first, the sharing of one body had been nearly unbearable for both of them—it wasn't exactly deliberate on Richard's part any more than on Wendell's, at least consciously. They grew accustomed to it surprisingly fast, once clear and detailed personal questions had established to each other that they were not crazy, after all. Gradually, if painfully, they adjusted to the situation. Their closeness as childhood companions helped immeasurably, as did their common aversion to social mixing and people in general.

Now the strain was growing.

Wendell gazed quietly. He was a Master Gamer now, an accomplished performer with a greater knowledge of his field than many military historians. Great civil decisions rode on his tides, and the Prairie Sector of the country followed. He was too young to remember the entry of the games into stalemated judicial disputes, though he had read about it later. The game sets had had only a few battles to choose from back then, though all had been classics. The technology was primitive.

And Wendell and Richard were two ostracized, introverted kids in an upstairs bedroom, setting up toy plastic knights. A carefully tumbled landscape of books, boxes, and blankets on the floor formed rugged peaks, treacherous valleys, and unscalable castle walls. Set aside, stacks of various histories provided countless scenarios and suggestions for their vivid visions.

"Okay," Richard announced, from his own side of the floor. He had his back to Wendell and was maneuvering nine thirteenth-century men in armor down the cascading folds of a blue blanket. "Mace-face is leading his puny band down into the valley now, sneaking up on the camp down there." Carefully, he lifted a large armored individual with an upraised mace, and knocked over a sentry with it.

"The Norman cavalry is having trouble," said Wendell, from his side of the room. He wheeled about seven toy knights, actually from the Wars of the Roses, and sent them into retreat. They didn't resemble Normal cavalry at all, but they did have horses and lances. "The Saxon shield-wall has held, and re-forms while the Normans regroup for another attack." He knew that Richard was listening with only the barest of attention, just as he was, but that didn't matter. This way, they could enact whatever battles and time periods and strategies they wanted. This included manipulating defeats into victories, and deciding on their own who would live or die. Both of them always won and the victories were always shared.

Richard sat back suddenly and considered. "All of these kinds of people were descended from Roman tradition—mixed up with the Franks and other barbarians, of course. I wonder what would have happened if some descendants of Carthage had lasted into medieval times."

"Yeah," said Wendell, without interest. He was trying to form a new shield-wall on the fold of a bedspread with nine Saxons and two temporary-converted Vikings, who looked similar enough, but they all kept falling down.

"No good, I guess," Richard continued. "Even if Carthage had survived the Romans, the Vandals went through later anyway. So did the Arabs, too, in the 700s." His voice grew pedantic. "Jebel Al-Tarik invaded Europe from Africa in 711—the easiest date to remember in all history."

"Hm." Wendell tried to fix the name in his memory, to go with the date, but he didn't know how to spell it. He had never been as good with dates as Richard, but he had a better grasp of concurrent events and their interrelation. Then Richard gave him an opening.

"I guess those Carthagians were doomed from the start," he said, and turned back to his half-completed battle.

"Carthaginians," Wendell corrected him.

Richard clenched his jaw and took on a firm look. "The city is Carthage—so, Carthagians, stupid. It's the easiest way to change it."

"I *read* 'Carthaginians' someplace," said Wendell. For them, the printed word was the last word.

"I presume," Richard said loftily, "that's C-A-R-T-H-A-G-I-N-I-A-N."

"Yep," said Wendell, thinking that Richard must be the only ten-year-old in the country who said "presume" out loud in sentences.

They looked at each other, and the undercurrent of childhood rivalry rose up in a mutual giggling ferocity that set them leaping at each other. Growling and yelling and laughing, they grappled and rolled in a narrow space of the floor that was still clear. Both were slender and limber, making them quick at close quarters. Richard had the reach, being considerably taller—and he looked thinner on account of it—but Wendell was more aggressive. As they rapidly approached their usual stalemate, someone's foot flicked into a battlefield and knocked over a few miniature stalwarts. Instantly, they both froze.

"Whose was it?" Richard panted, holding an awkward pose.

"Yours, I think." They untangled themselves gingerly and returned with extreme care to their battles. Fallen fighters were resurrected, to be killed according to plan instead of by accident. Although their backs were turned to each other, they repaired the damage with a shared reverence, and in silence.

The insomnia that night was no worse than usual. In nine years as a Master, Wendell had never slept the night after any of his twenty-six games. Unlike some Masters he knew, he slept easily and soundly on the nights preceding games, and on every other night. But after the games, he lay on his back in his huge blackened bedroom, staring from his circular bed into the gloom. Coupled with silence, the darkness seemed to be a giant void.

"I'm exhausted," Richard whined. *"Go to sleep. I can't stand this."*

"Me, too," thought Wendell with effort. His arms and legs felt like inorganic weights, attached to his torso by straps. In the total darkness, and his complete weariness, his mind felt detached from his body and yet trapped in it—floating in his skull like a—like a body in a suspension tank. Or a specimen in formaldehyde.

"Go to sleep," Richard said again. *"I'm . . . tired."*

"Shut up," Wendell answered, without force. "What are you? You might . . . not even be there. Just another voice in my head."

"What! Of course I'm here. We figured that out a long—"

"Yeah, I know . . . but what if I *am* just crazy, huh? What if you're *not* there?" Wendell spoke in a spiritless monotone that largely disarmed the words. Vaguely, he wished he could be firmer. Or maybe a farmer.

Richard made a sound of annoyed muttering. Wendell blinked, or tried to. In the darkness, without moving anything but his eyelids, he wasn't sure if his eyes were open or closed. If he couldn't tell, then it could hardly matter. But he wondered. He always wondered.

"Stupid game . . . no people involved," Wendell thought. "All machinery. No . . . heart to it. Circuits and moving lights. Dead. I should give it up . . . I hate it. It's empty, like, uh, my head." His tone lacked bitterness, even that required energy.

"If that's a joke, I resent it."

"Games. I've got games coming out of my ears. I haven't got any friends. I'm scared of them. All of them. Aiieee." He sighed inwardly. This was nothing new; the same thoughts went through his mind every sleepless, post-game night, after every urgent, killer-filled war game. He hated war, even his toy war. But he hated socializing more. The careful cultivation of a smooth, laconic speaking style camouflaged that fear, but it ruled his life.

For a moment, images of Terri rose up, laughing and talking with him earlier in the evening. Her hair bounced and swung as she moved. She looked at him when she smiled.

"Go to sleep," mumbled Richard.

Terri's face dissolved into blackness.

Wendell tried to blink again and see if he could tell. He stared at the darkness and gave up again. On the average, he supposed, he tried this ten or twelve times every sleepless night. If he ever reached a conclusion, he'd have to find something else to do. He tried it a third time. So tired.

"Aw, c'mon. Can't you take a pill or something?" Richard always made the same complaints and asked the same questions on these nights. Why not? There was nothing else to do.

Fear—that was the true source of Richard's coma. Fear of life. Fear of human contact. Fear of doing something stupid. Fear had sent him diving into the world of the phosphorous shine.

Wendell understood it all, because he shared it. He lived his life inside the electronic gamebox, killing and re-killing people centuries dead, to flex his embryonic courage against other Masters—people who might be just as weird and antisocial as he, if not exactly in the same way. He wasn't sure, but he suspected that the Masters' Guild was another of the many refuges for loners, cowards, and repressed crazies. If one could handle the occupation, it paid better than bookkeeping, running projectors, wandering carnival crowds, and the rest. An occasional normal like Terri or Kirk Emerald preserved the staid image.

Someday he would quit. He certainly wouldn't want anyone ever replaying his life, and improving upon it. How would Napoleon feel, seeing Wendell win Leipzig and Waterloo over and over again? It was a funny business.

The coma was a combination of electronic mishap and willful escape. Wendell had no idea how Richard's presence in his mind had really come about, but he was certain that some volition was involved in Richard's remaining there, even if it was all subconscious. Out of boredom, Wendell tried to imagine that he, motionless in the consuming black silence of his room, was also in a sort of trance. For a fleeting second, the escape had its attraction: no fears, no contests, and no irrevocability, like suicide. Then his physical exhaustion intruded upon his senses again, dissolving the respite. Not a trance, just old insomnia.

Until Crandall had mentioned the new tandem game that night, Wendell had hoped, guardedly, that their symbiotic relationship would reach an end soon. If Richard was as bored with it as he was, then the subconscious desire to maintain it would fade away. Now, the new game would bring another exciting dimension into their lives. And Wendell would never be able to request being left alone outright—not with his lifelong fear of others making that same request to him.

If Richard could listen to these thoughts, he gave no sign.

Shrugging away his serious concerns, Wendell took a deep breath. Without intending to, he began to visualize surroundings, somewhere out in the darkness. Then, amused, he began listing them in order from beyond his left ear, clockwise: alarm radio with voice-activated clock, set to light up when he gave the Clan Munro battle-cry in Gaelic; the controls to an elaborate sound system which was similarly started or stopped by listing the first three Plantagenet kings or the last three Capetians, respectively; a video desk and television receiver whose channels were selected by the names of certain standard military procedures in Sun Tze's *Art of War;* a desk with a combined telephone and dictaphone set rendered usable from across the room by reciting any two of the major military contributions of the Mongol armies of Genghis Khan; a small movie projector which, unfortunately, had to be operated manually; last, floor-to-ceiling bookshelves, totally filled, which covered an entire wall. They were his instant references, the ones most needed or the ones most rarely in libraries.

"Don't do it," sighed Richard. "There's too many."

Wendell did his blinking routine again. Afterward, ignoring Richard, he began to list every book on the shelves by title, author, and major value to his own purposes. When he had finished, his review of the room was complete. He was tempted to force energy into his voice and mutter, *"Caisteal Fòlais na Theine,"* at his clock, but he was afraid to know how early it still was. So tired. So dark.

The night had a long way to go. If he had been up, he would have activated his noise-making electric friends all at once, raising their volume in direct proportion to his loneliness. But now, in the darkness, in his weariness, he just lay there.

The foyer to Crandall's office was luxuriously furnished, and, ordinarily, both spacious and immaculate. Now, the new tandem machine, over twice the size of the old ones, stood in the center of the room, surrounded by the bright orange carpet. A coffee table and two easy chairs had been unceremoniously crowded into the far end of the room. The receptionist's desk had also been moved from its usual location, leaving deep impressions behind in the orange pile. The receptionist, stifling her annoyance, frowned at her papers and made a point of not looking up.

"Hot stuff," said Richard, *"Look at this place."*

"Quiet," thought Wendell. He swallowed nervously, anticipating the introductions.

"You know Master Emerald, of course," said Crandall, gesturing to a tall, well-dressed man at his side. The taller man was slender, with a full head of white hair and a slight tan.

"Of course." Wendell shook hands with him. Kirk Emerald was Director of the Trustees in the Gaming Masters' Guild. More than that, he was a codeveloper of the original game machine and the acknowledged champion of the early contests. The games in the first several series of machines had been slow and studied compared to the current ones. As the games grew faster, the best players became the younger ones. Kirk Emerald had already been middle-aged when the game was developed, and quickly found his reflexes too slow for the later models. Still, he commanded tremendous respect.

"Master Wei," said Emerald, nodding slightly. "This is a fine game, here. I was fortunate enough to participate in the quality control games, and enjoyed them very much."

"Do you know Master Kief?" Wendell said. "We've played each other twice, most recently last night. So we're somewhat familiar with each other's playing style." Hopefully, that would be enough small talk.

"That's part of teamwork," said Terri. She smiled at Emerald. "We've met."

"Ah." Emerald bowed slightly and smiled in return. "I remember."

Crandall, who had been shifting back and forth impatiently on his feet, waved a hand at the machine. "Shall we?" He grinned eagerly.

Wendell and Terri moved around it warily, like visitors at a zoo. Wendell trailed his fingers over the chair backs, looking at the double consoles—two keyboards, two screens—on each side. He tried to imagine working elbow-to-elbow in a fast maneuver, where he had to predict the combined moves and weaknesses of three other players instead of one.

Inside his head, Richard whistled appreciation.

"I envy your opportunity," said Emerald, hesitating between the other two chairs. No one doubted his sincerity. "Shall we begin?"

"What do you think?" said Richard.

"No telling yet, of course," Wendell thought back. "Shut up." Aloud, he said, "I'm ready. Uh. . . ." He looked from Emerald to Terri to Crandall.

Crandall took charge, putting a hand on Wendell's shoulder. "We'll take this side. Master Emerald, if you'll join Master Kief over there. Go easy, please," he added, laughing. "I can play, but I'm no Master."

Wendell sat down and felt the keyboard. The seat, the board, and the screen were still the standardized equipment he was used to—an important detail. Crandall eased his bulk into the adjacent seat. He pushed a button and the screen said: "Cannae. 216 B.C. Roman Cavalry." Officers' names, Victory Conditions, and odds for the battle were given below. The adjacent screen would be saying, "Roman Infantry." The opposing screens were the same, except "Carthaginian" in nationality. All four players laughed politely.

"I figured we'd start easy," said Crandall, chuckling.

"Coward," said Richard. *"Sniveller."*

Wendell relaxed a little as he waited for the minute of orientation to go by. This was a classic confrontation, which needed no forced recall. Kirk Emerald had built it into the very first machine for the first game, and it had been fought many times over. Its choice by Crandall was a subtle tribute to the elderly player seated across from Wendell, out of sight. Wendell guessed also that seating Emerald on the winning side was no accident, either, but it was a harmless bit of protocol. In fact, Wendell was glad. Kirk Emerald was a reigning monarch, but in a society of combatants, that was a step down from the fighting ranks. Master Gamers had a keen sense of passing time, possibly from their concern over history—and every Master was well aware that the rarest future this occupation offered was aging with dignity. With perhaps five good years left, Wendell was growing more conscious of the small amenities.

The screen blinked once and began to move. Wendell's Roman Cavalry were crimson units, while Crandall's Roman Infantry were burgundy. The Carthaginians were two shades of yellow. Wendell's shyness fell away as he took control of his forces. He advanced his lines slowly; there was not much maneuvering possible. Much of the Carthaginian victory had been decided by a highly favorable field, and the Gamers could not change that.

"Easy, that's it," said Richard. *"If we can avoid being routed, we'll be a step ahead. The only—"*

"Can it," Wendell thought. He was getting annoyed. "We both know this battle the same as each other's. . . ." He trailed off uncomfortably. The subject of sameness had little meaning when they shared everything.

Crandall was taking the Roman Infantry forward to their doom with wanton joy. Wendell could see, out of the corner of his eye, Crandall's delighted grin as he shared a battle with three genuine Master Gamers. Every contractor was a Gamer at heart.

Terri obligingly allowed the Carthaginian center to sag in, as Hannibal had planned, until her flanks, anchored on hillsides, could turn and encircle the enemy. Wendell grinned at Crandall's light-hearted slaughter of his own units, as the two cavalry forces closed with each other.

"What's Crandall doing? Is he crazy?" Richard demanded. His voice had a righteous ring.

"He's just enjoying himself. Forget it." Wendell frowned and his fingers leaped about the keyboard. The screen responded just as it should, and the keys felt fine. For several moments he concentrated on the struggle at hand, testing more intricate aspects of the machine. He was off his game from lack of sleep, but he managed with no trouble.

Wendell noticed suddenly that he had been gaining an upper hand. Surprised, he tried an experimental feint and watched the opposing units over-shift in response. He hesitated.

"C'mon, push the advantage." Richard was impatient. *"What's wrong with you?"*

Wendell turned his line slightly, exposing his flank. He could be a ruthless competitor, but not a cruel one. Emerald's reflexes were slow and his style rusty. Wendell could slice him to pieces and turn one of the greatest defeats of all time into something of a question. He found that he would not.

"Stop it," screamed Richard. *"You malevolent fool. Are you retarded?"*

"Shut up," thought Wendell. He could not let his forces fall apart, for Emerald would see through that, and be even more embarrassed than if he were soundly defeated. Carefully, Wendell kept his resistance stiff, but allowed himself to be forced backward. He could not honor Emerald from this role, but he could avoid humiliating him.

Mercifully, Crandall's reckless advance brought about a quick end to the battle. The screen froze with "Victory Conditions, Carthage," and the elapsed time. Wendell took a deep breath and leaned back.

Crandall threw back his head and laughed. "Wonderful!" he declared. His receptionist, in a far corner, glanced up and smiled slightly. Terri slid out of her chair and watched Crandall with amusement.

"I'm afraid you were easy on me, Master." Emerald smiled at Wendell as they both stood.

"No." Wendell shook his head, smiling back and then glancing at the other two. Crandall had probably not noticed the subtle change in the cavalry engagement, but Terri would have. "It's a good game, Master Emerald. I see no problems."

"Yes, I believe so. Lou, you have a certain, ah, flair for tactics."

Crandall grinned and turned his hands palm up. "I know when I'm licked."

"He licked himself pretty good," Richard snarled.

Crandall stood, joining the others.

"The machine is fine," said Terri. "The battle didn't offer much real interplay, though. It was almost two separate battles. I was under the impression that the whole point was—"

"My fault," said Crandall quickly. "I should have chosen a battle that would utilize that area better. Most of the scenarios will fully engage each player with the activities of the other three, I assure you."

Wendell glanced nervously at Terri, wishing he had thought to raise the point.

"I can vouch for that," said Emerald. "In most cases, the game becomes as complex as anyone could want."

Terri nodded and caught Wendell's eye. He sort of shrugged.

"How come his hair is never out of place?" demanded Richard. *"Think he glues it?"*

Wendell glanced up at Emerald's full mane of white hair, flowing back with a mixture of precision and naturalness that matched his stylish clothes. "I like him," Wendell thought to Richard.

"I hate him," Richard said firmly.

"I have contracts here," said Crandall, pulling them from his inside pocket. "The two of you may take and read them at leisure."

Emerald cleared his throat and looked at the floor, frowning.

"Three months away," said Wendell, glancing at the match date on the first page.

"Too short?" Crandall sounded concerned. "I know the usual is six months, but—"

"It's legal, all right," said Terri, nodding. She raised her eyebrows at him. "It's just, well, especially short when you consider that it's a completely new kind of game."

"I see," said Crandall. He made a jaw motion as though he were chewing a cigar. Then he glanced at Emerald.

Emerald frowned more deeply. "I must tell you that we're on the threshold of something here. The . . . principals named on the contracts are actually representatives." He paused for effect. "In reality, the principals are the governments of Portugal and Yugoslavia."

"Garbage," said Richard. *"Who cares?"*

"Shut up," thought Wendell.

"Wait a minute," said Terri, looking at Emerald. She stared for a moment, twirling a curl of dark hair on one finger. "Governments."

"Governments," Wendell repeated quietly. That was new.

Emerald nodded. "The true dispute is something small—some kind of mutual maritime rights. It's all in the contract hidden behind dummy corporations. The real point is, that no governments have ever before agreed to abide by a decision of this type. Individuals and corporations and internal governmental decisions all over the world—of course. But no two national governments."

Terri's voice was tight with excitement. "And this could set a precedent."

"Hmph," said Richard.

"It's all theoretical," Crandall put in, clearly enjoying Terri's interest. "But the Gaming Masters' Guild has a reputation for being selfish enough, cautious enough, international enough, and rich enough to be incorruptible. It's a start, at least, if matters hold up." He laughed and shrugged.

Wendell and Terri glanced at each other, grinning. A new challenge was rare for Masters in the top ten, and they had one with a double punch. Wendell thrust his hands in his pockets and looked from Terri to his feet.

"This will be the test case," said Emerald. "And the only item that could be a catch is the insistence of both governments that the dispute be decided by late autumn. Apparently it will affect their work in winter dry-dock."

"Under the circumstances," said Terri, "I think we can handle it in three months." She smiled and looked at Wendell.

"Yes, of course," he said. "But, uh, why did you wait?"

"To tell you?" Emerald smiled "Naturally, I'll trust your discretion in all of the foregoing. We weren't allowed to contact anyone at all until the last details of the agreement were finalized, early yesterday. Since both of you played under a contract of Lou's, he knew you weren't signed for the future, and he pounced."

"Of course he knew we'd accept," Richard complained. *"Any Master would jump at the chance to play tandem. I despise this manipulation."*

"I had you in mind for a long time," Crandall added. "The selection involved much more than availability, I assure you, though that was certainly important. Don't think I chose you at random. It was no accident." He let out a breath and looked around. "Are we set?"

Terri and Wendell both nodded. "We'll look over the contracts and be back tomorrow," said Wendell. "I expect no problems."

Terri nodded in agreement.

All four of them shook hands again, smiling all around. As the brief celebration ended, Kirk Emerald glanced wistfully at the game machine. "Anyone care to play again?" he asked.

The early weeks of preparation went quickly. The necessary rest sessions became the height of Wendell's day; time set aside for planning now offered conversation instead of rote memory work done in private. Before, he had always enjoyed the practice matches most out of the preparatory routine.

The elevator doors inside the Guild Hall opened into the heavily carpeted hallway. Wendell stepped from the elevator into an intricate, complex maze which offered thick, locked doors at intervals. These were the preparation rooms, where Masters would hone their skills for an upcoming game, normally by playing against the Guild Apprentices, or "spars." For the special tandem game, though, other Masters had agreed to act as spars for both teams. Wendell walked quickly, glancing at the door plates. Even after nine years, the maze sometimes still baffled him. He finally reached a door titled *"Dan no Ura,"* and sighed with relief.

"Japan by the western end of the Inland Sea," Richard recited. *"Year, 1185. Minamoto Clan eliminated Taira Clan."*

Wendell used his borrowed key in the door. Every week, they

changed their preparation room as well as their Master spars; this was to insure that opposing players would not accidentally identify each other through the pre-game routine. By custom, only the most functional and necessary conversation was carried out on this floor.

Inside the room, Terri greeted Wendell with a quiet smile. Away from the door, on the other side of the game machine, the two Master spars nodded at him. Wendell knew both of them by sight, but he had never spoken with either. As soon as Wendell was settled at his console, Terri activated the game.

The screen read: "Ain Jalut, 1260 A.D. Ilkhan Mongols." Several names followed, and a list of Victory Conditions and odds. Wendell was the second-in-command, leading one wing of cavalry.

"*Hulagu,*" said Richard, identifying the Ilkhan himself. "*The Mongols, as always, have a totally mounted force. Important: up to this point, they are undefeated. Consider an overconfidence factor programmed into the game.*"

"Right. Terrain?"

"*Mm—inconsequential to an all-mounted contest. Open desert country, slightly rolling.*"

Wendell's fingers wiggled nervously over the keyboard as the minute of orientation dragged by. This would be a rough one for him, demanding skill from his weak points. He felt like consulting Terri, but negotiations conducted through the contractors with the opposing team had produced the agreement that no talk would be allowed between partners. Speaking would eliminate the factor of on-field communication, which had always been important.

"*Opposition,*" said Richard. "*Victory by Mamluk Egypt, under Baibars. He himself is part Mongol and produces this first major trouncing of the Mongol army by utilizing their own style of war against them. Speed, surprise, mobility, discipline.*"

"Right." Wendell had all of this in him somewhere, but having it spoon-fed relieved him of both the pressure and energy of trying to recall it. He squirmed in his seat as the final seconds approached.

At least, the Mongol style of battle required a minimum of on-field communication. The general plan was discussed first, and the actual timing was coordinated as much by the judgment of the unit commanders as by conveying orders. Wendell and Terri, as any Masters, were prepared to utilize those plans and styles without discussion. In the last practice session, Terri and Wendell had commanded a loose confederation of Hindu forces at Tararori in 1192. Hamstrung by a disjointed command and strict Hindu religious laws, they had been easily overrun by Mohammed of Ghur. This clash, on the other hand, matched nearly identical fighting styles.

"*Go!*" screamed Richard.

The two sides closed fast and kept moving. Terri worked quickly and easily, setting up one side of a pincer movement. Wendell was ill at ease in the open, slash-and-run conflict. Repeatedly out-maneuvered, he failed to bring about the second wing of the pincer. She was probably annoyed, he thought, as she reconsolidated her wing.

"Back. Wheel about. Faster. No, faster." Richard's voice was quick and steady.

Wendell tried to set up a defensive posture, but the enemy's mobility on the open land could outflank any stand. "I'm still no good at this," he thought to Richard. Fleetingly, he remembered again: Richard was the undisputed number-one.

"Attack. What are you waiting for? C'mon!"

"Lemme alone," Wendell thought in a snarl. He brought his chaotic squads into reasonable order, trying to use Terri's more successful units as a buttress. She recognized the effort and helped with a long, sweeping charge which momentarily broke the enemy's pressure. The battle, made up of charges and sudden wheeling flights to regroup and charge again, rolled over wide areas of terrain, always moving. Lathered horses whinnied and screamed in the distant edges of Wendell's attention.

"Stop trying defense," Richard said angrily. *"Cavalry is an offensive weapon, you know that. Take—"*

"Shut up," Wendell thought. He took two good swipes at the enemy flank, but then a concerted enemy charge separated him completely from Terri. A second later he was in full retreat.

"Satisfied?" Richard growled. Terri's force quickly collapsed under the undiluted assault from the other side. Still, her facility with this command remained obvious, even in defeat.

"Victory Conditions, Mamluk Egypt," came on the screen. The elapsed time was remarkably short, even for this kind of battle. All four players audibly relaxed and leaned back, their faces bathed in the phosphor sheen of their screens.

Wendell smiled weakly at Terri, who shrugged. He flexed his fingers and looked at the frozen screen, feeling anger rise inside him. Yet Richard had clearly been right in his advice. Well, after a short break, they would go at it again. Silence reigned in his mind, as neither he nor Richard would speak.

"Tell me," said Terri, smiling over the short candle between them. "Did you invite me out to dinner just to make up for that first loss this morning?" The yellow light flickered over her smooth cheeks. "You realy didn't need to."

Wendell smiled shyly and stared into his empty bowl. "Oh, I dunno. I just felt like I should acknowledge it as my fault."

"You fool," said Richard.

Wendell tried to ignore him. He had not been in this sort of social situation before, with Richard. "Anyway, that type of fighting has always come hard for me."

Terri nodded. Her dark hair was almost lost in the dimness of the restaurant, but the candlelight shimmered on the curls around her face. "You're extremely tough defensively. The cavalry-to-cavalry attack just doesn't offer a stationary unit to work from."

"After this morning, I'm certain I've been lucky never to have fought Ain Jalut in a match. I did even worse than the real commander, and he lost badly."

"You're not kidding," said Richard. *"Very lucky."*

"I was the commander, today, don't forget." Terri laughed. "If you had fought a match, you would have been playing solo, and that's much easier. I'm serious about your defensive instincts, though. We just have to mesh our abilities better."

"Oh, I agree." Wendell leaned an elbow on the table, then changed his mind and took it off. "You think on your feet very well—adapt and respond while in motion."

Terri laughed again. "That comes from growing up in Queens—it's my New York paranoia showing."

"Oh, I didn't know where you were from."

"I left there quite a few years ago. Where are you from?"

"Right here—born and raised."

"Me, too," said Richard in a snide tone.

"Shut up," Wendell thought to him.

"Really?" said Terri.

"What?" Wendell blinked, in confusion.

Terri laughed and cocked her head to one side, studying him. "Aren't you paying attention? What's the matter?"

"I'm sorry. I—"

"Yeah. Tell her what's the matter, why don't you?"

"Stop it," Wendell thought back angrily, clenching his teeth.

"Wendell? Are you all right?" Terri brushed the curls from her eyes, frowning.

"Yes, I'm okay. Sorry." Wendell took a deep breath and tried to smile at her.

"Getting kind of crowded here, isn't it?"

Wendell controlled himself with tremendous effort. He could feel himself quivering. "It certainly is," he replied in his mind.

"No more personal questions," said Terri. "I promise."

"Oh—no, it's not, uh, not that, I—"

"That's all right. I wanted to tell you more about Ain Jalut, anyway."

"You don't need to, it's okay." Wendell had been hoping for more personal questions, really.

"It's just that when we fought Zama and Doryleum, you used your cavalry very effectively against me. Ain Jalut was just a certain kind of problem. And now I'll change the subject."

Wendell laughed. "All right. But you routed my cavalry at Zama—don't deny it."

"Oh, all right." Terri paused to take a drink of water. "But talking about different kinds of battles, weren't you one of the ones playing when Master Cohn's practical joke appeared in a match?"

"Ha! I sure was." Wendell grinned. "He paid for it, though—a year's suspension, just for inserting a Moopsball program into the game banks."

"That must have been quite a shock, when you were all primed for a serious match."

"Yeah, but to tell you the truth, I would have been just as happy to go ahead and play." Wendell made a grim face and drummed on the table as though it were a keyboard.

"I think I would, too." Terri smiled looking into the candle, and her teeth flashed white in the flickering light. "We're more alike than you think."

"Uh . . . you think?" Wendell blinked again and met her eyes. They were bright blue, with a corona of yellow streaks radiating from the pupils. His felt bloodshot, and he chuckled at making the comparison.

"What's so funny, huh?"

"I'm just having a good time. Would you like any dessert?"

"Naw—too fattening."

She excused herself, and the candle flame fluttered as she rose. Wendell sat back and watched her go.

Late one afternoon, they strolled through the Crown Center shops, unwinding from a hard-fought practice victory over Ferghana by Han Dynasty China in 102 B.C. Exhilaration had leveled off to a general simmer of satisfaction. Their teamwork was beginning to jell.

Terri stopped in front of a window that held a back-to-school display. Pencils and notebooks were strewn all over the green carpet, while two giant cardboard children grinned ferociously in the background, marching arm-in-arm. They were wearing matching red plaid outfits, and clean white shirts.

"Ugly kids," said Terri. "Their heads are too big."

"You suppose those plaids are anything?" Wendell frowned at them, trying to remember if they were familiar.

"Oh, I doubt they're tartans. Probably just ordinary, modern plaids."

The next window offered rows and rows of hand-made ceramics. Most of them were variations of brown and gray, for the coming fall.

"Ferghana," said Terri. "The T'ang Dynasty horses, that were immortalized in ceramic work."

"Same color," Wendell agreed. He shook his head. "I wonder what knowing all this is good for."

"It's good for a Master," said Terri. "Not for much else, if that's what you mean."

"I guess I'm just feeling futile these days. Too much practicing, probably."

Terri looked at him. "You almost quit once, didn't you? A long time ago. I heard about it."

Wendell nodded. "A long time ago." After the experience with Richard and the disastrous helmets.

"He's still in a coma, isn't he? Your friend?"

"Yeah." Wendell looked at the floor. Richard's collapse had been big news, back when it had happened.

Terri pursed her lips, seeing that she had touched on a bad subject. She started to move, then stopped.

Wendell was nodding to himself, staring at a brown pottery teapot. It seemed to have a faint Japanese flavor in its glazed design, but that might be an accident. "You ever consider quitting the Guild?" he asked abruptly, putting the thought into words before he had a chance to reconsider.

Terri looked up in surprise. "No, never. I mean until I have to on account of age, of course. Why, do you? Now?"

"Yeah, often—that is, whenever I win. I guess today it's from winning in practice session. I could never quit after losing; it'd have to be a victory."

Terri cocked her head to one side. "I see."

"Doesn't it ever seem odd that we keep reliving other people's lives, and killing them over and over? It's all such total fantasy. And kind of disrespectful to them."

Terri nodded. "Of course. It's just a game. Gaming Masters are some of the craziest fantasizers around. Isn't it obvious?"

"No," Wendell said slowly. "Maybe not to me. I knew it was true for me, but I guess I didn't think about how anyone else thought of it. It is disrespectful, though, don't you think? Kind of arrogant."

"We're all crazy that way. That doesn't mean it's serious."

"Yeah. Maybe." Wendell rocked on his heels, surveying the ceramics to avoid her eyes.

Terri slid her thumb under the strap of her shoulderbag and hoisted it. "Are you really serious about quitting?"

Wendell shrugged, still looking away. "I think if we score a victory, it'll be a good time. I'll be leaving at a sort of peak."

"I see." She studied him for a moment. "Well, you've been at this for a while longer than I have. I suppose, well, if you're sure you've had enough."

"I'm also afraid not to quit after a good victory—what if it's the last one, and I pass up the chance? I might *have* to go out in defeat, if I'm not careful." He glanced at her, sort of sideways.

Other doubts remained unspoken. If Richard was the best Master, and he advised Wendell, then was Wendell really any good at all? Would he win without Richard, the twenty-year-old prodigy? Or go down the drain?

Terri was silent a moment. "Okay," she said. "Okay, Master Wei. We'll make this a huge victory, and send you out in style. All right?"

Wendell smiled self-consciously. "Uh, all right." He cleared his throat and glanced at the store window once more as they moved on.

"All right," said Richard.

As the practice sessions progressed, one pattern became clear. The team could not work properly as a trio, not indefinitely, not even if Richard was the top of the field. The certainty grew in Wendell's mind that the official match itself would climax the entire situation. He suspected that Richard was somehow communicating the fact on a non-verbal level, but whatever the source, he accepted it. They conducted practice sessions with a grave civility between them which was more tense and calmly angry than even the silence, which now characterized nearly all the rest of the time.

Wendell's friendship with Terri bloomed quickly, watered by the familiar wasting of electronic blood. For the first time, now, he became less afraid that Richard's presence had been seriously warping his perceptions and relations with other people. Richard meanwhile went into a cold eclipse, only expressing himself with a mechanical precision during practice games that evinced a raw-nerved hostility.

On the night before the match, Wendell again slept deeply, without waking. Beside him, Terri stared fitfully into the blackness of his bedroom, trying to toss only very gently on the mattress. He noticed no movement, and did not stir at all. At one point, she raised herself up on one elbow to squint at the clock. She remembered Wendell telling her that a Scottish clan's battle-cry would activate it, but she couldn't remember which one. She whispered the war-cries of both Ross and Robertson before trying Munro, but even then, she said it in English instead of Gaelic, and nothing happened. Dropping back to the pillow with a tired sigh, she closed her eyes and started counting sheep-drawn chariots. After several minutes, they came upon a phalanx of Macedonians armed with giant blood-red sleeping pills. Instinctively, she drew them all up into battle formation. It was better than nothing.

* * *

The attendant finished his introduction to the audience and motioned to the open doorways on each side of him. At the scattered applause, the house lights dimmed. The sound of September crickets came faintly through the walls.

Wendell trembled slightly with nervousness as he walked to the game machine. He focused his eyes on his seat, ignoring the springy luxuriance of the carpet and the rows of privileged spectators, who had gathered to watch the first tandem game ever played—and, unknown to them, the first to decide an international issue between two governments. He was vaguely aware of Terri sliding into the seat beside him, and felt the familiar vibrations of the machine under his hands. Their opponents would be entering from the opposite door, and also seating themselves. The attendant stood by to await nods from all four Masters. When he had them, he pressed a lever on the screen and retired.

A fifteen-second red warning light went on, and Wendell just had time to glance at Terri with a quick smile. She smiled back while chewing on the inside of her cheeks.

"Here we go," said Richard, in a neutral tone.

The screen read: "Mount Badon. *Ca.* 490–503 A.D. Briton *Dux Bellorum,* Artorius."

"Mount Badon," Wendell whispered to himself, staring. This hadn't been in his Apprentice training. It was a recent addition to the military annals. "Mount Badon?"

Richard was there as always, but not without hesitation. *"Uh, Mount Badon. It was, um, a battle considered semi-legendary for almost sixteen centuries. Won by a Roman . . . Romano-British leader over waves of invading Saxons . . . yeah, that's right."*

"I need something useful," thought Wendell, with unaccustomed deference.

"The actual site was only discovered six or seven years ago." Richard paused, then continued with more certainty. *"Classic battle. We hold about five thousand infantry, stretched across the upper third of a gentle slope, facing down in three lines. Scouts and skirmishers have gone ahead. Experienced Briton commanders are joined in a confederacy under you, as Artorius. The decisive element is the heavy cavalry which you direct personally, numbering maybe a thousand. The Saxons want this slope to advance northward, divide the Celtic kingdoms, and control the horse-raising country. They must come to us."*

"Hold it," thought Wendell. "Look at the screen—that isn't right. Mount Badon began as a siege, didn't it? The Saxon host surprised Artorius with a small force atop Mount Badon and had him tripped."

"That was earlier," Richard said forcefully. *"This begins after reinforcements have arrived. The Saxons pulled back yesterday to avoid*

being attacked on two sides. Now they're on the advance again—start-ing here."

"All right, sorry," thought Wendell. "Let's see—steeper slopes pro-tect our flanks; we'll send the cavalry out from there, of course." He was musing to himself as much as to Richard. Checking the screen for Terri's *persona,* he found her as a Briton commander whose name was unknown, in charge of the irregular infantry confederation below that was modeled on portions of the old Roman legion. In the single games, her role probably would have gone to a computerized personality.

"Don't worry about your cavalry command. You have a defensive posture here. And remember, this is not the era of the heavy lance, with armored horse. Your mounts are vulnerable, and the weapons will be primarily spear and javelin. Charge in a series of rushes, not a single heavy line."

"Right." Wendell fastened his gaze on the screen, feeling a return of the confidence that he had momentarily lost. He recalled when the ar-chival discoveries had been made; it had been a tremendous find, and he had studied it avidly. But the information had never been absorbed as thoroughly as the battle facts he had learned as an eager apprentice.

The screen activated, and Wendell found himself on the right slope with all of the cavalry, still unpositioned.

"We're outnumbered by about three thousand," said Richard. *"But the Saxons have no cavalry. The real Mount Badon was a total slaughter of the Saxons; you'll have to do very well to equal that."*

"Right." Wendell looked out over the green valley beneath him. Far in the distance, the Saxon horde crawled like a giant, living carpet of blackness. Their van was fast approaching Terri's advance skirmishers, who would slowly fall back to merge with the main force. A thin rain of arrows would be arching sporadically from the woods on each flanking hill; these were also from scouts and harriers of the Briton force, sent to annoy the enemy, to put their march off stride, and to return with infor-mation. They would not do significant damage.

Terri held the three lines of infantry essentially motionless, making small adjustments. The infantry wings were comprised of light javelins and archers, and she pushed them forward slightly to increase their range. The Saxons were coming uphill, and every additional step they took cost them a little more breath. She began to move the standard-bearers some, building morale. As the Saxons approached, the calls of their sheep-horn trumpets preceded them in Wendell's mind, and the Britons answered with war-cries and old Roman trumpets and by beating on their shields with their weapons. The valley began to fill with the dull roar of massed voices, spiced with the shriek and bellow of the horns.

The Saxons were coming slowly, both to save their breath and to taunt the waiting Britons. Restraint, and a keen sense of timing, would decide the battle at many different junctures. Wendell also waited, trusting Terri not to break ranks early. In the fighting itself, if she could force the Saxon reserves into battle before he was forced to bring in the cavalry, all should be well. She, in turn, was trusting him to throw in the cavalry at the critical moment when she had held as long as possible—and no later.

"Position the cavalry." Richard's voice was firm and cool, perhaps even more authoritative than usual.

Wendell sent a third of the cavalry squads behind the crest of the slope, out of sight of the Saxons. They circled to the wooded area at the left of Terri's infantry and then stood there assembled, still hidden to the enemy. Wendell guarded his trumpeters carefully; only they could signal the left wing now.

Suddenly the Saxon advance lunged forward at a run. Spears and throwing axes would come seconds before the two front lines clashed bodily. As the yards between them quickly shrank, Terri surged forward with the front line of the Britons. The impact of striking shields sent a shock up and down the line. At first, the advantages of gravity and fresh breath carried Terri's line hard against the Saxons and pushed them back. As the Saxon line steadied, Wendell kept an anxious eye on the second line. Again, she would feel great temptation to throw them forward, but it was too early.

Slowly, the thrust of Saxon numbers began to push the line of combat up the hill. Behind them, the Saxon reserves followed restlessly, allowing their colleagues space to move, but little else. They gained the ground slowly, and Wendell judged that the cost was just slightly greater for the enemy. That would do for the moment.

The first line of Britons gradually backed into the second. The two merged and held. With renewed spirit, the new combined line even carried forward again and down the slope for a short time.

There was one more line to the rear of that.

Wendell studied the lay of the land again, finding the best paths for his three cavalry charges—to each flank of the enemy, and to its rear. When the Brittany Annal had first surfaced, deep in some Frankish stone cellar, it had proved to be an eleventh-century copy of a Celtic monk's personal journal. He had originally written in the mid-sixth century, when the memory of Mount Badon was alive but a generation old. Afraid that the glory of Artorius's victory would be forgotten, he had described the location and mechanics of the entire confrontation in great detail. Its reliability was accepted slowly, but its authenticity was verified by chemical analysis, and the content meshed completely both with known facts and learned conjecture. What the copy was doing in Brittany remained a mystery. The battle itself, almost identical to Cannae, was even closer to a pure theoretical example of that technique because of the Saxon need to advance up the slope for strategic objectives and because of their lack of cavalry. Wendell picked out his routes carefully, and felt Richard nod agreement.

The line of struggle began to recede up the slope once again. Wendell shifted in his seat and took a deep breath. The time for cavalry was coming, and Terri's positioning and execution so far had been nearly perfect. Quickly, Wendell cast about for any surprises, any twists that their opponents might have in readiness, but he could think of none. Their chances of winning lay not so much in besting Artorius and the Britons as in besting their actual Saxon predecessors.

"That won't be hard," said Richard. *"If they save almost anyone, they'll have done better."*

Wendell watched the struggle stretched across the slope with rising tension. Slowly, grudgingly, fiercely, Terri's line fell back and back. They held good formation, and the final line of reserves stiffened in readiness. All at once, Terri brought the front line back sharply, in an ordered retreat, and they melted into the rear line. As the Saxons continued forward, the one solid line of Britons fell hard down upon them again, and Wendell nodded in admiration. Victory was procured by compiling small moves, like this emphasizing the advantage of the slope. The Saxon line faltered and was forced back one more time.

"Here they come," thought Wendell, with a smile of anticipation. The Britons were pressing forward more quickly than before, with both psychological and gravitational momentum. The Saxon reserves could not back away, for fear of losing morale. So, as the line of combat came back down the slope into them, Terri was effectively forcing them into play before they wanted to go. "That's the way."

The Saxons reserves, greatly outnumbering the final line of Britons that was already in the struggle, were ordered forward. Once fully committed, they would have trouble turning to meet the charges of the cavalry. Grudgingly, the massive rear lines of the enemy came forward.

"Not yet," said Richard, sternly.

Intensely anxious, Wendell gave the signal. Trumpets sounded, and a third of the cavalry squads began to move on each flank of the battle.

"No!" yelled Richard. *"Too soon, stop it. Hold."*

"Too late," Wendell tossed back, without regret. Artorius began to take the final third of cavalry around the right flank, high on the shoulder of Mount Badon itself, at a fast trot. Their target was the Saxon rear, for the final blow.

Meanwhile, the heavy cavalry came charging down past the flanks of their own Briton line and took the Saxons hard on each side. The sheer weight and momentum of the charges carried them deep into what was becoming a blunt, curved mass of Saxons, with both flanks turned to form a horse-shoe shape.

"Look, will you? Stop," Richard hissed. *"Can't you see?"* Wendell stared. He had not allowed the Saxon reserves enough time to engage Terri's force. Although they had taken tremendous losses from the initial attack, they were wheeling about to maintain their curved lines, forming the horse-shoe with its open end facing back toward their own south. Instead of smashing the Saxon center and pinching out the strength that pushed against the Briton shield-wall, the two cavalry wings had simply re-aligned the struggle. The Saxon center still advanced in good order against Terri's line, and threatened to punch through.

"Attack. Straight down the slope," Richard ordered. *"Go."*

Wendell hesitated, then continued to push his squads farther on his own chosen path. "Their rear is still vulnerable. We'll hurry and—"

"No time, fool. Charge now, before anything changes. Hit the center. Fast." Richard's voice ended in a falsetto note. *"Go."*

Terri's line had no more reserves. The Saxon center pushed onward, forcing the Britons slowly toward the crest of the slope. If the Saxons attained the crest, all the mechanics of the battle would alter drastically, to their benefit. Wendell rushed his cavalry squads into a canter toward the far downward slope of Mount Badon.

"No!" Richard yelled again.

Wendell lurched forward suddenly in the seat with a wave of nausea. He momentarily lost his bearings and his grip on the keyboard. Badly shaken, he looked up at the screen, fighting panic. The keyboard was slick with sweat under his fingers.

"GARG'N UAIR DHUISGEAR," screamed Richard. As Wendell stared at the screen and pounded the keyboard, the cavalry broke from the path across Mount Badon and charged at full gallop for the enemy's flank.

The alert cavalry squads already on the field saw them coming and expertly parted to let them pass.

Wendell stared wide-eyed at the screen, clutching and punching at the keys. The units ignored him. In his mixture of panic and reflex, he couldn't tell if the keyboard wasn't functioning right or if his own hands were out of control.

"Garg'n uair dhuisgear," echoed again and again in Wendell's mind. The cavalry reserves thundered through the opened ranks of their comrades and crashed through to the heart of the Saxons. The tremendous power of the charge crushed the enemy center, and the other cavalry squads renewed their rushes on both sides of the collapsing Saxon horse-shoe.

Wendell looked back at Terri's line. They were holding fast, relieved of the intense pressure of greater numbers. Stability was needed now, and simple attrition. Confidence would sustain them.

Two squads of cavalry split off from the right flank, and swung wide around the struggling mass. They wheeled at the base of Mount Badon, and charged into the enemy rear. The Saxons were surrounded, jammed together, and partially divided into separate bands.

The outcome was decided.

"Victory Conditions, Britain," appeared on the screen. Wendell collapsed back in his seat, ignoring the statistics that were listed under the crucial phrase. He was soaked in sweat and sick to his stomach. Breathing heavily, he let his head roll to one side to see Terri. She was damp and flushed. As he watched, she brushed matted curls of hair from her eyes and smiled at him weakly. The attendants arrived, to help them into the back rooms. Wendell waved his away, gesturing a need to catch his breath.

"Made it," he thought. "Congratulations."

No answer. Wendell was too exhausted to wonder about it. He watched Terri leave the room on the arm of one attendant, while several more tried to keep back the crowd of excited spectators. The only voice in his mind was his own.

"Well," he thought, as his strength gradually gathered. "Gone, huh?" There was no doubt that Richard had won this game—the prodigy still reigned. "Wherever you are, congratulations, anyhow."

Far below the city, in a cavern edged with blue-white frost, the gangling body lay unmoving. The tank sparkled in the pale light. Deep within the silent cranium, a spark began to glow.

Wendell lay back in the seat, motionless, looking at the frozen screen without seeing it. He had tread too long on the subtle interface where dreams and dreams threatened to merge. His eyes suddenly focused on the screen, and he thought again of the phosphorous shine and its ethereal universe. Those lives belonged to the dead, but they had thrown a millennial shadow.

THEODORE R. COGSWELL
THE SPECTER GENERAL

1 "**S**ergeant Dixon!" Kurt stiffened. He knew *that* voice. Dropping the handles of the wooden plow, he gave a quick "rest" to the private and a polite "by your leave, sir" to the lieutenant who were yoked together in double harness. They both sank gratefully to the ground as Kurt advanced to meet the approaching officer.

Marcus Harris, the commander of the 427th Light Maintenance Battalion of the Imperial Space Marines, was an imposing figure. The three silver eagle feathers of a full colonel rose proudly from his war bonnet and the bright red of the flaming comet insignia of the Space Marines that was painted on his chest stood out sharply against his sun-blackened, leathery skin. As Kurt snapped to attention before him and saluted, the colonel surveyed the fresh turned earth with an experienced eye.

"You plow a straight furrow, soldier!" His voice was hard and metallic, but it seemed to Kurt that there was a concealed glimmer of approval in his flinty eyes. Dixon flushed with pleasure and drew back his broad shoulders a little further.

The commander's eyes flicked down to the battle-ax that rested snugly in its leather holster at Kurt's side. "You keep a clean sidearm, too."

Kurt uttered a silent prayer of thanksgiving that he had worked over his weapon before reveille that morning until there was a satin gloss to its redwood handle and the sheen of black glass to its obsidian head.

"In fact," said Colonel Harris, "you'd be officer material if—" His voice trailed off.

"If what?" asked Kurt eagerly.

"If," said the colonel with a note of paternal fondness in his voice that sent cold chills dancing down Kurt's spine, "you weren't the most completely unmanageable, undisciplined, overmuscled and under-brained knucklehead I've ever had the misfortune to have in my command. This last little unauthorized jaunt of yours indicates to me that you have as much right to sergeant's stripes as I have to have kittens. Report to me at ten tomorrow! I personally guarantee that when I'm through with you— if you live that long—you'll have a bare forehead!"

Colonel Harris spun on one heel and stalked back across the dusty plateau toward the walled garrison that stood at one end. Kurt stared after him for a moment and then turned and let his eyes slip across the wide belt of lush green jungle that surrounded the high plateau. To the north rose a great range of snow-capped mountains and his heart filled with longing as he thought of the strange and beautiful thing he had found behind them. Finally he plodded slowly back to the plow, his shoulders stooped and his head sagging. With an effort he recalled himself to the business at hand.

"Up on your dying feet, soldier!" he barked to the reclining private. "If you please, sir!" he said to the lieutenant. His calloused hands grasped the worn plow handles.

"Giddiup!" The two men strained against their collars and with a creak of harness the wooden plow started to move slowly across the arid plateau.

2   **C**onrad Krogson, Supreme Commander of War Base Three of Sector Seven of the Galactic Protectorate stood at quaking attention before the visiscreen of his space communicator. It was an unusual position for the commander. He was accustomed to having people quake while *he* talked.

"The Lord Protector's got another hot tip that General Carr is still alive!" said the sector commander. "He's yelling for blood; and if it's a choice between yours and mine, you know who will do the donating!"

"But sir," quavered Krogson to the figure on the screen, "I can't do anything more than I am doing. I've had double security checks running since the last time there was an alert, and they haven't turned up a thing.

And I'm so shorthanded now that if I pull another random purge, I won't have enough techs left to work the base."

"That's your problem, not mine," said the sector commander coldly. "All that I know is that rumors have got to the Protector that an organized underground is being built up and that Carr is behind it. The Protector wants action now. If he doesn't get it, heads are going to roll!"

"I'll do what I can, sir," promised Krogson.

"I'm sure you will," said the sector commander viciously, "because I'm giving you exactly ten days to produce something that is big enough to take the heat off me. If you don't, I'll break you, Krogson. If I'm sent to the mines, you'll be sweating right alongside me. That's a promise!"

Krogson's face blanched.

"Any questions?" snapped the sector commander.

"Yes," said Krogson.

"Well don't bother me with them. I've got troubles of my own!" The screen went dark.

Krogson slumped into his chair and sat staring dully at the blank screen. Finally he roused himself with an effort and let out a bellow that rattled the windows of his dusty office.

"Schninkle! Get in here!"

A gnomelike little figure scuttled in through the door and bobbed obsequiously before him.

"Yes, commander?"

"Switch on your thinktank," said Krogson. "The Lord Protector has the shakes again and the heat's on!"

"What is it this time?" asked Schninkle.

"General Carr!" said the commander gloomily, "the ex-Number Two."

"I thought he'd been liquidated."

"So did I," said Krogson, "but he must have slipped out some way. The Protector thinks he's started up an underground."

"He'd be a fool if he didn't," said the little man. "The Lord Protector isn't as young as he once was and his grip is getting a little shaky."

"Maybe so, but he's still strong enough to get us before General Carr gets him. The Sector Commander just passed the buck down to me. We produce or else!"

"We?" said Schninkle unhappily.

"Of course," snapped Krogson, "we're in this together. Now let's get to work! If you were Carr, where would be the logical place for you to hide out?"

"Well," said Schninkle thoughtfully, "if I were as smart as Carr is supposed to be, I'd find myself a hideout right on Prime Base. Everything's so fouled up there that they'd never find me."

"That's out for us," said Krogson. "We can't go rooting around in the Lord Protector's own backyard. What would Carr's next best bet be?"

Schninkle thought for a moment. "He might go out to one of the deserted systems," he said slowly. "There must be half a hundred stars in our own base area that haven't been visited since the old empire broke up. Our ships don't get around the way they used to and the chances are mighty slim that anybody would stumble on to him accidentally."

"It's a possibility," said the commander thoughtfully. "A bare possibility." His right fist slapped into his left palm in a gesture of sudden resolution. "But by the Planets! at least it's something! Alert all section heads for a staff meeting in half an hour. I want every scout out on a quick check of every system in our area!"

"Beg pardon, commander," said Schninkle, "but half our light ships are red-lined for essential maintenance and the other half should be. Anyway it would take months to check every possible hideout in this area even if we used the whole fleet."

"I know," said Krogson, "but we'll have to do what we can with what we have. At least I'll be able to report to sector that we're doing *something!* Tell Astrogation to set up a series of search patterns. We won't have to check every planet. A single quick sweep through each system will do the trick. Even Carr can't run a base without power. Where there's power, there's radiation, and radiation can be detected a long way off. Put all electronic techs on double shifts and have all detection gear double checked."

"Can't do that either," said Schninkle. "There aren't more than a dozen electronic techs left. Most of them were transferred to Prime Base last week."

Commander Krogson blew up. "How in the name of the Bloody Blue Pleiades am I supposed to keep a war base going without technicians? You tell me, Schninkle, you always seem to know all the answers."

Schninkle coughed modestly. "Well, sir," he said, "as long as you have a situation where technicians are sent to the uranium mines for making mistakes, it's going to be an unpopular vocation. And, as long as the Lord Protector of the moment is afraid that Number Two, Number Three, and so on have ideas about grabbing his job—which they generally do—he's going to keep his fleet as strong as possible and their fleets so weak they aren't dangerous. The best way to do that is to grab techs. If most of the base's ships are sitting around waiting repair, the commander won't be able to do much about any ambitions he may happen to have. Add that to the obvious fact that our whole technology has been on a downward spiral for the last three hundred years and you have your answer."

Krogson nodded gloomy agreement. "Sometimes I feel as if we were all on a dead ship falling into a dying sun," he said. His voice suddenly altered. "But in the meantime we have our necks to save. Get going, Schninkle!"

Schninkle bobbed and darted out of the office.

3   It was exactly ten o'clock in the morning when Sergeant Dixon of the Imperial Space Marines snapped to attention before his commanding officer.

"Sergeant Dixon reporting as ordered sir!" His voice cracked a bit in spite of his best efforts to control it.

The colonel looked at him coldly. "Nice of you to drop in, Dixon," he said. "Shall we go ahead with our little chat?"

Kurt nodded nervously.

"I have here," said the colonel, shuffling a sheaf of papers, "a report of an unauthorized expedition made by you into *Off Limits* territory."

"Which one do you mean, sir?" asked Kurt without thinking.

"Then there has been more than one?" asked the colonel quietly.

Kurt started to stammer.

Colonel Harris silenced him with a gesture of his hand. "I'm talking about the country to the north, the tableland back of the Twin Peaks."

"It's a beautiful place!" burst out Kurt enthusiastically. "It's . . . it's like Imperial Headquarters must be. Dozens of little streams full of fish, trees heavy with fruit, small game so slow and stupid that they can be knocked over with a club. Why, the battalion could live there without hardly lifting a finger!"

"I've no doubt that they could," said the colonel.

"Think of it, sir!" continued the sergeant. "No more plowing details, no more hunting details, no more nothing but taking it easy!"

"You might add to your list of 'no mores,' no more tech schools," said Colonel Harris. "I'm quite aware that the place is all you say it is, sergeant. As a result I'm placing all information that pertains to it in a 'Top Secret' category. That applies to what is inside your head as well!"

"But, sir!" protested Kurt. "If you could only see the place—"

"I have," broke in the colonel, "thirty years ago."

Kurt looked at him in amazement. "Then why are we still on the plateau?"

"Because my commanding officer did just what I've just done, classified the information 'Top Secret.' Then he gave me thirty days extra detail on the plows. After he took my stripes away that is." Colonel Harris rose slowly to his feet. "Dixon," he said softly, "it's not every man who can be a noncommissioned officer in the Space Marines. Sometimes we guess wrong. When we do we do something about it!" There was the hissing crackle of distant summer lightning in his voice and storm clouds seemed to gather about his head. "Wipe those chevrons off!" he roared.

Kurt looked at him in mute protest.

"You heard me!" the colonel thundered.

"Yes-s-s, sir," stuttered Kurt, reluctantly drawing his forearm across his forehead and wiping off the three triangles of white grease paint that marked him a sergeant in the Imperial Space Marines. Quivering with shame, he took a tight grip on his temper and choked back the angry protests that were trying to force their way past his lips.

"Maybe," suggested the colonel, "you'd like to make a complaint to the I.G. He's due in a few days and he might reverse my decision. It has happened before, you know."

"No, sir," said Kurt woodenly.

"Why not?" demanded Harris.

"When I was sent out as a scout for the hunting parties I was given direct orders not to range farther than twenty kilometers to the north. I went sixty." Suddenly his forced composure broke. "I couldn't help it, sir," he said. "There was something behind those peaks that kept pulling me and pulling me and"—he threw up his hands—"you know the rest."

There was a sudden change in the colonel's face as a warm human smile swept across it, and he broke into a peal of laughter. "It's a hell of a feeling, isn't it, son? You know you shouldn't, but at the same time there's something inside you that says you've got to know what's behind those peaks or die. When you get a few more years under your belt you'll find that it isn't just mountains that make you feel like that. Here, boy, have a seat." He gestured toward a woven wicker chair that stood by his desk.

Kurt shifted uneasily from one foot to the other, stunned by the colonel's sudden change of attitude and embarrassed by his request. "Excuse me, sir," he said, "but we aren't out on work detail, and—"

The colonel laughed. "And enlisted men not on work detail don't sit in the presence of officers. Doesn't the way we do things ever strike you as odd, Dixon? On one hand you'd see nothing strange about being yoked to a plow with a major, and on the other, you'd never dream of sitting in his presence off duty."

Kurt looked puzzled "Work details are different," he said. "We all have to work if we're going to eat. But in the garrison, officers are officers and enlisted men are enlisted men and that's the way it's always been."

Still smiling, the colonel reached into his desk drawer, fished out something, and tossed it to Kurt.

"Stick this in your scalp lock," he said.

Kurt looked at it, stunned. It was a golden feather crossed with a single black bar, the insignia of rank of a second lieutenant of the Imperial Space Marines. The room swirled before his eyes.

"Now," said the older officer, "sit down!"

Kurt slowly lowered himself into the chair and looked at the colonel through bemused eyes.

"Stop gawking!" said Colonel Harris. "You're an officer now! When a man gets too big for his sandals, we give him a new pair—after we let him sweat a while!"

He suddenly grew serious. "Now that you're one of the family, you have a right to know why I'm hushing up the matter of the tableland to the north. What I have to say won't make much sense at first. Later I'm hoping it will. Tell me," he said suddenly, "where did the battalion come from?"

"We've always been here, I guess," said Kurt. "When I was a recruit, Granddad used to tell me stories about us being brought from some place else a long time ago by an iron bird, but it stands to reason that something that heavy can't fly!"

A faraway look came into the colonel's eyes. "Six generations," he mused, "and history becomes legend. Another six and the legends themselves become tales for children. Yes, Kurt," he said softly, "it stands to reason that something that heavy couldn't fly so we'll forget it for a while. We did come from some place else though. Once there was a great empire, so great that all the stars you see at night were only part of it. And then, as things do when age rests too heavily on them, it began to crumble. Commanders fell to fighting among themselves and the Emperor grew weak. The battalion was set down here to operate a forward maintenance station for his ships. We waited but no ships came. For five hundred years no ships have come," said the colonel somberly. "Perhaps they tried to relieve us and couldn't, perhaps the Empire fell with such a crash that we were lost in the wreckage. There are a thousand perhapses that a man can tick off in his mind when the nights are long and sleep comes hard! Lost . . . forgotten . . . who knows?"

Kurt stared at him with a blank expression on his face. Most of what the colonel had said made no sense at all. Wherever Imperial Headquarters was, it hadn't forgotten them. The I.G. still made his inspection every year or so.

The colonel continued as if talking to himself. "But our operational orders said that we would stand by to give all necessary maintenance to Imperial warcraft until properly relieved, and stand by we have."

The old officer's voice seemed to be coming from a place far distant in time and space.

"I'm sorry, sir," said Kurt, "but I don't follow you. If all these things did happen, it was so long ago that they mean nothing to us now."

"But they do!" said Colonel Harris vigorously. "It's because of them that things like your rediscovery of the tableland to the north have to be suppressed for the good of the battalion! Here on the plateau the living is hard. Our work in the fields and the meat brought in by our hunting parties give us just enough to get by on. But here we have the garrison and the Tech Schools—and vague as it has become—a reason for remaining together as the battalion. Out there where the living is easy we'd lose that. We almost did once. A wise commander stopped it before it went too far. There are still a few signs of that time left—left deliberately as reminders of what can happen if commanding officers forget why we're here!"

"What things?" asked Kurt curiously.

"Well, son," said the colonel, picking up his great war bonnet from the desk and gazing at it quizzically, "I don't think you're quite ready for that information yet. Now take off and strut your feather. I've got work to do!"

4

At War Base Three nobody was happy. Ships that were supposed to be light-months away carrying on the carefully planned search for General Carr's hideout were fluttering down out of the sky like senile penguins, disabled by blown jets, jammed computers, and all the other natural ills that worn out and poorly serviced equipment is heir to. Technical maintenance was quietly going mad. Commander Krogson was being noisy about it.

"Schninkle!" he screamed. "Isn't anything happening any place?"

"Nothing yet, sir," said the little man.

"Well *make* something happen!" He hoisted his battered brogans onto the scarred top of the desk and chewed savagely on a frayed cigar. "How are the other sectors doing?"

"No better than we are," said Schninkle. "Commander Snork of Sector Six tried to pull a fast one but he didn't get away with it. He sent his STAP into a plantation planet out at the edge of the Belt and had them hypno the whole population. By the time they were through there were about fifteen million greenies running around yelling, 'Up with General Carr!' 'Down with the Lord Protector!' 'Long Live the People's Revolution!' and things like that. Snork even gave them a few medium vortex blasters to make it look more realistic. Then he sent in his whole fleet, tipped off the press at Prime Base, and waited. Guess what the Bureau of Essential Information finally sent him?"

"I'll bite," said Commander Krogson.

"One lousy cub reporter. Snork couldn't back out then so he had to go ahead and blast the planet down to bedrock. This morning he got a three line notice in *Space* and a citation as Third Rate Protector of the People's Space Ways, Eighth Grade."

"That's better than the nothing we've got so far!" said the commander gloomily.

"Not when the press notice is buried on the next to last page right below the column on 'Our Feathered Comrades,'" said Schninkle, "and when the citation is posthumous. They even misspelled his name; it came out Snark!"

5

$\mathbf{A}$s Kurt turned to go, there was a sharp knock on Colonel Harris' door.

"Come in!" called the colonel.

Lieutenant Colonel Blick, the battalion executive officer, entered with an arrogant stride and threw his commander a slovenly salute. For a moment he didn't notice Kurt standing at attention beside the door.

"Listen, Harris!" he snarled. "What's the idea of pulling that clean-up detail out of my quarters?"

"There are no servants in this battalion, Blick," the older man said quietly. "When the men come in from work detail at night they're tired. They've earned a rest and as long as I'm C.O. they're going to get it. If you have dirty work that has to be done, do it yourself. You're better able to do it than some poor devil who's been dragging a plow all day. I suggest you check pertinent regulations!"

"Regulations!" growled Blick. "What do you expect me to do, scrub my own floors?"

"I do," said the colonel dryly, "when my wife is too busy to get to it. I haven't noticed that either my dignity or my efficiency have suffered appreciably. I might add," he continued mildly, "that staff officers are supposed to set a good example for their juniors. I don't think either your tone or your manner are those that Lieutenant Dixon should be encouraged to emulate." He gestured toward Kurt and Blick spun on one heel.

"*Lieutenant* Dixon!" he roared in an incredulous voice. "By whose authority?"

"Mine," said the colonel mildly. "In case you've forgotten I am still commanding officer of this battalion."

"I protest!" said Blick. "Commissions have always been awarded by decision of the entire staff."

"Which you now control," replied the colonel.

Kurt coughed nervously. "Excuse me, sir," he said, "but I think I'd better leave."

Colonel Harris shook his head. "You're one of our official family now, son, and you might as well get used to our squabbles. This particular one has been going on between Colonel Blick and me for years. He has no patience with some of our old customs." He turned to Blick. "Have you, Colonel?"

"You're right, I haven't!" growled Blick. "And that's why I'm going to change some of them as soon as I get the chance. The sooner we stop this Tech School nonsense and put the recruits to work in the fields where they belong, the better off we'll all be. Why should a plowman or a hunter have to know how to read wiring diagrams or set tubes. It's nonsense, superstitious nonsense. You!" he said, stabbing his finger into the chest of the startled lieutenant. "You! Dixon! You spent fourteen years in the Tech Schools just like I did when I was a recruit. What for?"

"To learn maintenance, of course," said Kurt.

"What's maintenance?" demanded Blick.

"Taking stuff apart and putting it back together and polishing jet bores with microplanes and putting plates in alignment and checking the meters when we're through to see the job was done right. Then there's class work in Direc calculus and subelectronics and—"

"That's enough!" interrupted Blick. "And now that you've learned all that, what can you do with it?"

Kurt looked at him in surprise.

"Do with it?" he echoed. "You don't *do* anything with it. You just learn it because regulations say you should."

"And this," said Blick, turning to Colonel Harris, "is one of your prize products. Fourteen of his best years poured down the drain and he doesn't even know what for!" He paused and then said in an arrogant voice, "I'm here for a showdown, Harris!"

"Yes?" said the colonel mildly.

"I demand that the Tech Schools be closed at once, and the recruits released for work details. If you want to keep your command, you'll issue that order. The staff is behind me on this!"

Colonel Harris rose slowly to his feet. Kurt waited for the thunder to roll, but strangely enough, it didn't. It almost seemed to him that there was an expression of concealed amusement playing across the colonel's face.

"Some day, just for once," he said, "I wish somebody around here would do something that hasn't been done before.

"What do you mean by that?" demanded Blick.

"Nothing," said the colonel. "You know," he continued conversationally, "a long time ago I walked into my C.O.'s and made the same demands and the same threats that you're making now. I didn't get very far, though—just as you aren't going to—because I overlooked the little matter of the Inspector General's annual visit. He's due in from Imperial Headquarters Saturday night, isn't he, Blick?"

"You know he is!" growled the other.

"Aren't worried, are you? It occurs to me that the I.G. might take a dim view of your new order."

"I don't think he'll mind," said Blick with a nasty grin. "Now will you issue the order to close the Tech Schools or won't you?"

"Of course not!" said the colonel brusquely.

"That's final?"

Colonel Harris just nodded.

"All right," barked Blick, "you asked for it!"

There was an ugly look on his face as he barked, "Kane! Simmons! Arnett! The rest of you! Get in here!"

The door to Harris' office swung slowly open and revealed a group of officers standing sheepishly in the anteroom.

"Come in, gentlemen," said Colonel Harris.

They came slowly forward and grouped themselves just inside the door.

"I'm taking over!" roared Blick. "This garrison has needed a house cleaning for a long time and I'm just the man to do it!"

"How about the rest of you?" asked the colonel.

"Beg pardon, sir," said one hesitantly, "but we think Colonel Blick's probably right. I'm afraid we're going to have to confine you for a few days. Just until after the I.G.'s visit," he added apologetically.

"And what do you think the I.G. will say to all this?"

"Colonel Blick says we don't have to worry about that," said the officer. "He's going to take care of everything."

A look of sudden anxiety played across Harris' face and for the first time he seemed on the verge of losing his composure.

"How?" he demanded, his voice betraying his concern.

"He didn't say, sir," the other replied. Harris relaxed visibly.

"All right," said Blick. "Let's get moving!" He walked behind the desk and plumped into the colonel's chair. Hoisting his feet on the desk he gave his first command.

"Take him away!"

There was a sudden roar from the far corner of the room. "No you don't!" shouted Kurt. His battle-ax leaped into his hand as he jumped in front of Colonel Harris, his muscular body taut and his gray eyes flashing defiance.

Blick jumped to his feet. "Disarm that man!" he commanded. There was a certain amount of scuffling as the officers in the front of the group by the door tried to move to the rear and those behind them resolutely defended their more protected positions.

Blick's face grew so purple that he seemed on the verge of apoplexy. "Major Kane," he demanded, "place that man under restraint!"

Kane advanced toward Kurt with a noticeable lack of enthusiasm.

Keeping a cautious eye on the glittering ax head, he said in what he obviously hoped to be a placating voice, "Come now, old man. Can't have this sort of thing, you know." He stretched out his hand hesitantly toward Kurt. "Why don't you give me your ax and we'll forget that the incident ever occurred."

Kurt's ax suddenly leaped toward the major's head. Kane stood petrified as death whizzed toward him. At the last split second Kurt gave a practiced twist to his wrist and the ax jumped up, cutting the air over the major's head with a vicious whistle. The top half of his silver staff plume drifted slowly to the floor.

"You want it," roared Kurt, his ax flicking back and forth like a snake's tongue, "you come get it. That goes for the rest of you, too!"

The little knot of officers retreated still farther. Colonel Harris was having the time of his life.

"Give it to 'em, son!" he whooped.

Blick looked contemptuously at the staff and slowly drew his own ax. Colonel Harris suddenly stopped laughing.

"Wait a minute, Blick!" he said. "This has gone far enough." He turned to Kurt.

"Give them your ax, son."

Kurt looked at him with an expression of hurt bewilderment in his eyes, hesitated for a moment, and then glumly surrendered his weapon to the relieved major.

"Now," snarled Blick, "take that insolent puppy out and feed him to the lizards!"

Kurt drew himself up in injured dignity. "That is no way to refer to a brother officer," he said reproachfully.

The vein in Blick's forehead started to pulse again. "Get him out of here before I tear him to shreds!" he hissed through clenched teeth. There was silence for a moment as he fought to regain control of himself. Finally he succeeded.

"Lock him up!" he said in an approximation of his normal voice. "Tell the provost sergeant I'll send down the charges as soon as I can think up enough."

Kurt was led resentfully from the room.

"The rest of you clear out," said Blick. "I want to talk with Colonel Harris about the I.G."

6   There was a saying in the Protectorate that when the Lord Protector was angry, stars and heads fell. Commander Krogson felt his wabble on his neck. His far-sweeping scouts were sending back nothing but reports of equipment failure, and the sector commander had coldly informed him that morning that his name rested securely at the bottom of the achievement list. It looked as if War Base Three would shortly have a change of command. "Look, Schninkle," he said desperately, "even if we can't give them anything, couldn't we make a promise that would look good enough to take some of the heat off us?"

Schninkle looked dubious.

"Maybe a new five-year plan?" suggested Krogson.

The little man shook his head. "That's a subject we'd better avoid entirely," he said. "They're still asking nasty questions about what happened to the last one. Mainly on the matter of our transport quota. I took the liberty of passing the buck on down to Logistics. Several of them have been . . . eh . . . removed as a consequence."

"Serves them right!" snorted Krogson. "They got me into that mess with their 'if a freighter and a half flies a light-year and a half in a month and a half, ten freighters can fly ten light-years in ten months!" I knew there was something fishy about it at the time, but I couldn't put my finger on it."

"It's always darkest before the storm," said Schninkle helpfully.

7

"Take off your war bonnet and make yourself comfortable," said Colonel Harris hospitably.

Blick grunted assent. "This thing is sort of heavy," he said. "I think I'll change uniform regulations while I'm at it."

"There was something you wanted to tell me?" suggested the colonel.

"Yeah," said Blick. "I figure that you figure the I.G.'s going to bail you out of this. Right?"

"I wouldn't be surprised."

"I would," said Blick. "I was up snoopin' around the armory last week. There was something there that started me doing some heavy thinking. Do you know what it was?"

"I can guess," said the colonel.

"As I looked at it, it suddenly occurred to me what a happy coincidence it is that the Inspector General always arrives just when you happen to need him."

"It is odd, come to think of it."

"Something else occurred to me, too. I got to thinking that if I were C.O. and I wanted to keep the troops whipped into line, the easiest way to do it would be to have a visible symbol of Imperial Headquarters appear in person once in a while."

"That makes sense," admitted Harris, "especially since the chaplain has started preaching that Imperial Headquarters is where good marines go when they die—*if* they follow regulations while they're alive. But how would you manage it?"

"Just the way you did. I'd take one of the old battle suits, wait until it was good and dark, and then slip out the back way and climb up six or seven thousand feet. Then I'd switch on my landing lights and drift slowly down to the parade field to review the troops." Blick grinned triumphantly.

"It might work," admitted Colonel Harris, "but I was under the impression that those rigs were so heavy that a man couldn't even walk in one, let alone fly."

Blick grinned triumphantly. "Not if the suit was powered. If a man were to go up into the tower of the arsenal and pick the lock of the little door labeled 'Danger! Absolutely No Admittance,' he might find a whole stack of shiny little cubes that look suspiciously like the illustrations of power packs in the tech manuals."

"That he might," agreed the colonel.

Blick shifted back in his chair. "Aren't worried, are you?"

Colonel Harris shook his head. "I was for a moment when I thought you'd told the rest of the staff, but I'm not now."

"You should be! When the I.G. arrives this time, I'm going to be inside that suit. There's going to be a new order around here, and he's just what I need to put the stamp of approval on it. When the Inspector General talks, nobody questions!"

He looked at Harris expectantly, waiting for a look of consternation to sweep across his face. The colonel just laughed.

"Blick," he said, "you're in for a big surprise!"

"What do you mean?" said the other suspiciously.

"Simply that I know you better than you know yourself. You wouldn't be executive officer if I didn't. You know, Blick, I've got a hunch that the battalion is going to change the man more than the man is going to change the battalion. And now if you'll excuse me—" He started toward the door. Blick moved to intercept him.

"Don't trouble yourself," chuckled the colonel, "I can find my own way to the cell block." There was a broad grin on his face. "Besides, you've got work to do."

There was a look of bewilderment in Blick's face as the erect figure went out the door. "I don't get it," he said to himself. "I just don't get it!"

8

Flight Officer Ozaki was unhappy. Trouble had started two hours after he lifted his battered scout off War Base Three and showed no signs of letting up. He sat glumly at his controls and enumerated his woes. First there was the matter of the air conditioner which had acquired an odd little hum and discharged into the cabin oxygen redolent with the rich, ripe odor of rotting fish. Secondly, something had happened to the complex insides of his food synthesizer and no matter what buttons he punched, all that emerged from the ejector were quivering slabs of undercooked protein base smeared with a raspberry-flavored goo.

Not last, but worst of all, the ship's fuel converter was rapidly becoming more erratic. Instead of a slow, steady feeding of the plutonite ribbon into the combustion chamber, there were moments when the mechanism would falter and then leap ahead. The resulting sudden injection of several square millimicrons of tape would send a sudden tremendous flare of energy spouting out through the rear jets. The pulse only lasted for a fraction of a second, but the sudden application of several G's meant a momentary blackout and, unless he was strapped carefully into the pilot seat, several new bruises to add to the old.

What made Ozaki the unhappiest was that there was nothing he could do about it. Pilots who wanted to stay alive just didn't tinker with the mechanism of their ships.

Glumly he pulled out another red-bordered IMMEDIATE MAINTENANCE card from the rack and began to fill it in.

Description of item requiring maintenance: "Shower thermostat, M7, Small Standard."

Nature of malfunction: "Shower will deliver only boiling water."

Justification for immediate maintenance: Slowly in large, block letters Ozaki bitterly inked in "Haven't had a bath since I left base!" and tossed the card into the already overflowing gripe box with a feeling of helpless anger.

"Kitchen mechanics," he muttered. "Couldn't do a decent repair job if they wanted to—and most of the time they don't. I'd like to see one of them three days out on a scout sweep with a toilet that won't flush!"

9 It was a roomy cell as cells go but Kurt wasn't happy there. His continual striding up and down was making Colonel Harris nervous.

"Relax, son," he said gently, "you'll just wear yourself out."

Kurt turned to face the colonel who was stretched out comfortably on his cot. "Sir," he said in a conspiratorial whisper, "we've got to break out of here."

"What for?" asked Harris. "This is the first decent rest I've had in years."

"You aren't going to let Blick get away with this?" demanded Kurt in a shocked voice.

"Why not?" said the colonel. "He's the exec, isn't he? If something happened to me, he'd have to take over command anyway. He's just going through the impatient stage, that's all. A few days behind my desk will settle him down. In two weeks he'll be so sick of the job he'll be down on his knees begging me to take over again."

Kurt decided to try a new tack. "But, sir, he's going to shut down the Tech Schools!"

"A little vacation won't hurt the kids," said the colonel indulgently.

"After a week or so the wives will get so sick of having them underfoot all day that they'll turn the heat on him. Blick has six kids himself, and I've a hunch his wife won't be any happier than the rest. She's a very determined woman, Kurt, a very determined woman!"

Kurt had a feeling he was getting no place rapidly. "Please, sir," he said earnestly, "I've got a plan."

"Yes?"

"Just before the guard makes his evening check-in, stretch out on the bed and start moaning. I'll yell that you're dying and when he comes in to check, I'll jump him!"

"You'll do no such thing!" said the colonel sternly. "Sergeant Wetzel is an old friend of mine. Can't you get it through your thick head that I don't want to escape. When you've held command as long as I have, you'll welcome a chance for a little peace and quiet. I know Blick inside out, and I'm not worried about him. But, if you've got your heart set on escaping, I suppose there's no particular reason why you shouldn't. Do it the easy way though. Like this." He walked to the bars that fronted the cell and bellowed, "Sergeant Wetzel! Sergeant Wetzel!"

"Coming, sir!" called a voice from down the corridor. There was a shuffle of running feet and a gray-scalp-locked and extremely portly sergeant puffed into view.

"What will it be, sir?" he asked.

"Colonel Blick or any of the staff around?" questioned the colonel.

"No, sir," said the sergeant. "They're all upstairs celebrating."

"Good!" said Harris. "Unlock the door, will you?"

"Anything you say, colonel," said the old man agreeably and produced a large key from his pouch and fitted it into the lock. There was a slight creaking and the door swung open.

"Young Dixon here wants to escape," said the colonel.

"It's all right by me," replied the sergeant, "though it's going to be awkward when Colonel Blick asks what happened to him."

"The lieutenant has a plan," confided the colonel. "He's going to overpower you and escape."

"There's more to it than just that!" said Kurt. "I'm figuring on swapping uniforms with you. That way I can walk right out through the front gate without anybody being the wiser."

"That," said the sergeant, slowly looking down at his sixty-three inch waist, "will take a heap of doing. You're welcome to try though."

"Let's get on with it then," said Kurt, winding up a roundhouse swing.

"If it's all the same with you, lieutenant," said the old sergeant, eyeing Kurt's rocklike fist nervously, "I'd rather have the colonel do any overpowering that's got to be done."

Colonel Harris grinned and walked over to Wetzel.

"Ready?"

"Ready!"

Harris' fist traveled a bare five inches and tapped Wetzel lightly on the chin.

"Oof!" grunted the sergeant cooperatively and staggered back to a point where he could collapse on the softest of the two cots.

The exchange of clothes was quickly effected. Except for the pants—which persisted in dropping down to Kurt's ankles—and the war bonnet—which with equal persistence kept sliding down over his ears—he was ready to go. The pants problem was solved easily by stuffing a pillow inside them. This Kurt fondly believed made him look more like the rotund sergeant than ever. The garrison bonnet presented a more difficult problem, but he finally achieved a partial solution. By holding it up with his left hand and keeping the palm tightly pressed against his forehead, it should appear to the casual observer that he was walking engrossed in deep thought.

The first two hundred yards were easy. The corridor was deserted and he plodded confidently along, the great war bonnet wabbling sedately on his head in spite of his best efforts to keep it steady. When he finally reached the exit gate, he knocked on it firmly and called to the duty sergeant.

"Open up! It's Wetzel."

Unfortunately, just then he grew careless and let go of his headgear. As the door swung open, the great war bonnet swooped down over his ears and came to rest on his shoulders. The result was that where his head normally was there could be seen only a nest of weaving feathers. The duty sergeant's jaw suddenly dropped as he got a good look at the strange figure that stood in the darkened corridor. And then with remarkable presence of mind he slammed the door shut in Kurt's face and clicked the bolt.

"Sergeant of the guard!" he bawled. "Sergeant of the guard! There's a *thing* in the corridor!"

"What kind of a thing?" inquired a sleepy voice from the guard room.

"A horrible kind of a thing with wiggling feathers where its head ought to be," replied the sergeant.

"Get its name, rank, and serial number," said the sleepy voice.

Kurt didn't wait to hear any more. Disentangling himself from the headdress with some difficulty, he hurled it aside and pelted back down the corridor.

Lieutenant Dixon wandered back into the cell with a crestfallen look on his face. Colonel Harris and the old sergeant were so deeply engrossed in a game of "rockets high" that they didn't even see him at first. Kurt coughed and the colonel looked up.

"Change your mind?"

"No, sir," said Kurt. "Something slipped."

"What?" asked the colonel.

"Sergeant Wetzel's war bonnet. I'd rather not talk about it." He sank down on his bunk and buried his head in his hands.

"Excuse me," said the sergeant apologetically, "but if the lieutenant's through with my pants I'd like to have them back. There's a draft in here."

Kurt silently exchanged clothes and then moodily walked over to the grille that barred the window and stood looking out.

"Why not go upstairs to officers' country and out that way?" suggested the sergeant, who hated the idea of being overpowered for nothing. "If you can get to the front gate without one of the staff spotting you, you can walk right out. The sentry never notices faces, he just checks for insignia."

Kurt grabbed Sergeant Wetzel's plump hand and wrung it warmly. "I don't know how to thank you," he stammered.

"Then it's about time you learned," said the colonel. "The usual practice in civilized battalions is to say 'thank you.'"

"Thank you!" said Kurt.

"Quite all right," said the sergeant. "Take the first stairway to your left. When you get to the top, turn left again and the corridor will take you straight to the exit."

Kurt got safely to the top of the stairs and turned right. Three hundred feet later the corridor ended in a blank wall. A small passageway angled off to the left and he set off down it. It also came to a dead end in a small anteroom whose farther wall was occupied by a set of great bronze doors. He turned and started to retrace his steps. He had almost reached the main corridor when he heard angry voices sounding from it. He peeked cautiously around the corridor. His escape route was blocked by two officers engaged in acrimonious argument. Neither was too sober and the captain obviously wasn't giving the major the respect that a field officer usually commanded.

"I don't care what she said!" the captain shouted. "I saw her first."

The major grabbed him by the shoulder and pushed him back against the wall. "It doesn't matter who saw her first. You keep away from her or there's going to be trouble!"

The captain's face flushed with rage. With a snarl he tore off the major's breechcloth and struck him in the face with it.

The major's face grew hard and cold. He stepped back, clicked his calloused heels together, and bowed slightly.

"Axes or fists?"

"Axes," snapped the captain.

"May I suggest the armory anteroom?" said the major formally. "We won't be disturbed there."

"As you wish, sir," said the captain with equal formality. "Your breechcloth, sir." The major donned it with dignity and they started down the hall toward Kurt. He turned and fled back down the corridor.

In a second he was back in the anteroom. Unless he did something quickly he was trapped. Two flaming torches were set in brackets on each side of the great bronze door. As flickering pools of shadow chased each other across the worn stone floor, Kurt searched desperately for some other way out. There was none. The only possible exit was through the bronze portals. The voices behind him grew louder. He ran forward, grabbed a projecting handle, and pulled. One door creaked open slightly and with a sigh of relief Kurt slipped inside.

There were no torches here. The great hall stood in half darkness, its only illumination the pale moonlight that streamed down through the arching skylight that formed the central ceiling. He stood for a moment in awe, impressed in spite of himself by the strange unfamiliar shapes that loomed before him in the half-darkness. He was suddenly brought back to reality by the sound of voices in the anteroom.

"Hey! The armory door's open!"

"So what? That place is off limits to everybody but the C.O."

"Blick won't care. Let's fight in there. There should be more room."

Kurt quickly scanned the hall for a safe hiding place. At the far end stood what looked like a great bronze statue, its burnished surface gleaming dimly in the moonlight. As the door swung open behind him, he slipped cautiously through the shadows until he reached it. It looked like a coffin with feet, but to one side of it there was a dark pool of shadow. He slipped into it and pressed himself close against the cold metal. As he did so his hipbone pressed against a slight protrusion and with a slight clicking sound, a hinged middle section of the metallic figure swung open, exposing a dark cavity. The thing was hollow!

Kurt had a sudden idea. "Even if they do come down here," he thought, "they'd never think of looking inside this thing!" With some difficulty he wiggled inside and pulled the hatch shut after him. There were legs to the thing—his own fit snugly into them—but no arms.

The two officers strode out of the shadows at the other end of the hall. They stopped in the center of the armory and faced each other like fighting cocks. Kurt gave a sigh of relief. It looked as if he were safe for the moment.

There was a sudden wicked glitter of moonlight on axheads as their weapons leaped into their hands. They stood frozen for a moment in a murderous tableau and then the captain's ax hummed toward his opponent's head in a vicious slash. There was a shower of sparks as the major parried and then with a quick wrist twist sent his own weapon looping down toward the captain's midriff. The other pulled his ax down to ward the blow, but he was only partially successful. The keen obsidian edge raked his ribs and blood dripped darkly in the moonlight.

As Kurt watched intently, he began to feel the first faint stirrings of claustrophobia. The Imperial designers had planned their battle armor for efficiency rather than comfort and Kurt felt as if he were locked away in a cramped dark closet. His malaise wasn't helped by a sudden realization that when the men left they might very well lock the door behind them. His decision to change his hiding place was hastened when a bank of dark clouds swept across the face of the moon. The flood of light that poured down through the skylight suddenly dimmed until Kurt could barely make out the pirouetting forms of the two officers who were fighting in the center of the hall.

This was his chance. If he could slip down the darkened side of the hall before the moon lighted up the hall again, he might be able to slip out of the hall unobserved. He pushed against the closed hatch through which he entered. It refused to open. A feeling of trapped panic started to roll over him, but he fought it back. "There must be some way to open this thing from the inside," he thought.

As his fingers wandered over the dark interior of the suit looking for a release lever, they encountered a bank of keys set just below his midriff. He pressed one experimentally. A quiet hum filled the armor and suddenly a feeling of weightlessness came over him. He stiffened in fright. As he did so one of his steel shod feet pushed lightly backwards against the floor. That was enough. Slowly, like a child's balloon caught in a light draft, he drifted toward the center of the hall. He struggled violently, but since he was now several inches above the floor and rising slowly it did him no good.

The fight was progressing splendidly. Both men were master axmen, and in spite of being slightly drunk, were putting on a brilliant exhibition. Each was bleeding from a dozen minor slashes, but neither had been seriously axed as yet. Their flashing strokes and counters were masterful, so masterful that Kurt slowly forgot his increasingly awkward situation as he became more and more absorbed in the fight before him.

The blond captain was slightly the better axman, but the major compensated for it by occasionally whistling in cuts that to Kurt's experienced eye seemed perilously close to fouls. He grew steadily more partisan in his feelings until one particularly unscrupulous attempt broke down his restraint altogether.

"Pull down your guard!" he screamed to the captain. "He's trying to cut you below the belt!" His voice reverberated within the battle suit and boomed out with strange metallic overtones.

Both men whirled in the direction of the sound. They could see nothing for a moment and then the major caught sight of the strange menacing figure looming above him in the murky darkness.

Dropping his ax he dashed frantically toward the exit shrieking: "It's the Inspector General!"

The captain's reflexes were a second slower. Before he could take off, Kurt poked his head out of the open faceport and shouted down, "It's only me, Dixon! Get me out of here, will you?"

The captain stared up at him goggle-eyed. "What kind of a contraption is that?" he demanded. "And what are you doing in it?"

Kurt by now was floating a good ten feet off the floor. He had visions of spending the night on the ceiling and he wasn't happy about it. "Get me down now," he pleaded. "We can talk after I get out of this thing."

The captain gave a leap upwards and tried to grab Kurt's ankles. His jump was short and his outstretched fingers gave the weightless armor a slight shove that sent it bobbing up another three feet.

He cocked his head back and called up to Kurt. "Can't reach you now. We'll have to try something else. How did you get into that thing in the first place?"

"The middle section is hinged," said Kurt. "When I pulled it shut, it clicked."

"Well, unclick it!"

"I tried that. That's why I'm up here now."

"Try again," said the man on the floor. "If you can open the hatch, you can drop down and I'll catch you."

"Here I come!" said Kurt, his fingers selecting a stud at random. He pushed. There was a terrible blast of flame from the shoulder jets and he screamed skywards on a pillar of fire. A microsecond later, he reached the skylight. Something had to give. It did!

At fifteen thousand feet the air pressure dropped to the point where the automatics took over and the face plate clicked shut. Kurt didn't notice that. He was out like a light. At thirty thousand feet the heaters cut in. Forty seconds later he was in free space. Things could have been worse though; he still had air for two hours.

10   Flight Officer Ozaki was taking a cat nap when the alarm on the radiation detector went off. Dashing the sleep out of his eyes, he slipped rapidly into the control seat and cut off the gong. His fingers danced over the controls in a blur of movement. Swiftly the vision screen shifted until the little green dot that indicated a source of radiant energy was firmly centered. Next he switched on the pulse analyzer and watched carefully as it broke down the incoming signal into components and sent them surging across the scope in the form of sharp-toothed sine waves. There was an odd peak to them, a strength and sharpness that he hadn't seen before.

"Doesn't look familiar," he muttered to himself, "but I'd better check to make sure."

He punched the comparison button and while the analyzer methodically began to check the incoming trace against the known patterns stored up in its compact little memory bank, he turned back to the vision screen. He switched on high magnification and the system rushed toward him. It expanded from a single pin point of light into a distinct planetary system. At its center a giant dying sun expanded on the plate like a malignant red eye. As he watched, the green dot moved appreciably, a thin red line stretching out behind it to indicate its course from point of first detection. Ozaki's fingers moved over the controls and a broken line of white light came into being on the screen. With careful adjustments he moved it up toward the green track left by the crawling red dot. When he had an exact overlay, he carefully moved the line back along the course that the energy emitter had followed prior to detection.

Ozaki was tense. It looked as if he might have something. He gave a sudden whoop of excitement as the broken white line intersected the orange dot of a planetary mass. A vision of the promised thirty-day leave and six months' extra pay danced before his eyes as he waited for the pulse analyzer to clear.

"Home!" he thought ecstatically. "Home and unplugged plumbing!"

With a final whir of relays the analyzer clucked like a contented chicken and dropped an identity card out of its emission slot. Ozaki grabbed it and scanned it eagerly. At the top was printed in red, "Identity. Unknown," and below in smaller letters, "Suggest check of trace pattern on base analyzer." He gave a sudden whistle as his eyes caught the energy utilization index. 927! That was fifty points higher than it had any right to be. The best tech in the Protectorate considered himself lucky if he could tune a propulsion unit so that it delivered a thrust of forty-five per cent of rated maximum. Whatever was out there was hot! Too hot for one man to handle alone. With quick decision he punched the transmission key of his space communicator and sent a call winging back to War Base Three.

11

Commander Krogson stormed up and down his office in a frenzy of impatience.

"It shouldn't be more than another fifteen minutes, sir," said Schninkle.

Krogson snorted. "That's what you said an hour ago! What's the matter with those people down there? I want the identity of that ship and I want it now."

"It's not Identification's fault," explained the other. "The big analyzer is in pretty bad shape and it keeps jamming. They're afraid that if they take it apart they won't be able to get it back together again."

The next two hours saw Krogson's blood pressure steadily rising toward the explosion point. Twice he ordered the whole identification section transferred to a labor battalion and twice he had to rescind the command when Schninkle pointed out that scrapings from the bottom of the barrel were better than nothing at all. His fingernails were chewed down to the quick when word finally came through.

"Identification, sir," said a hesitant voice on the intercom.

"Well?" demanded the commander.

"The analyzer says—" The voice hesitated again.

"The analyzer says what?" shouted Krogson in a fury of impatience.

"The analyzer says that the trace pattern is that of one of the old Imperial drive units."

"That's impossible!" sputtered the commander. "The last Imperial base was smashed five hundred years ago. What of their equipment was salvaged has long since been worn out and tossed on the scrap heap. The machine must be wrong!"

"Not this time," said the voice. "We checked the memory bank manually and there's no mistake. It's an Imperial all right. Nobody can produce a drive unit like that these days."

Commander Krogson leaned back in his chair, his eyes veiled in deep thought. "Schninkle," he said finally, thinking out loud, "I've got a hunch that maybe we've stumbled on something big. Maybe the Lord Protector is right about there being a plot to knock him over, but maybe he's wrong about who's trying to do it. What if all these centuries since the Empire collapsed a group of Imperials have been hiding out waiting for their chance?"

Schninkle digested the idea for a moment. "It could be," he said slowly. "If there is such a group, they couldn't pick a better time than now to strike; the Protectorate is so wobbly that it wouldn't take much of a shove to topple it over."

The more he thought about it, the more sense the idea made to Krogson. Once he felt a fleeting temptation to hush up the whole thing. If there were Imperials and they did take over, maybe they would put an end to the frenzied rat race that was slowly ruining the galaxy—a race that sooner or later entangled every competent man in the great web of intrigue and power politics that stretched through the Protectorate and forced him in self-defense to keep clawing his way toward the top of the heap.

Regretfully he dismissed the idea. This was a matter of his own neck, here and now!

"It's a big IF, Schninkle," he said, "but if I've guessed right, we've bailed ourselves out. Get hold of that scout and find out his position."

Schninkle scooted out of the door. A few minutes later he dashed back in. "I've just contacted the scout!" he said excitedly. "He's closed in on the power source and it isn't a ship after all. It's a man in space armor! The drive unit is cut off, and it's heading out of the system at fifteen hundred per. The pilot is standing by for instructions."

"Tell him to intercept and capture!" Schninkle started out of the office. "Wait a second; what's the scout's position?"

Schninkle's face fell. "He doesn't quite know, sir."

"He *what?*" demanded the commander.

"He doesn't quite know," repeated the little man. "His astrocomputer went haywire six hours out of base."

"Just our luck!" swore Krogson. "Well, tell him to leave his transmitter on. We'll ride in on his beam. Better call the sector commander while you're at it and tell him what's happened."

"Beg pardon, commander," said Schninkle, "but I wouldn't advise it."

"Why not?" asked Krogson.

"You're next in line to be sector commander, aren't you, sir?"

"I guess so," said the commander.

"If this pans out, you'll be in a position to knock him over and grab his job, won't you?" asked Schninkle slyly.

"Could be," admitted Krogson in a tired voice. "Not because I want to, though—but because I have to. I'm not as young as I once was, and the boys below are pushing pretty hard. It's either up or out—and out is always feet first."

"Put yourself in the sector commander's shoes for a minute," suggested the little man. "What would you do if a war base commander came through with news of a possible Imperial base?"

A look of grim comprehension came over Krogson's face. "Of course! I'd ground the commander's ships and send out my own fleet. I must be slipping; I should have thought of that at once!"

"On the other hand," said Schninkle, "you might call him and request permission to conduct routine maneuvers. He'll approve as a matter of course and you'll have an excuse for taking out the full fleet. Once in deep space, you can slap on radio silence and set course for the scout. If there is an Imperial base out there, nobody will know anything about it until it's blasted. I'll stay back here and keep my eyes on things for you."

Commander Krogson grinned. "Schninkle, it's a pleasure to have you in my command. How would you like me to make you Devoted Servant of the Lord Protector, Eighth Class? It carries an extra shoe ration coupon!"

"If it's all the same with you," said Schninkle, "I'd just as soon have Saturday afternoons off."

12

As Kurt struggled up out of the darkness, he could hear a gong sounding in the faint distance. *Bong!* BONG! *BONG!* It grew nearer and louder. He shook his head painfully and groaned. There was light from some place beating against his eyelids. Opening them was too much effort. He was in some sort of a bunk. He could feel that. But the gong. He lay there concentrating on it. Slowly he began to realize that the beat didn't come from outside. It was his head. It felt swollen and sore and each pulse of his heart sent a hammer thud through it.

One by one his senses began to return to normal. As his nose reassumed its normal acuteness, it began to quiver. There was a strange scent in the air, an unpleasant sickening scent as of—he chased the scent down his aching memory channels until he finally had it cornered —rotting fish. With that to anchor on, he slowly began to reconstruct reality. He had been floating high above the floor in the armory and the captain had been trying to get him down. Then he had pushed a button. There had been a microsecond of tremendous acceleration and then a horrendous crash. That must have been the skylight. After the crash was darkness, then the gongs, and now fish—dead and rotting fish.

"I must be alive," he decided. "Imperial Headquarters would never smell like this!"

He groaned and slowly opened one eye. Wherever he was he hadn't been there before. He opened the other eye. He was in a room. A room with a curved ceiling and curving walls. Slowly, with infinite care, he hung his head over the side of the bunk. Below him in a form-fitting chair before a bank of instruments sat a small man with yellow skin and blue-black hair. Kurt coughed. The man looked up. Kurt asked the obvious question.

"Where am I?"

"I'm not permitted to give you any information," said the small man. His speech had an odd slurred quality to Kurt's ear.

"Something stinks!" said Kurt.

"It sure does," said the small man gloomily. "It must be worse for you. I'm used to it."

Kurt surveyed the cabin with interest. There were a lot of gadgets tucked away here and there that looked familiar. They were like the things he had worked on in Tech School except that they were cruder and simpler. They looked as if they had been put together by an eight-year-old recruit who was doing the first trial assembly. He decided to make another stab at establishing some sort of communication with the little man.

"How come you have everything in one room? We always used to keep different things in different shops."

"No comment," said Ozaki.

Kurt had a feeling he was butting his head against a stone wall. He decided to make one more try.

"I give up," he said, wrinkling his nose, "where'd you hide it?"

"Hide what?" asked the little man.

"The fish," said Kurt.

"No comment."

"Why not?" asked Kurt.

"Because there isn't anything that can be done about it," said Ozaki. "It's the air conditioner. Something's haywire inside."

"What's an air conditioner?" asked Kurt.

"That square box over your head."

Kurt looked at it, closed his eyes, and thought for a moment. The thing did look familiar. Suddenly a picture of it popped into his mind. Page 318 in the "Manual of Auxiliary Mechanisms."

"It's fantastic!" he said.

"What is?" said the little man.

"This," Kurt pointed to the conditioner. "I didn't know they existed in real life. I thought they were just in books. You got a first echelon kit?"

"Sure," said Ozaki. "It's in the recess by the head of the bunk. Why?"

Kurt pulled the kit out of its retaining clips and opened its cover, fishing around until he found a small screwdriver and a pair of needle-nose pliers.

"I think I'll fix it," he said conversationally.

"Oh, no you won't!" howled Ozaki. "Air with fish is better than no air at all." But before he could do anything, Kurt had pulled the cover off the air conditioner and was probing into the intricate mechanism with his screwdriver. A slight thumping noise came from inside. Kurt cocked his ear and thought. Suddenly his screwdriver speared down through the maze of whirring parts. He gave a slow quarter turn and the internal thumping disappeared.

"See," he said triumphantly, "no more fish!"

Ozaki stopped shaking long enough to give the air a tentative sniff. He had got out of the habit of smelling in self-defense and it took him a minute or two to detect the difference. Suddenly a broad grin swept across his face.

"It's going away! I do believe it's going away!"

Kurt gave the screwdriver another quarter of a turn and suddenly the sharp spicy scent of pines swept through the scout. Ozaki took a deep ecstatic breath and relaxed in his chair. His face lost its pallor.

"How did you do it?" he said finally.

"No comment," said Kurt pleasantly.

There was silence from below. Ozaki was in the throes of a brain storm. He was more impressed by Kurt's casual repair of the air conditioner than he liked to admit.

"Tell me," he said cautiously, "can you fix other things beside air conditioners?"

"I guess so," said Kurt, "if it's just simple stuff like this." He gestured around the cabin. "Most of the stuff here needs fixing. They've got it together wrong."

"Maybe we could make a dicker," said Ozaki. "You fix things, I answer questions—Some questions that is," he added hastily.

"It's a deal," said Kurt who was filled with a burning curiosity as to his whereabouts. Certain things were already clear in his mind. He knew that wherever he was he'd never been there before. That meant evidently that there was a garrison on the other side of the mountains whose existence had never been suspected. What bothered him was how he had got there.

"Check," said Ozaki. "First, do you know anything about plumbing?"

"What's plumbing?" asked Kurt curiously.

"Pipes," said Ozaki. "They're plugged. They've been plugged for more time than I like to think about."

"I can try," said Kurt.

"Good!" said the pilot and ushered him into the small cubicle that opened off the rear bulkhead. "You might tackle the shower while you're at it."

"What's a shower?"

"That curved dingbat up there," said Ozaki pointing. "The thermostat's out of whack."

"Thermostats are kid stuff," said Kurt, shutting the door.

Ten minutes later Kurt came out. "It's all fixed."

"I don't believe it," said Ozaki, shouldering his way past Kurt. He reached down and pushed a small curved handle. There was the satisfying sound of rushing water. He next reached into the little shower compartment and turned the knob to the left. With a hiss a needle spray of cold water burst forth. The pilot looked at Kurt with awe in his eyes.

"If I hadn't seen it, I wouldn't have believed it! That's two answers you've earned."

Kurt peered back into the cubicle curiously. "Well, first," he said, "now that I've fixed them, what are they *for?*"

Ozaki explained briefly and a look of amazement came over Kurt's face. Machinery he knew, but the idea that it could be used for something was hard to grasp.

"If I hadn't seen it, I wouldn't have believed it!" he said slowly. This would be something to tell when he got home. Home! The pressing question of location popped back into his mind.

"How far are we from the garrison?" he asked.

Ozaki made a quick mental calculation.

"Roughly two light-seconds," he said.

"How far's that in kilometers?"

Ozaki thought again. "Around six hundred thousand. I'll run off the exact figures if you want them."

Kurt gulped. No place could be that far away. Not even Imperial Headquarters! He tried to measure out the distance in his mind in terms of days' marches, but he soon found himself lost. Thinking wouldn't do it. He had to see with his own eyes where he was.

"How do you get outside?" he asked.

Ozaki gestured toward the air lock that opened at the rear of the compartment. "Why?"

"I want to go out for a few minutes to sort of get my bearings."

Ozaki looked at him in disbelief. "What's your game, anyhow?" he demanded.

It was Kurt's turn to look bewildered. "I haven't any game. I'm just trying to find out where I am so I'll know which way to head to get back to the garrison."

"It'll be a long, cold walk." Ozaki laughed and hit the stud that slid back the ray screens on the vision ports. "Take a look."

Kurt looked out into nothingness, a blue-black void marked only by distant pin points of light. He suddenly felt terribly alone, lost in a blank immensity that had no boundaries. *Down* was gone and so was *up*. There was only this tiny lighted room with nothing underneath it. The port began to swim in front of his eyes as a sudden, strange vertigo swept over him. He felt that if he looked out into that terrible space for another moment he would lose his sanity. He covered his eyes with his hands and staggered back to the center of the cabin.

Ozaki slid the ray screens back in place. "Kind of gets you first time, doesn't it?"

Kurt had always carried a little automatic compass within his head. Wherever he had gone, no matter how far afield he had wandered, it had always pointed steadily toward home. Now for the first time in his life the needle was spinning helplessly. It was an uneasy feeling. He had to get oriented.

"Which way is the garrison?" he pleaded.

Ozaki shrugged. "Over there some place. I don't know whereabouts on the planet you come from. I didn't pick up your track until you were in free space."

"Over where?" asked Kurt.

"Think you can stand another look?"

Kurt braced himself and nodded. The pilot opened a side port to vision and pointed. There, seemingly motionless in the black emptiness of space, floated a great greenish-gray globe. It didn't make sense to Kurt. The satellite that hung somewhat to the left did. Its face was different, the details were sharper than he'd ever seen them before, but the features he knew as well as his own. Night after night on scouting detail for the hunting parties while waiting for sleep he had watched the silver sphere ride through the clouds above him.

He didn't want to believe but he had to!

His face was white and tense as he turned back to Ozaki. A thousand sharp and burning questions milled chaotically through his mind.

"Where am I?" he demanded. "How did I get out here? Who are you? Where did you come from?"

"You're in a spaceship," said Ozaki, "a two-man scout. And that's all you're going to get out of me until you get some more work done. You might as well start on this microscopic projector. The thing burned out just as the special investigator was about to reveal who had blown off the commissioner's head by wiring a bit of plutonite into his autoshave. I've been going nuts ever since trying to figure out who did it!"

Kurt took some tools out of the first echelon kit and knelt obediently down beside the small projector.

Three hours later they sat down to dinner. Kurt had repaired the food machine and Ozaki was slowly masticating synthasteak that for the first time in days tasted like synthasteak. As he ecstatically lifted the last savory morsel to his mouth, the ship gave a sudden leap that plastered him and what remained of his supper against the rear bulkhead. There was darkness for a second and then the ceiling lights flickered on, then off, and then on again. Ozaki picked himself up and gingerly ran his fingers over the throbbing lump that was beginning to grow out of the top of his head. His temper wasn't improved when he looked up and saw Kurt still seated at the table calmly cutting himself another piece of pie.

"You should have braced yourself," said Kurt conversationally. "The converter's out of phase. You can hear her build up for a jump if you listen. When she does you ought to brace yourself. Maybe you don't hear so good?" he asked helpfully.

"Don't talk with your mouth full, it isn't polite," snarled Ozaki.

Late that night the converter cut out altogether. Ozaki was sleeping the sleep of the innocent and didn't find out about it for several hours. When he did awake, it was to Kurt's gentle shaking.

"Hey!" Ozaki groaned and buried his face in the pillow.

"Hey!" This time the voice was louder. The pilot yawned and tried to open his eyes.

"Is it important if all the lights go out?" the voice queried. The import of the words suddenly struck home and Ozaki sat bolt upright in his bunk. He opened his eyes, blinked, and opened them again. The lights *were* out. There was a strange unnatural silence about the ship.

"Good Lord!" he shouted and jumped for the controls. "The power's off."

He hit the starter switch but nothing happened. The converter was jammed solid. Ozaki began to sweat. He fumbled over the control board until he found the switch that cut the emergency batteries into the lighting circuit. Again nothing happened.

"If you're trying to run the lights on the batteries, they won't work," said Kurt in a conversational tone.

"Why not?" snapped Ozaki as he punched savagely and futilely at the starter button.

"They're dead," said Kurt. "I used them all up."

"You what?" yelled the pilot in anguish.

"I used them all up. You see, when the converter went out, I woke up. After a while the sun started to come up, and it began to get awfully hot so I hooked the batteries into the refrigeration coils. Kept the place nice and cool while they lasted."

Ozaki howled. When he swung the shutter of the forward port to let in some light, he howled again. This time in dead earnest. The giant red sun of the system was no longer perched off to the left at a comfortable distance. Instead before Ozaki's horrified eyes was a great red mass that stretched from horizon to horizon.

"We're falling into the sun!" he screamed.

"It's getting sort of hot," said Kurt. "Hot" was an understatement. The thermometer needle pointed at a hundred and ten and was climbing steadily.

Ozaki jerked open the stores compartment door and grabbed a couple of spare batteries. As quickly as his trembling fingers would work, he connected them to the emergency power line. A second later the cabin lights flickered on and Ozaki was warming up the space communicator. He punched the transmitter key and a call went arcing out through hyperspace. The vision screen flickered and the bored face of a communication tech, third class, appeared.

"Give me Commander Krogson at once!" demanded Ozaki.

"Sorry, old man," yawned the other, "but the commander's having breakfast. Call back in half an hour, will you?"

"This is an emergency! Put me through at once!"

"Can't help it," said the other, "nobody can disturb the Old Man while he's having breakfast!"

"Listen, you knucklehead," screamed Ozaki, "if you don't get me through to the commander as of right now, I'll have you in the uranium mines so fast that you won't know what hit you!"

"You and who else?" drawled the tech.

"Me and my cousin Takahashi!" snarled the pilot. "He's Reclassification Officer for the Base STAP."

The tech's face went white. "Yes, sir!" he shuttered. "Right away, sir! No offense meant, sir!" He disappeared from the screen. There was a moment of darkness and then the interior of Commander Krogson's cabin flashed on.

The commander was having breakfast. His teeth rested on the white tablecloth and his mouth was full of mush.

"Commander Krogson!" said Ozaki desperately.

The commander looked up with a startled expression. When he noticed his screen was on, he swallowed his mush convulsively and popped his teeth back into place.

"Who's there?" he demanded in a neutral voice in case it might be somebody important.

"Flight Officer Ozaki," said Flight Officer Ozaki.

A thundercloud rolled across the commander's face. "What do you mean by disturbing me at breakfast?" he demanded.

"Beg pardon, sir," said the pilot, "but my ship's falling into a red sun."

"Too bad," grunted Commander Krogson and turned back to his mush and milk.

"But, sir," persisted the other, "you've got to send somebody to pull me off. My converter's dead!"

"Why tell me about it?" said Krogson in annoyance. "Call Space Rescue, they're supposed to handle things like this."

"Listen, Commander," wailed the pilot, "by the time they've assigned me a priority and routed the paper through proper channels, I'll have gone up in smoke. The last time I got in a jam it took them two weeks to get to me; I've only got hours left!"

"Can't make exceptions," snapped Krogson testily. "If I let you skip the chain of command, everybody and his brother will think he has a right to."

"Commander," howled Ozaki, "we're frying in here!"

"All right. All right!" said the commander sourly. "I'll send somebody after you. What's your name?"

"Ozaki, sir. Flight Officer Ozaki."

The commander was in the process of scooping up another spoonful of mush when suddenly a thought struck him squarely between the eyes.

"Wait a second," he said hastily, "you aren't the scout who located the Imperial base, are you?"

"Yes, sir," said the pilot in a cracked voice.

"Why didn't you say so?" roared Krogson. Flipping on his intercom he growled, "Give me the Exec." There was a moment's silence.

"Yes, sir?"

"How long before we get to that scout?"

"About six hours, sir."

"Make it three!"

"Can't be done, sir."

"It will be done!" snarled Krogson and broke the connection.

The temperature needle in the little scout was now pointing to a hundred and fifteen.

"I don't think we can hold out that long," said Ozaki.

"Nonsense!" said the commander and the screen went blank.

Ozaki slumped into the pilot chair and buried his face in his hands. Suddenly he felt a blast of cold air on his neck. "There's no use in prolonging our misery," he said without looking up. "Those spare batteries won't last five minutes under this load."

"I knew that," said Kurt cheerfully, "so while you were doing all the talking, I went ahead and fixed the converter. You sure have mighty hot summers out here!" he continued, mopping his brow.

"You what?" yelled the pilot, jumping half out of his seat. "You couldn't even if you did have the know-how. It takes half a day to get the shielding off so you can get at the thing!"

"Didn't need to take the shielding off for a simple job like that," said Kurt. He pointed to a tiny inspection port about four inches in diameter. "I worked through there."

"That's impossible!" interjected the pilot. "You can't even see the injector through that, let alone get to it to work on!"

"Shucks," said Kurt, "a man doesn't have to see a little gadget like that to fix it. If your hands are trained right, you can feel what's wrong and set it to rights right away. She won't jump on you anymore either. The syncromesh thrust baffle was a little out of phase so I fixed that, too, while I was at it."

Ozaki still didn't believe it, but he hit the controls on faith. The scout bucked under the sudden strong surge of power and then, its converter humming sweetly, arched away from the giant sun in a long sweeping curve.

There was silence in the scout. The two men sat quietly, each immersed in an uneasy welter of troubled speculation.

"That was close!" said Ozaki finally. "Too close for comfort. Another hour or so and—!" He snapped his fingers.

Kurt looked puzzled. "Were we in trouble?"

"Trouble!" snorted Ozaki. "If you hadn't fixed the converter when you did, we'd be cinders by now!"

Kurt digested the news in silence. There was something about this superbeing who actually made machines work that bothered him. There was a note of bewilderment in his voice when he asked: "If we were really in danger, why didn't you fix the converter instead of wasting time talking on that thing?" He gestured toward the space communicator.

It was Ozaki's turn to be bewildered. "Fix it?" he said with surprise in his voice. "There aren't a half a dozen techs on the whole base who know enough about atomics to work on a propulsion unit. When something like that goes out, you call Space Rescue and chew your nails until a wrecker can get to you."

Kurt crawled into his bunk and lay back staring at the curved ceiling. He had thinking to do, a lot of thinking!

Three hours later, the scout flashed up alongside the great flagship and darted into a landing port. Flight Officer Ozaki was stricken by a horrible thought as he gazed affectionately around his smoothly running ship.

"Say," he said to Kurt hesitantly, "would you mind not mentioning that you fixed this crate up for me? If you do, they'll take it away from me sure. Some captain will get a new gig, and I'll be issued another clunk from Base Junkpile."

"Sure thing," said Kurt.

A moment later the flashing of a green light on the control panel signaled that the pressure in the lock had reached normal.

"Back in a minute," said Ozaki. "You wait here."

There was a muted hum as the exit hatch swung slowly open. Two guards entered and stood silently beside Kurt as Ozaki left to report to Commander Krogson.

13

The Battle fleet of War Base Three of Sector Seven of the Galactic Protectorate hung motionless in space twenty thousand kilometers out from Kurt's home planet. A hundred tired detection techs sat tensely before their screens, sweeping the globe for some sign of energy radiation. Aside from the occasional light spatters caused by space static, their scopes remained dark. As their reports filtered into Commander Krogson he became more and more exasperated.

"Are you positive this is the right planet?" he demanded of Ozaki.

"No question about it, sir."

"Seems funny there's nothing running down there at all," said Krogson. "Maybe they spotted us on the way in and cut off power. I've got a hunch that—" He broke off in mid sentence as the red top-priority light on the communication panel began to flash. "Get that," he said. "Maybe they've spotted something at last."

The executive officer flipped on the vision screen and the interior of the flagship's communication room was revealed.

"Sorry to bother you, sir," said the tech whose image appeared on the screen, "but a message just came through on the emergency band."

"What does it say?"

The tech looked unhappy. "It's coded, sir."

"Well, decode it!" barked the executive.

"We can't," said the technician diffidently. "Something's gone wrong with the decoder. The printer is pounding out random groups that don't make any sense at all."

The executive grunted his disgust. "Any idea where the call's coming from?"

"Yes, sir; it's coming in on a tight beam from the direction of Base. Must be from a ship emergency rig, though. Regular hyperspace transmission isn't directional. Either the ship's regular rig broke down or the operator is using the beam to keep anybody else from picking up his signal."

"Get to work on that decoder. Call back as soon as you get any results." The tech saluted and the screen went black.

"Whatever it is, it's probably trouble," said Krogson morosely. "Well, we'd better get on with this job. Take the fleet into atmosphere. It looks as if we are going to have to make a visual check."

"Maybe the prisoner can give us a lead," suggested the executive officer.

"Good idea. Have him brought in."

A moment later Kurt was ushered into the master control room. Krogson's eyes widened at the sight of his scalp lock and paint.

"Where in the name of the Galactic Spirit," he demanded, "did you get that rig?"

"Don't you recognize an Imperial Space Marine when you see one?" Kurt answered coldly.

The guard that had escorted Kurt in made a little twirling motion at his temple with one finger. Krogson took another look and nodded agreement.

"Sit down, son," he said in a fatherly tone. "We're trying to get you home, but you're going to have to give us a little help before we can do it. You see, we're not quite sure just where your base is."

"I'll help all I can," said Kurt.

"Fine!" said the commander, rubbing his palms together. "Now just where down there do you come from?" He pointed out the vision port to the curving globe that stretched out below.

Kurt looked down helplessly. "Nothing makes sense, seeing it from up here," he said apologetically.

Krogson thought for a moment. "What's the country like around your base?" he asked.

"Mostly jungle," said Kurt. "The garrison is on a plateau though and there are mountains to the north."

Krogson turned quickly to his exec. "Did you get that description?"

"Yes, sir!"

"Get all scouts out for a close sweep. As soon as the base is spotted, move the fleet in and hover at forty thousand!"

Forty minutes later a scout came streaking back.

"Found it, sir!" said the exec. "Plateau with jungle all around and mountains to the north. There's a settlement at one end. The pilot saw movement down there, but they must have spotted us on our way in. There's still no evidence of energy radiation. They must have everything shut down."

"That's not good!" said Krogson. "They've probably got all their heavy stuff set up waiting for us to sweep over. We'll have to hit them hard and fast. Did they spot the scout?"

"Can't tell, sir."

"We'd better assume that they did. Notify all gunnery officers to switch their batteries over to central control. If we come in fast and high and hit them with simultaneous fleet concentration, we can vaporize the whole base before they can take a crack at us."

"I'll send the order out at once, sir," said the executive officer.

The fleet pulled into tight formation and headed toward the Imperial base. They were halfway there when the fleet gunnery officer entered the control room and said apologetically to Commander Krogson, "Excuse me, sir, but I'd like to suggest a trial run. Fleet concentration is a tricky thing, and if something went haywire—we'd be sitting ducks for the ground batteries."

"Good idea," said Krogson thoughtfully. "There's too much at stake to have anything go wrong. Select an equivalent target, and we'll make a pass."

The fleet was now passing over a towering mountain chain.

"How about that bald spot down there?" said the Exec, pointing to a rocky expanse that jutted out from the side of one of the towering peaks.

"Good enough," said Krogson.

"All ships on central control!" reported the gunnery officer.

"On target!" repeated the tech on the tracking screen. "One. Two. Three. Four—"

Kurt stood by the front observation port watching the ground far below sweep by. He had been listening intently, but what had been said didn't make sense. There had been something about *batteries*—the term was alien to him—and something about the garrison. He decided to ask the commander what it was all about, but the intentness with which Krogson was watching the tracking screen deterred him. Instead he gazed moodily down at the mountains below him.

"Five. Six. Seven. Ready. FIRE!"

A savage shudder ran through the great ship as her ground-pointed batteries blasted in unison. Seconds went by and then suddenly the rocky expanse on the shoulder of the mountain directly below twinkled as blinding flashes of actinic light danced across it. Then as Kurt watched, great masses of rock and earth moved slowly skyward from the center of the spurting nests of tangled flame. Still slowly, as if buoyed up by the thin mountain air, the debris began to fall back again until it was lost from sight in quick rising mushrooms of jet-black smoke. Kurt turned and looked back toward Commander Krogson. *Batteries* must be the things that had torn the mountains below apart. And *garrison*—there was only one garrison!

"I ordered fleet fire," barked Krogson. "This ship was the only one that cut loose. What happened?"

"Just a second, sir," said the executive officer, "I'll try and find out." He was busy for a minute on the intercom system. "The other ships were ready, sir," he reported finally. "Their guns were all switched over to our control, but no impulse came through. Central fire control must be on the blink!" He gestured toward a complex bank of equipment that occupied one entire corner of the control room.

Commander Krogson said a few appropriate words. When he reached the point where he was beginning to repeat himself, he paused and stood in frozen silence for a good thirty seconds.

"Would you mind getting a fire control tech in here to fix that obscenity bank?" he asked in a voice that put everyone's teeth on edge.

The other seemed to have something to say, but he was having trouble getting it out.

"Well?" said Krogson.

"Prime Base grabbed our last one two weeks ago. There isn't another left with the fleet."

"Doesn't look like much to me," said Kurt as he strolled over to examine the bank of equipment.

"Get away from there!" roared the commander. "We've got enough trouble without you making things worse."

Kurt ignored him and began to open inspection ports.

"Guard!" yelled Krogson. "Throw that man out of here!"

Ozaki interrupted timidly. "Beg pardon, Commander, but he can fix it if anybody can."

Krogson whirled on the flight officer. "How do you know?"

Ozaki caught himself just in time. If he talked too much, he was likely to lose the scout that Kurt had fixed for him.

"Because he . . . eh . . . talks like a tech," he concluded lamely.

Krogson looked at Kurt dubiously. "I guess there's no harm in giving it a trial," he said finally. "Give him a set of tools and turn him loose. Maybe for once a miracle will happen."

"First," said Kurt, "I'll need the wiring diagrams for this thing."

"Get them!" barked the commander and an orderly scuttled out of the control, headed aft.

"Next you'll have to give me a general idea of what it's supposed to do," continued Kurt.

Krogson turned to the gunnery officer. "You'd better handle this."

When the orderly returned with the circuit diagrams, they were spread out on the plotting table and the two men bent over them.

"Got it!" said Kurt at last and sauntered over to the control bank. Twenty minutes later he sauntered back again.

"She's all right now," he said pleasantly.

The gunnery officer quickly scanned his testing board. Not a single red trouble light was on. He turned to Commander Krogson in amazement.

"I don't know how he did it, sir, but the circuits are all clear now."

Krogson stared at Kurt with a look of new respect in his eyes. "What were you down there, chief maintenance tech?"

Kurt laughed. "Me? I was never chief anything. I spent most of my time on hunting detail."

The commander digested that in silence for a moment. "Then how did you become so familiar with fire-control gear?"

"Studied it in school like everyone else does. There wasn't anything much wrong with that thing anyway except a couple of sticking relays."

"Excuse me, sir," interrupted the executive officer, "but should we make another trial run?"

"Are you sure the bank is in working order?"

"Positive, sir!"

"Then we'd better make straight for that base. If this boy here is a fair example of what they have down there, their defenses may be too tough for us to crack if we give them a chance to get set up!"

Kurt gave a slight start which he quickly controlled. Then he had guessed right! Slowly and casually he began to sidle toward the semicircular bank of controls that stood before the great tracking screen.

"Where do you think you're going!" barked Krogson.

Kurt froze. His pulses were pounding within him, but he kept his voice light and casual.

"No place," he said innocently.

"Get over against the bulkhead and keep out of the way!" snapped the commander. "We've got a job of work coming up."

Kurt injected a note of bewilderment into his voice.

"What kind of work?"

Krogson's voice softened and a look approaching pity came into his eyes. "It's just as well you don't know about it until it's over," he said gruffly.

"There she is!" sang out the navigator, pointing to a tiny brown projection that jutted up out of the green jungle in the far distance. "We're about three minutes out, sir. You can take over at any time now."

The fleet gunnery officer's fingers moved quickly over the keys that welded the fleet into a single instrument of destruction, keyed and ready to blast a barrage of ravening thunderbolts of molecular disruption down at the defenseless garrison at a single touch on the master fire-control button.

"Whenever you're ready, sir," he said deferentially to Krogson as he vacated the controls. A hush fell over the control room as the great tracking screen brightened and showed the compact bundle of white dots that marked the fleet crawling slowly toward the green triangle of the target area.

"Get the prisoner out of here," said Krogson. "There's no reason why he should have to watch what's about to happen."

The guard that stood beside Kurt grabbed his arm and shoved him toward the door.

There was a sudden explosion of fists as Kurt erupted into action. In a blur of continuous movement, he streaked toward the gunnery control panel. He was halfway across the control room before the poleaxed guard hit the floor. There was a second of stunned amazement, and then before anyone could move to stop him, he stood beside the controls, one hand poised tensely above the master stud that controlled the combined fire of the fleet.

"Hold it!" he shouted as the moment of paralysis broke and several of the officers started toward him menacingly. "One move, and I'll blast the whole fleet into scrap!"

They stopped in shocked silence, looking to Commander Krogson for guidance.

"Almost on target, sir," called the tech on the tracking screen.

Krogson stalked menacingly toward Kurt. "Get away from those controls!" he snarled. "You aren't going to blow anything to anything. All that you can do is let off a premature blast. If you are trying to alert your base, it's no use. We can be on a return sweep before they have time to get ready for us."

Kurt shook his head calmly. "Wouldn't do you any good," he said. "Take a look at the gun ports on the other ships. I made a couple of minor changes while I was working on the control bank."

"Quit bluffing," said Krogson.

"I'm not bluffing," said Kurt quietly. "Take a look. It won't cost you anything."

"On target!" called the tracking tech.

"Order the fleet to circle for another sweep," snapped Krogson over his shoulder as he stalked toward the forward observation port. There was something in Kurt's tone that had impressed him more than he liked to admit. He squinted out toward the nearest ship. Suddenly his face blanched!

"The gunports! They're still closed!"

Kurt gave a whistle of relief. "I had my fingers crossed," he said pleasantly. "You didn't give me enough time with the wiring diagrams for me to be sure that cutting out that circuit would do the trick. Now ... guess what the results would be if I should happen to push down on this stud."

Krogson had a momentary vision of several hundred shells ramming their sensitive noses against the thick chrome steel of the closed gun ports.

"Don't bother trying to talk," said Kurt, noticing the violent contractions of the commander's Adam's apple. "You'd better save your breath for my colonel."

"Who?" demanded Krogson.

"My colonel," repeated Kurt. "We'd better head back and pick him up. Can you make these ships hang in one place or do they have to keep moving fast to stay up?"

The commander clamped his jaws together sullenly and said nothing.

Kurt made a tentative move toward the firing stud.

"Easy!" yelled the gunnery officer in alarm. "That thing has hair-trigger action!"

"Well?" said Kurt to Krogson.

"We can hover," grunted the other.

"Then take up a position a little to one side of the plateau." Kurt brushed the surface of the firing stud with a casual finger. "If you make me push this, I don't want a lot of scrap iron falling down on the battalion. Somebody might get hurt."

As the fleet came to rest above the plateau, the call light on the communication panel began to flash again.

"Answer it," ordered Kurt, "but watch what you say."

Krogson walked over and snapped on the screen.

"Communications, sir."

"Well?"

"It's that message we called you about earlier. We've finally got the decoder working—sort of, that is." His voice faltered and then stopped.

"What does it say?" demanded Krogson impatiently.

"We still don't know," admitted the tech miserably. "It's being decoded all right, but it's coming out in a North Vegan dialect that nobody down here can understand. I guess there's still something wrong with the selector. All that we can figure out is that the message has something to do with General Carr and the Lord Protector."

"Want me to go down and fix it?" interrupted Kurt in an innocent voice.

Krogson whirled toward him, his hamlike hands clinching and unclinching in impotent rage.

"Anything wrong, sir?" asked the technician on the screen.

Kurt raised a significant eyebrow to the commander.

"Of course not," growled Krogson. "Go find somebody to translate that message and don't bother me until it's done."

A new face appeared on the screen.

"Excuse me for interrupting, sir, but translation won't be necessary. We just got a flash from Detection that they've spotted the ship that sent it. It's a small scout heading in on emergency drive. She should be here in a matter of minutes."

Krogson flipped off the screen impatiently. "Whatever it is, it's sure to be more trouble," he said to nobody in particular. Suddenly he became aware that the fleet was no longer in motion. "Well," he said sourly to Kurt, "we're here. What now?"

"Send a ship down to the garrison and bring Colonel Harris back up here so that you and he can work this thing out between you. Tell him that Dixon is up here and has everything under control."

Krogson turned to the executive officer. "All right," he said, "do what he says." The other saluted and started toward the door.

"Just a second," said Kurt. "If you have any idea of telling the boys outside to cut the transmission leads from fire control, I wouldn't advise it. It's a rather lengthy process, and the minute a trouble light blinks on that board, up we go! Now on your way!"

14   Lieutenant Colonel Blick, acting commander of the 427th Light Maintenance Battalion of the Imperial Space Marines, stood at his office window and scowled down upon the whole civilized world, all twenty-six square kilometers of it. It had been a hard day. Three separate delegations of mothers had descended upon him demanding that he reopen the Tech Schools for the sake of their sanity. The recruits had been roaming the company streets in bands composed of equal numbers of small boys and large dogs creating havoc wherever they went. He tried to cheer himself up by thinking of his forthcoming triumph when he in the guise of the Inspector General would float magnificently down from the skies and once and for all put the seal of final authority upon the new order. The only trouble was that he was beginning to have a sneaking suspicion that maybe that new order wasn't all that he had planned it to be. As he thought of his own six banshees screaming through quarters, his suspicion deepened almost to certainty.

He wandered back to his desk and slumped behind it gloomily. He couldn't backwater now, his pride was at stake. He glanced at the water clock on his desk, and then rose reluctantly and started toward the door. It was time to get into battle armor and get ready for the inspection.

As he reached the door, there was a sudden slap of running sandals down the hall. A second later, Major Kane burst into the office, his face white and terrified.

"Colonel," he gasped, "the I.G.'s here!"

"Nonsense," said Blick. "I'm the I.G. now!"

"Oh yeah?" whimpered Kane. "Go look out the window. He's here, and he's brought the whole Imperial fleet with him!"

Blick dashed to the window and looked up. High above, so high that he could see them only as silver specks, hung hundreds of ships.

"Headquarters *does* exist!" he gasped.

He stood stunned. What to do . . . what to do . . . what to do—The question swirled around in his brain until he was dizzy. He looked to Kane for advice, but the other was as bewildered as he was.

"Don't stand there, man," he stormed. "Do something!"

"Yes, sir," said Kane. "What?"

Blick thought for a long, silent moment. The answer was obvious, but there was a short, fierce inner struggle before he could bring himself to accept it.

"Get Colonel Harris up here at once. He'll know what we should do."

A stubborn look came across Kane's face. "We're running things now," he said angrily.

Blick's face hardened and he let out a roar that shook the walls. "Listen, you pup, when you get an order, you follow it. Now get!"

Forty seconds later, Colonel Harris stormed into the office. "What kind of a mess have you got us into this time?" he demanded.

"Look up there, sir," said Blick leading him to the window.

Colonel Harris snapped back into command as if he'd never left it.

"Major Kane!" he shouted.

Kane popped into the office like a frightened rabbit.

"Evacuate the garrison at once! I want everyone off the plateau and into the jungle immediately. Get litters for the sick and the veterans who can't walk and take them to the hunting camps. Start the rest moving north as soon as you can."

"Really, sir," protested Kane, looking to Blick for a cue.

"You heard the colonel," barked Blick. "On your way!" Kane bolted.

Colonel Harris turned to Blick and said in a frosty voice: "I appreciate your help, Colonel, but I feel perfectly competent to enforce my own orders."

"Sorry, sir," said the other meekly. "It won't happen again."

Harris smiled. "O.K., Jimmie," he said, "let's forget it. We've got work to do!"

15

It seemed to Kurt as if time was standing still. His nerves were screwed up to the breaking point and although he maintained an air of outward composure for the benefit of those in the control room of the flagship, it took all his will power to keep the hand that was resting over the firing stud from quivering. One slip and they'd be on him. Actually it was only a matter of minutes between the time the scout was dispatched to the garrison below and the time it returned, but to him it seemed as if hours had passed before the familiar form of his commanding officer strode briskly into the control room.

Colonel Harris came to a halt just inside the door and swept the room with a keen penetrating gaze.

"What's up, son?" he asked Kurt.

"I'm not quite sure. All that I know is that they're here to blast the garrison. As long as I've got control of this," he indicated the firing stud, "I'm top dog, but you'd better work something out in a hurry."

The look of strain on Kurt's face was enough for the colonel.

"Who's in command here?" he demanded.

Krogson stepped forward and bowed stiffly. "Commander Conrad Krogson of War Base Three of the Galactic Protectorate."

"Colonel Marcus Harris, 427th Light Maintenance Battalion of the Imperial Space Marines," replied the other briskly. "Now that the formalities are out of the way, let's get to work. Is there some place here where we can talk?"

Krogson gestured toward a small cubicle that opened off the control room. The two men entered and shut the door behind them.

A half hour went by without agreement. "There may be an answer somewhere," Colonel Harris said finally, "but I can't find it. We can't surrender to you, and we can't afford to have you surrender to us. We haven't the food, facilities, or anything else to keep fifty thousand men under guard. If we turn you loose, there's nothing to keep you from coming back to blast us—except your word, that is, and since it would obviously be given under duress, I'm afraid that we couldn't attach much weight to it. It's a nice problem. I wish we had more time to spend on it, but unless you can come up with something workable during the next few minutes, I'm going to give Kurt orders to blow the fleet."

Krogson's mind was operating at a furious pace. One by one he snatched at possible solutions, and one by one he gave them up as he realized that they would never stand up under the scrutiny of the razor-sharp mind that sat opposite him.

"Look," he burst out finally, "your empire is dead and our protectorate is about to fall apart. Give us a chance to come down and join you and we'll chuck the past. We need each other and you know it!"

"I know we do," said the colonel soberly, "and I rather think you are being honest with me. But we just can't take the chance. There are too many of you for us to digest and if you should change your mind—" He threw up his hands in a helpless gesture.

"But I wouldn't," protested Krogson. "You've told me what your life is like down there and you know what kind of a rat race I've been caught up in. I'd welcome the chance to get out of it. All of us would!"

"You might to begin with," said Harris, "but then you might start thinking what your Lord Protector would give to get his hands on several hundred trained technicians. No, Commander," he said, "we just couldn't chance it." He stretched his hand out to Krogson and the other after a second's hesitation took it.

Commander Krogson had reached the end of the road and he knew it. The odd thing about it was that now he found himself there, he didn't particularly mind. He sat and watched his own reactions with a sense of vague bewilderment. The strong drive for self-preservation that had kept him struggling ahead for so long was petering out and there was nothing to take its place. He was immersed in a strange feeling of emptiness and though a faint something within him said that he should go out fighting, it seemed pointless and without reason.

Suddenly the moment of quiet was broken. From the control room came a muffled sound of angry voices and scuffling feet. With one quick stride, Colonel Harris reached the door and swung it open. He was almost bowled over by a small disheveled figure who darted past him into the cubicle. Close behind came several of the ship's officers. As the figure came to a stop before Commander Krogson, one of them grabbed him and started to drag him back into the control room.

"Sorry, sir," the officer said to Krogson, "but he came busting in demanding to see you at once. He wouldn't tell us why and when we tried to stop him, he broke away."

"Release him!" ordered the commander. He looked sternly at the little figure. "Well, Schninkle," he said sternly, "what is it this time?"

"Did you get my message?"

Krogson snorted. "So it was you in that scout! I might have known it. We got it all right, but Communication still hasn't got it figured out. What are you doing out here? You're supposed to be back at base keeping knives out of my back!"

"It's private, sir," said Schninkle.

"The rest of you clear out!" ordered Krogson. A second later, with the exception of Colonel Harris, the cubicle stood empty. Schninkle looked questioningly at the oddly uniformed officer.

"Couldn't put him out if I wanted to," said Krogson, "now go ahead."

Schninkle closed the door carefully and then turned to the commander and said in a hushed voice, "There's been a blowup at Prime Base. General Carr was hiding out there after all. He hit at noon yesterday. He had two-thirds of the Elite Guard secretly on his side and the Lord Protector didn't have a chance. He tried to run but they chopped him down before he got out of the atmosphere."

Krogson digested the news in silence for a moment. "So the Lord Protector is dead." He laughed bitterly. "Well, long live the Lord Protector!" He turned slowly to Colonel Harris. "I guess this lets us both off. Now that the heat's off me, you're safe. Call off your boy out there, and we'll make ourselves scarce. I've got to get back to the new Lord Protector to pay my respects. If some of my boys get to Carr first, I'm apt to be out of a job."

Harris shook his head. "It isn't as simple as that. Your new leader needs technicians as much as your old one did. I'm afraid we are still back where we started."

As Krogson broke into an impatient denial, Schninkle interrupted him. "You can't go back, Commander. None of us can. Carr has the whole staff down on his 'out' list. He's making a clean sweep of all possible competition. We'd all be under arrest now if he knew where we were!"

Krogson gave a slow whistle. "Doesn't leave me much choice, does it?" he said to Colonel Harris. If you don't turn me loose, I get blown up; if you do, I get shot down."

Schninkle looked puzzled. "What's up, sir?" he asked.

Krogson gave a bitter laugh. "In case you didn't notice on your way in, there is a young man sitting at the fire controls out there who can blow up the whole fleet at the touch of a button. Down below is an ideal base with hundreds of techs, but the colonel here won't take us in, and he's afraid to let us go."

"I wouldn't," admitted Harris, "but the last few minutes have rather changed the picture. My empire has been dead for five hundred years and your protectorate doesn't seem to want you around any more. It looks like we're both out of a job. Maybe we both ought to find a new one. What do you think?"

"I don't know what to think," said Krogson. "I can't go back and I can't stay here, and there isn't any place else. The fleet can't keep going without a base."

A broad grin came over the face of Colonel Harris. "You know," he said, "I've got a hunch that maybe we can do business after all. Come on!" He threw open the cubicle door and strode briskly into the control room, Krogson and Schninkle following close at his heels. He walked over to Kurt who was still poised stiffly at the fire-control board.

"You can relax now, lad. Everything is under control."

Kurt gave a sigh of relief and pulling himself to his feet, stretched luxuriantly. As the other officers saw the firing stud deserted, they tensed and looked to Commander Krogson questioningly. He frowned for a second and then slowly shook his head.

"Well?" he said to Colonel Harris.

"It's obvious," said the other, "you've a fleet, a darn good fleet, but it's falling apart for lack of decent maintenance. I've got a base down there with five thousand lads who can think with their fingers. This knucklehead of mine is a good example." He walked over to Kurt and slapped him affectionately on the shoulder. "There's nothing on this ship that he couldn't tear down and put back together blindfolded if he was given a little time to think about it. I think he'll enjoy having some real work to do for a change."

"I may seem dense," said Krogson with a bewildered expression on his face, "but wasn't that the idea that I was trying to sell you?"

"The idea is the same," said Harris, "but the context isn't. You're in a position now where you have to cooperate. That makes a difference. A big difference!"

"It sounds good," said Krogson, "but now you're overlooking something. Carr will be looking for me. We can't stand off the whole galaxy!"

"You're overlooking something too, sir," Schninkle interrupted. "He hasn't the slightest idea where we are. It will be months before he has things well enough under control to start an organized search for us. When he does, his chances of ever spotting the fleet are mighty slim if we take reasonable precautions. Remember that it was only by a fluke that we ever happened to spot this place to begin with."

As he talked a calculating look came into his eyes. "A year of training and refitting here, and there wouldn't be a fleet in the galaxy that could stand against us." He casually edged over until he occupied a position between Kurt and the fire-control board. "If things went right, there's no reason why you couldn't become Lord Protector, Commander."

A flash of the old fire stirred within Krogson and then quickly flickered out. "No, Schninkle," he said heavily. "That's all past now. I've had enough. It's time to try something new."

"In that case," said Colonel Harris, "let's begin! Out there a whole galaxy is breaking up. Soon the time will come when a strong hand is going to be needed to piece it back together and put it in running order again. You know," he continued reflectively, "the name of the old empire still has a certain magic to it. It might not be a bad idea to use it until we are ready to move on to something better."

He walked silently to the vision port and looked down on the lush greenness spreading far below. "But whatever we call ourselves," he continued slowly, half talking to himself, "we have something to work for now." A quizzical smile played over his lips and his wise old eyes seemed to be scanning the years ahead. "You know, Kurt; there's nothing like a visit from the Inspector General once in a while to keep things in line. The galaxy is a big place, but when the time comes, we'll make our rounds!"

16

On the parade ground behind the low buildings of the garrison, the 427th Light Maintenance Battalion of the Imperial Space Marines stood in rigid formation, the feathers of their war bonnets moving slightly in the little breeze that blew in from the west and their war paint glowing redly in the slanting rays of the setting sun.

A quiver ran through the hard surface soil of the plateau as the great mass of the fleet flagship settled down ponderously to rest. There was a moment of expectant silence as a great port clanged open and a gangplank extended to the ground. From somewhere within the ship a fanfare of trumpets sounded. Slowly and with solemn dignity, surrounded by his staff, Conrad Krogson, Inspector General of the Imperial Space Marines, advanced to review the troops.

CHARLES SHEFFIELD

FIXED PRICE WAR

As the sun set, the first line of at-
tackers came silently over the brow of the hill. They were the scouts,
shadowy figures moving with no apparent coordination down to and
across the river, on to the waist-high savannah scrub on the near side.
When the last man was across, the second wave appeared, a line of
hover-tanks with chopper cover, advancing at no more than walking
pace. The counterattack waited until the tanks had reached the river.
Then a bright mesh of ruby pulsed-laser beams lanced out from the
nearer hillside, probing for the soft underskirts of the hover-tanks and
the chopper rotors. Yellow and red tracers replied. The air became a
multicolored confusion of stabbing pencils of light, smoke from burning
vegetation and the fitful glare of crippled tanks and choppers.

Suddenly the whole hillside was lit by an intense blue-white fireball,
spreading from a point close to the river bank. It grew rapidly, changing
color to a greenish-yellow.

Merle Walters gave a grunt of surprise, leaned forward and hit a
button on the console in front of him. The display stopped, frozen with
the fireball about forty meters across. He swiveled in his chair and
pressed the intercom. "Franny, get Alex Burns on the line. I think I've
finally caught him."

He waited impatiently as the connection to Redondo Beach was made,
looking at his watch as he did so. Eight-thirty, that made it five-thirty in

California. Alex would still be around. When the intercom buzzed he reached out his right arm to pick up the phone. The left sleeve was empty, pinned to his dark jacket. As he placed the receiver to his ear, the screen lit up to show a trim, ruddy-faced man in his early forties.

"Alex, I think you've finally goofed." Walters grinned in triumph at the man on the screen. "If I had another arm I'd be rubbing my hands together here. I'm reviewing the simulation you've done for Exhibit Three of our proposal. One of your boys has gone wild and thrown in a tactical nuke. You know that's right out."

"Mr. Walters, I invite your attention to Page 57 of the Work Statement of the Request For Proposal." Burns answered in the careful speech of an Inverness Scot, unchanged after sixteen years in Southern California. "The RFP very clearly states, and I quote: 'Although nuclear weapons may not be employed, clean imploders up to 1,000 metric tons TNT equivalent may be used. No more than three such devices will be available in any single engagement.' The fireball that you are looking at in Exhibit Three is a new Morton Imploder, type four, one hundred and fifty TNT tons equivalent."

Alex Burns's face showed the slightest trace of a smile. Merle Walters looked at the display screen, thumbed rapidly through his copy of the Request For Proposal, and swore. "Alex, you Gaelic bastard, you did that on purpose. Don't deny it. I've known you too long not to recognize your touch there. Tell your lads the simulations are damn good—but I'd like them a lot better if you'd put some faces on the attackers. All I can see is blobs."

Burns nodded gloomily. "I know, Mr. Walters. I feel the same way. But the people at GSA won't say who we're fighting and I can think of at least four possibles. Maybe you can get something for me at the bidders' conference."

"I'll give it a try, Alex—but don't hold your breath waiting for it. I'll be honest with you, that won't be my top priority at this bidders' session. There's something else I have to get an answer on. The Contracts Office have been like a bunch of clams on this one. Jack's trying a little line of his own to get information—we'll tell you tomorrow how it works out."

Burns nodded again. "Goodnight, Mr. Walters. Maybe I could suggest that you should call it a day. You're looking very tired. Trouble with the résumés?"

"As usual. We need two or three good production men, all we can find is a bunch of retired colonels and generals. Keep up the good work on the simulations, Alex, and I'll call you about noon—our time—tomorrow."

Merle Walters broke the connection and leaned back in his chair. He rubbed his hand over the top of his bald, furrowed forehead. Alex was right. He was damn tired. Alex couldn't usually catch him that way. And with just ten days to go before the proposal was due, with all the costing still to be done, he'd better keep something in reserve for next week. He spoke again into the intercom.

"Franny, I'm cutting out. Pull a bunch of those résumés together for me as bedside reading, will you? Remember, I won't be in first thing in the morning. Jack and I will be down at 18th and E Streets, at the Bidders' Conference. I can't be reached there."

He levered himself to his feet and walked to the outer office, limping slightly. He could disguise it if he tried, but it was pointless in front of Franny. She knew him better than he knew himself. She had the résumés all ready for him—probably had them ready two hours ago. Her plump, pretty face was set in what he thought of as her "take your medicine like a good little boy" expression.

"Mr. Walters, I discussed this earlier with Mr. Tukey." She held out a locator. "If you'd carry this about with you, it would be so much easier for us to get messages to you. Look, this new one only weighs an ounce—and it's only an inch wide, it wouldn't be any trouble."

He looked at it, then peered at Franny from under his thick, grizzled eyebrows—his sternest expression. "Franny, I've told you once and I'll tell you again. I'm not going to wear a damned beeper. It's an invasion of privacy. When you see Jack Tukey tomorrow, you tell him exactly what he can do with that thing. Tell him it's only an inch wide, so he shouldn't have any trouble." His gray eyes twinkled beneath the bushy brows. "Goodnight, Franny, and thanks for another day."

He went slowly out into the chilly November evening. Ten minutes later, Franny locked up and left also. The Washington office of WAWD Corporation was closed for the night.

The Bidders' Conference was scheduled for 9 A.M. in the biggest Conference Room of the old Interior building. Merle Walters was there by 8:45, watching the arrivals. About a hundred people. Say two per company. So fifty groups interested in the procurement. Merle knew the real competition like the back of his hand. Three groups, and WAWD. The other forty-six were innocents, flesh-peddlers, or companies looking for subcontract work. When Tolly Suomi of VVV Industries arrived at two minutes to nine, Merle followed him in and sat in the same row. Suomi looked his way and inclined his head. Merle had no doubt that Tolly knew the real score as well as he did.

Biggest Conference Room, so more than a twenty million dollar job. Coffee served, so more than fifty million. Merle read the signs almost subconsciously, the pricing signals that only the pros could read. Then Petzell would be running the Government side, for a job over five hundred million dollars.

Merle was sitting smugly on that train of thought when the senior government man came forward to the podium. Instead of Petzell it was his deputy, Pete Wolff. Merle sat up and took notice. What the hell was going on? He'd been tracking this procurement for a year, sniffing it and sizing it. He'd been pegging it at about a billion two. Surely they couldn't have missed the mark so badly? He leaned forward to catch the opening remarks, ignoring the stab of pain in his left side.

"Good morning, ladies and gentlemen." Wolff looked around at the sea of faces, old friends and old enemies. "I want to begin by running over the procedures we will be following on questions and answers. First, though, I should tell you that I'm deputizing today for Howard Petzell." He looked around with a slight smile. "He is home today with a bad case of the 'flu."

Merle leaned back, then looked across at Suomi. He was sitting there with a half-smile on his face, stroking his gray beard with one finger. Chalk one up to VVV's intelligence service. Suomi had known about Petzell's illness in advance.

Wolff closed the opening preamble with the usual warning about staying away from the technical men in the Government until the award was announced. Well, why not? Anybody who didn't have all his sources lined up well before the Request For Proposal hit the streets was a dead duck anyway.

Wolff came at last to the guts of the meeting. "We will now answer the questions from prospective bidders. All questions have been submitted in writing in advance. All answers will be given in writing to all attendees. Will you please identify yourselves as you read your questions. First question, please."

"Jim Peters, Consultec. How will you be applying the Equal Employment Opportunity Clause in this job?" The speaker was well-known to Merle. From his Baltimore offices, Peters could be relied on to find a few hundred talented mercenaries for any job.

"As far as feasible. We know it's not easy for any of you. We don't expect an exact split, but we do want to see some WASPs in there. We can't accept a bid that's all blacks and Puerto Ricans. And we'd really like to see some minorities up near the top of your team, not just a bunch of retired West Pointers. That answer it?"

Peters shrugged. Wolff and the other government men knew his problem well enough.

"Next."

"Oral Jones, Rockdonnell Industries. It's not clear from the Request For Proposal how much Government Furnished Equipment we should assume. Can you give us any guidance?"

"It's been left open. It's up to you. Use GFE for anything, weapons, food, medical supplies, if you want to. Bid it yourselves if you think you can get it cheaper. We'll be happy to give you our price lists so you can see what we pay."

Merle sniffed. Dumb question. Nobody could undercut Government prices on supplies, unless they were buying stolen goods. GSA insisted on the best prices in town from everybody. Merle waited for the real action to start.

"Warren McVittie, Lockheed. I have a question on types of bid."

Merle noticed that the Lockheed and the Rockdonnell reps were sitting in pairs. Jack Tukey was over on the left-hand side, well away from Merle, where he could keep an eye on Suomi's crack salesman, Vince Menoudakis, and also on the men from Lectron Industries and Lockheed. He and Merle were careful to remain well apart, to get independent views of the meeting, and Tolly Suomi and Vince Menoudakis followed the same logic. Merle also noticed that the Lectron and Lockheed men were not their most senior reps. Suomi's presence confirmed Merle's own feelings—that this meeting was going to be a real groundbreaker. Top men should be there. Score one point against Lectron and Lockheed.

"The bid request is not clear," went on McVittie. "On Page 24 of the RFP, there's a note to say that bidders may choose to quote cost-plus or fixed price. That's a new clause for this kind of procurement. Are you actually inviting Fixed-Price bids for the whole job?"

The action had arrived. Merle Walters leaned forward intently. This was one of the questions he had come to hear an answer to. Wolff looked a little uneasy, and paused before he replied.

"Just what it says. Bid it cost-plus-fixed-fee, cost-plus-incentive-fee, or fixed price. It's up to you. I think I should tell you that, other things being equal, fixed price bids will be favored." He stopped, then apparently felt obliged to add another comment. "I know it's new, but this will probably be our policy in the future on this type of project."

Fixed price. A whole new set of parameters to worry about. Merle sat, deep in thought, until he was roused by Jack Tukey's voice.

"Jack Tukey, WAWD Corporation. I'd like to ask about deliverables, especially in view of what you said about a preference for a fixed-price contract. What are the project deliverables, and how will they be evaluated?"

"If you bid fixed price, there's only one real deliverable. The overall tactical position at the end of the contract period must be acceptable in territorial holdings. We realize this gives you problems in bidding, since we can't at this time reveal to you the exact area where the engagement will be fought. However, this deliverable will be developed in detail during the final contract negotiation, when a vendor has been selected."

Nasty. In other words, you're bidding it blind, fellers. And if you won't play the fixed-price game, you probably lose outright. Some smartie in the Government was being super-tricky. Merle tried to fit it together.

"Vince Menoudakis, VVV Industries." The voice was soft, with a slight trace of a stammer. Merle awakened again from his trance. He always liked to see an artist at work, and Vince was one of the great ones. "Mr. Wolff, the geography makes a big difference to the cost of the action. You know that just as well as we do. Now, wouldn't it save the Government money if the bidders could be told the fighting area? There would be less work for you in negotiation, more precise bids from each of us, and a bigger effort on our part to get the really best strategies for the terrain. Where will the project be located, Mr. Wolff?"

Merle smiled to himself. In five or six sentences, Vince had somehow done his usual stroking job. How did he do it? Wolff was smiling and nodding, responding to some mysterious warmth in the questioner. Menoudakis, if he were available, would really be a catch for WAWD. Earlier tries proved that Tolly Suomi knew it. He had Vince pretty well locked in.

"Yes, it would certainly save time later. Our main area—" Wolff actually began to reply before he realized what he was doing. He stopped. "Our main area is—roughly in the latitude range 15 to 25 degrees, as it says in the Request For Proposal. That is as far as I can go—after all, Mr. Menoudakis, war has not yet been declared. We don't want to start an international incident here, do we?"

Nice try, Vince. Pulling an area out of Wolff wouldn't have helped VVV much—everybody else would share the information. Suomi had gone along with it just to rub in to the rest of them what a master Vince Menoudakis was. Jack Tukey had hit the nail on the head the first time he had met Menoudakis at a debriefing. "I don't remember what he said to me, Merle, but if he'd asked me to marry him I'd probably have agreed."

The meeting broke up at about 11:30. Merle and Jack Tukey shared a cab back to the WAWD offices on Wisconsin Avenue. They had lots to talk about. Jack had news on the evaluation procedure, straight from the horse's mouth: Petzell's secretary.

"Do you realize I was in the Embers with Lottie Mitchell until two o'clock this morning? I'm telling you, she nearly drank me under the table. I should be getting danger money for my liver. I had seven bourbons and then I just lost count—and Lottie didn't have a hair out of place. Then we went on over to her apartment, and you won't believe this but at half-past-three I found myself doing—"

"Jack, I should get money from you for introducing you to Lottie in the first place," interrupted Merle. "Stop stringing me out, and get to the point. I'm well aware that you do it on purpose."

Jack Tukey grinned. It was a pleasure to see Merle rise to the bait.

"All right, if you've got no romance in your soul. It's going to be a four-man review board. Technical evaluation will count 40 points, price 60 points. Now for the bad news. This one's going fixed price, or nothing. Lottie says there's no way they'll give it out on a cost-plus basis. Where does that leave us, Merle?"

Walters looked out at the leafless November trees on Pennsylvania Avenue. "In deep shit, my boy. In up to our necks." He spoke quietly, almost abstractedly. "You know, we've never tried to be the low dollar man on these bids. WAWD offers quality. But I don't know if we can do it this time. Six outfits underbid us. They'll not be a patch on us technically. But you heard those deliverables. Completely undefined. Have the status half-way right after a year, and you'll get paid. And an option to renew for another two years. Doesn't matter how shaky the field position is, as far as I can tell." He fell silent as they drove through the rutted streets of Georgetown. "I'm telling you, Jack. Some half-wit's dreamed this one up to make his name in the Government. We've got to think of some way around it. Fixed price war, is it? What's our edge now?"

He was silent again for a few minutes, then nodded. "When we get to the office, Jack, call up Lottie and make a date for tonight. Most of all, I have to know *where* this war will be fought. That's the top priority. Location, and combatants. We've got a six-month job ahead of us, and two weeks to do it in. You'll have to risk your kidneys again. And one other thing. I need to know how they'll be auditing this one. If it's genuine fixed price, there shouldn't be any Government audit of it at all."

Merle sat slumped in the car seat, staring into space. His right hand rubbed the shoulder of his empty sleeve and his blunt features were twisted in thought. Jack thought how much the old man was aging, how ill he looked. Maybe this effort was just too much to ask of him.

Merle glared at him, suddenly alive again.

"Stop gawping at me like a half-wit, Jack. When we get to the office, I want to talk to CBS and NBC. You handle ABC. Here's the way it goes."

Jack felt a surge of relief as Merle outlined his plans. Down but not out. As usual, Merle seemed to have found his angle.

"Can we price it low enough, Merle?"

"If it works out the way I'm hoping, we can underbid everybody in the business. I want you to fly out to the West Coast tomorrow night and bounce the main ideas off Alex Burns. He's key to this. I'll find somebody else to woo Lottie in your absence. Maybe I'll recruit Vince Menoudakis for the job."

Jack sniffed. "You'll be doing Lottie a disservice. You know these high power sales types. Lots of promises—until it's time to deliver.

Then they don't have what it takes. Tolly Suomi, he's the man for my money."

"You don't have that much money, Jack. Here, give me a hand to get my stiff leg out of the cab. I feel like Pinocchio today."

The air was full of gray sand and black smoke, blinding the soldiers and blotting out the fierce desert sun. Tanks were barreling forward through the dust, a group of men with combat lasers following each one. The long, high scream of an omniprojector was approaching along a dry wadi, and a Clarke neutralizer was turning to meet it, lobed antennae moving into exact phase for cancellation. The operators of the neutralizer were tunneling deep into narrow trenches in the sand, reading the strength of the omniprojector signal on the dials set in their helmet displays.

"Mr. Suomi calling on line one, Mr. Walters."

"At last." Merle grunted in satisfaction. He left the screen display running, reached over and picked up the receiver. Tolly Suomi's bland, unlined face appeared on the intercom screen.

"Perhaps I am calling at an inopportune time, Merle. It sounds as though you are tuned to the NBC news report. Should I call back later?"

"No. I've been trying to reach you all day. I asked your office to find you and give you the message to call me. Where are you, Tolly?"

"Newark, New Jersey."

"Can you be here in Washington, tonight?"

Suomi's face, as usual, betrayed no curiosity or surprise. "I can. By seven o'clock at the latest, perhaps by six-thirty."

"I'll be here." Merle broke the connection and leaned back in his chair, looking for a comfortable position.

On the screen, the Clarke neutralizer had been homed on by a seeking missile and was out of action. The omniprojector was advancing again. Men fell before it, flopping and convulsing like landed fish as the vibrations turned to their central nervous system frequencies.

Merle watched as the NBC newscaster summarized the day's fighting, the advances and retreats. It was on the nose with his own scratchpad estimates. He placed a call to Alex Burns and sketched out a scenario. Alex objected to some of the ideas, and they went at it hammer and tongs for the rest of the afternoon. When Suomi arrived they were still arguing. Merle waved him to a seat, fired a final salvo, and cut the connection.

"Never try and argue with a Scotsman, Tolly. Stubborn as donkeys. Must be the oatmeal."

Suomi smiled, smooth white in smooth ivory. "Alex Burns?"

Merle nodded. "You know him, do you? He's right again, blast him." He leaned back, his voice a bit too casual. "Had any chance to see much of Alex's work? I was wondering what you think of him."

"The same as you do, Merle. Not just the best, the very best." Suomi smiled the Tolly smile, a fraction of an inch elevation of the corners of his mouth. "Don't let's be coy, Merle. You know quite well I've tried to hire Alex Burns from you. Probably as many times as WAWD has tried to steal Vince Menoudakis—and with the same success. Nothing."

"Tolly, I don't own Alex. His job does. Get ahead of us on the simulations, and Alex would take a job with VVV tomorrow to find out how you do it. I couldn't hold him a day."

"And how to do that, when Alex Burns leads the world on simulation mock-ups." Suomi waved his arm at the display screen. "He's an artist with that thing. He can make it more real than reality. Burns is an artist the way Disney was, posing as something else. I'll tell you, Merle, I've needed an Alex in the past six months."

Merle nodded, his eyes averted. "Aye, it's been a hard time for all of us, Tolly."

The reaction was a Suomi maximum. One eyebrow raised a fraction of an inch. The sign of strong emotion. "Hard? When you've won the last four war jobs in a row? Merle, I'm not here for social reasons. I dropped everything to get here today—just as you knew I would. We've been running in circles since the November bidders' conference, trying to find out how you can price the way you do and still make money. We've got our sources in Contracts Departments, same as you—and we still don't know how you do it."

Merle smiled, rubbing his left shoulder in his habitual gesture. "You're not a poker player, Tolly. You show your hand."

"I'm a chess player, Merle. I can tell when somebody is planning seven moves ahead and the rest of us are playing six. We've been competitors for a long time, the two of us. For fifteen years we've been neck and neck. Now, what's your secret?"

"You know, don't you, that we sewed up the TV rights for the Trucial War with NBC? That was a twenty million dollar deal, just for special footage."

"I know. It was a neat idea, putting it on the same basis as the Olympics—but I know that's not your trick. We caught on to that last Christmas and now we use it in our bids too." Suomi placed his hands flat on the desk between them. "The real thing, Merle. What will it cost me to get it? You know I'll find out anyway, if I stick at it. And VVV won't go broke without it. But you have to know what it feels like to lose four big ones in a row. Name your price, I'll pay it."

A lengthening silence. Merle looked out at the gardens far below, dusk falling over the bursting azaleas of early May. "You seem sure of yourself, Tolly. Got an insider in our accounting department?"

"I don't need that, Merle. Look at this office." He gestured at the furniture. "The better you're doing, the cheaper and lousier the fixtures. I daren't sit down too hard on this chair in case it falls apart. Come on, Merle, let's get to it. What's your price?"

"I've got my price, Tolly. Here's the ticket I'm selling." He reached into his suit pocket and pulled out his wallet. From it he took a sheet of paper about seven inches square. "That came to me yesterday."

Tolly Suomi read through it, caught his breath, and read it again, slowly. At last he lifted his head and looked Merle Walters straight in the eye. "How long, Merle?"

"You tell me. The medics can't seem to agree. One month, six months, two years. From now on, it's a game of roulette. Good thing Jack Tukey's ready. He'll make a good president for WAWD." He paused expectantly. "Don't you agree, Tolly?"

Suomi hesitated, for the beat of a hummingbird's wing. "An excellent president, Merle. He has a good business head, he eats work, and he can pick the right people—and keep them, too. Jack will make a good president for WAWD—a great president. In ten years' time." His voice raised a little. "You see, Merle, we've met, what, thirty or forty times over the past fifteen years? But I think I know you as well as you know me. Jack Tukey has one failing, but it's one you can't live with. Jack doesn't hate war—yet—as Merle Walters hates it. He doesn't hate the stupidity of it, the cruelty of it, the very idea of it."

Merle bowed his head. "I'm a war hero, Tolly, didn't you know that? To a lot of people in this country I'm Mister War himself. Generals are proud to shake my hand. I got this—" he gestured at his empty sleeve and left leg, "—being a hero, forty years ago in the Pacific. Fighting your countrymen. No, it's Tolly Suomi that really hates war, I would say. You remember World War Two, Tolly?"

"I was eight years old when it finished, Merle. I remember it. I lost no arm, no leg. But I was on holiday in the country, when my family was home in Nagasaki. I remember that. And other things. I remember your cost-benefit study, showing that napalm is not a cost-effective weapon of war. How much did that study cost you, Merle?"

"Enough so no one would question our results. And VVV Industries' analysis, showing that antipersonnel fragmentation bombs aren't a good investment of war capital. How much did that one cost you, Tolly?"

"As you say, Merle, enough. Vince did a marvelous sales pitch on that one."

"The next president of VVV, Tolly? Would Vince want it?"

Suomi looked quizzically at Walters and waved the thought away. "You don't hire Liszt and ask him to move pianos. Vince is an artist, too. He has something we can't analyze—no place for it in chess or poker. People like him, he likes them, he sells them. Never fails. He's right where he is."

Merle nodded quietly, rubbing the side of his face with his hand. The two men sat in silence for several minutes. Finally Merle spoke.

"So now you can guess my price, Tolly. The price for the secret, the way we can underbid the market, every time, on the fixed price war jobs. Only one way I'll accept payment." He gestured at the photograph of Lyndon Johnson, hanging on the wall. "Know why I've got that picture up there, Tolly? I'll tell you. He's the man who turned me from a hawk to—what I am. I lost two sons in Vietnam. Two boys, too young to vote, to feed the ego of a man who wouldn't ever admit he was wrong.

"Merger, Tolly. Merger, with you at the top. Vince Menoudakis as VP of Sales, Alex Burns as VP of Production. And Jack Tukey, as Executive VP, waiting in the wings. Your time will come, too, Tolly, and Jack has to be ready. And maybe I'll be around here for a while yet, as a high-priced easy-life consultant for you—when you need stirring up a bit. Life's not chess, and life's not poker, but there's some of both in it. Merger, Tolly. Let's talk terms."

Suomi sat, face expressionless, one hand stroking his beard. "Perhaps. Perhaps. Would Jack Tukey work for me?"

"He thinks you walk on water, Tolly. So does Alex."

"Suppose I agree, find out how you operate, then back out?"

"That's tough titty for Merle Walters. A man either goes along with his judgment of people, or he's got nothing. That's the least of my worries, Tolly."

Suomi was nodding slowly. "My ancestry and education prepared me for this, Merle. There has been something that year by year has bound our fortunes tighter together, two caterpillars in one cocoon." He held out his hand. "Agreed in principle—details to be worked out. I hope we both live to see an end—to the lawyers putting the groups together. It will take a while. You control a stock majority, I hope?"

Merle nodded. "As you do. I did a little tracing of the lines on VVV this morning."

"Then it can be done. So now, Merle, tell me. Tell me something that has been on my mind every spare minute for six months. You are bidding fixed price and you are thirty percent lower than the rest of us. How are you doing it?" Suomi was leaning forward intently.

Merle opened the credenza behind him, pulled out a bottle and two glasses. "Champagne, Tolly. Let me savor the moment. You'll have to open it. It takes two hands."

"You were that sure of yourself?"

"Either way, I would drink the champagne. Take a look at this."

He turned on the display screen. The picture filled with scenes of battle, again in the desert. The heat, the smoke, the noise, the chaos, almost the smell seemed to spring from the screen.

"Now, Tolly, what are you seeing?"

"The Trucial War. I don't know which action. Last week's, maybe, up on the border."

Merle smiled and raised his glass. "You've got a great eye, Tolly. It's the Trucials, it's even a border skirmish—but it's next week, not last week. You said that Alex Burns is a genius. I agree. Half the battles in that war never happen. They're Alex's simulations. We ship the footage to NBC—they pay for it—and they weave the commentary around it. Much better for them, they don't have to keep a camera team out in the field. About half the footage is genuine fighting. The rest is Alex."

Suomi's eyes were flicking from the screen to Merle and back again. He was running rapidly through the difficulties, the possibilities. "How can you meet the deliverables? How can you pass an audit?"

"No audit. Fixed price war, remember? Deliverables? We maintain the lines we promised—you know, these aren't wars to win, they're to hold the status quo. We find the bidders on the other side, as early in the game as we can. We agree what will be fought, what will be simulated. They buy the simulations they need from us—a tidy profit there for WAWD. We have to mix it up, in case there are parties of journalists or junketing politicians. They see genuine battles. How can somebody tell if the other battles they see on the screen are real?"

"And you make a profit?"

"Thirty-five percent. No matter how much the simulations cost, or how much it takes to keep things going smoothly, *nothing* costs as much as a war—even a small one. One other thing, Tolly. Go and take a look at the war hospitals. There are still deaths, because there are still battles. We stopped the worst maiming a while back, the two of us, when we got rid of the worst weapons. Now, the injuries are down again—and WAWD gets credit for tactics and brilliant fighting."

Merle Walters raised his glass again. "Here's to the merger of WAWD Corporation and VVV Industries—the War leaders. You'll have to keep up the struggle now, Tolly, until some day maybe we'll get some sense. I'm not optimistic. We're aggressive animals, the lot of us. But here's to War, damn its soul."

Tolly Suomi was thoughtful. He flexed his shoulders, feeling a new weight there. At last he too raised his glass. "To the merger. And to our motto: War is much too serious a thing to be left to the Government."

The glasses clinked. On the screen in front of them, the battle raged.

ROBERT A. HEINLEIN

THE LONG WATCH

"Nine ships blasted off from Moon Base. Once in space, eight of them formed a globe around the smallest. They held this formation all the way to Earth.

"The small ship displayed the insignia of an admiral—yet there was no living thing of any sort in her. She was not even a passenger ship, but a drone, a robot ship intended for radioactive cargo. This trip she carried nothing but a lead coffin—and a Geiger counter that was never quiet."

> —from the editorial *After Ten Years,* film 38, 17 June 2009, Archives of the *N. Y. Times*

1   **J**ohnny Dahlquist blew smoke at the Geiger counter. He grinned wryly and tried it again. His whole body was radioactive by now. Even his breath, the smoke from his cigarette, could make the Geiger counter scream.

How long had he been here? Time doesn't mean much on the Moon. Two days? Three? A week? He let his mind run back: the last clearly marked time in his mind was when the Executive Officer had sent for him, right after breakfast—

"Lieutenant Dahlquist, reporting to the Executive Officer."

Colonel Towers looked up. "Ah, John Ezra. Sit down, Johnny. Cigarette?"

Johnny sat down, mystified but flattered. He admired Colonel Towers, for his brilliance, his ability to dominate, and for his battle record. Johnny had no battle record; he had been commissioned on completing his doctor's degree in nuclear physics and was now junior bomb officer of Moon Base.

The Colonel wanted to talk politics; Johnny was puzzled. Finally Towers had come to the point; it was not safe (so he said) to leave control of the world in political hands; power must be held by a scientifically selected group. In short—the Patrol.

Johnny was startled rather than shocked. As an abstract idea, Towers' notion sounded plausible. The League of Nations had folded up; what would keep the United Nations from breaking up, too, and thus lead to another World War. "And you know how bad such a war would be, Johnny."

Johnny agreed. Towers said he was glad that Johnny got the point. The senior bomb officer could handle the work, but it was better to have both specialists.

Johnny sat up with a jerk. "You are going to *do* something about it?" He had thought the Exec was just talking.

Towers smiled. "We're not politicians; we don't just talk. We act."

Johnny whistled. "When does this start?"

Towers flipped a switch. Johnny was startled to hear his own voice, then identified the recorded conversation as having taken place in the junior officers' messroom. A political argument he remembered, which he had walked out on . . . a good thing, too! But being spied on annoyed him.

Towers switched it off. "We *have* acted," he said. "We know who is safe and who isn't. Take Kelly—" He waved at the loudspeaker. "Kelly is politically unreliable. You noticed he wasn't at breakfast?"

"Huh? I thought he was on watch."

"Kelly's watch-standing days are over. Oh, relax; he isn't hurt."

Johnny thought this over. "Which list am I on?" he asked. "Safe or unsafe?"

"Your name has a question mark after it. But I have said all along that you could be depended on." He grinned engagingly. "You won't make a liar of me, Johnny?"

Dahlquist didn't answer; Towers said sharply, "Come now—what do you think of it? Speak up."

"Well, if you ask me, you've bitten off more than you can chew. While it's true that Moon Base controls the Earth, Moon Base itself is a sitting duck for a ship. One bomb—*blooie!*"

Towers picked up a message form and handed it over; it read: I HAVE YOUR CLEAN LAUNDRY—ZACK. "That means every bomb in the *Trygve Lie* has been put out of commission. I have reports from every ship we need worry about." He stood up. "Think it over and see me after lunch. Major Morgan needs your help right away to change control frequencies on the bombs."

"The control frequencies?"

"Naturally. We don't want the bombs jammed before they reach their targets."

"What? You said the idea was to *prevent* war."

Towers brushed it aside. "There won't be a war—just a psychological demonstration, an unimportant town or two. A little bloodletting to save an all-out war. Simple arithmetic."

He put a hand on Johnny's shoulder. "You aren't squeamish, or you wouldn't be a bomb officer. Think of it as a surgical operation. And think of your family."

Johnny Dahlquist had been thinking of his family. "Please, sir, I want to see the Commanding Officer."

Towers frowned. "The Commodore is not available. As you know, I speak for him. See me again—after lunch."

The Commodore was decidedly not available; the Commodore was dead. But Johnny did not know that.

Dahlquist walked back to the messroom, bought cigarettes, sat down and had a smoke. He got up, crushed out the butt, and headed for the Base's west airlock. There he got into his space suit and went to the lockmaster. "Open her up, Smitty."

The marine looked surprised. "Can't let anyone out on the surface without word from Colonel Towers, sir. Hadn't you heard?"

"Oh, yes! Give me your order book." Dahlquist took it, wrote a pass for himself, and signed it "by direction of Colonel Towers." He added, "Better call the Executive Officer and check it."

The lockmaster read it and stuck the book in his pocket. "Oh, no, Lieutenant. Your word's good."

"Hate to disturb the Executive Officer, eh? Don't blame you." He stepped in, closed the inner door, and waited for the air to be sucked out.

Out on the Moon's surface he blinked at the light and hurried to the track-rocket terminus; a car was waiting. He squeezed in, pulled down the hood, and punched the starting button. The rocket car flung itself at the hills, dived through and came out on a plain studded with projectile rockets, like candles on a cake. Quickly it dived into a second tunnel through more hills. There was a stomach-wrenching deceleration and the car stopped at the underground atom-bomb armory.

As Dahlquist climbed out he switched on his walkie-talkie. The space-suited guard at the entrance came to port-arms. Dahlquist said, "Morning, Lopez," and walked by him to the airlock. He pulled it open.

The guard motioned him back. "Hey! Nobody goes in without the Executive Officer's say-so." He shifted his gun, fumbled in his pouch and got out a paper. "Read it, Lieutenant."

Dahlquist waved it away. "I drafted that order myself. *You* read it; you've misinterpreted it."

"I don't see how, Lieutenant."

Dahlquist snatched the paper, glanced at it, then pointed to a line. "See? '—except persons specifically designated by the Executive Officer.' That's the bomb officers, Major Morgan and me."

The guard looked worried. Dahlquist said, "Damn it, look up 'specifically designated'—it's under *'Bomb Room, Security, Procedure for,'* in your standing orders. Don't tell me you left them in the barracks!"

"Oh, ño, sir! I've got 'em." The guard reached into his pouch. Dahlquist gave him back the sheet; the guard took it, hesitated, then leaned his weapon against his hip, shifted the paper to his left hand, and dug into his pouch with his right.

Dahlquist grabbed the gun, shoved it between the guard's legs, and jerked. He threw the weapon away and ducked into the airlock. As he slammed the door he saw the guard struggling to his feet and reaching for his side arm. He dogged the outer door shut and felt a tingle in his fingers as a slug struck the door.

He flung himself at the inner door, jerked the spill lever, rushed back to the outer door and hung his weight on the handle. At once he could feel it stir. The guard was lifting up; the lieutenant was pulling down, with only his low Moon weight to anchor him. Slowly the handle raised before his eyes.

Air from the bomb room rushed into the lock through the spill valve. Dahlquist felt his space suit settle on his body as the pressure in the lock began to equal the pressure in the suit. He quit straining and let the guard raise the handle. It did not matter; thirteen tons of air pressure now held the door closed.

He latched open the inner door to the bomb room, so that it could not swing shut. As long as it was open, the airlock could not operate; no one could enter.

Before him in the room, one for each projectile rocket, were the atom bombs, spaced in rows far enough apart to defeat any faint possibility of spontaneous chain reaction. They were the deadliest things in the known universe, but they were his babies. He had placed himself between them and anyone who would misuse them.

But, now that he was here, he had no plan to use his temporary advantage.

The speaker on the wall sputtered into life. "Hey! Lieutenant! What goes on here? You gone crazy?" Dahlquist did not answer. Let Lopez stay confused—it would take him that much longer to make up his mind what to do. And Johnny Dahlquist needed as many minutes as he could squeeze. Lopez went on protesting. Finally he shut up.

Johnny had followed a blind urge not to let the bombs—*his* bombs! —be used for "demonstrations on unimportant towns." But what to do next? Well, Towers couldn't get through the lock. Johnny would sit tight until hell froze over.

Don't kid yourself, John Ezra! Towers could get in. Some high explosive against the outer door—then the air would whoosh out, our boy Johnny would drown in blood from his burst lungs—and the bombs would be sitting there, unhurt. They were built to stand the jump from Moon to Earth; vacuum would not hurt them at all.

He decided to stay in his space suit; explosive decompression didn't appeal to him. Come to think about it, death from old age was his choice.

Or they could drill a hole, let out the air, and open the door without wrecking the lock. Or Towers might even have a new airlock built outside the old. Not likely, Johnny thought; a *coup d'état* depended on speed. Towers was almost sure to take the quickest way—blasting. And Lopez was probably calling the Base right now. Fifteen minutes for Towers to suit up and get here, maybe a short dicker—then *whoosh!* the party is over.

Fifteen minutes—

In fifteen minutes the bombs might fall back into the hands of the conspirators; in fifteen minutes he must make the bombs unusable.

An atom bomb is just two or more pieces of fissionable metal, such as plutonium. Separated, they are no more explosive than a pound of butter; slapped together, they explode. The complications lie in the gadgets and circuits and gun used to slap them together in the exact way and at the exact time and place required.

These circuits, the bomb's "brain," are easily destroyed—but the bomb itself is hard to destroy because of its very simplicity. Johnny decided to smash the "brains"—and quickly!

The only tools at hand were simple ones used in handling the bombs. Aside from a Geiger counter, the speaker on the walkie-talkie circuit, a television rig to the base, and the bombs themselves, the room was bare. A bomb to be worked on was taken elsewhere—not through fear of explosion, but to reduce radiation exposure for personnel. The radioactive material in a bomb is buried in a "tamper"—in these bombs, gold. Gold stops alpha, beta, and much of the deadly gamma radiation—but not neutrons.

The slippery, poisonous neutrons which plutonium gives off had to escape, or a chain reaction—explosion!—would result. The room was bathed in an invisible, almost undetectable rain of neutrons. The place was unhealthy; regulations called for staying in it as short a time as possible.

The Geiger counter clicked off the "background" radiation, cosmic rays, the trace of radioactivity in the Moon's crust, and secondary radioactivity set up all through the room by neutrons. Free neutrons have the nasty trait of infecting what they strike, making it radioactive, whether it be concrete wall or human body. In time the room would have to be abandoned.

Dahlquist twisted a knob on the Geiger counter; the instrument stopped clicking. He had used a suppressor circuit to cut out noise of "background" radiation at the level then present. It reminded him uncomfortably of the danger of staying here. He took out the radiation exposure film all radiation personnel carry; it was a direct-response type and had been fresh when he arrived. The most sensitive end was faintly darkened already. Half way down the film a red line crossed it. Theoretically, if the wearer was exposed to enough radioactivity in a week to darken the film to that line, he was, as Johnny reminded himself, a "dead duck."

Off came the cumbersome space suit; what he needed was speed. Do the job and surrender—better to be a prisoner than to linger in a place as "hot" as this.

He grabbed a ball hammer from the tool rack and got busy, pausing only to switch off the television pick-up. The first bomb bothered him. He started to smash the cover plate of the "brain," then stopped, filled with reluctance. All his life he had prized fine apparatus.

He nerved himself and swung; glass tinkled, metal creaked. His mood changed; he began to feel a shameful pleasure in destruction. He pushed on with enthusiasm, swinging, smashing, destroying!

So intent was he that he did not at first hear his name called. "Dahlquist! Answer me! Are you there?"

He wiped sweat and looked at the TV screen. Towers' perturbed features stared out.

Johnny was shocked to find that he had wrecked only six bombs. Was he going to be caught before he could finish? Oh, no! He *had* to finish. Stall, son, stall! "Yes, Colonel? You called me?"

"I certainly did! What's the meaning of this?"

"I'm sorry, Colonel."

Towers' expression relaxed a little. "Turn on your pick-up, Johnny, I can't see you. What was that noise?"

"The pick-up is on," Johnny lied. "It must be out of order. That noise—uh, to tell the truth, Colonel, I was fixing things so that nobody could get in here."

Towers hesitated, then said firmly, "I'm going to assume that you are sick and send you to the Medical Officer. But I want you to come out of there, right away. That's an order, Johnny."

Johnny answered slowly. "I can't just yet, Colonel. I came here to make up my mind and I haven't quite made it up. You said to see you after lunch."

"I meant you to stay in your quarters."

"Yes, sir. But I thought I ought to stand watch on the bombs, in case I decided you were wrong."

"It's not for you to decide, Johnny. I'm your superior officer. You are sworn to obey me."

"Yes, sir." This was wasting time; the old fox might have a squad on the way now. "But I swore to keep the peace, too. Could you come out here and talk it over with me? I don't want to do the wrong thing."

Towers smiled. "A good idea, Johnny. You wait there. I'm sure you'll see the light." He switched off.

"There," said Johnny. "I hope you're convinced that I'm a half-wit—you slimy mistake!" He picked up the hammer, ready to use the minutes gained.

He stopped almost at once; it dawned on him that wrecking the "brains" was not enough. There were no spare "brains," but there was a well-stocked electronics shop. Morgan could jury-rig control circuits for bombs. Why, he could himself—not a neat job, but one that would work. Damnation! He would have to wreck the bombs themselves—and in the next ten minutes.

But a bomb was solid chunks of metal, encased in a heavy tamper, all tied in with a big steel gun. It couldn't be done—not in ten minutes.

Damn!

Of course, there was one way. He knew the control circuits; he also knew how to beat them. Take this bomb: if he took out the safety bar, unhooked the proximity circuit, shorted the delay circuit, and cut in the arming circuit by hand—then unscrewed *that* and reached in *there,* he could, with just a long, stiff wire, set the bomb off.

Blowing the other bombs and the valley itself to Kingdom Come.

Also Johnny Dahlquist. That was the rub.

All this time he was doing what he had thought out, up to the step of actually setting off the bomb. Ready to go, the bomb seemed to threaten, as if crouching to spring. He stood up, sweating.

He wondered if he had the courage. He did not want to funk—and hoped that he would. He dug into his jacket and took out a picture of Edith and the baby. "Honeychile," he said, "if I get out of this, I'll never even try to beat a red light." He kissed the picture and put it back. There was nothing to do but wait.

What was keeping Towers? Johnny wanted to make sure that Towers was in blast range. What a joke on the jerk! Me—sitting here, ready to throw the switch on him. The idea tickled him; it led to a better: why blow himself up—alive?

There was another way to rig it—a "dead man" control. Jigger up some way so that the last step, the one that set off the bomb, would not happen as long as he kept his hand on a switch or a lever or something. Then, if they blew open the door, or shot him, or anything—up goes the balloon!

Better still, if he could hold them off with the threat of it, sooner or later help would come—Johnny was sure that most of the Patrol was not in this stinking conspiracy—and then: Johnny comes marching home! What a reunion! He'd resign and get a teaching job; he'd stood his watch.

All the while, he was working. Electrical? No, too little time. Make it a simple mechanical linkage. He had it doped out but had hardly begun to build it when the loudspeaker called him. "Johnny?"

"That you, Colonel?" His hands kept busy.

"Let me in."

"Well, now, Colonel, that wasn't in the agreement." Where in blue blazes was something to use as a long lever?

"I'll come in alone, Johnny, I give you my word. We'll talk face to face."

His word! "We can talk over the speaker, Colonel." Hey, that was it—a yardstick, hanging on the tool rack.

"Johnny, I'm warning you. Let me in, or I'll blow the door off."

A wire—he needed a wire, fairly long and stiff. He tore the antenna from his suit. "You wouldn't do that, Colonel. It would ruin the bombs."

"Vacuum won't hurt the bombs. Quit stalling."

"Better check with Major Morgan. Vacuum won't hurt them; explosive decompression would wreck every circuit." The Colonel was not a bomb specialist; he shut up for several minutes. Johnny went on working.

"Dahlquist," Towers resumed, "that was a clumsy lie. I checked with Morgan. You have sixty seconds to get into your suit, if you aren't already. I'm going to blast the door."

"No, you won't," said Johnny. "Ever hear of a 'dead man' switch?" Now for a counterweight—and a sling.

"Eh? What do you mean?"

"I've rigged number seventeen to set off by hand. But I put in a gimmick. It won't blow while I hang on to a strap I've got in my hand. But if anything happens to me—*up she goes!* You are about fifty feet from the blast center. Think it over."

There was a short silence. "I don't believe you."

"No? Ask Morgan. He'll believe me. He can inspect it, over the TV pick-up." Johnny lashed the belt of his space suit to the end of the yardstick.

"You said the pick-up was out of order."

"So I lied. This time I'll prove it. Have Morgan call me."

Presently Major Morgan's face appeared. "Lieutenant Dahlquist?"

"Hi, Stinky. Wait a sec." With great care Dahlquist made one last connection while holding down the end of the yardstick. Still careful, he shifted his grip to the belt, sat down on the floor, stretched an arm and switched on the TV pick-up. "Can you see me, Stinky?"

"I can see you," Morgan answered stiffly. "What is this nonsense?"

"A little surprise I whipped up." He explained it—what circuits he had cut out, what ones had been shorted, just how the jury-rigged mechanical sequence fitted in.

Morgan nodded. "But you're bluffing, Dahlquist. I feel sure that you haven't disconnected the 'K' circuit. You don't have the guts to blow yourself up."

Johnny chuckled. "I sure haven't. But that's the beauty of it. It can't go off, *so long as I am alive*. If your greasy boss, ex-Colonel Towers, blasts the door, then I'm dead and the bomb goes off. It won't matter to me, but it will to him. Better tell him." He switched off.

Towers came on over the speaker shortly. "Dahlquist?"

"I hear you."

"There's no need to throw away your life. Come out and you will be retired on full pay. You can go home to your family. That's a promise."

Johnny got mad. "You keep my family out of this!"

"Think of them, man."

"Shut up. Get back to your hole. I feel a need to scratch and this whole shebang might just explode in your lap."

2 Johnny sat up with a start. He had dozed, his hand hadn't let go the sling, but he had the shakes when he thought about it.

Maybe he should disarm the bomb and depend on their not daring to dig him out? But Towers' neck was already in hock for treason; Towers might risk it. If he did and the bomb were disarmed, Johnny would be dead and Towers would have the bombs. No, he had gone this far; he wouldn't let his baby girl grow up in a dictatorship just to catch some sleep.

He heard the Geiger counter clicking and remembered having used the suppressor circuit. The radioactivity in the room must be increasing, perhaps from scattering the "brain" circuits—the circuits were sure to be infected; they had lived too long too close to plutonium. He dug out his film.

The dark area was spreading toward the red line.

He put it back and said, "Pal, better break this deadlock or you are going to shine like a watch dial." It was a figure of speech; infected animal tissue does not glow—it simply dies, slowly.

The TV screen lit up; Towers' face appeared. "Dahlquist? I want to talk to you."

"Go fly a kite."

"Let's admit you have us inconvenienced."

"Inconvenienced, hell—I've got you stopped."

"For the moment. I'm arranging to get more bombs—"

"Liar."

"—but you are slowing us up. I have a proposition."

"Not interested."

"Wait. When this is over I will be chief of the world government. If you cooperate, even now, I will make you my administrative head."

Johnny told him what to do with it. Towers said, "Don't be stupid. What do you gain by dying?"

Johnny grunted. "Towers, what a prime stinker you are. You spoke of my family. I'd rather see them dead than living under a two-bit Napoleon like you. Now go away—I've got some thinking to do."

Towers switched off.

Johnny got out his film again. It seemed no darker but it reminded him forcibly that time was running out. He was hungry and thirsty—and he could not stay awake forever. It took four days to get a ship up from Earth; he could not expect rescue any sooner. And he wouldn't last four days—once the darkening spread past the red line he was a goner.

His only chance was to wreck the bombs beyond repair, and get out —before that film got much darker.

He thought about ways, then got busy. He hung a weight on the sling, tied a line to it. If Towers blasted the door, he hoped to jerk the rig loose before he died.

There was a simple, though arduous, way to wreck the bombs beyond any capacity of Moon Base to repair them. The heart of each was two hemispheres of plutonium, their flat surfaces polished smooth to permit perfect contact when slapped together. Anything less would prevent the chain reaction on which atomic explosion depended.

Johnny started taking apart one of the bombs.

He had to bash off four lugs, then break the glass envelope around the inner assembly. Aside from that the bomb came apart easily. At last he had in front of him two gleaming, mirror-perfect half globes.

A blow with the hammer—and one was no longer perfect. Another blow and the second cracked like glass; he had tapped its crystalline structure just right.

Hours later, dead tired, he went back to the armed bomb. Forcing himself to steady down, with extreme care he disarmed it. Shortly its silvery hemispheres too were useless. There was no longer a usable bomb in the room—but huge fortunes in the most valuable, most poisonous, and most deadly metal in the known world were spread around the floor.

Johnny looked at the deadly stuff. "Into your suit and out of here, son," he said aloud. "I wonder what Towers will say?"

He walked toward the rack, intending to hang up the hammer. As he passed, the Geiger counter chattered wildly.

Plutonium hardly affects a Geiger counter; secondary infection from plutonium does. Johnny looked at the hammer, then held it closer to the Geiger counter. The counter screamed.

Johnny tossed it hastily away and started back toward his suit.

As he passed the counter it chattered again. He stopped short.

He pushed one hand close to the counter. Its clicking picked up to a steady roar. Without moving he reached into his pocket and took out his exposure film.

It was dead black from end to end.

3

Plutonium taken into the body moves quickly to bone marrow. Nothing can be done; the victim is finished. Neutrons from it smash through the body, ionizing tissue, transmuting atoms into radioactive isotopes, destroying and killing. The fatal dose is unbelievably small; a mass a tenth the size of a grain of table salt is more than enough—a dose small enough to enter through the tiniest scratch. During the historic "Manhattan Project" immediate high amputation was considered the only possible first-aid measure.

Johnny knew all this but it no longer disturbed him. He sat on the floor, smoking a hoarded cigarette, and thinking. The events of his long watch were running through his mind.

He blew a puff of smoke at the Geiger counter and smiled without humor to hear it chatter more loudly. By now even his breath was "hot"—carbon-14, he supposed, exhaled from his blood stream as carbon dioxide. It did not matter.

There was no longer any point in surrendering, nor would he give Towers the satisfaction—he would finish out this watch right here. Besides, by keeping up the bluff that one bomb was ready to blow, he could stop them from capturing the raw material from which bombs were made. That might be important in the long run.

He accepted, without surprise, the fact that he was not unhappy. There was a sweetness about having no further worries of any sort. He did not hurt, he was not uncomfortable, he was no longer even hungry. Physically he still felt fine and his mind was at peace. He was dead—he knew that he was dead; yet for a time he was able to walk and breathe and see and feel.

He was not even lonesome. He was not alone; there were comrades with him—the boy with his finger in the dike, Colonel Bowie, too ill to move but insisting that he be carried across the line, the dying Captain of the *Chesapeake* still with deathless challenge on his lips, Rodger Young peering into the gloom. They gathered about him in the dusky bomb room.

And of course there was Edith. She was the only one he was aware of. Johnny wished that he could see her face more clearly. Was she angry? Or proud and happy?

Proud though unhappy—he could see her better now and even feel her hand. He held very still.

Presently his cigarette burned down to his fingers. He took a final puff, blew it at the Geiger counter, and put it out. It was his last. He gathered several butts and fashioned a roll-your-own with a bit of paper found in a pocket. He lit it carefully and settled back to wait for Edith to show up again. He was very happy.

He was still propped against the bomb case, the last of his salvaged cigarettes cold at his side, when the speaker called out again. "Johnny? Hey, Johnny! Can you hear me? This is Kelly. It's all over. The *Lafayette* landed and Towers blew his brains out. Johnny? *Answer me.*"

When they opened the outer door, the first man in carried a Geiger counter in front of him on the end of a long pole. He stopped at the threshold and backed out hastily. "Hey, chief!" he called. "Better get some handling equipment—uh, and a lead coffin, too."

"Four days it took the little ship and her escort to reach Earth. Four days while all of Earth's people awaited her arrival. For ninety-eight hours all commercial programs were off television; instead there was an endless dirge—the Dead March *from* Saul, *the* Valhalla *theme,* Going Home, *the Patrol's own* Landing Orbit.

"The nine ships landed at Chicago Port. A drone tractor removed the casket from the small ship; the ship was then refueled and blasted off in an escape trajectory, thrown away into outer space, never again to be used for a lesser purpose.

"The tractor progressed to the Illinois town where Lieutenant Dahl-

quist had been born, while the dirge continued. There it placed the casket on a pedestal, inside a barrier marking the distance of safe approach. Space marines, arms reversed and heads bowed, stood guard around it; the crowds stayed outside this circle. And still the dirge continued.

"When enough time had passed, long, long after the heaped flowers had withered, the lead casket was enclosed in marble, just as you see it today."

ISAAC ASIMOV

THE MACHINE THAT WON THE WAR

The celebration had a long way to go and even in the silent depths of Multivac's underground chambers, it hung in the air.

If nothing else, there was the mere fact of isolation and silence. For the first time in a decade, technicians were not scurrying about the vitals of the giant computer, the soft lights did not wink out their erratic patterns, the flow of information in and out had halted.

It would not be halted long, of course, for the needs of peace would be pressing. Yet now, for a day, perhaps for a week, even Multivac might celebrate the great time, and rest.

Lamar Swift took off the military cap he was wearing and looked down the long and empty main corridor of the enormous computer. He sat down rather wearily in one of the technician's swing-stools, and his uniform, in which he had never been comfortable, took on a heavy and wrinkled appearance.

He said, "I'll miss it all after a grisly fashion. It's hard to remember when we weren't at war with Deneb, and it seems against nature now to be at peace and to look at the stars without anxiety."

The two men with the Executive Director of the Solar Federation were both younger than Swift. Neither was as gray. Neither looked quite as tired.

John Henderson, thin-lipped and finding it hard to control the relief he felt in the midst of triumph, said, "They're destroyed! They're destroyed! It's what I keep saying to myself over and over and I still can't believe it. We all talked so much, over so many years, about the menace hanging over Earth and all its worlds, over every human being, and all the time it was true, every word of it. And now we're alive and it's the Denebians who are shattered and destroyed. They'll be no menace now, ever again."

"Thanks to Multivac," said Swift, with a quiet glance at the imperturbable Jablonsky, who through all the war had been Chief Interpreter of science's oracle. "Right, Max?"

Jablonsky shrugged. Automatically, he reached for a cigarette and decided against it. He alone, of all the thousands who had lived in the tunnels within Multivac, had been allowed to smoke, but toward the end he had made definite efforts to avoid making use of the privilege.

He said, "Well, that's what *they* say." His broad thumb moved in the direction of his right shoulder, aiming upward.

"Jealous, Max?"

"Because they're shouting for Multivac? Because Multivac is the big hero of mankind in this war?" Jablonsky's craggy face took on an air of suitable contempt. "What's that to me? Let Multivac be the machine that won the war, if it pleases them."

Henderson looked at the other two out of the corners of his eyes. In this short interlude that the three had instinctively sought out in the one peaceful corner of a metropolis gone mad; in this entr'acte between the dangers of war and the difficulties of peace; when, for one moment, they might all find surcease; he was conscious only of his weight of guilt.

Suddenly, it was as though that weight were too great to be borne longer. It had to be thrown off, along with the war; now!

Henderson said, "Multivac had nothing to do with victory. It's just a machine."

"A big one," said Swift.

"Then just a big machine. No better than the data fed it." For a moment, he stopped, suddenly unnerved at what he was saying.

Jablonsky looked at him, his thick fingers once again fumbling for a cigarette and once again drawing back. "You should know. You supplied the data. Or is it just that you're taking the credit?"

"*No,*" said Henderson, angrily. "There is no credit. What do you know of the data Multivac had to use; predigested from a hundred subsidiary computers here on Earth, on the Moon, on Mars, even on Titan. With Titan always delayed and always that feeling that its figures would introduce an unexpected bias."

"It would drive anyone mad," said Swift, with gentle sympathy.

Henderson shook his head. "It wasn't just that. I admit that eight years ago when I replaced Lepont as Chief Programmer, I was nervous.

But there was an exhilaration about things in those days. The war was still long-range; an adventure without real danger. We hadn't reached the point where manned vessels had had to take over and where interstellar warps could swallow up a planet clean, if aimed correctly. But then, when the real difficulties began—"

Angrily—he could finally permit anger—he said, "You know nothing about it."

"Well," said Swift. "Tell us. The war is over. We've won."

"Yes." Henderson nodded his head. He had to remember that. Earth had won so all had been for the best. "Well, the data became meaningless."

"Meaningless? You mean that literally?" said Jablonsky.

"Literally. What would you expect? The trouble with you two was that you weren't out in the thick of it. You never left Multivac, Max, and you, Mr. Director, never left the Mansion except on state visits where you saw exactly what they wanted you to see."

"I was not as unaware of that," said Swift, "as you may have thought."

"Do you know," said Henderson, "to what extent data concerning our production capacity, our resource potential, our trained manpower—everything of importance to the war effort, in fact—had become unreliable and untrustworthy during the last half of the war? Group leaders, both civilian and military, were intent on projecting their own improved image, so to speak, so they obscured the bad and magnified the good. Whatever the machines might do, the men who programmed them and interpreted the results had their own skins to think of and competitors to stab. There was no way of stopping that. I tried, and failed."

"Of course," said Swift, in quiet consolation. "I can see that you would."

This time Jablonsky decided to light his cigarette. "Yet I presume you provided Multivac with data in your programming. You said nothing to us about unreliability."

"How could I tell you? And if I did, how could you afford to believe me?" demanded Henderson, savagely. "Our entire war effort was geared to Multivac. It was the one great weapon on our side, for the Denebians had nothing like it. What else kept up morale in the face of doom but the assurance that Multivac would always predict and circumvent any Denebian move, and would always direct and prevent the circumvention of our moves? Great Space, after our Spy-warp was blasted out of hyperspace we lacked any reliable Denebian data to feed Multivac and we didn't dare make *that* public."

"True enough," said Swift.

"Well, then," said Henderson, "if I told you the data was unreliable, what could you have done but replace me and refuse to believe me? I couldn't allow that."

"What did you do?" said Jablonsky.

"Since the war is won, I'll tell you what I did. I corrected the data."

"How?" asked Swift.

"Intuition, I presume. I juggled them till they looked right. At first, I hardly dared. I changed a bit here and there to correct what were obvious impossibilities. When the sky didn't collapse about us, I got braver. Toward the end, I scarcely cared. I just wrote out the necessary data as it was needed. I even had the Multivac Annex prepare data for me according to a private programming pattern I had devised for the purpose."

"Random figures?" said Jablonsky.

"Not at all. I introduced a number of necessary biases."

Jablonsky smiled, quite unexpectedly, his dark eyes sparkling behind the crinkling of the lower lids. "Three times a report was brought me about unauthorized uses of the Annex, and I let it go each time. If it had mattered, I would have followed it up and spotted you, John, and found out what you were doing. But, of course, nothing about Multivac mattered in those days, so you got away with it."

"What do you mean, nothing mattered?" asked Henderson, suspiciously.

"Nothing did. I suppose if I had told you this at the time, it would have spared you your agony, but then if you had told me what you were doing, it would have spared me mine. What made you think Multivac was in working order, whatever the data you supplied it?"

"Not in working order?" said Swift.

"Not really. Not reliably. After all, where were my technicians in the last years of the war? I'll tell you, they were feeding computers on a thousand different space devices. They were gone! I had to make do with kids I couldn't trust and veterans who were out-of-date. Besides, do you think I could trust the solid-state components coming out of Cryogenics in the last years? Cryogenics wasn't any better placed as far as personnel was concerned than I was. To me, it didn't matter whether the data being supplied Multivac were reliable or not. The *results* weren't reliable. That much I knew."

"What did you do?" asked Henderson.

"I did what you did, John. I introduced the bugger factor. I adjusted matters in accordance with intuition—and that's how the machine won the war."

Swift leaned back in the chair and stretched his legs out before him. "Such revelations. It turns out then that the material handed me to guide me in my decision-making capacity was a man-made interpretation of man-made data. Isn't that right?"

"It looks so," said Jablonsky.

"Then I perceive I was correct in not placing too much reliance upon it," said Swift.

"You didn't?" Jablonsky, despite what he had just said, managed to look professionally insulted.

"I'm afraid I didn't. Multivac might seem to say, Strike here, not there; do this, not that; wait, don't act. But I could never be certain that what Multivac seemed to say, it really did say; or what it really said, it really meant. I could never be certain."

"But the final report was always plain enough, sir," said Jablonsky.

"To those who did not have to make the decision, perhaps. Not to me. The horror of the responsibility of such decisions was unbearable and not even Multivac was sufficient to remove the weight. But the point is I was justified in doubting and there is tremendous relief in that."

Caught up in the conspiracy of mutual confession, Jablonsky put titles aside. "What was it you did then, Lamar? After all, you did make decisions. How?"

"Well, it's time to be getting back perhaps but—I'll tell you first. Why not? I did make use of a computer, Max, but an older one than Multivac, much older."

He groped in his own pocket for cigarettes, and brought out a package along with a scattering of small change; old-fashioned coins dating to the first years before the metal shortage had brought into being a credit system tied to a computer-complex.

Swift smiled rather sheepishly. "I still need these to make money seem substantial to me. An old man finds it hard to abandon the habits of youth." He put a cigarette between his lips and dropped the coins one by one back into his pocket.

He held the last coin between his fingers, staring absently at it. "Multivac is not the first computer, friends, nor the best-known, nor the one that can most efficiently lift the load of decision from the shoulders of the executive. A machine *did* win the war, John; at least a very simple computing device did; one that I used every time I had a particularly hard decision to make."

With a faint smile of reminiscence, he flipped the coin he held. It glinted in the air as it spun and came down in Swift's outstretched palm. His hand closed over it and brought it down on the back of his left hand. His right hand remained in place, hiding the coin.

"Heads or tails, gentlemen?" said Swift.